Seeds of Destruction

Seeds of Destruction

JOE KENNEDY AND HIS SONS

RALPH G. MARTIN

G. P. PUTNAM'S SONS
NEW YORK

G. P. Putnam's Sons
Publishers Since 1838
200 Madison Avenue
New York, NY 10016

Library of Congress Cataloging-in-Publication Data

Martin, Ralph G., date.
Seeds of destruction : Joe Kennedy and his sons / Ralph G. Martin.
p.   cm.
ISBN 0-399-14061-1
1. Kennedy family.   2. Politicians—United States—Biography.
3. Kennedy, Joseph P. (Joseph Patrick), 1888–1969—Family.
I. Title.
E747.M37   1995   94-48357 CIP
973.9'092—dc20
[B]

Printed in the United States of America
1   3   5   7   9   10   8   6   4   2

Book design by Julie Duquet

ACKNOWLEDGMENTS

Seeds of Destruction really began in 1959 with my first fascination with the Kennedys. It was then that Ed Plaut and I wrote *Front Runner, Dark Horse,* a political analysis of how John Kennedy and Stuart Symington ran for the Democratic presidential nomination.

Kennedy was still a young Senator, and so there were no available archives, no libraries of oral histories. We plowed fresh ground with original interviews and personal observations.

Front Runner began on a negative note. Kennedy already had arranged for an authorized biography of himself and did not want any un-authorized book before the 1960 Democratic convention that might make unfavorable revelations. He managed to persuade our publisher to cancel the proposed contract by saying that he would not cooperate with us. We then took the book to another publisher, who was not so easily intimidated.

What happened then was typical of the Kennedy technique: When power fails, use charm. Ed and I received the full force of Kennedy personality. JFK invited us to visit his home at Hyannis and to travel on his small plane when he made a political tour of the primary states.

He then made himself freely available to us for interviews and offered access to his family, staff, and friends. We took full advantage. He even flattered us by asking our advice. Soon his father complained to Ed Plaut that Jack was spending too much time with us when he should be talking to him. My most vivid memory is of JFK and me in a

Piper Cub heading for a rally somewhere in Indiana. With a passion I had never seen before, he told me all the things he planned to do when he became President of the United States. Nevertheless, my feeling about the Kennedys then was that politics was much more important to them than principle.

When I wrote *A Hero for Our Time,* I had the great advantage of going back to interview family and staff whom I knew well, to ask more searching questions. My friendships with some of them meant they talked to me more freely than they had talked to others.

The question of dynasty stayed with me as something to be explored further. I remember my first meeting with a very young Robert Kennedy, on a Stevenson campaign plane; he came as a shy observer, talking to few people. I saw him evolve into a brash, arrogant prosecutor on a Congressional committee, and then become his brother's right hand in his presidential campaign. When Bob ran for the U.S. Senate in New York State, I was invited to work on his campaign, but I refused because the early impression of his arrogance had remained. Later I had reason to regret that decision. Bob, like Jack, had emerged into an area of strong emotional involvement in such issues as civil rights.

As for Ted, I recall being so moved by his early memories of his brothers, and by their tight friendship, even when they competed against each other. I saw how their deaths almost destroyed him, but how he came out of his playboy world and his personal tragedies to become one of the most important United States Senators.

I now felt ready to write the final chapter of the original dynasty: *Joe Kennedy and His Sons.* Assisting me enormously was the JFK Library, a huge repository of more than 1,500 oral histories and countless public and private papers. In addition, it contained a growing oral history project on Robert Kennedy. And there were other important archives across the country, and in London.

To help me on *Seeds of Destruction,* as she had on so many of my books, Tina Martin has been as much a part of this project as I. She has done almost all the archival research, finding sources previously unavailable, as well as marvelously fresh material in television and radio interviews of key Kennedy people, some of whom talked more freely to the microphone and the camera than they had to print reporters or authors.

Tina is an excellent writer and editor, and many of her comments on different parts of the book have been incorporated intact into the text. She was the first to read and edit the manuscript and her criticism has been sensitive and superb. I hope to collaborate with her as a co-author in any future work.

Among the most important archives are the Special Collections of the Mugar Memorial Library at Boston University—and that's not just because my own papers are stored there. Its director, Dr. Howard Gotlieb, has collected an impressive archive of the twentieth century. For my purpose, the most important papers were those of Laura Bergquist, Fletcher Knebel, and David Halberstam. I am grateful to Dr. Gotlieb and his researcher Charles Niles, who has an encyclopedic memory.

The Lyndon Baines Johnson Library in Austin, Texas, has been a source of many valuable oral history interviews, and the Sarah McClendon Papers have been especially interesting. Similarly, the oral history interviews on the Kennedys at Columbia University in New York City have added many insights, and I am particularly grateful to its director, Ronald J. Grele. Several other archives of special importance are the American Heritage Center at the University of Wyoming, which contains the interviews and papers of Clay Blair, Jr., among others. I am grateful to its director, Michael Devine, for his special help and to Michael J. Bell, who helped in research. At Brown University, the Harold Tinker Papers were most interesting. And in the House of Lords Library in London, I found valuable correspondence between Lord Beaverbrook and Joseph Kennedy.

Some of the richest material again came from papers privately held. Among the most important were those of Patricia Coughlan, the widow of Robert Coughlan, who wrote an autobiography of Rose Kennedy. There was a treasure trove of many family interviews. His research also included copies of family letters as well as the manuscript of an unpublished book on the Kennedys, from which his widow generously allowed me to quote. Patricia Coughlan not only made all this available but also gave us the hospitality of her home.

Some of my friends, too, opened their private files to me. Merle Miller gave me his pertinent interviews prepared for his biography of Lyndon Johnson; Charles Roberts, who had covered the Kennedy White House for *Newsweek,* made his files available, as did John Sharon, a longtime Kennedy friend and associate. Joe McCarthy, who had co-authored *Johnny We Hardly Knew Ye,* let me have all his taped interviews with the Kennedy family and friends. So did Lester David, who has written so extensively on the Kennedys. I am particularly indebted to Richard J. Whelan, for giving me access to his many interviews for his book on the Founding Father.

Other authors and researchers who have been helpful include Peter Collier, Hank Searls, Stephen Corsaro, Harvey Rachlin, Peter Wyden, Robert Donovan, Frank Waldrop, Hugh Sidey, and Warren Rogers.

Noted psychologist Dr. Murray Krim, of the William Alanson White Institute, and prominent psychiatrist Dr. Leon Tec gave me the benefit of their expertise in the area of sibling relationships.

My thanks, also, to Claire Quigley and to the Reference Room staff of the Westport Public Library, including Kathy Greidenbach, Marta Campbell, Barbara Murphy, Sylvia Schulman, and Joyce Vitali. At the Valley Cottage Library, Tina Martin thanks Michael Kavich, Marion Gimpel, and Caroline Bailey; at the Nyack Library, Sandy Rosoff, Kim Weston; and at the Finkelstein Library, Ruth Geneslaw. My special thanks to the librarian at the Century Association, W. Gregory Gallagher.

My great appreciation to the staff of the John F. Kennedy Presidential Library in Boston, particularly its director, William Johnson, as well as Ron Whealen, June Payne, Maura Porter, Susan D'Entrement, and Allen Goodrich. James Hill, particularly, was patient and helpful to a degree above and beyond the call of duty, especially in the final stages of picture selection for the book.

I am always grateful to dear friend and former co-author Ed Plaut, for all his help and wisdom; Richard Kroll, for a variety of willing assistance, including some research; Daniel Greenbaum, for his emergency technical help; Steve Goethner, for being invaluable in keeping my computer in working order; Fred Wasserman, for his own private insight; Kim Kastens and Will Ayres, Robert and Edna Brigham, Arthur and Edna Greenbaum, Paul and Shirley Green, Pearl and Lionel Bernier, Guyo Tajiri, Ruth and Larry Hall, Max Wilk, and as always, John and Chica Weaver.

My dear friend Mari Walker, who has translated so many of my notes and interviews for so many books, once again proved indispensable. Lisa Meiners was also most important in recording the computer database, and my thanks also to Janice Murray and Lydia Virvo.

A special vote of thanks to the friendly staff of Golds for all their willing assistance.

I am deeply indebted to Phyllis Grann, who has been unstinting in her support and friendship; my superb editors, Andrea Chambers and Eileen Cope, both of whom have helped shape this book into what it is, and have done it with taste and expertise; David Groff for his added help; my copy editor, Fred Sawyer, who was a model of a perfect copy editor—concerned and sensitive. My thanks again, as always, to my agent, Sterling Lord, who could not have been a better friend. To my wife, Marjorie Jean, my continuous gratitude for all her support.

In the course of writing these three books, there have been hundreds of interviews. Some of the most important people interviewed are named below: Joseph Alsop and Susan Mary Alsop, Jake Arvey, Letitia Baldrige, George Ball, Martha and Charles Bartlett, Lucius Battle, Betty Beale, Phoebe and Edgar Berman, Laura Bergquist, Governor James Blair, William McCormack Blair, Jr., Congressman Hale Boggs and Congresswoman Lindy Boggs, Richard Bolling, Joan Braden, Benjamin Bradlee, Richard and Ginny Paul, Sam Brightman, McGeorge Bundy, Quentin Burdick, Igor Cassini, Oscar Chapman, Marquis Childs, Blair Clark, Joseph Clark, Ted Clifton, Clark Clifford, Ray Cline, Nancy Coleman, Charles Collingwood, Bill Connell, Frank Cormier, Ralph Coughlan, Robert Coughlan, Jill Cowan, Kenneth Crawford, Mark Dalton, Lester David, Mary Davis, Joe De Gulielmo, Jim Deakin, Governor Michael DiSalle, Nancy Dickerson, Irving Dilliard, John Donovan, Robert Donovan, Senator Paul Douglas, Ralph Dungan, Fred Dutton, Rowland Evans, Myer Feldman, John Fenton, Phil Fine, Joel Fisher, Gerald T. Flynn, Helen Fuller, Governor Foster Furculo, Anthony Gallucio, John Gardner, General James Gavin, Jean Gildea, Stanton Gilderhorn, Roswell Gilpatric, Arthur Goldberg, David Hackett, Bill Haddad, John R. Hahn, Mark Halloran, Lord Harlech (David Ormsby-Gore), Joe Healy, Mrs. William Randolph Hearst, Jr., Richard Helms, Bruce Hopper, Lawrence Houston, Hubert H. Humphrey, William Hundley, Gardiner Jackson, Alexis Johnson, Max Kampelman, Joe Kane, Senator Estes Kefauver, Carroll Kilpatrick, Harvey Klemmer, Patricia and Victor Lasky, Ernest Leiser, General Lyman Lemnitzer, Evelyn Lincoln, Ben Loeb, Louis Lyons, Norman MacDonald, Torbert MacDonald, Robert Manning, Carl Marcy, Earl Mazo, Eugene McCarthy, Joe McCarthy, Frank

McNaughton, General Godfrey McHugh, Porter McKeever, Edward McLaughlin, Sarah McLendon, Robert McNamara, Marianne Means, Jim Meredith, Cord Meyer, Abe Michelson, Ed Michelson, Fishbait Miller, Newton Minow, Edward Morgan, Patsy Mulkern, Debs Myers, Senator Richard Neuberger, Larry and Sancy Newman, Paul Nitze, John Nolan, Angie Novello, Lawrence O'Brien, Kenneth O'Donnell, Congressman Thomas "Tip" O'Neill, Judge Louis Oberdorfer, Frederic S. Papert, Claiborne Pell, Phil Potter, Dave Powers, Hy Raskin, Jack Raymond, Timothy Reardon, James Reed, Harold Reis, Abraham Ribicoff, Dave Richardson, Frank Riley, Charles Roberts, Warren Rogers, Ed Rooney, Eleanor Roosevelt, Franklin D. Roosevelt, Jr., James Roosevelt, Eugene Rostow, James Rousmaniere, James Rowe, Jim Rowse, Pierre Salinger, Arthur Schlesinger, Jr., Senator Hugh Scott, John Sharon, Admiral Tazewell Shepherd, Abba Schwartz, Eric Sevareid, Sidney Shore, Eunice Kennedy Shriver, Robert Sargent Shriver, Hugh Sidey, Marvin Sleeper, Senator George Smathers, Stephen Smith, Theodore C. Sorensen, Charles Spalding, Adlai Stevenson, Michael and Nina Auchincloss Straight, Jim Sundquist, James Symington, Dave Talbot, General Maxwell Taylor, Herbert Trask, Frank Thompson, Esther Tufty, Sander Vanocur, Frank Waldrop, William Walton, Bill Welsh, Edward Welsh, Theodore White, Thomas Winship, Peter Wyden, Adam Yarmolinsky, and Sam Zagoria.

For my grandchildren,
Eleanor and Max; Amelia, Maya and Alexander; and Abigail;
and any others en route

CONTENTS

PROLOGUE

On a golf course in Palm Beach in 1936, a friend asked Joseph Patrick Kennedy, Sr., "What are you doing these days, Joe?" Without taking his steely-blue eyes from the ball, he replied, "My work is my boys."

It wasn't just his work—it was his life, his immortality. Kennedy's multimillions had helped him become the American Ambassador to the Court of St. James, but he had been forced to resign with a badly battered reputation because he liked Hitler too much and democracy too little. The driving dream of his life had been to become President of the United States. With that dream dead, Joe zeroed in on his four sons to do the things he could not do, to reach the political prize he could not reach. He shaped them in his image, instilled in them his principles and ideas. When Jack became a first-term Congressman, he explained his conservatism, saying, "I'd just come out of my father's house at the time, and these were the things I knew."

From their father, the four sons learned how to manipulate people and events, how to court the press and create an image. He taught them that money was the mother's milk of politics and that politics was just another form of show business. Most of all, he poured into them, from their childhood, that they must win, win, win—no matter what the cost.

To help them win, he freely made available his vast fortune, great influence, and conniving mind. So completely did Kennedy Sr. merge his life with his sons' that their successes became his successes. In doing this, Kennedy Sr. would not be deterred by obstacles of morality or law.

Had Joe Sr. left them alone to live their normal lives, Joe Jr. might have become a commercial pilot; Jack, an English teacher; Bobby, a social worker; and Teddy, perhaps a playboy. Instead, their father directed their lives, almost step by step, with a combination of arrogance and loyalty and love.

In time, the four would carve out their own standards and their own clannish dependence on each other. In all of American history, the four Kennedy brothers are unique, both in their success and in their tragedy. And the roots of their success, the seeds of their destruction, were not only shaped by their parents and their heritage—but by each other.

Clare Boothe Luce once said of the Kennedys that their lives were like a soap opera. "Where else but in Gothic fiction, where else among real people, could one encounter such triumphs and tragedies, such beauty and charm and ambition and pride and human wreckage, such dedication to the best and lapses into the mire of life; such vulgar, noble, driven, generous, self-centered, loving, suspicious, devious, honorable, vulnerable, indomitable people. . . . No wonder the American public, their audience—for that matter much of the world—has been fascinated by them."

———————

WHAT MATTERED MOST to the four sons, in their early years, was their competition for the love and applause of their father. If their mother, Rose Fitzgerald Kennedy, provided the sense of what it meant to be a family, Joe supplied much of the emotional intensity. When they were small they came to him for the physical love they rarely got from their mother. Like all his brothers, John Kennedy always embraced and kissed his father—even when he became President of the United States.

It was Joe who saw them for what they were as individuals, and had the clear vision of each of their capabilities. Joe was always there to decide who would run for what, and when—sometimes even whom they would marry. From the beginning, the father's pride was the eldest son. When young Joe graduated with honors from Choate, his father full of praise, Jack watched with painful envy. Afterward, Jack bitterly confided to his best friend that he knew he was brighter than his older brother, and one day he would prove to his father that he was better. When Jack became a war hero—with the great help of his father's public relations machine—young Joe was found crying uncontrollably in his room because he was no longer the family star. The next day he would fly to the European battlefields to outdo his brother, and die doing so.

The father then selected the reluctant Jack to replace Joe in a political career. He later helped his third son, Bobby, emerge into the national limelight as a dynamic prosecutor and his brother's eventual successor. And he disregarded everybody's protests by insisting that the youngest, Teddy, become Senator as soon as he was old enough. The father also predicted that all three sons would be President, and if young Joe had lived it would have been four. Then he gloated that this was better than the Adams family, who had only two Presidents.

When his three brothers were dead, and his father silenced by a stroke, Ted found their heritage too difficult to live with, and stumbled badly before finding himself.

Although the competition between the four brothers proved deadly, their relationship was threaded tightly with love. The eldest brother, Joe, was a loving surrogate father to the youngest brother, Ted. And, when Joe died, Jack took over his role. Jack had a leather jacket with the presidential seal, and when he was killed, Bob wore it—and even dived into a stormy sea to recover it. And when Bob died, Ted wore it.

———————

AS THE FAMILY force, Joseph Patrick Kennedy was a strange mix. He had a hot heart and a cold head which created a special animal vigor, a boundless self-confidence, and an awesome ego. Yet, no matter how handsome his varied houses, no matter how powerful his government positions, people always saw him as a pushy outsider, a crass Catholic. All of this built up into a growing resentment that Joe Kennedy would not forget or forgive—and which he passed on to his sons. It became the touchstone of his life.

As one of the richest men in the country, he decided that money had meaning only when it bought power. And the more power he got, the more he wanted.

He had no problem in dealing directly with Chicago gangsters importing liquor during Prohibition, or using them to buy votes for a son in a presidential primary. To get what he wanted, he could be vicious, cruel, a man without morality.

A United States Supreme Court Justice said of him, "Isn't the most evil man you ever met, the most evil of the entire lot, Joe Kennedy?"

Those who try to justify Joe's code of behavior note that he had been brought up in an age of "robber barons" and political bosses who controlled cities and states. Joe Kennedy's father, known as "P.J.," was a political boss who knew all about buying votes. P.J. was a cheerful, pleasant man, and it was said of Joe that "he had inherited his father's business acumen, but not his soul."

Joe's soul was not based on his faith or even his heritage, because he seemed eager to run away from both. He was a Catholic because he was born a Catholic, and he followed the basic rituals, but he never paraded it as a badge of honor—until it became politically profitable. Since he had no private ambitions for his five daughters, he let their mother send them to Catholic schools, but he supervised his sons' education at secular schools.

Self-interest was Joe's motivating force. His judgments were black and white, and quick, and he believed more in himself than in his God. Nor did he parade the Irish roots his sons would later prize. More than anything else, he wanted to be assimilated and respected by the WASP world.

Basically he was a loner, pragmatic and bitter, and he was not an easy man to talk to. "He'd call everybody a son of a bitch except the man he happened to be having dinner with at the moment," said Henry Luce. This did not translate into easy friendships, and Joe had few friends who were not on his payroll.

Joe felt democracy was decadent and dying, and said so. In a speech to some movie men in Hollywood in 1941, he urged them not to make any more anti-Hitler pictures because Hitler was going to win. And after he resigned as Ambassador to Great Britain, he was quoted as saying, "I hate all those goddamned Englishmen—from Churchill on down."

As a public figure, Kennedy's greatest liability was his tactlessness. When he spoke, he could be passionate and brilliant, but, too often, and at critical times, he sounded ugly and bigoted. And yet, despite all this, he could be charismatic and utterly charming. He had a contagious laugh, a vitality that magnetized a room. "It's not what you are that counts," Joe Kennedy told his sons, "but what people think you are."

Joe's sons later demonstrated varying degrees of his charm, vitality, and magnetism, yet they also showed some of his dark side. Jack had no qualms in sharing the mistress of a Mafia boss, and even using his help in a presidential election; Bobby, as his brother's campaign manager, had no hesitation in lying to destroy the reputation of a respectable political opponent; Teddy, filled by his father with beliefs in Kennedy invincibility, found it easy to cheat on a Harvard exam, try to bribe a rival not to oppose him in a Senate race, and leave the scene of a woman drowning in his submerged car without calling the police for many hours.

The sons also absorbed their father's standards about women. Joe Sr. consumed women like food, but he seldom seemed to savor them. When he was a Hollywood magnate, he brought a parade of mistresses home while his wife was there. When his sons grew older, he gave them a motto which helped taint their lives: "A day without a lay is a day wasted."

His sons often provided women for him on request, and he even tried to make some of their conquests his own. Copying his pattern, the four sons felt free to raid each other's women.

———

IN THE LONG run of their lifetime, none of these negative things about their father ever really mattered much to these sons—because they truly loved him and they knew he truly loved them.

For them, he was the fount of constant encouragement. The father said often that all his ducks were swans, and he believed it. More important, he made his sons believe it. No matter what they did, no matter how wrong they sometimes were, he made them all think they were wonderful, that they were part of an untouchable dynasty.

Such arrogance was an arrogance of invulnerability, an arrogance that began with immense wealth, and was capped with a driving ambition and sometimes a sparkling brilliance that propelled them beyond themselves into the limelight of the world and into the myth of history.

1

THE YOUNG YEARS

Joseph Patrick Kennedy, Jr., the eldest child, was born in a rented cottage close to the sea, at Nantasket, Hull, Massachusetts, on July 28, 1915, alert, dimpled, almost ten pounds. Young Joseph would become the family golden boy.

At birth, his maternal grandfather, John Francis "Honey Fitz" Fitzgerald, a former mayor of Boston, was quick to predict to the press: "Well, of course, he is going to be President of these United States . . . his mother and father have already decided."

Rose Kennedy then had no such pretensions.

"When you hold your baby in your arms the first time, and you think of all the things you can do and say to influence him, it's a tremendous responsibility. What you did with him and for him can influence not only him but everyone he meets; not for a day, a month or a year, but for time and eternity."

Hers was a warm memory of her young son Joe "running into my arms and snuggling into my lap." Simply thinking of him, she said, "could produce a happy feeling in my heart."

Later Kennedy children might accuse her of a lack of real warmth, but this was never true of young Joe. She lavished her love on him.

Joe and the brood that followed were bearers of a powerful legacy. The flamboyant Honey Fitz, a three-term Congressman, was a dapper Dan of a man who wore a black derby and boutonniere and became the first child of Irish immigrants to serve as the city's mayor. Fitz's wife, Josie Hannon, was more interested in religion than in politics, and so Rose often took her mother's place as First Lady of Boston.

The pretty, outgoing Rose fell in love with a sandy-haired, blue-eyed Joseph Patrick Kennedy when she was sixteen. They had first met when she was five and he was seven, and their fathers were bitter political rivals. Joe's father, P.J., was the powerful East Boston ward boss, but Honey Fitz still regarded him as shanty Irish because he had been a former saloonkeeper.

Honey Fitz would have preferred other suitors for his daughter but found it difficult to protest because his own reputation was being blemished by a threatening scandal over his relationship with a cigarette girl named Toodles Ryan.

At the time of his wedding to twenty-four-year-old Rose, twenty-six-year-old Joe Kennedy managed to graduate from Harvard and become the first Irish bank inspector in Boston. Then he took over the presidency of the Columbia Trust Company, which his father had helped organize in 1895. As the youngest bank president in the country, he announced that he would earn his first million before he was thirty-five—and so he would. The marital promise was bright, but it soon darkened. Rose believed in God and children, but not lovemaking. She preferred separate bedrooms, and was adamant about minimal sexual relations even when her husband embarrassed her in front of friends and threatened to tell their priest. But nothing would change Rose's mind.

Submitting to sex primarily for procreation, Rose would produce nine children in quick succession.

Her second son, John Fitzgerald Kennedy, was born on May 29, 1917, a month after the United States declared war on Germany. Joe Jr. was a sturdy boy, but Jack was sickly from the start. He had trouble with his infant feeding, and his mother reported that he "always did have a funny tummy like me."

With two babies, and the expectancy of many more, the young couple made their first penetration into a Protestant suburb by paying $6,500 for a gray, two-and-a-half-story, nine-room clapboard house with a front porch, the last house on Beale Street in exclusive Brookline. Those Irish who remained in Boston referred to these deserters to the suburbs as "two-toilet Irish." They were also known as "the cut glass Irish," which was a level higher than the "lace curtain Irish"—those who had fruit on the table even when nobody was sick.

Joe Sr. was now a self-assured young man with the bright, alert eyes of a powerful bald eagle. Joe had no patience for people who could not understand problems quickly. He was blunt, decisive, came quickly to essentials. If he wanted to make a strong statement, he extended his right index finger and punched each point home. And he had sharp opinions on almost everything—some sound, some ridiculous, but almost all of them stimulating.

"I've always been controversial," Joe told a reporter. "And if I'd been worried about whether people agreed with me or not, I'd still be back in East Boston, right where I started. My father told me that if, when I died, I could count my friends on the fingers of one hand, I'd be lucky. I have more than that."

But not many more. A Boston politician, Wilton Vaugh, claimed Joe kept friends "dependent enough to know that they must remain loyal. He can make a man a slave, for example, by making him a generous loan."

Rose felt Joe's tough-mindedness came from his mother, Mary Hickey. She came from a respectable, energetic, and ambitious family: one brother would be a police captain, another a doctor, and still another the Mayor of Brockton. She had a good contralto voice, sang in the church choir, and was an immaculate and severe housekeeper. When the Kennedy children visited their grandparents' house they had to sit and not speak unless spoken to, be careful not to spill anything, and weren't "even allowed to wink."

WITH THE WAR over in 1918, their two sons were joined by a sister, Rosemary. Rose said she first knew her daughter was retarded "because she couldn't steer a sled." For most of her young years, her slowness was a family secret. Rose spent long hours tutoring her, and gave her more maternal love than any of the other children. Rosemary was eventually diagnosed as mildly retarded, which Joe regarded as an imperfect smudge on an otherwise picture-perfect clan.

Shortly afterward, the family picture became more imperfect. It had been said of Rose that she had developed "a salted heart." She shocked her friends and family by abruptly going home to her parents. For

Rose, trained to be a good Catholic wife, this was a desperate move. But she was embittered and hurt by the constant gossip of her husband's "showgirls," by the fact that she so seldom saw him because he claimed to be so busy working. She came home for her father's counsel on how to settle her fate.

Rose adored Honey Fitz and saw him as a man of sunshine and magic who had twirled her in the air, taught her to swim, even bought her a horse and carriage when she was twelve. She quoted him so often that friends nicknamed her "Father-Says."

It was her father who persuaded her to return home to her husband after three weeks. "What is past is past. The old days are gone. . . . You've made your commitment, Rosie, and you must honor it now," he told her.

Her father's compelling argument was that she could not turn her back on her obligations as a Catholic wife and Catholic mother. And divorce was then out of the question for a Catholic wife. Deeply conflicted, but a creature of ritual and duty, Rose returned to Joe and the making of a family.

Rose named her next baby Kathleen, soon nicknamed "Kick," which suited her. Still nursing Kick, Rose kept a bedside vigil for two-year-old Jack, who almost died from scarlet fever. A priest was brought for the final sacraments, and, in his own prayers, father Joe had promised to contribute half his current wealth to the church if his child recovered. Joe Sr. kept his promise, but managed to minimize his contribution by first signing over much of his assets to his wife.

A million Americans were preparing to join the American Expeditionary Force in France in World War I, and this included most of Joe's Harvard class of 1912. But not Joe. He turned the management of Columbia Bank to his father and took a job as assistant general manager at the Fore River shipyard, building ships for Bethlehem Steel. It gave him a draft status exempting him from the war—and also the local reputation as a coward. The combination of pressured work and guilt gave him an ulcer.

After the war, Joseph Kennedy became manager of the stock department of the Boston office of Hayden Stone and Company, increasing his fortunes managing other people's money as well as his own. "It's easy to make money in this market," he said as the stocks skyrocketed. "We better get in before they pass a law against it."

Joe soon replaced the Locomobile with a Rolls Royce and a chauffeur. Extravagance came naturally to him. "For the Kennedys," he said, "it's the outhouse or the castle, no in-between." So the family moved to a fourteen-room house with a wraparound porch on an acre in Brookline. To their new neighbors, the Kennedys were still the Catholic family living in a sea of Protestants.

"The children came very fast," explained Rose Kennedy. "And even when I had one in the baby carriage on the porch, there were usually two or three others around. So we used to go to the neighborhood stores while the nursemaid was washing the diapers. . . . I was usually home at lunchtime to see that the children ate properly. And at suppertime, I sat with them and then had my dinner later. My great ambition in those days was to have my children morally, physically, and mentally as perfect as possible."

Rose gave birth to her fifth child—and her third daughter—a little over a year after Kick was born. She named her Eunice, after her own sister. Eunice would become the strongest of the daughters. In a family where women had small expectations except to get married, Eunice came closest to becoming another Kennedy brother.

Joe Kennedy became an independent Wall Street operator in 1922, speculating in both stocks and real estate. Two years later, he was so successful that he was asked to save the Yellow Cab Company from financial raiders. He spent more than a month with a battery of phones in a hotel suite issuing buy and sell orders with brokers scattered around the country, confusing the raiders until the stock price stabilized. And, meanwhile, he multiplied his own fortune.

Rose remembered that when her husband returned home "the children met him—filling the Rolls Royce . . . with heads sticking out of the windows, yelling 'Daddy, we've got another baby!' and other passengers looked as though they thought he already had plenty." Patricia was a month old before her father had even seen her.

Watching her mother cope with a large family and a traveling husband had made a memorable impact on Rose. Her mother, Josie, before her marriage had worked as a seamstress, on the edge of poverty, but had such great expectations that it gave her a haughty, almost regal air. After her marriage to Honey Fitz, reporters called her "the Grand Duchess" because she dressed in black lace and her fingers were heavy with rings. Detached from domestic chores, she lived a life of pride, dignity, arrogance, and emotional indifference. It was later said of her that she found it easier to give God to her children than to give of herself. The same would be said of Rose.

"I would give up everything I've ever been given," said Rose, ". . . and I have been given a lot—health, wealth, family—I would give all of that up, but I would never give up my faith."

———————

ROSE HAD NOTED carefully how her mother required absolute solidarity among all six children. From living with a father whose life was politics, Rose had learned the dire need of family unity to face constant attack. It was said of Rose Kennedy that she had "a mind with the simple, functional strength of a crowbar," and that she was "half Irish charm and all business." Her card file became one of the most publicized card files in the world. It included the names and birthdays and vital statistics about each child, including dates of inoculations. She had an obsession about weight and weighed her children every Saturday night. Children losing weight would be given more food. When they went swimming, they all wore bathing caps of the same color so she could quickly count them.

She trained her children how to stand correctly. "You stand up straight, and keep your right hand away from your body; it makes you look thinner," she told them, "and keep your feet close together, so that your clothes hang right—put your shoulders back, just slightly. . . . Remember how it was with the Greek statues? You see how they stand? See how the clothes flow, just correctly?"

She had additional rules on appearance and conduct for her sons: "Suit-sleeves short enough to have shirt-cuff hang below sleeve one inch. . . . Don't say 'Hi' to people when addressing them, but particularly don't use it when greeting Cardinal Cushing, James Forrestal, Arthur Krock, or the like. Important to keep a daily diary. Always allow the ladies to leave the dining-room first."

"Mother was a strict disciplinarian," remembered her son Ted. "Lunch was at one, prompt. If you were late, you missed the course. Every Thursday we went to the public library to get books. We had tennis lessons, swimming lessons, all of us for seven years. . . . You had to be in the house when the lights went on. We had to pick up our clothes. We had to appear at a meal table five minutes early. We were computerized at an early age, but fortunately by a very compassionate computer.''

Sometimes it was not so compassionate. Rose was quoted as saying that she did not hesitate to use physical punishment with her children, ''because when they're very young, that's the only thing they understand.'' But she added, ''I always spanked my children with their britches on and never hit bare skin.''

If a child was found playing with a sharply pointed instrument, the point was pressed into his skin until he understood thoroughly the painful risks of sharp objects. If he seemed to want to explore the kitchen stove despite commands not to, his finger was held over a lighted burner until he felt a memorable uncomfortable amount of heat. Rose had a ruler in her desk that she often used for spanking, but believing that punishment if needed should be applied at once, to make a lasting connection between cause and effect, she resorted to whatever was within reach.

''I think they said Bobby put pillows so he wouldn't be whacked so hard, but that was always a question, whether he got the pillows in on time or not,'' said Rose Kennedy. But that was just for little things.

Her children knew her as iron-willed, dogmatic. Many years later, John Kennedy confided that he never wanted to have a large family because it involved ''institutionalized living, children in a cell block.''

Physically and temperamentally, John Kennedy may have resembled his mother, but he still felt a distance from her. He later told his good friend William Walton, speaking with great feeling: ''My mother never hugged me . . . never . . . never!!''

A childhood visitor, Henry Fowler, recalled that he never saw Rose even pat a child's head. Rose Kennedy got little physical affection from her own prim mother who, it was said, ''brought gloom into the house the minute she entered it.''

A family friend who knew them all well talked about the Kennedys as a tribe: ''I don't know how much real love there was in their childhood. Certainly they got very little love from their mother, Rose. Even if there is love, when you have a large family, it's hard to share equally, and there are always some who feel deprived. But I don't think there was much love after young Joe.''

It was said of the Kennedy family that the floating base was the father, but the trouble was that the father floated too much. He would always find time for his oldest son, but his mind was often elsewhere. Once he pulled young Joe on a homemade soap-box sled without noticing that the boy had fallen off. Young Joe was not found until later. Still, Joe was always, at heart, the proud, concerned father. His secretary Ethel Turner remembered, "One day, shortly after Joseph Jr. had started school, JPK brought in a few papers and said 'Put these in the Safety Deposit Box. They are Joe's first works of art, and I'd like to show them to him later.' "

ROSE KEPT HER children close to home. She was accustomed to looking toward her extended family to provide most of her social life. Unused to the company of other children, young Joe suddenly found himself in a large kindergarten class in Edward Devotion School. It was said of him then that he "sometimes cried in frustration." He always had been a favorite child; now he was simply part of a crowd.

In the coming year, his brother Jack joined him. With Jack there, young Joe soon emerged from his original nervousness into a cheerful kind of toughness. Having brother Joe at school helped Jack, but not for long. Jack was absent most of the kindergarten year because of assorted illnesses.

As his first grandson, young Joe was clearly the Honey Fitz favorite. "No sweeter personality ever lived," Fitz would say, and add, "What a laugh . . . what a boy! . . . sincerity was spelled all over him. He loved life. He liked to meet people. . . . He was courageous . . . ambitious . . . persistent. He was everything a grandson could ever be." It was said of young Joe, "As a little boy, he threw his heart and soul and every ounce of energy into the job at hand."

Fitz told stories about taking grandson Joe with him when he was campaigning for governor in 1922, a race he lost. Seven-year-old Joe went along with him in Fitz's chauffeur-driven Locomobile to some of the political rallies. Young Joe soon learned to interrupt at appropriate points with applause. Fitz once took Jack backstage at the Boston Opera and Jack remembered how his grandfather captivated everyone. If they were ever stopped by a cop, Fitz would simply say, "I'm John Fitzgerald," and the cop would smile, salute, and wave them on their way. It was his first lesson in political power.

Young Joe and Jack marveled at grandpa Fitz. He could talk for fifteen minutes on any subject at 200 words a minute without letting anyone else speak more than once or twice, and briefly. Grandson Jack would later say of Fitz, "You didn't talk to grandpa. You listened. Grandpa was interested in grandpa."

———————

THE BOYS ENTERED the real world of prejudice late in 1924 when their father transferred them to a posh private school, Noble and Greenough, a bastion of the Boston old rich. Another student, Augustus Soule, recalled the snobbery of the place. "Almost everybody was a Protestant." To call somebody "a Catholic" or "Irish" was an epithet. Their families considered the Kennedys as simply "unsavory."

The boys soon developed their own methods of protection. When young Joe was chased by a covey of his Protestant schoolmates, he ran to a nearby Catholic church, turned and faced them, and said, "This is a shrine! You can't touch me here!" And they didn't.

Joe was soon fully adjusted to his new school. He was bright and quick and robust—surplus energy made him shine. But there was also a darker side to him.

A Cape Cod neighbor observed that he was cracked on the head by the Sisters with a catechism book so often "it was a wonder the top of his head wasn't flatter than a pancake." For him, bloody fights were not an unusual occurrence.

Jack didn't have that kind of aggression. He stayed on the sidelines while his brother fought. Friends claimed that when Jack spoke, they would hear his mother's voice. But the influence went even deeper. He had her sense of calm and distance from others. His mother was concerned how thin he was and saved his extra meat juice. However, young Joe still remained his mother's real pride. He was not only her first child, but she saw in him a younger version of her husband, the one she had fallen in love with—the same potential, and fewer faults. When the school IQ test showed that Jack had a higher intelligence than Joe, the mother refused to believe it, and later insisted to Robert Coughlan, "Joe had the higher."

With so many young noisy children, the family scene was frenetic with bustling maids and governesses trying to keep some order. Rose presided as supervisor, instilling God and good manners. She had a way of keeping chaos out of the dinner table when her husband wasn't home, which was often. But there was still a lot of laughter in the house, a lot of giggling from the girls, and constant horseplay from the older ones. If it was a highly organized home, it was still a happy one.

A chauffeured car delivered the sons to school, and picked them up. Rose Kennedy never appeared at that school. Her husband only occasionally came. But he told the children's nurse, "Miss Cahill, don't hesitate to interrupt me, whether I am at a meeting, in conference, or visiting with friends, if you wish to consult me about my children."

But business was still primary. His classmates at the Boston Latin School had made a remarkable prediction about Joseph Patrick Kennedy in their yearbook—that he would make his fortune "in a very roundabout way." He made most of it by acquiring an expertise in manipulating the rise and fall of specific stocks. There were then few stock market regulations. Joe would buy options on inactively traded stocks, organize a pattern of buying and selling those stocks to create an artificial picture of activity until the public began buying, pushing up the stock price. Then Joe would sell everything and the price would sharply fall, and only the "suckers" would be hurt. Some called it "legalized swindling."

"He was shrewd and tough and self-confident," said Harvard classmate and friend Arthur Goldsmith, "but Joe had a unique sense of timing, a special sense of when to move. . . . And then there was the Kennedy luck."

———

ROBERT FRANCIS KENNEDY was born in November 1925, when Rose was thirty-five—the seventh child and third son. The older sons had been sent by that time to boarding school and Jack later recalled, "The first time I remember meeting Bobby was when he was three-and-a-half, one summer at the Cape."

By then, his father at age thirty-eight had become a motion picture magnate, buying the Film Booking Office, which handled American rights to British movies. Young Joe became even more popular with his classmates when his eleventh birthday party included a private showing of Charlie Chaplin's Gold Rush. But Joe Sr. could give little more than such rewards to his family at that time. He now seemed always en route to London or Paris or Hollywood.

When he was in London, Rose wrote him, "I am praying that I shall see you soon. Do pray too, and go to church, as it is very important in my life that you do just that."

She was particularly concerned, however, about her children's religious training. Rose drilled them on the liturgy of the Mass, and waited at the bottom of the stairs on Sunday morning to hand each of the girls white gloves and a prayer book as they raced away for Sunday Mass. When Patricia had her appendix removed, her mother "walked up and down my room, holding a crucifix, trying to comfort me. She stayed right there—I think it's worse than being operated on, having to watch it."

"We always had a rosary on our beds," said Patricia. "And of course, she'd hear our prayers, and our catechisms, which we learned every week."

Of her boys, she seemed to concentrate her religion on Bobby. "Bobby wanted to be an altar boy; and I used to go in his room, to hear his Latin," said Pat. "Then mother would either come in, or he'd go into mother's room, and show her how much he'd learned."

In Joe's absence, Rose also tried to deal with her children's secular education. "If father gave us the competitive spirit," said Eunice, "mother gave us a love for books and discussion of world issues. She made American history come alive at the dinner table, in our trips to the Old North Church and Concord Bridge. . . . She read countless bedtime stories to us and read to us for hours at a time when we were sick. . . . She took us for walks in our strollers and piled us into the family station wagon to go swimming at Walden Pond or for an outing on Cape Cod."

Jack fondly recalled her history lessons, but had a different overall memory of his mother during their young years, suggesting, perhaps, that Eunice's view may have been clouded by memory and wishful thinking. Jack said that his mother was not around much, that "she was either at Paris fashion shows or on her knees in some church."

———

WHENEVER THE FATHER was there, everything was programmed. The clock dictated daily life. Time, like money, was not to be wasted. Minutes counted because life was too short. They often heard the reminder that Lord Nelson attributed his success to the fact that he was always fifteen minutes ahead of time. Latecomers found their father staring at them over the top of his glasses, and "his eyes would just pitch you right out of the window," said Lem Billings.

"I grew up in a very strict house," John Kennedy later said, "and one where . . . there were no free riders, and everyone was expected to do, give their very best to what they did. . . . There was a constant drive for self-improvement."

Yet Father Joe realized that keen competition had its limits.

"Even when we were six and seven years old Daddy always entered us in public swimming races in the different age categories, so we didn't swim against each other," said Eunice. . . . "The big thing we learned from Daddy: *Win, don't come in second or third, that doesn't count, but win, win, win.*"

Once the young Kennedys were all sprawled around the Hyannis lawn, stretched out on chaise longues, sipping Cokes, sunning. Suddenly the Kennedy chauffeur appeared with the word that their father was landing at the airport. Almost instantly the scene changed. Everybody scrambled. They started playing tennis, football, readying the sailboat. When their father arrived, he surveyed the scene. He liked to see them all busy, and they knew it.

Joe himself preferred a powerboat, but he would boast that his sons would rather sail than eat. They sailed races in the Wianno Junior Class and soon had three sixteen-foot sloops and a larger twenty-five-footer for overnight trips. Young Joe was a gut sailor who seemed to sense the winds just before they came alive, and was willing to take more risks to win than most of his peers would. He soon had a collection of silver cups.

If they came in second in a race, father Kennedy would say, "What was wrong? If the sail was too loose, tighten it, if the hull isn't good enough, change it, but the next time come in first."

"He could be pretty caustic when we lost," said Jack Kennedy. "He scared some of my contemporaries who visited the house."

Eunice compared her father to "a tidal wave" that carried everything with him. But she insisted that he used his many talents to discover and release in other people energy and ability they never knew they had, helping them to achieve heights they never dreamed possible. His son Bobby similarly insisted much later that his father was not the devouring kind, that he did not see himself as a puppetmaster and that he did not visualize himself as a sun around which satellites would circle. "He wanted us, not himself, to be the focal points."

But family retainer Katie Flynn, who had been with the family for years, described "the savage domination of Joe Kennedy over those children. . . . A *savage* domination." "We don't want any crying in this house," the father would say—a proposition his children came to render, somewhat sardonically, as "Kennedys never cry."

John Hersey noted how deeply set this Kennedy tradition was. On Martha's Vineyard, years later, Hersey was there when Rose's grandchildren slept in sleeping bags outside in the chilly, foggy night. "One of the kids came inside . . . fell to the floor, whining and carrying on. His mother stood up and said, 'On your feet!' And the child stood at attention in front of her, and she said, 'Now, you know how to behave. Go out there and behave as you know you should.'

"Well, this seemed to me to be symbolic—to be symbolic of the Kennedy code to endure discomfort and pain . . . that is so powerfully ingrained."

When Bobby broke a toe when an old radiator dropped on it, he was more worried about the family reaction than about his pain. "For almost an hour he bore his anguish, refusing to remove his shoe. When he did, the blood was spotted and Bobby was rushed to a doctor."

What was always understood to the Kennedys was that their codes, their values, were the right ones. The Kennedys were insular and self-contained, a family unit that functioned perfectly well without the outside world.

"They almost didn't need anyone else," said Dave Powers, a long-time friend and aide to Jack. "When they were together, they seemed all the same. You had to get them apart to see how different they were. They lived on each other. Each of them would rather have another Kennedy say, 'Nice play!' than get a compliment from a Pope or a President."

"You hear a lot about togetherness," said Joe Sr. "Long before it became a slogan, I guess we had it." Most of the Kennedy children did not marry before their late twenties. That, in those days, was unusual. They simply preferred staying home. Even after marriage, they still kept together in a family compound.

Some felt that Joe Sr. kept the ancient Irish village concept of family, with all the values and prejudices, with all its power of unity and heroes and legends. "The origin of the Kennedy sense of family is the holy land of Ireland, priest-ridden, superstitious, clannish," wrote Gore Vidal. "It flourished a powerful sense that the family unit is the only unit that could withstand the enemy, as long as each member remained loyal to the others, regarding life as a joint venture between one generation and the next."

"They use such people as are useful to them," said family friend Norman Macdonald, "but they warn, 'Let no one use us.' "

Rose had strong feelings on the togetherness theme. "Children in a large family learn to be alone. Surprisingly, they are better at it than the only child, who gets used to constant attention. They learn to share, to sacrifice their individual desires, to consider the feelings of others, to adjust to adversity. It is no accident that when the Navy was looking for men for PT-boat duty—one of the most difficult assignments in World War II, requiring the closest kind of teamwork—it chose men from large families."

BOTH JOE AND Rose believed in the oldest son as a model and a surrogate. "Most important," Rose said, "was to bring up the oldest one the way you want them all to go. If the oldest one comes in and says 'good night' to his parents or says his prayers in the morning, the younger ones think that's the thing to do and they will do it." She also took Joe to Mass most mornings as a model to the others.

In maintaining this favored peer position, trying to set a good example for the others, Joe had to suppress his anger, and some of his individuality.

At fourteen, young Joe already had found the first love of his life, the thirteen-year-old daughter of a California Unitarian minister visiting an old Cape Cod family with her mother. He wrote to her: "I've been thinking about you ever since you went away. I was going to kiss you good-bye, but you didn't give me any encouragement. When I see you, I will, if you don't mind. Really, I love you a lot."

In his father's pattern, he would soon love a lot of girls a lot. As he grew older, young Joe echoed more of his father's personality and character, including his advertisement of his masculinity, his need to excel, his recklessness, the energy and ambition as well as the sudden fury. When he was irritated or angry, he was even a finger-pointer like his father. He also organized and systematized like him, examined all sides of a question before he made his move. He was better at facts than imagination. And he was always in motion. Jack would write of Joe, years later, "Even when still, there was always a sense of motion forcibly restrained."

The elder Kennedy was still on the move all over the country, all over the world, making more money. What Joe recalled about his Catholic confirmation was not the gifts from his grandfathers—a five-dollar gold piece P.J. gave him, the signet ring he got from Honey Fitz—but rather the fact that his father couldn't be there. For a birthday card for his faraway father, Joe sent this:

> No father was ever so dandy before
> They just don't make them and don't anymore
> For there's only one you, and there hasn't been since
> A dad who could touch you, because you're a prince.

There was a sharp point in the picture on the birthday card. It featured the back of an armchair, only a pipe showing. The father was invisible.

When his father was away, young Joe spent time with his grandparents, the Fitzgeralds, at their third-floor suite at the old Bellevue Hotel. All his grandchildren would refer to Honey Fitz as the greatest grandfather and pal.

Honey Fitz would take young Joe on fishing trips, train trips, to baseball games, to the zoo at Franklin Park. He and Joe would take long walks in Boston Common and visit the historic sites of the American Revolution. It was Fitz, the fifty-four-year-old grandfather, who gave young Joe his first swimming lessons.

Fitz would also tell some of the family history.

His father, Thomas ("Cocky Tom") Fitzgerald, the first Fitzgerald in Boston, a powerfully built man, was a farmer who wanted to pioneer in the American West. He got as far as Lexington, some twenty-five miles from Boston, where he worked as a farmhand. When Tom's wife, Rose Mary, didn't want to live on a farm, he joined his brother in a grocery store.

Had the store failed, Cocky Tom would have headed west and there would have been no Kennedy dynasty. Instead, the store started selling whiskey, and prospered. His wife died pregnant at forty-five, leaving him with nine children, all boys. Cocky Tom died six years later. Honey Fitz, then in Harvard Medical School, quit to become the family provider.

Joe Jr. also went to see his other grandpa, P. J. Kennedy, usually every other Sunday. An impressive-looking man with a handlebar mustache, P.J. had started as a stevedore, soon owned saloons and real estate, became founding director of a bank as well as a ward boss. In good weather, P.J. had come to Brookline, always with a bag of penny candies for the grandchildren. Joe Jr. and Jack remembered him as "a venerable figure, not given to displays of emotion but quietly interested."

Joe Sr. was even too busy in Hollywood to make his own father's funeral. P.J. was well-loved and his funeral was attended by a great mix of people—from bankers to bums. At his death, he had canceled debts from all those who owed him money, and there were many. From Hollywood, Joe Kennedy wrote his son Joe a note of appreciation for representing him at the funeral. "I have heard such lovely reports."

———

THE KENNEDY FAMILY had seen dramatic changes in fortune over the past years. Yet, with all his new millions, and even though he no longer "talked Mick" to the Boston elite, Joseph Kennedy was still a bartender's son. It was time to make a change. He said of Boston, "I felt it was no place to bring up Catholic children."

What he really meant was that he couldn't assimilate socially. The catalyst came when he was blackballed for membership in the Cohasset Yacht Club on Cape Cod—where they spent summer holidays. "Since I think the greatest motivating thing in this world is social status, a far greater force than sexual attraction," Joe told Betty Beale—he was going to move elsewhere and "show those bastards."

He felt, as Rose did, that no matter how "high Irish" she became, no matter how well she rode a horse or spoke French, she could never expect to break the wall into the Brahmin world of Boston. Joe Sr. would one day bristle at being referred to in print as a Boston Irishman: "I was born here. My children were born here. What the hell do I have to do to be an American?"

In September 1927 he took his family, chauffeur, cook, and nurse to their new home in Riverdale, New York. The legend is that they made the trip in a private railway car that awaited them on a siding in Boston and deposited them near their new home. The fact is that it was a standard Pullman in which they occupied all the compartments and most of the seats. They were accompanied by a small mountain of luggage and nursery equipment, and by hampers full of sandwiches, fruit, milk, and Boston cream pie, and eased the trip by having a picnic much of the way. Joe Sr. was the first of his family to leave Boston.

But, socially, the Kennedys in New York were as unacceptable as they were in Boston, because they were still trying to assimilate into Protestant neighborhoods. Riverdale was then more rural than suburban, a town of wealthy estates. The Kennedys lived in a wooded area in a manor house within view of the Hudson. The children's school in Riverdale was similar to the one in Brookline—athletic and progressive. In 1929 the Kennedys settled into an even larger mansion in nearby Bronxville, a redbrick colonial with white columns and twenty rooms on six acres, with a cottage for the gardener and the chauffeur. They soon also owned a fifteen-room white frame Cape Cod house in Hyannis Port, with nine bathrooms, on two acres, right on the beach.

"It's beyond any of my wildest dreams or anybody's dreams that he would succeed so tremendously and so quickly," said Rose Kennedy. "We had one maid, and then we had three or four maids . . . and a couple Rolls Royces, so it just went on and on. And then we had a motor-boat, and we took a trip round the world. Then we met presidents and dukes, kings and queens. So you know, it couldn't last. As I said, it was perfect existence for anybody to expect in this world."

Robert Coughlan, who ghosted almost all of Rose Kennedy's autobiography, once asked her: "Of all these thousands and thousands of people you've met and had association with, who stands out most in your mind?"

"We never grew very intimate with any of them. Joe had his own friends . . . and he'd keep them on his own personal payroll. He would always have someone with him, someone he could trust."

It was significant that all the "friends" she mentioned for herself and her husband were on their payroll. Moreover, although Rose had an assortment of acquaintances in the Pondfield Road neighborhood and St. Joseph's parish, there seem to have been no friends. Certainly no one cultivated her. Proper Bronxville, white-Anglo-Saxon-Protestant and wealthy, was far more amused than impressed. Their general feeling about the Kennedys was: "How unchic, how Irish Catholic!"

It was fortunate for Rose that she had an inner self-sufficiency. In fact, she loved to be alone. Her husband, on the other hand, always needed people. So did his sons. But to Joe, who struggled as an outsider in a Protestant world, his family would remain the place where he would always belong.

And the family kept growing. In 1928, Jean was born. Young Joe was her godfather. Rose had gone back to Boston to have the child, the first of her children to be born in a hospital. "My husband had all my meals sent to me from the Ritz in a taxi. So every day if I had any guest in they used to rave about the food in the hospital."

Jean, like the other daughters, was relegated to Rose's supervision. Most of the girls later expressed resentment at being second-class to the boys in the family. But while there were several rebels among the girls, including Jean, there were none among the boys. The risks of disapproval were too great. Everything depended on it.

In the ten years they lived in Bronxville, the elder Kennedy insisted to Sargent Shriver that he ate dinner at home with his family every single night. But that was one of his myths. His office was now in New York, but his business was with the world, and he still traveled widely.

"I never traveled very much with my husband on long trips . . . there were no airplanes like today, and California was three days and two nights from Boston . . . if the children got a cold or fever, they could be dead and buried before I could get back."

And Joe was more than happy to be on his own.

"Joe knew what to use his money for . . . how to have fun with it," said Henry Luce, the founder of Time-Life. "Joe bought all those houses. He made all of those movies. He played golf and whatnot. He understood about buying himself positions in government. . . . Most businessmen are pretty stupid about that. It doesn't cost you very much to buy those jobs. He even knew how to handle all those church appointments.

"There's one more thing that he knew about money," added Luce. "He knew how to use money to push his children along, as fast as they could be pushed. What was his secret with his children? That's the great mystery. How did he get them all so set on the political line? Of course you know he intended for Joe Jr. to be President. He told me once that he didn't think Jack would get very far and indicated he wasn't very bright. But he never believed in starting his kids at the bottom. He said, 'I'll send my girls to Catholic schools and colleges to believe, but I'll send my men to the marketplace to know better.' "

Joe called Hollywood "a gold mine." And so it was, for a while. He made a series of cheap, second-rate action films that sold well. Then, in November 1927, he met Gloria Swanson, probably the sexiest, most glamorous actress in Hollywood. Kennedy was determined to absorb her, economically, artistically, and physically. It hardly mattered that she was already married to a French marquis.

In a seduction scene in her hotel suite—which he had filled with orchids—he overcame her protestations with, "No longer, no longer, *now!*" Yet it was hardly a rape, as one writer suggested. Swanson did not object too much, because Joe had painted the bright promise of a financial partnership. If there was a later rape, it was only of her finances.

For Joe, getting Gloria was the brass ring, the ultimate, the most celebrated actress of her time. It was not surprising that this feeling would be echoed by Jack years later—and even more so by Bobby—in their affair with Marilyn Monroe.

Swanson soon became so intimate with his family that when Jack was nine, he sent "Aunt Gloria" a letter thanking her for the rocking horse.

In her autobiography, Swanson wrote, "He didn't resemble any banker I knew. His suit was too bulky, and the knot of his tie was not pushed up tight. With his spectacles and prominent chin, he looked like any average, working-class person's uncle . . . he still retained a certain boyishness. I usually got bored to death talking about pictures, but not with him. He had the most ambitious view of pictures I've ever encountered; in fact, he seemed to see them precisely as a means of attaining not only wealth but also power. Like his father and his father-in-law, whom he mentioned over and over again, he was intrigued by the manipulation of people and events."

One evening Joe Kennedy told Swanson that he had a surprise for her and unveiled a portrait depicting himself the way he must have told the artist he wanted to look—"severe and elegant, very much the chairman of the board, perhaps even a touch of royal family. I had to smile, to see Joe's face glow with pleasure as he studied this other self from his seat on the couch. . . . That night was the first time I truly believed that Joe's dream of power exceeded far beyond that of being president of some huge corporation. He lingered before the painting, and said he was planning to open an office in Washington, and probably build a house there, near the real figures of power in this country."

That same day, Joe "blurted out that he had been faithful to me. 'How can we be faithful, Joe? We're both married.' And he stunned me by telling me proudly that there had been no Kennedy baby that year. What he wanted more than anything, he continued, was for us to have a child. 'You can't ask that of me,' I said. 'I refuse to discuss it.' "

In November 1928, Kennedy decided to make a monumental epic movie starring Swanson, called *Queen Kelly*. It was a disaster. Celebrated director Erich von Stroheim seemed to be filming forever and dipping endlessly into the Kennedy millions. *Queen Kelly* was too lurid, too long, and too dull, and was never released in this country.

Gloria Swanson recorded how Kennedy reacted to their film's failure. She said he sounded like "a wounded animal whimpering in a trap . . . little high-pitched sounds escaped from his rigid body. Then his voice became quiet and controlled and he said, 'I've never had a failure in my life!' "

The film's failure seemed to have no obvious impact on the Kennedy-Swanson romance. Swanson filed for divorce from the Marquis Henri de la Falaise de la Coudraye, known as "Hank." Then Joe visited Cardinal O'Connell to try to dissolve his marriage with Rose so he could marry the movie star, but the Cardinal refused. Kennedy then asked Church permission to live apart from his wife so he could live with Swanson. The Cardinal insisted this was impossible.

In her autobiography, Gloria Swanson told of a visit from the Cardinal. "I am here to tell you to stop seeing Joseph Kennedy. Each time you see him you become an occasion of sin for him."

Gloria suggested that he tell this to Joseph Kennedy.

"I think only a Roman Catholic could possibly describe how you could be amoral and still religious . . . by penitence. . . . It was . . . the way of his world," said Arthur Krock. "The fact that Kennedy had girls around as houseguests. . . . It never bothered me at all, because Rose acted as if they didn't exist, and that was her business, not mine."

Gloria arrived in Hyannis Port in August 1929, in a Curtiss amphibian plane that flew her up from the Hudson River in New York City. Peering neighbors remembered that she was flawlessly coiffed despite the breeze. Bringing her home to his family was more than a matter of pride. It was as if Joe dared his wife to say anything. That evening Joe took his wife and Gloria to an elegant local supper club, La Goleta, and introduced Miss Swanson as his most important business associate, and Rose's friend. Rose even arranged for her parents to visit—it was their fortieth anniversary—to meet Gloria. Of Rose Kennedy, Swanson wondered whether she was "a saint or a fool or just a better actress than I was."

Rose's rationale was simple: she didn't want to lose her husband, her family, her way of life. This, then, was a price she was willing to pay. Gloria even traveled to Europe with them. Rose explained that Joe and Gloria had a lot of work to do aboard ship, so "I stepped aside."

But nobody was fooled. Gossip columnist Hedda Hopper speculated in print, "It must have been a mighty trying trip for Mrs. Kennedy. I often wondered how she weathered it."

Rose's daughter Eunice insisted to Robert Coughlan that her mother "never heard about this supposed romancing until twenty years later. There was never any jealousy by Mother about Gloria Swanson." In his notes on the interview, Coughlan wrote, "This is absurd."

Adept at denial, Rose Kennedy also insisted that "we never had a husband-and-wife fight. It was not difficult as we had the same religious background. Irish-Americans of the third generation. Our education was similar. We were about the same age, we liked the same people, we enjoyed athletics, college football games, we like symphony concerts and we had a similar political background, and enjoyed meeting stimulating people. We never fussed about non-essentials, which I think some people do."

Eunice didn't buy this. "Do you really believe that everyone will believe that you and Dad never had one fight during all the years of your marriage?"

But Rose was adamant. "He was wonderful to me. . . . He let me go on trips whenever I wanted to. . . . When we went to a party he would come home and say, 'You were the best-looking woman there . . . you stole the show.' He had sent her an anniversary cable calling her "the eighth wonder of the world."

Friend and neighbor Nancy Coleman once asked Rose, "Haven't you showed iciness to your husband?"

"Yes, I have," Rose replied. "And I made him pay for that iciness—I made him give me everything I want: clothes, jewels, and everything else. You have to learn how to use that iciness."

She later enumerated "some of the ecstasies" in her marriage: "Oh, little things like getting my first mink coat, reading in the newspaper that my husband was worth fifty, or was it a hundred million dollars."

But then she added, "Whenever I wanted to do anything, I always could do it. . . . There never was anything to fight about. . . . I was really spoiled and really perfectly happy, as he was."

Such was the illusion.

Joe and Rose gradually led separate lives and the children seldom saw them together. When one was home, the other was usually traveling.

The children, years later, asked her why they had not spent more time together.

Just being together wasn't the meaning of marriage, she said, and added that they had enriched each other by working together in close relationship for their mutual good.

"I think it's very selfish of a woman sometimes to demand or be cross with her husband when he doesn't come home," Rose later added. "He never felt that he had to get home. . . . If I were ill, if I had a temperature, I never would tell him. If he went to California, I would never say, Joe Jr.'s got a temperature of a hundred, and have him worried." When her children were grown and gone, she even had an emergency appendectomy without notifying her husband.

Later, she came to regret her behavior. "I was always calm and collected, and never complaining—that was a great mistake. A lot of things I wanted to complain about. I resent that."

Rose was both a product of her era and a product of her home: a prim mother and a philandering father. Having suffered the scandal of her father and Toodles Ryan, her husband's flagrant affairs were not unexpected. This image of marriage was deeply embedded in the children—especially the boys—and helped destroy some of their own marriages.

———

GLORIA SWANSON RETURNED to Hyannis with Joe several times in 1929. Neighbor Nancy Coleman, "Aunt Nan," recalled how Joe brought Gloria into the house while Rose was still there. But the next year Rose Kennedy went off to Paris for her fashion shows during Gloria visits. Aunt Nan observed Joe's perfect timing. "Almost to the second . . . Rose Kennedy would be driving out to the airport in her Rolls Royce, and, almost simultaneously, Joe Kennedy would be driving in with Gloria Swanson and move into the big house. . . . The children were still home. . . . Gloria Swanson would stay in a guest-room."

They were not always the most discreet. On one visit, Joe and Gloria decided they wanted to spend a few hours by themselves on the family sailboat. Ironically, it was named after his wife, Rose Elizabeth.

A Kennedy neighbor later revealed that twelve-year-old Jack had hidden himself below deck. When Jack peeked up and saw what was happening between his father and "Aunt" Gloria, the horrified, bewildered boy jumped overboard and started swimming out to sea. His father dove in after him and rescued his son. Gloria left for New York soon afterward.

For Jack, the impact of what he saw was surely enormous, and lifelong. Besides Gloria, there was a small parade of women, all young, all attractive, who arrived at their home at different times with their father. Young Joe and the other sons learned to consider their father's promiscuity as an inherent masculine right.

For Kennedy Sr., as later with his sons, women were a game and a challenge. He saw them as trophies for display, and the excitement of the chase and the challenge never stopped. The wife at home was put on a pedestal, while other women were available for private pleasure. There was little question that the elder Kennedy enjoyed himself fully with little guilt. In everything, he had always made his own rules.

To give his prolific affairs some cover of discretion, Joe Sr. used a "beard," his old sidekick and golfing partner, Joseph Francis Timilty. A bachelor, Timilty came with Kennedy, ostensibly as the date for any woman his friend was squiring on the town that night. Timilty, a former Boston police chief, was a constant fixture at Hyannis and Palm Beach. He was later assigned to help young Joe get his baptism into politics. An intimate friend, Dr. Paul O'Leary, once asked the elder Kennedy, "Joe, now that the kids are growing up and noticing things, what are you going to tell them if they ask you about your outside extramarital activities?" "They won't ask me," Joe replied with complacency.

"But suppose they do?"

Joe's eyes became cold. "Well, if they do, I'll tell them to mind their own goddamn business."

The father had set an example. The Kennedy brothers would expect their wives to put up with everything "as long as the fame and glory are pouring in."

Joseph Kennedy had a movie studio in the Kennedy basement where they showed the latest films once a week for family and friends. "Along the bottom-stairs, they had three wicker chairs in the back, where the old man would sit with two people," Nancy Coleman recalled. "In the front seats, before him, everybody else sat. The servants would come in, and maybe sit on the sides. Rose Kennedy would always come in late, and usually sit on the side with the servants. She never sat up in the wicker chairs with her husband. He'd always pick a pretty girl to sit on each side of him. It was not an invitation any of them relished because it became a well-circulated fact that anyone sitting alongside Joe Kennedy could expect to get her pretty bottom pinched, and often. One young woman ruefully showed her friends that her bottom had been pinched black and blue."

Told of another incident of his father chasing a young woman at a racetrack, Jack Kennedy later said, "When I'm sixty, I hope I'm just like my father."

The boys learned that their grandfather Honey Fitz, in his sixties, was similarly active with young girls. His niece remembered that he had taken her to the theater, put his hand on her thigh, and started exploring elsewhere until she kicked him in the shins.

————————

EDWARD MOORE KENNEDY ("Teddy") was born in February 1932. Rose was then forty-one, her husband forty-three.

"Joe was not necessarily around for the births of the children, something a woman has to go through, which is difficult," said Rose. "When Ted was born, I told Joe to go to Palm Beach for his regular holiday, his rest and relaxation. I was with my parents, perfectly happy and well cared for. When all was over, we notified him, he came home.

"People said I was crazy to have children after the age of forty. . . . People said why do you want to have nine children, you have had eight. You are over forty years old and you will be all tired out and you will lose your figure and looks, why do you want to pay any attention to those priests?

"And it turned out to be a stroke of genius. Yes it did, as Fate decreed that all my other sons were taken. That, of course, is a puzzle—is a question, too—why God took three sons who were equipped and wanted to work for the government and for humanity, and left my daughter who is incapacitated. But, as I said, that is one of those things about life we cannot understand—God's ways we can't always understand."

————

JOHN KENNEDY, THEN almost fifteen years old, wrote, "Dear Mother, It is the night before exams so I will write you Wednesday. Lots of Love. P.S. Can I be Godfather to the baby." A month later, Jack arrived in a dark blue suit at his brother's baptism to make the Profession of Faith.

Years later, Teddy would keep that letter framed on his office wall.

"You wonder if the mother and father aren't quite tired when the ninth one comes along," said Rose Kennedy. "There were seventeen years between my oldest and youngest child, and I had been telling bedtime stories for twenty years. When you have older brothers and sisters, they're the ones that seem to be more important in a family, and always get the best rooms and the first choice of boats and all those kinds of things, but Ted never seemed to resent it.

"I admit that with Teddy I did things a little differently than I did with the other children," Rose later said. "He was my baby and, I think every mother will understand this, I tried to keep him my baby." Teddy's sisters also seem to have often mothered him. Ted once commented, "It was like having an army of mothers around me. While it seemed I could never do anything right with my brothers, I could never do anything wrong so far as my sisters were concerned."

Someone coined an awful phrase for the chubby little boy, "Tubby Teddy." In fact, later, he often signed his childhood letters "Fat Ted."

Yet behind his cheerfulness was a quick temper. Teasing Teddy was a ritual with his older brothers. Every time he poked his head into a brother's room, he would be hit with a pillow. Bobby, five years older, who was watchful of his oversize baby brother, did his own share of teasing him, but was always there to help.

One of Joe Jr.'s friends remembered driving to the Cape with him. "The minute we got out of the car, Teddy came running up. Joe grabbed him, kissed him like a father would, and hoisted him up on his shoulder. They were like father and son." Whenever Joe returned home from school, the first room he would visit was Teddy's. Joe felt less responsibility as a role model for Teddy because of the age gap—so he could relax and enjoy him.

It was young Joe who had decided to call the family's new sixteen-foot sloop *Onemore* after his youngest brother. Ted made his first trip on that sailboat as an infant, wrapped in blankets. When Teddy was seven years old, he begged to be allowed to sail with brother Joe. It was a race and Joe told Teddy to pull in the jib. Ted didn't know what he was talking about, and the other boats were getting farther ahead. Joe suddenly leaped up, and grabbed the jib, seized Teddy by the pants, and threw him into the water. "I was scared to death practically," said Teddy. "I then felt his hands grab my shirt, and he lifted me onto the boat. We continued the race, and came in second. He got very, very mad in the race."

On the way home from the pier, Joe told Teddy to be quiet about what happened. He had a family image to maintain for his father.

———

WHEN HER HUSBAND happened to be home from his travels, Mrs. Kennedy became invisible, acted almost like a servant. "A quiet maid in the background," observed a neighbor.

"When he was there," said Eunice, "it was his personality that dominated. Our mother . . . let him take over." And, when Mrs. Kennedy interrupted to ask one of the older children a question, she would often be ignored.

"Jack loved his mother and he tried to stand up for her against the old man," said a family friend. "But on the other hand he recognized that she'd been beaten down so long that she'd become sort of empty. I think it colored his idea of what women were, and what relationships with the opposite sex were all about."

"My mother is a nothing," Jack once told his friend, Mary Gimbel.

But he also had said, "She was the glue that held our family together."

Rose said she put up her separate little cottage to get away from the noise of a large family, "because all my life I have had a great many people around me." It was a single prefabricated room with a small desk and a porch "where I could go and write, or rest, or read in peace and comfort." She called it a place of study and prayer. In an odd way, Rose had somehow combined marriage and the convent. She had her responsibilities as a Catholic wife, but she also had this cottage as her private chapel.

————

ON WEEKENDS, WHEN he was home, the father would often take his children to ride through the woods of Sleepy Hollow, or to take some of them to lunch at Longchamps in New York City and a movie at Radio City Music Hall. His Sunday-afternoon ritual included a long afternoon walk with his wife.

The children with problems most often came to him for solutions—not to their mother. In fact, nurse Luella Hennessey remembered his telling her to bring all the children's complaints to him, not to Mrs. Kennedy. They admired him, feared him, but also adored him. They counted on him to pick them up, hug and kiss them. When they did something wrong, he was the one to forgive them and hold them.

Whenever their father was available, "the boys would listen intently to his every word; to be with him, to talk with him, to do things with him—all that was pleasure beyond imagining," recalled Rose's lifelong friend Marie Greene.

And when he was away, all of them would write him about everything they were doing and thinking and how much they missed him and wanted him to hurry home. And he would answer every letter with the same warmth.

Typical was this complaining letter from his son Jack:

My recent allowance is forty cents. This I used for aeroplanes and other playthings of childhood, but now I am a scout and I put away my childish things. Before I would spend twenty cents of my forty cent allowance and in five minutes I would have empty pockets and nothing to gain and twenty cents to lose . . . and so I put in my plea for a raise of thirty cents.

When Joe and Jack had the measles, they received a telegram: "I have had them myself and I know how you feel. . . . Visit me in California and I will give you a good horse and a complete outfit to use. Your pal, Tom Mix." Tom Mix was then the most popular cowboy in the movies. Their Dad, of course, had arranged the telegram.

As the children grew, Rose became an even more insatiable traveler. Her father had once taken her on a whirlwind tour of Europe before enrolling her in the convent school. Later "Rambling Rose" traveled with him to South America, playing piano for him while he sang "Sweet Adeline." The Boston *Herald* wrote that Honey Fitz was the only man who could sing that song sober and get away with it.

All this gave Rose an excitement for travel she never lost, and now that she had plenty of nursemaids and other servants, and her husband's encouragement, she took a long trip abroad after the birth of every baby, and often in between. The timing of her trips says a lot about her emotional relationships with her children. She usually traveled with her sister Agnes. Starting in 1929, Rose went abroad seventeen times in the next seven years.

"Mr. Kennedy used to like to go on a boat of the United States line, and go on the same ship every year," she said. "I used to like to go on a different ship; the German line, French line, the British line. Because I like to experience different things, eat different foods. I never got into any difficulty.

"If I wanted to go someplace after he got home," she added, "I would go. It worked out very well. . . . While I was gone, the children had the measles, but he managed to get them through that. He never complained but took care of them very adequately, so I was saved any bother."

———

IT WAS SAID of the Kennedys that they were responsible "for stimulating an obsessive public curiosity about themselves."

"Not our idea," said Rose Kennedy. But the fact was that the Kennedys were constantly sending clippings of themselves to each other, were keenly conscious of public image. Joe Kennedy allied himself early to Arthur Krock to advise about their public relations. The family had a strong sense of the power of publicity long before it was commonly understood outside of Hollywood. But Rose became fearful of this publicity after the kidnapping of the Lindbergh baby in 1932, and she asked Time-Life publisher Henry Luce to feature them less often in his magazines.

When Joe was away, it was Joe Jr., bright and winning and without fear, with a strong sense of ownership and responsibility, who played father substitute.

It put him on a strange plateau. Joe Jr. somehow was expected to exact obedience from his younger brothers and sisters and maintain the approval of his parents. Knowing how much his mother depended on him, he had learned to suppress his natural rage and jealousy, walling off a part of himself.

But this responsibility brought with it a premature maturity and an obvious tension. The family record is that Joe obeyed his parents completely, fully accepted their direction and discipline. "His friends thought him oddly lonely at times, and they were touched at the way he would slip away from the chaos of his own home, to sit eating and talking with their parents."

Young Joe was generally gentle and considerate with his sisters, but he could be cruel with Jack. He would pitch a baseball so hard to him that his younger brother often winced and dropped the ball. He would slam a football into Jack's stomach so forcefully that Jack often doubled up in pain, and Joe would walk away laughing. He and Jack once raced their bikes around the block in the front of their house, in opposite directions, on a collision course at the finish line. Jack went to the hospital for twenty-eight stitches, while Joe escaped without a scratch. "Jack always lost in these contests; he always kept trying."

The fights were so fearful that the walls would shake, frightening the smaller children, "especially Bobby, who stood crying with his hands over his ears." Bobby would never forget it.

"They tried to knock each other's brains out," said family friend Ralph Horton.

In the family dynamics, Jack was determined to assert himself. Meanwhile, Joe's mean streak deepened, perhaps partly because Jack would not stay the younger weakling. Jack often had an impulsive courage.

"Joe's appetite was enormous; he liked roast-beef and Margaret's orange-meringue, but most of all he liked chocolate pie," Hank Searls reported. "When that was served for dinner, he would flash the grin at a maid, and ask for his piece early, just to look at it. It would be placed on display by his plate. One noon, Jack snatched it, stuffed it into his mouth, and took off at a dead run. With Joe in pursuit, he dived off the breakwater into Lewis Bay. Joe waited, in implacable anger, until his brother finally emerged, shivering with cold, and then there was a free-swinging brawl, for keeps. The lesson was clear to Jack: To embarrass young Joe before an audience was a dangerous affair."

In "the Kennedy clan"—a term Joe Jr. had started using—seniority alone among the boys was not the ultimate test of leadership. Bravery was. Winning was. Jack's later thesis was that Joe Jr. was not dominant in the family because he was the oldest son but because he was the strongest. If he, Jack, could prove stronger and braver, then he believed he would replace Joe's leadership in the family. And he knew Joe sensed that he was resourceful and cunning enough to be a constant threat.

2

SCHOOL AND SEX

The Choate School is situated in the beautiful rolling countryside of central Connecticut, with eighteen tennis courts, Choate is a prestigious boys' preparatory school, founded in 1896 by Episcopalians. Modeled after Eton College, Choate promises parents that the school will provide "efficient teaching, manly discipline, systematic exercise and association with boys of purpose."

Arriving at Choate in September 1929, at the age of fourteen, young Joe found himself in a sea of favorite sons. Instead of being in the center of the circle, as he was at home, he was on the far fringe. This was primarily a Protestant school, and the few Catholics were not warmly embraced. Joe was lonely. He missed his family, his father's constant support and affection, and the adoration of his sisters and the fun with his brothers. Here he was hazed, derided, and, what was worse, often overlooked.

His academic beginnings were not brilliant. Joe barely passed French, did poorly in Latin, only a little better in English. The one subject in which he did well was algebra. The next semester, he improved somewhat, despite a D in public speaking. His report indicated, "Joe is bright enough to finish quickly his day's assignment . . . but he is too easily satisfied, and does not go that second mile that would make him a real student. Joe is still somewhat superficially childish. We like Joe so much that we want his best, and Joe himself really wants to give it to us."

If Joe Jr. didn't, his father would correct that. From Joe Sr. came a continuous stream of encouraging letters that provided incentive: he could not disappoint his father.

Joe soon acclimated to Choate. He learned to utilize both his natural aggression and affability, and developed a flair for student politics. He was described by classmates as "a hell of a guy!" The headmaster described Joe as "one of the most worthwhile people in the world. He has a high Academic Quotient, big heart and a young boy's way of doing things. I am betting on him a hundred percent."

"Joe was the golden guy," said the headmaster's son, Seymour St. John. "He was big, athletic, he was a good student, disciplined, did everything right. On the Student Council. Just a great guy. On the football team. You know, that all-around combination. He was one of the strong people in the school."

What was surprising was that his parents—with all their obvious and declared love for him—never came to visit him at Choate. The headmaster finally wrote to Mr. Kennedy how much Joe hoped he would come to visit on Father's Day, "though Joe and I understand how it is." The father, however, was still migrating to California, making movies and money. Joe Jr. never reprimanded his father, but to the absent Rose he delivered one of his rare caustic comments. "I can easily understand how busy you must be buying antiques and clothes."

While her husband was elsewhere, and could not veto the idea of a Catholic prep school, Rose sent Jack to Canterbury, twenty-five miles away—the only Catholic school he ever attended. He wrote her that he expected to return home "quite pius [sic]."

Younger and shyer than Joe, Jack found the transition to boarding school even more difficult. He was even lonelier than Joe had been. What had inspired Joe and gave him more determination to survive was the special incentive he received from his father. Jack had less of everything, and to complicate matters he was now sick more often.

Jack wrote his uncle that "it's a pretty place but I was pretty homesick the first night. . . . You have a whole lot of religion and the studies are pretty hard. The only time you can get out of here is to see the Harvard–Yale."

Young Joe visited Jack, at his father's request, reported that Jack seemed all right, but still didn't have a roommate. Jack's grades were also poor. After Joe left, Jack wrote home: "Send me up a pair of gray pants like Joe's please."

Rose would later say of Jack that the reason he wasn't as good a student as Joe was that he wasn't as disciplined. "He did the things he liked to. Reading a lot of books and a lot of history."

Jack was taken out of Canterbury School after an appendicitis operation, and never returned. At home, he was hospitalized for further tests. The concern then was that he had anemia.

Longtime friend Kay Halle recalled that father Joe took her with him to visit Jack. "He couldn't have been more than twelve or thirteen. Jack was lying in bed, very pale, which highlighted the freckles across his nose. He was so surrounded by books I could hardly see him. I was very impressed, as at that point this very young child was reading '*The World Crisis*,' by Winston Churchill."

WHEN HE WAS fourteen, Jack followed Joe to Choate in 1931. The start was not a happy time for him. In a sense, it was even worse than Canterbury. At Choate, with its strict social standards, there were no shortcuts to popularity or prominence. You had to measure up the hard way. What made it worse was that the shadow of his brother loomed large. And so, the expectations for Jack by faculty and students seemed unreachable.

"It reminds me a little bit of my older brother and myself," said Seymour St. John. "I was the middle son, as Jack was. Jack came along. He was scrawny, didn't have the size of Joe, and that hurt him because . . . he had all the ambition. He wanted to be at the top. But he had no way of getting there, no easy way. . . . He did poorly in his studies. . . . He wasn't organized."

A senior proctor, Richard Pinkham, was assigned to show Jack around the Choate campus and explain some of the basic rules and customs. As Jack tagged along and listened, Pinkham formed a mediocre impression of him. Joe Jr. was becoming a campus celebrity, a star, "and here was this scrawny kid brother who didn't seem to have much. We had standards; it was a selective school, and by Choate standards he was unimpressive."

"I never had that drive at Choate," Jack admitted. "I was just a drifter there."

JACK DID MAKE an attempt at celebrity by running for freshman class president—but he ended far down in the field of twenty-nine.

Consciously or subconsciously, in his heightened rebellion, knowing he could not duplicate his brother's status, Jack now took the opposite course. Where Joe was impulsive, Jack became more cautious. If Joe was serious at school, Jack became lazy. If Joe was neat, Jack was sloppy.

"I regard the matter of neatness or lack of it on Jack's part as quite symbolic," reported housemaster J. J. Maher, "for he is casual and disorderly in almost all of his organization projects. Jack studies at the last minute, keeps appointments late, has little sense of material value, and can seldom locate his possessions."

"My brother is the efficient one in the family," Jack admitted, "and I am the boy who doesn't get things done. . . . If my brother were not so efficient, it would be easier for me to be efficient. He does it so much better than I do."

There was a kind of melancholy in his admission.

"Everybody admired him, respected him, and liked him," said Seymour St. John of Joe. "But Jack, nobody really admired what he did nor respected what he did, but they liked his personality. When he flashed his smile, he could charm a bird off a tree. He was a very appealing kind of guy."

His Choate transcript shows that JFK flunked Latin and French. In a letter to the school, Jack's father wrote that his son's "happy-go-lucky feeling doesn't fare well."

To his father, Jack wrote: "My studies are going pretty hard. . . . Do you think you can come up some week-end. It would be swell if you could come up for Father's weekend which is about the 28 of October."

Once again, the father never came.

It was not that his feeling for his sons had lessened. It never would. But his time was severely limited. He could only give his children short intense spurts of himself. In a crisis, he was always there. Mrs. Kennedy never visited Jack at Choate, or any other school he attended. She was relishing her privacy and her travels. There were so many children. Her concentration was on the pragmatic and more practical dynamics of their lives. As far as Jack was concerned, Rose would always worry about his low weight.

Jack was then at a low ebb. He was keenly conscious of the small expectations his parents had for his future—and it is likely that Jack was beginning to feel the pressure from them. To make matters worse, his older brother again stole the family spotlight by acting as chauffeur in the family Rolls Royce for a famous aviator in a town parade. Joe Jr. afterward announced that he too would one day be a famous pilot.

If ever John Kennedy needed a friend, he needed one now, and so did Kirk LeMoyne Billings.

It is difficult to fully understand the character of Jack Kennedy without knowing the quality of his relationship with Lem Billings. Jack, like all his brothers, would never have many intimate, personal friends, but Lem Billings would serve as a battalion.

Like Jack, Lem was also a second son, whose older brother had achieved an outstanding record at Choate, and Lem felt a similar family pressure. This, as much as anything, initially brought them closer together.

In many ways, Billings was a counterpoint to Kennedy: no money, unattractive to women, and uninterested in them. He traced his ancestry to the Mayflower. His mother's family included a French physician and a noted abolitionist who founded several colleges for blacks in Memphis. Lem's father, a founder of the Children's Hospital in Pittsburgh, died during the Depression after losing the family funds.

Lem was a scholarship student, sixteen years old, with a piercing, prissy, nasal voice that turned "yes" into "yas," and didn't seem to fit his six-foot-two, 175-pound frame. He was strong but not coordinated.

Jack called Lem "Billy" (because they discovered they both had liked boys' books about a mischievous goat named Billy Whiskers) as well as "Lemmer," "Leem," or "Moynie," and sometimes "Le-Moan," "Delemma," or "The Walking Ape Man." Lem called Jack "Johnny" or "Ken" or "Kenadosus." A 1935 yearbook photograph of them roughhousing in a snowdrift was captioned "Leem and Rat-Face."

Jack inscribed one of his photographs: "To Lem, A neat guy and a swell gent your aces with me Best Luck Now + Always You horse's ass."

Undeniably, Lem was a mama's boy. Ethel Kennedy later reminisced that "his eyes filled with tears when he spoke of his mother. And she doted on him: when Lem arrived home, all her social obligations were automatically canceled so she could be at his beck and call." Lem designed and made a pair of shoes for his mother with the tallest heels ever manufactured.

"Lem was clearly *very* effeminate," said one of Jack's close friends, who quickly added, "I don't know whether or not he was homosexual." Others, like George Terrien, who married Ethel Kennedy's sister and knew Billings well, insisted that Billings was, indeed, gay, and that "everybody knew . . . everyone!"

In his early Choate years, Jack was hardly the stereotypical male either. "He *pretended* to be macho," said good friend Henry James. "He worked hard at it . . . I think Jack had more of the feminine in him than he'd ever admit—he was heartily *ashamed* of them, they were a mark of effeminacy, of weakness which he wouldn't acknowledge. I think all that macho stuff was compensation—all that chasing after women—compensation for something that he hadn't got, which his brother Joe had. Joe was truly macho, truly a man's man. Jack was not. Jack was a woman's man *and* a man's man."

Lem and Jack soon roomed together. What made the Kennedy-Billings relationship even more unusual is that not only did they room together, but Billings even postponed his own graduation to room with Jack for another year.

One of those who strongly recommended that they should not room together was housemaster John J. Maher. Irritated by their "silly and giggling" intimacy, especially in the showers, he felt that "they cannot regain a position of respect . . . among the boys on my corridor." He was overruled.

A later college classmate and sailing companion of Jack described Lem as "a toady . . . most unpleasant . . . not very bright . . . and I never could see what Jack saw in him."

What Jack saw in Lem was uncritical friendship, absolute loyalty and, most of all, adoration and love. What also connected them was a sense of fun. Jack had the wit and Lem the ready energy and a passionate willingness to do whatever necessary. But, most paramount, was that Jack could talk to Billings more intimately than he could talk to his brothers.

The phrase several friends used in describing the Billings-Jack relationship was that Lem "glued himself to Jack." Lem was so possessive about Jack that he tagged along with Jack and his date, even though he didn't have his own date during Choate's Festivities Weekend. A friend described Lem as "sitting alone in a corner while Jack and his date smooched in his car."

For a man who only wrote a single letter of courtship to his future wife, Jack Kennedy later wrote hundreds of letters to Billings, confiding in him in a way that he never did with anyone else. What brought them together even closer was a full month's summer vacation touring Europe. Later, when Kennedy went into politics, Billings was there to volunteer in each campaign. When Kennedy became President, Billings was his only friend who had his own room in the White House where he kept his clothes, invariably arriving on weekends. When the President made any foreign trips, Lem usually went with him.

Jack invariably brought Lem home to Hyannis and Palm Beach whenever he returned for holidays and summers.

"I was ten months old and Jack was sixteen when he brought his roommate down from Choate to see us in Palm Beach," said Ted Kennedy. "As Dad liked to say, with some exasperation, Lem Billings and his battered suitcase arrived that day and never really left."

Patricia also commented later, "Actually, I was three years old before it dawned on me that Lem wasn't one more older brother. . . . He kept more clothes than Jack did in the closets at Hyannis Port, and, in self-defense, Mother said she'd have to sew on Lem Billings labels, too."

At a costume party at Wianno Yacht Club in Hyannis, Jack decided to dress up as Mahatma Gandhi, and LeMoyne and four girls were costumed as Gandhi's wives. "Getting Lem to dress as a wife was hilarious," said Nancy Coleman. "He couldn't keep his glasses in place and he was helpless without them. The sheet he was wrapped in slipped in every direction. To make matters worse, we had to hide his belt and remove his trousers. Jack was to be first in the lineup, then the four girls and LeMoyne. . . . As we got close to the judges' stand, LeMoyne couldn't control himself any longer. His glasses flew off, the sheet slipped off and there he was in his underpants, roaring, perspiring, and talking. The end result: we all went home and changed our clothes and returned to have a fine time."

———

IN HIS LATER correspondence with Lem—one letter forty pages long—Kennedy revealed much of himself: his conflict with parents, his physical pain, but mostly his frustrating competition with his brother. Joe and Jack were two classes apart at Choate and their contact was spasmodic, but competition between them remained a constant. Lem later recalled, "Many times I saw it happen: Joe getting at Jack about his attitude or grades or something, cutting him up—'for his own good,' of course—and Jack trying to be nonchalant. One day I was in Jack's room, Joe came in and started needling. Jack became very upset in spite of himself. When he lost control of his temper he could be fierce. He jumped up from the bed where he had been sitting—and he was blazing. And Joe grabbed him. Joe was enormously strong, the strongest person I've ever encountered for his size and weight, and Jack was wiry but thin and not too well and simply no match for him. Joe stood there and held him and smiled with that somewhat crooked smile he had, while Jack flailed around but couldn't really do anything. Joe made a few more remarks, then turned and left the room. Jack sat on the edge of the bed. And he began crying from sheer frustration."

Jack was not reluctant to use sarcasm. In a letter to his father about Joe: "He was rough-housing in the hall, a sixth-former caught him. He led him in . . . and all the sixth-formers had a shot at him. Did the sixth-formers lick him? O, Man. He was all blisters, they almost paddled the life out of him. What I couldn't have given to be a sixth-former." Jack also observed that Joe felt so sick afterward that he couldn't even eat his Thanksgiving dinner, and then Jack added, mockingly, "Manly youth."

Jack was willing to do anything he could to weaken his father's image of young Joe and heighten his own. Joseph Kennedy Sr. was conscious of the competition and encouraged it.

Betty Young, who met Jack during that time at a Bronxville Field Club dance, recalled how obsessed Jack was with his brother Joe, how Jack talked about him all the time, saying, "Joe plays football better, Joe dances better, Joe is getting better grades."

"Joe just kind of overshadowed him in everything," said Young.

A Choate friend later reminded Jack, "Joe set the pace . . . you tagged along."

————

AT THE CHOATE graduation ceremony, Jack predicted to Lem that Joe would get a major award. In fact, Joe received the Harvard Trophy, a small bronze statue of a football player given to the graduating sixth-former who best combined scholarship and sportsmanship. Lem recalled that Jack was "very pleased for his brother," but at the same time, "when he saw the look of pride bursting from his father's face, he felt a little sad."

After the ceremony there was a concert by the glee club on the chapel steps, followed by a supper under a large tent on the lawn. Jack led Lem on a long walk across the muddy campus to the athletic field, where they sat together for several hours under a large tree and talked openly about the pain they each experienced on account of their older brothers. Jack confided to Lem that "underneath it all he believed he was smarter than Joe but that no one understood this, least of all his parents. His intelligence, he believed, simply worked along different lines—more questioning perhaps, and more imaginative, but less organized. Nor did he really believe that Joe was the better athlete. To be sure, Joe had, by far, the healthier body but he was not necessarily more coordinated. Yet whatever remaining confidence Jack possessed, it had been shaken that day as he watched his parents race up to Joe with arms outstretched and looks of wonder on their faces. Nor could he help but wish that someday the roles would be reversed, that someday he would achieve supremacy in a family in which he had for so long felt himself in a subordinate role."

Jack's friend James Rousmaniere had another view. He felt that Jack seemed relieved that Joe was his father's number one son, facing the obligation of his father's ambition—something he himself preferred to avoid, giving Jack a sense of space and obscurity and independence "that he valued."

After young Joe had left Choate, headmaster George St. John wrote to Joe Sr. in Jack's junior year that he was seriously worried about Jack but that he was sure that in the next two years Joe Sr. would be as proud of Jack as he was of Joe. The headmaster saw Jack's mind as "a harder mind to put in harness than Joe's," but he felt that when Jack learned "to use his individual way of looking at things as an asset instead of a handicap, his natural gift of an individual outlook and witty expression are going to help him."

What Jack needed, he said, was a period of adjustment but that period of adjustment would take time and patience.

Joe wrote a prompt letter to his son:

Now, Jack, I don't want to give the impression that I am a nagger, for goodness knows that is the worst thing a parent can be. After long experience in sizing up people, I definitely know you have the goods, and you can go a long way. Now aren't you foolish not to get all there is out of what God has given you? . . .

"I am not expecting too much, and I will not be disappointed if you don't turn out to be a real genius, but I think you can be a really worthwhile citizen with good judgment and understanding."

Jack informed him:

I thought I would write you right away as LeMoyne and I have been talking about how poorly we have done this quarter, and we have definitely decided to stop any fooling around. . . . I really feel that we will get something done this quarter as LeMoyne seems to feel the same way I do.

But Jack was still having too much fun.

Lem and Jack roomed near the dining hall, and Jack's Victrola made it a popular place for students going to dinner. Jack and Lem then decided to limit the use of their room to eleven of their closest friends who would share the exclusive privilege of listening to Kennedy's Victrola. They called themselves The Muckers and their emblem was a little gold shovel. Jack's great-grandfather Patrick had been a mucker who shoveled manure. Jack's Muckers had lighter concerns.

One of the milder pranks for Mucker Jack was to fill a boy's room with pillows so when he opened the door he couldn't get in. The headmaster in chapel called a Mucker "the worst kind of boy."

Lem later proudly recalled, "Jack and I were labeled public enemies number one and two of the school, in that order."

"Well, I have two things to do," wrote the exasperated headmaster to Kennedy Sr. "One to run the school, another to run Jack Kennedy and his friends."

The headmaster finally expelled the Muckers—and Joe Sr., who had never found time to visit his son, now arrived to fight for him.

It took considerable pressure on the headmaster to cancel the expulsion.

What was important for Jack in all this was his father's attitude toward him. There was no bitterness or anger but a wink and a joke. Said his father: If the muckers had been his club, "you can be sure it wouldn't have started with an M."

To the father, Jack was a pale reflection of his older son, but he was still a Kennedy. Jack seemed to be heading for failure, and Kennedy Sr. would not recognize failure. "When the air had cleared," said Harold Tinker, "Jack was a changed boy."

———

IN THE NEXT months, Jack studied hard and got better grades.

In 1933 Joe Sr. bought a seven-bedroom house, on North Ocean Boulevard in Palm Beach. At none of their homes did the Kennedy children have their own rooms or their own pictures. On arriving, a Kennedy child was simply assigned to any available space, and it was seldom the same space from a previous visit.

Lem was still Jack's constant companion, guest, and roommate. Lem would always do almost anything Jack wanted. Kennedy offered the impoverished Lem a hundred dollars if he would take off all his clothes and walk into the Off Limits study of his father, and declare, "Hi, Dad—I know you've always wanted me to call you Dad," and then sing Mae West's song "I'm No Angel."

As much as Lem needed the money, he refused, and with good reason.

At his proud best at the dinner table, exercising his love of control, Kennedy Sr. was too formidable. Joe guided all conversation. As Jack remembered, "Only the boys could talk at the table." The father not only pitted the boys against one another, but he would encourage them to argue with him, always taking an opposite view, coming in on them "like a destroyer." The conversation would often be insulting, deprecating. "He'd look at you; you'd wonder if he knew what color underwear you were wearing."

Jack later felt that the table discussions had been "greatly exaggerated." "We didn't have opinions in those days. At first, in the early years, they were mostly monologues by my father."

The elder Kennedy insisted that he never organized the dinner-table discussions. "No, I never asked opinions of each of the children on a question of the day. We talked about personalities of the day. It's a natural thing to do—to talk about the people that you know and the people that you read about."

His mother had her own complaints: "I was always reading the wrong thing, I would read *Life* and *Time* and they would discuss *Newsweek* . . . or something else."

Many years later, Ted would say of these dinner discussions that they were on "a rather high level. It necessitated that if you were going to get involved in it, you would have to do more reading or be involved in some kind of undertaking—travel or reading or doing something. Otherwise, you wouldn't have something to say; or nobody would be very interested."

Their father was a man interested in almost everything, and his curiosity was contagious. He would listen to what his children said, but seldom changed his mind. Choate classmate Ralph Horton remembered how he answered all his children's questions in the greatest detail, no matter how simple or how stupid the questions might seem. "However, if an outsider, such as myself, would have asked him a question, he'd be practically ignored."

In the end, the children mostly absorbed their father's opinions as their own. Neighbor Sancy Newman noticed how the old man worked on his children to shape them his way. He would ask a question, then suggest an answer, and finally make it a must.

———

KENNEDY SR. FELT certain in his mind that his son Joe would be a political leader in the coming generation. To prepare him for it, he did something surprising: he contacted a man with whom he thoroughly disagreed, yet respected, a man much too liberal for his taste, Felix Frankfurter, the eminent lawyer who would become a United States Supreme Court Justice.

"I have two lads," he told Frankfurter, "and I'm wondering—and it was suggested to me that I should talk with you—consult you. . . . Do you think they're too young to go to Harvard?"

"If they were mine, I know what I would do," Frankfurter replied. "I would send them to London to spend a year with Harold Laski, who is, in my opinion, the most stimulating teacher in the world. . . ." Some of the best students in the Law School were products of Harold, who had been an instructor in Political Science at Harvard.

Kay Halle found it fascinating that father Joe wanted his sons trained to serve their country in the British tradition, which would give them the social and educational stamp of British aristocrats. "That is what's so strange, that the advantaged classes in England should have imprinted itself upon an Irishman, and such an Irishman as Joe. This is a curious paradox. I think there are paradoxes in the whole family, except for the girls. I think the girls are really very typically Irish."

In a way, it was not so paradoxical. Whether he had a problem, or his children did, Joseph Kennedy automatically went to the expert— the best source available. He trained his sons to do the same.

Frankfurter later wrote Joe Sr. how impressed he was with young Joe's sense of what was important and unimportant, and his ability to absorb experience wisely. He predicted young Joe would take the fullest advantage of his year in London.

Frankfurter did not have the same confidence in Joseph Sr. Neither did President Roosevelt. In anticipation of the repeal of Prohibition, Kennedy had exploited Roosevelt's eldest son James for entrée in England to get exclusive franchises to distribute the valuable British brands of liquor, and Joe got all the huge profits while James had difficult getting his expenses paid.

A frustrated Joseph Kennedy, Sr., waited a long time to be admitted into the Washington power circle. Kennedy finally told the President, "I'll take any job you want me to, and even work for nothing, so long as it's interesting. I never want to be bored."

Kennedy wrote his son Joe, saying he did not desire a position with the Government unless it really meant some prestige to his family.

Finally, in 1934, President Roosevelt appointed Joe Kennedy head of the newly created Securities and Exchange Commission, a bipartisan agency to protect the public from investing in unsafe securities.

Roosevelt felt obligated to Kennedy not only because he had been a big fund-raiser but because he had been important in Roosevelt's nomination at the Democratic National Convention of 1932. The California delegation was then critical, and newspaper publisher William Randolph Hearst was the political key. Joe had swung him to Roosevelt.

The Boston *Post* headlined: BIG SACRIFICE FOR CHILDREN'S SAKE.

It wasn't much of a sacrifice. He insisted he was taking the job mainly because he wanted his children to be proud of him.

"Joe wanted the Treasury," said Roosevelt brain-truster Tom Corcoran, "but FDR wouldn't give it to him." The SEC was the second-best job but it had the power to purge. "He could take the money men in New York and sweep them into the sea."

FDR reportedly told a friend, in discussing Kennedy, "It takes a crook to catch a crook." A lot of New Dealers thought it was like putting the wolf in charge of Red Riding Hood.

A consensus of economists afterward felt that Kennedy had done a good job in reviving the country's financial markets and reestablishing private capital for private industry. As New Dealer Tom Corcoran said of him, "He has a hot heart and a cold head. This is what makes the steam in him."

Young Joe was also full of steam. Shortly after he arrived at the London School of Economics and Political Science in 1933–1934, for the year before he entered Harvard, he wrote his father that he was not only reading all the conservative newspapers, but also the Socialist ones, "so that I can get both points of view . . . and not be like a dumb ham." His father replied that young Joe was exceeding his fondest expectations and "I feel definitely sure that this year may be the turning point in your whole life."

Professor Laski found young Joe "adorably young and still more adorably unsophisticated." What also impressed Laski was young Joe's astonishing vitality as well as his astonishing capacity for enthusiasm coupled with a smile that was "pure magic." Laski was also intrigued with Joe's profound interest in politics, his declared intention to have a political career.

"My husband would finish discussing some point," said Mrs. Laski, "and then he would turn to Joe, sitting on the floor, and say, 'Now, Joe, what will you do about this when you are President?' "

As young Joe put it, he wanted to be the first Irish-Catholic

President of the United States—if his father didn't get there before him.

Laski's Sunday teas had become famous at the school. Students would sit on the rug in the little room above the garden and discuss everything in a room thick with smoke.

"Joe would always come to the teas," Frida Laski remembered. "He was tall and very good-looking. And argumentative, and very bright, but of course he was at a disadvantage." Joe's roommate, Aubrey Whitelaw, has described Joe's usual response from a room full of experts. "Dead silence for only a second, and then Joe would tackle the problem in a completely logical manner, and struggle through it until he had answered—not batting an eye or retreating from the established positions, either."

Harold Laski was then forty years old. "I'm a Socialist," he told his students, "though from time to time I shall prescribe other books as an antidote to my poison. If you disagree, come along to my study, and tell me where I'm wrong."

During one discussion, Frida Laski made some observations about the Catholic Church which were rather difficult to answer and finally Joe said, "I don't know the answers to all those questions but I know the Catholic Church is right, anyway!" The amused Mrs. Laski later told Mrs. Kennedy about it.

Laski was invited to lecture at the University of Moscow in the summer of 1934, and he and his wife invited young Joe to accompany them. Joe took along his tennis racket, but didn't use it much. He talked to a man on the train who said that he only had four meals of meat per year before the revolution. And Frida Laski recalled that Joe got a headache when they visited the Anti-Religious museum and said he didn't want to argue.

Back in London, with the help of his father's British friends, Joe found a flat overlooking a garden at Earl's Court. He invited Whitelaw to share it, but Whitelaw realized it was more than he could afford. Joe asked him to pay only what he was already paying elsewhere.

Whitelaw noted that the Kennedy family photograph was a living room centerpiece, "like a shrine." Joe would tell "Whitey" in great detail about each of his brothers and sisters and what they planned to do.

Joe had letters of introduction to movie people from his father, and the apartment filled at tea time with starlets from the British studios. Whitey knew when to tactfully disappear. He remembered their visit to the estate of wealthy whiskey distiller John Dewar, who took them on a tour of his vast estate across the moors at high speed in his Rolls Royce, and then explained the lineage of scores of fine-blooded horses. Whitey recalled that he and Joe could barely smother their laughter at the pomposity. It was a curious response, given his own lavish upbringing.

———

ON A SUMMER holiday, Joe and Whitelaw bought a Chrysler convertible in London for a trip to Rome to "see the Pope." Finding no lodging in Rome, he and Whitey were taken in by an Italian family, for the equivalent of ninety cents a day, including breakfast. Whitey remembered Joe dragging him along to see all the sights his mother had told him to see: the Catacombs, the Colosseum, St. Paul's, the Forum, San Pietro in Vincoli, Santa Maria Maggiore, John Lateran, where—he wrote home—he had "climbed the Holy Stairs on my knees."

Wherever Joe went in Europe, there were always available women. Whitelaw remembered the moon beaming down on a beautiful blonde with Joe in the middle of the Colosseum. There were even newspaper rumors that he had become engaged to the world figure-skating champion, Megan Taylor, but his father insisted to the press, "He's not engaged to anybody. He's going back to Harvard in the fall."

From Munich, in April of 1934, Joe wrote his father about the despondent German people, and how Hitler used the Jews as a scapegoat to blame for their predicament. "It was excellent psychology, and it was too bad that it had to be done to the Jews." Then he added, "It is extremely sad, that noted professors, scientists, artists . . . should have to suffer, but as you can see, it would be practically impossible to throw out only a part of them. . . . As far as the brutality is concerned, it must have been necessary to use some, to secure the whole-hearted support of the people. . . . Hitler is building a spirit in his men that could be envied in any country. . . . This spirit would very quickly be turned into a war spirit, but Hitler has things well under control. . . . I am sending this to you, Dad, to see how you think I have sized it up. . . . I would not like to discuss it with Laski. . . . Laski would probably give me examples which might change me back again."

Not surprisingly, young Joe echoed his father's opinion on most issues. For one thing, Joe Sr. did not particularly like Jews, and in fact had even expressed his dissatisfaction to President Roosevelt that "they have surrounded you with Jews and Communists." Joe Sr.'s assistant, Harvey Klemmer, once returned from Germany to report the bitter persecution of Jews. Kennedy told him curtly, "Well, they only have themselves to blame—they brought it on themselves."

Some time later, when young Joe was in the war, an Irish-Catholic squadron mate recalled that "he was just like me. He didn't like kikes, but some of his best friends were Jews."

Rose Kennedy even speculated to Robert Coughlan that her husband picked up the concept of tight family togetherness from some of his Jewish friends. "I always thought that he got the idea from some of the big picture people at that time . . . the Warner Brothers, for instance . . . because I believe in the Jews there is a close family relationship."

Whitelaw had a different memory of their time in Germany. "In Munich, we watched this Brown Shirt parade, and everybody was 'Heil-Hitler-ing,' except Joe and me, and some guy nudged him on the other side to get his hand up. Joe didn't pay any attention, and the guy nudged him again. I saw Joe's fist come back, and I grabbed it, or they probably would've kicked the hell out of us. He hated the Nazis as much as I did."

If Whitelaw's memory is accurate, it seemingly contradicts Joe's letter to his father. The odds are that Joe was telling his father what he felt his father wanted to hear. Young Joe's anti-Nazi reaction with Whitelaw was surely more instinctual. It seems he had absorbed much from the Laski lectures.

Joe reshaped his views on Germany after that trip. While in Poland, he had conversations with key officials about their fear of the war with Germany. His father forwarded his son's report to President Roosevelt and later confided to a Polish diplomat, "You cannot imagine to what extent my eldest boy was able to influence the President. I should say the President believes him more than he does me."

———

EXCEPT FOR HISTORY and English, Jack's grades at Choate were still poor. And he always seemed to spend considerable time in the infirmary, with assorted viral complaints. Billings later said that if he ever wrote Jack's biography, they would call it "John F. Kennedy: A Medical History." In January 1934 he developed a blood condition so serious that students were told to pray for him in the evening chapel. His mother, then at Palm Beach, still felt no urgent need to visit him. He was hospitalized more than a month, then sent to Palm Beach to recuperate. He wasn't there long before he was again ill, and was sent to the Mayo Clinic in Rochester for further diagnosis. They never did discover what was wrong with him, and finally sent him home.

His letters to Billings from there were full of obscenities, sexual fantasies, and persistent frustration. "Have you laid pussy yet?" he asked Billings. Perhaps his sexual boasting was also Jack's way of urging Billings to follow his lead. Years earlier, Lem even let Jack persuade him to go to a Harlem whorehouse, in full evening dress, to lose their virginity to the same whore. Lem told the story afterward of waiting at the door, wearing his bowler hat. When Jack was finished and came out, it took considerable pressure to force Lem to go into that same room. Breaking their virginity with the same Harlem whore became the older boys' version of being "blood brothers," and deepened their inseparability. Afterward, concerned about venereal disease, they sought out a doctor to check them. Later, at Harvard, Jack did get venereal disease and was treated at the Leahy Clinic.

———————

YOUNG JOE, NOW home from Europe, was then taking strong opposition to many of his father's views. In a letter to Billings, Jack wrote, "Joe came back three days ago and is a communist. Some shit, eh!" But when sixteen-year-old Jack saw young Joe making a stand against old Joe, he quickly sided with his brother.

Joe's defiance of his father was surprising. It seldom ever had happened. Jack's reaction was more expected. It made him feel more grown up to side with his brother against their father.

"That was a completely new experience for my husband and me, to listen to that point of view," said Rose Kennedy. According to Rose, this did not bother her husband at all.

"My husband had to argue with the boys and say that he had made his money, success and happiness and more or less depended on the capitalist system and that is what he believed in. He said, 'If I were their age I probably would believe what they believe. . . . I don't care what the boys think about my ideas. I can always look out for myself. The important thing is that they should stand together.' ''

The elder Kennedy also had said, ''I made my choice among the philosophies offered when I was young. Each of them will have to make his or her choice.'' He later told editor John Seigenthaler, ''I don't want my enemies to be my sons' enemies, or my wars to be my sons' wars.''

What became destructive were that the goals he set for his sons and himself combined a sense of personal omnipotence with crusading mission. And regardless of what he intended, that money still persuaded his sons to further their father's ambitions for them.

But Kennedy Sr.'s own sense of purpose was changing. He confided to a friend, ''I find myself much more interested in what young Joe is going to do than with the rest of my life.''

RETURNING HOME FROM London, Joe entered Harvard in September 1934. A Harvard friend described Joe then as ''a good-looking, clean-cut chap, athletic, all-American type, with a wonderful smile . . . he knew the yard policemen at Harvard, the valets, and Snowball and everybody. . . . If I were asked to name but one of his attributes, I would say it was his innate understanding of human nature. This faculty enabled him to grasp every situation as though it were a photograph; and his genial approach and ability to think on his feet took care of the rest. Frequently, at college and even at law school, one of the boys would pose the question, ''How can one guy do so many things well?''

Joe felt he had to exceed his father's record at Harvard. Academically, this wasn't difficult. Ironically, Joe Sr. had done so poorly in a course on banking and finance at Harvard that he changed his major from economics to music ''because I wanted to be sure I would graduate.'' And, despite his charm and persistence, he was still turned down by the top social clubs. Joe Sr.'s social failure at Harvard was so strong and so deep that it shaped his lifelong desire to conquer the society which had snubbed him. His sons would be his way to accomplish this. ''You can go to Harvard and it doesn't mean a damn thing.'' he later said. ''The only thing that matters there is money.''

Most of his father's best friends at school were athletes. Joe Sr. had tried football, unsuccessfully, but his prime aim at Harvard was to earn his letter in baseball. He could earn this by playing against Yale. Team captain Charles McLaughlin was told by two of P.J.'s ward heelers that if this happened, McLaughlin would get a business permit for a movie house after graduation. Joe earned his letter and repaid the favor by pocketing the ball in the final play of the game—which traditionally went to the team captain. "Joe played the game his own way—and for keeps—and didn't give a damn what anybody thought." McLaughlin's angry memory of Joe: "If he wanted something badly enough . . . he didn't much care how he got it. He'd run right over anybody."

———

JACK WAS SEVENTEEN when he graduated from Choate in June 1935. The yearbook listed his activity in football, basketball, baseball, always on the second team. His classmates voted him "most likely to succeed."

Jack was desperate about winning the "succeed" title. His Choate record had been so bad for so long that he needed it to impress his father. Although, academically, he surely did not deserve it, he and Billings campaigned and maneuvered intensively to ensure the result. Years later, telling *Time* reporter Hugh Sidey about it, Jack chuckled and said "my old buddy Billings counted the votes."

In 1935, Joe Sr. had resigned from the SEC after a year of service, and decided to go to England on business, taking Jack with him. Jack had been accepted at Harvard but Kennedy Sr. now wanted him to spend a year with Harold Laski, as young Joe had done.

Jack wrote Billings from the ship, "There is a fat Frenchie aboard who is a 'homo' . . . He has had me to his cabin more than once and is trying to bed me." Then he added, "Tonight is the Captain's Ball— don't be dirty, Kirk, I am not discussing his vital organs."

It was on the *Normandie* that Jack's father introduced him to two brothers who were then two of the top officials at General Motors "because I want you to see what brothers can do who work together."

Before Jack could attend any Laski lectures, he was hospitalized in London with a "mysterious illness." One doctor even felt he was "near death." Billings had enrolled at Princeton and Jack's letters to him were all about erections and sexy nurses. Lem, in turn, wrote how he could now name all the presidents and their wives and the kings and queens of England in order and a contest he won by shaving the fastest without a cut and another for putting the most sticks of chewing gum in his mouth. In order to make money at Princeton, Lem gave out free samples of Juicy Fruit gum.

Allowed to leave the hospital, Jack decided not to go to Harvard, where he had been admitted, and enrolled in Princeton. He knew he was defying the family tradition, but he had other concerns. "I know he went there mainly to be with Billings," said James Rousmaniere. More significantly, his act of defiance was to get away from his brother's shadow and his father's pressure.

Billings was overjoyed and cabled him at the Hotel Claridge: NOTH-ING COULD POSSIBLY SOUND BETTER SO HURRY HOME.

He and Billings were again roommates and it was again great fun— but it didn't last long. Only six weeks later, Jack was again sick and was sent back to his Boston doctor for further diagnosis. He was hospitalized for several months, and Billings was a frequent visitor.

After a rest in Palm Beach, Jack was brought back to Boston for two more months of medical tests. In that interim, he visited Joe at Harvard. Jack wrote Billings that Joe had brought back an alligator from Palm Beach and kept it in the bathtub. He himself, he wrote, had found better use for a bathtub. "B.D. came to see me today in the hospital, and I laid her in the bath-tub."

Jack was particularly proud of Joe's becoming an item in Walter Winchell's nationally syndicated column: "Boston romance—J. P. Kennedy Jr., the Wall Streeter's lad, and Helen Buck of the Boston Back-Bay bunch are keeping warm." Jack's footnote to Lem was that "keeping warm" meant "fucking."

Kennedy family friend Arthur Krock was in Palm Beach with Joseph Kennedy, who was obviously worried about sickly Jack. Krock suggested a stay at his friend's ranch might improve his health. His friend Jack Speiden was a former New York banker, a Yale graduate, a defeated Republican Congressman. He owned the 43,000-acre Jay Six Cattle Ranch, with a thousand head of cattle, outside Benson, Arizona, near the Mexican border.

Jack and his Choate friend Smokey Wilde signed on as paid ranchhands for a dollar a day, living in a bunkhouse with the others. Speiden described the boys as soft when they arrived, tough when they left. Besides making adobe bricks to build some ranch offices, the boys also learned how to doctor cattle and repair fences. "I worked the hell out of them," Speiden recalled.

On Saturday night, Jack and Smokey rode the ranch truck to the border town of Nogales. As Jack wrote to Billings, "Got a fuck and a suck in a Mexican hoar-house for 65 cents so am feeling very fit and clean."

After Arizona, Jack journeyed to Hollywood, where he met and enjoyed some starlets. He'd have more stories to tell Joe, whom he had arranged to meet later in Chicago.

The boyhood fights were finished. The age gap had disappeared. The skinny Jack was now a toughened ranchhand. That summer of 1936, the two brothers sailed in the races at Hyannis. Neighbor Pat Gardner Jackson remembered the Kennedy boys using a metal centerboard when the rules specified it had to be wooden, and also a larger set of sails than regulation. This showed their common need to win, but, another time, another incident revealed more of the brotherly bond. Jack took his Choate friend Charles Wilson in the family powerboat to watch brother Joe in a sailing race with Herb Merrick. When Merrick started to pass Joe, Wilson observed, "Jack gunned our boat in front of Herb to slow him down."

WHEN JOE CAME to Dillon Field House at Harvard to be outfitted for football, coach James Farrell recalled that he didn't have a real athletic build "but he worked hard, stayed on the field longer than anybody else, and built himself up into a good athlete." He was on the squad for four years.

His father had encouraged him, "being out for the team gives you a great chance to meet a lot of fellows, and after all, that is the first requisite of a successful college education—learning how to meet people and getting along with them."

Joe practiced every night after regular practice, running, jumping, throwing, catching. He broke an arm during his freshman year, and hurt his knee during his sophomore year badly enough to require an operation. Joe persisted in playing because he was determined to earn a Harvard letter as his father had.

After visiting young Joe in the hospital, his father changed his tune. He predicted that the knee operation would "certainly put an end to all football activities, but that fact does not bother me at all.

"I know how anxious you are to make your letter, but after a fellow has been banged up the way you have and as you have only one more year to go before you go out in the world, you should think very seriously whether it is worthwhile or not. I do not want to be in the position of telling you not to, but all my judgment urges me to at least ask you to give it grave consideration."

Joe listened intently to anything his father said, and they had an easy relationship. It was easy enough so that young Joe could write, "By the way, Barbara Cushing and a friend of hers who was out with you in New York hearing Toscanini, Persian Room etc. till 3 o'clock were up here and gave me the lowdown on you. They said they nearly went South." (Barbara Cushing was a Boston socialite and the sister of James Roosevelt's wife, Betsy. Apparently, Kennedy had spontaneously invited the two girls to Palm Beach.) "I think Mother ought to keep a better eye on you!" Responding by return mail, Kennedy told him not to worry too much, "as 21 or 22 is still a little too young for me."

In the fall of 1936, Jack finally acceded to his father's pressure and his brother's urging and transferred to Harvard.

Jack now once again had to contend with his brother's looming shadow.

Faculty adviser Dr. Payson Wild remembered their first conversation: "He came to my office in Winthrop House, sat down on the sofa, tousled head, and he said, 'Dr. Wild, I want you to know that I'm not bright like my brother Joe.' He was very much under the spell of his older brother . . . Joe was then a very, very bright, outgoing young man. He could dance all night until 5 o'clock and go back and get A's . . . Jack was an individual who had to work more solidly to get done, but he was far more thorough."

Many of the friends Jack collected around him were jocks—like his brother's friends. But even though Jack's preference in friends was changing to athletes, his friendship with Lem remained strong. According to Rousmaniere, who shared an adjoining room, Lem would visit Jack often on weekends and Jack would go to Princeton for football games and occasional parties.

Early on, Jack determined to rival his brother in football. Whenever they played touch football with the family at Hyannis, Jack would always play on the opposite team from Joe. Jack's roommate Torby MacDonald, who became Harvard football captain, recalled a tense scene after practice one day. Joe Jr. came up to Jack and offered advice: "Jack, if you want my opinion, you'd be better off forgetting about football. You just don't weigh enough and you're going to get hurt." Jack's face flushed with anger, but he did not respond. At this point, MacDonald decided to get involved. "Come off it, Joe," he said. "Jack doesn't need any looking after." But, to MacDonald's surprise, Jack whirled on him, saying, "Mind your own business! Keep out of it! I'm talking to Joe, not you!"

"His brother was six-two and weighed 185 or so," Torby added. "He was a natural athlete and a good football player . . . varsity. Jack was six feet and weighed 150 and of only average ability. Jack wasn't big enough for the line and he wasn't fast enough to be a back and he wanted to be a football player; so he went out for end. He didn't make the first team but he stayed on the squad as freshman. After practice was over he'd have me throw the ball for him and he'd practice snagging them."

Jack himself told the story of his freshman year in football when he had not played until the Yale game was almost over. And he walked up to the coach, tapped him on the shoulder, and said, "Coach, what about putting me in?" And, as Jack put it, after six weeks of working out there as a freshman, "the coach turned to me and said, 'Who the hell are you?' "

Jack sidelined in showgirls and airline hostesses and models, mainly one-night stands. His friend George Smathers later described him as a lousy lover—"in-and-out." One woman said, "I was fascinated by him at the time, but our lovemaking was so disastrous that for years later I was convinced I was frigid. He was terrible in bed."

Jack's sexual conquests were one of the few ways he could compete with his brother and earn easy praise from his father.

"I thought his reputation was so promiscuous—that this suggested an immaturity to me, a lack of confidence in the man, who through the years had to prove himself every day," said friend Betty Beale. Another friend traced it back to an unloving childhood, remarking that Jack

needed to be close to someone and to feel loved. Jack's Harvard friend
Vic Francis detailed Jack's lack of respect for women. He remembered
Jack's invitation of a New York model to a weekend ball. Francis met
her on Jack's behalf at Boston's South Station, but Jack never appeared.
When Francis called brother Joe and explained, Joe moaned, "Oh no!
Not again!" Joe then escorted the model to the ball, but Jack never
appeared all weekend.

In reprisal, Joe felt it fair game, and even fun, to poach his young
brother's dates. Once he saw Jack with a beautiful woman at the Stork
Club in New York. Joe had him paged, and while Jack was at the
telephone, picked her up and took her home. Another time, Joe cut in
more directly on Jack's date, telling him, "Get lost, baby brother." The
fuming Jack did not get lost and the lovely singer, Gertrude Niesen,
was delighted to have two Kennedy escorts.

Like his father, Joe could exercise his charm or turn it off quickly. But
Rousmaniere recalled that to him "Joe had no sense of humor. To have
Joe tell a joke on himself was an aberration. Joe was not an easy person
to get along with . . . he did not ingratiate himself with people . . . Joe
never had any softness. Jack did. Jack had some of his mother's softness.
He didn't begrudge anybody anything. He had all the money he wanted.
He had all the girls he wanted. If he ran into a problem, he'd just change
direction and do something else. . . . I can't think of a single person Jack
ever antagonized. But if anybody started to put Joe down in his presence, Jack would say, 'Well, Joe was right in this case.' Jack would stand
up for Joe in many, many ways . . . his loyalty was intense . . . and this
loyalty was mutual."

———

MANY OF JOE'S friends saw him surrounded by an aura of inevitable
success. "Very aggressive and very forceful, fearless. He was always the
politician of our group," said Charles Garabedian. George Taylor,
whom Joe called his "gentleman's gentleman," was later asked, "Do
you think Joe could have become President?"

"Oh, I do think so."

But if you asked Arthur Schlesinger, Jr., young Joe's classmate at
Harvard, he said: "I'd find it hard to see the Joe Kennedy whom I knew
as President of the United States. I don't think he had quite the

intellectual acuteness, or the inwardness, the introspective quality, that both Jack and Bobby had. On the other hand . . . who knows? You can never tell about the Kennedys; they're late-bloomers anyway."

Jack had been privy to much of his brother's presidential ambitions. But as for his own future, Jack himself had only the vaguest idea of what he might want to do. On a double date in Hyannis, he asked his young woman, "Would you vote for me when I run for Governor?"

"No," she said. "We're Republicans."

––––––––

NO ONE KNOWS how seriously Jack Kennedy considered his political options at that time. Perhaps he was just speculating with the ambitions of Joe and his father. Mutual friends saw a greater potential in Jack than in Joe, but one classmate was more critical. "I don't remember ever taking Jack Kennedy's views very seriously. No, I didn't think he was very profound. I thought he was a *fils à papa,* as the French say, his father's son."

While his father's prime focus was clearly on Joe Jr., he did not ignore Jack. Jack later told his brother-in-law Steve Smith, "You know, when I was just trying out for the freshman team at some of these meets, my Dad was always there; he was *always* there. He did the same for all his kids." Smith added, "His father was a one-man cheering squad."

––––––––

JOE AND JACK had their own separate circles, and did not often intermingle. The top ten clubs were extremely restrictive, as they were the core of Harvard's social environment. Neither the Kennedy father nor his son Joe were able to get into any of them.

Spee, in snob terms, was high on the social pecking order. Joe had been turned down because he was Boston Irish and Spee was dominated by New York Protestants. Rousmaniere, who was New York society, was solicited by a number of clubs but made a pact with their mutual friend Bill Coleman "that we wouldn't join any club that wouldn't take Jack Kennedy. . . . We just told them that," said Rousmaniere. "Well, that was a black mark at nine of the clubs, but Spee finally took us all."

For Jack, it was a major achievement. It was the first real time he had outdistanced his brother. Rousmaniere remembered that Joe was not pleased when Spee took Jack. "Joe really took a bit of umbrage."

Yet, he did try to help his brother when he could. As chairman of the House Student Committee, Joe recommended that swimming be made a major sport mainly because he knew Jack was trying out for the swimming team. He even stopped by to talk to swimming coach Harold Ulen about Jack. Swimming was one of the few sports where Jack felt equal or better than Joe. But what was key here was that Joe Jr. never stopped being the watchful, concerned surrogate father.

———

WINTHROP WAS CALLED "Jock House" because so many athletes roomed there. Jack's roommate was Torbert MacDonald, who became football captain. "Torby was a very rough diamond and Jack was a smooth diamond," said Rousmaniere, "but they mated up very well."

Torby was the exact counterpart of Billings. A tough kid who came out of the Boston public school system, Torby had many of the qualities Kennedy was now reaching for. It is interesting that both Torby and Billings would court Kathleen Kennedy—and neither would win her. Lem later took her to the World's Fair, and to the Cotton Club in Harlem on a double date with Jack. When the father learned of the Harlem visit, he exploded.

"What fun I had!" recalled Billings. "I think I probably fell in love with her right then and there. She opened up a side of me that no woman ever reached."

And what was Lem trying to prove when he dated Jack's sister Kathleen? Primarily friendship for the female Kennedy who most resembled Jack. Kathleen was the closest image to Jack. Lem described her as "a unique girl. She had this amazing vitality . . . warm, a tremendous success." It wasn't long before Lem started a correspondence with her that lasted until her death. Kick saw Lem as her very dear platonic friend. He later examined all her suitors and suggested whom she should marry, but then jokingly added, "I've always known after you've had your girlish fling you'll settle down with me and sell Coca-Cola in Bridgeport."

———

IN 1936 KENNEDY Sr. had produced a book, *I'm for Roosevelt*.

"He had the idea . . . I gave him the title for his book," said Arthur Krock. "I wrote a good deal of the book and edited the rest. . . . I took no pay for this."

Jack Kennedy later told Charles Houghton that his father had paid Krock $25,000 to keep the Kennedy name in the papers. In his own papers, Krock only mentioned the Kennedy offer at Christmas of a limousine, which he described as "a coarse bribe" and said he refused.

In his book, Kennedy mildly objected to some of the President's tax proposals and fiscal policies, but generally the book served as loud applause for Roosevelt. Critics generally snickered when Kennedy wrote that he had "no political ambitions for myself or my children." Nobody questioned his statement in the book that "the future happiness of America" meant to him "the future happiness of my family."

As in FDR's previous campaign, Kennedy worked hard for Roosevelt's reelection. Kennedy praised FDR in a nationwide radio address, then said that the President had given the American people "a Christian program of social justice."

FDR later nominated Kennedy as chairman of the United States Maritime Commission, to develop and maintain a Merchant Marine. Joe had done a commendable job at the Securities and Exchange Commission, but FDR always considered Kennedy a loose cannon, ready to explode in any direction. He never truly trusted him. Both Joe and Rose felt he should have received something better.

———

THOUGH HE WAS once again deeply embroiled in his life in Washington, father Joe kept a keen eye on any exposure or experience that would help young Joe. During the school holidays, he arranged for trips abroad, even paid the expenses of Joe's school adviser Harry Greaves to go with him to the Disarmament Conference in Geneva. Joe wrote a paper on that conference which received praise back in the States.

One of young Joe's teachers, Professor John Galbraith, described him as "every faculty member's favorite." Of Jack, Galbraith then said, "unlike Joe . . . he was given to varied amusements, much devoted to social life and affectionately to women. One did not cultivate such students."

William Randolph Hearst, Jr., recalled young Joe visiting the Hearst family ranch on the McCloud River at the foot of Mt. Shasta in California. He had come with a Harvard friend. "I remember it principally because the river there is really just melted snow and literally as cold as ice. Ever since my brothers and I could remember, we were warned to stay out of it, as it was so cold you could get a numb feeling in your fingers just by sticking them in the water for a minute. This didn't seem to faze these two, because the next thing I knew, they had swum across it." Kennedy Sr. would have approved, and Joe Jr. knew it. Jack had the same need for his father's acceptance, but, generally, felt himself an ignored understudy to his brother. As for Bobby, he was virtually invisible to his father during this period. He was sometimes even invisible to his mother. Returning home after a trip, and expecting a warm welcome, Bob saw his mother, who simply stared at him and asked, "Bobby, have you seen Jack?"

Once when someone was praising the young Kennedys and Bobby's name came up, his sister Eunice blurted out: "Bobby? Forget it. Let's talk about the other boys."

Things were not easy for Bobby. He was slight and small, looking very much like the runt of the litter. His older brothers were so tall and handsome and personable and had done so much already. How could he ever compete?

"He was number seven," said his mother, "and Bobby was surrounded by girls, there were three girls older, one girl younger than he was. He was with them a good deal, because he was their age. He was with the governess. His grandmother was always afraid he would grow up to be a sissy."

Somebody said that Bobby looked like a bird in a storm when he walked, his head way down, his hands in his pockets, looking out from underneath his bushy hair. He looked shy and awkward. Even when he danced, he would pump his right arm up and down.

Bobby *was* awkward. Racing down to dinner one night—his father frowned on lateness—he forgot the glass partition separating the living room and the dining area and crashed into it, and shards of falling glass cut him all over his body. Another time, Eunice had tossed a plate of chocolate frosting at him, hitting him squarely in the face, and everybody laughed. Bobby chased her, cornered her, shut his eyes and charged toward her head-on. Eunice sidestepped and Bobby crashed into a table and needed stitches.

Reminiscing later about his boyhood, Robert Kennedy told Jack Newfield, "What I remember most vividly about growing up was going to a lot of different schools, always having to make new friends, and that I was very awkward. I dropped things and fell down all the time. I had to go to the hospital a few times for stitches in my head and my leg. And I was pretty quiet most of the time. And I didn't mind being alone."

Yet, he did, according to Eunice, who felt Bobby was more dependent emotionally than his brothers, "more anxious for affection and approval and love."

Bobby once wrote his father: "Why don't you write me a letter, the way you write to Joe and John?"

Lem Billings commented to Joseph Kennedy on Bobby's exceptional generosity with possessions. Bobby's father grunted, "I don't know where he got that." Luella Hennessey, who joined the household as the children's nurse when Bobby was twelve, called him "the most thoughtful and considerate of all the Kennedy children."

"I think he had just a natural connection to the underdog," said his close friend David Hackett. "If he saw an old lady trying to cross the street, he would go and help her. We'd think it'd be good to do that; but he'd actually *do* it. That was what was unique about him."

BOB WAS AN obedient boy, according to the Counselors' Report at Camp Winona, but he was inclined to do only what was expected of him and not much more. Only occasionally did he show a flash of leadership. Nor did he read very much. What Bob did do, when he started reading more, was to copy quotes that he liked and repeat them. One that he liked then was, "To strive, to seek, to find and not to yield."

Beneath the Boy Scout was a savage individuality. And beneath the most religious boy in his class was "the dirtiest fighter," a school friend remembered. He proved this later when he campaigned for Jack.

"I think he was a misfit at school," said Hackett, "and I think he was a misfit all through his whole career, in a way, in the best sense of the word."

He was a misfit because he was not what he wanted to be. He was his mother's altar boy and his sisters' pet, but most of all he wanted to be with his older brothers. When he was very small, young Joe would grab him and throw him in the air, and, sometimes, so would Jack. But now that he was a teenager, he was in between. His father didn't yet consider him seriously, and his older brothers were too busy with their college years. It was then that he reached for Teddy.

Like his three older brothers, Teddy was sent away to school as a young boy. He, too, felt the loneliness, and at times, the bitterness over losing the security of home. Many years later, he would confide to a friend, "My mother shipped me off to boarding school when I was seven." Rose would later explain, "This is a very involved household, with two or three houses, and my own problems."

Teddy was deposited at Portsmouth Abbey Priory, a Benedictine school in Portsmouth, Rhode Island. Because he was so young, ordinarily Teddy would not have been admissible at the Priory, but Rose insisted because Bobby was also there.

Bobby was not always helpful to his brother. When Teddy was in a fight with a bigger boy, and being pounded, flat on his back, he later recalled, Bobby came along, took one look, and refused to help, telling him, "You'll just have to look out for yourself." Father Damian recalled that he didn't succeed in this. After three months, Teddy was transferred to the Riverdale Country School for Boys in the Bronx. Teddy would transfer in and out of ten schools in his early years, since the family migrated so often.

During a later family vacation on the Riviera, young Joe and Jack were urging Teddy to jump off a thirty-foot cliff at Eden Roc into the Mediterranean. Rose was concerned but didn't interfere because she felt they were all having a good time and Joe would be there to rescue him.

"They would be swimming down below—I think it was Joe for the most part—and would encourage me to jump off the rock—I could barely swim at that point," Teddy remembered. "I'd jump in the water and grab ahold of them. . . . I did this several times. I think I was pretty scared, but they all seemed to be doing it."

When Teddy made a very poor showing in the final swimming

contest, brother Joe coached him carefully, and the next year he did very well.

Rose was most pleased with Teddy's religious attitude: "Teddy served Mass twice last Sunday . . . and is studying to be an altar boy and made his initial appearance yesterday morning at nine o'clock Mass. He is still strong for family spirit, because the other day after the teacher had confided to the class the heavy responsibility of Class Treasurer and had asked for nominations, Teddy stood up and said, 'I nominate Jean Kennedy.' "

Teddy never had the opportunity then to spend time with Joe Jr. and Jack. "My oldest brother Joe had been in Russia by the time I was five, and Jack had been in Poland when I was six," said Teddy. He also recalled the exciting table talk of the time, sensed that he would be doing his own traveling "when I was old enough." Joe Sr.'s expectations were quite different for his youngest son.

All his life, Teddy had heard his father tell Jack and Bob, "You can do better than that." To him, his father would say, "Gee, Teddy, you got it right! What a smart kid!"

His father's fond eye for him never hardened:

I was terribly sorry not to be with you in swimming at Cape Cod this summer, but I am sure you will know I wanted to be, but couldn't leave here while I had work to do. However, I am looking forward with great pleasure to our swims at Palm Beach this winter. . . .

Well, old boy, write me some letters and I want you to know that I miss seeing you a lot, for after all, you are my pal, aren't you?

In a memorial book Teddy later produced about his father, Ted wrote, "Dad wanted us to be natural, and able to smile no matter how tough things were. He wouldn't let any of his children feel sorry for himself, and expressed his frequent dislike of 'sour-pusses.' Yet he was also quick to scold a child who tried to smile too readily, or to charm his way through life. 'Remember,' he would say, 'a smile and a dime can only get you a ride on a streetcar. . . . You are going to need a lot more than that to get somewhere in life.' "

Compared to his older brothers, Teddy always saw himself as stupid and inadequate. Remarkably, each of the Kennedy brothers felt the same compared to older brothers. Teddy would spend his lifetime trying to overcome this. "The way it worked," observed Garry Wills, "was that the old man would push Joe, Joe would push Jack, Jack would push Bobby, Bobby would push Teddy, and Teddy would fall on his ass."

3

WAR AND DEATH

Joe Sr. now geared his immediate ambition to an unlikely quest.

When her husband came home from Washington for weekends, Rose Kennedy told Robert Coughlan, "I would ask him, 'What has the President said? Couldn't you tell him what you want?'

"Joe said to me, 'Well, I can't just walk into the office of the President of the United States and say, 'I want to be Ambassador to England.' "

When James Roosevelt reported to his father what Joe Kennedy wanted, "he laughed so hard, he almost toppled from his wheelchair." At Hyde Park, with dinner guests, Roosevelt said that appointing a Boston Irishman to the Court of St. James was "a great joke, the greatest joke in the world."

FDR, still beholden to Kennedy, told Henry Morgenthau that he considered Kennedy "a very dangerous man," and would regard it as an interim six-months appointment that would repay all political debts. An ambassador serves at the pleasure of the President.

When Kennedy came to see him, FDR asked him to please drop his pants. James Roosevelt recalled that a puzzled Joe Kennedy slowly obliged.

Roosevelt examined him critically. "You are just about the most bowlegged man I have ever seen," he said. "Don't you know that the Ambassador to the Court of St. James has to go through an induction ceremony in which he wears knee breeches and silk stockings? When photos of our new ambassador appear all over the world, we'll be a laughingstock.''

After the announcement, a friend sent him a word of warning. ''The job of Ambassador to London needs skill brought by years of training, and that, Joe, you simply don't possess. If you don't realize that soon enough, you're going to be hurt as you were never hurt in your life.''

The Ambassador used his natural genius at public relations to exploit whatever advantages he did have. One of those distinct assets was his photogenic and charismatic family.

On arrival in Britain, the new Ambassador announced to the British newsreels: ''Well, not wishing to add to the housing problem of England and make it any worse than it is, I'm bringing my children over in installments—five, two and two.'' The Ambassador had told his aide not to take too much luggage to London because they would only stay there long enough ''to get the family in the Social Register.''

Rose was thrilled. She had often complained, ''When will the nice people of Boston accept Catholics?'' And now she was happily basking in the royal limelight. For the children, it was an exciting adventure: an ocean liner, a new country. A British newsreel reporter tried to interview six-year-old Teddy, but he was speechless. Then he tried twelve-year-old Bobby, and Rose warned, ''Don't get him excited.''

''It's my first trip to Europe,'' Robert said, ''and I couldn't even sleep last night.'' He then added, ''I want to go to day school, so I can be home at night.''

Ambassador Kennedy left his own stamp on British protocol. When presented to King George VI at Buckingham Palace in 1938, Ambassador Joseph Kennedy did not wear breeches.

At the royal presentation of the Kennedys, Eunice described the walk along red-velvet-covered floors: ''countless footmen whose appearance in white knee breeches, red tail coats and powdered wigs led one to believe that these men served the English King of 1555 rather than 1939. . . . Fans of tinted ostrich feathers were carried, and as each one curtsied before Their Majesties . . . I had the honor of being the first debutante presented.''

––––––

ROSE LATER HAD her own private chat with the Queen. ''The Queen asked me if I got up in the morning to see the children off to school," said Rose Kennedy, "and I said I did unless I was out very late the night before. She said she got up and then hopped back into bed again."

This breathtaking closeness to royalty, and her husband's ambitions, gave Rose an urgency toward investigating, and possibly enhancing, her own genealogy. She claimed that the Fitzgerald family had originated in Italy eight centuries before, where their name was Gheraldini. The Gheraldinis reportedly helped William the Conqueror defeat England, and were awarded a castle and title. By the time the family settled in Ireland, the name had been transformed into Fitzgerald. The name itself was as distinguished as "Kennedy" was common. There were noble branches, and two of the most famous revolutions had been led by them, including the one by Lord Edward Fitzgerald that brought the Wexford uprising.

Rose wanted to show her children that they did not merely emerge from Irish peasants. This vision of herself as future American royalty was perfect for Rose. It gave sanction to the removed way she dealt with people.

Observing the British royals carefully, Rose gave suggestions on behavior and posture and manners to her children. "I would remind my sons," she later told Coughlan, "how well trained the royal family has been to remember such things, which are so important in public life."

Rose was brought back to quick reality later when her parents came for a visit to share the excitement. Soon after arriving at the embassy residence, seventy-five-year-old Honey Fitz mailed invitations—on official stationery, which he found on desks—to hundreds of his cronies back in Boston to come to tea on a date five days hence: which, of course, in those steamship days, made it impossible for them. But he thought they would enjoy being invited. "Joe was away at the time," Rose noted, "and was irritated when he came back and found out later . . . but what could he do?"

———

AT HIS FIRST press conference, the Ambassador Extraordinary and Plenipotentiary to the United Kingdom of Great Britain and Northern Ireland shocked the British newsmen by putting his feet on the desk ("You don't expect me to develop into a statesman overnight"). It reflected Joe Sr.'s instinct for public relations, a calculated ploy of casualness.

New York Times correspondent James Reston reported that the new Ambassador observed at his first press conference that the American people were more interested in the Boston Braves than in foreign policy.

"He was then in his fiftieth year," said Reston, "a recklessly charming, intelligent handsome man who seldom let his official responsibilities interfere with his personal pleasure. He worked hard and had many other admirable qualities, but judgment wasn't one of them. . . . He never met a man—or a woman, for that matter—he didn't think he could conquer, but he couldn't keep his mouth shut or his pants on."

Meanwhile, the British press commented favorably on the Ambassador's gusto and zest in squeezing dry the orange of life, and predicted that his time there would not be boring.

When Kennedy paid his respects to the austere, aloof Prime Minister Neville Chamberlain he promptly called him "Neville," according to a British observer, "and Chamberlain's Adam's apple would work up and down convulsively three or four times before he could emit a forced 'Joe.' "

The British press constantly reported everything about the Kennedys, including Teddy taking an upside-down picture of the changing of the guard, and Bobby's awkward attempts to begin a conversation with Princess Elizabeth at a party. "We became practically public property," Rose later said. "I almost began to feel that we had been adopted as a family, by the whole British people."

Ambassador Kennedy soon became known as "Jolly Joe, the nine-child envoy." "Who would have thought that the English could take into camp a red-headed Irishman," President Roosevelt wondered aloud to Morgenthau.

———

THEY QUICKLY SETTLED in the six-story embassy at 14 Princes Gate. Bobby, serious and intense, acted as a restraining influence on Teddy, who gleefully operated the elevator, commandeering the servants to play department store. Before this, Jean had said of herself and Ted that they were the babies, "kind of the last gasp, so we don't remember the close family life the other children had."

Their nurse Luella Hennessey recalled that "the boys had always been close, but in London they were together most of their free time. I could see that they truly liked each other, which is rare between brothers. So many other siblings bicker and shut one another out from their games." After school the young Kennedys used the private house telephones as an intercom to arrange which of the thirty-six rooms to gather in for backgammon and checkers.

Bobby and Teddy were sent to the Sloane Street School for Boys, and then to the more exclusive Gibbs. They wore traditional clothes of upper-class schoolboys: maroon jackets, gray flannel trousers (shorts in the summer), and small skullcaps. When a classmate told Teddy that he wanted to be his "best friend," Teddy said that he already had one, his brother Bobby.

Their nurse would pick up the boys to walk them home. When they passed a Catholic Church, Bobby would say, "Let's stop in and pay a visit to the Lord," and they would go in and pray for a few minutes.

Master Robert Kennedy even represented his father at a cornerstone ceremony of the Temple of Youth at the First Clubland Church before an expected audience of a thousand people. The Ambassador's press secretary, James Seymour, wrote some remarks: "I hope the house that this stone helps to build will make ever so many English boys and girls happy for ever and ever so long. . . . When I'm a man—it will be grown up, too. And I know it will be fine and strong—and doing wonderful things for lots of other boys and girls who aren't born yet."

Teddy would often be in his father's room in the morning when the servant was preparing the Ambassador's clothes. Later in the day he'd repeat anything he heard there. If his father talked about the English Channel, Teddy would later start talking about the English Channel.

The two younger brothers, the intense Bobby and the easygoing Teddy, needed each other more than ever. Their older brothers were still in the United States, and the two young boys felt surrounded by their sisters. The six months they had together before their big brothers came was the most important bonding time in their lives.

There was a big park behind the embassy, and sometimes Teddy, his father, and Bobby would go riding together. Bobby also taught Teddy how to ride his first two-wheeler bicycle. It was a downhill run between two trees and Teddy recalled crashing at the bottom.

When Bobby and Teddy would spend time with their father briefly early every evening, Bobby would talk about school and ask serious questions about current events. "When Teddy's turn came, however," the governess recalled, "the atmosphere in the room would completely change. Teddy was lighting up everything in sight and keeping his father young. Through the corridors you could hear them laughing as Teddy jumped up and down on his father's bed until he was exhausted."

Even with the demands of his new position, Joe kept close track of his family. The Kennedys regularly had pajama dinners for their family, where everybody including the Ambassador wore pajamas and robes. A guest observed how the Ambassador required each child to report on their details of the day, including their current weights. To her amazement, he even found a discreet way of inquiring whether they had a bowel movement.

Ambassador Kennedy made a trip back to Washington to report to the State Department in the summer of 1938. His main reason, he confided, was to be at his son Joe's graduation from Harvard. When the Ambassador arrived, the Boston *Herald* reporter described the hectic scene aboard the ship and the suite crowded with reporters. Suddenly, young Joe appeared, "big, square-shouldered athlete with tousled bronze hair . . . good-natured, grinning son with smiling eyes that were always determined, looking at his idol—his father."

Young Joe was proud of his honors thesis on the isolationist movement and the Spanish Civil War. And so was his father. His major was government, and he listed his intended vocation in the class album as business. But his goal was still the presidency.

Kennedy took both Joe and Jack back with him to England. Felix Frankfurter, who had recommended to the elder Kennedy that young Joe study under Harold Laski, this time suggested that Joe join his father at the British Embassy as his assistant.

On the journey to England, Arthur Krock remembered the shipboard romance between young Joe and a beautiful actress. Jack also was staying up late with a young woman he had met. Kennedy had carefully calculated his sons' futures and worried about the serious intentions of the young women, and so imposed a midnight curfew on his sons. The two boys arrived at their father's suite on schedule the first midnight, but then Krock arranged to let them out the back door, "and I don't know whether the old man found out about it or not."

In a threatening Europe, London seemed casual and unconcerned. Prime Minister Chamberlain still felt he could negotiate peaceful relations with Adolf Hitler while Hitler was planning to absorb as much of Europe as rapidly as possible. The British, meanwhile, were enjoying the Kennedys as an interesting interlude.

For young Joe, London was revisiting old territory in very new surroundings; for Jack, it was a brief whirl of excitement before returning to school. Except for holidays, this was the first time the whole Kennedy family had been together in a single house since Joe had left for Choate.

Pamela Harriman, who would later become Ambassador to France, felt young Joe was "magnificent." In contrast, she then regarded Jack as "a scrawny kid." His sister Kick called Jack "John of Gaunt." If Jack seemed shyer about asking questions, everybody admitted that he had a more appealing manner than Joe and a lightning reflex.

Young British aristocrats found Jack more attractive than Joe, less abrasive, with more finesse. Joe would cut in on dance partners at a ball, and do it curtly, as he did at Harvard. This kind of sexual aggressiveness was not appreciated in Britain. There were some exceptions. One of them was Virginia Gilliat, who had been listed earlier among the debutantes as "Popular Girl Number One."

Tall, vivacious Virginia Gilliat, later to become Lady Sykes, and mistress of Sledmere House, later admitted that she was very keen on young Joe. One night, after a date, she invited him in for a nightcap in the drawing room. "The lights were dim. We were very young, there was a good deal of kissing going on, but nothing more than that. Well, my father walked in. Joe was absolutely covered, all over his face, with lipstick. Father put all the lights on. My father had the most beautiful manners, and he just made incredibly polite conversation with Joe, and asked him how he liked being in England. . . . And there was Joe beaming, all over lipstick, and tears in my eyes, and my father not concerned, as if it were nothing, you know? Poor Joe!"

Lorelle Hearst, war correspondent and former showgirl, was a charming and beautiful woman who later became one of his closest friends. She remembered that Joe was "sweet . . . but sometimes could be cruel. He never would have married anyone who wasn't socially prominent, mostly virginal, and Catholic."

Young Bobby had been waiting impatiently for his older brothers.

He didn't like being different, and when his father suggested he join the Boy Scouts in Britain, he said no because it would mean that he'd have to swear allegiance to the King. His father understood and arranged that Bobby become an American Boy Scout with visiting privileges to the British scouts.

Bobby loved his older brothers and was perfectly willing to be bullied by them. He happily trailed after them—when they let him. Bobby and Jack would have late discussions, and Jack would often walk around the embassy grounds with Bobby, who was always ready with a barrage of questions which he always patiently answered.

It was difficult to adopt any formal behavior, despite nurses and nannies, especially for the younger Kennedys. They acted as they always had acted at Hyannis, carefree and a little crazy. Their father could crack down, and they would listen, but now he was too busy. Their mother would try to discipline, but she was now part of a frenetic social whirl. So the younger boys had a considerable amount of leeway with a beleaguered nurse trying to keep pace with them, and not often succeeding. And what made it so interesting for Bobby and Teddy and their sisters was how the British servants always catered to them so respectfully as if they were aristocrats.

Joe and Jack worked for their father. Their duties were nominal, which Jack described as those of a glorified office boy. Joe was more serious and attentive, but Jack often had his own way of keeping his father at arm's length, and enjoying life. The Ambassador would sometimes send his sons to represent him at various functions when he had other appointments—often with women.

One of the staff stories was that Ambassador Kennedy brought with him to Britain a particularly lovely secretary—he always had pretty ones. Most of them had an extracurricular involvement with their boss. When word got back to President Roosevelt, he reportedly called Kennedy and told him to get rid of this particular secretary immediately. Kennedy's answer, which may be apocryphal, was, "I'll get rid of her when you get rid of Missy LeHand." Missy LeHand was Roosevelt's attractive secretary who, it was later revealed, had been his mistress.

Aide Klemmer recalled the Ambassador boasting of an affair with the Duchess of Kent, but added, "He would lay anything in sight and was always talking about who was the best lay in the United States and who was second best.'' Lady Maureen Fellowes, a friend of Kick's, described the Ambassador as ''a filthy old man.''

The American Embassy's public relations director, James Seymour, served as the Ambassador's surrogate in watching over his sons. Seymour had been a public relations director at Harvard Business School. Joe Kennedy had hired him to come to Hollywood and write the story line for his film *Gold Diggers of 1933*. An attractive and personable man, Seymour was also a man of considerable courage. He had earned the Croix de Guerre in World War I.

It was no secret among their London friends that Jim Seymour was seriously smitten with Rose Kennedy. Seymour said he and Rose would discuss the arts and the world of culture and recite poetry. When Rose Kennedy was returning from a trip, Seymour would always go to meet her. Seymour told author Ed Plaut of the time when the weather was too bad for the ship to dock so he took the pilot ship in the storm to be with her. Seymour spent that night aboard ship with Rose, and without giving details described it as one of the highlights of his life. No one knows what transpired that night.

If there was any romantic feeling at all in this relationship, it may well have been one-sided with Seymour. With her husband's constantly flaunting his affairs, it would be easy to understand any possible receptiveness by Rose, although her religion dictated otherwise.

Seymour stayed in England for another thirty-five years before briefly visiting the United States. He confided that it was for the sole purpose of seeing Rose again.

EUROPE WAS IN turmoil, and Spain became a preview of the war to come. The Republican government found itself faced with a civil war, an uprising by the fascist forces of General Franco. Hitler and Mussolini sent troops and planes to fight alongside Franco, and the Soviet government sent aid to the Loyalist government. The United States declared an embargo on all arms to Spain.

Returning to London from a short trip, the Ambassador found a cable from his son Joe: SORRY I MISSED YOU. ARRIVED SAFELY IN VALENCIA. GOING TO MADRID TONIGHT. REGARDS, JOE.

Jack had tried to get into Spain earlier that summer when he toured Europe with Lem, but couldn't get in. He had stayed with a Harvard classmate on the border, listening to Loyalist stories of Franco's bloody persecution.

It was now different with Joe. Madrid was under siege, but the Spanish government was anxious to cater to the son of an American ambassador, still hoping that the United States might lift their arms embargo. They provided young Joe with a private bus, but he often preferred to walk the streets. They gave him a rich luncheon of mutton and cognac while the average Madrid citizen was rationed to a few slices of bread a day. The Kennedys retained their privilege wherever in the world they happened to be.

Human life was cheap there and Joe was even escorted by the underground through the various sectors of the city, held by different forces, all of them quick to kill.

"I remember thinking then of how brave Joe was," wrote Kathleen, "when different Spaniards told me of how he, the only American, used to walk about during the bloody, horrible days of the siege."

Clearly, young Joe was moved by what he saw in Republican Madrid. In a letter to the *Atlantic Monthly*, he described the devastated Valencia: "Every house within a radius of a half-mile was in literal wreckage. It's just plain suicide to stay there any length of time. Incredibly, some people still live there, but it's like a deserted village . . . it's been battered to death by bombs."

In discussing the spirit of the people in Madrid, young Joe never faulted Franco as being responsible for the siege. Instead, he saw the Franco fascists as the bastion of the Catholic faith. That, to him, was the determining factor. And he knew this was also how his father felt.

"Good night, Dad, and much love to all of you. Somehow, this must be prevented from happening to any of you."

Ambassador Kennedy reread these letters so often that he could quote parts of them, which he did once at a small dinner given by Prime Minister Chamberlain at Ten Downing Street. The Ambassador was then closely tied with the isolationist Cliveden set. Anne Morrow Lindbergh described how proudly the Ambassador read his son's letter and looked "like a small boy, pleased and shy . . . like an Irish terrier wagging his tail (a very nice Irish terrier)."

———

THE BRITISH ATMOSPHERE was changing. It seemed like a bubble about to burst. People were increasingly nervous, and the younger ones saw it as a time to live to the hilt.

The world was moving closer to war when Prime Minister Chamberlain flew to Berchtesgaden to appease Hitler. Chamberlain agreed to all of Hitler's territorial demands, including Sudetenland, Austria, and democratic Czechoslovakia. In *Mein Kampf*, Hitler had outlined his plan for a German empire that would include all of Europe, an empire, he said, that would last a thousand years.

Britain was not ready to fight, and neither was Ambassador Kennedy. He had passed on to the Prime Minister a memo from Charles Lindbergh that the Luftwaffe could beat the combined air forces of Britain, France, and Russia. At a dinner at which Winston Churchill and columnist Walter Lippmann attended, Kennedy said that war was inevitable and the Allies would be defeated. An indignant Churchill bristled: combat instead of surrender, faith instead of fear.

"Joe thought war was irrational and debasing," said a friend. "War destroyed capital. What could be worse than that?" Or, as an American correspondent in London explained it: "He not only thought that wars were bad for business, but what was worse, for *his* business." Even more personally, Joseph Kennedy felt that if war came, America would soon be part of it. "I have four boys and I don't want them killed in a foreign war."

———

THE AMBASSADOR OPPOSED the "destroyers-for-bases" deal whereby the U.S. government gave Britain fifty "overage" warships in return for ninety-nine-year leases in British territories for military bases. It was negotiated through the embassy in Washington with Kennedy merely being kept informed in a routine way. Kennedy cabled Hull, "I am very unhappy about the whole position and of course there is always the alternative of resigning." Hull replied that "the President and I appreciate the magnificent way in which you and your staff are carrying on your work." They persuaded him not to resign. FDR wanted him in Britain because he felt he would be more of a political problem in the United States in the upcoming presidential election.

———

KENNEDY INTIMATE JOE Kane told a fantastic story about the Ambassador and a plan he hatched with the Prime Minister. Kennedy was to go to Germany and make a proposition to Hitler: England would help restore German possession of its territories if Germany would stay off the continent. They took the idea to King George, who quickly called FDR. "First thing Kennedy knew he was explaining it to FDR, who said, 'I'm against it.' "

Many at that time felt Kennedy sympathized with Germany. Max Aitkin, the son of Lord Beaverbrook, told Ed Plaut that he thought one of the reasons Kennedy was so fervently pro-Nazi was that the German Embassy provided him with a steady flow of very lovely German girls, especially one who was later revealed as a spy.

———

KENNEDY, WHO SAW himself as the center of growing animosity and danger, then announced he was coming home. He did not want to represent a country whose views on the war he could not accept. Roosevelt ordered him to stay, and he did.

Time later reported that the Ambassador wrote a book on his career in the administration in which he lambasted FDR. Kennedy compatriot Mike Ward claimed that the book was written and scheduled for publication when FDR phoned the Ambassador and told him, "Buster, you publish that book and here's your tax blank." Kennedy leaked the story of this threat of an Internal Revenue tax investigation to columnist Westbrook Pegler, who printed it. But he did not publish the book.

Prime Minister Chamberlain signed his pact with Hitler, surrendering Czechoslovakia, but taking a stand on Poland. He called it "peace in our time." Rose Kennedy echoed her husband when she said that everyone felt relieved and happy and that war was now out of the question. Meanwhile, the British were busy digging trenches.

———

WITH THE WAR again threatening because of Hitler's new demands on Poland, the Kennedys took a final vacation on the Riviera. They always stayed at the Hôtel du Cap d'Antibes because Kennedy had a long relationship with its owner, André Sela. Between swims in the blue Mediterranean, Kennedy often spent hours with Sela discussing the international situation. One day, Sela asked Kennedy: "Do you think we are going to have war?"

Kennedy replied: "When I am called back, you will know that war is imminent." On August 29, 1939, Kennedy suddenly left the Hôtel du Cap, and André Sela was alone to enjoy his last swim before World War II.

JACK AND JOE had already traveled a great deal and now possessed the charm and informality that would enable them to mingle with all kinds of people. They were now writing long reports every week or two for their father on what they had seen and heard and what they thought. Both were observant and wrote well—except for Jack's spelling, which remained atrocious.

"But the main point of the whole exercise was not to inform him but to educate them for the important roles in public affairs that he envisioned for them in years ahead," remarked Coughlan.

In Paris, one of Ambassador William Bullitt's senior staff assistants later recalled to Coughlan, "Jack was sitting in my office and listening to telegrams being read or even reading various things which were actually none of his business, but since he was who he was we didn't throw him out." Then, as nearly as he can be tracked, he went on to Germany and Poland, Lithuania, Latvia and Estonia, to Russia, Turkey, Palestine, Egypt, back to Europe to visit Romania and Yugoslavia. At most stops he was preceded by a message such as this to Arthur Bliss Lane, the Ambassador to Belgrade from the Ambassador in London: "Will appreciate any courtesy. My son arriving today."

From Palestine, Jack wrote his father with views his father applauded, "The sympathy of the people on the spot seems to be with the Arabs . . . after all, the country has been Arabic for the last few hundred years, and they naturally feel sympathetic. After all, Palestine was hardly Britain's to give away." His proposal for a fair solution was to "arbitrarily force the partition plan to be accepted."

Another ambassador, George Kennan, recorded in his memoirs of the advancing Germans and closing frontiers and the confusion of war.

In the midst of this, he noted, he received a telegram from Ambassador Kennedy that he was sending "one of his young sons (John) on a fact-finding tour around Europe, and it was up to us to find a means of getting him across the border and through the German lines so that he could include in his itinerary a visit to Prague. We were furious. . . . The idea that there was anything he could learn or report about conditions in Europe which we did not already know and had not already reported seemed (and not without reason) wholly absurd."

Despite this, arrangements were made.

This "inquisitive nuisance of a boy" would one day as President call Kennan out of retirement to serve as Ambassador to Yugoslavia.

———

NAZI TROOPS AND tanks swept into Poland on September 1, 1939.

Kennedy had told *New York Times* correspondent James Reston, "I don't care if Germany carves up Poland. . . . I'm for appeasement one thousand percent." And he had been telling this to Chamberlain, "every chance I had every day for more than a year."

He also wrote the King and Queen a note, which sounded strange coming from someone who firmly believed the Nazis would beat Britain: "Of this you may rest assured, whatever strength or influence I possess will be used every hour of the day for the preservation of *that life* we all hold so dear, and in which cause you and your gracious Queen help to lead the world."

But the British pact with Poland had no loopholes.

Two days later, Kennedy sat in the Strangers' Gallery of the House of Commons with Rose and Joe Jr., Jack, and Kick, listening to the Prime Minister, noticeably bent and frail, make his declaration of war, a speech he had read two hours earlier at Ten Downing Street. It had been written in Spencerian script, "His Most Excellent Majesty George the Sixth by the Grace of God, of Great Britain, Ireland, and of the British Dominions beyond the Seas, King, Defender of the Faith, Emperor of India, is constrained to announce that a state of war exists with Germany."

Chamberlain had said: "Everything that I have worked for, everything that I have believed in during my public life has crashed in ruins." Given the choice between shame and war, said Churchill, Chamberlain "chose shame and got war!"

Few felt as bitterly as the Ambassador. His sons would be in this war after all. Earlier he had told a friend: ''There's a big storm coming up . . . my Joe might be flying through that storm. If anything ever happened to one of my boys, I'd die.''

Running for cover on the way home from the House of Commons, as air raid sirens began to howl, Rose later said she knew ''it was time to get our children back home.''

Ambassador Kennedy, whom the British public had adopted, was now publicly persona non grata, and it hurt. His pro-Nazi sympathies were bitterly resented.

Sir Robert Vansittart expressed the view of many British leaders when he wrote in 1940, ''Mr. Kennedy is a very foul specimen of a double-crosser and defeatist.''

Young Joe defended his father in a note to his mother. ''Dad cannot be blamed for misreading Hitler's intention. Almost everybody did too, including the State Department.''

JACK VOLUNTEERED AS an air raid spotter at the American Embassy, which requested unmarried men and suggested ''unguessable potential dangers,'' said the Ambassador's aide, James Seymour. ''Jack had to go to the roof with binoculars, steel helmet and gas mask and keep watch until All Clear sounds. When they see or hear anything approaching which seems to endanger the building, they sound buzzer warning officer at Front Door Information desk. At departure of said danger they will sound buzzer twice,'' said Seymour. ''If the buzzer didn't work, they were supposed to wave a white flag on a pole if they saw enemy planes approaching their area.''

London was now a vastly different place. The social life was stilled; the talk somber and the reality hard. Young men and women were rushing into uniform. The public talk concerned air raid shelters, rations, and grim hope.

The Kennedy family had a final dinner together at a borrowed estate outside London. A visiting friend, Tom Egerton, remembered how gay they all were, how they never stopped talking.

Joe sent his family back to the United States in September 1939, in separate batches to spread the risk, because there were six Nazi submarines lurking nearby in the Atlantic. Rose went home first with

Bobby and two girls. Eighteen-year-old Eunice wrote how packed the ship was, people even sleeping in the swimming pool. "Bob is rushing around trying to get Tilden, Budge, and Montgomery's autographs, but today two people asked him for his, so at present he is feeling very important."

Joe and Jack stayed behind helping Americans desperately trying to get home. When the first civilian ship was sunk by Nazi torpedoes off the Scottish coast, with some 300 American passengers, the Ambassador sent Jack as his surrogate to help the survivors. He was a skinny twenty-two, looking years younger, and he toured the hospitals and hotels, telling surviving Americans that he had talked to his father and that the government had "plenty of money for you all." The survivors were not impressed and demanded a convoy home. Jack hurried back with this recommendation, but his father turned it down.

Jack expected to be late to register for the new term at Harvard but an empty plane seat materialized for the Ambassador's son, and he arrived in time.

The Ambassador wrote a sad note to Krock about saying goodbye to his children, "for how long God only knows. . . . Maybe never to see them again."

Kennedy could hardly have resigned when war came, because it would be stamped as cowardice and ruined his reputation. But he did stock his air raid shelter and included Gruyère, twenty-four bottles of Malverne water, and 144 bars of chocolate. He also persistently reminded the Secretary of State that the embassy needed more air raid protection.

The Ambassador was at the embassy when he learned that a young aide's father had died. Joe Sr. urged her to call her mother and she did. When she finished, she came to the Ambassador to thank him. He said, "God, I'd give anything to talk to my mother"—she had been dead for years. And then he added confidingly, "I've had a wonderful life." He said that if he died now, he could leave each child a million dollars. And then he added, "And you know they'd never never have an exciting time as I've had."

––––––––

WITH THE RESIGNATION of Chamberlain, Winston Leonard Spencer Churchill became Prime Minister of Great Britain. He promised to fight on the beaches with beer bottles if they had to, never to surrender.

"Churchill phoned Roosevelt so often—during the night in USA— that an extra hand was put on his clock where he worked so he would know the time in USA and not disturb the President unnecessarily," said Rose Kennedy.

Ambassador Kennedy said of Churchill, "He drinks too much. I don't have any confidence in a man who is always sucking on a whiskey bottle." The Ambassador, who didn't drink at all, nevertheless had no qualms about telling his aide Harvey Klemmer to reserve valuable cargo space in outgoing vessels for 200,000 cases of whiskey for his importing company.

———

JOE STILL STRONGLY followed his father's isolationist line about keeping out of the war. War could bring chaos to the world and then maybe bolshevism. Young Joe, who returned to Harvard Law School in 1939, wrote a friend that the Germans were a marvelous people and "it would be tough to keep them from getting what they want." He suggested we should try to get along with Hitler.

He also soon formed the Harvard Committee Against Military Intervention. He appeared on the same platform with Senator Robert Taft, at Boston's Ford Hall, saying that the United States would be better off accepting Nazi domination of the continent than plunging into a war that would strain American economy beyond its limits, which would unleash the forces of radicalism.

The British press reacted by calling young Joe "a smart-aleck of a boy, who will not help his father's standing."

However, the Ambassador had nothing but praise for his eldest, and wrote him:

It was a terribly tough thing to go back to that kind of work, after a year in Europe, and the fact that you stuck with it is a great tribute to you. Hoping and praying I would be back, so that I could be with you on your 25th birthday, because on that day you take over your interest in the Trust, and you become owner of a considerable amount of securities and money. In addition, you are now arriving at the point where you have responsibilities to the family. Of course, I am completely confident nothing is going to happen to me in this mess, but one never can be sure, and you don't know what satisfaction it is for me to know that you've come along so well, and I have such confidence that come what may, you can run the show.

For Jack, much had changed dramatically. Now a junior, he seemed more interested in academic history. One of his professors, Bruce Hopper, noted that Jack came back from Europe much more mature, with a subject for his thesis well blocked out.

In it, some of his ideas now seemed to veer away from those of his father.

Jack would later tell his friend Rousmaniere, "You know, my brother Joe is like my father, and my father does try to tell us how to do things, and I just have to rebel against this every so often." But then he added, "When my father pushes too hard, why then Joe and I get together."

As much as they admired their father, he sometimes could be very arbitrary and difficult with them. At that point Joe and Jack sometimes aligned together against him. "That never came out in public," said James Rousmaniere. "They were pretty careful not to be too bitter about it."

———

NINETEEN FORTY WAS a presidential election year and the big question still was whether or not Franklin Delano Roosevelt was going to run for a third term. If he decided against it, then Joseph Kennedy Sr.'s dream of the presidency would be alive again.

In a quiet time of reflection, Joe Kennedy told a friend, "Six or seven times in my life, the pendulum swung my way. If it had fallen favorably to me, life could be quite a bit different."

In May 1938, *Liberty* magazine had a story headline, WILL KENNEDY RUN FOR PRESIDENT? It created a flurry of national editorials. Krock, whom Kennedy had invited to England (and paid for his passage), later said that Kennedy fully expected to be nominated for president in 1940, "without any question."

Many Americans agreed with Kennedy's appeasement, and a Washington *Post* article said that Ambassador Kennedy had an excellent chance to be the first Catholic President. A May 1940 public-opinion poll put Kennedy fifth among Democratic presidential possibilities if Roosevelt didn't run.

But FDR, who had not yet announced his decision to run for a third term, quickly indicated his displeasure at the Kennedy boomlet. The power of FDR's judgment on this was absolute. To cut off Kennedy's ambitions and eliminate possible opposition, the President called the Ambassador to tell him how much the Democratic Committee wanted him to run Roosevelt's upcoming presidential campaign, "but the State Department is very much against you leaving England . . . they were very anxious to have you and you know how happy I would be to have you in charge, but the general impression is that it would do the cause of England a great deal of harm if you left there at this time."

What Roosevelt had, and Kennedy didn't, was a broad vision of public purpose. Roosevelt saw power as "the fulfillment of self, rather than the preservation of self." Kennedy wanted status and Roosevelt wanted change. However, Arthur Krock insisted, "Kennedy knew the human race pretty well, and he knew its weaknesses and strengths and pretensions and hypocrisy, and he went right to the nut. He would have made a hell of a President."

Kennedy had taken private polls which were not promising. Too many people remembered what he had said in Britain. It wasn't long before *The New York Times* reported that the Ambassador had been approached to run and had refused. Joe Kennedy later explained to Clare Boothe Luce why he had changed his mind and strongly endorsed FDR for reelection. "I simply made a deal with Roosevelt. We agreed that if I endorsed him for president in 1940, he would support my son Joe for governor of Massachusetts in 1942." According to Jack Kennedy, his father also had the promise from Roosevelt to support the senior Kennedy for the Democratic presidential nomination in 1944. In view of FDR's real feelings about the elder Kennedy, this seems unlikely.

———

JACK HAD WRITTEN his father that his Harvard courses were "really interesting this year" and that he was doing a thesis on British foreign policy. "Everyone is getting much more confident about staying out of the war." He also noted that Mother looked very well and was even taking some college courses.

Joe Jr. also wrote their father:

> The Easter vacation is just about over and soon back to law school for the last two months of the grind. . . . Teddy is fatter than ever and looks as healthy as it is possible to look. Jack finished his thesis. . . . It looks like Dewey will get the Republican nomination OK, and it is still a mystery as far as the Democratic one goes. At the present time it doesn't seem that anyone could be elected except Roosevelt. . . . Farley has come out and said that his name will be presented at Chicago regardless of what happens.

Joe wrote to his father that "Jack rushed madly around last week, with his thesis—'Appeasement at Munich,' an explanation of England's foreign policy since 1931—and finally, with the aid of five stenographers, the last day got it under the wire. He seemed to have some good ideas, so it ought to be very good."

Two professors called Jack's thesis "badly written" and "defective" but it was finally graded "cum laude." Young Joe suggested that Jack ask Krock to read it, too.

"I am sending my thesis," Jack wrote his father. "I'll be interested to see what you think of it, as it represents more work than I've ever done in my life. Arthur Krock read it and feels that I should get it published. He thinks that a good name for it might be Why England Slept, as sort of a contrast to Churchill's While England Slept. . . . Please let me know what you think about the thesis as soon as you can. . . . The chief questions are: 1. Whether it is worth publishing if polished up. 2. If it can be published while you're still in office."

He added a note he hoped might please his father: "Just got back from the South . . . three girls to every man—so I did better than usual." And he had another comment about Bobby: "Bobby has increased in strength to such a degree that I seriously believe he will be bouncing me around plenty in two more years . . . he has improved immensely as everyone has noticed in every way. He looks 100% better too."

His father replied promptly how anxious he was to read his son's thesis. "Whether you make a cent out of it or not, it will do you an amazing amount of good, particularly if it is well received. You would be surprised how a book that really makes the grade with high-class people stands you in good stead for years to come."

Replying, Jack added, "I should get it out before the issue becomes too dead. . . . What should I do about a publisher—keep Krock's agent or can you fix it?"

Joe gave the manuscript to Harvey Klemmer to rewrite. "I had to rewrite the whole thing, including the final sum-up paragraph. It was terribly written and disorganized, and even the spelling was bad, the sentences ungrammatical." Klemmer later said of Jack, "I did not think he was a very bright young man and I certainly did not think he was a very good writer." But, once again, Kennedy would do anything, use anybody to advance his sons.

Up to then, young Joe was clearly the ascendant son. There was no question of this, and nobody admitted this more quickly than Jack. But now, suddenly, with this book, Jack emerged into the family limelight. For Jack, it was a heady thing; for young Joe, it was a hard blow. Nor was he graceful about it to his father, to whom he wrote: "It seemed to represent a lot of work, but didn't prove anything." The Ambassador then persuaded Henry R. Luce to write the foreword. Luce agreed. Both his foreword and the book seemed to run counter to some of Joe's pro-Nazi views. It seemed that the father had put his son's rising future above his own principles. But also, in promoting his son, he was illustrating his own power.

———

IN THE HARVARD yearbook, Jack Kennedy gave his "intended vocation" as "Law," mainly, his friends said, because he had to put down something, and his brother was in law. But, at graduation, under his cap and gown, he expressed his independence by wearing dirty saddle shoes. His father, who had attended Joe's graduation, did not come to Jack's, but cabled from London: TWO THINGS I ALWAYS KNEW ABOUT YOU, ONE THAT YOU ARE SMART AND TWO THAT YOU ARE A SWELL GUY.

When Jack's book was published in 1940, the elder Kennedy sent copies to everybody he knew, including the King and Queen. The younger Kennedy donated the British royalties on his book to help rebuild the bombed city of Plymouth—and used the American royalties to buy a car.

IT WAS NOW Joe's turn, and the Ambassador gave Klemmer a batch of thirty-six letters from Joe and told him to make a book out of it with his suggested title "Dear Dad." A literary agent pointed out that Jack's book, *Why England Slept*, had become a best-seller and had "stolen, quite innocently, to be sure . . . the thunder of Joe's courageous stand."

"Once I said to Old Man Kennedy that I thought Jack was a more serious young man than Joe," said Klemmer. "The old man bristled at this, and said, 'Why do you say that?' He was obviously annoyed. . . . I think that's because young Joe looked more like him and was probably the young man that the old man would have liked to be."

The Ambassador also kept contact with his youngest son, Teddy, thanking him for a radio message. "You are a great little cheer leader, and that Hip! Hip! Hooray! couldn't have been better." He also added:

> I certainly don't get all those letters you keep telling me you write. . . . You and Bobby are the worst correspondents I have in the family. . . . I don't know whether you would have had much excitement during these [air] raids. I am sure you wouldn't be scared, but if you heard all of these guns firing every night and the bombs bursting you might get a little fidgety . . . it is really terrible to think about all those poor women and children and homeless people down in the East End of London all seeing their places destroyed.
>
> I hope when you grow up you will dedicate your life to trying to work out plans to make people happy instead of making them miserable, as war does.

Americans in London who stayed in London during the blitz now regarded Kennedy as a coward because he had rented the seventy-room former Dodge mansion, about twenty-five miles from London, and disappeared to it regularly to avoid the bombing.

On the first night of the blitz, the Ambassador had walked down Piccadilly with Klemmer and said, "I'll bet you five to one—any sum—that Hitler will be at Buckingham Palace in two weeks." Nor did he seem to be depressed at the prospect. He told this to everyone, even calling Henry Luce on an open phone line, saying the jig was up for England. "You just don't do that kind of thing. The British never forgave him for that."

Ambassador Kennedy seemed to be right. The Nazis rolled through Europe and destroyed the French army. Paris fell on June 14, 1940, and the French surrendered a week later. Hitler's invasion of Great Britain seemed imminent.

Joe Jr. reported to his father the changing American opinion on the war and the feeling that the United States would soon be in it. He even added that he was investigating the possibility of joining the Reserves of the Navy or Army Air Corps, "so that if anything happens I won't be a private." With Grandfather Honey Fitz's help, he was also planning to become a delegate to the upcoming Democratic National Convention. He already had hired a speech teacher.

Bobby made his own family report: "Joe has . . . been giving all his speeches around here. They are pretty good. Last week, Jack was telling us all about himself, now Joe is telling us about himself."

The elder Kennedy was not unhappy when Joe became a delegate for James Farley for President at the Convention. Joe wrote his father on July 22:

> Even before the delegation left Boston, there were arguments as to whom they would support, Farley or Roosevelt. . . . We had a caucus the first night, and it was the stormiest session that I've ever seen. They called each other liars and thieves. . . . Of course, someone demanded a poll of the delegation so I gave my vote orally. A lot of people came up to me afterwards and said that they thought I had done the right thing, and now I am more than ever convinced that it was the right thing.

Roosevelt expected to be nominated by acclamation, which meant that not a single ballot could be cast against him. "The pressure was very strong on Joe Kennedy," said Krock, "because he was told among other things that his father's political future was at stake and if he stayed by his Farley instructions—that he would be doing his father an injury." But young Joe stood up on the convention floor and announced, "I came pledged for Farley and I'll vote for Farley."

Jim Farley cabled Ambassador Kennedy in gratitude for young Joe's "manly and courageous stand." The Ambassador replied how delighted he was that his son had refused to change his vote. "After all, if he's going into politics, he might just as well learn now that the only thing to do is to stand by your convictions. Am most happy to say he needed no prompting in this respect." This, however, was a practice to which Joe Sr. seldom adhered.

Joseph Patterson, president of the New York *Daily News*, who also had seen young Joe at the Democratic Convention, added his own footnote: "I am sure he can have a political future if he wants one."

Even though Jack had been excited when Grandpa Honey Fitz took him and Joe to meet President Roosevelt, he still reflected his father's private feeling about FDR. Jack passed on to Billings the joke about sexy actress Mae West telling FDR that if he was as good at screwing women as he was at screwing the country, he should "come up and see her sometime."

The Ambassador had covered his tracks with a speech for Roosevelt which he paid for himself: "My wife and I have given nine hostages to fortune. My children and your children are more important than anything else in the world. The kind of America that they and their children will inherit is of grave concern to us all. In light of these considerations, I believe that Franklin D. Roosevelt should be elected President of the United States."

Joseph Kennedy, Sr., was a pragmatist who found no problem in switching political gears from being pro-Nazi to pro-Democrat. The elder Kennedy was always ready to compromise on his convictions and his principles when it conflicted with his ambition. His only ideology was achievement, and this, too, he instilled in his sons. It became theirs just as it was always his. He saw what needed to be done and made sure it happened. The next step for Joe was the governorship of Massachusetts—with the President's promised support.

"For Joe," Lem Billings recorded, "Harvard was simply a way station, for he already had his heart set on a political future and he was so closely tied with his father's ambitions for him that there was little room for anything else."

————

IF JACK STILL felt at the outside edge of his father's relationship with young Joe, fourteen-year-old Bobby was on a distant rim, watching enviously, admiringly. It was his mother who played out her own ambitions for her sons through young Bobby. When Rose returned to the States with her sons, she registered Bobby and Teddy back at Portsmouth Priory, the Catholic boarding school in Rhode Island. Joe, back in London, was too involved and too far away to object. Rose was determined to expose her sons to the same religious education she had received. Bobby would become more religiously devout than her other sons.

One day, Bobby had been away studying and returned to find Jack deep in conversation with a girl. As Bobby mounted the staircase, obviously deeply hurt and troubled, he turned toward his brother and said, "Aren't you glad to see me?" Jack just smiled and said, "I'm always glad to see you."

Of all the brothers, Bobby had the toughest fight to get out of his mother's orbit and into his father's. But Bobby was too young for his father to consider him seriously. And, as Bobby learned in London, his older brothers were also too busy to give him much time. But, as a teenager, Bobby craved their recognition. Desperate to be accepted by them, he followed them around. Most of all, he wanted to be like them. They were the primary standard against which he measured himself. Only when they died could he break loose from that standard, and even then, not completely.

———

WITH HIS FATHER still in London, and his book a best-seller, Jack felt at loose ends after graduation. He was marking time. One of his brother's roommates, a former student body president at Stanford, had impressed Jack with how great it was there—the beautiful coeds, the lovely campus, the perfect weather. Jack considered it only as an interval until war came, when he expected to be drafted.

At Yale or Harvard, he would have been absorbed into campus life despite his book's success, but at Stanford, he was considered a celebrity, even interviewed by the *Stanford Daily*.

He audited graduate classes in business and political science, lived in a comfortable cottage on campus, and bought a green convertible. Susan Imhoff, one of the women he took for drives, recalled that Jack didn't enjoy cuddling, was bossy, arrogant, "loved to laugh," and "talked endlessly about his father." Another Stanford student, Harriet

Price, remembered talking to Jack about marriage and how he said he wasn't ready for it, and she recalled that he also talked a lot about his father's infidelities, which he seemed to consider the true measure of a man, an example to be learned.

When the blindfolded Secretary of War picked the draft numbers, Jack was in the first batch. He didn't want to go, "and yet if I don't, it will look quite bad."

Joe Sr. was now talking to Jack more and more as an equal. His father had written him, "When I hear these mental midgets in U.S.A. talking about my desire for appeasement and being critical of it, my blood fairly boils. What is this war going to prove? And what is it going to do to civilization? The answer to the first question is nothing; and to the second I shudder even to think about it." His sons, and the rest of America, were now veering away from this view.

The German blitz of Britain intensified, even damaging Buckingham Palace. A bomb fell just 300 yards from the Ambassador's home. In another narrow escape, several cottages were destroyed on an estate near his country home. The walls of his house trembled, and the lampshades fell across his bed while he was occupying it. The Ambassador insisted he had been in 244 air raids in London, but had been in a bomb shelter only twice. To his son, the Ambassador mentioned that his friend's house had been "blown right off the map," and that "some people are beginning to break down" but that he didn't have "the slightest touch of nervousness."

Rose said she planned to go back to London to be with him but decided against it because "if both of us were together in London and were bombed, it would have left nine orphans under the age of 25."

To his friend Arthur Krock, the Ambassador wrote: "The job is terribly boring and with all the family back in America, I am depressed beyond words."

Ambassador Kennedy once again wrote Washington requesting to come home, saying that his usefulness seemed reduced to a minimum," and mentioning, "Continuous London air raids have now lasted two months."

———

FOR ALL HIS brilliance, few question that Ambassador Kennedy was full of unpredictable opinions. Many commented on his flaws, but his confidence in his own judgment was almost infinite. Let someone challenge him and he could become caustic enough to say anything.

He did just that in an interview with Louis Lyons of the Boston *Globe*. One week after making his report to President Roosevelt in the White House, the Ambassador told Lyons, "Democracy is finished in England." He also clearly intimated that democracy was probably finished in the United States too. Kennedy was also finished as Ambassador. He had submitted his resignation to the President three days before. His position in Britain had become untenable and FDR accepted his resignation.

The Lyons article was a bombshell. The Ambassador made it worse when he added later that he didn't care if people "hated my guts." He did, however, resent attacks on his family.

He also had said earlier, "I've got nine children, and the only thing I can leave them that will mean anything is my good name and reputation." And, as Coughlan noted on this: "He failed."

Joe Sr. was fifty-two when he told his daughter Kick that he thought his life was over. His biographer Richard Whelan had written, "He was embarked on the darkest episode of his life, which would end in humiliation, defeat and eclipse for the name of Kennedy."

Commenting on this, Rose Kennedy said, "I never felt it! And I never heard him voice any such sentiments. He was always too busy with the next exciting new venture to dwell too long on past defeats. His favorite expression, 'Do the best you can and then to Hell with it!' "

————

THE AMBASSADOR HAD stopped off in San Francisco in November and told Jack that the President would accept his resignation as soon as he found a successor. He wanted Jack to draft an outline of an article, for his signature, in favor of appeasement. In view of his own conflicting sentiments, Jack was highly reluctant. His book had been more evenhanded than his father would have liked, and since then Jack was moving more strongly to support President Roosevelt.

But he couldn't refuse his father. What he did do was urge his father to support aid to Britain to avoid the curse of being an appeaser. "Of course I do not mean that you should advocate war—but you might explain . . . how vital it is for us to supply England. You might work in how hard it is for a democracy to get things done unless it is scared and how difficult it is to get scared when there is no immediate menace. We should see that our immediate menace is not invasion, but that England may fall—through lack of our support."

Jack delayed writing the article but his father pressed him on it. In his article, Jack finally wrote, for his father's signature:

> Rumours have sprung that I am a defeatist . . . that I hold views unacceptable to 90% of the American people. I do not think that I do . . . I must confess . . . that I am gloomy and I have been gloomy since September, 1938. . . . It is not easy for me to discuss what should be our attitude towards England without emotion. . . . I have seen the spirit of the Londoners through 244 air raids. . . . therefore, it is not easy for me to discuss the situation from a purely American point of view but I feel I must, I feel that the situation today is so fraught with peril and disaster for us we must take the course, for many it may be the hardest, of looking at the situation completely from the point of view of what is best for America.

Concerned that his views might hurt his son's future, the Ambassador finally agreed to advocate military aid to England—as long as we did not enter the war.

It was a dramatic crossroads for John Kennedy. For the first time, this second son, unfavored and shunted off to the side, had now not only served his father well, but had somehow managed to change his mind and moderate a major decision.

Despite his new position, a New York *Herald Tribune* editorial said that the Ambassador's resignation would let the country breathe more easily.

If Jack could not go along with his father's original views, young Joe sensed that his father's revised views didn't represent his basic belief. That's why, at a Foreign Policy Association meeting in Boston, young Joe continued to speak against convoying food and supplies to Britain. He still felt—as he knew his father did—that the sinking of one ship might propel us into war.

———

IN VIEW OF the uncertainty of the impending draft, Jack left Stanford. After more medical tests, the doctors ordered him to rest. Restless in

Palm Beach, he accepted his father's suggestion that he tour South America.

If his popularity dimmed elsewhere, the senior Kennedy was still the focus of his family. Charles Spalding vividly recalled a Kennedy family dinner in the summer of 1940. As he walked up on the porch, "there was an uproar of voices, laughter and insults pouring from every room."

For Spalding, the fever excitement of the family was unforgettable. Everybody seemed to be vitally involved in something, and on the move: Spain, South America, the Ambassadorship. Everybody bubbling, happy, opinionated, all unafraid to disagree, even with their father, whom they adored and admired.

"On the way home, I went over the evening in my mind and wondered about what had made it so good. There was the excitement of the unusual achievement of the house coupled at the same time with a complete lack of pretense. There was the constant spur of competition which brought out an intense appreciation of excellence. There was the feeling shared by everybody that anything was possible and the only recognized problem was that there would never be enough time. And this combined to produce the most heightened group of people, much less one family. I thought to myself—that's the best I've seen."

———

AFTER RETURNING FROM South America, with no word yet on the draft, Jack had planned to work in his father's former bank for the summer and then, if he was still not called, go to Yale Law School.

Meanwhile, Joe Jr. decided to skip his final year at law school and enlist as a Naval air cadet. As he explained to his father, "I think that Jack is not doing anything, and, with your stand on the war, the people will wonder what the devil I am doing back at school, when everyone else is working for national defense."

He was not going into the war because he believed in it, but because it would help his father's image. Nor did his father seem to object. His image was always his vital concern, with or without the presidential possibility. Joe would not only fight in this war for his father, but he would become the hero his father always wanted him to be. War provided the simplistic heroism Joe Jr. always had craved. He now didn't have to worry about right or wrong. It was enough to be brave.

When young Joe worried about the delay in his physical examination, the Ambassador quickly contacted Captain Kirk, the Director of the Office of Naval Intelligence, who had been his naval attaché in London. Very shortly, a physical was arranged. "They took great care of me and rushed me right through," Joe later wrote.

Joe enlisted in the Naval Reserve in June 1941, a Seaman Second Class at the Naval Aviation Cadet Selection Board. After qualifying, he was sent to the Naval Air Station in Jacksonville, Florida.

The personal pressure on Jack to enlist was now stronger. What predominated was the envy and competitiveness with his brother and the need to elevate his prestige with his father and the rest of the family. Most of all he needed to prove his own worth. As did Joe Jr., Jack felt the need to fight the war his father never fought.

"Jack had a high regard for courage and what he inescapably had to do, but he was no romantic about war," said Charles Spalding. "He still was distrustful of everything that was being said about saving the world for democracy. He used the phrases in a chiding and humorous way, never convinced by them at all." But, soon, this too started changing. In view of Russia's stand against the Nazi invasion, Jack now felt that American aid to Britain could be decisive, "and if a quick victory could be achieved I would favor America going in."

Both the Army and Navy had turned Jack down because of his back injury. He then built up his back through exercise. The Ambassador again contacted Captain Kirk. Kirk arranged an examination by a friendly doctor he knew. Jack finally passed the Navy physical, became an ensign in the U.S. Naval Reserve in September 1941, bypassing any need to go to Officers' School. There is little question that the father could have prevented Jack's entry into the war but chose not to.

For him, it would be far better for Jack to go for the family's war glory while he kept young Joe ripe—and safe—for his political career.

Young Joe reacted badly to his father's success in making Jack a naval officer. He rationalized his bitter envy by telling Lorelle Hearst about his brother's bad back, and that his father should have kept Jack out of uniform. Now, when the two brothers posed for a photograph, both wearing Navy uniforms, Joe, with his single ensign stripe, was junior to his younger brother. It was a hard blow at his pride. To win back that status would destroy him.

It was the last time the two brothers met.

———

KATHLEEN AND A friend were flying together to visit friends and the plane stopped at Jacksonville. "Kathleen got all dollied up," said her mother, "and got off the plane and was enfolded in the arms of this very attractive cadet who was of course Joe Jr. but the other woman didn't know it was her brother. Then Kathleen got on the plane and then they stopped again at Virginia someplace. Kathleen again got all beautiful and got off the plane with another officer who clutched her in his arms—and was Jack. . . . So this woman was perfectly fascinated by this girl who seemed to have a devoted beau at every station."

Training was tough and many cadets washed out. Joe finished in the bottom tenth of his cadet class. The flight instructor, who had qualified Joe as safe for primary solo, noted, "This student does not absorb instruction readily. . . . He cannot remember things from one day to the next. . . . The student does not look where he's going. . . . Student is afraid of inverted spins; consequently, recovery is uncertain." The instructor later admitted, however, that Joe had a feel for stunt-flying. Joe was also certified by another instructor as having an aptitude for flying at night. He graduated to his first real airplane, the SNJ low-wing, metal monoplane, and showed "average ability in adapting himself to a strange plane." At the end, though, he was finally evaluated as "good officer material."

Father Maurice Sheehy, chaplain at the base in Jacksonville, and also its public relations officer and editor of its newspaper, developed a close relationship with Joe. He recalled that the young man practically had taken over his office. Sheehy commented on his inviting smile and hungry mind, and how he insisted on arguing about everything from politics to theology. One of young Joe's joking comments was picked up by the Associated Press: It suggested the Lend-Lease law should be extended to American girls.

Young Joe heard with amusement that Jack was cavorting with a girl named Bunny and he expected further news about the girl's father with a shotgun giving brother Jack "a shot of lead up the ass." He signed it "Best from Brother."

While Joe was stationed in Florida, it was rumored that he was seriously involved with a Protestant girl; and his father wrote him: "You wouldn't think this is very important but it definitely is, and I am thoroughly convinced that an Irish-Catholic with a name like yours and with your record, married to an Irish-Catholic girl, would be a push-over in this state for political office. They just wouldn't have anything to fight about. It seems like a silly thing, but I can't impress it on you too strongly."

———

A NOTE FROM Billings informed Jack that his application as an ambulance driver for the American Field Service had been approved. Pat Kennedy said that she "nearly fell over backwards when I heard. . . . It doesn't seem the kind of thing Lem would do." A letter of recommendation from the elder Kennedy had been decisive, and Billings had been assigned to North Africa. Kick was throwing a party for him in New York and Lem sent Jack a poignant plea. "Try and make NY next weekend—altho I hardly expect it."

With the older boys part of a coming war, the others scattered in schools, the Bronxville house was silent, and the Kennedys sold it, "so today I feel quite relieved and very free with nothing on my mind except the shades of blue for my Palm Beach trousseau."

Kathleen, still always known as "Kick," had gone to work on the Washington *Times-Herald*, writing a column called "Did You Happen to See?" Shortly after she went to work, Ambassador Joseph Patrick Kennedy had lunch with Managing Editor Frank Waldrop "and fixed me with his bright blue eyes as he told me how pleased he was to trust his daughter to my care . . . I read him and put Kathleen at a desk in the city room just outside my door. And kept the door open. On the telephone she was faultless, and good, too, at translating a 'no,' 'yes,' or 'stall,' from me into proper little notes for callers. Her typing was pitiful."

Kick was not really pretty. She was slightly plump and had broad shoulders, but a Frenchman who had met all the Kennedy daughters said, "Eunice is the most intellectual, and Pat's the prettiest, but Kathleen's the one you remember."

Arthur Krock said Kathleen was Rose with a more released spirit. She looked like her mother, the same brow and nose, but her mother had a fixed smile and Kick's smile was always joyous and infectious. Her mother had sent her to the Sacred Heart Convent school in Connecti-cut, where they wore brown wool uniforms and woke at six to go to

Mass, and then to the Holy Child Convent in Neuilly outside of Paris. But as soon as she came home, all her brothers' friends started dating, and falling in love with her. They loved the way she laughed uncontrollably at her own jokes, before she even got to the punch line. Her favorite was the one she'd heard about an American who tells an Englishman that his favorite breakfast is "a roll in bed with Honey."

Her father wrote her a perceptive note, which he could also have written to Jack: "With you, popular opinions are frequently accepted as true opinion. There is nothing particularly wrong in this, it's safe and you've got plenty of company, which you like. But I think you'll find that the majority are only occasionally well-informed and that your own judgment is frequently better. . . . So don't bum rides on other people's opinions. It's lazy at best—and in some cases it's much worse."

The Jack–Kick closeness was typified by the way Spalding heard him bawling her out for the "extravagant, irresponsible use she was making of her great charm. She'd be sitting in this chair . . . always twisting her hair. . . . He's awfully hard on the kid . . . he'd really slice her up . . . for not being sincere."

She wrote him afterward: "As for your words of advice Brother I'll take 'em. Boy the only persons you can be sure of are your own flesh and blood and then we are not always sure of them."

Jack Kennedy began work on the *Daily Digest* in the office of the chief of Naval Operations at the end of 1941. About that time, he met Inga Arvad Fejos, the former Miss Denmark. Frank Waldrop also had put her to work on the Washington *Times-Herald* at the behest of his friend, *New York Times* columnist Arthur Krock.

Jack wrote rave reports to Billings about Inga, about her very blue eyes, and very blond hair, and how she wowed people when she entered a room. Soon their affair became serious.

Billings had heard about "the big Romance that has been rocking Washington circles. That one of the Kennedy boys is madly in love with a very beautiful and ravishing Danish reporter—but that fortunately the girl has been married several times—so that it will be difficult for her to marry him."

This affair with Inga Binga, as Jack called her, was one of the longer-lasting, more intense relationships of his life. To the still-callow Jack, Inga represented a sophistication that was exciting. She had stories and gossip about all kinds of prominent people that titillated him. It was exciting making love to someone who had been in bed with some of the top Nazi leaders, maybe even Hitler. She was older and wiser than he was, and being married young and more than once, there were few things about sex she didn't know.

Hearst columnist Walter Winchell noted in his January 12, 1942, column, "One of Ex-Ambassador Kennedy's eligible sons is the target of a Washington columnist gal's affections. So much so she has consulted her barrister about divorcing her exploring groom. Pa Kennedy no like."

The next time the senior Kennedy visited the *Times-Herald,* Waldrop overheard him telling his son, "Damn it, Jack, she's already married."

"The boy said he didn't care," Waldrop remembered.

But was Jack really falling madly in love? No. He would never fall madly in love with anyone. The challenge for Jack was not Inga herself, but the fact that she was off limits, and prohibited by his father. Defying his father on Inga represented another turning point for Jack.

On December 7, 1941, Jack and Lem were returning from a football game at Griffith Stadium in Washington, when they heard the news that would change their lives: the Japanese had attacked Pearl Harbor. Germany soon also declared war on the United States and World War II had begun.

Jack informed Lem that "Inga-Binga" was heading for Reno. "It would certainly be ironical if I should get married while you were visiting Germany."

Waldrop meanwhile had received word that Inga once had been taken to dinner in Berlin by Hermann Goering and that Hitler had described her as the "perfect Nordic beauty." Waldrop also learned that Inga was now under surveillance by the FBI as a possible Nazi spy. Joe Sr. was promptly informed.

The next day, Jack was transferred to the Sixth Naval District Security Office, in Charleston, South Carolina. Inga saw in this the power hand of the father, and wrote Jack that "big Joe has a stronger hand than I" and added, "You belong so wholeheartedly to the Kennedy-clan, and I don't want you ever to get into an argument with your father on account of me. As I have told you a dozen times, if I were but 18 summers, I would fight like a tigress for her young, in order to get you and keep you. Today I am wiser."

Inga had intimately known many men of power and money but most of the important ones were older and not interested in marriage. She knew she had bedazzled Jack Kennedy, who was not only rich and handsome but could be anything his father wanted. And she sensed he might marry her, but they would have to do it secretly and present the father when the deed was done. There was also the possibility of getting pregnant as a means of trapping Jack. She told Jack that one of their friends had asked, "Have you started making the baby yet?"

Meanwhile she knew the FBI was tapping their phones. The FBI file of February 6, 1942, put her in the same hotel room with Jack Kennedy in Charleston for three nights. Kennedy seemed aware of her past because he wrote her, "I've returned from an interesting trip about which I won't bore you with the details, and if you are a spy, I shouldn't tell you."

For Jack, the whole affair had an intoxicating quality of forbidden fruit, dancing with danger, defying his father, never knowing what would happen next. Never before was he involved with anything that had this kind of fever pitch.

Years later, Kennedy, then President, told Timothy Seldes, a Doubleday editor, that he couldn't fire FBI Director Hoover because he had all the tapes of him and Inga.

Inga saw her man clearly. She described Jack then as "full of enthusiasm and expectations, eager to make his life a huge success. He wants the fame, the money—and what rarely goes with fame—happiness . . . when you talk to him or see him you always have the impression that his big white teeth are ready to bite off a huge chunk of life. . . . He has two backbones: His own and his father's."

Yet she would also write him, "Maybe your gravest mistake, handsome . . . is that you admire brains more than heart, but then that is necessary to arrive. Heart never brought fame—except to Saints. . . . You haven't lost the tough hide of the Irish potatoes. . . . Put a match to the smoldering ambition and you will go like wild fire . . . the unequaled highway to the White House."

Inga's son later commented that his mother "thought old Joe was awfully hard—a really mean man. He could be very charming when she and Jack were with him but if she left the room he'd come down on Jack about her and if Jack left the room, he'd try to hop in the sack with her. He did that one weekend at the Cape, she said. She thought it was a totally amoral situation, that there was something incestuous about the whole family."

Neighbor Nancy Coleman suggested that Big Joe was romancing Inga to break up any idea of her marriage to Jack. There may be some truth to this. Although he had done this before to some of Jack's dates, it is just as likely he was indulging his usual sexual appetite. He had once mocked one young woman readying herself for an outing with Jack, "Why don't you get yourself a *live* one?" And one of Jack's dates even testified that he had tried to bribe her into bed with him.

Whatever went on between Joe and Inga didn't stop her from writing to Kick, "Please tell big Joe that I never enjoyed any man's brains and cleverness as much as his. Jack has plenty, but your father naturally is matured perfection." It was Kick who later informed her friend John White that her father hired private detectives to watch his children and check out their friends.

There is no evidence that he succeeded in smashing the Inga–Jack romance. But Jack told his friend Ted Reardon that "they shagged my ass out of town to break us up," and he was scheduled to go to Panama when he called his father and insisted he wanted action, "and the next day, just like that, the very next day, I had orders sending me to his PT outfit in the Pacific." Unlike Joe, Jack expressed no wish to be a hero. He had been propelled into the move by his relationship with Inga.

Before Jack left the country, Inga wrote that she wanted him back from the war "with your young handsome body intact . . . with the wishes both to be a White-House-Man and wanting the ranch—somewhere out West. So, Dear . . . whatever happens, let us have lunch together the first day you are ashore, shall we? That of course provided that you are not married, your wife maybe wouldn't understand . . . but if not, if you are still free . . . I think we can always find something to talk about."

And she added, "And wherever in the world I may be—drop in."

The romance would linger long after Jack returned from the war. Some of the women Jack knew were just as beautiful and bright and willing as Inga, but Inga had more mystery, more promise of greater excitement. And she always knew how to intrigue him.

In some ways, Inga was also motherly. She seemed to know his needs and insecurity and frustration. Betty Coxe, a friend of Kathleen's, wondered whether "men have to get rid of their mothers somehow, grow past them . . . they work out this mother business with . . . a particular woman. That seems to me, in many ways, what Inga was for Jack."

Inga even later confided to her son what she had said before, that Jack Kennedy was "a lousy lover."

Arthur Krock told the Blairs that Inga, whom he also knew intimately well, had confided that Jack loved as a boy, not as a man, that he was intent on achieving ejaculation rather than prolonging it for a woman's pleasure. She described him as "awkward and groping and unsure." "I don't think he ever really made love to a girl!" said one of his college friends. "He wasn't in it for the cuddling."

Said Henry James, "I mean he admitted that to me! He told me that! He said, 'I'm not interested—once I get a woman, I'm not interested in carrying on, for the most part. I like the conquest. That's the challenge. . . . It's the chase I like, not the kill!' "

Angie Dickinson would sum it up sardonically as "the most memorable fifteen seconds of my life."

In view of Inga's many affairs and past marriages, and her own obvious sensuality, it seemed almost axiomatic that she would release in Jack any inhibitions he may have had. And, surely, from their many passionate letters, from the talk of possible marriage, their mutual feeling was intense. And, yet, here was her description of Jack as "a lousy lover"—a description that Kennedy would earn repeatedly from all the many women he had romanced, who would talk about it, yet remain entranced with him despite that.

Despite their sexual problems, Inga also told her son something that "blew my head right off." She told him that she was already pregnant before she remarried, and she wasn't certain whether her son's father was Jack or Tim (McCoy, a cowboy actor). But she told her son he most reminded her of Jack—the way he acted and the way his mind worked.

Inga earlier had written to Kick: "Tell young Kennedy that I got his letter, that it was the longest he ever wrote, that I am saving it for my great grand-children—whom I hope will look like him."

———

YOUNG JOE GOT his "wings" as an ensign in his father's presence in April 1942. The former Ambassador was supposed to give a speech to the graduating class of naval aviators, but he was too choked with emotion to finish it. The odds are good that his choked emotion had little to do with any latent patriotism. His negative view of the war had never changed. His emotion was for the son he loved, the son who might fight, the son who might die.

Joe was sent with a squadron attached to the Atlantic fleet, flying on antisubmarine missions from Puerto Rico with a squadron of gull-winged PMP Mariner reconnaissance planes. He loved flying. In piloting a plane, he dominated his own world for a time as he otherwise never could. There is no feeling that he saw the larger meaning of this war. Flying to him was a personal thrill, a camaraderie with an elite group of peers. And it would help politically.

Joe always thrived on family adulation, and he could expect none from Jack, but he got a constant dose of clear hero-worship from his younger brother Bobby. In his late teens, Bobby was increasingly restless about being too young to enlist and wrote often. Talking about some jokes Bobby had sent, Joe replied, "They certainly are wows, and if you didn't get any more than those out of the school, I think you may regard your years spent there as most valuable. If you hear any more good ones, air mail them on, the base is going crazy for more."

Young Joe wrote Bobby about completing precision landing acrobatics, graduating into larger planes "with millions of gadgets," and soloing the fastest planes they have around here, "which go about 180."

He also said that he might get back to the air base in Palm Beach for a few days, and he hoped Bobby might visit him there "as you would really enjoy seeing the station. . . . That's about all the news, Robert, keep in touch."

When Bobby did visit his air base, Joe smuggled him onto his plane and even let him take the controls once they were in the air.

Bobby then had a real problem in his lack of self-confidence. He was sixteen, and had been transferred to Milton Academy, a nonsectarian school. As a junior, he was not doing well academically. "I don't know where I got my brains," Bobby wrote his father, "but it's quite evident that I received them from neither my father nor my mother."

"I think everything he did was very difficult for him," said Bobby's closest friend, David Hackett. "Athletics for him—which he loved—were always difficult. Studies, the same thing. And also, I think, with his social life. . . . I don't think he ever had anything easy."

Hackett also noted another problem: Bobby was one of the few Catholics in the school.

Bobby's clothes reflected his own defiance: a checkered coat, loud ties, white athletic socks. Hackett regarded him as unusual. "He talked differently . . . held himself differently. . . . We both felt sort of picked on and persecuted. My first impression of him is that we were both, in a way, misfits. . . . We became bonded friends very quickly."

It was revealing that the *Orange and Blue* Milton Academy yearbook listed Bobby's nickname as "fella." "I think, if you talked to most of the people who knew him at that time . . . very few would have said that he'd be a remarkable person."

He was intense—the most intense of the brothers, highly introspective, and restless. Even when he was relaxed, he seemed to be in a hurry, but he didn't know where he was going. His mother still wanted him to be a priest—she later had that same ambition for Teddy—and his father still had made no plans for him. All Bobby wanted to be was like his much-admired brothers. All he wanted to be was a hero.

Bobby was still too slight to make the varsity football team. His three brothers were all about six feet tall, and Bobby was much smaller, and very conscious of his height. His body was well developed but his legs were short. What he lacked in height, he made up in feistiness. On the football field, Bobby was fiercely competitive, but still only rated at Milton as a fourth-string quarterback. The coach, however, let him sit in on the game plan sessions.

In response to a question on what play he would call under certain conditions, the third-string quarterback said he would call for an end run to gain a few yards. The coach then turned to Bobby with the same question. "I'd go for a forward pass and a touchdown."

Despite his lack of confidence, Bobby was always going for a touchdown.

Bobby needed David Hackett for a friend just as young Joe needed Ted Reardon and Jack needed Lem Billings. Dave was a highly principled and gifted young man who would do anything for Bobby. But even though Dave was "truly his best friend . . . I just don't think Bob was the kind of guy that poured his heart out to anybody."

What he did have was "a savage individuality," observed Arthur Krock. He also seemed to have a natural compassion for people. It was

Bobby, too, who kept a brotherly concern for younger Teddy, who was then also doing badly in his studies, getting paddled for mischief, and, like Bobby, Ted was lonely. He had been transferred to so many schools that they began to blur. "That was hard to take," he said. "I finally got through school where I spent some time trying to find out where the dormitory and the gym were located."

"My brothers and sisters were all away, and dad and mother were in New York." said Ted later. "Bobby was the one who used to call me up to see how I was getting along. On the two or three weekends I was able to get off from school, if I couldn't get home, he'd spend the weekend with me. I'll never forget how we used to go to the big empty house at Cape Cod—just the two of us rattling around alone. But Bobby was in charge, taking care of me and always making sure I had something to do."

Bobby wasn't being just brotherly with Teddy. Bobby needed Teddy as much as Teddy needed him. They energized each other.

"Bobby also had a marvelous sense of humor," said Teddy. "It was a different type of humor from Jack's and mine. Bobby had a wry, caustic wit that often poked fun at himself—but he didn't like you to join him. He didn't have a hearty laugh, but he laughed a lot at irony. Or at the broad things, like somebody slipping on a banana peel. He could be droll, sometimes telling jokes in a slightly startled voice as if he was surprising himself. In fact, his only class distinction at Milton was the four votes he received for being 'most humorous.' "

Despite his shyness, he had a warm twinkle in his eyes. He invariably was at his best with Teddy, when they were both poking fun at each other. Young Joe's fun-poking had more bite—he would kid Teddy about being fat.

But Teddy was good-natured, happy-go-lucky, and irrepressible. "He'd try to bring everyone together by making them laugh," said Eunice. Teddy had a loud laugh, described as "a laugh of joy, the kind of laugh that makes you feel better about life."

Bobby, particularly at this lonely time of his life, needed Teddy's laughter. Teddy recalled: "I did more things with Bobby than I did with Jack—they were different types of relationships—perhaps because there was such a difference in years."

Reflecting on his own loneliness as a boy, Teddy would say years later that his brothers also had gone to prep school "and they were lonesome too, so I shouldn't complain."

"I remember Teddy at ten or eleven," said Billings, "and he was a kind of wise-ass fresh kid, kind of fat, not terribly appealing—then suddenly, when he was twelve or so, this terrific appeal, his personality emerged and overcame the rest. His sense of humor couldn't be equaled, it was very adult for his age, he took part in everything, the family games you always played after dinner. He became . . . just damn good company. His older brothers and sisters began to appreciate him." As far as his sisters were concerned, he knew he could do no wrong. He compared them to an army of mothers.

———

WHEN HIS FATHER had Jack transferred to possible combat, he hoped that it wouldn't be "too deadly," but was still willing to sacrifice him to the danger. But as far as Joe was concerned, his father wasn't interested in him getting anywhere near the war. This was the son he wanted as President. Young Joe was then flying Liberators to Norfolk from the factory in San Diego, making five uneventful cross-country trips in eight days. He also had volunteered as an instructor to accumulate more flight hours. He was a dashing figure wearing a white scarf with his leather jacket, and smoking cigars.

Rose Kennedy observed later that this was the first time Jack had won such an advantage by such a clear margin. "I daresay it cheered Jack, and must have rankled Joe Jr." Young Joe already had been rankled because Jack was an officer and he was not.

The flight surgeon diagnosed young Joe as "tense and preoccupied," with "accumulated stresses," and recommended a week's leave of absence. Joe needed to talk to his father. He needed to impress how much he wanted to see action.

Young Joe was at the Washington airport when his father was due to arrive and he pushed through the crowd. His friend Tom Shriver heard an armed guard shout at young Joe, "Halt or I'll shoot!" but Joe simply shoved him aside and embraced his surprised father.

The senior Kennedy was not moved by his son's urgency for combat. Kennedy's long-range plan for his son Joe was now well established and now President Roosevelt had tampered with it by handpicking an attractive young Irish-Catholic congressman, Joseph Casey, to run against incumbent Senator Henry Cabot Lodge, Jr., for the Massachusetts governorship in 1942. The senior Kennedy saw Casey as a potential threat to his son. He considered running against Joseph Casey himself in the Democratic primary, but didn't meet the residency requirement. Looking around for a proxy, he saw the perfect candidate in Honey Fitz. Kennedy knew his seventy-nine-year-old father-in-law had one more campaign in him, and got his cousin and political handyman, Joe Kane, to organize it. "Honey Fitz is throwing his hat into the ring as a candidate for the Senate," Jack wrote to Lem Billings. "He told me confidentially that he would win in a breeze, and he does have a good chance. It seems his opponent had a baby six months after he got married, and the Catholic women . . . are busy giving him the black-ball for it."

Honey Fitz once approached his political opponent and said indignantly, "I understand you are going around accusing me of being an octogenarian!"

"Well," asked Casey, "how old are you?"

Fitz retorted, "I am seventy-nine!"

Honey Fitz lost the primary, but bloodied Casey badly, and Lodge easily beat him. "The message came through loud and clear in Washington," wrote Peter Collier and David Horowitz in their book *The Kennedys: An American Drama.* "The President might control the destiny of the nation, but Massachusetts was Kennedy turf."

———

IN APRIL 1943, Lieutenant (j.g.) John F. Kennedy became commanding officer of USS PT-109, assigned to the Solomon Islands. A PT boat was an eighty-foot plywood vessel powered by three engines. PT boats, which carried a crew of thirteen, were usually sent to "slots" of water looking for Japanese destroyers.

For Jack, it had been a remarkable exposure. His crew represented a cross section of people, the kind of people he had never known at Choate or Harvard. Most of them had led ordinary lives. And now their lives were his to command.

In a letter home about war, Jack didn't gripe much about conditions but mentioned everybody's constant urgent wish to come home, and he counseled his older brother not to be impatient about coming there into action because "he will want to be back the day after he arrives." At the same time, he advised Bobby to stay in V-12 training as long as he could because "the fun goes out of war in a fairly short time."

At Blackett Strait in August 1943, at 2:30 in the morning, the man forward in PT-109 shouted, "Ship at two o'clock." As Lt. John Fitzgerald spun the wheel to turn, in came a Japanese destroyer, straight at them, and cut them in half. Jack remembers thinking, "This is how it feels to be killed."

Two of the dozen drowned. Jack swam from man to man and helped to get some of them onto the floating hulk until it started to turn over.

Ted Reardon later met one of Kennedy's crew, a radioman, at a VFW convention. The man remembered that after the ship had been sliced up, Kennedy told the surviving crew then hanging on to the wreckage, "I know I'm the skipper of this PT crew and I can still give you orders, but most of you men are older than I am. I have nothing to lose, but some of you have wives and children and I'm not going to order you to try to swim to that shore. You'll have to make your own decision on that."

The island was three miles southeast. Some swam, some floated in on loose timber, and Kennedy towed in the one badly burned man—who didn't know how to swim—by taking one end of the long strap of the man's Mae West life jacket, gripping it in his teeth, and swimming the breaststroke. It took five hours to reach the island.

"When the enemy seemed to be coming closer, they moved to a larger island, and this time it took three hours, Kennedy again towing his crewman with his teeth. After days of hunger, searching, and danger, Kennedy found some friendly natives and scratched a message on a coconut: ELEVEN ALIVE NATIVE KNOWS POSIT AND REEFS NAURU ISLAND KENNEDY. Then he told the natives, "Rendova, Rendova," where the PT base was.

And several days later, picked up by a PT boat, the crew of 109 sang a hymn they all knew. "Jesus loves me, this I know."

———

"TED, I'M NOBODY," Kennedy told Theodore M. Robinson, the PT-boat executive officer who rescued him, "but my father does have a pretty good job so I've had a little experience with reporters. . . . I'm afraid that someday, somewhere, perhaps after I'm dead, somebody who didn't understand the blackness of Blackett Strait and those appalling conditions will misunderstand."

There would be one report which "almost depicts Kennedy as a coward." Another report detailed that Kennedy got lost, failed to join an attack on a Japanese convoy, then was rammed by the Japanese destroyer while some of his crew were sleeping on deck. But to his crew, he was a hero.

Kennedy would always keep the coconut on his desk.

Edward McLaughlin, who met him in a privy on Guadalcanal, remembered when they brought Kennedy in, all scratched up from coral poisoning. "He was very skinny, had a *great* smile and a great sense of humor."

"Sure I remember him," said former Navy man Joseph Alecks. "Thin, in khakis with no insignia, looked sick, probably had malaria on top of everything else and he looked awful young. I said to him, 'If my father was an Ambassador I wouldn't be in this goddamn place.' I thought he had a lot of moxie. With his father he coulda had a desk job."

Joseph Kennedy, Sr., was driving his car on the Cape when he heard the news on the radio that Jack had been rescued. "Ted and I were not with him at the time," said his nephew Joe Gargan, "but he told us that he was so excited that he drove the car off the road and into a field. He had known for days that Jack was missing in action; yet he had told no one, not even Aunt Rose."

Dr. Janet Travell, later to become John Kennedy's personal doctor, suggested that the PT-boat incident had far-reaching effects on his health. "One of the common things that happens is hemorrhage under conditions of stress, hemorrhage into the adrenal glands. . . . I can picture that following the boat explosion and his period on the island that he really was very low in ascorbic acid intake. This would favor easy rupture of blood vessels. . . . I think that this adrenal insufficiency was a condition which started following the extreme stress in the Pacific . . . it was practically a death sentence."

———

YOUNG JOE HAD learned about the incident from a friend several hours before he saw it in the papers "and got quite a fright." But he never called home about it, and finally got a reprimand from his father that he'd been "considerably upset that during those few days after the news of Jack's rescue we had no word from you. I thought that you would very likely call up to see whether we had any news as to how Jack was." It was a rare reprimand. One can only explain Joe's behavior as a mix of concern and envy.

When Joe learned that his brother had been rescued, crewman Sunshine Reedy found him proud of his brother's courage and coolness in the water. But now Jack was not only a combat veteran, but a full-fledged naval hero who managed to save his crew.

Chief Degman, on the base with Joe, sensed a subtle change. "When news came about brother John's PT-boat activities, I think it inspired him to try harder. I don't think anyone was more intent on seeking out the enemy and meeting him than Joe Kennedy." Navigator Gene Martin, still unimpressed with Joe, complained that "when I tried to make casual conversation, I got the positive impression that I was talking about firecrackers to a man valiantly trying to perfect the atom bomb."

Joe's homecoming on leave was not the welcome he had once hoped for. He was not the hero—his brother was. And when one of the guests toasted the Kennedy patriarch on his fifty-fifth birthday, he added, "father of the hero, of our own hero, Lieutenant John F. Kennedy of the United States Navy."

Family friend Boston Police Commissioner Joseph Timilty shared a bedroom for the weekend with young Joe and later reported that he had found Joe crying in his room. Young Joe suddenly sat up in his bed, oblivious of Timilty's presence, and began clenching and un-clenching his fists in a rage, muttering, "By God, I'll show them." Three weeks later, he was on his way to England. Jack meanwhile had written home that he hoped his brother Joe would still be around when he came back.

Young Joe replied:

I understand that anyone who was sunk got 30 days' survivor-leave. How about it? Pappy was rather indignant that they just didn't send you back right away. . . . If you give me a rough idea of your itinerary, I will try to fit in a few enjoyable evenings for you en route. If you ever get around Norfolk, you will get quite a welcome if you mention the magic name of Kennedy, so I advise you to go incognito.

Joe then discussed a former girlfriend of Jack's:

After you burst into the front pages . . . she doesn't think you will ever speak to her now. She was looking extremely well, having taken off about 15 pounds. I was tempted to take her out myself, but knowing how you feel about that sort of thing, and knowing what a swell job you're doing in winning the war, I decided to lay off.

Buoyed up by all the patriotic fervor surrounding the action of both older brothers, seventeen-year-old Robert enlisted as a seaman apprentice in the United States Naval Reserve.

Jack wrote him:

The folks sent me a clipping of you taking the oath. The sight of you up there, just a boy, was really moving, particularly as a close examination showed you had my checked London coat on. I'd like to know what the hell I'm doing out here, while you go strolling around in my drape coat, but I suppose that what we are out here for—or so they tell us—is so that our sisters and younger brothers will be safe and secure. Frankly I don't see it quite that way—at least if you're going to be safe and secure, that's fine with me, but not in my coat, brother, not in my coat.

Kick had quit her job on the Washington *Times-Herald* to go to work for the Red Cross in London, practicing Red Cross bandages on anybody available. There was small secret that Kick wanted to be near her boyfriend, William Cavendish, Marquis of Hartington, eldest son of the Duke of Devonshire, and heir to over 180,000 acres, with estates all over England, and revenues of over a quarter million pounds a year. "Billy," as she called him, was six-foot-two, a graceful cricket player, a placid, gentle man with a coltish charm.

Father Joe made certain that Kick's Red Cross job was highly publicized. The London *Daily Mail* photographed her in uniform coming to work on a bicycle, and Joe Sr. circulated it all over the United

States. There was some resentment at the Red Cross that Kick's father had pulled strings to get her stationed in London. The elder Kennedy wrote Frank Waldrop about Kick: "There are no two ways about it, she still thinks the British are the second-best people on earth."

On Joe's flight to England, one of the squadron planes developed engine trouble over the ice cap in Greenland. Joe told the troubled pilot off his wing, "You better not ditch here, Jeff, I can't stick around and circle. I've got a crate of eggs for my sister."

He brought six dozen eggs from home for Kick. It wasn't until months later that a member of his crew asked her, "I certainly hope you enjoyed those eggs. There wasn't anything Mr. Kennedy didn't make our plane do on the excuse that those eggs should arrive fresh and unbroken."

"We were away from home and in a foreign land," said Kick. "To each other, we symbolized the happy family we had left in America."

That year together in England, Joe and Kick became very close. Kick provided dates for her brother whenever he needed any, made certain that his social life was filled when he had any leave in London. She wrote home of one of her parties where Joe Jr. brought his entire squadron "who were feeling no pain." The next day she and Joe rode horses together on Rotten Row. She found him in wonderful spirits. "One feels one must pack all the fun possible into the shortest space of time."

On one of his leaves in London, Joe and Kick were invited to dine at The Savoy with William Randolph Hearst, Jr., then a war correspondent. Joining them was General Robert Laycock, head of the British Commandos, and his wife, Angela, and Joe's old girlfriend, Virginia Gilliat, now married to Sir Richard Sykes. Virginia had asked along Patricia Wilson.

The daughter of an Australian sheep rancher from Cootamundra, New South Wales, Pat was seventeen when she came with her mother to London. Less than a year later, she had married George Child-Villiers, the twenty-one-year-old Earl of Jersey. She divorced him in 1937 and married Robin Filmer Wilson, a banker in his late thirties. Pat had three small children from her two marriages. In 1943 her husband was a British major in Libya and had been away for more than two years.

Pat was a beauty with black hair, blue eyes, lovely figure, a rich, infectious laugh which favorably compared to the reticence of most Englishwomen of her class. She lived in a tile-roofed gardener's cottage called Crastock Farm, in Woking, about an hour from London. She called her home "charming beyond belief." She had chickens on the tennis court, and even a cow (which her chauffeur milked).

Her house had become a social center for Billy Hartington and Kick and Frank Moore O'Ferrall, a horse breeder serving in the Irish Guards who was a good friend of Joe's. She invited Joe to join them.

They rechristened the house "Crashbang." Each arrived with some contribution of food or drink borrowed or stolen from some commissary or kitchen. They played records, tennis, gin rummy or poker for stakes. And there was a little wooded glen behind the cottage where Joe and Pat fell in love. Woking was on the same train line as Taunton, in Somerset, where Joe was stationed. They were soon spending most weekends together. For Joe, it was the first serious love affair of his life.

In a way, Pat and Inga were a parallel. Both were already married and had been previously married. Both would be clearly unacceptable to religious Rose and politically minded Joe.

For Joe and Jack, the forbidden nature of these affairs surely heightened their excitement. For Joe, it was his first flagrant rebellion against the tight family discipline.

But Pat Wilson gave Joe a center of gravity, of belonging, of understanding that no other woman had given him, just as Inga had done for Jack.

There was great question that Pat would ever divorce her husband for Joe. If she did, and married Joe, her friends felt that Pat would be ostracized by many for marrying an Irish-Catholic. As for Joe, those close to him did not believe he would sacrifice his political ambitions by marrying a twice-divorced Protestant.

For Joe, this love was a sweeping experience, heightened, of course, by the war. Every day he made it a ritual to cycle down to the nearest private phone to call Pat from his air base.

Angela Laycock, who had been one of Joe's ardent admirers in London, later revealed something rather remarkable about Joe's political ambitions. He had told her that his brother Jack, and not he, would ultimately be President of the United States. Not only was Jack perhaps more clever than he, Joe explained to her, but Jack was now a war hero and he was not. And that would be the political payoff.

Whether this was an odd mix of envy and realism, and whether he truly believed this, he certainly didn't act like it. If he had, he would have relaxed and enjoyed the love of his life. The chance to be near Pat was one of the reasons he volunteered for an extra month's duty after completing the forty missions which would have sent him home. But the other primary reason he stayed was soon to become obvious: he still had a desperate urge to rival his brother as a hero and reclaim his previous status in the family.

Jack was scheduled to go to the naval hospital in Chelsea, Massachusetts, for surgery on his spine. The surgery was not successful and he found it painful even to stand. Jack was in the hospital for eight weeks and his weight fell from 160 to 125 and his skin yellowed. Only afterward was he able to visit occasionally at Hyannis.

Joe wrote to Jack, saying he had read in *The New Yorker* about the PT-109 incident. The story was written by John Hersey, who had married Florence Ann Cannon, one of the few women about whom Jack had seemed to be serious. Joe then wrote:

Tell the family not to get excited about my staying over here. I am not repeat not contemplating marriage nor intending to risk my fine neck . . . in any crazy venture. I trust your back is OK at this point. Most of the letters from home are filled with bulletins about the progress of your back and stomach. I should be home around the first of Sept. . . . should be good for about a month's leave. Perhaps you too will be available at that time, and will be able to fix your older brother up with something good.

I have already sent a notice home about my greying hair. I feel, I must make a pretty quick move, so get something that really wants a tired old aviator. My congrats on the Medal. To get anything out of the Navy is deserving of a campaign medal in itself. It looks like I shall return home with the European campaign medal if I'm lucky.

Your devoted brother Joe

The last sentence from the devoted brother revealed much: *It looks like I shall return home with the European campaign medal if I'm lucky.* The self-pity and bitterness was blatant.

Jack meanwhile was still getting a hero's welcome at rallies and award ceremonies in Boston, and his father beamed at him as never before, seemed bursting with pride. It was heady stuff and may well have been the beginning of his thoughts of a political future.

Robert Kennedy had reported to the Navy V-12 unit at Harvard, permitting him to get his college degree and become a Navy officer.

Bobby wrote Joe Jr. in England that "at this point you are about the only one of us many that has the good graces of the head of the family but I give you about four days after your arrival in this country before you'll join the rest of us. I am constantly jacking things but the hope still remains in the family that the Navy will make a man of me." He added, "We haven't really had too much action here in Harvard Square but we're on the alert at every moment for an attack and I'm sure when that time comes we will conduct ourselves according to Navy Standards."

————

JACK WROTE BILLINGS that he had heard from his brother Joe about the heavy casualties in his squadron. "I hope to hell he gets through OK." He also continued to try to persuade brother Bobby not to follow Joe into aviation, and he asked Billings to help him by also writing to Bobby. "It would be just his luck to get hit when old worn out bastards like you and me get through with nothing more than a completely shattered constitution."

Billings had been riding his ambulance during General Montgomery's decisive victory at El Alamein, and returned home in November with minor shrapnel wounds. What was particularly distressing to Lem was that "I got scarlet fever, and ended up at the same hospital with Jack but I couldn't see him; I was quarantined."

Again, with the help of Ambassador Kennedy, Lem now received a commission as an ensign in the U.S. Naval Reserve. He had orders for sea duty aboard the attack transport U.S.S. *Cecil*, soon to depart for the South Pacific "for the duration." Meanwhile he and Jack had their reunion in Palm Beach.

Kick wrote to Lem, wondering if he and Jack were "lounging on the beaches of Palm Beach . . . recounting your war experiences to each other while we had the most active air raid since the Battle of Britain. To be quite frank with you . . . I was slightly nervous and when I say slightly I may be guilty of understatement." Joe and Kick were fighting emotional battles of their own. Joe and Pat were in love, so were Kick and Billy Hartington. Kick wrote about it to Jack, telling him that she never expected him to give in about the religious issue, "and he knows I never would. . . ."

> It's really too bad, because I'm sure I would be a most efficient Duchess of Devonshire in the post-war world, and I'd have a castle in Ireland, one in Scotland, one in Yorkshire, and one in Sussex, I could keep my old nautical brothers in their old age. But that's the way it goes. . . . I can't understand why I like Englishmen so much, as they treat one in quite an offhand manner, and aren't really as nice to their women as Americans, but I suppose it's just that sort of treatment that women really like. That's your technique, isn't it?

Rose Kennedy was bitter about the possible marriage because they might not be married in the Church or swear that their children be raised as Catholic. In one letter, Jack wondered aloud that if Kick did marry Hartington, would that mean that he would also get some kind of title? Pragmatic Eunice summed up some of the family feeling, "It's a horrible thing—but it will be nice visiting her after the war, so we might as well face it."

When Joe realized that Kick had made up her mind, he stood by her. Kick showed all the independence, all the feistiness and freedom that Joe may well have secretly wished for himself, and he could not stand by and see her crushed. For Joe, it was almost as if, in his support for Kick, he had suddenly grown up.

He tried to mediate with the family, and wrote home: "Billy is crazy about Kick . . . and I know they are very much in love. . . . I think he really has something on the ball. . . . He is ideal for Kick. . . . As far as Kick's soul is concerned, I wish I had half her chance of seeing the pearly gates. As far as what people say, the hell with them. I think we can all take it. It will be hardest on Mother; and I do know how you feel, Mother, but I think it will be all right."

In another letter home, Joe added, "I told her that she would have to decide whether she thought her life would really be broken up if she didn't marry him. . . . If this is the love of her life, and she will not be happy with anyone else, then she will probably be unhappy the rest of her life for not having done it." Perhaps, here, Joe was making his own case for his own relationship with Pat—and their possible marriage.

Rose did not relent but several days before the wedding, her father cabled his blessing: WITH YOUR FAITH IN GOD, YOU CAN'T MAKE A MISTAKE. REMEMBER YOU ARE STILL AND ALWAYS WILL BE TOPS WITH ME. Rose also sent a cable: HEARTBROKEN. FEEL YOU HAVE BEEN WRONGLY INFLUENCED.

Religion had been the strong key to her life, and Rose saw this marriage as a clear breach of faith.

On Saturday, May 6, only two days after notice of her engagement, Kathleen, with her brother Joe, entered the small redbrick building of the Chelsea Register's office. She was wearing a very pale-pink matte crepe street-length dress. Joe gave away the bride; and Joe and the Duke of Devonshire signed as witnesses. The day after the wedding took place, Joe Jr. sent a cable to his father: THE POWER OF SILENCE IS GREAT.

It was a cable of criticism of his parents, and an enormous act of confrontation. Never before had he done this. It was almost as if—in support for Kick—at long last he was his own man. Reporters in Boston queried Rose Kennedy for her comment but she said nothing. She privately denied that she had first heard of the wedding from a friend who had heard it on the radio. She was later seen burying her head in her hands.

In a note to Billings, who had courted Kick, Jack wrote: "Your plaintive howl . . . was certainly evident that you weren't irked so much by her getting married as by her failure to inform you."

On D-Day, June 6, 1944, Allied forces launched their invasion of Europe along the Normandy coast. Joe flew during the D-Day invasion. Disregarding orders, he flew so close to German fortifications on the Isle of Guernsey that his plane was hit frequently with flak. Some of his crew talked about unnecessary recklessness. Joe was gambling on everything. In July he was promoted to lieutenant and transferred to Bombing Squadron 110.

Joe had volunteered for ten extra missions, completed them, and again volunteered to stay on longer. From his hospital bed, a concerned Jack urged his older brother to come home. It hardly helped Joe's morale to receive a batch of clippings from his parents about Jack's heroism.

Joe had written Jack: "I am really fed up, but the work is quite interesting. The nature of it is secret, and you know how secret things are in the Navy."

The "buzz bomb," the German V-1 rocket, was a small, pilotless gyrostabilized aircraft that could travel 350 miles an hour and deliver a devastating explosive charge. The first hit London on June 13, two days after Jack received his Navy–Marine Corps medal for heroism. Of the three hundred V-1s launched on the Dutch and Belgian coasts, seventy-three struck London, causing enormous damage.

Volunteers were requested to destroy the launching sites. None of the first four missions proved successful, and the Army planes were lost. The Navy organized its own mission which they code-named Aphrodite. A special plane was loaded with almost ten tons of explosives. The pilot would approach the target, set the plane to crash, and then parachute out of it at the last possible minute. Joe's outfit already had been rotated back to the States, and his family anxiously awaited him. Joe Sr. had written his friend Beaverbrook in May, "Although he's had a large number of casualties in his squadron, I'm still hoping and praying we'll see him around the first of July." A friend recalled that Joe's gear had been packed and ready to go when he heard about Aphrodite, and volunteered.

After hearing the details, Joe felt he had a 50–50 chance of survival. To him, these were odds that seemed worth taking, especially since he was given to understand that if his mission succeeded, he would get the Navy Cross, the Navy's highest honor.

————

"I THINK I was the last person, outside of his immediate colleagues, who saw Joe Kennedy alive," said his friend Frank O'Ferrall. "I was with him on the night before he died. We had a party. And he told me that he hoped to be back in London again the following night, but he had to go on some mission the next morning. . . . He said he couldn't tell me anything about it, it was on the secret list, but he didn't anticipate any trouble."

Joe seemed restless, even nervous, at the barracks later that evening, and was irritable when an official refused to let him cycle to a public phone and make a goodbye call to Pat Wilson. The two of them now had almost decided that they would marry, and soon.

That evening Joe even said he was sorry he had volunteered. He had talked about it to Ensign John Demlein, who was to trail him in another plane. "I just wonder about this damn mission," said Joe.

"What the hell, there's nothing to it," said Demlein. "You're going to bail out, and in a couple of weeks you're going to get married and be off on your honeymoon. Everything's going to be great guns for you, and we've got to go over there."

"Yeah," Joe said quickly, "I guess you're right."

Joe was more determined when electronics officer Earl Olsen asked him to postpone his flight because he wanted to make some circuit change in the electrical system. Otherwise, Olsen said, the danger was so heightened that Joe might be risking his neck for nothing. Joe refused. "I think I'm gonna fly it."

His mother would later say that her oldest son "was a gambler."

————

AS THEY LEFT the briefing, Joe handed Demlein the Army parachute-knife he'd been issued to cut himself free if his shrouds became tangled. "You take this; I won't need it."

"You'd better keep it," warned Demlein. "Christ, I won't need it."

"No," insisted Joe, "if anything happens, I've got my own little knife. If I get stuck in a chute, I know how to work that better than this knife."

He had made a last call to his sister, leaving the message for her to call Pat and tell her he'd be a day late meeting her in Yorkshire. He added that he was "about to go into my act. If I don't come back, tell my dad . . . that I love him very much."

Not his mother, but the one who meant the most to him, his father.

The plane was called *Zootsuit Black*. "I was in the plane testing and double checking three minutes before takeoff," recorded Ensign James Simpson, USN. "I shook hands with Joe and said, 'So long and good luck, Joe. I only wish I were going with you.' He answered, 'Thanks, Jim, don't forget, you're going to make the next one with me. Say, by the way, if I don't come back, you fellows can have the rest of my eggs.' We never saw him again."

Joe and his copilot, Bud Wiley, were in the air only twenty minutes when Joe switched over to remote radio guidance. Elliott Roosevelt, son of the President, was flying photoreconnaissance, taking pictures of the mission, when he heard two explosions and saw the plane disintegrate, scattering fragments over a mile-wide area. It could only have been an electrical malfunction. No parts of their bodies were ever found.

Joe was twenty-nine. His death came almost exactly a year after his brother Jack's PT boat was sliced in half. The connection of events was tangible. Jack had never tried to be a hero, never really considered himself one. Joe was desperate to be one.

It was later discovered that the missile sites had been abandoned some time before our planes were sent to destroy them.

THE NEWS ARRIVED in Hyannis on August 13, 1944. "I remember it was Sunday afternoon," recalled Rose Kennedy, "and we all had lunched outside, picnic-style on our big porch at Hyannis Port. It was about two in the afternoon, and Joe Sr. had gone upstairs for a nap. The younger children were in the living-room, chatting quietly so as not to disturb their father; I sat reading the Sunday paper. There was a knock at the front door. When I opened the door, two priests introduced themselves and said they would like to speak with Mr. Kennedy.

"This was not unusual: priests and nuns fairly often came to call, wanting to talk with Joe about some charity or other matter of the Church in which he might help. So I invited them to come into the living-room and join us comfortably till Joe finished his nap. One of the priests said that the reason for calling was urgent. That there was a message both Joe and I must hear. Our son was missing in action and presumed lost.

"I ran upstairs and awakened Joe," recalled Rose Kennedy. "I stood for a moment with my mind half-paralyzed. I tried to speak but stumbled over the words. Then I managed to blurt out that the priests were here with that message. He leapt from the bed and hurried downstairs, I following him. We sat with the priests in a smaller room off the living-room, and from what they told us we realized there could be no hope, and that our son was dead."

The whole family was then home, Jack on weekend leave from Chelsea Naval Hospital, Robert home from the Navy ROTC. Their father went out on the porch and told them. They were stunned. He said they must be brave; that's what their brother would want from them. He urged them to go ahead with their plans to race that day, and most of them obediently did so. But Jack could not. Instead, for a long time he walked on the beach in front of our house.

"There were no tears from Joe and me, not then," said Rose. . . . "We sat awhile, holding each other close, and wept inwardly, silently. Then Joe said: 'We've got to carry on. We must take care of the living. There is a lot of work to be done.' "

Then Joe went to his room and shut the door. A friend said that Joe, a teetotaler, had taken a bottle of Scotch and belted it down. Never before had he lost something that he valued so tremendously, never before had he suffered such a severe shock.

It was not true that Rose more easily coped with the death of her firstborn son. Young Joe had been the repository of all her ambitions, and her official biographer, Robert Coughlan, observed: "and she could never really accept Jack—quirky, unusual Jack—as a successor."

But she had her faith in God, and would tell her daughter-in-law, Jacqueline, "Nobody's ever going to feel sorry for me." "We both decided we should carry on 'our regular life' . . . we had movies during the rest of the month as usual."

The next day, Jack told Eunice, "Let's go for a sail—that's what Joe would have wanted us to do."

While they were sailing, and his wife was praying, Joe Sr. called his sister Mary Loretta. "For an hour and a half he cried," she recalled, "terrible terrifying sounds welling up out of some dark place of eternal sadness, cry as he would never cry in front of his own wife."

Joe's death was a monumental event for the Kennedys. For Kick, it was despair and disaster. Joe had been her family anchor, her constant support, no matter what. She always came to him for advice and judgment. For Teddy, Joe had been a central figure in his life, and his death was incomprehensible. Bobby seemed to take it the hardest. He was bewildered, crushed. For him, Joe had been the family god.

Asked by a family friend soon afterward how many brothers and sisters he had, young Bobby named them all, including Joe.

"Where is Joe?" asked a friend, John Hooker, Jr.

Bobby looked at Hooker without the slightest embarrassment or the slightest hesitation, and said almost matter-of-factly, "He's in heaven."

For Jack, the trauma would take time to penetrate. Back at Chelsea Hospital, shortly after getting the news, Jack told James Reed, "You know, the waste of this man who had so much and who was gonna be President of the United States, dying the way he did . . ." Reed remembered Jack saying this almost in a dispassionate way. But George Taylor recalled Jack talking about it later and "we both sat down, we both had a good cry together."

Forgotten were the bitter fights with an overbearing brother. Now he would say he never knew anyone with a better sense of humor than Joe or anyone with whom he would rather have spent an evening or played golf "or in fact done anything."

In a loose-leaf notebook, Jack began collecting assorted clippings and quotes about Joe for a memorial book. An inventory of all of Joe's gear included two St. Christopher medals and sixteen books, including *War and Peace* and *So Little Time*.

One of the quotes was from Winston Churchill, on the death of Raymond Asquith in France, in 1915: "The War, which found the measure of so many men, never got to the bottom of him, and when the grenadiers strode into the crash and thunder of the Somme, he went to his fate, cool, poised, resolute, matter-of-fact, debonair." The other quote, from John Buchan's *Pilgrim's Way*: "He loved his youth, and his youth has become eternal. Debonair and brilliant and brave, he's now part of the immortal England which knows not age or weariness or defeat."

————

THE WAY YOUNG Joe had lived his life, the upward flowing pattern of it, had let everyone who knew him feel that he would always have luck in his life. But just before the war, young Joe told his friend Clem Norton, not once but twice, that he had a premonition that he would be killed flying in the war. Then he had added, "But don't you dare tell Dad."

There is no knowing if Joe Sr. ever felt any guilt for his son's death. What was absolute was the father's grief, not only for his son but for himself. His son was to be everything he could not be. He also felt deeply for the young man with Joe, Bud Wiley, and not only put Wiley's children through college, but contributed monthly support until they were grown.

"One morning, Joe called me from the Boston Ritz-Carlton," said Jack Dowd, who headed a Boston advertising firm which had done much work for the senior Kennedy. Arthur Krock had informed the former Ambassador that the long-withheld news of the circumstances surrounding the death of Joe Jr. in England was being released at noontime by the Navy Department. The elder Kennedy asked Dowd if there was a place they could hear the report in privacy. Dowd arranged for an audition room at Radio Station WNAC to hear the program.

"For a long time he had the look on his face of someone who has seen something frightening and can't get it out of his mind," said Lem Billings.

"When the young bury the old," Joe Sr. explained to his friend Bunny Green, "time heals the pain and sorrow; but when the process is reversed the sorrow remains."

Joe Sr. had regained a kind of composure when a final letter arrived from his son Joe, written just before he had gone on his mission. "There was something about receiving that letter," Rose later recalled, "that simply tore Joe apart." He wrote them that he couldn't share with them the secret details of his mission, but he was sure that they would understand why he had volunteered. "Don't get worried about it . . . as there is practically no danger."

"Joe simply threw the letter on the table," Rose recalled, "and collapsed in his chair with his head in his hands, saying over and over that nothing would ever be the same again, that the best part of his life was finished."

Many years later, a friendly interviewer, Robert Considine of International News Service, asked Joseph Kennedy to characterize his children. The father talked about each with great pride and Considine finally asked if he wanted to speak about Joe Jr.

"One of the top financiers of the age, a man known in many fields as cool beyond calculation under fire, suddenly and terribly burst into tears at the luncheon-table, and for five full minutes was wracked with grief that cannot be described. 'No,' he finally was able to say. 'No,

Mrs. Kennedy can, but I'll never be able to.' He later told Considine, 'Every night I say a prayer for him. Joe is now and always will be part of my life.' "

In his will, Joe Jr. left his estate to his father. His father set up the Joseph P. Kennedy, Jr., Foundation to help children in need—children from orphanages or from institutions for the mentally retarded.

His father also made certain that the Navy Cross was awarded posthumously to his son.

For extraordinary heroism and courage in aerial flights as Pilot of a United States Navy Liberator Bomber on August 12, 1944. Well knowing the extreme dangers involved and totally unconcerned for his own safety, Lieutenant Kennedy unhesitatingly volunteered to conduct an exceptionally hazardous and special operational mission. Intrepid and daring in his tactics and with unwavering confidence in the vital importance of his task, he willingly risked his life in the supreme measure of service and, by his great personal valor and fortitude in carrying out a perilous undertaking, sustained and enhanced the finest traditions of the United States Naval Service.

For the President
James Forrestal

Secretary of the Navy Forrestal would later name a 2200-ton destroyer the USS *Joseph P. Kennedy Jr.* Bobby, then in Naval Reserve Officer Training at Harvard, promptly quit and enlisted as a seaman on the destroyer named for his brother. A letter from Bobby indicated it was his father's idea, and he wasn't sure how he could cope with it. The constant reminder could not have been too easy. "Bobby wasn't allowed to go overseas during the war because the Government didn't allow it, after his brother was killed. So he'd joke about not being allowed outside the ten-mile limit."

Rose received a letter from Pat Wilson, a letter she never acknowledged. It read:

Loving him as much as I did, I can understand a little the agony you, as his mother, must be going through. Although Joe would hardly admit anything at all flattering to himself, he did tell me he thought you loved him the best of your sons maybe—so I can truly realize how unhappy you must be, and I long to be able to give you comfort. My thoughts and my deepest heartfelt sympathy are with you, and because I loved him so much and we were so happy together, I pray and believe that they will reach to your heart from mine. . . . Please forgive me, even if you blame me for loving him so much that he wanted to stay here and took this job. He would have taken some job anyhow, and the only way I could have made him go back to America would have been to say I didn't love him—which he would not have believed. Here are some photographs (and letters). . . . Perhaps if you would like it, I will write to you again and send you more.

Joseph Kennedy, Sr., sent Pat a cable, suggesting that his wife would not welcome any further communication.

———

SEVERAL WEEKS AFTER Joe's death, Jack had a Labor Day weekend get-together at Hyannis for some of his PT-boat buddies. Bobby was still a "scrawny little guy in a white sailor suit," taking a Midshipman's course at Harvard. He resented being on the sidelines and threatened to tell his father that they were drinking his Scotch. The housekeeper recalled that Kathleen had talked Bobby out of doing that. Meanwhile, Jack and his friends were roaring with laughter over some reminiscences when Jack heard the bellowing voice of his father from upstairs, "Jack, don't you and your friends have any respect for your dead brother?"

This was cruel, because Rose Kennedy already had set the family tone: no tears, life must go on. They even continued showing movies on their screen for the rest of the month.

All of his life, Jack would retain that special sensitivity, the emotional inequity that marked his early years. Joe had been everything his parents had wanted in a son. There was little question that if they had to choose to lose a son, it would not have been Joe. For them, he could never measure up to Joe.

All his life, Jack envied the family role Joe was playing. Now that the role was his, he would no longer need to copy his brother. He could be himself. Jack himself later said, "For a long time, I was Joseph Kennedy's son, then I was Joe's brother . . . someday I hope to be able to stand on my own feet." If his brother's death opened a new area of achievement for Jack, it also put him on the road to danger.

4

EARLY POLITICS

The elder Kennedy confided to his friend Krock that his son's death had brought him to the edge of madness. He had put too much of himself into his son and the ache was now enormous, the bitterness intense. When President Roosevelt, running for his fourth term in 1944, replaced his Vice President, Henry Wallace, with Senator Harry S Truman, Joseph Kennedy approached Truman in Boston, and his tone was vicious. "Harry, what are you doing campaigning for that crippled son of a bitch that killed my son Joe?" He blamed the wrong person, but it was too unbearable to blame himself.

Writing to his friend Arthur Houghton, Kennedy confided that "all my plans for my own future were all tied up with young Joe, and that has gone smash." And, to Jack Knight of the Miami *Herald,* who lost his own son years later, Kennedy wrote: "You never really accept it. You just go through the motions. . . . You think of what he might have done with a few more years, and you wonder what you're going to do with the rest of yours." When a former roommate of Joe Jr.'s visited Hyannis, the father burst into tears. "I feel bad that I was away so much when the boy was growing up. I didn't know him like I should have. I cheated him."

Whatever guilt he had, it was soon buried. A Joe Kennedy motto was: don't look back. He was a man who always moved on, and he had other sons to focus on.

Jack later wrote that it was impossible for a younger brother "to look at an older brother with any degree of objectivity.'' But Jack did not have the easy flow of his father's tears or the hard faith of his mother. ''He was never pushed off this hard, sensible center of his being.'' At Joe's death, Jack was quoted as saying, ''It was a matter of statistics. His number was up.''

Still, it seemed to increase his bitterness about the war, and he echoed his father's slanted view. In a letter to a teacher at Choate, he wrote, ''This war makes less sense to me now than it ever made and that was little enough—and I should really like—as my life's goal—in some way and at some time to do something to help prevent another.''

———————

FEW SAW AN open emotion in Jack about Joe's death. But there was a talk he made at an American Legion breakfast, where he used the quote: ''Greater love than this hath no man, than to lay down his life for his friend.''

''Of course, he was speaking about his brother, Joe,'' said his friend Edward McLaughlin. ''And the tears rolled right down his face; it broke the whole place up. . . . No, I never saw tears on his face, before or after—just that one day.''

When Jack produced a memorial volume about his brother, some saw it as paying a kind of penance for his mixed feelings. *As We Remember Joe* was privately printed, with family reminiscences. Joseph Kennedy confided to an interviewer, ''I've never read that book. . . . I've tried, many times. And once I even got to about page 25. But I couldn't go on. I just couldn't bring myself to it.''

Several weeks after Joe's death, Kick was again plunged into mourning. Her husband of four months was killed while leading his regiment of Coldstream Guards into action.

Kick was much like Jack. ''I am a Kennedy,'' she said, ''I know that we've all got the ability not to be got down.''

She did not rush home to Hyannis. She had made her break for freedom and there was no going back. Her mother had never forgiven her. When Kick did come home for the holidays, Jack was the only family member to meet her when she got off the plane—and she rushed into his arms. They were very much alike in spirit, humor, personality, and Joe's death had made them even closer.

Jack was still convalescing at Chelsea Naval Hospital, skinny, sallow, with intermittent pain. In the flow of condolence letters to him about Joe, there was a memorable one from an old Harvard friend, Michael Grace. Grace reminded Jack that Joe had been their model in almost everything, that his speechmaking had even persuaded them to take a course in public speaking.

At that time, Grace said, he had thought that "Joe will carry on the Kennedy fame, but Jack is the heart behind the name." Now, said Grace, it was plain that "Joe was the heart behind your name. . . . Joe has left behind to you a great responsibility—for when God calls one of us away from a job, it is so another can do it alone."

All of Jack's life, he had wanted to be just like his brother. His brother was his paragon, his model of perfection. His brother had it all. There was no way he could be as perfect as his brother. Now he didn't need to be. His brother's death had released him.

"I don't know what would have happened," said Jack. "It's always difficult for the younger ones and it would have been difficult for me that way if my brother had lived, just as I make it difficult for Bobby and we both make it difficult for Teddy and if Teddy doesn't do something why then he's just high tit on us and so he will try to do something and I suppose that's what contributes to the drive in each of us. What else?"

There is serious question whether Jack would have emerged without Joe's death. If Joe had gone on to political stardom, Jack, as he often said, would probably have eased into some quiet academic life. He had no intense ambition for anything else at that time. Because his father regarded him as unsuited, there would then have been no family attempt to draft him into politics. If young Joe had lived and gone into national politics, and if the father then started thinking of a dynasty, he would have reached out for Bobby, and even Teddy—but not Jack.

Now Jack could be his own man. In London, he had learned the power of his charm. He could charm people individually without losing his reserve. He had a talent for fellowship, almost a kind of magic the way he made people like him. He needed that affection more than most. Jack also discovered he thoroughly enjoyed adulation, despite his natural bent for privacy. His health was still not good. But if the path of his life was still uncertain, he now felt a stronger ability to cope with it, whatever it was. Meanwhile, he would not be his brother, but he would take his brother's place.

His mother later observed that when Joe was alive, Jack "was apt to goof off in debonair fashion," but when Joe was killed, "Jack took on the responsibility for the younger children."

Teddy still mourned. At a party at Hyannis after his brother's death, the whole family was proposing toasts, and the father asked fourteen-year-old Teddy if he had something to say. Teddy held up his water-glass and said, "I would like to offer a toast to our brother who is not with us."

Jack now felt ever more paternal toward Teddy, who had not done well academically at his various schools. But, now, at the Palm Beach Private School, he seemed to bloom—even being elected seventh-grade president and named captain of the basketball team.

"I was in school when Jack came down there as a PT-boat instructor," Ted Kennedy recalled, "and he used to smuggle me aboard a PT boat and take me for rides. We used to chew tobacco and spit and have a great time. He taught me to ride a bicycle, throw a forward pass and sail against the wind." Jack even introduced Teddy to his private passion, the roller coaster.

Bobby envied the closeness between Jack and Teddy. Family friend Mary Gimbel recalls a scene in which the three Kennedy brothers were getting ready to be photographed. "Jack and Teddy put their arms around Bobby and said sort of kiddingly, 'We three!' Bobby slipped out of the embrace and said in a way that was lighthearted but still made it clear how different he felt from them in certain ways: 'No. You two!' "

Bobby always had felt a distance between him and his older brothers, but he had developed a closeness to Joe. The age gap seemed great then. He still felt the gap with Jack. That gap didn't matter between Jack and Teddy because Jack saw Teddy not so much as a friend but as a mascot. Bobby wanted the same intimacy, but on a different level than Teddy.

Cousin Joe Gargan noted how often Bobby and Teddy went sailing together. They would spend "hour after hour of one-on-one in bathing suits on the Kennedy beach sand, practicing football pass patterns, which leg ended up in front when you left your feet laying down a cross-body block."

AFTER MONTHS IN and out of hospitals, two operations, innumerable tests, and persistent pain, Jack finally received a medical discharge from the Navy. It was almost as if he could breathe free again. "He didn't have the luxury of feeling well day after day," said Spalding, "so that when he came to his friends, he was in a euphoric state, and he was always the greatest, greatest company . . . so bright and so restless and so determined to wring every last minute that he just set a pace that was abnormal." At Palm Beach, he could indulge himself with parties and young women. The future was too remote to think about, especially when he had no compulsions, no plans, not even any dreams.

His father sent him to Castle Hot Springs Hotel in Arizona to fatten up, breathe fresh air, and ride horses. Jack described it to a friend as the place "where self-panickers come to die." Jack again took a side trip to Hollywood, where, as he wrote to Billings, "I expect to tangle tonsils with Inga Binga among others." Inga Binga was then working for MGM, and now had other romantic interests, but, as she had written him before he left for war—she would always have time for him when he returned.

Understandably, Jack kept close to Billings, and always would. It was with Billings, who truly knew him, that Jack could always be himself. Jack's letters to him continued in a constant stream, much of it still filled with pornographic references.

Billings was quick to tease: "Haven't you found any girl that will have you, Kennedy? It seems to me you are destined to never fall in love with anyone unless she's married or a divorcee—You know you're no spring chicken any longer—28 in a couple of weeks—as I recall—when I last saw you your hair line was receding conspicuously. . . . So what the hell have you? Take it from me you'd better cut out being so particular—you're on the road down—Leaving you with that in mind, I remain looking very well with a bronzed and stern appearance—"

Billings, however, was highly critical of any woman Jack went with. He continued to visit Jack often at Hyannis and Palm Beach, where he still kept his clothes.

There is the story that several days after his son's death, Joe Sr. called a family meeting and dramatically told Jack that he must now pick up the political torch of his older brother. "I was not present," said family friend Edward Gallagher, "but . . . I recall strong discussion to that effect took place in the home, at Hyannis Port, that Jack made up his mind that day, that that's what his father wanted and I think he set out to do it."

Jack later confided to Walter Cronkite that he did not feel obligated to go into politics to carry out Joe's unfulfilled ambitions, but admitted that Joe's death was indeed a decisive factor in his choice of a political career, simply because it cleared that path which had been previously reserved for the Kennedys' eldest son.

Cronkite pointedly asked, "Was it a conscious feeling on your part, of taking Joe's place?"

"No," Jack said. "But I never would have run for office if he had lived. I never would have imagined before the war that I would become active in politics." When discussing politics, he once admitted to a friend, "Sometimes we all have to do things we don't like to do." He was saying he was not enthusiastic about going into politics, but he was doing it for one reason: "I was drafted. My father wanted his eldest son in politics. 'Wanted' isn't the right word. He demanded it. You know my father," Jack told reporter Bob Considine.

His father afterward told an interviewer quite bluntly, "I got Jack into politics, I was the one. I told him Joe was dead, and that it was therefore his responsibility to run for Congress. He didn't want it. He felt he didn't have the ability . . . but I told him he had to."

"I'm certain he never forgets he must live Joe's life, as well as his own," wrote Choate headmaster George St. John to Jack's mother.

But it was more than Joe's life that he had to live; he had to live his father's life.

"When we lost our oldest son and Jack assumed his mantle . . . I thought that it was great," said Rose Kennedy. . . . "I was surprised at the leap to go over to Congress first thing because my father had gone up through legislature but his [Jack's] father always believed in getting the top place, if you could. That was the thing to strive for."

It was interesting that Rose Kennedy used the phrase "assumed his mantle"—the royal family concept. Although she denied that she considered the Kennedys an American royal family, she loved the idea.

———

JACK'S SISTER EUNICE wondered whether her frail brother was ready for politics. "Daddy, do you really think Jack can be a Congressman?"

"You must remember," her father replied, "it's not what you are that counts, but what people think you are."

Both Rose and Joe had definite ideas on what the Kennedy name meant and they would ingrain it in their family. Joe was not enthused about Jack's political qualities, but felt that whatever his son lacked could be compensated by the family millions and by his own political experience.

Although Joe saw little political potential in his second son until Joe's death, it wasn't long before he changed his mind. Meanwhile, there were more immediate things to consider to pave the way.

Father Joe had learned that Congressman James Michael Curley— Honey Fitz's old enemy—might be induced to run again for mayor if his debts were paid. The colorful seventy-one-year-old Curley already had been mayor three times, a governor, and four-term Congressman. To the people of Boston, there remained an intense loyalty to Curley unaffected by the fact that he had been convicted of mail fraud. If Curley was again elected mayor, the Eleventh Congressional District would need another Congressman. Who would be a more likely candidate than John Fitzgerald Kennedy? Kennedy Sr. put up a quick $12,000 to pay Curley's immediate debts and promised much more once the campaign began.

In the meantime, Jack needed a job.

Arthur Krock suggested to Joe the idea of finding Jack a position on a newspaper. Joe arranged a job on the Chicago *Daily American* and Jack was promptly assigned to report to San Francisco, where the United Nations was being officially born. When Krock saw him there, "he was having much more of a good time as a young man, however, than he was as a young reporter. He was not terribly diligent there. . . . It seems that one night in San Francisco, during the UN organization meeting, Johnny King and Chuck Spalding were sitting in Jack Kennedy's suite at the Palace Hotel, and he was supposed to be preparing an article for the Chicago *American*. As Johnny King describes it, when they entered the suite, Jack Kennedy was stretched out on the bed with his dinner-suit pants on, and his evening socks, and his black tie, beautifully tied . . . and he was talking on the telephone . . . and it was perfectly clear in a couple of minutes that he was trying to reach the managing editor of the paper he was supposed to be doing a piece for that day. . . . King said he heard Kennedy say, 'Well, then, give him a message: "Kennedy will not be filing tonight." ' ' "

A note from Billings kept Jack in balance: "Bobby tells me you are now writing up the San Francisco Conference for some Chicago papers—Why are they trusting you with so important a job? I do not know—it must be rather an unimportant paper."

From brother Bob came another gentle poke: "Everyone evidently thinks you're doing a simply fine job out there, except mother who was a little upset that you still mixed 'who' + 'whom' up. Get on to yourself."

It was in San Francisco that Jack told his friend Spalding, "I'm going into politics."

"That's great," said Spalding, "you'll go all the way."

"Do you really think so?" asked Kennedy.

"Yes, I do."

His father had made clear that this reporting was only an interlude until the upcoming congressional election. His pressure had been unrelenting.

"I can feel Pappy's eyes on the back of my neck," Jack told his friend Red Fay. He talked about "Dad trying to parlay a lost PT boat and a bad back into a political advantage. I tell you, Dad is ready right now and can't understand why Johnny boy isn't 'all engines ahead.' "

———

DURING THIS INTERIM, Jack wrote "very good, very clear" articles for Hearst. When he wrote an article for the *Atlantic Monthly*, the editor turned it down. Then Joe Sr. intervened with some friendly pressure on the publisher, and the editor decided the Kennedy story was pretty good after all.

Jack's next assignment was the 1945 election in Great Britain, and his father arranged a meeting for him with British publisher Max Beaverbrook, who had remained an important friend to all the Kennedy boys.

Britain was a happy place for Jack. Kick was there and had a few girls lined up for him, including the love of his brother's life, Pat Wilson. Whether he was commiserating with Pat or dating her on his own is not certain.

Thinking of the upcoming Congressional election, his father urged him to visit Ireland. He cabled him: THINK IT MOST IMPORTANT THAT YOU GO AND COVER THE SITUATION . . . PAPERS AND MAGAZINES WILL BE VITALLY INTERESTED.

Jack and Kick stayed at the Devonshire family castle in County Waterford, Ireland, along with Anthony Eden and Randolph Churchill and his wife, Pamela—who had dated young Joe.

Pamela remembered: "One morning Jack said rather quietly, rather apologetically, 'Would you mind coming on an expedition with me to find the original Kennedys?' He said that before leaving America he'd done certain research and discovered which village they came from and it was about 200 miles north. . . . So he and I started off one morning . . . in a station wagon. Well, a station wagon in Ireland then, in Europe in fact, was an absolutely marvelous thing. Nobody had ever seen them and it was the height of luxury."

Pamela and Jack took the station wagon and headed for County Wexford, where they found a little white house crowded with pigs and chickens and children. The parents seemed dignified but suspicious. Jack changed the mood when he gave the children a ride in his station wagon around the village.

Jack recalled that the house had a thatched roof, with a great open hearth, and was near a stream. "The farmer did say that a Patrick Kennedy from Boston, who of course was my grandfather, had come to visit the home some thirty-five years before, when the farmer was a boy. It sounded from their conversation as if all the Kennedys had emigrated. I figured that they were my third cousins.

"I spent about an hour there and left in a flow of nostalgia and sentiment. This was not punctured by the English lady turning to me as we drove off and saying, 'Just like *Tobacco Road.*' She had not understood at all the magic of the afternoon."

There wasn't time for a long stay in Ireland because Secretary of the Navy James Forrestal, a friend of the elder Kennedys, had invited Jack to join him en route to Berlin for the Potsdam Conference. President

Roosevelt had died and the new President, Truman, would meet Stalin and Churchill for a summit conference.

Jack, who had been in Berlin as a young college student, seeing the hysteria of Hitler, now saw the city rubbled by war.

Not only were major governments in transition, but the world had altered dramatically when the atomic bomb was dropped on Hiroshima in August 1945. The Japanese had surrendered and the war was over.

While Jack was away, his father had arranged to become chairman of the Governor's Committee on Commerce. This required crisscrossing some 1300 miles in the state, making twenty-six speeches in eight days. Most important, he felt he was preparing political contacts for his son's future—an idea which backfired because the public response to him was so negative, partly because of his wartime reputation.

However, there were other ways he could pave the way for Jack. Kennedy wrote Beaverbrook that he was selling his profitable liquor business. It was obviously not the kind of business that a political candidate's father should have.

————

FOR A POTENTIAL Congressman, Jack then had few strong views of his own. Mostly, Jack's early political positions reflected his father's views. It was not surprising. They had been drummed into his head at the dinner table since he was a boy.

"We went for a walk along the beach," said his Harvard friend Blair Clark, "and we talked about things. And he made a big attack on the Wagner Act. You know, I was the old Liberal, and gave him a short lecture on how much that meant, and how it didn't go far enough. We argued back and forth. Finally, I said, 'Jack, you ought to break with your old man. We've all got to break with our fathers, or we're not grown up!' Well, I can't remember what he said . . . but it was the worst advice that anybody could have given him, from the point of view of his career. He would have gotten nowhere, without the old man."

Few thought much of John Kennedy as a candidate. Thomas "Tip" O'Neill, who would later represent the same congressional district, said, "To be perfectly truthful, this pasty-faced-looking kid didn't look any more like a Boston politician that was going to go to Congress than the man in the moon."

A reporter later asked Jack, "Why didn't you stay as a reporter?" Jack said, "Reporters and writers have to stay up in the stands, and be observers. I'd rather be an activist, down on the field."

He probably would rather have been the observer. All his life, even while looking comfortable in a crowd, he had been a loner, an outsider. His friends felt he thrived on the sidelines watching everyone, especially himself. Now he saw himself choosing politics for a complicated mix of reasons: duty, ambition, power, and excitement. And, of course, to win his father's approval.

Jack described his decision: "Suddenly, the time, the occasion and I all met. . . . I moved into the Bellevue with my grandfather. . . . I started to run, and I've been running ever since!"

Grandfather Honey Fitz was then past eighty, but Jack's campaign now put a new spring in his step, a fresh lilt to his "Sweet Adeline." His grandson was not only filling his shoes but living just down the hall from him at the hotel. That was called being a "mattress voter."

Jack was not Fitz's favorite. Young Joe had kept closer to his grandparents than Jack had, and was the golden boy. Still, Jack was Honey Fitz's namesake and Fitz had given Jack, the boy, much love and private time. Now Jack, the man, listened hard when Fitz talked serious, basic politics. Shortly before Jack announced his candidacy, Honey Fitz introduced Jack to a wiry little man whose life was politics: Patsy Mulkern. Mulkern reminded him of the state law that a candidate must be a registered member of his party twenty days before formal declaration. Had Jack ever registered and voted before? His answer was no.

So, as his mother recorded, "Jack hustled down to City Hall and quietly joined the Democratic Party." They slipped him into the City Hall Annex and got his name on the Democratic rolls several days after the deadline.

Ed Plaut, who was co-authoring a political book on Jack, later photocopied the signed declaration from the files at the Town Hall, proving that Kennedy had filed too late to qualify for that primary. Plaut later discovered that this bound file had disappeared from Town Hall, the only volume that was missing, and nobody seemed to know what had happened to it. Had all this been revealed at that time, there might not have been any Kennedy candidacy, at least not in 1946.

WHEN ASKED ONCE by a reporter about his influence on Jack, Joe Sr. smiled broadly and said, "No, I didn't advise Jack at all."

He didn't advise; he commanded. It was true that the father exerted more pressure than inspiration, and the leverage was money. Campaign worker Anthony Gallucio asked Jack Kennedy what his old man would do in the campaign. Jack rubbed his thumb with the other four fingers, meaning "money."

"You know, you can be a candidate, you can have the issues, you can have the organization," said Tip O'Neill, "but money makes miracles and money did miracles in that campaign. . . . Why they even had six different mailings . . . *nobody* had *any* mailings in that district."

It took his father's money to hire the advertising agency and pay its many bills, rent meeting halls, dining rooms and ballrooms, supply most of the expenses for the volunteers and professionals. His father brought in most of the old pros to help. The fund-raising follow-up for the "Back Jack" campaign included how-to-do-it booklets plus a sample sell for telephone solicitation with answers to possible questions.

"With the money I spent on that campaign, I could have elected my chauffeur," the father told an interviewer.

JACK WANTED THE celebrity and excitement of politics, but he hated the grit of it: the handshaking, the backslapping, the phony smile, the small talk. For all these reasons, cousin Kane, who was teaching him these fundamentals, did not consider him prime political material, as young Joe had been. Jack seemed weak, too willing to accept the ideas of others, hardly able to defy his father on anything. He was obviously not happy campaigning, did not enjoy crowds, and he had little confidence in himself.

Jack told Kane, "I wish Joe was around. Joe would have been Governor by now." Or Jack would tell friends, "I'm just filling Joe's shoes. If he were alive, I'd never be in this."

Jack knew he would never be "Daddy's Joe." In all his talks with his father, there was maximum critique, minimum approval. His father had told Tip O'Neill that Jack was too soft. "You can trample all over him, and the next day he's there for you with loving arms."

Jack had growing difficulty in dealing with his brother's death. He almost never referred to brother Joe in public. He also never made any political profit off his brother's death, never said, "My brother, who was killed while fighting valiantly in World War II." It would not have been classy. Nevertheless, his campaign headquarters in various storefronts did have all kinds of pictures of Jack in uniform, including his medals and awards. And there were some discreet photos of Joe in uniform, even a few in the campaign literature.

Many politicians still saw him as "a little boy dressed up in his father's clothes." In his speeches, his voice was high-pitched and scratchy. Reardon remembered how Kennedy raced through a formal speech, barely pausing. "I talk too fast because I just do not believe the clichés a politician must utter," he later told a reporter. "A speech where you ascribe only the good to yourself and only the bad to your opponent has a synthetic quality that throws me—I find it difficult to give it conviction. These guys who can make the rafters ring with hokum—well, I guess that's okay, but it keeps me from being an effective political speaker." He had sent a copy of a speech to an old friend with the note, "It's the old bullshit with a new twist." His younger brothers would go through that same process.

He could always speak quickly and glibly and amusingly at any time, but it took him a long time to develop a style of his own. The man who influenced him most, according to Charles Spalding, was Winston Churchill. Jack had gone to listen to him when the great British leader addressed the joint session of Congress in December 1941.

———————

JACK WAS STILL uneasy and uncertain with his politicking. But the family pressure intensified. James Reed, a war buddy, recalled one night at Hyannis, sitting on the open porch with Jack and his father and grandfather Fitzgerald, and a few close friends. "One of them said to me, 'Jim, you're going to be the President of the United States one day.' With that, Jack piped up and said, 'After me.' Whereupon Honey Fitz stood up, looked right at Jack, and very seriously proposed a toast: 'To the future President of the United States, my grandson, John Fitzgerald Kennedy.' Whereupon we all stood up and drank a toast. . . . And I think that everyone there thought that Jack would be President of the United States."

It was exhilarating stuff. He was a young man entering a new world with an unimaginable ultimate prize. But what was most immediately important was that he had become the absolute focus of his whole family. All his life he had wanted to earn their pride. It was more important to him then than almost anything else. His future no longer seemed uncertain. But before he could be elected to the Congress, he had to be nominated.

There were ten contenders for that congressional seat. "It cost Old Joe a million dollars to buy Jack a seat in the House," insisted columnist Robert S. Allen. "McCormack was the Speaker then and a political force in Massachusetts but he sputtered and hemmed and hawed about the Kennedy race, but there was nothing he could do. . . . They just bought out all the opposition."

But Joe Kane afterward had a footnote: "Jack could have gone to Congress like everyone else for ten cents." What he meant was that Jack didn't need all that money because 1946 was a great year for veterans, and Jack was a hero.

At first, Jack minimized the hero label. "It was involuntary. They sank my boat." But soon he basked in the glory. At the same time, he evolved from a hesitant candidate to a determined one. It took hard concentration for Jack to develop a way to work his easy charm on crowds. But the tingling ebullience of the campaign, the reaction of people to *him*, had become contagious and hard to deny. He was caught. The promise of power was a glittering thing.

COMING FROM SUCH overpowering family intimacy, it wasn't easy to seek outside friendships. Like his father, he kept close only to those people he trusted completely. He suspected everybody else's motives, especially the people who might be close to being zealous. The more excited they were, the more suspicious he became.

Few outsiders could ever enter into his intimate circle. It seemed impenetrable. During the congressional campaign, out of necessity, it expanded. One of the new insiders was Dave Powers.

"My first tip-off on the kid is great," reflected Powers later. Jack had knocked on his door in Charlestown while Powers was baby-sitting for his sister's nine children. Jack introduced himself and Powers explained that he was supporting a friend of his who grew up with him.

"And I'm thinking, 'A millionaire-type from Harvard, they're gonna laugh at!' "

But then Jack said he didn't know anybody in Charlestown and would Powers come with him to a meeting with the Gold Star Mothers at the American Legion Hall. Powers agreed. These were the mothers who had lost their sons in the war, and there were several hundred of them in the hall. "And he's makin' the world's worst speech! And I'm getting nervous as hell," said Powers. "And then, he looked out at all these ladies—and I say today, the greatest line of his life was—'I think I know how you feel, because my mother is a Gold Star Mother, too.' And in all the years I've been in politics, I've never seen such a reaction. He's immediately surrounded by these wonderful Charlestown ladies. . . . I can hear 'em saying, 'He reminds me of my own son,' the son that they had lost.

"We come out of there; he's solemn as hell. He said, 'How do you think I did?' And I said, 'You were great.' And he put out his hand, 'Then you will be with me?' In the excitement . . . I shook his hand, and said, 'I will.' "

From then on, Dave became Jack's "pal." Dave was different from Billings. Lem was Jack's most intimate friend, his confider and confessor, his blood brother. Dave was his political mentor, his watchful friend.

Patsy Mulkern described a typical Kennedy campaign day: "We'd start Jack out in the morning early, what they call street work . . . meet the city worker, meet the cabby, meet the waitress, wander in and say, 'My name is John Kennedy, I'm running for Congress.' Some would say, 'I knew your grandfather Honey Fitz,' and another would come up an' say, 'I knew your other grandfather, PJ,' or 'I knew your mother, Rose Fitzgerald.' He didn't have to talk nothin'. They might ask him about his war record, but nothin' 'bout issues.

"He kept goin'. Never ate much. Great frappe drinker. He had the biggest rallies ever held in the North End . . . rallies, house parties, dances. . . . Every girl you met thought she was going to be Mrs. Kennedy."

Campaign worker Wilton Vaugh also felt that Jack's secret was the women—they all either fell in love with him or wanted to mother him. "And they'd feel he's a nice boy and he's a good boy and he's intelligent; and he needs somebody to help him," Vaugh noted. "So they all went out and helped him by voting for him. I think that the relatives of some of the candidates running against him actually voted for him."

What John Kennedy also had was something he learned from Grandpa Honey Fitz—the Irish Switch: the ability to shake hands with one person while talking to another and looking ahead at a third person. But it was a real handshake, and he had a way of looking into a person's eyes, saying just the right words and at the same time keeping that line moving fast. Said a newsman: "He's beautifully disciplined. And behind that generous smile is a cool, calculated machine that is constantly saying, 'What's in it for me?'"

Jack took time out for women. His brother Joe would not have taken any chances that might self-destruct. But for young Joe, politics was a passion and a calling. For Jack, it was not. One of the great perks of politics for Jack was that it increased the availability of women.

"What Jack did like to do was to take a few days off and go to New York," Larry Newman recalled. "We once walked back to the Park Lane, and on the way back Mort [singer Morton Downey] was giving him hell for going out with two or three girls from Broadway—showgirls. Mort told Jack, 'You know, you damn fool, if you ever want to get any place in politics, you'd better cut out this nonsense with those long-stemmed beauties from Billy Rose's place!' Jack said, 'Oh, Jesus, I'm in love with this girl.' And Mort said, 'You've been in love with every girl you've ever met since I've known you!' And they laughed."

When Arthur Krock complained to Kennedy Sr. about Jack's sexual exploits, the father bristled and replied, "The American people don't care how many times he gets laid."

One of Jack Kennedy's conquests that year was actress Gene Tierney. He met her at a Hollywood party when she was separated from her husband. "Jack took me to dinner at El Morocco," she recalled. "We danced that night for hours and hours. He was a superb dancer. He held a girl like a real man should—softly on the shoulder, and firmly but not aggressively around the waist. When we kissed good night, I knew that we'd be seeing each other again." She added that she was soon deeply in love with him "and would have married him in a minute if he had been able to ask me." But Jack knew that his family would never allow him to marry a divorced actress and they slowly drifted apart.

Gene Tierney had a retarded daughter from a previous marriage. Jack told Tierney about his retarded sister, Rosemary, but Tierney noted that the subject was awkward for him. " 'Gene,' he said, after a silence had passed between us, 'in any large family you can always find something wrong with somebody.' " Rosemary had become emotionally difficult, and in 1941, Joe decided—without consulting his wife—on a lobotomy. It was not successful. Instead of being mildly retarded, she became a human vegetable.

The longtime Kennedy silence on Rosemary was part of the family tradition of minimizing any physical handicap, disease, accident, pain. Imperfection was a kind of shame.

Jack's mother was also soon involved in the campaign. Rose Kennedy was then fifty-six years old and looked twenty years younger. She was born in that ward and was better known in the 11th Congressional District than anybody. She could call people by their names, and she had gone to school with many of them at Dorchester High.

When Rose spoke, she was something she could never be at home—the star of the show. She told people what they wanted to hear from her—mostly about the glamorous people she had known and the places she had visited. She always got a standing ovation.

"I remember showing up—and we were running late in Brighton," said Powers. "She was just finishing. . . . I came up the stairs with Jack . . . and he's listening to her. And he was so overwhelmed that his mother could talk that well, to an audience, that she was a 'natural.' And as she came off the stage, she introduced him, and he said, 'Mother, they really love you, here in Boston.' If he wasn't a Kennedy, he'd say, 'Oh God, thank you for making that speech for me.' But Kennedys are funny about saying things like that."

This was a mother he never knew, and he was deeply impressed. He was also grateful. She did make him feel, however, that she was the pro and he was the amateur. But now when she said something he listened. He asked her whether or not he should wear a hat, because some said he would look older if he wore a hat. She glared at him and replied that it was more important for him to be on time, that his father didn't like to be kept waiting, nor keep other people waiting, and neither did she.

ROBERT FRANCIS KENNEDY was then twenty years old, looking much younger in his sailor suit. He was waiting for his discharge. He seemed terribly shy when he arrived at his brother Jack's rooms at the Bellevue Hotel, in Boston.

Jack had come out of one of his frequent tub baths—he needed the wet heat for his bad back—and had a towel around his middle when he introduced Bobby to Dave Powers, adding, "He's on a destroyer."

While Jack was changing, Bobby asked, "Dave, how do you think old Jack will do?"

Powers told him that young veterans were coming home, and the quality that they looked for in a person was courage. "They admire a guy with a lot of guts."

"And I can always remember," said Powers, "Bobby's face lighting up and looking like a big kid. And he said, 'Jack has more courage than any man I ever met.' "

Courage was the key Kennedy word. Bobby's great regret was that he could not prove his courage in war as his brothers did.

Jack was dubious about what Bobby could do to help him. As he told his Navy buddy Red Fay, "It's damn nice of Bobby wanting to help, but I can't see that sober, silent face breathing new vigor into the ranks." Jack suggested that the best thing was a publicity picture of the two brothers for the press. "Then you take Bobby out to the movies."

Fay found it a disconcerting experience. Bobby was unenthusiastic, almost expressionless. His total conversation was an occasional yes or no. After the film, there was vaudeville, and Fay thought the comic was hilarious. "But Bobby looked as if he might have been paying his last respects to his closest friend." Fay finally asked Bobby whether he wanted to leave and Bobby quickly got up, and the two of them filed out in absolute silence.

Bobby had written to his friend David Hackett a bit earlier that he was "my usual moody self. I get very sad at times."

It was a difficult time for Bobby. He longed to be as close to Jack as Joe had been. He wanted to earn his brother's respect. One way to become close was to prove himself indispensable to Jack's campaign.

He asked for the toughest place to work. They sent him to Cambridge, a stronghold for one of the rival candidates. Jack also sent

Billings there, telling him, "Whatever you do, Lem, don't tell anyone you went to Choate." Lem, who had known Bobby since he was a little boy, was now put in charge of him.

Bobby later admitted, "I had very little to do with that campaign. I spent a few weeks in three wards of East Cambridge. My job was to meet as many people as possible, hoping to reduce the vote against us there from five to one to four to one. Actually that's what that campaign consisted of: contacting people."

Bobby's office was in the poorest part of Cambridge. He worked hard, beginning each day at 8:30 in the morning to open the headquarters, then went from one precinct to the other, and was always the last to leave.

"You could disagree with Jack," said friend Charles Houghton, "yet walk away from him liking him. . . . Jack had this tremendous ability to have people like him. . . . Whereas Bobby: you'd disagree with him, and go away hating him. . . . I'm sitting in Jack's headquarters, late one evening, with Bobby, and Teddy. There was some talk about how all the real Massachusetts pols were critical of Bobby—I'll always remember what Bob said then—and it's so typical of his life that was dedicated to the success of Jack. He said: 'They don't have to like me; I only want them to like Jack.' "

But Jack's early supporter, Councilman Joe De Gulielmo, saw another side of Bobby: the way he went across the street to play softball with the kids, as if he were just another kid himself—and part of him was. It tore down any feeling in the area that the rich Kennedys were high-hat. With the kids, Bobby was a Navy veteran, and any veteran was a hero. With the kids, he could be bigger than he was.

And Powers testified to Bobby's intensity. "Bobby took all the chances for Jack, and assumed all kinds of responsibility. . . . We were riding over to Charlestown, and he pointed to a bridge coming from North Station and he said, "That'd be a great place for a Kennedy sign! . . . I'll send a sign over."

The huge sign read: ELECT JOHN F. KENNEDY . . . HE WILL DO MORE FOR MASSACHUSETTS.

Bobby came by a couple of days later, and the sign wasn't up because the ladder wasn't tall enough. Then Bobby himself stood on the top rung of a ladder, hammering in nails. Down below, Dave Powers was thinking, "If I had this fellow's money, I'd be sitting in a rocking chair on Cape Cod. . . . But that's what made them great." Powers also told the story of Bobby, with a load of Kennedys in a station wagon, honking his horn for Dave to join them on a Sunday morning—his only day off in the campaign—to deliver brochures in a Republican neighborhood.

Eunice was the natural politician in the family. Her father had said that if she had balls, she would have been President. Eunice beamed when someone told her she looked like Jack. Jean wanted to know whom she looked like. Told she looked like Bobby, she protested that she didn't want to look like Bobby—she also wanted to look like Jack. It's interesting how the Kennedy women worshiped their brothers, wanted to share their excitement, wanted to be like them. Being themselves was not enough because in their family it meant their horizons would be limited. Eunice felt this more than the other sisters.

Teenage Teddy was still a bit chubby, still gorged cookies, still was affectionate, and also worked eagerly in the campaign as office boy, messenger, coffee-and-tea boy. It was his first exposure to practical politics. He was then in ninth grade at Milton Academy, a highly respected prep school, ten miles south of Boston. He had gone to Milton because "Bobby liked it and thought I would."

Milton, like Choate, was considered a way station to Harvard, but was not quite as competitive. Milton promoted the principle: It's not whether you're better than anyone else that's important—it's whether or not you tried.

Arthur Hall, a head football coach as well as teacher, regarded Teddy as "a very good-humored, fun sort of kid but he was not a good student. It took a tutor to enable Teddy to pass and graduate. He was a straight-C student."

Teddy and Honey Fitz were frequent companions. "When I was going to school, I'd get Sunday lunch off and I'd go on into the Bellevue Hotel and have Sunday lunch with him . . . and he would take you all through the kitchen and introduce you to all of the waitresses. On several occasions, I remember Bob was there—and he would join us. And then in the afternoon he'd take us for a walk through the Boston Common and we'd go down to the Old North Church and sit outside in a chair and look up at the steeple and view the architecture. . . .

Once in a while we'd start out the door to go and view these various historic sights and he'd get wrapped up in conversation with friends and we'd never get there. . . . I heard my first off-color story from Grandpa. He was laughing so hard."

———————

THE GREAT KENNEDY political machine triumphed. Jack won, polling 40.5 percent of the total vote against nine other Democratic candidates in the primary. It helped him when cousin Kane persuaded an unknown candidate named Joseph Russo to enter the race. Since there was already a candidate with the same name, it split the Russo vote and ensured the Kennedy victory. In another election for a local office, years later, the Kennedy name was so popular that a John F. Kennedy won overwhelmingly before the public realized he was a foreman in a razor-blade factory.

When it was time for the November election, Jack defeated the Republican candidate, receiving 71.9 percent of the popular vote. When his eighty-three-year-old grandfather Honey Fitz heard the news, he climbed on a table and sang.

A *Harvard Crimson* interview with the new Congressman Kennedy indicated that he didn't have any specific platform for action and seemed to have a lack of knowledge of government affairs and issues "and tells you to look at his record in two years to see what he stands for." The one thing Kennedy seemed vehement about was that Russian Communistic expansionist policies were a real threat to peace that must be stopped no matter what the cost. The *Crimson* headline had read: JOE KENNEDY'S BOY.

He still was Joe's boy. What he said about Russia were his father's words. His election victory was largely his father's victory and the exhilaration was mostly his father's exhilaration. What was Jack's own was his sense of personal struggle. It would have been different if his father had forced him to do something when he had some dramatic desire to do something else. But that wasn't it. Whatever career ideas he otherwise had were vague. He did not yet have the strength of personality to defy his father, nor did he want to—because he had no surging alternative to offer. So he let his father shape him, direct him.

Lem Billings, who knew Jack best, explained his candidacy: "He was running because it was required, but he was also running because he thought he might be able someday, somehow to locate *himself* in the middle of this complex mix of duty, expectation, and all the rest of it."

His personal struggle was *not* to be Joe Jr., but, as much as possible, to be himself. To do this, he knew, deep within, that he would have to begin edging away from his father. He knew the day would come when he would be his own man.

Young Joe's influence on Jack was still so strong that he selected young Joe's best friend at Harvard, Timothy Reardon, as his administrative assistant.

Jack was twenty-nine when he was sworn into the Eightieth Congress. On the first day of his first congressional term he showed up not only late—which would become a habit—but dressed in tan cotton chino pants and an open collar shirt, tennis shoes, no jacket. It was his own rebellion showing, his way of exerting his independence.

When Congressman John Kennedy was mistaken as one of the page boys, House doorkeeper Monroe Melletio announced that all congressional page boys must wear blue uniforms. Reardon had to impress on Kennedy that his time was important, "so whenever you want anything, push your buzzer and don't walk out there and drape yourself over your secretary's desk every time you want anything. But he still continued to come out and people would close in on him and he would go over to them with his face-splitting smile, his gray eyes looking friendly, casual but alert."

ROBERT SARGENT SHRIVER became an intimate part of the Kennedy household. A handsome Yale graduate, former *Newsweek* editor Shriver had been asked by the senior Kennedy to read young Joe's diaries to see whether they were publishable. Shriver suggested they were outdated and that they be published privately. In turn, Kennedy Sr. invited him to breakfast and asked him to run his newly bought Merchandise Mart building in Chicago. Shriver, who knew nothing about real estate, took the job because he found Kennedy Sr. "extremely appealing because he was very direct. Practical, down to earth. No pomposity. . . . He always used to say that money isn't important in itself, it's only the power it gives you to do something more important."

Eunice, who had been working on juvenile court cases, got the job of organizing a national committee to combat juvenile delinquency. Kennedy Sr. asked Shriver to go and help her.

Jack and Eunice shared a townhouse in Georgetown, and Shriver remembered "seeing all four of the Kennedy girls, all dressed in long evening dresses, standing in front of the fireplace. They were just talking to each other. I can remember thinking that if you were a father and had four girls as pretty, congenial, interesting as these four . . . every one a knockout . . . you could say your life was a success. To produce a family of nine that were so happy, warm-hearted, close—I think that's a fantastic achievement."

Shriver recalled that at many of the parties at Jack and Eunice's, there were games because the Kennedys loved them. In one game Eunice had everybody close their eyes, put their hands on the shoulders of the person in front of them and follow the leader, and not open their eyes until told. When they all opened their eyes, they found themselves in front of the door, the hostess there to say goodnight.

But, as one friend put it, "if you stay overnight, you don't get a nightcap. You get a glass of milk before going to bed."

———

IT WAS TRADITIONAL for a freshman Congressman to find a political mentor in the House, and stay under his wing for a while, somebody he could go to whenever he was in trouble. But not Jack. It would have been expected that he would seek out Representative John McCormack of Massachusetts, a good friend of his father and grandfather. He didn't do it. "It wasn't because he didn't like McCormack, it wasn't that at all," said Reardon. "It's just that this goes against his grain. He's an independent and likes to keep himself that way."

Jack's initial legislative stamp was generally regarded as more conservative than liberal—again reflecting his father. One thing he did not know were economic issues. On this, Congressman Kennedy still listened hard to his father. Reflecting on Kennedy's vote on a St. Lawrence Seaway issue, *New York Times* correspondent John Fenton felt it was motivated by the father's financial interests in that area at that time.

But Jack soon realized the importance of selecting an experienced staff.

Kennedy hired Theodore Sorensen, a brilliant young liberal who became his prize speechwriter and "intellectual blood-bank." Sorensen soon knew the mind of Kennedy better than almost anyone. Kennedy considered him indispensable. "I want to keep Ted with me wherever I travel. You need somebody whom you can trust implicitly, trust his judgment, his loyalty, his intelligence." Sorensen was soon able to speak for him on any issue.

He also became the Congressman's key social conscience, giving him something he never got from his father. All this did not break the bond, not even bend it, but perhaps slowly stretched it a little more.

For example, Kennedy began to take some controversial opinions such as attacking the American Legion leadership for their opposition to the housing bill. Kennedy also opposed the Taft-Hartley Act, a law designed to curb labor unions—something his father would have favored. "He came back to the office that day, sort of waving his hands," said Reardon, and saying, "Well, I'm dead now. I'm politically finished, dead."

———

AFTER NINE MONTHS in Congress, Jack's recurrent ailments brought him back to the hospital on a stretcher. His father was the first to arrive and take over. Few realized Jack's constant struggle with his back pain. Spalding suggested that he controlled the pain within himself so that he could cope with the outside world, that there were stretches of time when he was just out of commission. It was later offered as an explanation why he was not considered a hard worker in Congress, and also an explanation for his high absentee record. This was only partially true.

Kennedy liked politics, but not the daily detail of legislation. It bored him. Fellow Congressmen claimed he would come to the House and give a speech on a subject, a good speech, written for him, that would get all the publicity, but a subject about which he knew little if anything. This was the same accusation later leveled at Bobby—but not Teddy.

Jack Kennedy wasn't one of those young Congressmen who worried overmuch about any bill he'd introduced. He saw himself as a freshman Congressman at the bottom of the totem pole, and he didn't like it.

What Jack did have—besides a good staff—was his father's organized mind and memory. "We could be sitting in a car talking about some important things," said Reardon, "and he would suddenly drop in a footnote about something else and ask me to look into it and then switch back to our important subject. Maybe I didn't have a pencil, and maybe I forgot about it, we'd talk about so many things. But he didn't forget. It could be weeks, maybe months later, and he might suddenly bring it up again, and ask what I did about it. He had a lot of guys doing a great many different things, but he was always on top of all of them. He really had such an organized mind that it sometimes frightened me."

Bobby had this same kind of memory.

Bobby was then twenty-one. His short time on a ship as a seaman had changed him because it gave him the same exposure to ordinary people that his brothers had in war. It softened some of his smugness. The short experience in the campaign had further broadened him, but, more than that, alerted him to the excitement of politics.

His father had not yet zeroed in on him as a political possibility. But, deeply religious as he was, he had decided not to be the priest his mother wanted. There was the vague idea of law—Joe Jr. had gone to law school. And there was the vaguer idea of journalism—Jack had worked as a reporter.

Of Harvard, Bobby later said, "I didn't go to class very much, to tell you the truth. I used to talk and argue a lot, mostly about sports and politics." He admitted his academic inadequacy to his parents: "I'm certainly not hitting the honors like my older brothers."

Bobby didn't read as much as Jack did. But Jack read more because he was ill so much. Bobby didn't study as hard as young Joe did. But young Joe studied more because their father was watching so intently, and because he had a sharply defined goal. Bobby had no goal. Nothing was forcing Bobby to search himself and settle on something. "He was a terrible student at Harvard," said Hackett. "Went out with the jocks."

Bobby did so for the same reason Jack went out with women—to prove his manhood. Though he weighed only 154 pounds, Bobby still played varsity football. His teammate Ken O'Donnell recalled that "after the war, there were eight men on the team, all high school stars, all-scholastic or all-prep. Some had returned from the war bigger and stronger. They used to knock Bobby down then, and he'd be right up again and make a tackle." His high point came in 1947 when he caught a scoring pass from Ken O'Donnell against Western Maryland. He had smashed his leg against a bench in a scrimmage session but kept on playing. Three days later X rays showed the leg was broken. Dave Powers called it "Bobby's great second effort. . . . Yes, he had more of that kind of intensity than Jack or Teddy. . . . He had a barrel of guts."

"Bob tried to do everything the other boys did," said Hackett. "He was just not much of an athlete . . . but Bobby's father didn't care, as long as Bobby tried. Bobby was not gifted at really anything. Not being a gifted athlete or student and I think he did try harder than anybody at anything he took on." Hackett added later, "Nothing came easily for him. What he had was a set of handicaps and a fantastic determination to overcome them. The handicaps made him redouble his effort . . . and we loved him for it."

Bobby also followed Jack on the Harvard swimming team. The swimming coach remembered Jack for his "float ability," and recalled Bobby as being "heavy in the water. . . . He would sink, sink quite easily." Some saw this as "a good metaphor for the difference between the brothers. Jack's sensibility was buoyantly literary; Bobby's was heavily moral, however inchoate. Bobby sought responsibility as compulsively as Jack tried to evade it."

That was a patent difference in their personalities, and it lasted their lifetimes. The moral, responsible Bobby, and the easygoing, more charming, more intellectual Jack. It was this difference that perhaps kept them from being socially close, but also so greatly enriched them later as a working team.

———

WHEN ROBERT KENNEDY graduated from Harvard in 1948, his father gave him renewed attention. "He is just starting off," Joe wrote his old friend Beaverbrook, "and he has the difficulty of trying to follow two brilliant brothers, Joe and Jack. That in itself is quite a handicap, and he is making a good battle against it."

As part of the battle, father Kennedy put Bobby in the same sequence he had earlier arranged for Jack and Joe—he got him a job on the Boston *Post* and arranged to send Bobby abroad. He also gave him letters of introduction from Cardinal Spellman, among others, and a letter of credit from the National City Bank of New York. And when he learned that Beaverbrook would be sailing on the same ship as Bobby, he urged them to get together.

Beaverbrook then reported to Kennedy Sr., "I wined and dined with Robert. He is a remarkable boy. He is clever, has a good character, energy, a clear understanding and a fine philosophy. You are sure to hear a great deal of him if you live long enough and from what I hear of your health it seems that you will outlive the lot of us. Certainly you will outlive me."

Robert was traveling with a college friend, George Terrien. Joe Sr. had paid for his trip. Said Terrien, "Bobby was very capable, but Joe wanted someone with a lot of seasoning to baby-sit for him."

It is interesting that none of the Kennedy brothers ever traveled alone. Neither did their father. They all needed people. They had been part of a bustling, laughing family, and they needed people who would laugh and admire and approve. Loneliness was only a time for brooding and mourning.

The Middle East was at war and Bobby decided to go there. In Palestine, he talked to a British soldier who was sympathetic to the Jews and admitted responsibility for much of the terrorism. Bobby described the hatred of the British by Arabs and Jews, described the Jews as fighting with "unparalleled courage," that they had an undying spirit the Arabs would never have, and said a Jewish state would be the "only stabilizing factor" in the Middle East. Of the Arabs, he added that "I just wish that they didn't have that oil." Bobby also found a Jew in a kibbutz who had made speeches in Boston for Honey Fitz.

Bobby's father had a different attitude about Jews, and his reputation as a Nazi sympathizer threatened to outlive him. A 1200-page document released by the State Department, summarizing captured Nazi documents, quoted the German Ambassador in the United States in 1938 passing on to Hitler that Ambassador Kennedy had said that "it was not so much the fact that we wanted to get rid of the Jews that was harmful to us, but rather the loud clamor with which we accompanied this purpose."

The senior Kennedy, however, despite his anti-Semitic remarks, had written to Charles Lindbergh that he felt the Nazis had gone too far in their persecution of Jews, and he had tried, unsuccessfully, as Ambassador, to help arrange a Jewish homeland in Africa.

Later, Bobby was in Rome recovering from a case of jaundice when Jack called him about Kick. In May 1948, Kathleen Kennedy, now the widowed Lady Hartington, had gone back to London because she was in love with the handsome thirty-seven-year-old Lord Peter Fitzwilliam, whose family was Church of England. Rose Kennedy warned Kick that if she once again married outside the Catholic Church, she would never speak to her again and would cut off all relations with any other Kennedy who did.

Joseph Alsop, years later, asked John Kennedy which side he would have been on. Jack replied quickly, "With Kick, of course." His brother Joe would have said the same. And both sons would feel that, deep down, their father would have ultimately sided with Kick too. It was easier for the brothers to break with their mother than with their father.

Kick and Peter were flying to the Riviera in a chartered two-engine plane when it crashed in a storm over the mountains. There were no survivors. "When I awakened him and told him," said the Ambassador's friend, Boston Police Commissioner Joseph Timilty, "he couldn't utter a word."

Jack was in Hyannis listening to Ella Logan singing "How Are Things in Glocca Morra," from *Finian's Rainbow*, when the call came. Billy Sutton took the call reporting the crash. Jack grimly asked if there was confirmation, and Sutton said no. The record kept playing. Then came the confirmation.

"They say that Kennedys don't cry," said Sutton, "but don't you believe it. Jack's eyes were full of tears."

In a sense, Kick's death was a deeper hurt for Jack than Joe's death. With Joe, it was love/hate, but with Kick, it was always pure love. They were so close in personality, in their joy of life, in their wit and laughter. Spalding had said of Kick that she was like Jack, without the drive. Not that Jack had much drive then either. What Kick could do, that Jack yet couldn't, was to stand up against the whole family for what she loved and wanted. She refused to compromise, and that Jack admired but couldn't copy. Of course, Kick had less at stake. She didn't need anything from her father—except his love.

Kick and Jack and Joe had been a kind of royal trio in England during the war. Everybody wanted them because of their zest for life and sense of fun. Until then, Jack and Joe had seldom been happier. Later, at a more reflective time, Jack would tell James MacGregor Burns, "The thing about Kathleen and Joe was their tremendous vitality. Everything was moving in their direction—that's what made it so unfortunate. If something happens to you or somebody in your family who is miserable anyway, whose health is bad, or who has a chronic disease or something, that's one thing. But for someone who's living at their peak, then to get cut off—that's the shock."

The engraving on her tombstone read JOY SHE GAVE AND JOY SHE HAD. She reportedly was pregnant at the time.

The imprint of Kick's death on Jack was deep and lasting. He went to England to settle his sister's estate, and visited Kathleen's housekeeper, probing all her memories. Then he said simply, "We will not mention her again."

Bobby and Terrien were still touring Europe when Jack called to tell him of Kick's death. Terrien remembered that Bobby "broke down like a little kid." When Bobby came to London, he also talked to Kick's housekeeper and made a similar statement about not mentioning her again.

It was strange, this decision for silence. It was as if it was unmanly for the Kennedys to show grief. But, besides that, the Kennedys found deep emotion excruciating. It would always be that way for Jack, as it would be for Bobby. Their father more easily showed emotion than any of them. Kick's death had deepened Joe's bitterness and he now saw the world as "a horrible mess" with little hope on the horizon.

"I never saw Dad here in England," Robert Kennedy wrote his sister Patricia, "but everyone said he looked terrible. I talked to him on the phone, and he was no laughs, to use an old expression. All these people love Kick so much, it's really impressive."

Bobby felt strongly enough about his dead sister to name his oldest daughter Kathleen Hartington Kennedy. However, there was a family stipulation that the new Kathleen must never be known as Kick.

The family made no privately printed book of reminiscences for Kick, as they did for Joe, set up no scholarships in her honor. What was finally done was a donation to build a gymnasium to be named after Kathleen at Manhattanville College, a Catholic college in Purchase, New York. She had never gone to that college, or any other Catholic college. It was, perhaps, a final defiant declaration by her mother, who had never forgiven her marriage to a non-Catholic. Rose once had described Kathleen matter-of-factly to a family friend as "the only one of her nice children eager to leave home."

But it was probably more than that. In this male-oriented family, only the sons got memorial volumes.

Bobby had continued his grand tour after Kick's death, but not with the same zest. He saw the war-torn rubble of Nazi Germany, the "dazed silence" of the people, but noted that the majority of those Germans he interviewed didn't feel any regret, and one veteran still thought that Hitler was worthy of being in heaven.

Of the British he met, Bob wrote home, "Between you and me, except for a few individuals, you can have the bunch."

One of his exceptions was a twenty-one-year-old lovely blond actress named Joan Winmill. "It was love at first sight," she said. Shortly after they met, Bobby told Terrien, "Ethel's fun, but she's just a girl; Joan's a real woman." And Joan would say of Bobby, "He was very romantic . . . very passionate."

Joan was sexy, sophisticated, and a Protestant. Bobby told her, "Nothing will break us up," but he was still careful to keep their romance out of the public eye.

It was a romance that lasted several months, and Bob then had to go to graduate school. But he told her, "I can't stay away from you," and promised to come back. He sent her food packages, letters, and finally a note, "I am getting married." In retrospect, Joan said, "if I was to have eleven children as Ethel did, I would never have made it."

Bobby now had achieved his romantic rite of passage. Both his older brothers and his father had been involved with pretty Protestant actresses, and now he felt he had passed some kind of entrance test into the Kennedy circle.

———

AFTER SIX MONTHS abroad, Bobby did not seem to agree with his father that the United States should stop minding other people's business. Travel had changed his views of the world.

When Bobby returned home, there was some serious question of what next. Since he saw no special alternative, he had decided on graduate school. "I just didn't know anything when I got out of college," he said later. In a choice between business or law, Bobby chose law, like his brother Joe. And, since his grades were not good enough for Harvard, he decided on the University of Virginia, in the picturesque city of Charlottesville, within sight of the Blue Ridge Mountains. Even there, he had to take a special aptitude test to get in, and the admissions people were not enthusiastic.

He arrived at college dressed in an old pair of khakis, driving an old Chrysler convertible, a gift from his father. Bobby moved into a tiny tenant house so close to the railroad tracks that the whole place shook every time a train went by. He soon had a dog—he always had a dog.

His friend Gerald Tremblay remembered Bobby as a "crash-artist" at studying, a relatively good student who especially disliked a class called Legal Bibliography because he figured if he ever practiced law he would have somebody else looking up things in the legal library. Like his brothers, Bobby felt that the Kennedys were all very special, earmarked for some glory in the world.

Some things had not changed. Bobby never missed going to church every morning, and would even volunteer as altar boy.

———————

THE CONSENSUS OF his classmates was that Bob was highly introverted, sensitive to criticism, seldom ever relaxed, more of a listener than a talker, still sometimes seemed moralistic and arrogant in his certainty, rushed to judgments much too fast, and once he made up his mind, it was impossible to shake him from his convictions. His classmate Endicott Peabody Davison would ask him, "Now, Bobby, how do you know all these facts? Aren't you making too many assumptions?" Bob would just answer stubbornly: "I'm right. I know I'm right."

Perhaps this was partly because Bobby, the boy, was so overshadowed by the older ones at home that he had to fight to make himself heard at all. Ted gave this as a reason he stumbled so often when he spoke. Here at Virginia, he could always make himself heard, and he was now just as arbitrary to others as his brothers had been to him. It was as if his insecurities made it necessary for him to act twice as sure of himself as he really was—which made him seem so stubborn.

The high point of his academic career at Virginia was a research paper on Yalta which echoed his father's postwar views. His professors described his scholarship as "sheer persistence." One of the coups of his student career came when he persuaded the celebrated Dr. Ralph Bunche of the United Nations to address the student body.

The limits he set with close friends remained unchanged.

"To my knowledge," said Tremblay, who knew him well, "he never had anybody, like a friend you might discuss a pretty intimate problem with, maybe about your love life." Dave Hackett, too, had emphasized this.

His social life with women on campus was almost zero. "At law school, the students would work very hard and then there would be a big party," recalled Davison. "Some of the women there were pretty loose. He was disgusted with them and would say so."

It was not simply that he was a Puritan, still in the strong grip of his mother's religious morality, but because he was in love. She was twenty-two-year-old Ethel Skakel, a roommate of his favorite sister, Pat, at Manhattanville College. They met when Ethel volunteered to work for Jack's campaign.

Ethel was seriously considering becoming a nun. But she was too restless, too vivacious. She was a bubbling, talkative, impulsive young woman. "Ethel was really something else. She was funny; she said what was on her mind, without any ifs, ands, or buts. Had no hesitancy about it; would joke and kid quite a bit," said Stanton Gilderhorn. And she was an extrovert who enjoyed doing what she wanted to do, including an unexpected tap dance. The Manhattanville yearbook described her: "An excited hoarse voice, a shriek, a peal of screaming laughter, the flash of shirttails, a tousled brown head—Ethel! Her face is at one moment a picture of utter guilessness and at the next alive with mischief."

She was exactly what Bob needed to pull him out of his stuffy, sober loneliness—and he knew it.

It was at Hyannis where Bobby could really relax with Ethel. The family passed around copies of widely publicized Rules for Visiting the Kennedys, written by his close friend Dave Hackett. They enjoyed quoting from it: "Prepare yourself by reading the Congressional *Record*, *U.S. News & World Report*, *Time*, *Newsweek*, *Fortune*, *The Nation*, *How to Play Sneaky Tennis*, and the *Democratic Digest*. Anticipate that each of the Kennedys will ask you what you think of another Kennedy's (a) dress, (b) hairdo, (c) backhand, (d) latest public achievement. Be sure to answer, 'Terrific.' Now for the football field. It's touch but it's murder. If you don't want to play, you'll be fed in the kitchen and nobody will speak to you. Don't let the girls fool you. Even pregnant, they can make you look silly. Don't suggest any plays. . . . Don't appear to be having too much fun. They'll accuse you of not taking the game seriously enough. Don't criticize the other team. It's bound to be full of Kennedys, too, and the Kennedys don't like that sort of thing."

At Hyannis one could expect only one drink (unless they sneaked upstairs for another one). Then the bell rang for dinner. In fact, the senior Kennedy didn't smoke and rarely drank. He repeated often, and proudly, to interviewers that he gave each child a thousand dollars for not smoking or drinking until the age of twenty-one. He put it on the honor system, no questions asked. "I got that idea from the Rocke-fellers," said Rose Kennedy, "and I told Joe."

"I didn't really care whether they smoked or drank," Joseph Ken-nedy later told author Joe McCarthy. "I was just trying to teach them a little responsibility and how to be honest with themselves. Two of our children handed the checks back to me."

Later, John Kennedy would drink moderately, a beer or a daiquiri. Bobby drank even more moderately. Teddy later turned out to be the one who liked to drink.

JOHN KENNEDY RAN unopposed for reelection to Congress in 1948. Harry Truman was elected President for his first full term. Honey Fitz celebrated his eighty-sixth birthday at a dinner in his honor at which Massachusetts governor Paul Dever called him "an outstanding citizen of all New England." Honey Fitz would die within the year and the funeral procession would be headed by 200 firemen, with 3500 mourners filling the cathedral. One of the men at the funeral ex-plained, "I went to his funeral to make sure they buried the bastard." Rose Kennedy, in Paris for her annual fashion show, was unable to return in time for her father's funeral.

The next year marked the first marriage of a Kennedy son.

Bobby was in his second year at law school and still looked like a teenager when he married Ethel. "We had a party the evening before, a bachelor's party at the Harvard Club in New York," recalled Ken O'Donnell. They almost wrecked the banquet room on the third floor. "John Kennedy agreed that he had never seen such an outrageous, irreverent group of characters in his life. . . . The in-laws, the Skakel family, were horrified by all of his friends, not so much the father, who . . . joined right in with the fun, but the mother. She couldn't understand where Bobby got these characters that were around him, who all weighed 250 pounds, and were Greeks, Armenians, Italians."

They were married in a garden setting of white peonies, lilies, and dogwood in St. Mary's Roman Catholic Church in Greenwich, Connecticut. Pius XII sent an apostolic blessing. The bride wore a white satin gown made with a fitted bodice finished with an off-the-shoulder neckline embroidered with pearls. Representative John F. Kennedy was best man for his brother. LeMoyne Billings and Teddy were ushers; Jean, Pat, and Eunice were bridesmaids.

At the wedding party dance floor, all the Kennedy men took turns cutting in on their new sister-in-law, and this included Joe Sr. Rose would say that she had doubts about their marrying so young, but that she never had doubts about Ethel. Ethel was even more pious than she was. No other wife became a Kennedy more completely or more quickly than Ethel.

Robert blossomed. "I like marriage," he later said. "I like being married. Liking someone is the thing. It's liking someone that matters. I find it hard to like anyone for long. I like her and I like that. It's nice."

For the shy, nonverbal Robert, it said volumes. The fact was that Bobby, more than any of his brothers, was hungry for affection and recognition and support, and Ethel gave him all of that, always and unstintingly. Ethel would complete his life in countless ways. She refreshed his humor, brought out his sensitivity, and gave him goals.

———

EDWARD KENNEDY WAS eighteen in 1950 when he graduated from Milton Academy. His father delivered the commencement address. Following the family tradition, Teddy enrolled in Harvard.

His school grades were barely passing. Dr. Arthur N. Holcombe, who taught all the Kennedy boys at Harvard, admitted that he didn't think Teddy "was in the same class as his older brothers," but added, "I have no doubt that Edward could have graduated with high distinction if he had wanted to."

Physically, Teddy was transformed. The pudginess was long since gone and now he was lean and tall—taller than any of his brothers— and handsome, probably the most handsome of them all.

When it came to parties and dances, Ted was much in demand. He still maintained his private system of grading his dates from A to E. And a long parade of them seemed ready and willing to be classified.

"College girls who went out with him reported that he made his expectations clear early and with undisguised feeling, and took it more as a curiosity than an affront if his straightforward-enough offer was not instantly accepted."

Ted later described a reprimand from his father about a special horn he had on his car at Harvard, a horn that sounded "like a cow's anxious call." His father had written:

> I heard in my roundabout way that you are using that bell of yours on your car. I don't want to be complaining about things you do but I want to point out to you that when you exercise any privilege that the ordinary fellow does not avail himself of, you immediately become the target for display and for newspaper criticism.
>
> It's all right to struggle to get ahead of the masses by good works, by good reputation and by hard work, but it certainly isn't by doing things that people could say, "Who the Hell does he think he is."

Teddy had not paused long enough then to consider who he was, except that he was rich, privileged, handsome, and happy. The lonely fat little boy in all those different schools was now a memory. Now he was on a pleasure ride.

Teddy even earned points with his mother when he became a religious policeman at school, waking his roommates at seven to go to Mass every day during Lent. His brother Joe had done the same thing when he was in the Air Force.

He particularly starred in football. Coach Henry Lamar, who had coached all the four brothers, would say that "while Ted was not what I would call a natural athlete, he was an outstanding player, the kind that carried out his assignments to the letter. . . . I've never seen any of them really excited but Teddy, in particular, would respond to a hard knock by playing harder. . . . He was that kind of kid. The harder you played against him, the harder he'd play against you. But he never got mad or complained to the referee. Lamar felt that Teddy was the easiest to know—more open and outgoing." Other coaches agreed that Ted developed into the best football player of all the brothers.

It was a great satisfaction to be better than all his brothers at something so specific as football. And this was something that earned all their praise and envy. It was the only time it would happen to him.

––––––––

AT THIRTY-THREE, John Kennedy was easily reelected to his third term, in 1950. Congressman Richard Bolling said of him afterward, "I thought he was a third-rater. I don't mean a second-rater either. I mean third-rater."

Many of the views he had shifted even further from his conservative father. Primarily, Jack was a strong internationalist while the father was still a fervent isolationist.

Kennedy Sr. told Arthur Krock, "Of course Jack is saying many things I don't believe in." But, as Krock remembered it, it didn't seem to bother old Joe too much. "He was rather proud of that." The Ambassador was more irritated when he told Coughlan, "Jack and I see eye to eye on practically nothing." Later Jack would say, "I disagree with everything my father says, but what can I do?"

Washington hostess Kay Halle remembered "one very vivid instance when we were all at a cocktail party in the garden of Drew and Luvie Pearson. . . . In one corner of the garden, father Joe, Jack and I were talking together. Suddenly Joe said, 'Kay, I wish you would tell Jack that he's going to vote the wrong way.' I can't even remember what bill it was, but Joe said, 'I think Jack is making a terrible mistake.' Then he told him, 'Jack, I know you're going to vote on this bill this week and I think you're wrong. I'd like to discuss it and we can get Kay's independent judgment on it.'

"And then I remember Jack turning to his father, giving him a long look, then saying quietly, 'Now, look here, Dad, you have your political views and I have mine. I'm going to vote exactly the way I feel I must vote on this. I've great respect for you, but when it comes to voting, I'm voting my way.' Then Joe looked at me with that big Irish smile, and said, 'Well, Kay, that's why I settled a million dollars on each one of them, so they could spit in my eye if they wished.' "

If the young Congressman was trying to increase the political distance from his father, the social distance was still close.

"I was at some posh restaurant in Washington," said Halle, "and the waiter brought me a note inviting me to join friends at another table. It was Joe and his two sons Jack and Bobby. Jack was a Congressman then. When I joined them, the gist of the conversation from the boys was the fact that their father was going to be in Washington for a few days and needed female companionship. They wondered whom I would suggest, and they were absolutely serious!"

It was not so outlandish. The boys had been privy to their father's frequent dalliances with other women. They had witnessed their mother's acceptance of these women whenever their father brought them home. It was simply their father's way of life. The father worked the situation differently with his daughters and daughters-in-law in Washington. He asked each of them to arrange a dinner for eight, on different nights of the week. On the basis of the best food, wine, ambiance, conversation, and the quality of the extra women they provided for him, he would decide on the winner, and give her a thousand dollars.

Nancy Dickerson told of getting such a call from Ethel Kennedy to be the extra woman. "I'm sure glad I got to you before Eunice did," Ethel told her.

What interested Congressman Kennedy most was foreign affairs, and he had made a study of Britain's rearmament program in 1951. On his various tours of Europe, Representative Kennedy talked with General Eisenhower and everybody from the Pope to Prime Minister David Ben-Gurion in Israel. Bobby was with him when he was with Prime Minister Jawaharlal Nehru of India, discussing the country's food shortage. "Nehru had them to dinner but gazed, bored, at the ceiling as if he did not know why he was wasting his time." Only their pretty sister roused him from languid condescension. "He hardly spoke during dinner," Robert noted in his journal, "except to Pat." In a real sense, this trip provided the two brothers with the first chance to spend some concentrated time together. Their eight-year difference had been a large gap. It now mattered less and less.

———

TEDDY SUDDENLY HAD a major problem. He was doing badly in Spanish and he paid another student to take the exam in his place. He was caught and suspended. The youngest Kennedy was shocked. His life had been based on the concept that the Kennedys were superior and invulnerable and everything always worked out. His father was mainly concerned that his son had been caught. Rose Kennedy recalled how quickly her husband forgave him.

Teddy received an unexpected note of support from his father's friend Max Beaverbrook: "When a man is put in a corner on an act of indiscretion at 18 . . . he always gets the benefits over difficulties."

The father's further reaction was strange, yet typical. He had always impressed on his sons the need to win, no matter how. He now hired the young man who had taken the exam for his son. He later also "quietly aided thirty-one West Point cadets who were expelled in the cribbing scandal of 1951. Through the Joseph P. Kennedy Jr. Foundation, set up in memory of his oldest son, the senior Kennedy arranged for the ex-cadets to enter other colleges, and paid their tuition fees."

"I was told I had to do something if I wanted to come back into Harvard," said Ted Kennedy. "It seemed that if I went into the Army then for two years, if I had a good record, it would . . . strengthen the case of trying to come back."

Teddy thought he had enlisted for a two-year term, but it turned out to be four years. His father was furious. "Don't you even look at what you're signing?" Fearful that Teddy could be sent to Korea, the father made phone calls to the draft board and cut the four-year hitch in half. He also got Teddy attached to a military police unit in Paris.

In a letter home, Teddy reported that on the rough ocean trip, "your ninth was so busy washing the total of twenty-five thousand trays during the voyage that he didn't have much time for anything else."

As an enlisted man, Teddy got his first full exposure to a humanity he never knew. Like all his brothers, Ted now lived with young men from a variety of social and economic backgrounds who knew nothing of the advantages he always had taken for granted. All his life, Teddy had lived in a privileged cocoon. He had been cloistered, insulated. Private schools, tennis, sailing, parties. Suddenly he was scraping food off metal trays and sleeping in a barrack with young men who spoke a different language of a different world. It was probably one of the most important experiences that had ever happened to him. It would redirect his life into a real world.

In a letter home from Germany, soldier Teddy also reported that he had discovered there were eight other Massachusetts boys in his outfit and he had persuaded all of them to send in their absentee votes for Jack.

————

BACK IN CONGRESS after his foreign trips, Congressman Kennedy was again restless. He told Hale Boggs of Louisiana, the Democratic House majority leader, that he wanted to run for the U.S. Senate "because he was bored by the House." Boggs replied, "You don't know the House well enough to be bored by it; you haven't been here long enough."

George Smathers told Kennedy, "I hope, if you run, you know exactly what you're doing. It would be terrible to lose you altogether."

"Do you think I've got a chance?"

"Well," Smathers said, "I wouldn't know."

Kennedy paused, then added, "Well, I don't really think I've got a chance."

Kennedy knew his record in the House of Representatives was not good. But he also knew he had a lot of assets in Massachusetts, particularly his name and family, and the celebrity publicity largely generated by his father.

"Everyone thought Jack was crazy . . . said he could not win, but Dad said yes," Rose Kennedy recalled. "They said Jack was a nice young man but to run against Henry Cabot Lodge in Massachusetts was suicide, politically."

"The guy who really had the vision, and the guts, and the prestige to make it stick was Mr. Kennedy," remembered Shriver. "I'm not minimizing what Jack did; that's not the point. But Mr. Kennedy had such confidence in his own judgment, that if Jack ever thought, in the middle of the night, 'I can't beat Cabot Lodge,' there was always this terrific force behind him, saying, 'You can! . . . You can do it. . . . You're the best. You can't fail.' "

Discussing Lodge, the father told his thirty-five-year-old son, "When you've beaten him, you've beaten the best. Why try for something else?" Francis Morrissey, who was there, recalled that the Ambassador also told his son that when he did beat Lodge, "I will work out the plans to elect you President."

This was the first time his father had said this directly to him. He had heard it before from his grandfather Honey Fitz, and he even had said it himself, in jest, to friends. Now, when his father said it, it suddenly became viable. He knew his father. He knew his fanatic determination. And he could see now, for the first time, how thoroughly his father had finally transferred his own ambition to him.

If any of the four boys ever questioned themselves, it wasn't for long. They rarely lingered on a negative thought. The Kennedy credo was: Just tell me the good things.

Kennedy doctor Henry Betts saw the essence of that as some kind of Greek tragedy: "You cannot live like that. You cannot always just repress everything—but with their sense of destiny and feeling that they are different—and they all really feel that they are different— they made a stronger effort at repression than anybody I've ever seen."

They didn't like to face failure. If they lost at something—whether it was a game or an election—they kept at it until they won. Success was not simply a prize . . . it was a need.

––––––––

ON FEBRUARY 19, 1952, the senior Kennedy wrote to Beaverbrook saying that Jack was a probable candidate for the U.S. Senate and "I am finding myself with plenty to do."

The Ambassador made sure that the way was paved "for Jack to make an impression, for the spotlight to fall on him during the Democratic National Convention in Chicago in 1952," recalled Ralph Coughlan, "and he brought Sargent Shriver for the purpose."

Jack was interviewed everywhere, with noteworthy frequency. "The more you study them the more you realize it," said Abe Michelson. The Kennedys leave *nothing* to chance."

As Eunice recalled, their father told them, "Jack is going to run for the United States Senate. All of you think of what you can do to help him."

"We started talking about sex appeal," said Kennedy friend Anthony Gallucio, making observations about both Lodge and Jack, and pointed out that Lodge really had it, too. The old man dismissed Jack's appeal, said only old ladies liked him. Jack got embarrassed as hell. It was his father's way of cutting him down, keeping him in line, showing everybody he was still really the boss.

In the same way, especially at home, the father still enjoyed playing patriarch, telling everyone where to sit, what to do—and everybody listened, including Jack. "They were just children in that house."

Whenever the father was presiding, everybody seemed to be a little on edge. Jack, particularly, was fidgety, tapping a front tooth with a finger and stroking his jawbone. Or else his fingers would drum a tabletop, or grab a pencil to twirl it, beat it, tap it. Or else he liked to massage his ankles. His hands moved ceaselessly.

Larry O'Brien remembered Joe bawling out Jack. Guest Norman McDonald saw the Kennedy father then as a vindictive, harsh person who "disciplined Jack like a Jesuit. When the father was around, Jack couldn't invite any friends he wanted to their summer home in Hyannis Port. Jack had to submit a guest list and schedule to his father, could invite only people who were useful."

There was one time when Jack got a bit of his own back. During the talk about who would work doing what in the campaign, there came the question of getting the money. Almost mockingly, Jack said to his father, "We concede you that role."

––––––––

JACK ESTABLISHED RESIDENCE in a small apartment near the statehouse, but probably never spent the night there. He preferred his room at the Ritz. "Probably not a guy in American history was ever elected to the Senate who didn't even have a valid mailing address in the state he represents until young Kennedy," said Norman McDonald.

The campaign slogan was one they had used before: "He will do *more* for Massachusetts."

The father was the one who said "more" should be underscored, as a way to hit Lodge, who had concentrated on foreign affairs in the Senate.

"As far as the running of the campaign, Joe absolutely dominated Jack," said Tip O'Neill. "As I understand it, a log was made every day and every day that log was checked by Joe Kennedy and Joe Kane to see if he was seeing the proper people."

Joe Kennedy operated an iceberg operation, orchestrating everything out of sight, planning everything—or trying to, hiring most of the people, holding daily strategy sessions in his apartment. He also had his star spies reporting back to him on the campaign—Frank Morrissey and former police chief Joe Timilty.

Television was the great difference between the congressional and Senate campaigns.

Shriver credited Joseph Kennedy's instincts about TV to his great success in the motion-picture industry. "For one reason, he had a fantastic knack for knowing what the public was interested in. That's how he made money, too. . . . He was spooky, brilliant at it. . . . He figured that TV was going to be the greatest thing in the history of politics. He set out studying TV, and how should Jack utilize it most effectively. . . . The whole strategy of that campaign came from him— the whole, bloody damn thing.

"I remember one night eight of us were in Mr. Kennedy's apartment watching Jack make a TV speech," said Shriver. "There was the guy that wrote the speech and the guy from the advertising agency and all the yes men sitting there with Mr. Kennedy smack in front of the tube. After it was all over, Mr. Kennedy asked what they thought of it. They gave these mealy-mouthed answers and all of a sudden Mr. Kennedy got ferocious, I mean ferocious. . . .

"He said, 'I tell ya, that TV program was the worst goddamn thing I ever saw—a disgrace! Everybody in this room should have the guts and intelligence to know that it was a fiasco. And I never want to see my son on TV, making such an ass of himself as he made tonight. And I'll tell you (pointing his finger at the guy) that was the lousiest writing I've ever seen on any show. And I've been in show business for thirty years. It stunk!' "

He felt his son was earnest enough, but too stiff and a little pompous, that he should be more informal, more direct.

He said, "Get the hell out of here. We'll meet tomorrow morning at ten, and I want a whole new TV program. 'Cause we're wrecking this boy. We've got the most precious political asset in the world, and you stupids just don't know how to use it.

"Half an hour later, Jack called and Mr. Kennedy said, 'Boy, Jack, you were great, Triffic.' "

Tom Cochran, a political friend of Joe Kennedy, said: "The sheer

animal vitality of the man. . . . He lost his favorite daughter and son—
even God's against you—it takes sheer vitality to rise again."

———

JACK WAS ON the early quiz shows and "Meet the Press." The father
not only predicted the questions and helped phrase the answers but he
told Jack what to wear and even how to comb his hair. Pat Jackson
recalled how carefully Jack brushed his hair, saying, "Pat, isn't it
amazing what a man will do to get votes."

Jack quickly mastered TV. He would get angry when a TV crew was
sent in without giving him preparation time. And he sent friends to
view films in advance to check how he appeared. When Ken O'Donnell once reported that a particular TV report was not flattering,
Kennedy managed to persuade the network to kill it.

"I have heard so much about the so-called charisma of the Kennedys,
whatever it is," said Rose Kennedy. "My father had it, too, the appeal
to the masses, he brought a spirit of excitement, he had a close
relationship and empathy with the other people. When I first saw Jack
on TV, I could see the same kind of appeal . . . my husband sensed it
too, he said TV would be a better medium for Jack than billboards or
newspaper ads."

A friend of actor Clark Gable's once said that when he walked along
Fifth Avenue in New York with Gable, women of all ages, recognizing
Clark, would stop dead in their tracks and gasp, as if they had been
suddenly punched in the belly. It was the same with Kennedy.

"Jack and I spent hours talking about it," said Charles Spalding. "His
magnetism, did he have it or didn't he?"

———

WITH ALL THIS business expertise and television exposure, the early
start of the campaign was a disaster. Mark Dalton was the official
campaign manager when the senior Kennedy moved in.

When Pat Gardner Jackson prepared a cautiously worded newspaper
ad for Jack to separate himself from the smearing attacks of Senator
Joseph McCarthy, Jack finally agreed. The ad was headlined:
MCCARTHYISM AND COMMUNISM—BOTH WRONG. But when Jackson
read the ad—at Jack's request—to the elder Kennedy, "he jumped to

his feet with such force that he tilted the card table over against the others and he stood there shouting at me, 'You're trying to ruin Jack . . . you and your sheeny friends.' "

Later, Jack tried to explain his father to Jackson: "My father's one motive that you can understand, Pat, is love of family . . ." And then he paused, and added very quietly, "Although sometimes I think it's really pride."

———

KEN O'DONNELL CALLED his old friend Bobby to tell him that the campaign was "a shambles," that the elder Kennedy hadn't been privy to Massachusetts politics for twenty years and knew nothing about the current situation, and that he was such a strong personality that nobody had the courage to defy him—including the campaign manager.

The idea was that only Bobby could talk to his father and make things work. "But without that, we're just in an impossible situation."

Bobby then was working for the Department of Justice in New York, and wasn't interested, claimed he didn't know enough about Massachusetts, and told O'Donnell, "I'll screw it up . . . I just don't want to come." Some felt that Bobby just didn't look forward to a summer arguing with his father. O'Donnell then called Jack, repeated everything, and added, "You're not gonna win it." It wasn't long before Bobby called O'Donnell: "I suppose I'll have to do it."

———

THE REMARKABLE THING was that it was Jack who made the ultimate decision to bring Bobby into the campaign. And what did Jack see in Bobby besides his ability to talk to his father? After all, when Bobby worked in the congressional campaign, he was just a kid in a sailor suit, working on the fringes, making a minimal contribution. But Jack and Bob had taken an overseas trip together, and spent a lot of time talking and listening to each other. Marriage had matured Bobby and given him more dimension and self-confidence. If Jack had none of his brother's workaholic intensity, he did have a great perception of people and talent potential, and he sensed it in Bobby. And he was right.

It was a defining time for Bobby. He had been on the family sidelines. Now his brother needed him, badly. And now he knew how much he could help.

In a sense, this was the chance Bobby always had wished for—to be a vital part of his brother's life. He was doing it now because he had no choice. To prove himself, he had to do things nobody else would do, solve problems without hesitation. "The real camaraderie between them began when he joined the campaign," said Hackett.

Robert Kennedy explained later that his object was to get a little work out of as many people as possible instead of a lot of work out of a few. He organized ethnic committees, professional committees, keeping them small to make everyone feel he or she was contributing something important.

Bobby told the Smith College volunteers, who were covering the town of Weston, "If you hand that tabloid of my brother's life to someone, they'll read it. If it comes in the mail, with all the junk mail, it goes right in the wastebasket."

"So this was hand-delivered, one hell of a task."

"We worked from eight in the morning," said Kennedy niece Mary Jo Clasby. "We all lived in the same rooming house on Marble Street and we used to go to the Ritz and we would be covered with mimeograph ink and really not looking the ritzy type and we'd go and have cream puffs with ice cream and chocolate frosting . . . and go to bed at twelve. Then we would get up at eight the next morning and the woman who ran the rooming house couldn't figure out what was going on. . . . We just had a wonderful summer. Kenny and Bobby would go out at night and make speeches."

Bobby was also the only reliable intermediary with his brother. When somebody wanted to inform Jack about a sensitive problem, "too sensitive for one of us to mention to him . . . Bobby could tell him about it and bring back an answer. When Jack was in one of his inaccessible moods, Bobby could always reach him and make him listen to reason."

"Jack tended to be a little bit fey, a little offhand around his father," said Steve Smith. It was more than that. At that time, he simply didn't want to confront him. "Bobby could handle the father," said O'Donnell, "and no one else could have. . . . It was Bobby with whom Joseph Kennedy would discuss family matters." Billings later said that the father "suddenly found he had another able son, which I don't think he realized."

For the elder Kennedy, it was an awakening, a dramatic one. When he concentrated on young Joe, he thought little about Jack. When he concentrated on Jack, he thought little about Bobby. Now he saw Bobby in a fuller perspective. This was a son who had more of his own toughness than Jack did. He could work hard. He could make decisions. He could crack heads.

The more heads Bobby cracked, the more decisions he made, the more orders he barked, the more his self-confidence grew. His great strength was simply getting things done. Bobby, like his father, felt there was nothing that couldn't be done. Arthur Schlesinger, Jr., pinpoints the "ruthless Bobby" concept as being born during that campaign.

Stewart Alsop called it a "sweet-and-sour brother act. . . . Jack uses his charm and waves the carrot and then Bobby wades in with the big stick."

Jack was later quoted as saying that Bobby had taken on all the campaign dirty work, allowing him to remain "a virgin." He also told someone—but not Bobby—that he "had a hell of a brother."

Bobby was almost abrasively busy during the campaign. At one point he told Governor Paul Dever that he had committed an error that could hurt Jack's campaign and should be more careful in the future. The Governor then told Joe Sr.: "I know you're an important man around here and all that, but I'm telling you this and I mean it: Keep that fresh kid of yours out of my sight from here on in."

"Every politician in Massachusetts," John Kennedy said, "was mad at Bobby after 1952 but we had the best organization in history." "If Bobby hadn't come in, we'd have lost the campaign," O'Donnell insisted. "Bobby pulled the whole thing together."

If this campaign was important to John Kennedy, it was equally important to Bobby. It not only burnished his image with his father and his family, but it suddenly put him on the same level with his big brother. And, best of all, he realized he had his own special quality, and his own horizons.

———

A FRESH RELATIONSHIP was emerging between Jack and Bobby. They still had different personalities, different tastes in men and women. They laughed at dissimilar things and had contrasting lifestyles. Governor Dever called Jack Kennedy "the first Irish Brahmin; Bobby is the last Irish Puritan."

At that time, most politicians were men. Robert Kennedy felt, like his father and brothers, that women were mothers or sexual objects, but never, never working partners. In a campaign, women licked envelopes, delivered pamphlets door to door, made telephone calls, and were given little or no work which suited their skills.

However, this was not quite true of the Kennedy women. They were not involved in the political plans and programs, but they were allowed to extend their reach. Even though they were women, they were still Kennedys, which made them more qualified and more special on family campaigns.

Rose Kennedy and her daughters would sort out assignments. If they were meeting a group from Lebanon, Rose remembered, "we would have a poll and see who had been in Lebanon. Well, Eunice had been in Lebanon. They would have a French meeting, then I would go to the French meeting. . . . So it was just an army of Kennedys that invaded every precinct."

"Eunice was really almost Jack's twin, in many ways," said Charles Spalding. "Really inclined to political battling, political exposure, and political success. Every one of the girls knew how great power was . . . but Eunice could taste it."

Bobby worked his sisters harder than anyone else. He had them hosting teas all over the state to overflow crowds. He even had them make speeches.

The family campaign story of that election was Bobby's wife. She was always there with Bobby, working hard. One night Ethel made a speech in Fall River, then drove to Boston, where she went into a hospital and had their first child before morning.

As usual, Rose was the best of them, the professional. "When she speaks to wealthy Irish women out near Boston College in the Chestnut Hill section," wrote *New York Times* correspondent John H. Fenton, "she'd dress up with a set of matched pearls, a diamond bracelet and lovely mink stole, all decked out like Mrs. Astor's plush horse and she would speak to them as the wife of the former Ambassador to the Court of St. James. Then she'd get in the car and drive over to a rally or a party in the Dorchester section—the corned beef and cabbage section—and she'd remove the stole and speak to them as the daughter of Johnny Fitz, Irish girl who made good. Then she'd go up to the North End and she'd strip off her rings and her pearls and bracelet and put on a simple crucifix and a simpler hat and she'd address them as the mother of nine children and a gold star mother."

Although Bobby was developing many skills, speechmaking was not one of them. During one event, Jack and his mother and three sisters were on various speaking platforms, leaving Bobby for an unfilled engagement so he simply stood up and said, "My brother Jack couldn't be here. My mother couldn't be here. My sister Eunice couldn't be here. My sister Pat couldn't be here. My sister Jean couldn't be here. But if my brother Jack were here, he'd tell you Lodge had a very bad voting record. Thank you." And he sat down.

Even their father broke with his precedent of staying silent during the campaign. He once reluctantly agreed to substitute for Jack. But when he spoke about his sons, his voice broke, and this blasé worldly figure simply became a proud and sad father. Proud because of Jack; sad because it wasn't Joe.

Teddy also came to work. When Jack was told by the Bellevue Hotel clerk that Ted was coming up, he put his hand over the receiver and warned the others in the room, "Let's watch our swearing and our language. . . . Remember—he's not a part of this yet, he wouldn't understand."

When father Joe complained that he didn't see many "Vote for Kennedy" bumper stickers, it was Ted who drove to the entrance of the Sumner Tunnel, announcing, "I'm Ted Kennedy. Do you mind if I put a bumper sticker on your car for Senator Kennedy?"

James King explained to Burton Hersh, "When Ted came to the western part of the state everybody was glad to get him out, keep him busy. I myself found him challenging and delightful. Partly, I think, because he was such an eager campaigner; he really loved the pace of campaigning. You'd go to one fire station in Springfield, and then he had to go to all the others. So you'd have fourteen hours of visiting fire stations that day. I remember once we got stalled in a traffic jam and he jumped out and started going from car to car shaking hands and attaching bumper stickers to every car they'd let him. He loved campaigning, you couldn't hold him down."

Teddy was quick to catch the excitement of it. It made all his grandfather's campaign stories come freshly alive. Teddy saw it as simply fun.

THE WOMEN'S VOTE was key to Kennedy. He told of Grandfather Honey Fitz saying that "if only" women had the right to vote, he would have defeated Henry Cabot Lodge in their Senate race. After telling this story, John Kennedy would smile charmingly at his female audience and say, "Ladies, I need you."

He definitely did.

Reporters of *The Capitol News* in Washington chose John Kennedy as the handsomest member of Congress. Kennedy was delighted that there were more women than men in Massachusetts "and they live longer," and felt it would help him win the election.

Jack Kennedy was not an intellectual, although he liked to think he bordered on it. He read a lot and could analyze things well. He had more feeling for the masses than for the individual. And he was more pragmatic than passionate about principle. He got angry at stupidity but not at injustice. He still had some of his father's impatience and assumption of superiority. All the Kennedy brothers had that—Bobby most of all.

Typical of the Kennedy superiority was the story of the Boston *Globe* and the Boston *Post*. Joe Kennedy reportedly pulled a million dollars' worth of advertising from the Boston *Globe* because it was not keen on Jack.

The stranger story was the so-called $500,000 editorial at the Boston *Post*. Publisher John Fox planned to endorse Lodge for Senator in 1952, but in a quick turnaround came out in support of Kennedy. Shortly afterward Fox received a loan of $500,000 from Joseph P. Kennedy. Both Kennedy and Fox insisted the loan was "purely business."

When *Look* reporter Laura Bergquist confronted Jack with that statement, he simply grinned and said, "We didn't have a single major paper in Massachusetts. Hell, we had to buy that paper."

Jack was more explicit with his Harvard classmate Fletcher Knebel, Bergquist's husband: "You know, we had to buy that fucking paper, or I'd have been licked."

THE NIGHT BEFORE the election, the three brothers found themselves together in Mattapan, just outside Boston. The speaker before them talked interminably. John Seigenthaler remembered: "Finally, in sort of a sweat, he began to wind up his speech, and he said to that audience, in which there was *nobody* that night who was *not* Jewish: 'Furthermore, I'm telling you that if you go out and bring home the Democratic Party tomorrow, the Democratic Party is going to bring home the bacon for you for the next four years.' "

"Bacon" was not a proper, diplomatic word for that audience.

"That's the way he ended," said Seigenthaler. "I mean it was like . . . peeing in the punch bowl. The place was just like a graveyard, and then somebody started to clap. And then nobody clapped. And then two or three people clapped, and somebody started to laugh. The poor master of ceremonies got up and said, 'Ladies and gentlemen, I'd like to introduce the next Senator from Massachusetts, the Honorable John F. Kennedy.' You just couldn't imagine a situation worse for a politician. Well, he walked up to that microphone and he said, 'Ladies and gentlemen, everything that has been said and everything that could have been said in this campaign has been said.' And they roared! He said, 'Instead of that, the brothers Kennedy are going to sing a song.' He said to the bandleader, 'Do you know "They're Breaking Up That Old Gang of Mine"?' The other brothers got up, and they started singing. This was the first time I ever realized that Bob Kennedy couldn't carry a tune in a bucket. . . . But Teddy and Jack carried him, and they did very well. When they got through . . . they had everybody in the hall singing with them, literally turning it into a great rally."

Democratic presidential candidate Adlai E. Stevenson lost to Republican Dwight D. Eisenhower, but John Kennedy defeated three-term Senator Henry Cabot Lodge by a plurality of more than 70,000 votes. He became only the third Democrat ever elected to a Senate seat from Massachusetts. Powers would always insist that Jack got more joy out of beating Lodge than any other election because the odds then were so much stronger against him.

Ken O'Donnell recalled the immediate aftermath of the 1952 Senate fight. "We had done the impossible; we had whipped Henry Cabot Lodge and we were relaxing at the Cape. The Ambassador was a very gracious host. Nothing was too good for us—for two days. On the third day he said to Bob: 'When are you people going back to work? You've been here three days. Are you going to lie around and live forever off one campaign?' And that was it. We went back to work."

"People say, 'Kennedy bought the election. Kennedy could never have been elected if his father hadn't been a millionaire.' Well, it wasn't the Kennedy name and the Kennedy money that won that election," Jack insisted in an interview. "I beat Lodge because I hustled for three years. I worked for what I got. I worked for it."

And yet it was his father's money that had made his name a Massachusetts legend. That money had given the war hero Congressman a drenching statewide publicity; that money had taken a fast-moving, seemingly amateur operation and given it just enough professional polish in the necessary places to win.

After the victory, Ted Kennedy bet a friend named Carey $500 that Jack would one day be President of the United States. Ted's father held the bet in a sealed envelope.

5

SENATE SPOTLIGHT

With Jack's victory, Bobby was now at loose ends. It was the Kennedy patriarch who had caustically told his third son, "Are you going to sit on your tail end and do nothing now for the rest of your life? You better go out and get a job."

The elder Kennedy had offered to open a law office for Bobby anywhere he wanted, or get him placed in a major law firm. Bobby refused. After the excitement of managing his brother's Senate campaign, law work seemed pallid. Bobby sensed that his time had come, and he was now pushing to make his own entrance onto stage center.

The man who would help him do that was Republican Senator Joseph McCarthy of Wisconsin, who later galvanized America's anti-Communist hysteria. The elder Kennedy had contributed heavily to his friend's campaigns. Besides courting Eunice in Georgetown with Joe Kennedy's approval, McCarthy was also a regular guest at Hyannis, and played shortstop on the Kennedy family's "Barefoot Boys" softball team. Later, when McCarthy married, his wife, Jean, became an intimate friend of Ethel Kennedy's and the two attended the McCarthy hearings regularly or watched them on television together. McCarthy would become godfather to Bobby and Ethel's first child.

McCarthy headed the Senate Permanent Subcommittee on Investigations, reporting to the Committee on Government Operations. The subcommittee cut a broad swath, but McCarthy sharpened it as the spearhead for a witch hunt for Communists. McCarthy was a demagogue who knew how to appeal to fear of the threatened Soviet Communist expansion in the world—the Red scare. In this hunt, he painted Communists and liberals with the same Red brush. Caught in the sensational, often unfounded charges, many innocent people were smeared, others fled the country, and some even committed suicide. Few had the courage to confront McCarthy. Even the enormously popular President Eisenhower refused to defend his own hero, the highly respected General George Marshall, when McCarthy called him a traitor. Eisenhower's advisers had persuaded him that defying McCarthy at that time was politically inadvisable. McCarthy repeatedly claimed long lists of known Communists in government but never produced any of them.

George Nelson, a lobbyist for the Machinists, recalled drinking whiskey and eating steaks with McCarthy, in his house one rainy night, "when a knock came at the door and in came Joe Kennedy. . . . He said, 'I've got one who's a Senator, and the other's driving me crazy . . . put him on your payroll.' " He added that Bobby wasn't giving him any peace, that he wanted to work for McCarthy. "He believes passionately in what you're doing." And Senator McCarthy had said, "My pleasure . . . he's a bright young fella. Fine."

Joseph Kennedy afterward called McCarthy's general counsel, Francis "Frip" Flanagan. "Hey, Frip, Joe Kennedy here. . . . I just want you to know that by God you won't have any trouble with him [Bobby]. But if you do, I'll give you my private number, and just give me a call."

His brother Jack had not been keen on Bobby working for McCarthy. He told Sorensen earlier that he hoped Bobby would not take that job. He knew the intensity of feeling that McCarthy had stirred. As Sorensen observed, John Kennedy felt Bobby's presence on the committee would be bad for political, not ideological, reasons.

Bobby was twenty-seven when he became an assistant counsel on McCarthy's subcommittee. Bobby's first job for McCarthy was to investigate homosexuals in the State Department. What made this particularly interesting was that the committee's majority counsel was Roy Cohn. Cohn and Kennedy were soon at a hot point of friction. Kennedy also resented the fact that the younger Cohn, only twenty-five, had the job he felt should be his.

When a friend observed to the Kennedy father that his son Bobby was now traveling with "pretty tough company," the elder Kennedy replied, "Well, put your mind at rest about that. Bobby is just as tough as a boot-heel."

He was tough, but it wasn't enough. After being a full-charge campaign manager, it was too much of an adjustment to be a minor wheel on a major committee. "He's just too damn greedy," Hubert Humphrey later said of Bobby, "like a kid who wants to be captain or he won't play."

Ted Sorensen saw Bobby then as "intolerant, opinionated, somewhat shallow in his convictions . . . more like his father than his brother." What kept Bobby from quitting, or being fired, was the close relationship that he and Ethel had with Joe McCarthy and his wife, Jean.

In addition to his other duties Bobby was soon busy investigating trade of strategic materials with Communist China by American allies. The United States was then at war with the Communists in Korea, who were supported by the Chinese. The Kennedy report on his investigation was factual, not inflammatory, but McCarthy called it "blood trade."

"No question in my mind about Bob's feelings on McCarthy," said Al Spivak. "Because on one occasion he took a group of journalists— he and his wife—for a boat ride on the Potomac . . . a boat owned by Ethel's parents. . . . We got into a conversation about McCarthy. . . . Bob was just incredulous. 'Why do you reporters . . . feel the way you do? . . . OK, Joe's methods may be a little rough, but after all, his goal was to expose Communists in government—a worthy goal. Then why are you reporters so critical of his methods?' "

Bobby soon became increasingly concerned about McCarthy tactics. Earl Mazo, national political correspondent for the New York *Herald Tribune,* recalled, "Bobby would call McCarthy after hearings to say, 'Now Joe, you shouldn't have done this.' "

Bobby warned McCarthy that he was "headed for disaster," that he was destroying himself "just to get his name in the paper." Bobby also later said that he felt McCarthy was on a toboggan. "It was so exciting and exhilarating as he went downhill that it didn't matter to him if he hit a tree at the bottom."

Kennedy Sr. became a persistent caller for progress reports on his third son. Roy Cohn reported one such call from the elder Kennedy, with Senator McCarthy listening and finally scribbling him a note: "Remind me to check on the size of his campaign contribution. I'm not sure it's worth it."

Bobby, too, wondered whether the job was worth it. McCarthy's hit-and-run tactics were becoming increasingly vicious. Bobby discussed all this with Jack years later, and admitted that he was wrong in thinking McCarthy was making a serious contribution in fighting Communism. Bobby was proud of his one report on trade with China, for which he was named one of America's "ten outstanding young men of the year" by the Junior Chamber of Commerce. But he now felt the whole experience was mostly a waste.

It would prove much more than a waste. It would prove a political albatross that would haunt him through his political life. He resigned from the committee in May 1953, after only six months.

———————

DURING THAT TIME Senator John Kennedy had made three major speeches on the Senate floor on the business decline in New England and the federal actions that could alleviate it. "His instincts were all very, very conservative. Business, financial, fiscal—just gut instincts. . . . He had all of Papa Joe's basic fiscal instincts," said Washington business correspondent Hobart Rowen.

But he also did things Papa Joe would not have done. He cosponsored a bill providing for the protection of civil rights in employment, called on Congress to use offshore oil revenue for education and national defense, and urged amendments to increase quotas on refugees who could enter this country.

Even though John Kennedy seemed much more serious as a Senator than he ever was as a Congressman, one of his staff members, Mary Davis, felt he was just marking time in the House.

While paying minute attention to Jack's progress, Joe had not forgotten his oldest son.

The French government posthumously awarded the Legion of Honor to Joseph Kennedy, Jr., one of many honors the father would arrange for his sons in the coming years. It was not that his sons didn't deserve the honors; it was simply that this father knew how to help make them happen.

He also helped his wife to receive the title of Papal Countess by

Pope Pius XII "for her exemplary life." Beaverbrook wrote the former Ambassador Kennedy that an American priest had described Rose as "an uncanonized saint in a Dior dress." Joe Kennedy took some of the credit for both the sainthood and the Dior dress by telling Beaverbrook, "Besides being assistant manager of my children's affairs, I am third assistant manager of my wife's."

Joseph P. Kennedy was appointed as one of the eleven commissioners of the Second Hoover Commission on Organization of the Executive Branch of the Government by his friend Speaker of the House Joseph Martin. Presided over by former President Herbert Hoover, then eighty, it directed task forces of some eighty-five men, mostly older men, presumably searching for ways to improve government.

Bobby went to work there in August 1953, as his father's assistant. Once again he was not happy with the position. On the Senate campaign, he had begun willingly as his father's surrogate and then gradually branched out on his own. But here at the Hoover Commission, it was the first time father and son had worked so closely together on a regular basis. Lem Billings commented that it was tough on Bobby because, despite the Senate campaign, "the old man . . . still considered him a child."

He was twenty-eight years old and he saw himself surrounded by "a squabbling among septuagenarians." Bobby felt it was a job of no importance and was going nowhere.

Senator McCarthy was still fulminating loudly, but the three Democratic members finally won the right to appoint a Minority Counsel. They offered it to Robert Kennedy, who quickly accepted. As Minority Counsel, representing the Democrats, he could needle Cohn all he wanted by phrasing the sharp questions his Senators would ask.

McCarthy, riding high, now made the serious mistake of accusing the American Army of being riddled with Reds. The televised hearings enabled the whole country to see the brutality of the interrogation. Questions from Kennedy and the highly respected special counsel Richard Paul ridiculed McCarthy. It so incensed Roy Cohn that he provoked a fistfight with Bobby.

Bobby sought advice from Jack. Jack would never have lost his cool; would never have worked for McCarthy either.

The whole McCarthy affair was causing tensions in the Kennedy family. Many of them, especially the father, still saw the McCarthys as friends. Bobby always would.

"I liked him," said Bobby, "and yet, at times, he was terribly heavy-handed. He was a very complicated character. . . . He was sensitive and yet insensitive . . . he would get a guilty feeling and get hurt after he had blasted somebody. He wanted so desperately to be liked."

Bobby might have been describing himself.

————

JACK, HOWEVER, WAS edging away from McCarthy.

Larry Newman recalled a Kennedy family party attended by both Father Cavanaugh and Senator McCarthy. "Joe McCarthy asked, 'Well, Father, what do you think of the work I'm doing with the Communist conspiracy?' And Cavanaugh looked at him a long time before he said, 'Well, Joe, about the only way I can answer that is this way: if you came to Confession, and I knew it was you, I wouldn't give you absolution.' " Cavanaugh then turned and left.

"This would be right when Joe McCarthy was at his peak—It was long before anybody else ever attacked Joe," said Newman. "Nobody had ever said anything like this to him before. John Kennedy was there to work his charm in relieving the tension. . . . It gave you an idea, that night, of how tough and how cold JFK could be. . . . There was no percentage in him getting involved."

And yet Jack had defended McCarthy. At the hundredth anniversary of the Harvard Spee Club, one of the speakers had said how happy he was that the Spee Club had not produced a Joe McCarthy or an Alger Hiss. In a voice full of anger, John Kennedy said, "How dare you couple the name of a great American patriot with that of a traitor?" And he stalked out of the party.

Kennedy really considered McCarthy a great American patriot. When he talked about him to William Douglas he discussed him as "a screwball guy who needed help." But despite everything Kennedy considered McCarthy a family friend who deserved his loyalty.

————

EUNICE KENNEDY FINALLY agreed to marry Robert Sargent Shriver, in May 1953, after a "fantastically dogged" courtship of seven years. "I searched all my life for someone like my father," she said, "and Sarge came closest."

William McCormick Blair, a strong Stevenson supporter and a friend of the Kennedys, remembered: "I sat next to some bridesmaid, who asked me what I thought of Joe McCarthy. I guess I raised my voice—I didn't realize my voice would carry—and Bobby, at the other end of the table, said, 'That's a goddamn lie!' Mr. Kennedy walks over, and says, 'Now, now, this isn't the time.' And I apologized; that was the end. But Bobby never forgot. As luck would have it, he was the usher who took me to my seat, and he put me behind a post, where I couldn't see anything."

One of the wedding guests, Walter Gridley, saw Eunice and Sarge at the airport the next day, en route to Portugal. Teddy Kennedy was with them, and Gridley remarked how nice it was of Teddy to say goodbye to them.

"Oh, Ted is coming with us," said Eunice.

"But not on your honeymoon trip," said Walter.

"Why, of course," Eunice replied. "Ted wanted to do it with us a long time ago. It was always arranged and decided."

Sarge Shriver never became a Kennedy brother—he had his own mind and his own ambitions. But he was always there when needed.

———

SENATOR KENNEDY SEEMED increasingly consumed with politics. "Not more than ten minutes after the wedding ceremony, Jack had a sympathetic group of guests corralled into the next room telling them about political campaigns—that's how obsessed he is," said Washington editor Helen Fuller.

John Kennedy was still "The Senate's Gay Young Bachelor" at thirty-six, according to a *Saturday Evening Post* article in June 1953. "He never talked very much about getting married when we lived together," said Eunice. "Then I got married."

When a friend discussed his planned marriage, Jack asked seriously, "Do you really want to get married? There are so many unhappy marriages."

"I guess some people do think of me as a cold fish," said Jack Kennedy. "I think I get along fine with people on a personal intimate basis. . . . As far as backslapping with the politicians, I think I'd rather go somewhere with my familiars or sit alone somewhere and read a book. I think it's more of a personal reserve than a coldness, although it may seem like coldness to some people.

"No, I don't think I ever react emotionally to a problem rather than in a reasoning way, but that doesn't mean I'm unemotional," Jack Kennedy said. "It simply means I reason problems out and apply logic to them. We are all the product of our conditioning. I don't know why it is. I probably have as many emotions as the next person. I have emotional feelings about my family. You can see the way we feel about each other. . . . My brothers and my sisters and I see a lot more of each other than many people who don't see other members of their families for long periods of time and then well up. I don't do that. This causes people to say Kennedy is a cold fish. I'm not a cold fish."

He was not a cold fish, but he *was* cool. There is much evidence of that. Coldness implies an underlying contempt or callousness or cruelty. He had none of that. What he did have was a highly developed persona of a very controlled man, a very private, pragmatic man.

Schlesinger had written of Kennedy that "only the unwary could really conclude that his coolness was because he felt too little. It was because he felt too much and had to compose himself for an existence filled with disorder and suffering." Commenting on that, Harris Wofford added, "Perhaps, but over time I concluded that Kennedy's coolness was because he was cool."

If Jack was cool, Bobby was warm. Jack had a natural reserve and found it difficult to communicate his feelings. Bobby had so much more of an emotional commitment to things. He was now personally *moved* by the plight of the poor. He had so much empathy, in listening and dealing. Jack, in a comparable situation, was more remote, and intellectual. He *understood* these issues in a statistical way. "But I never had the feeling it 'got him here,' " said Jim Sundquist. "I never saw Jack get carried away in his life—on anything."

Jack's future wife would defend him on that by quoting one of his favorite lines from one of his favorite books, *Pilgrim's Way* by John Buchan: "He disliked emotion, not because he felt lightly but because he felt deeply." She had underlined that line for *Look* correspondent Laura Bergquist and had written, "This is a classic description of JFK."

It was the pragmatism in him that spurred the idea of marriage. His father made the inarguable point that any ambitious political leader must have a wife and family. The question then became: who?

Jacqueline Lee Bouvier had been selected as the most beautiful debutante of the year in 1948 when she made her debut in both Newport and New York. Her wide, hazel-gray eyes had long lashes beneath well-marked brows. A dainty nose, lovely mouth, clear, fair complexion, luxuriant, softly waved brown hair, Jacqueline also carried herself beautifully.

"I think she was the most interesting girl he'd ever met, really," said Eunice. "I'm sure of that. Of all the girls I ever saw, she was the brightest. Different. She could handle him. Something he never found, very often. Somebody as bright as he was, or as clever."

When Jacqueline graduated from Miss Porter's School, she listed her life ambition: "Not to be a housewife." Jacqueline attended Vassar, the Sorbonne, and graduated from George Washington University. She was of French descent on her father's side. Her father, "Black Jack" Bouvier III, was a swarthy, swashbuckling stockbroker, who had inherited a big fortune and made it into a little fortune. He was wistfully described by his daughter after his death in 1957 as "a most devastating figure."

Her father, whom she adored, gave her some advice about men: Be hard to get. To be tantalizing you must always be exasperating. He also told her never to be aggressive and pay attention to everything a man says. "Fasten your eyes on him like you were staring into the sun." His advice clearly reflected the attitudes of his own life and his own era. Jackie took his advice to heart.

Arthur Krock, a friend of both Black Jack and Joe Kennedy, called Frank Waldrop, editor of the Washington *Times-Herald*, and asked if there were any jobs available for a round-eyed, clever girl who was "a wonder." Waldrop asked her, "Do you really want to go into journalism or do you just want to hang around here until you get married?"

"I want to make a career," she said.

He took Jacqueline on at $42.50 a week as the newspaper's inquiring photographer.

Although the press loved to report that she first met John Kennedy when she photographed him for her Inquiring Photographer column in the *Times-Herald* in February 1952, it wasn't true. "Actually, it wasn't nearly so romantic as that. I met him casually at a party."

John Kennedy's memory of their first meeting was, "I leaned over the asparagus and asked her for a date." Jacqueline smiled at that. "There was no asparagus."

When she did write about him, Miss Bouvier quoted a Capitol page on Senator Kennedy: "He always brings his lunch to the office in a brown paper bag . . . and he's always being mistaken for a tourist by the cops because he looks so young. The other day he wanted to use the special phones and they told him 'Sorry, mister, these are reserved for Senators.' "

Jacqueline was twelve years younger than Jack Kennedy. She liked French films and he preferred Westerns. She loved art books and ballet and he liked to read seventeenth-century English history and James Bond thrillers. But she found him exciting and unpredictable.

"He and Jackie were both alike, both lonely in the crowd, and both brought up in that same kind of loneliness," suggested William Walton, who had known Jacqueline before Jack did. "It was one of the things that probably attracted them to each other."

John Kennedy had no interest in marrying a woman like his mother. And Jacqueline Bouvier wanted very much to marry a man like her father.

The one she loved best among the Kennedys was Jack's father. They spent a lot of time talking about everybody from Gloria Swanson to Cardinal Spellman. He made her laugh a lot and absolutely charmed her. She called him "amazing, vigorous, colorful, how he filled every minute with some activity." She affectionately recalled how immersed he was one day in teaching a little girl how to hop on one leg.

"I used to think of him as a tiger mother, swatting his cubs when they were out of line, and drawing them in with his paw when they were troubled," Jacqueline once wrote of her father-in-law. "When you married into his family, you became one of those cubs: as loved, as protected, as chastised, as much an object of pride as one of his own. I have never seen that anywhere else . . . he could have been my enemy, but he was my greatest and my closest friend. So few people, when you see them, make your heart light up. That is what I always felt when I saw him."

She found Rose Kennedy more nervous, slightly distant and forbidding, and a little scatterbrained. But Jacqueline still observed, "Of course, none of it could have run without her."

Jacqueline also thought that Rose Kennedy had been brought up with the maxim: don't reveal yourself . . . it's dangerous. She noted that Jack followed his mother's maxim to the fullest: "I'd say Jack didn't want to reveal himself at all."

Neither did Jacqueline. It was a tough bit of business trying to merge with the Kennedys at Hyannis and still survive as an individual. She followed her father's dictum to submerge the steel and concentrate on her aura.

On her first visit to Jack's house, she made the initial mistake of overdressing for dinner, and was quickly teased. Teasing was a fun game at the Kennedys' and the gibing jokes came fast, testing your cool. The trick was to return with your own wit, giving as much as you got, without losing your temper. Nor could you go away and hide. They would find you.

The real Jacqueline was hard to find. She hid behind the picture of being a little breakable, with a very soft, intimate speaking voice that seemed unreal. She described herself as more solitary, more introverted. And a friend said of her, "Jackie was really prepared for one eventuality in life—to be exquisite."

Behind that exquisite fragility was steel. A friend said that if you put her in a boat in the middle of the Atlantic with one paddle, she'd somehow manage. Jack, the keen observer, saw all this and liked it. He needed a survivor. He needed someone who understood his father and could cope with him. His longtime friend John Sharon predicted that he would marry the first woman who said no to him. This was a woman who could do that.

"There was a Senator Kluger who had been trying to get Jack fixed up with a young woman he might marry," recalled noted Washington attorney Joel Fisher. "And Jack told him, 'Look, you might as well know, I talked to my dad, and he told me that now is that time to get married'—and Jack added that his father preferred Jackie. 'For a lot of reasons. I mean, she's a perfect hostess; she's got the background; and she's Catholic.' "

He later added that she had a very retentive memory, spoke many languages, was more indirect than his sisters, and "You might even call her fey."

In his usual understatement, he made it sound more of a marriage of convenience. But, whatever it was, it was not a sweeping romance.

Frank Waldrop called in Jacqueline. "I understand you're running around with Kennedy?"

Jacqueline admitted she was dating him.

"I want to tell you something," said Waldrop. "He's older than you and smarter than you and he's been around and a half a dozen women have had their shot at him, so watch yourself."

She said "yes sir" and left.

"The next thing I knew I got an invitation to the wedding," said Waldrop.

There was no whirlwind courtship. Jack sent her a single picture postcard from Bermuda: "Wish you were here. Cheers. Jack." And he proposed to her by telephone while she was in England reporting on Queen Elizabeth's coronation.

Lem Billings did not encourage the marriage. He warned Jacqueline that Jack was "set in his ways," twelve years older, had a history of serious illness and an active record of female conquests.

The age difference didn't bother her. As Jack later told Chuck Spalding: Jackie had a "father crush." Neither did Jack's womanizing faze her. "I don't think there are any men who are faithful to their wives. Men are such a combination of good and evil."

Lem still was skeptical. "I couldn't visualize him actually saying 'I love you' to somebody and asking her to marry him. It was the sort of thing he would have liked to happen without having to talk about it."

Billings knew him best. Even in marriage, this was not a man who could surrender himself, or change.

Congresswoman Lindy Boggs, a friend of both, described Jacqueline as a woman "full of love and full of hurt. . . . When she really loved something, she gave herself completely. . . . But I don't think he could love anyone too deeply."

A month before the wedding, Jack was en route to Europe and propositioned some five women on the ship. Marquis Childs later heard about it from one of the women, and commented, "Maybe it's just a hobby, like collecting stamps . . . part of his arrogance . . . to assume his charm and physical attraction was so great, that no one could say NO to him.''

———

JACQUELINE SAID SHE hoped to have ''a simple and very small wedding,'' but father Kennedy had other plans. The church was filled to capacity and many of the invited guests were key political figures. Robert Kennedy was his brother's best man.

The bride and groom stood in a reception line for two hours and shook hands with most of the 1400 wedding guests. A crowd of 3000 persons broke through police lines and nearly crushed the bride. The father had provided a truck to deliver the champagne and two trucks to take away the wedding presents. The four-foot wedding cake was so elaborate that it had to be delivered in two sections.

Archbishop Richard J. Cushing conducted the nuptial Mass, with a special blessing from Pope Pius XII. Jacqueline's father was too drunk to walk his daughter down the aisle, so her stepfather did. One of the guests also reported later that John Kennedy's father ''even made a play for one of the bridesmaids.''

The Boston *Globe* headline on the wedding story was: EXIT PRINCE CHARMING, and the story began, ''Yesterday was a difficult day for the American women. . . . The price of hope is just a little higher today.''

''Just the night before the wedding,'' said James Reed, ''I said to Jackie, 'When did you first discover that you were in love with Jack?' And she answered very coolly, 'What makes you think I'm in love with Jack?' ''

Her half sister and maid of honor, Nina Auchincloss Straight, thought that Jack and Jackie loved each other deeply. But, after reflection, she qualified that. ''Let's say that they fascinated each other. There was some love, but it couldn't have been too deep.''

Part of the fascination, perhaps, was the excitement of an unknown puzzle. ''You have a hard time getting to the bottom of that barrel,'' Ethel Kennedy said of Jacqueline, ''which is great for Jack, who is so inquisitive. The wheels go round constantly in Jackie's head. You can't pigeonhole her.''

''Jack and I both have inquiring minds,'' said Jacqueline. ''That's the reason we chose each other. I have always felt so alive with him.''

John Kennedy later confided to Priscilla McMillan at a dinner party: "I only got married because I was thirty-seven years old. If I wasn't married, people would think I was queer."

———

THE NEWLYWEDS WANTED a different kind of family than Bobby and Ethel did. "They weren't going to have ninety-nine kids," said Spalding. Her father had taught her how to catch a husband; he did not explain how to make a marriage work. That was not within the scope of his credentials.

The great difficulty of the marriage, as Lindy Boggs said, was that they were two private people, two cocoons married to each other, trying to reach into each other. And, since he was so much older than she was, she felt that it was up to him to reach out more than she did. But he couldn't.

Even more apt than the cocoon analogy was Jacqueline's description of her husband and herself as icebergs—"the public life above the water and the private life submerged." The iceberg diagnosis was apt. There were very few people with whom Jack Kennedy felt intimately comfortable with or felt he could confide in. Even those few were not intimate with each other.

Part of it was his basic lack of trust in most people, that he never felt safe enough to reveal himself. Also, perhaps, he was disdainful because so few people measured up to his expectations—especially women.

When an author asked Kennedy if he ever had talked to his wife about politics, he looked at her and said, "What are you, one of those feminists?"

In one of his greatest uses of hyperbole, the junior Senator from Massachusetts later said, "I'm quite sure once we're married, she'll become just as interested in Massachusetts and international problems as I am." But Jacqueline had freely confessed her minimal interest in politics. "You see, I never voted until I was married to Jack. I guess my first vote was probably for him for Senator, wasn't it?"

When *Look* reporter Laura Bergquist wanted to talk to Jacqueline, a surprised Jack said, "What do you want to talk to my wife for?"

"I don't think he regarded women for their brains," Bergquist continued. "No, that sounds wrong. He was beguiled by women, he loved being around them. But when it came to serious talk, he preferred talking to the guys. . . . There are men who really like women or who think of women as equals, with ability. . . . But I don't think Kennedy was that way."

"She wasn't really interested in the struggles he had in the Congress," said Jack's secretary, Evelyn Lincoln. "I think Jackie would've enjoyed it if he was royalty, and she would have been very good at it."

But she was wise enough to know her husband's priorities. She wrote a poem for Jack soon after they were married, part of which read:

> He would find love
> He would never find peace
> For he must go seeking
> The golden fleece.

Part of the peace came in the home she created for him. As a teenager, she had been described as a sloppy kid. But she knew how a house should work and she wanted to make it work for him. Not simply having the laundry done and the beds made, but giving it a cozy feeling with a touch of elegance. She wanted to give him a home he had always envied elsewhere. And she did.

Jack admitted, after five months of marriage, "Being married, I get more done."

Doodling on a pad for Bergquist, to indicate the difference between himself and his wife, Jack drew a straight, horizontal line for himself and a wavering, intersecting line for Jacqueline.

The intersecting line not only spelled out her own uncertainty in this marriage, but his own. What he most wanted from her was to create a home he never had and give him children. While he didn't want her to be like his mother, he wanted her to wear blinders, as his mother did—so that, like his father, he could live his separate sexual life.

He had his own arrogance about his contribution to her life. When Charles Spalding came to visit, Kennedy told him, "See that smile on her face? . . . I just put it there."

———

ALTHOUGH BOBBY, LIKE Jack, had his own private reserve, his denial of intimacy—he never had it with Ethel. With Ethel, it was a storybook romantic marriage, complete with handholding and starry-eyed looks.

Bobby and Ethel had a fresh naiveté. "When I first met Bob," said his secretary Angie Novello, "he looked so young. He looked like he stepped out of high school, his shirttails hanging out, heels needing repair, hair never combed. His mother would write him nasty little notes about, 'Please comb your hair, Bobby' . . . or 'Tuck your shirt-tail in.' "

The two young couples were not a social foursome. Jack and Bobby found it difficult to be at ease together socially. Jack was always seeking to relax and Bobby was often tense, too serious. As for Ethel and Jacqueline, they belonged to two different worlds.

Bobby also had a different concept of marriage than Jack. Bobby discussed everything with Ethel. He was a reasonably faithful husband. When Jacqueline was visiting her mother at Newport, a gossip item reported Jack at a nightclub with another woman.

His Senate staff was aware of all this. "The staff thought there was an early strain between Jack and Jackie. . . . Most of us didn't understand it," said Ralph Dungan. "I always said that was the way that class lives—like the Edwardians . . . but I found it very odd. . . . I saw all these gals after him . . . you'd have to be a saint to avoid it. Jackie would have to be blind not to be aware of all the women."

———

PATRICIA KENNEDY MARRIED actor Peter Lawford, son of a British general, in April 1954. Generally regarded as the most attractive of the Kennedy women, Patricia was also considered artistic as well as strong-willed, a renegade independent who had worked in the business end of television. Some even had suggested she run for Congress. If Eunice was Jack's favorite sister, Patricia was Bobby's. They were very much alike.

Lawford often sat in on Kennedy family discussions "with my ears and my mouth open, listening." He would never come close to being a Kennedy. He was of a different species. In helping provide John Kennedy with willing women, his relationship could not have been more personal—but, still, never intimate, never family, never brotherly. Years later, when he was in a drug-induced decline, he sold the story of his role as his brother-in-law's procurer for ladies to a tabloid magazine. He said of his brother-in-law that he would examine women "like he was admiring some fine china."

Of his own wife, Lawford said, "I always felt that her love for her father took precedence in a funny way over her love for me. . . . She worshipped him."

––––––––

"AT THE WEDDING, when we were in the can and talked about everything," said Larry Newman, "I said to Jack, 'Well, it's all downhill from now on.'

" 'What do you mean?' said Kennedy.

" 'Well, the next stop is the White House.'

" 'I think you're right,' said Kennedy."

The hurdles were many. The dominating thing in Jack's life then, about which he said nothing to anyone—except Billings—was the physical pain, which never left him. He scheduled his needed spinal surgery, a double fusion operation to correct a ruptured disk. It also appeared to be the time when the Senate was to vote on their censure of Joe McCarthy. Correspondent Phil Potter felt that Kennedy deliberately scheduled his operation to get himself out of town because he didn't want to take a stand on the issue.

Spalding was with Kennedy in the hospital just before surgery. Kennedy told him, "You know, when I get downstairs, I'll know exactly what's going to happen. . . . Those reporters are going to lean over my stretcher. There's going to be about ninety-five faces bent over me with great concern, and every one of those guys is going to say, 'Now, Senator, what about McCarthy?' . . . You know what I'm going to do? I'm going to reach back on my back, and I'm going to yell, 'Ow-w-w-w-!' And then I'm going to pull the sheet over my head and hope we can get out of there."

"What was I to do, commit hara-kiri?" Kennedy later asked a reporter. "I had all these family pressures. . . . Then I thought that McCarthy would eventually fade away. . . . And you must understand, too, that I had never known the sort of people who were called before the McCarthy committee. I agree that many of them were seriously manhandled, but they all represented a different world to me. What I mean is, I did not identify with them, and so I did not get as worked up as other liberals did."

Reminiscing about it afterward, Senator Kennedy added, "I was caught in a bad situation. My brother had been working for Joe. I was against it; I didn't want him to work for Joe, but he wanted to. And how the hell could I get up there and denounce Joe McCarthy when my own brother was working for him? So it wasn't so much a thing of political liability as it was a personal problem."

The United States Senate finally voted 67 to 22 to censure McCarthy.

————

AFTER JACK'S SURGERY, in which he was given a bone graft and metal plate in his back, his wound became badly infected. When he was released from the hospital, it was raw and oozing. Jack asked Lem Billings to check his wound: "Is it still open? Is stuff still running out? Does it smell bad?" There was serious question whether he would ever walk again.

"He was bitter and low," said Billings. "We came close to losing him. I don't just mean losing his life. I mean losing him as a person. . . . It was a terrible time."

Two months later Jack was back in the hospital again, for another operation at the Hospital for Special Surgery in New York City. The surgery was seriously complicated by Kennedy's continuous bout with Addison's disease, which hinders the body's ability to heal properly.

After the operation, his condition became so critical that Father Cavanaugh was called in to deliver Last Rites. Arthur Krock remembered Joe Kennedy coming to his office to tell him that Jack was dying, "and he wept sitting in the chair opposite me."

Kennedy survived, but with a greater need for crutches. He would use his crutches, as he used his glasses—whenever he was out of political view.

Kennedy's Addison's disease of the adrenal glands had been diagnosed in 1947 and was considered fatal then. It was later discovered that pellets of corticosteroid hormones implanted in the thigh would extend life expectancy by five to ten years. Only later did oral medication promise a normal life. Cortisone had a bloating effect on Kennedy's face and may have stimulated both his libido and stamina, though there is still no definitive opinion on this. According to doctors, Jack would not have survived without it.

Politically, Jack felt it imperative to deny the disease, as did Bobby. This was not the first or last time his brother would lie for him. Had the American people been told that Jack had suffered for thirteen years from an incurable, potentially fatal disease, he would have been politically dead.

During his time in the hospital, Bobby was the one to call a friend and say, "Jack's feeling sort of lousy; come down." Even Grace Kelly was drafted to come to Jack's room, dressed as a nurse. Grace would later become a friend, and, some said, a lover.

Jack's physician, Dr. Janet Travell, remembered when Jack came to her office after his six months' leave from the Senate:

"He was thin, he was ill, his nutrition was poor, he was on crutches. There were two steps from the street into my office and he could hardly navigate these. His major complaint was pain in his left low back with radiation to the left lower extremity, so that he couldn't put weight on it without intense pain. But he also had an old football injury to his right knee which was, at that time, very stiff and painful. . . . There was no doubt but what, in my mind, that the operation in special surgery in October 1954 made him worse. . . . I would like to say at this point what I have never said before: what I really thought had happened to his back. He was born with the left side of his body smaller than the right; the left side of his face was smaller; his left shoulder was lower."

———

EXCEPT FOR THE father's emotional outburst to Krock, the Kennedys contained their concern, as always. Stoicism had been bred into them. Jacqueline called it something else.

"All the Kennedys have a gallantry . . . what's so incredible about them is their gallantry—so impressive," Jacqueline told Robert Coughlan. "You can be sitting down to dinner with them; and so many sad things have happened to each—maybe something sad even happened that day. And you can see that each one is aware of the other's suffering—has this sad thing in mind. And then, each one will start to make this conscious effort to be gay, or to be funny, or to raise the others' spirits. And finally you find it is infectious. Everybody's doing it. And you just think, 'Look at these people—the effort they're making!' Nobody ever sits and wallows in their self-pity. It's just so gallant . . . it really makes you proud to think you're even in the Compound.''

The Kennedy women generally congregated at the "big house" in the late afternoon. The big house was not really that big—six rooms and a servants' wing—but it was the home of the patriarch father. Their own homes clustered nearby, all on the water's edge, in what was called the Kennedy Compound.

"It was really Mr. Kennedy who wanted to keep everybody here," said Jacqueline. "I was against it . . . I wanted to get away from the Compound. And he had this house for us for two years, before we lived in it."

Jacqueline knew when to assert her independence. At Hyannis, at the end of a day of sizzling outdoor fun and games, one of the sisters cried: "Now we're all going over to the big house."

"*You're* going over to Joe's," replied Jacqueline firmly. "*We're* having guests for dinner."

She now could also be more abrupt with interviewers: "Oh, please, don't ask me about Jack's complexes, like all the others. All they ask me is: 'Doesn't Jack have a complex about his father, and isn't Bobby driven by his complexes about Jack?' How silly, and how dreary!" Nevertheless, Bobby, like Jack, was driven by these complexes. And the forces behind that drive were becoming more complicated.

The perceptive Ben Bradlee regarded Bobby as more interesting than Jack because he was totally unpredictable compared to the highly controlled Jack. If the two of them had been presented to him as puzzles, added Bradlee, Jack was the one he might have hoped to solve someday, "Bobby never."

———

BOBBY SAW HIMSELF in a kind of limbo after McCarthy's downfall. As campaign manager for Jack during the Senate race, he had a strong start. Then came his jobs with Hoover and McCarthy, and his self-confidence had plunged.

He was happier when his brother returned to Washington. Jack was very understanding about Bobby. "Some people don't like him because he's too curt and too competitive," said Jack, "but I can understand why. As I said, he's got to fight himself out of my shadow."

Bobby not only had to fight out of his brother's shadow, but out of his father's shadow, and out of the family shadow. His chance soon came.

That November 1954 election swept the Democrats back in control of the Senate, and John L. McClellan replaced McCarthy as chairman of the Senate Permanent Subcommittee on Investigations. Robert Kennedy, age thirty, became its new Chief Counsel and staff director. The committee under McClellan was scheduled to investigate corruption in labor unions. Joe Sr. had contributed liberally to McClellan's campaign.

The committee was still geared to investigate Communist infiltration in government and fraud in Army contracts, but they were no longer matters that attracted press attention.

"Bob and Ethel would come by and say, 'We're going to the movies; come with us.' So I'd drop the dishes and mop," said his secretary, Angie Novello, "and run, and go to the theater with them. It'd always have to be a Western—Bob loved Westerns. Then we'd stop and have a bite to eat, on the way home." This was not something Jack and Jacqueline would ever do with his secretary.

———

JACK RETURNED FROM his surgery a much changed man. His closeness to death had intensified his search for private pleasure. One of the new diversions he discovered was painting. Churchill, whom he so greatly admired, had painted as a pastime. Jack had bought his wife a painting set for Christmas in 1954 in Palm Beach, and then started using it himself. "That painting was a godsend for him," said Jacqueline. "That first day he worked right through from morning until eleven that night."

"I was at Harvard when he came back from the hospital," said Ted Kennedy, "and we both did a lot of painting then," Ted said. "We'd start out in the morning and pick out something to paint— we'd both paint the same thing. Then, by suppertime, we'd have a daiquiri and get a visiting friend to decide which of our paintings was the best."

His brush with death had somewhat dimmed Jack's drive to be President. He seemed somewhat adrift, and became increasingly lackadaisical about his Senate work. "He really had a second- or third-rate record as a Senator," Justice William Douglas commented. And even

Sorensen later admitted, "His contribution as a freshman Senator was too modest to be included in what I have termed the Kennedy legacy."

His father made certain that Jack did work hard on some things. Joe Kennedy once told Senator George Aiken the advice he had given Jack for political success: "Be against everything that your old man has stood for—in business, government, and philosophy." But he didn't really mean it. There were some issues he felt too strongly about, and demanded Jack's help.

As chairman of the Senate's Reorganization Subcommittee, Senator Kennedy held hearings on thirty of the fifty-five Hoover Commission proposals—with which his father had been so involved. He introduced ten bills providing for implementation of the Hoover recommendations. Bobby kept his father updated on his brother's progress, and his father now decided Bob needed some foreign exposure. He arranged for him to travel to Soviet Russia for five weeks with Supreme Court Justice William O. Douglas.

"Bobby didn't want to go," recalled Bergquist, "but he went because his father wanted him to."

For Bobby, it was an adventure that included the historic city of Bukhara, where Marco Polo met the emissaries of the Great Kublai Khan. They would also cross the highest mountain pass, called the "Gate of Timur." Bob traveled with a camera, a diary, a suitcase, and a Bible. He later said that he and Douglas convinced themselves that "the wires in all the rooms we stayed in were tapped" by Communist spies.

Bobby brought his own food and water and prejudices, but Douglas still felt that the trip created a "transformation in Bobby." Now in his post-McCarthy days, Bobby saw the Russians as "people with problems" instead of "soulless fanatics."

Still, Bobby had been bred on his father's bitter anti-Communist views, and so he ended his trip as he began it—critical and suspicious. He told Harris Wofford, "It can only be suicidal for us during this period, on the basis of smiles, to strengthen Russia and weaken ourselves." Kennedy said he saw life behind the Iron Curtain as a form of slavery.

———

DURING HIS RECUPERATION, Jack Kennedy, with the great help of his key aide, Ted Sorensen, researched and wrote *Profiles in Courage,* a book about Senators who took gallant but unpopular positions on controversial issues. When family friend Arthur Krock suggested that the book might win a Pulitzer Prize, Kennedy was spurred to finish.

Krock had been on the Pulitzer board and knew most of the board members. "There was such log-rolling that I thought it had better be taken in hand by somebody and it might as well be me," said Krock. "So we log-rolled under my direction." What Krock did was simply to talk persuasively with all his friends on the board. Some of them, he later implied, owed him some favors. There was never any scandal about it because nobody ever knew about it then.

Profiles in Courage won the Pulitzer prize.

Then came a different scandal. National columnist Drew Pearson said on the ABC network that Kennedy had not written the book.

Jack then went to see his personal lawyer, Clark Clifford, who had been adviser to President Truman. While Jack was there, his father called, in rage, and told Clifford, "I want you to sue the bastards for fifty million dollars. Get it started right away. My boy wrote the book. This is a plot against us."

When Joe Kennedy got off the phone, Jack told Clifford, "Well, that's just Dad. Let's deal with this thing."

ABC, after examining the Kennedy notebooks, apologized for the Pearson statement. Pearson also retracted his statement, adding, "I'm still dubious as to whether he wrote too much of it in the final draft himself."

The notebooks indicated that Jack, indeed, had been involved in the book, had made extensive notes, and had done some of the writing. There is no question that Sorensen had done a considerable amount of the research and the final writing. Jack was a reasonably good writer but Sorensen gave it the professional polish. It was a good book, and interesting, but perhaps would not have earned a Pulitzer without the extra push. As for the ABC lawsuit, it was not the kind of publicity they needed—it was simpler to settle.

John Kennedy later told Clifford that they had decided to fight the question of authorship because the issue "could have destroyed my candidacy."

Even after the book was published, Jack's editor, Evan Thomas, was getting the heavy brunt of complaint from Joseph Kennedy Sr. about the quality and quantity of promotion for his son's book. Evan finally asked Jack if he could moderate the intensity of his father's objections. Evan's father was Norman Thomas, the prominent Socialist and a frequent candidate for President, and Jack asked him if he always agreed with his own controversial father. Evan said no. Kennedy asked, "But you love him, don't you?"

"Yes, I do."

"Well, so do I," said Kennedy. "Let's not get upset. My father thinks he's helping me."

In reality, Joe Kennedy's help for his sons often translated into dollars. But, curiously enough, he was never able to give his sons a sense of money, especially the ability to manage their money. "Listening to them talk about money," said Charles Spalding, "was like listening to nuns talk about sex."

The often-told story is that Kennedy set aside trust funds of millions for each child "because I want them to be independent of me and free to make their own decisions."

This, however, was not true. He would try to shape their lives and decisions as long as it was physically possible. Jack once explained that the real reason for the trust funds was that his father was in a highly speculative stock market, just before the crash, "and his health was not too good at the time, and that was the reason that he did it. There was no other reason."

One day Joe summoned George Smathers. "George, I understand my boys don't know how to handle money. . . . I had to struggle, and I know what a dollar is, how to make it and how to keep it. But none of my children do. I wanted them not to have this particular problem, and have been fortunate enough so that they do not have to do that. However, I think they're getting old enough now—now that my oldest boy's been killed, and Jack is now head of the family . . . to look at these trusts. I know that you're a lawyer, and you're his friend, and our friend. I'd like you to advise him. I want him to become more familiar with what money's all about, what expenses are."

Smathers found it a difficult job. "I never could get Jack to listen; he was just totally uninterested. Joe was right . . . Jack would always ask me one question: 'Have we got enough?' I'd say, 'You've got enough.' . . . Nothing more to it; that's all he'd say."

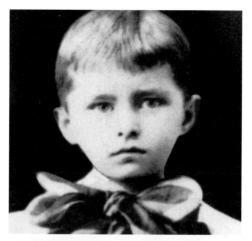

As a toddler and as a young cadet, Joseph Patrick Kennedy, Sr., showed the set jaw and the determined stance that would become his trademarks. (BOTH PHOTOGRAPHS: JOHN F. KENNEDY LIBRARY)

*Patrick Joseph "PJ" Kennedy (top), and Josephine and John F. "Honey Fitz" Fitzgerald
in Palm Beach (bottom).* (TOP: JOHN F. KENNEDY LIBRARY; BOTTOM: UPI/BETTMANN)

Joseph P. Kennedy and his bride, Rose. (BOSTON GLOBE PHOTO)

Joe Sr., with Joe (left) and Jack (right), offered great affection to his children.
Rose, with (left to right) Rosemary, Jack, and Joe Jr., was more concerned with manners.

Sometime rivals Joe Jr. (left) and Jack (right), here in 1925, were always pals.

Joe Jr. with Teddy: The older brothers were surrogate fathers to their young siblings. (BOSTON HERALD)

Like all the other Kennedys, Bobby and his favorite sister, Jean, loved the water.

(JOHN F. KENNEDY LIBRARY)

Family portrait in Hyannis, 1928. (Left to right) Bobby, Jack, Eunice, Jean, Joe Sr., Rose, Kathleen (in front of Rose), Pat, Joe Jr., and Rosemary. (JOHN F. KENNEDY LIBRARY)

Jack with his best friend, Lem Billings.

(JOHN F. KENNEDY LIBRARY)

Jack at his Choate graduation, 1935.

(JOHN F. KENNEDY LIBRARY)

Sports were a favorite Kennedy proving ground. Joe excelled at football, Jack at swimming.

An American royal family goes to London. (Left to right) Rose, Teddy, Rosemary, Joe Jr., Ambassador Kennedy, Eunice, Jean, Jack, Pat, Bobby, and Kathleen. (© GILBERT ADAMS)

Joe (left) and Jack flanking their favorite sister, Kathleen ("Kick"), in London. (JOHN F. KENNEDY LIBRARY)

Bobby and Teddy as British schoolboys.
(UPI/BETTMANN)

The Ambassador and his two favorite assistants, Jack (left) and Joe (right).
(ARCHIVE PHOTOS)

*London, 1939. Family tragedy would make this the last portrait of the entire Kennedy family.
(Left to right) Eunice, Jack, Rosemary, Jean, Joe Sr., Ted, Rose, Joe Jr., Pat, Bobby, Kathleen.*

PT boat commander John F. Kennedy (left)
and fighter pilot Joseph P. Kennedy, Jr., were both heroes. (PICTORIAL PARADE)

Joe Jr. insisted on volunteering for a highly dangerous bombing mission in 1944. (JOHN F. KENNEDY LIBRARY)

Aboard the destroyer USS Joseph P. Kennedy, Jr., *a proud father greets new sailor Robert F. Kennedy.* (JOHN F. KENNEDY LIBRARY)

PT boat commander John F. Kennedy (left)
and fighter pilot Joseph P. Kennedy, Jr., were both heroes. (PICTORIAL PARADE)

*Joe Jr. insisted on volunteering for a highly dangerous
bombing mission in 1944.* (JOHN F. KENNEDY LIBRARY)

Aboard the destroyer USS Joseph P. Kennedy, Jr., *a proud father greets new sailor
Robert F. Kennedy.* (JOHN F. KENNEDY LIBRARY)

At the unveiling of a portrait of Joe Jr. after his death, Jack and Joe Sr. eulogized the family's first martyr. (JOHN F. KENNEDY LIBRARY)

After Joe's death, Jack became the role model for his younger brothers Bobby and Teddy.
(JOHN F. KENNEDY LIBRARY)

A gathering of the Kennedy clan in Hyannis after the war. (Left to right) Jack, Jean, Rose, Joe, Teddy (in front), Pat, Bobby, and Eunice. (JOHN F. KENNEDY LIBRARY)

IT WAS TRUE that Joe's short-term influence would wax and wane with his boys, but on the vital issues he could play God with the key decisions of their lives. He never took his eyes from the main prize. The constant pressure for the Presidency came from him. In the fall of 1955, he sent a letter to Senator Lyndon Johnson, part of which read:

> As I told you in our telephone call awhile back, both Jack and I are ready to support you in 1956, if you decide. . . . Jack shares my respect for you, and feels he owes a debt to you, but especially to the country. . . .
>
> I guarantee we'll be behind you all the way. . . . Jack wants to remind you of his support for you when you went for the Senate minority leadership in 1953. He also speaks of his admiration and personal regard for you, and the guidance you have given him along the way in both the House and in his early days in the Senate. As you already know, Jack is his own man, and his actions in all matters are without any pushing from "Big Joe." I get damn tired of reading how I tell him everything to do. He is impossible to handle by me or anyone else, once he digs into a situation and sets his mind to it. We have our battles, but in the decision on 1956 we have agreed from the start. Jack is a tough fighter, and I like to think he got some of that from his old man. More often than not, he is out in front of me in most political situations, and his loyalty to those he respects rarely wavers. His decision in supporting you in 1956 was his own, and for a change agreed with my long-time feelings.

Johnson replied, and explained that he deeply appreciated their interest, but he felt that the country wasn't ready for a southern President, and that he thought it would be very divisive in the party. The Kennedy letter served a purpose anyway. It picked up a strong ally who paid off at a future convention.

Asked who was the most qualified person to be President, Jack said, "No question, Senator Johnson, but he can't become President [because he is a Southerner]." Then he said, "I'm the next best."

Some months before the 1956 Democratic National Convention, *Newsweek* Washington editor Ben Bradlee had some guests at his Georgetown home, including Jack and Jacqueline and William McCormick Blair, best friend and closest adviser of Adlai Stevenson. Blair made an impassioned pitch for Jack Kennedy to make a serious try for the vice presidency. Kennedy listened hard and said little, but Jacqueline turned to Ken Crawford of *Newsweek* and said in her soft voice, "Why is Bill trying to persuade Jack to run for Vice President when Jack really wants to be President?"

She was right, of course, but premature. Jack's interest in the vice presidency—even as a nomination—was that he saw it as an entry into the national political limelight. He had conferred with Stevenson on the subject in December 1955, even though he privately felt that Stevenson could never beat Eisenhower. Kennedy called Congressman Tip O'Neill to get Bobby named a delegate to the national convention, "in case lightning strikes."

———

AS HIS BROTHERS contemplated yet greater expansion of the family's power, Teddy had been reinstated at Harvard, partly because of his good Army service record. A reporter asked the elder Kennedy, "Where will Teddy go when he completes school?" "That's up to him," the father said, but he hoped Teddy might possibly be the one to get involved with some of the family business enterprises that had been neglected by his other sons. "Somebody has to watch the store."

Teddy had spent the summer in Europe, taking his Thunderbird with him, working hard at the playboy image. At Harvard, he soon was busy with football and girls, seldom dating the same girl twice. Teddy still had his wild side. Like Jack, he drove recklessly. He apologized for a speeding ticket, pleaded guilty, and added, "I am afraid I can offer no excuses." His brother Bob represented the family at Teddy's graduation from Harvard, and Bob reported to his father how surprised he was that Teddy had managed to graduate "considering everything about him," and then he added, "I guess Joe's, Jack's and my record at Harvard was a big help to him." That same year Harvard gave John Kennedy an honorary Doctor of Laws degree, making him one of the youngest alumni to be so honored.

Ted would always remember his first visit to the United States

Senate. "I'd come down to visit Jack on the night train, getting in early, and I arrived at his office at about 7:30 in the morning. No one was there. So I sat down on my suitcase out in the hall. Next door was the office of the Vice President, and just then Nixon came along. He introduced himself and invited me into his office. It was the first time I'd ever met him. We had a pleasant talk, sparring about who gets in first in the morning and that sort of thing. Later, my brother showed me all around the Senate. I was tremendously impressed."

He was impressed enough to apply for a summer intern job at the U.S. Senate.

"I talked with him," said Carl Marcy, aide on the Senate Foreign Relations Committee, "and explained we didn't take interns at that time because by the time they were properly cleared and knew their way around, the summer was over. . . . The fellow was very polite, and stood up to leave. And his name was Kennedy. On his way out, I said, 'Are you by any chance related to Jack Kennedy—Senator Kennedy on the committee?' He said, 'Yes, I'm his brother Teddy.' So he turned and left. No, he hadn't mentioned it till I asked it."

"Yes, that's the way it happened," Ted later said, "and that's the last time I ever applied for a job without using my brother's name!"

————

AT A PANEL on "Face the Nation" in 1955, Senator Kennedy said he would be honored to accept the vice-presidential nomination but gave four reasons making it unlikely: he was a Catholic; at thirty-nine, he might be considered too young; a southerner might bring a better balance to the ticket; and his vote in favor of the flexible farm support program had been unpopular. He hoped, though, "that no one would vote for a Catholic for Vice President because he was a Catholic or vote against him because he was a Catholic."

The fascination of a political convention comes from the constant air of unpredictability that hangs over it. The unexpected announcement can create a bandwagon psychology mixed with a sense of circus that can overturn the tightest political clique. Such was the announcement at the Democratic Convention of 1956 that the presidential nominee, Adlai Stevenson, would let the delegates choose their own vice-presidential nominee. Jack told Bobby to tell his father what he already suspected, that he was going to make a run for it. Ken O'Donnell was with Bobby when the call came through. "The Ambassador's language was loud and blue. He called Jack an idiot for ruining his career. The connection broke and Bobby hung up quickly. 'Whew!' Bobby said. 'Is he mad!' "

"The only advice I ever gave him was not to run for the vice presidency in 1956, but he didn't take that," said Joe. "I told him it was a terrible mistake and then I went over to Europe and I stayed there so there was no question of my interference. I knew Stevenson didn't have a chance. I felt that if Jack ran with him it would be a terrible mistake because it was hopeless."

But what was extraordinary about John Kennedy's decision was that for the first time he was fighting his father on a major political decision. Joe had denied him on some specific legislation, but never on anything so politically important. This conflict with his father had become cumulative, and easier to make—especially since his father had left the country.

If it was an important time for Jack, it was an equally important time for Bobby. Jack had been at the edge of his father's orbit when young Joe was alive, and it somehow seemed easier to edge away. But Bobby was always under his father's complete control. Only since his marriage did Bobby exercise a growing independence. But never, never before had he so openly sided with his brother against his father.

But now Bobby saw Jack representing adventure, a new world of excitement. They were caught in a political ferment that was irresistible. They saw a clear chance to win. More than anything else that had happened between them, joining forces against their father's wishes would create a lasting bond as brothers and as partners.

"Jack's campaign for the vice presidency followed exactly the same pattern as his '52 race and his other campaigns," said reporter Abe Michelson, who had kept close to Kennedy from the early days. "It was expensive and well-planned, but made to look amateurish and given that appearance of crusade zeal. The expenses were well hidden and God knows how you'd ever document them, but, if you were there at the time, you could see the money. They had space and telephones and operators and stenographers and money to entertain. Joe Kennedy was on the Riviera but he was on the phone repeatedly to John McClellan and Lyndon Johnson saying, 'How's my boy doing? What else should he be doing?' "

Joe called his son "an independent cuss," and had been violently against Jack's decision, but once it was made, he closed ranks and went to work.

Since the convention was in Chicago, Joe Sr. told officials of his Merchandise Mart there to help in any way they could. He also called former political cronies of the Roosevelt administration who were at the convention.

Jack's opponent, Senator Estes Kefauver (D. Tenn.), was nationally known, a strong liberal.

"I'll never forget Bobby Kennedy during the balloting," said North Dakota's Quentin Burdick, "standing in front of our delegation with tears in his eyes, pleading for our support. It didn't do any good. Jack had voted for sliding-scale supports and they don't like sliding-scale supports in our state."

After the zigzag close voting, Kefauver had won. Watching the returns from his hotel suite, Stevenson uttered an uncharacteristic word: "Shit." As much as he saw the Kennedy negatives, he disliked Kefauver much more.

"Something I'll never forget," said a dedicated Kefauver worker, "was Nancy Kefauver and the beautiful Jackie Kennedy in their boxes during the voting. There was no one around Nancy, and Jackie was surrounded by people. Then Estes won and suddenly there was no one with Jackie. She was left by herself at the end. She was pregnant and she just stood there and she was a very sad and forlorn figure."

"I remember Kennedy going to the podium to call for a unanimous vote for Kefauver," former Senator Abe Ribicoff told editor Woody Klein. "When he came down and shook my hand, I told him, 'Jack, next time we go all the way.' "

TV coverage of conventions was still something fresh and surprising in 1956, and a hundred million Americans were watching. They saw a young Senator on the podium before a packed national convention, listening to the roar, picking at some invisible dust on his boyish, handsome face, nervously dry-washing his hands, waving to yelling friends nearby, his smile tentative but warmly appealing, his eyes slightly wet and glistening.

John Kennedy spoke without notes, and his words were short, gallant, and touching. For the TV audience, it was a moment of magic they would not forget.

America was feeling its youth and vitality and Jack Kennedy reflected it. "I think he happened to hit TV at a time when TV was looking for a Jack Kennedy," said Ken O'Donnell.

————

"AFTER JACK LOST," said Smathers, "I went back with him and Jackie to their hotel room. I've never been to an Irish wake before, but I guess maybe this was it. All of Jack's buddies, Dave Powers and Kenny O'Donnell were there, Bobby, Eunice, Pat and Jean—a lot of the family was there. It was pretty crowded. Jackie shed a few tears—and Kennedy really showed more emotion than I'd really seen him display up to that point. . . . We were there about an hour and a half and all Jack could think of were all the different things he might have done that might have made the difference. He was hurt, deeply hurt. The thing is, he came so close. He's like all the Kennedys—once they're in something, they don't like to lose."

Bob said to him, "You're better off than you ever were in your life, and you made the great fight, and they're not going to win. You're going to be the candidate the next time."

Kennedy bristled. "This morning all of you were telling me to get into this thing, and now you're telling me I should feel happy because I lost it."

Jack never before had failed to get anything he really wanted. In public, he had been so graceful in defeat, but in private he was angry. Bob was bewildered. The great adventure had fizzled. Should they have listened more to their father? Bob had built up an image of his brother's invincibility, and now suddenly he saw him more as a human being. Still, he tried to be supportive. He also realized that his brother now needed him more than he had ever needed him.

"Coming back from the convention," said reporter Dave Talbot, "I was sitting right next to Bobby on the plane. He was pretty bitter. He said that they should have won and somebody pulled something fishy and he wanted to know who did it."

"If I had been there," said the father later, "I would have won that nomination for Jack. How? I would have had a recess after the first ballot, and that would have given us enough time to organize and win."

Afterward, Jack reflected on how things would have gone if his brother Joe had made the race instead of him. "Unlike me, he would not have been beaten. Joe would have won the nomination . . . and then he and Stevenson would have been beaten by Eisenhower, and today, Joe's political career would be in shambles, and he would be trying to pick up the pieces."

He was speaking matter-of-factly, but it would have been understandable if there had been a smirk in his voice. In the family competition, Jack was rapidly emerging more and more on his own, now far ahead of where the prize older brother had been, or even might have been.

———

ALTHOUGH JACK AND his wife barely had time to talk during the convention—she had stayed with the Shrivers all week—Jack and brother Teddy took off for a sailing vacation in the Mediterranean right after it ended, leaving behind a very pregnant Jackie. The premise was that he needed a vacation after all this, and she was too pregnant to go with him. The fact was that, even with the pregnancy, the marriage was floundering.

At her mother's Hammersmith Farm in Newport, in August 1956, Jacqueline had severe cramps and began to hemorrhage. She was rushed to the hospital and underwent an emergency cesarean section. The fetus was a stillborn girl.

When she recovered consciousness at two in the morning, Jacqueline found her brother-in-law Bob at her bedside, summoned by Janet Auchincloss. Jack was still on his yacht somewhere near Capri and nobody could contact him. "One of the things I've heard often in Boston," said columnist Marquis Childs, "is the story of how Jack and brother Teddy were on this ship in the Riviera with two whores just about the time Jackie was having her miscarriage of their first child."

Smathers finally contacted Jack, who seemed reluctant to cut short his sailing trip—especially, he said, since the miscarriage had already happened. But Smathers told him, "If you are ever planning to run for political office, get here in a hurry." He did.

It was Bob, not Jack, who arranged to bury the child. His brother had not arrived in time. Jacqueline said of Bob later, "You knew that if you were in trouble, he'd always be there."

Jacqueline went into a deep depression after the miscarriage. She was bitter at Jack for not being with her when she needed him most.

She was biting her nails now with an intensity, walking past old friends without seeming to see them. When Jack returned, one of their friends overheard an argument that ended with her saying, "You're too old for me."

"You're too young for me," he replied.

A newspaper friend, Paul Mathias of *Paris-Match*, described Jacqueline then as being erratic and out of control. She was later reported as a patient in Valleyhead, a private psychiatric clinic in Carlisle, Massachusetts.

"Joe Kennedy told me he had offered Jackie a million dollars not to divorce Jack," said columnist Igor Cassini. When she read Cassini's column, Jacqueline reportedly called her father-in-law and asked, "A million? Why not $10 million?" Jacqueline Kennedy later denied that story.

———

AT TWENTY-FOUR, Edward Kennedy, unlike his brother Joe, did not have good enough grades to get into Harvard Law School. And so he followed in his brother Robert's footsteps and enrolled at the University of Virginia Law School.

There was some initial problem of admission because he could not sign the initial pledge of new students, "On my honor, I have neither given nor received aid on term papers or examinations." He was finally admitted after a heated faculty vote.

Professor Neil Alford, who taught both Kennedys at the University of Virginia, noted, "I'd hate to compare the two," but felt that the records might show Bob "a little smarter." But Ted worked hard. Librarian Frances Farmer recalled that Ted and his friend Varick Tunney "would come in at eight o'clock in the morning, study until it was time for class, then return and sit just outside my office until it was time to close the doors."

"I've got to go at a thing four times as hard and four times as long as the other fellow . . . just to keep up," said Ted Kennedy. It was not surprising that he was treated for an ulcer while he was there.

One way he relieved the pressure was by drinking. Unlike his father and brothers, Teddy discovered he enjoyed alcohol. When he was arrested for drunken driving, convicted and fined $35, the story received national publicity. Teddy appeared penitently before his father, who said gruffly, "I don't care about the publicity, so long as they spell the name right." The old man apparently thought it more important at this point to assure his son of family solidarity. He would forgive much in Teddy that he did not in other sons.

For Joe, his youngest child was now the family joy. When Teddy came home for the holidays, he "would come into the room and pick up his mother from behind and twirl her, saying, 'How's my girl?' and then look over and say, 'Hi, Dad, you having any fun?' " When Teddy came home, everyone noticed how his father's face would beam.

Ted was growing up. The Harvard Spanish scandal had been a testing time, but then so was his service in the Army and his entrance into the real world. The hardworking success of Bob on the Labor Committee and Jack's catapult onto the national scene via TV at the convention were all stirring things in this young man. So was the fascination of politics. And threaded through it all was the renewed interest in him by his father.

His father realized that this playboy was no businessman, but that he was smart enough to be more than a playboy and that he must have his chance.

Joe and Jack had come of age when their father was often absent making his millions. The pressure for them was to compete for his praise. The pressure for Bob, growing up among a gaggle of girls, was to prove his worth as a tough man in a tough world. But for Teddy, written off as a playboy, the pressure was even more enormous. He had to deny himself, deny his personality, deny his love of fun and pleasure, and succeed when no one expected him to.

Like Bob, Teddy also became president of the Student Legal Forum. When he invited Bob as a speaker, Bob promptly poked fun at him for his traffic ticket. "My mother wants to know what side of the court my brother is going to appear on when he gets out of law school, attorney or defendant."

Joe Sr. did not concern himself with Ted's drinking or Jack's women—since he had his own history of assorted sins. He felt that success made any sin invisible, particularly when it came to himself and his sons.

The brothers were interested in that place within themselves where adventure left off and fear began. All of them tested these limits. Bob and Joe did it in the traditional male way: flying planes, running rapids, climbing mountains, going down dangerous ski slopes. Jack and Ted tested it in a different way. They tested the limits of social mores and propriety with drinking, reckless driving, having affairs. It provided a very similar thrill to see how far you could go without being caught.

Jack and Bob also tested those limits in the way they later would handle physical danger on the campaign trail. It was a crazy kind of Russian roulette. It's because of this kind of risk-taking on so many levels that people continue to be fascinated with the Kennedys and how much they would get away with. We all are intrigued with that part of the Kennedys (and ourselves): "How far would *I* go?"

Between semesters at law school, Ted attempted to scale the Matterhorn with Varick Tunney, a son of the former heavyweight champion. On Rimpfischhorn, Ted slipped, dangled over a 3000-foot chasm, and fell to a ledge. "Anybody else," Tunney recalls, "would have called it a day, but Teddy ate an orange and five minutes later we were climbing again and went on to the top."

Teddy's summer jobs ranged from being a crewman in a trans-Pacific yacht race to Honolulu, to being a forest ranger. He also did a summer at the International Law School in The Hague. Again, following in his brothers' footsteps, he reported for International News Service on the two months he spent with the French Army in Algeria.

When Teddy returned from Algeria, he and Jack and Laura Bergquist had dinner and Jack "was asking all these rapid-fire questions about Algeria . . . pumping Teddy like crazy about what the Algerian situation was, which Jack knew a great deal about, to my surprise. . . . Teddy wasn't a brain-picker."

Bob, like Jack, *was* a brain-picker. Adlai Stevenson named Joseph P. Kennedy an honorary cochairman of his National Business Council in 1956 and appointed Robert Kennedy as a special assistant on his campaign staff. This was a favor to the Kennedy father, who was still a contributor. "Joe thought Jack would eventually run and anything that Bob could learn from Stevenson's campaign would be useful," said Rose Kennedy.

"What struck me about Bob was that he was very young and quite aloof, really, and self-contained, and he didn't miss a single thing," said Harrison Salisbury of *The New York Times*. "The questions he asked were always very much to the point—about things that would directly concern him and his brother. It seemed to me he had very few friends in the campaign entourage. Nor did he try to make friends with these people, although later on many of them came over and joined the Kennedy group. I had the feeling that Bobby knew every single thing there was to know about a campaign. He just squeezed all that absolutely dry."

"I used to thank God at every stop that Stevenson hadn't picked my brother as his vice-presidential nominee because I knew that this whole Stevenson campaign was nothing but a great disaster area," Bob said. "He had to lose. I was learning what not to do in a presidential campaign for Jack in 1960."

John Kennedy also campaigned for Stevenson. "You know, Jack really was a very shy man," said Representative Hale Boggs. "We were riding along. . . . These Louisiana French people were all quite demonstrative. 'Hey, Jack! Hi, Jack! . . .' And I said to him, 'Look, either wave at the people or quit pulling those socks up. And the next time we come down here, for God's sake, get yourself a pair of garters or something! You can't ride around here with all these people and spend half your time pulling up your socks. . . .' It was one way he got rid of tension. As I told you, he never otherwise showed tension."

He showed it in all kinds of ways. News pictures almost invariably showed Kennedy with his hands stuffed into his side pockets. He kept his hands there to keep from giving in to nervous habits. "Kennedy is a knuckle rubber (fourth finger, left hand), forelock brusher, tie-knot shifter and teeth tapper," reported *Time* in 1961.

———

POLITICALLY, JACK HAD come a long way, and fast, but even he had no concept how much his political pace would speed up.

"I was having dinner with Jack and Jackie and a man named Smith and his wife," recalled Bill Walton. "Smith was a Republican and ambassador to Cuba, and his wife Flo was a former girlfriend of Jack's—she previously had been married to John Hersey. This was January 1957 and the Smiths were going to the Eisenhower inaugural and they were all dressed up in evening clothes. The rest of us were just sitting around in our everyday clothes to watch the inaugural on television.

"Jack and Jackie and I talked about this often, because only four years later—*four years later*—we were the ones going to the *Kennedy* inaugural."

Lem Billings recalled an equally memorable moment that year. It was at Palm Beach and he and Jack were laughing about some sexual adventures when the Kennedy father fiercely interrupted. "You're not to speak like that anymore," he told Lem. "There are things you just can't bring up anymore, private things. You've got to forget them. Forget the 'Jack' you once knew. Forget he ever existed. From now on you've got to watch everything you say. The day is coming, and it's coming soon, when he won't be 'Jack' anymore at all—not to you and not to the rest of us either. He'll be 'Mr. President.' And you can't say or do anything that will jeopardize that."

THE EIGHTY-FIFTH Congress opened in January 1957. Jack retained his position on the Labor and Public Welfare Committee and was also made a member of the Foreign Relations Committee. He had been chosen over Senator Estes Kefauver, even though Kefauver had seniority. Many saw the influential hand of the Kennedy father with Majority Leader Lyndon Johnson. Perhaps his earlier letter of presidential support for Johnson had paid off.

Senator Fulbright was then chairman of the Foreign Relations Committee. "One day, Fulbright came to me," said Carl Marcy, "and said, 'Carl, can't you get a quorum over here? . . . Call up that Jack Kennedy . . . I got him on the Foreign Relations Committee and all he does . . . if you ever get him here . . . is . . . autographing pictures of himself.' "

As Chief Counsel of the Second Investigating Committee, Robert Kennedy now directed his attention to labor racketeers. The committee was soon known as the Rackets Committee.

"Other congressional committees had looked into the Teamsters Union, but they'd all been fixed," said Walter Sheridan, who worked with Bob for four years. "The fixers also tried to move in on this committee, too. Whenever they'd go to John Kennedy, he'd say, 'Go see Bob.' They'd go to Bob, and he'd throw them out."

"Bobby was pretty green," recalled Arthur Goldberg, then general counsel for the AFL-CIO. "I remember when Bobby wanted to go after a union because the union paid the expenses of a staff member who was transferred from the West Coast to New York. He thought it was corrupt. I thought it was utter nonsense."

While Bobby was on the committee, he told Goldberg of the advisability of a bill giving him authority to tap the phones of labor leaders. "I said, 'You're out of your mind!' "

A headline read: MILLIONAIRE TO RUN SENATE RACKET PROBE.

And the story: "The big burden of this year's Senate 'spectacular' probe of labor racketeering—is on the shoulders of the shy-looking Boston millionaire with five children and an unruly head of hair."

Senator McClellan soon gave Bobby a fairly free hand, although some Senators felt it was too free. They complained that Bobby kept such tight personal control of his investigations that few of the minority members of the committee knew what he was doing. "Rarely had any Chief Counsel taken such complete charge of a Senate Committee's activities," said committee member Senator Barry Goldwater. "Bobby didn't consult us. We would arrive for hearings and there we would find witnesses called by the Kennedys without our knowledge."

Listening to witnesses, the brothers sat side by side, looking much alike, almost like a mirror act, the same infectious grin, the same twirling of hair around a finger, their glasses atop their heads, conferring constantly. It was the first time in their six years of public life that the Senator shared the limelight with his brother. Reporters, however, observed that Jack Kennedy seldom questioned witnesses. He stayed in the background to let Bob shine in the tough questioning, and repeatedly gave him public credit.

Bob's persistent grilling of the labor hoods absorbed the TV audience, and Bob now overshadowed his big brother as a national figure. As Chief Counsel, he was now the star, and his brother was simply another Senator on the committee. Their hearings were soon packed, often standing-room only.

It was a dramatic new setting for Bob. After being anonymous, so young and completely uncertain of his direction or goal, he now suddenly had the full focus of celebrity. For a man basically shy and unsure, this was strongly stimulating. "For the first time in his life he was happy," said Billings. "He'd been a very frustrated young man, awfully mad most of the time, having to hold everything in and work on Jack's career instead of his own."

Bobby still was quoted as saying Jack was heading for the top, and that his own number-one ambition was to advance Jack's career, his own progress taking second place. Sargent Shriver sent Bob some clippings with the note, "Your name is already becoming synonymous with something. Hope it is good." But Shriver was concerned enough about his brother-in-law Bob's performance to suggest that his father-in-law attend some of his son's hearings to get his own impressions.

Joseph Kennedy Sr. did not like what he saw and heard. He felt it would turn the labor movement against the Kennedys, particularly against Jack's presidential prospects. It resulted in the first heated confrontation between father and son. Bobby held his ground even when Joe drafted Justice Douglas to intervene. Bobby had considerable respect for Douglas but he still would not yield. He told Douglas that his new position represented "too great an opportunity."

To say no to Douglas, no to his father, and even place his new future ahead of his brother's future was a remarkable step for Bobby.

Jack was now concerned enough to discuss it with his good friend in the labor movement, Arthur Goldberg: "I think I'm gonna get the nomination. I'm well aware of the power of the labor movement. My record on labor matters is outstanding; but I'm caught in a very peculiar position. . . . Bobby is counsel. . . . I'm a member of that committee, too. And I don't want to get the reputation of being anti-labor."

"You can perform an important role," Goldberg told him. "You can see to it that the committee and your brother do not follow an anti-labor path. I think you can stand up to them, and should."

"I'll talk to Bobby," Jack replied.

————

IF ANYTHING, NOW there was perhaps an overeagerness about Bobby. He was impatient for results. The disgraced McCarthy was still a Senator, and called Bobby to denounce one of Bobby's staff appointments. After Bobby slammed down the receiver, he said, "Joe McCarthy, you're a shit."

"Almost day by day, you could see him developing," said his secretary Angie Novello. "All the other men on the committee were so much older than he. But interestingly, they now all called him 'Bob' . . . Nobody called him 'Bobby' on the Committee. . . . It was hard for us to say 'Bobby,' and the older men felt the same way—just a feeling of respect."

If "Bob," as he now was often called, still saw relationships in simplistic terms, then so did the public. They preferred political issues neatly packaged in black and white, good and bad. The public admired this young Kennedy trying to expose racketeering in the International Brotherhood of Teamsters, the country's most powerful union. They admired this intense young man attacking Jimmy Hoffa, the most powerful and most feared labor leader in the country.

His brother Jack didn't need causes, but Bob did. Jack saw Hoffa as an annoying phenomenon of corruption that existed in many other places. Bob Kennedy saw it as a matter of moral outrage. He saw it as a crusade and he was leading the movement.

"If Bob hadn't gotten into politics, he'd have been a Catholic crusader," claimed Fred Dutton. Alice Roosevelt Longworth envisioned Bob as a revolutionary priest.

"You should be in the hills with Castro and Che," photographer Stanley Tetrick once told him.

Bob thought, and after a long pause, said, "I know."

———

BOB WAS NOW getting more speaking requests (215 in 1957, of which he accepted only eight). He even had three fan clubs, including one in Brooklyn. From them he received the message: "We think you are the living end and a real doll."

The reaction that meant the most to Bobby was from his family. His favorite sister, the tall, chestnut-haired Pat, whom he called "Patticake," sent a telegram: WE DIDN'T THINK YOU HAD THAT MUCH KNOWLEDGE IN YOUR PIN-BALL MACHINE HEAD.

The press picked up the drama of the Hoffa vendetta. His defenders said Bob was trying to be a fair investigator, but that the technique of questioning was an art and he wasn't yet experienced at it. His critics saw an insolence in his manner and used words such as "browbeating," "bullying," "badgering," and even "vicious." When a Chicago lawyer called him a vicious little monster, Bob replied to the Associated Press: "Tell them that I said I'm not so little."

"Compared with this guy [Bobby]," said author Wilfrid Sheed, "Jack was all heart."

Bob admitted that his most obvious fault was his rudeness. "My biggest problem as counsel is to keep my temper. I think we all feel that when a witness comes before the United States Senate he has an obligation to speak frankly and tell the truth. To see people sit in front of us and lie and evade makes me boil inside. But you can't lose your temper—if you do, the witness has gotten the best of you."

During the Teamster hearings, Kennedy Sr. observed, "I doubt if Jack ever makes any enemies. But Bobby might make some. Not that Jack isn't just as courageous, but Bobby feels more strongly for or against people than Jack does—just as I do." What made this ironic was that Bob was attacking some of the same people his father had done business with. In some odd way, in attacking Hoffa, Bob was fighting aspects of his own father.

"Bob, who had an underlying distaste for the kind of people his father used to buy, recognized the devil in Hoffa," said columnist Murray Kempton. "Something absolutely insatiable and wildly vindictive. . . . Hoffa and Kennedy had feelings about each other of an intensity that can hardly be described."

When Hoffa was finally brought to trial for misusing union funds, Robert Kennedy recalled vividly how Hoffa's eyes burned into him as if they were burning holes with contempt and hate.

It wasn't long before Bob received threatening phone calls: "Lay off or we'll throw acid in your kids' faces." His wife was then pregnant with their seventh child.

Kempton told the story that Hoffa never turned the light off at his Teamster headquarters—which faced the old Senate Office Building where Bob Kennedy worked. Hoffa explained that if Bob left to go home and saw Hoffa's light on, he would immediately say to himself, "I'm not going to go home any earlier than that bastard." There was in both of them a passion for the other's discomfort.

How much Bobby accomplished was illuminated by the AFL-CIO vice chairman, who claimed that if Bob Kennedy had not done what he did on the Senate Investigating Committee, the Mafia would have controlled the labor movement within ten years.

Bobby sent Pierre Salinger to see Hoffa, at Hoffa's request. After more than an hour's wait, Salinger and an associate "were ushered into Hoffa's office and seated in low chairs in front of his desk. Hoffa, his own chair placed, like Mussolini's, on a slightly raised platform, stared down at them. Five union officials, clutching subpoenas, stood uncomfortably in a semicircle behind. In an apparent rage, Hoffa rose, grabbed the subpoenas from their hands, and waved them furiously at the men from the Rackets Committee. "You can tell Bobby Kennedy for me that he's not going to make his brother President over Hoffa's dead body."

———————

IN THE SENATE campaign, Jack and Bob had become politically close but now their political relationship was joined like the strands of a rope. More and more they now relied on each other as equals.

Yet they had reached an age when they began to compete—as they would for the rest of their lives. It would not have the tension of the Joe-Jack rivalry. The envy was there, but age gap and difference in temperament made the admiration stronger and deeper. And the loyalty was absolute. When it came to crisis, they were a single unit, one fierce force against the world.

After drafting a new labor bill, Jack told Ralph Dungan, "Let Bobby take a look at that draft." Even on a proposed labor speech, the Senator said, "Show it to Bobby."

"He turned to Bobby, to do things for him," said Dungan, "and tell him the hard facts when he needed to know them, but he did the real thinking."

"I don't think you can *overstress* the relationship between those two," said Washington correspondent Esther Tufty. "If one has a passion about education for Indians, they both had it . . . they were kind of more alert, because they were together. 'What I can't handle, you can.' "

"They did not need anyone else in the world," said Dave Powers. "They lived on each other."

A big question was: which brother had more impact on the other? As the older, with a broader, more sophisticated view of the world, Jack might well have softened Bob, perhaps made him more tolerant, more willing to compromise. Surely he also passed on his views on policy, personal philosophy, and commitment. More and more, their views became almost indistinguishable. But, in the later years, it would be the more emotional Bob who would have the greater impact on Jack on social issues.

Jack and Bobby began to have more fun together. They even raced each other in their cars over a bridge that crosses into Washington. There were some friends who watched Bob Kennedy drive so fast and furiously that they wondered if he would ever reach his next birthday.

Jack drove the same way. "I recall driving to the Washington airport in Kennedy's convertible, to catch a flight, with him at the wheel," said Bergquist. "Jackie was along, and she was amused by my terror at his driving. He drove very fast, as if he were gunning a PT-boat, weaving in and out of traffic."

Bob, who had skipped lightly and quickly through his books at college, saw his brother as the family intellectual, and deeply admired him for it. He saw Jack's enormous natural charm, which he could only envy but never imitate. And now he saw his brother on a clear path to the presidency, a path he could not even dream about for himself.

———

WHEN SENATOR JOSEPH McCarthy died in May 1957, it was symbolic in some ways, because Bob had moved so far away from his influence. But he still called in his staff "and stood in front of his desk—with his head down," said Novello, "and told us that he was going to close the office for an hour or two, out of respect for McCarthy. . . . It was the only time I saw tears in his eyes."

Robert Kennedy was the only Kennedy to attend McCarthy's funeral. Reporter Eddie Bayley observed that Bob stayed in the background, and afterward asked a favor of the reporter: "In your article, please don't mention that I was here."

"I remember later when we saw McCarthy's widow," said Laura Bergquist. "Bobby went over to her and embraced her, but Jack kept clear. Perhaps because I was there; but I don't think he would have embraced her, anyway."

———

JACQUELINE KENNEDY'S FATHER, John Vernon Bouvier III, died in August 1957, and her relationship with Joseph Kennedy Sr. grew closer than ever. In that whole family, he alone served as her anchor. "They would talk about everything, their most personal problems," said Bill Walton. Friends remember a very pregnant Jacqueline sitting for hours by her father-in-law's side, seeking from him all the attention her own father had given so sporadically.

Three months after Black Jack's death, on November 1957, Jacqueline finally gave birth to her first child, Caroline Bouvier Kennedy. After Caroline was born, the marriage improved. Motherhood made Jacqueline a more typical wife of the Kennedy tribe. Jack would quote one of his father's favorite, and much repeated, quotations, which he had used at the start of World War II: "He who has a wife and child gives hostages to fortune."

The new family was promptly featured in a *Life* cover story, and Jack was both envied and criticized by many. Among them was a Wisconsin Congressman who complained, "People will come out to see him the way they will to see a movie star, but they're not for him for President. He's not a President, he's a boy. The people don't want a boy for President in these times. Those crowds don't mean a thing."

Jack hadn't even proclaimed himself as a presidential candidate. But he was always acting like a candidate and kept telling friends that the time was now. The vice-presidential race had pulled John Fitzgerald Kennedy into the circle of power.

After the *Life* story appeared, a pretty high-school editor at a press conference for young people asked the Senator, "Do you have an 'in' with *Life*?" When the laughter subsided, Kennedy replied, "No, I just have a beautiful wife." After *Time* also had a flattering cover story on John Kennedy, his father wrote to Beaverbrook, "Weren't you surprised that *Time* went as far out as it did for Jack on his article?"

The father was not surprised. He was close to the Luces. He had recruited Henry Luce to write the foreword to Jack's first book. He had given Luce's son a job on his Hoover Commission. But, more than that, the Kennedy candidacy was picking up a glow of its own, and naturally the press wanted to cover it.

Columnist Rowland Evans and John Kennedy were walking along the street one day. They saw some women's magazines, and almost every one had Jack on the cover. Evans said, "Gee, Jack, you must be getting sick of all that stuff—all these magazines, what do they write about? Aren't they all writing about the same thing?"

"Yes, I am getting a little sick of it," Jack replied, "but what do you want me to do about it? Tell the magazine writers not to write about me and send them back to their office empty-handed? Of course not. Besides"—and he paused—"these stories about me do have one effect. They help take the 'V' out of 'V.P.' "

Joe had told Ed Plaut that the main reason magazines put Jack on their cover was that his face sold a record number of copies. "There is no answer to Jack's appeal. I can't explain that."

PUBLICLY, JACK KEPT denying any presidential ambitions. But, as his wife later admitted, "he was running, running, running."

Meanwhile, Joseph Kennedy Sr. wanted more than a Senate reelection victory for Jack—he wanted an overwhelming victory—the largest margin of victory in the history of the state—as a prelude to the presidential campaign."

"So I developed a campaign," said Larry O'Brien. "It would include a carefully planned, perceptibly vigorous, aggressive campaign on the part of the candidate."

Part of the reason for the vigorous schedule was to counteract any impression of Jack's physical weakness since the surgery. O'Donnell described the "feverish schedule, from 6 A.M. till 12 o'clock at night . . . cruel . . . but this is the toughest young guy you ever met in your life." Joe, however, was not impressed with the campaign. "It's terrible; throw it out." Jack quietly replied, "Dad, why don't we try out the first phase of this, just to see how it goes?"

Joe later told O'Brien, "You know, Larry, Jack is destined. He'll be President of the United States. He's destined to be President."

"I accepted that," O'Brien later recalled to an interviewer, "except as I'm winding my way around the towns that day, it did enter my mind that if destiny is the determining factor here, I'm wasting a lot of my time, for there's no need for any of this."

WHEN JACK'S COLLEGE classmate Torby MacDonald, then a Congressman, complained about being known as a Kennedy protégé, Jack told him, "I had to live under my father's name for thirty years. I outgrew it and I guess you can outgrow me."

In a large sense, he had outgrown it. When he differed with his father on certain issues, he voted his own way. In each instance, his father would protest, but not insist. It is also surely true that if young Joe had lived to be Senator, his liaison with his father would have been smoother because their opinions were cut from the same cloth, their attitudes and opinions much the same, and equally intense. But most of all, because no son ever tried harder to please and copy his father.

Jack still needed his father: his father knew how to market a product, and Jack was now the product. Publicity was key. His father told Tommy Corcoran that by the time the next Democratic National Convention opened, "Jack's name will be known to everybody in the country and there won't be a place in America where he isn't familiar." His father said that Jack would be a celebrity prince, the only presidential candidate a woman would read about while sitting under a hair dryer.

Corcoran told Richard Whalen, "Joe sent his girls to the Church to believe, and his sons to the marketplace to know better. He thought like a king and kings aren't nice guys."

The father sharply respected the power of print. It had destroyed his own career and would catapult his son's. He passed on to his sons the political wisdom of cultivating newspapermen. Jack, particularly, played the press with special skill.

Haynes Johnson, a young reporter with the Washington *Star* in 1957, was prepared to dislike Jack Kennedy when he first met him. "Everything I knew about him put me off," he later remembered. "The robber-baron-type father, the supposedly ruthless younger brother . . . the suffocating sense of family dynasty.

"He was tall, slim, deeply suntanned. He had a shock of reddish-brown hair . . . somewhat startling in its luxuriance. A broad smile crossed his face. He moved quickly, with an easy grace, straight toward the press table and directly at me. His blue eyes were sparkling as if he and I shared a secret joke. He held out his hand, and said, in a broad Boston accent, 'How *are* you?' He pumped my hand vigorously as if genuinely delighted at meeting an old friend, all the while smiling that mischievous smile. We had never met. He knew it, and what's more, he knew that I knew it. You son of a bitch," I said to myself. "You've got me."

Some insisted that Kennedy's relationship with the press was the greatest con game in the world.

Many admittedly found it hard to maintain their skepticism and independence when confronted with his personal charm and youth. "It was almost as if one of our own had made it," said *New York Times* correspondent Jack Raymond. Laura Bergquist found him "one of the smartest, quickest, funniest human beings I'd ever met. . . . He had such a curious mind, was so open to discussion that you could talk to him about almost anything without him getting angry. I felt, if I was deeply interested in a specific issue, and talked to him long enough, that I might even change his mind about it. At least he made me *feel* I could do that. He made you feel important." She also added, "If he thought you had something, he listened. If he didn't, he could kick the crap out of you with a few words."

Others felt he was too young, that he did his homework on some issues but lacked heart, that he had too many of his father's wayward habits.

"But unlike his father," said James Reston, "he knew the world was round, and he was loyal to his party and to his allies. He was a little too clever and fancy for my taste, but he was intelligent, half Irish and half Harvard, irresistibly witty, and like all the Kennedys, recklessly handsome."

———

IT ALL SEEMED to be going so smoothly. He had much of the press on his side. As his father had predicted, he was becoming a celebrity prince. Joe Kennedy should have been delighted.

Charles J. Lewin, editor of the influential New Bedford *Standard-Times,* recalled something surprising. "Joseph Kennedy said something which amazed me: Joe said he got down on his knees every night and prayed Jack wouldn't have to take the job."

Close Kennedy friends Charles Bartlett and Red Fay both remembered "the old man" telling them that Jack was running for the presidency too soon, that his timing was all wrong—the economy under Eisenhower was too good and there wasn't any threat of war. Besides, he was too young and would have to fight the Catholic issue. "He won't have a chance," the father told the two men. "I hate to see him and Bobby work themselves to death and lose."

"Then Jack walked in," said Bartlett, "and the Ambassador switched gears flip-flop. He was ebullient, enthusiastic, told Jack he would sweep the election."

When a reporter asked Joe whether young Joe might have been a presidential contender if he had lived, Joseph Kennedy now said, "Oh no. None of my other sons have Jack's universal appeal. Joe didn't have Jack's universal appeal."

Historian Arthur Schlesinger, Jr., who knew young Joe, agreed with the father. "I doubt whether young Joe, for all his charms and gifts, would have been President."

Jacqueline Kennedy agreed. "Jack does have the potential for a President. He knows how to pick smart people to do things and he thinks things out for himself. . . . No matter how many older brothers and fathers my husband had, he would have been what he is today—or the equivalent in another field."

But New Hampshire publisher William Loeb told reporter Sarah McLendon that he had paid a visit in Massachusetts to old man Kennedy during the campaign. "Joe pointed up on the wall to a portrait of his son Joe Jr. and said, 'That is the boy that should have been President. . . . That's the one—he'd make a wonderful President . . . and this one would've been a college professor."

There was a small incident illustrating a difference between Jack and Joe, and how it reflected in the father's feelings. Joseph P. Kennedy had three or four cars to take his friends to the 1955 Harvard–Yale football game, and ordered the police to sound the sirens all the way to the stadium. Jack crouched hidden down in the back while his father mocked him. Young Joe, of course, would have sat up proudly alongside his father.

At Palm Beach, the father pointed to Jack swimming in the pool and told Spalding, "I just can't understand that fellow . . . I don't know where he comes from. He's not like me, at all. Bobby's like me, but Jack . . . I couldn't do what he's done."

"I don't want to be a grasping father," Joe Sr. later added. "They'll make it on their own. They don't need me to fight my fight again. . . . I don't want my enemies to be my sons' enemies or my wars to be my sons' wars. I lived my life, fought my fights, and I'm not apologizing for them. And I don't want my son to apologize for any of my fights or my wars."

He later told Bob Considine, "My day is done . . . now it's their day."

Jack knew his father's liabilities. When London *Sunday Times* correspondent Henry Brandon asked to see his father, Kennedy replied, "Henry, if you do, you'll never speak to me again."

But to another reporter Jack responded, "If I need somebody older, there's no need to go outside the family. I can always get my father."

6

THE BIG PRIZE

Jack was invited one evening to the Georgetown home of columnist Joseph Alsop to present his views on the state of the Democratic Party at the next presidential election. Kennedy made an eloquent point of saying that the Democratic Party had better change its ways or it would end up without a single Catholic vote. When Kennedy was leaving, Alsop said he felt assured that Kennedy would be offered the vice-presidential nomination at the next Democratic National Convention. Kennedy barely smiled and replied, "But you have to remember that I am completely against vice in all forms."

He was even more firm about it talking to this author in a Piper Cub, en route to a speech. John Kennedy then explained why he felt the time was now. It was now for him, he said, because he felt he was at his peak. If he didn't go for it this time, another Democrat might get in and stay for eight years, during which time all kinds of fresher faces might emerge. "Otherwise I'd rather concentrate on being a good Senator. And being a good Senator has more importance for me than being Vice President. That's a dead job. VP with Adlai? No, he's a fuss-budget about a lot of things and we might not get along. Anyway, I think I'd see a lot more action and have more fun in the Senate."

"What you need in there at the top," Jack's father said, "is a man who has the knowledge and the courage to make cold decisions without being influenced by friendship or emotion, a man who respects only the objective facts. Most of the President's work and his big responsibility is settling fights between the Secretary of State and the Secretary of Defense, between the Treasury and the Federal Reserve system, between the Army and the Air Force. The President has to lay down the law in such arguments and make it stick. I may be prejudiced because he's my son, but I think Jack has both the wide factual knowledge and the cold dispassionate decisiveness that the job requires, more so than any other candidate. If I thought he was just a glamour boy with a good appearance and a nice way with people, I wouldn't be for him—and that's no baloney."

But John Kennedy once told New York *Post* publisher Dorothy Schiff, "You know, if I were running on the Communist ticket, my father would be working just as hard."

"Piecing it all together, I'm confident that the father does a great deal that Jack isn't aware of," said Anthony Gallucio. "I believe that the father pays people right on Jack's staff to con Jack into doing things the father couldn't persuade him to do by the direct approach, that the father manipulates things, pays for things, goes ahead with plans without Jack's knowledge. Jack simply lacks the backbone to read his old man the riot act."

Jack would never do so because he knew how much he needed Joe Sr. Jack told author Joseph McCarthy that Lyndon Johnson had Franklin Roosevelt and Sam Rayburn behind him on the way up. Symington had Harry Truman. Kennedy observed that he had nobody but his father.

JOE KENNEDY HAD told him, "This country is not a private preserve for Protestants. There's a whole new generation out there, and it's filled with the sons and daughters of immigrants and those people are going to be mighty proud of one of their own running for President. And that pride will be your spur, it will give your campaign an intensity we've never seen in public life."

For obvious political reasons, John Kennedy always minimized his father's influence. "People can't advise you on how to run your campaign," he said. "I get all kinds of advice every day. The decisions have to be made on the spot. Advice can't be given from a distance."

And, more often now, without confrontation, Jack did step in to stop his father. On one occasion the father called the clan together with a select group of political associates. Jack briskly called off the meeting. The rest of the family, used to unquestioning obedience to the old man's wishes, were stunned, but old Joe agreed without protest. Jack also fired a few people because he suspected them of being his father's men and not his own.

Myer "Mike" Feldman was part of Jack's inner circle on economic issues. When he issued a press release for a higher minimum-wage law, Joe accused him of destroying the campaign. At a staff meeting the father was there when Jack asked, "Well, Mike, what do you think? Think that's the best way to do it?"

"Sure."

"Okay, we'll go with it."

———

WHEN HIS FATHER brought a big contribution from one of his less savory friends, Jack returned it as too hot to keep.

"If Jack had known about some of the telephone calls made on his behalf to Tammany-type bosses, his hair would have turned white," said O'Donnell. "You know, the old man is hurting you," a friend once told Jack. "Can't you keep him out of the picture?"

"What do you want me to do?" Jack replied. "My father is working for his son. Do you want me to tell my father to stop working for his son?"

He would even joke about it. He told the Washington correspondents at their annual Gridiron dinner, "I have just received a cable from Dad. It says, 'Dear Jack. Don't buy a single vote more than necessary—I'll be damned if I'm going to pay for a landslide.' " One of the reporters had written fresh lyrics to "My Heart Belongs to Daddy." One line went: "Just send the bill to Daddy."

The family member with the greatest administrative skills was brother-in-law Steve Smith. "Eleven months before JFK even declared for President, Smith had a smooth operation going in the Esso building," said David Hackett. "He did everything from handling the money to chiding the girls when they overspent the coffee allowance. He scheduled trips and did the boring, painstaking, unglamorous work—like keeping card files on nearly 30,000 Democrats who might be for us. . . . Steve filled the gap of technician. He could be mighty tough, too, in knocking heads together.''

Until he married Jean Kennedy, Steve Smith had done nothing more political than be elected secretary of his class at Georgetown. Sitting quietly, unobserved as usual, slim, unflustered, Smith was unsung and underestimated. Somebody described him as ''a younger JFK crossed with a younger Frank Sinatra.'' The son of a wealthy tugboat owner in New York, Smith was boyish-looking, blue-eyed, a smooth dresser, and the best dancer in the Kennedy family. He could go under a mambo bar, knees first, with his head only two feet off the floor. He was also a nearly professional mimic, specializing in German submarine commanders.

Smith was also described as ''a Kennedy before the mold has hardened.'' No in-law came closer to being a Kennedy brother. Unlike Lawford, Smith was anonymous. ''There's no advantage for me to talk about myself to the papers.'' Unlike Shriver, he was not ambitious. ''I'm not running for anything. I'm not contemplating running for anything.''

Joe took to Smith immediately. What the elder Kennedy liked was Smith's description of his position on the hockey team at Poly Prep in Georgetown: ''I played attack.''

Smith not only clearly matched the Kennedy competitive instincts, but he had something all the brothers lacked: he was very good with finances. His wife feelingly remarked on this, ''Thank God.''

Steve Smith said that once a week he went through every one of Jack's suits to collect all the cash and checks, and used them for the campaign. Kennedy would accept contributions and forget about them. Steve collected thousands of dollars every week.

Jimmy Breslin later told of a fund-raiser that resulted in checks for $60,000 plus $45,000 in cash. When Ken O'Donnell reported this to the candidate, Jack said, ''You keep the checks, I'll take the cash.'' He put it in his pocket and walked out. In fund-raisers there were always those who preferred to give cash, to keep it off the record, especially those who gave to both sides.

One of the reasons the brothers liked to carry large sums of cash, according to Ted Kennedy's aide in later years, Richard Burke, was to pay expenses for a visiting woman—something they did not want to put on their credit cards.

————

AT THE GOVERNORS' Conference in Florida in May 1958, Abraham Ribicoff of Connecticut urged the election of John Kennedy as President in 1960. Privately, Ribicoff confided that "Kennedy could never be President because he is so frail. He lives on pills. He has blue pills for this and pink pills for that."

For Jack Kennedy, the pain was a constant. "He was on crutches two-thirds of the time," said his friend Larry Newman. "Inside the house, and around the yard, he would be on crutches almost constantly. . . . When he wanted to get out, he'd only go out after he had the Novocain shots. . . . To the very end, he'd never mention much about it, but he'd say to me, 'Pick your daughter up and put her on my lap.' Because he couldn't reach down . . . and she was just a little thing. His back was that bad."

————

WHILE SMITH DIRECTED the undeclared race for the presidency, Jack selected Ted to manage his campaign for his reelection to the Senate—and he and Jacqueline went to Europe.

Ted Kennedy was twenty-six, still in law school, and hardly knew the state. But there was no risk in this reelection. Besides, his father wanted Ted to have the experience of a major campaign. Larry O'Brien and Kenny O'Donnell would be there for professional help. Both O'Brien and O'Donnell, however, would also be concentrating on plans for the upcoming presidential election.

"Teddy Kennedy was better with people he didn't know, even better than Jack Kennedy was ever to be," said Edward McCormack. "Jack didn't really like adulation, open flattery embarrassed him, but Teddy was already a free-wheeler, a swinger, he liked to be with people, good with the glad hand, the big smile, the slap on the back."

If Joe had much to do with Jack's final proposal to Jacqueline, he was less successful with his son Ted. For Ted, the senior Kennedy originally selected Jacqueline's stepsister, Nina Auchincloss. Nina later married a liberal Republican Congressman.

Ted's future bride was handpicked by his sister, Jean. When Ted Kennedy first came to Manhattanville College to help dedicate a new gym, Jean steered Joan Virginia Bennett to him and said, "I want you to meet my little brother."

"I expected to see a small boy, and instead I found myself looking up at a six-foot-two, two-hundred-pound, and I must say darn good-looking fellow," said Joan. "It was just lucky that I was in my senior year, because only seniors were invited to the tea following the dedication to meet the Kennedy family and Cardinal Spellman."

Virginia Joan Bennett later described herself as a quiet, studious Girl Scout, a "little Miss Goody Two-Shoes." She also happened to be strikingly blond and beautiful. Joan was then a virgin, and intended to remain one until she married. She told friend and former employer Marcia Chellis the reason she "caught" Ted was that "he couldn't get me any other way."

After Joan graduated from Manhattanville that June, Ted invited her to Hyannis for the weekend to meet his mother. Rose quickly put Joan at ease. "My dear, I said the Rosary every night. You were an answer to my prayers—the girl I dreamed of my son marrying."

Rose later called Mother O'Byrne to inquire about Joan Bennett's grades and her behavior at school.

Joan met Joe after his usual summer holiday on the Riviera. "I'd heard terrifying stories about him—I was scared to death to meet him. I'll never forget it—he sat in this big wing chair at the far end of the large living room and I went in all by myself. I sat at his feet on an ottoman. . . . First thing he asked me was, 'Do you love my son?' I thought it a rather needless question at the time, but looking back, there were lots of girls who would have wanted to marry his son, and he wanted to be sure my intentions were honorable!

"My first impressions were that he was a very shrewd man, not unloving, but a man who penetrated every situation and asked the right questions. . . . Poor guy, he was barely home when he was hit with the news about his son's intentions to marry. But his priorities were right. He knew I was leaving the next day, so he wanted to meet with me right then. When the interview was over (and it was an interview) he said if we wanted to get married, we had his blessing. . . . He may have been tough, but he did make you feel at ease."

Because of Ted's new role as campaign manager, Joan said, "We didn't see each other from the time of his proposal until the engagement party.''

At the engagement party, she still didn't have an engagement ring. "Ted's father knew Ted had to give me a ring, so he bought one and had it sent over to my father's office." Joan's father passed on the package to Ted, who handed it to Joan as they descended the staircase for the party—he hadn't even unwrapped the box to look at the ring—a huge emerald-cut diamond engagement ring, so big that Joan called it her "skating rink."

As the date of their wedding approached, Ted suddenly got a case of cold feet, and he called Joan to ask if she would consider postponing it. She would not. "If you don't marry me the day we planned," she told him firmly, "you'll never see me again." They had been courting for almost a year, and finally married in 1958.

On the surface, they were well matched. Both were Catholic, socially prominent, beautiful people. But each needed a spouse with special strength, and neither was strong enough. Both had lived soft lives, cushioned from reality by strong families with much money. Her father, Harry Bennett, was a highly successful advertising man who doted on his two daughters. Joan fully expected life to continue that way, with her husband supplying added dollops of romance and excitement. Teddy needed a wife who was more of a partner, somebody to push and encourage him, quash his constant doubts, act as a buffer when needed. Joan could never be a buffer, just as Teddy could never be a protective romantic. Both were highly vulnerable.

Ted's reluctance to marry may well have imitated Jack's reluctance. Ted was then twenty-six, and Jack had not married until he was thirty-seven. It was true that Bobby and Ethel were perfectly happy, but Ted knew he was more like Jack in personality. They had chased women together on the Riviera even when Jacqueline was pregnant.

Then, too, Ted had always been the irresponsible, babied member of the family; now he would have new responsibilities and expectations. He also wanted to be treated with more respect by his brothers, so he had to act older. Marriage was the first step toward growing up.

Since he was so busy campaigning, and she hardly saw him, Joan herself had last-minute questions about postponing the wedding. Her father met with Teddy and Joe Sr. Teddy might well have been willing, but "Joe Sr. was furious," said Joe's sister, Mary Lou McCarthy, "and said they're not going to put in the papers that my son is being tossed over. He forced the issue. He was God.''

Francis Cardinal Spellman celebrated the nuptial Mass at St. Joseph's Church in Bronxville and Jack served as best man.

"JPK wanted to invite every political crony he'd ever met, and others he wanted to impress," said Joan.

A friend filmed the ceremony, and Joan's father slipped in a microphone to help record it. "Later, when Ted told Jack about the 'bug,' Jack was really embarrassed," said Joan, because when they were behind the altar, he was giving Ted a big-brother-to-little-brother talk about marriage! Jack blushed scarlet when he found out [this was edited out of the film].''

It was Ted's last year at the University of Virginia Law School. "Ted's roommate moved out and I moved in," said Joan. After graduation she found an apartment in Boston, while her husband joined his brother's campaign.

"I told my daughters-in-law, because they were not brought up in politics, that they might get anonymous letters," said Rose Kennedy, "or they might hear scandal about members of the family, and if they did they should just tell Mr. Kennedy, and then he would turn it over to the detectives to take care of it. It was nothing to be alarmed about, so they would understand it from the beginning, otherwise they might be very unhappy.''

Joan soon saw the reality of her own future problems. "I suppose he will always be a magnet for women," she said of her husband. "No one ever wants to hear about two people in love, though," she added somewhat wistfully. "They'd rather hear about hanky-panky.''

Jack was always very protective of Joan. "Jackie could take care of herself," he said. "Joan couldn't.''

————

DOCTORS ONCE HAD told Jack Kennedy that he would be dead by the time he was forty. But he was now forty and had survived Last Rites three times. Thanks to medical discoveries, doctors now told him that his Addison's disease was no longer fatal and could be carefully controlled. Since he wasn't doomed to die soon, he saw the presidency as a clearer course.

As he told neighbor Nancy "Aunt Nan" Coleman at the Hyannis

Circus Dance, "I not only goddamn *want* to be President, but I goddamn *will* be President." And when his good friend John Sharon mentioned that, after all, he was still very young, still had plenty of time to try again, "his whole face contorted, and he almost banged his fist and leaned his face close to mine and said, 'I must get it *now, now!*' "

That November he was reelected to a second term in the Senate by nearly three quarters of a million votes—the largest margin in the history of Massachusetts.

Friends noted a definite transformation. Right after the war, Jack had joked about being a hero just because his boat was sliced in half. Now friends noticed he wore a tie clip with a very big silver PT boat on it, and his office was decorated with pictures and models of PT boats. They also observed that he seemed bored by any subject except politics.

Jack was now obsessed with the presidency.

———

ROBERT KENNEDY HAD resigned from the Rackets Committee in September 1959 to write a book about it—*The Enemy Within*—with the help of John Seigenthaler. The book detailed his battle with labor racketeers, and was well received. Since election night 1958, when they had watched the returns together, Bob had not been much involved in his brother's push for the presidency.

He did prod Jack. Friend Paul "Red" Fay recalled Bobby then asking, "All right, Jack, what are you doing about the campaign? I mean, have you done anything about the campaign yet? What sort of organization have you arranged? And where are we going? I don't hear anything about what you're doing and what you're saying about the campaign." Jack leaned over to Fay and said, "How would you like to hear that raspy voice in your ear for the next six months?"

But Jack soon admitted to his friends, "I need Bobby."

He needed Bobby as his presidential campaign manager, not only because they sparked each other and fitted perfectly together but because Bobby was one of the very few people who could safely tell him to go to hell when he believed Jack was wrong.

Jack respected his brother's mind and judgments and was willing to give him much more responsibility than he would give anybody else.

Bobby made the tactical decisions; Jack made the strategic decisions. In this, it was much like that Senate campaign. Jack concerned himself with policies, principles, and speeches, while Robert organized and staffed the campaign. Bobby concentrated on the daily details, Jack on the long-term ideas.

What Jack knew was that if he lost, it would be largely blamed on his Catholicism and he would be politically dead. This was his one big shot. It gave the campaign an added intensity. For Bobby it was a multiplied pressure.

Jack and Bobby worked out an unwritten, three-phase program for the campaign: an organizational phase that ended on Labor Day, a second phase that concentrated on issues, and a final phase that would be tough, no-holds-barred.

Jack could be choleric but seldom vindictive; Bobby was often both. "I'm going to see that he never gets another job!" Bobby would say about a campaign worker who had failed them in some way. "Now, Bobby," interrupted his brother, "we don't want to get into that. Let's just fire him and forget it."

Bobby would neither forget nor forgive.

"Anybody who'd ever been against his brother, or who wasn't a hundred percent for his brother, was on Bobby's Absolute Shit-List, the 'kill list,'" observed *Newsweek* Washington editor Ken Crawford.

As in the Senate campaign, the brothers saw each other seldom, but talked to each other almost every night, wherever they were. They discussed strategy, problems, personnel, and ideas for speeches. If Jack had a bad day, Bobby was full of reassurance—as their father always was. Like his father, Bobby was also more aggressive and decisive than Jack.

Both were impulsive with their ideas and anxious for action. But Jack was "smooth as silk, considerate," asking, "Would you mind doing that?" Bobby would say, "Do it! I want you to have that done immediately; bring it back to me!"

Occasionally Jack would step in to stop his brother. "I saw him get mad one time, about Bobby, on the campaign," said Hugh Sidey. "He read a story about Bobby's attacking somebody, some Democrat. . . . Kennedy was tired, I guess; and he kinda blew up. 'God, Kenny, will you just tell Bobby to lay off this stuff? We don't need this. . . . Don't waste his energy! Attack Republicans!'"

Later, Ed Plaut asked him, "Has your brother helped or hurt you?" Jack quickly replied, "I'll take all his enemies if I can have all his friends too."

When Pierre Salinger came to work as the campaign publicity director, Jack made it very clear to Salinger that "he was hiring me strictly because Bobby has asked him to." Salinger had worked for Bobby on the Rackets Committee. Shortly after that, Bobby told Salinger to issue a statement on something, and Salinger did. The next day, candidate Kennedy angrily told Salinger, "Check those things with me. . . . You're working for me now, not for Bob."

But Jack would always defend his brother to others. "I understand you don't like Bobby," Jack said to one writer, who said he had never met Bobby. "I know Bobby rubs some people the wrong way, but you'll like him when you get to know him."

Jack knew that Bobby was fighting for him with all his boundless energy. He knew that no matter how much Bobby was being hit and hurt by others, it would never slow him down. What Bobby was now giving of himself was irreplaceable, something money could not buy. The money Joe had spent on his son's Senate race was small compared to what was needed now. Fortunately, money still wasn't a problem.

Fortune listed Joseph P. Kennedy as one of the sixteen richest people in the United States. His fortune was approximated at $400 million. When he left the movie industry, Kennedy Sr. had a fortune of $5 million and was thirty-two pounds underweight. But he had stock market tickers in all his homes where he sunned himself and waited for the market to recover. Then he gained some weight and multiplied his fortune.

Money couldn't pay for the intense loyalty of family and hundreds of close friends, but it gave the Kennedy name a glamour that pulled in volunteers by the thousands. Sometimes money could even buy the press. "For a fee of some hundred thousand dollars," said Charles Bartlett, "a man named Benjamin Sonnenberg [a major New York public relations man] practically guaranteed a *Life* cover. And, indeed, Jack's picture appeared there when he didn't even know it was going to happen." Of course, it might well have been a coincidence.

Beaverbrook suggested to Joe that this was the year he would get "the reward you so richly deserve—your son in the White House." Max added a postscript that Joe had surely contemplated often:

"Looking back on your own career, I am convinced that, had you not had to strive so hard in your early days for money to pay living expenses, you would have devoted yourself to politics. In that case, you would have had a term or two in the White House yourself."

———

JACK FELT INCREASINGLY that he understood the current world better than his father did. As his own self-confidence swelled, it left less room for his father's ego. "He can't run my campaign sitting out in Nevada or on Cape Cod, and he doesn't. He's really had less to do with the campaign than any other members of my family."

This, of course, was hardly true. His father was busier than ever.

In a family gathering, Hugh Sidey asked Red Fay about Joe Kennedy's impact. Fay discussed the father's crucial importance until he saw Jack run a finger across his throat to cut him short. Jack later told him, "God, if I hadn't cut you off, Sidey would have headed his article 'A Vote for Jack Is a Vote for Father Joe.' This is just the material *Time* would like to have—that I'm a pawn in Dad's hands. That it's really not Jack himself who is seeking the presidency but his father. That Joe Kennedy now has the vehicle to capture the only segment of power that has eluded him."

Ted Sorensen summed it up well: "The Ambassador was never present, but his presence was never absent."

———

"JOE KENNEDY IS a twisted disreputable man," said columnist Marquis Childs. "Some people have told me that one of the reasons they're afraid of Jack getting to be President is that the old man has such a long shit-list of people to get back at, and he will."

"I'm beginning to believe a little bit the story that the old man has somebody in every state now," said Washington editor Helen Fuller. "And I don't think it bothers Jack one bit. . . . I don't think he cares what's being done for him, as long as he doesn't know all about it, doesn't have to touch his fingers with it. Jack wants this nomination awful bad."

The pressure to support Jack was heavy everywhere. A furious, bitter Democratic state committeeman privately protested, "When the Kennedy people say they want to see you, it's not an invitation and it's not a request—it's an order. You don't say no to the Kennedy people.'' A Missouri state chairman asked a writer whether he had been bought up by Joe Kennedy. "Everybody else has been . . . they'll stop at nothing.''

————

AS JACK PREPARED to announce his candidacy, two authors were collaborating on a political book to be called *Front Runner, Dark Horse*, comparing the campaigns of Senators John Kennedy and Stuart Symington of Missouri. The Kennedys were concerned that this book might feature some facts the Kennedys would rather forget. Besides, they already had approved an authorized biography to appear before the convention. John Kennedy managed to kill the *Front Runner* contract negotiations by personally informing the publisher he would never cooperate with the authors. Their next publisher, Doubleday, was not so easily intimidated. Kennedy then decided to cooperate.

One of the authors, myself, arrived at Boston's Logan Airport at midnight to join the twin-engine Convair that was leaving on the campaign tour the next day. All was dark inside except a spacious compartment in the rear with a couch that opened into a bed, and two chairs, one riveted to the floor. The candidate stood to shake the author's hand, and his first words were, "I understand you're checking into my sex life.'' I laughed loudly and said, "I don't give a damn about your sex life. This is a political book.''

Kennedy looked at me as if he were examining me for nits or wrinkles, then said slowly, "Of course I screwed around a lot before I was married, but you don't think I'd be crazy enough to do that now, do you?'' And then he added, in a voice that had some fury in it, "It's just a book to you, but to me, it's my life, my whole future.''

But even on his personal plane he was "crazy enough.'' The stewardess was a contribution of father Kennedy—his former secretary, a beautiful young woman of part-French descent. Reporters noted that she obviously performed in other capacities—particularly when Jacqueline was not traveling on the plane. She was seen to enter Jack's compartment, draw the curtains, and linger with him for more than a half hour before exiting. "I think if you'll check old Joe's will, you'll find that he left this young woman some oil leases in Louisiana,'' said Charles Roberts of *Newsweek*.

Priscilla McMillan, a Kennedy researcher, once asked him, "Jack, when you're straining every gasket to be elected President, why do you endanger yourself by going out with women?

"He looked at me a long second and said, 'Because I just can't help it.' "

Joe Kennedy told his friend J. Edgar Hoover that he should have gelded Jack when he was a small boy.

Of course, Jack operated with the assumption that sex was a subject that the press would not report.

Still, there were exceptions. When reporters did plan to write something, reporter Frank Riley intimated that "the old man might have paid them off. . . . If the paper had only 25 readers, Jack would want it stopped because he's the most thin-skinned man in politics. He can't stand criticism or opposition, or even a friendly difference of opinion."

Respected columnist Marquis Childs reflected on some of this: "It's strange, isn't it, how many people in Boston automatically start telling you about Jack's sex life. But anybody who tells you anything about Jack is automatically afraid, almost looking over their shoulder as they say it because the Kennedys are the total power in Boston and in Massachusetts."

———

ON THE CAMPAIGN plane, writer Ed Plaut was struck that Teddy seemed lost, bored. He carefully noted that Teddy and Jack barely spoke to each other, that Teddy wandered aimlessly up and down the aisle, and when the pilot instructed passengers to fasten seat belts, Ted would stand up, even during the landings. When reporters questioned him about anything, he seemed sullen and withdrawn. Seated with Ted and some others at a dinner table, Plaut tried to draw Ted into the group, saying that Ted was the last man to score a touchdown for Harvard in the Yale Bowl. Ted simply said, "That's right," and turned away.

"Teddy wanted to be one of the group," said Sorensen. "There was a big difference in years. And he took a lot of razzing and kidding and chastening. I'm sure he was not brought into the inner circle, in the early days. But he paid his dues."

Here he was, a married man with a pregnant wife. He had run his brother's reelection campaign to the Senate. He had earned his points of respectability and expected more from his brothers—whom he envied.

Teddy felt frustrated as Bobby had felt earlier, as Jack had felt with young Joe—as if he were watching from the sidelines. His brothers' prominence, never important before, now seemed enormous.

———

JACQUELINE WAS THEN quiet, shy, and pregnant, and not much interested in politics. But when her husband was making a speech in Indianapolis—the same speech he had made several times before—this author suggested they go somewhere and talk. They lunched at the airport, then went onto the empty plane, where she mixed the drinks and they talked for the rest of the afternoon.

After several drinks, she lost her little-girl voice and said with some anger and much passion, "I wish Jack wouldn't call me 'Jackie.' How I hate that name! . . . My name is *Jacqueline. My name is Jacqueline!*" She also confided she hated touch football, found her mother-in-law difficult to deal with, and felt most of the politics was superficial. "It's so boring," she said, "when we keep going to places where everybody loves Jack, but on a trip like this where we're going to Humphrey territory and there are the questions of whether he's going to enter this primary or not, it makes things more fun, more challenging."

In the course of that afternoon, this author—who had not expected to like Jacqueline very much—discovered that here was a highly intelligent, very sensitive young woman with a full awareness of herself and of the public world into which she was now moving at such speed. It was not a pattern she would have selected, but it was a part of her husband, and so she would somehow make it part of herself.

———

THE DAY FINALLY arrived. On January 2, 1960, Senator Kennedy held a press conference in the caucus room of the Senate Office Building. "I am announcing today my candidacy for the Presidency of the United States." He promised to bring "more vital life to society" and would enter the New Hampshire primary in March. Under no circumstances would he accept the vice presidency. He called Eisenhower "a weak leader," and saw his own image of America "as fulfilling a noble and historic role as the defender of freedom in time of peril."

Most of the previous Presidents had white hair, and this one was young and handsome, born in this century. "For once I'd like to see a young President, coming in young enough so that at the end of his eight years, he would spend a working day as fresh and full of fight as when he came in," said Democratic liberal leader Oscar Chapman. "You have to have that final energy, otherwise your enemies keep crowding in on you."

Jack was also a symbol of grace, and Mark Dalton added, "Isn't it possible that there is something in Jack's chemistry or personality that makes people transfer their own views to him?" The fascinating essence of this idea was that this candidate was a mirror. Conservatives who liked Jack wanted to think he was a conservative; liberals wanted to think he was a liberal. It was because they wanted to think they belonged with him.

Jack was the front-runner for the nomination. He knew the difficulty and danger of that position, but at the same time he loved it. He loved it when his friends talked openly and glowingly about him in front of him. When the talk ebbed away from him during an interview, he said, only partly in jest, "Let's get back to me!"

"Nobody enjoyed politicking as much as he got to," said Dave Powers. "It was work . . . but then when he realized his own magnetism, his political charm, he wanted to exercise it as often as he could. And afterwards, it was amazing—he couldn't understand why everyone was not with him. And that is the way he campaigned. He had the feeling that he could go into any state and carry it, if he could give enough time to it. He had this great, great confidence."

Before, he was simply intense about winning the presidency—now he was increasingly compulsive.

"The thing about Jack now is that politics takes precedence over family, over religion, over everything," said Ben Bradlee. "It's his overwhelming drive."

A *Time* reporter followed Kennedy on a typical day: "Landing in Jackson, Kennedy read the local papers—and in them, a challenge from the Mississippi Republican State Chairman for him to state his views on integration and segregation. It was a tender topic. A wrong phrasing or a strong statement could kill him here politically. While he kept an overflow reception crowd waiting in the Roof Room of the Heidelberg Hotel, Jack Kennedy hid out in his room, lolling in a warm bath while he thought through a revised version of his speech. . . .

"Kennedy arose before a sell-out audience," the reporter wrote, "boyishly tugged at his ear, tweaked his nose, ran a finger around the inside of his shirt collar, and announced bleakly: 'I am particularly happy to be here tonight.' The crowd sat silent, waiting. 'The thing I said in my own city of Boston [was] that I accept the Supreme Court decision [on integration] as the supreme law of the land. I know that we do not all agree on that issue, but I think most of us do agree on the necessity to uphold law and order in every part of the land.'

"Kennedy paused, and for a brief, desperate moment there was more silence. Then he quickly added: 'And now I challenge the Republican chairman to tell us where he stands on Eisenhower and Nixon!' The crowd came to its feet, alive, roaring and stomping its approval: Jack Kennedy had won it by his own display of courage and by turning all good Democrats against the odious Republicans. . . .

"I never thought I'd see anybody in Central Mississippi speak up for integration and get a standing ovation," wrote the *Time* reporter. It was a rare instance of principle over pragmatism.

Reporter Laura Bergquist also told of a trip with Kennedy to South Carolina, which gave another southern reaction on the integration issue: "We met a publisher of a South Carolina paper. . . . In the course of the conversation, it was obvious that the publisher was both anti-black and anti-Semitic; and I asked him how he could see himself clear to supporting Kennedy as strongly as he did, if he believed all those things he told me? 'Well,' he said, 'we know Papa Joe. And Papa Joe will keep him in line.' "

———

JOHN KENNEDY HAD a strong and worthy Democratic primary opponent in Senator Hubert H. Humphrey (D. Minn.). Humphrey was one of the most effective members of the Senate, an exciting speaker, a longtime liberal, and a man of wit and warmth. He had stamped his image strongest on the issue of civil rights. Humphrey and Kennedy had a close relationship in the Senate. Senator Stuart Symington was a formidable dark horse candidate with an impressive Senate record. And Senator Lyndon Johnson, whom Kennedy and his father had both urged as their 1956 candidate, also had edged into the race.

Symington's son James recalled, "We all looked with some awe, envy, and a kind of muted anger at the way the Kennedy forces were marshaling strength. . . . Why the anger? You'd get a delegate you were pretty sure was yours. Then you'd find him in tears, and he couldn't tell you why . . . and it was because of some kind of pressure that had been applied. They knew much more about all the delegates than we did. They knew all about their families, and where all the pressure points were—and they used them."

Jacqueline accompanied her husband during some of the campaign, but it was clearly not her preferred activity. Months before, Jacqueline had startled a Democratic politician when he asked her where she thought the party should hold its 1960 convention.

"Acapulco," she replied with her wide smile.

Unlike Muriel Humphrey, Jacqueline took no part in her husband's political planning. "Jack wouldn't—couldn't—have a wife who shared the spotlight with him," she said.

Jack won easily in the New Hampshire primary, the nation's first, with more than 85 percent of the vote.

Bob advised Jack not to go into Wisconsin, which bordered on Humphrey's native Minnesota. A major problem was that the border counties were made up of German mothers and fathers, who'd never voted for a Catholic.

His father felt this could be overcome. According to *Newsweek*, the former Ambassador persuaded his son to enter the Wisconsin race by telling him, "Jack, you've got to go into Wisconsin, otherwise they'll say you're yellow." He repeated often that if they won Wisconsin, they would win the nomination.

The father touched a nerve. The decision of Wisconsin was "go," and it was a family project. Lady Bird Johnson once said that a politician "should be born a foundling and remain a bachelor." The Kennedys proved her wrong.

One of the first to arrive in Wisconsin was Lem Billings, assigned to coordinate activity at the Third Congressional District. John Seigenthaler, who liked Billings, regarded him as disorganized and inept. "I put my finger in the dike a thousand times trying to stop mistakes that he made in Wisconsin." Bobby trod carefully on Lem's feelings. He was quick to criticize anybody but he never would bawl out Billings. He knew Lem was one of his brother's closest friends and practically a member of the family.

Bobby seemed to be everywhere. He said, "You know something is wrong with the campaign if the campaign manager has time to ride in the motorcade with the candidate."

Lem now took Teddy in tow. After graduation from law school in June 1959, Teddy and Joan had moved to Boston, and Teddy quickly plunged into the campaign. At a Wisconsin ski jump event before some 10,000 people, Teddy asked the officials if he could speak to the crowd over the public address system in favor of Jack's candidacy. The officials told him they would allow him to speak—if he made the Olympic 180-foot ski jump himself.

Ted, who had never jumped before, said later, "I wanted to get off the jump, take off my skis or even go down the side. But if I did, I was afraid my brother would hear of it. And if he heard of it, I knew I would be back in Washington licking stamps and addressing envelopes for the rest of the campaign."

After he survived the jump, an anti-Kennedy politician said admiringly of him—what had been said at one time or another of all the brothers—that he had more guts than brains.

Joan was also busy. After their daughter Kara was born, she fully expected to be with her infant, but was soon informed by Jacqueline that, baby or no baby, all Kennedy women were supposed to be campaigning. Joan soon learned that Jacqueline meant business. "I felt totally unprepared. Jackie, who was pregnant, heard me say I didn't have the proper clothes for campaigning, and she insisted on lending me many of hers," Joan recalled.

Ethel was chagrined at how quickly Joan learned political tactics. The two shared a dais in Denver and Joan asked, "Ethel, what do you say when you get up to speak?"

"Like a fool, I told her," Ethel later complained. "So when she got up, she recited my speech verbatim. What a memory that girl has."

Ethel was unflappable in crowds, shaking everybody's hand, ignoring a fallen hairdo or a run in her stocking. "Just call me Ethel. Everyone else does," she would say. JFK dubbed her "Miss Perpetual Motion of

1960," but she later said that she had gone to Indiana, Kentucky, Colorado, Utah, Montana, California, and Virginia, "and we lost every one."

Bobby asked each of his three sisters to attend nine house parties a day in every town over a period of two weeks. "One Kennedy employee cracked that he could make an easy living just following the girls around and picking up misplaced jewels, whose value often goes into five figures." The women moved so fast that Eunice Kennedy once called an office secretary to ask, "Where was I yesterday?"

"We found out that it was easier to talk a housewife into giving a party if we told her that Peter Lawford's wife, Pat, would be coming to her house," recalled one of the hostesses. "Peter Lawford had a weekly comedy show on television then, and he was a much bigger celebrity in Wisconsin than Jack Kennedy."

Bobby asked *Time* correspondent Robert Ajemian for his reaction to his sisters' campaigning abilities. "Eunice was a little stodgy," Ajemian began, "and Pat was a little too flippant—" Before he got any further, Bobby snapped at him: "If you say anything more, I'm leaving the table!"

Eunice loved campaigning. A long, leggy woman with wiry grace and soft blue eyes, she could grab a microphone with both hands to tell Texas voters how her brother had fought alongside Texans in the war, how her brother Joe had a Texas boy in his plane when he was killed, and how much all the Kennedys admired Lyndon Johnson, and that's why they should all vote for her brother.

Eunice became her brother's confidante. "I think Jackie may have resented Eunice a bit because of it," Washington hostess Joan Braden said. "Almost every time I was there, Eunice called." "My sister Eunice is a lot like me," said John Kennedy. "She's full of nervous energy. She's always calling me up asking if she can go here or there for me. She's just as competitive as the boys."

Humphey said he felt like an independent store competing against a chain: two brothers, three sisters, three brothers-in-law, several sisters-in-law and cousins. "They're all over the state," Humphrey quipped. "They all look alike and sound alike so that if Teddy or Eunice talk to a crowd, wearing a raccoon coat and a stocking cap, people think they're listening to Jack. I get reports that Jack is appearing in three or four different places at the same time." JFK enjoyed that comment. In the Lutheran country of northern Wisconsin, at the N-Joy Cafe in Cornell, John Kennedy munched some cake with two dozen curious people, thanked them for coming, and added, "I'd like you to know that my sister will be here tomorrow to say hello to you, and my brother will be along on Monday."

"Muriel and I and our 'plain folks' entourage were no match for the glamour of Jackie Kennedy and the other Kennedy women, for Peter Lawford and Sargent Shriver, for Frank Sinatra singing their commercial, 'High Hopes.' Jack Kennedy brought family and Hollywood to Wisconsin. The people loved it and the press ate it up," said Humphrey.

Reporters described crowd reaction as a magnetic field: "Little girls with bare legs ran screaming alongside his car. Once a teen-age girl touched his hand, and ran off in semi-hysteria, crying, 'I touched him, I touched him!', and then fainted in another girl's arms. These female partisans were classified by reporters as teeterers, jumpers, loafers, bouncers, or leapers. In a press-bus, a newsman would sing out the score in the last village: '15 jumpers, 5 bouncers, 85 leapers. This burg is mostly leapers.' "

"I can literally remember Catholic nuns jumping up and down in tandem, holding hands," said Jim Deakin.

Kennedy won a surprising victory in Wisconsin, defeating Humphrey by more than 100,000 votes. But he had not won all seven counties, and that meant he and Humphrey would still fight it out in West Virginia.

———

WEST VIRGINIA WAS Humphrey country, a key primary for Kennedy, as Joe Kennedy explained to Beaverbrook. "Only about 3 percent of the state is Catholic, probably the smallest percentage in the United States."

Kennedy Sr.'s concern was whether West Virginia would bury its prejudice or bury his son's political future. Ben Bradlee sat in on a family session in Palm Beach when the subject of West Virginia came up. "Joe Kennedy argued strenuously against JFK's entering: 'It's a nothing state and they'll kill him over the Catholic thing.' "

At staff meetings, Jack still would often say, and respectfully, "Well, Dad says . . ." His father had urged Jack to enter the California primary, and he refused; then, when his father felt strongly that he had to go into the Wisconsin primary, he did. Now his father wanted him to stay out of West Virginia, and he was going in. He took his advice when he agreed with it.

Bobby soon discovered what his father was talking about on the Catholic issue in West Virginia. Prejudice there was like nothing the Kennedy brothers had ever experienced. "When Bobby came down to West Virginia to file his papers—and I was with him—he got the coldest reception any human being ever got," said Ken O'Donnell. "They actually shrank up against the wall, as if such a Catholic might be contagious. I looked at Bobby," said O'Donnell. "He seemed to be in a state of shock. His face was as pale as ashes. When we left the meeting, Bobby went to a telephone booth and called Jack in Washington. Our only hope of avoiding an ugly religious brawl, Bobby told Jack, was to persuade Hubert Humphrey to withdraw. It was a reasonable request to make because we had defeated Hubert in a fair and square contest in Wisconsin and he had nothing to gain in West Virginia anyway. . . . Jack was taken aback by Bobby's discouragement. 'It can't be that bad,' he said, and reminded Bobby of the favorable Harris poll. Bobby said, 'The people who voted for you in that poll have just found out that you're a Catholic.' "

A newspaper story reported Bobby denouncing the charge that the patriotic allegiance of Catholics was suspect. Bobby had talked about his older brother's death during the war, then was too overcome to continue, and sat down. In reading the article, Jack said softly, "Bobby must be getting tired."

"Come back to Washington for a few days," Jack told Bobby, "and we'll see what we can do."

Humphrey had no intention of quitting the race.

Asked by a reporter if he thought his own background would be brought into his son's campaign, Kennedy Sr. replied brusquely, "Me an issue? Let's not con ourselves. The only issue is whether a Catholic can be elected President."

On August 18, 1960, about twenty-five leaders of American Protestantism met privately in Montreux, Switzerland, and discussed how they could block the election of John F. Kennedy. The host was the Reverend Billy Graham; the most prominent guest was the Reverend Dr. Norman Vincent Peale. "They were unanimous in feeling that the

Protestants in America must be aroused in some way, or the solid bloc Catholic voting, plus money, will take the election." Had the Kennedys known of the meeting, it would only have spurred them on.

One of the things they quickly did was to bring in Franklin Roosevelt, Jr. Joe and Rose Kennedy invited young Franklin to Palm Beach. "Joe and I reminisced with him about FDR," said Rose Kennedy, "sent flowers to his wife whom he had left behind and cajoled him into going into West Virginia for Jack." Young FDR Jr. agreed only because he and Jack were friends.

In his enthusiastic introduction of Kennedy, young Roosevelt—who would later become Kennedy's Assistant Secretary of the Navy—held his fingers crossed in the air and declared, "My father and Jack Kennedy's father were just like this!" FDR would have groaned.

"Franklin Roosevelt was fantastic," said Ken O'Donnell. "He invoked his father's famous name, which was beloved in the state of West Virginia." Even in the tarpaper shacks of the poorest miners, the picture of President Roosevelt was on the wall like an icon. Old miners even affectionately referred to him as "Rosie." It wouldn't be long before Jack's face would join him.

The Kennedy staff had found copies of letters requesting draft deferment for Humphrey, but decided it would be distasteful to use them. Franklin Jr., however, revealed them in a speech. It was said that FDR Jr. would retract it at a press conference, but he never did.

Bobby also continued the attack, which he had begun in Wisconsin, implying that Jimmy Hoffa was contributing money to the Humphrey campaign to beat the Kennedys. Humphrey had vigorously denied this, saying, "Whoever is responsible deserves a spanking. And I said spanking because it applies to juveniles."

Everything was for sale in West Virginia, and everybody got paid. If this was true elsewhere, it was more obvious here. The black bag was full of money and nobody asked where it came from. It is common knowledge that Kennedy had a bigger black bag than Humphrey did.

A Baltimore *Sun* correspondent reported that he himself had seen money changing hands in exchange for votes. Charles D. Hylton, Jr., editor of the *Logan Banner*, said the rate of exchange was "anywhere from two dollars and a drink of whiskey to six dollars and two pints of beer for a single vote." Congressman Tip O'Neill told how a Kennedy man, Eddie Ford, went there with a suitcase full of money. "And they passed money around like it was never seen." As one sheriff told Bill Connell, "You gave us five and Kennedy came in with ten."

What Robert Kennedy did not know was the family relationship with the mob world. Since his early involvement in the liquor industry, before and after Prohibition, the elder Kennedy had dealt with top gangsters and Mafia members. FBI files later revealed that the elder Kennedy earlier that summer had been visited by many "gangsters with gambling interests."

In fact, at the height of the campaign, Joseph Kennedy reportedly met with an assortment of organized crime bosses at Felix Young's restaurant in New York. "I took the reservations," said the hostess at Young's, "and it was as though every gangster chief in the United States was there. I don't remember all the names now, but there was John Rosselli, Carlos Marcello from New Orleans, the two brothers from Dallas, the top men from Buffalo, California, and Colorado. They were all top people, not soldiers. I was amazed Joe Kennedy would take the risk."

The father reportedly made arrangements with some of them to buy the political support for his son from some of the key political figures throughout West Virginia. The idea was to use money and other pressure. The FBI files on John Kennedy reveal that Frank Sinatra also solicited his Mafia friends for help in the West Virginia primary.

Sam Giancana and Mafia compatriot John Roselli, who was Joe Kennedy's golfing friend, would later be overheard on an FBI wiretap discussing the "donations" they had made during the West Virginia primary. One thing they did do was to send Paul "Skinny" D'Amato to West Virginia to use his influence with local politicians who gambled in D'Amato parlors.

Judith Campbell, a beautiful young woman who described herself as an aspiring actress, had been introduced to Jack by Frank Sinatra— with whom she had also had a love affair. Campbell also happened to be the mistress of Mafia boss Sam Giancana. She would soon be sharing her bed with both Giancana and Jack Kennedy. She later admitted that she had served as a courier of sealed envelopes during the 1960 campaign, and that she had once arranged a short meeting between John Kennedy and Giancana at the Ambassador Hotel in Chicago. She said she left the two men alone, and went into the bathroom and sat on the tub until they were finished. What was so ironic was that Giancana was not only deeply involved with the CIA since the Eisenhower administration, but had invoked the Fifth Amendment when called to testify before the Senate Select Committee in June 1959.

Years later, Campbell told Larry King on Cable News Network of a dinner at Jack's home in Georgetown. He asked her to take a suitcase full of money to Giancana and told her, "It's a great deal of money. . . . I think he can help me with the campaign." She would be watched and guarded, he told her. "You won't be looking over your shoulder." Campbell told Larry King, "Now through wiretaps and things that are available now, we know that it went to West Virginia."

West Virginia was critical in establishing Kennedy as a viable candidate, despite his Catholicism. A defeat there would have crippled his candidacy.

––––––––

WHEN JOHN KENNEDY lost his voice in Clarksburg, he gave Dave Powers a note: "Get Ted." "We're all on the platform, and there's a great crowd," said Powers. "Oh, what a great speech Ted made that day. He was goin' like mad. Ted had copied all the flourish and rapid-fire of his brother's speech, and even his phrases. 'Do you want a man who will give this country leadership? Do you want a man with vigor and vision?' "

Peter Lisagor remembered that Teddy "spoke terribly fast . . . racing through everything . . . just like his brother did."

Ted told his audience the story about two brothers who went fishing. One brother caught all the fish and the other caught nothing. The next morning, the one who caught nothing decided to fish alone. He fished for hours without catching anything and, finally, a fish stuck its head out of the water and asked, "Where's your brother?" Teddy then told the crowd, "Well, here's my brother." Jack Kennedy took the microphone to whisper, "I'd just like to tell my brother that you can't be elected President until you are thirty-five years of age."

Despite the optimistic predictions of several reporters, Bob recalled that even at the end of the West Virginia primary, the Kennedys were certain they had lost—not only the primary, but the campaign. "Damn that Hubert Humphrey," Robert Kennedy said.

"When the returns came in, and Kennedy had clobbered Humphrey [with more than 60 percent of the vote], we couldn't believe it," said

O'Donnell. "They all look back and say, 'We all knew it,' but we sat in the lobby of the Connaught Hotel, and not one person there thought John Kennedy was going to win. . . . From then on in, we knew we had the nomination."

Senator Kennedy was in Washington on election eve, and Ben Bradlee was with him. There was a message to call Charleston. "It was Bobby again, and a grin split Kennedy's face," said Bradlee. "His hand was shaking. He asked only a few short questions—what percentage of the vote was in, should he come down there, was there any talk of conceding. He put down the phone and let out a very unsenatorial war-whoop. He was in. The champagne cork popped, but he only sipped at his glass. He called his brother-in-law Steve Smith and asked if the plane and crew were available, rushed upstairs to change his clothes. Kennedy then called his old man in Massachusetts—'What do you think, Dad? Looks pretty good . . . OK, Dad. . . . Thanks a lot, Dad.'

"The old man, who had been in contact with Bobby constantly, never let on to Jack that he already knew the result. He had already talked to Bobby. Old Joe said he'd known his son was going to win all along." On the plane Jack told Bradlee, "How the hell can they stop me now!"

Congratulated on the campaign victory, Bob quipped to the press, "I couldn't have done it without my brother."

Humphrey made a gracious concession statement, telling his weeping audience of supporters that he planned to quit the race. Joe Rauh called Bobby and read it to him. Several minutes later, a call came from downstairs to say that Mr. Kennedy was on his way up. The Humphrey people expected it was a courtesy call from Jack Kennedy, but not Bobby, whom they saw as the devil incarnate.

"The door opened. Bobby walks in," said Joe Rauh. "It was like the Red Sea opening for Moses. Everybody walked backwards, and there was a path from the door to the other side of the room where Hubert and Muriel were standing. I'll never forget that walk if I live to be a hundred. Bobby walks slowly, deliberately, over to the Humphreys. He leaned in and kissed Muriel." "Muriel stiffened, stared, and turned in silent hostility, walking away from him, fighting tears." Bobby then flung an arm round Humphrey's shoulders and took him off to hear his brother's victory speech. It was the right thing for Bobby to have done, said Rauh, "very nice and very gracious . . . but at that moment, it was sure something."

———

MANY YEARS LATER, long after the President and his brother were both dead and Hubert Humphrey was Vice President of the United States, Humphrey had dinner with Cardinal Cushing, a great friend of the Kennedys. "I keep reading these books by the young men around Jack Kennedy and how they claim credit for electing him," said the Cardinal in his Boston Irish accent. "I'll tell you who elected Jack Kennedy. It was his father Joe, and me, right here in this room. . . . We decided which [Protestant] church and preacher [in West Virginia] would get $200 or $100 or $500. . . . What better way is there to spend campaign money than to help a preacher and his flock? It's good for the Lord. It's good for the church. It's good for the preacher, and it's good for the candidate. . . . Joe Kennedy and I sat and discussed the strategy of that campaign. . . . Joe Kennedy and me! Sitting right here! We sat here and also decided what magazines were gonna get the money, and what newspapers."

Winning the West Virginia primary, Rauh said, "licked the Catholic issue forever, in my judgment, or any religious issue. So I think that's a cornerstone in American history, really."

The strange thing was that John Kennedy would not win West Virginia in the final election. He was clearly the front-runner, expecting to be nominated for President at the Democratic National Convention. Adlai Stevenson, who had lost twice to Eisenhower, still had an enormous emotional support in the country. When Kennedy won the Oregon primary, he went to Illinois to persuade Stevenson to side with him. Driving back to the airport after the meeting, Jack told Blair, "Why won't he be satisfied with Secretary of State?"

On his arrival in Los Angeles, the elder Kennedy stayed at the same hotel as his sons. "I remember his father was angry because Jack didn't check in with him when he came to the hotel," said Charles Spalding. "When I told Jack this, he said, 'Dad's got to realize that things are not the same anymore. I'm going to be the President of the United States.' And then he got an impish grin in his eye. His father's suite was on the floor just below his. He said, 'Let's drop our shoes on his ceiling.' "

Joe Kennedy did not sit and wait. He discussed possible deals for delegates at the California Governor's Mansion; talked to Stevenson supporter Senator Eugene McCarthy about giving grants to any Catholic hospitals McCarthy might recommend—as joint gifts from Gene and Jack, if Gene would switch to them. None of it worked, but he tried.

Jack once said with considerable understatement, "We were interested not so much in the ideas of politics as in the mechanics of the whole thing."

Former President Harry Truman was still adamantly opposed to Jack. He announced on national television that he would not attend the Democratic National Convention "because it was a pre-arranged affair controlled by the Kennedys." Delegates would have "no opportunity for a democratic choice." Truman called on Kennedy to put aside personal ambition and withdraw from the race so that the President in these troubled times should be "someone with the greatest possible maturity and experience."

Truman earlier had confided, "I'm not against the Pope, I'm against the Pop." Kennedy Sr. had embittered Truman by opposing his Truman Doctrine, which aided countries threatened by Communism. Joe Kennedy was basically an isolationist who believed we should not give any aid to anybody outside this country.

Joseph Kennedy now moved to Marion Davies' posh villa, eleven miles from Los Angeles. Davies had been the movie-star mistress of newspaper magnate William Randolph Hearst. She lived on twelve manicured acres behind a ten-foot-high iron grille fence. There Joe called friends who owed him favors, political bosses with whom his son had never felt comfortable. These party bosses could tip the balance at a convention. And Joe knew them intimately.

Candidate Lyndon Johnson might not have recalled posing for a photograph with John Kennedy when Kennedy was a Congressman—a photograph Kennedy had framed and kept on his wall because Johnson had autographed it and inscribed, *This young man destined to go far.* He hadn't realized then how far Kennedy would go, and how fast, and how Jack's future would be linked with his own. If nobody won on the first ballot, Johnson thought he had a strong chance on the second ballot.

Johnson saw Tip O'Neill and said he knew that O'Neill was "with the boy," as any Massachusetts delegate had to be, but he would appreciate O'Neill's vote for him on the second ballot. "You don't know the Kennedys," said O'Neill. "There won't be any second ballot." Johnson was incredulous.

Johnson bitterly complained, "Jack was out kissing babies while I was passing bills." He then sharpened his attacks. LBJ's good friend J. Edgar Hoover supplied material from his FBI files for any possible use to damage Kennedy. Hoover's key aide, Cartha DeLoach, recalled, "They knew all about Kennedy's desires for sex, and the fact that he would sleep with almost anything." A friend of Johnson's approached respected reporter Theodore H. White at the convention and "offered to get me pictures of Jack and Bobby Kennedy in drag at a gay party in Los Angeles if I would promise to publish them." White refused.

FAR BEHIND, WITH nothing to lose, Lyndon Johnson challenged Kennedy to a TV debate. Senator Ernest Hollings advised Kennedy to do it. "If you don't, Johnson's really gonna give it to you." The elder Kennedy said his son would be "a damn fool if he goes near him. It's all sewed up."

Jack felt it was a challenge he couldn't refuse. But when he walked on the stage for the debate, he turned to Bobby and asked, "What shall I say?" Jack and Bob sat on the stage together. "And I remember seeing that pant-leg fluttering there, as he waited for Johnson," said Hugh Sidey. "I thought he was shaking. I reported it to my office that way, but I guess it was a nervous twitch. . . . And we all thought that Johnson had done superbly well. Bob had whispered a couple of things to Jack as he waited. We wondered how Kennedy could top Johnson's performance, and he did. Kennedy just cut him to ribbons with a few quick thrusts of humor. I remember that kind of sly look that the brothers, Bob and Jack, gave each other when Senator Kennedy sat down after having thoroughly demolished Johnson's argument. He and his brother almost grinned. When he sat down, his leg no longer twitched."

Kennedy people afterward made much of the fact that Johnson had an almost-fatal heart attack in 1955 while Kennedy described his own health as "excellent" and that he was "the healthiest candidate for President in the country"—even though he was still unable to lift his daughter up in the air. John Kennedy again denied that he had Addison's disease, and Robert echoed that his brother "does not now nor has he ever had . . ." And his father joined in, denouncing "unfounded and disturbing rumors."

Kennedy's adrenal specialist, Dr. Eugene Cohen, was highly reluctant to sign a certificate establishing that Kennedy was healthy enough to be President. "I sat down at the typewriter and we went over it," said Dr. Janet Travell, Jack's personal physician. "We fought over every word of it. We spent three or four hours on it. I typed it out. Gene Cohen said he would sign it provided that it should not be released with his name, with our names on it. I said, 'All right.' "

Dr. Cohen had reason for concern. His office was ransacked twice "and his patients' records were thrown all over," said Travell. "They just sliced the door and they tried to break the lock." The fact that there was an attempt made at the same time on the offices of both Cohen and Travell clearly indicated that they were after Kennedy's medical records on Addison's disease.

"They wouldn't have found anything," said Travell. "I tracked down almost everything that was available. They were all under lock and key." Had Kennedy's condition been made public, it probably would have killed his candidacy.

After his death, two pathologists discovered that Kennedy's adrenal glands had so atrophied that they were almost completely gone. They were sworn to secrecy for almost thirty years.

Meanwhile, Bobby was busy squeezing delegates. He sat at a small table near a window overlooking Pershing Square, in one of four rooms of Suite 8315 at the Biltmore. He had learned much since Jack's Senate race. Forty professionals, who made up the organization hard core, collected in his office every morning for specific instructions on how hard to push whom. The Kennedy card files—blue cards, four inches by six—kept in a file reverently known as "the box"—included all the detailed data about each of the 4509 delegates and alternates, including their hobbies, habits, and children's names. This gave them enormous leverage in dealing with delegates. Ben Bradlee described Bob as tough and tireless when he got within smelling distance of a delegate. Joe Kennedy taught his boys to hire detectives if necessary to check on the past life of a man before dealing with him—just as he had done with many of his children's questionable companions. These careful prior investigations now enabled them to locate delegates who would vote for him before the Los Angeles convention. "Bobby really steers the

Kennedy machine," said Bradlee. "Counting delegates, talking to delegates, tracking delegates, blitzing delegates."

Unlike any of his brothers, Bobby had none of the gift of charming small talk with delegates. "In the art of small talk," observed Dick Schapp, "Bobby is, at best, a few steps in front of the late Harpo Marx." Stevenson said of Bobby, "That young man never says please . . . never asks for things . . . he demands them."

At the morning sessions, Bobby would snap out crisp orders for his staff of forty to check and double-check delegates at different meetings, ensuring that they were packed with Kennedy people.

Bobby was so precise in his delegate count that he told Teddy to get a commitment from the Wyoming chairman to release four votes for Kennedy if that was the margin needed for nomination on the first ballot. The Wyoming chairman was unbelieving that they could be so confident of their count, but finally agreed. The Wyoming delegates would ultimately make the final difference.

Humphrey was out of the race, but still controlled his Minnesota delegation, among others. Bobby now brusquely demanded, "Hubert, we want your announcement and the pledge of the Minnesota delegation today or else." To which Humphrey replied: "Go to hell."

Eighty telephone lines provided instant communications to strategic people. At least once an hour Bob would be on the line to Jack.

––––––––––

KEN O'DONNELL DESCRIBED Senator Eugene McCarthy's nominating Adlai Stevenson as McCarthy's finest hour. Jack called Bobby at the convention, then called his father. "Dad, Adlai has everything but delegates."

He was right. John Kennedy won the Democratic Party nomination for the presidency on the first ballot.

"I remember that frantic ride," recalled Sidey. "We went to the convention at over 70 miles per hour, and in the great crush we couldn't get in. The cops barred some of us, and I remember I did slip in. . . . I remember seeing he and Bob go off by themselves—this was the first time they'd met since they had won it—and walked off into this corner, and Bob, with his head bowed, as he usually did. And I remember Bobby—his only show of emotion was in hitting his open palm of his left hand with the fist of his right hand repeatedly, as they talked. And a kind of a smile on John Kennedy's face: the ultimate satisfaction. The thing went so smoothly, and they were within a few votes of what they said they were going to be."

But John Kennedy remembered all the details, and smilingly prodded Bobby: "You son of a bitch. . . . What happened to our two votes from Montana?"

"Some people say that Jack called Jackie right after his nomination, but he didn't," said Evelyn Lincoln. "While he talked to his Dad, I was calling Jackie."

Novelist Gore Vidal, Jacqueline's stepbrother, was standing with Peter Lisagor outside the convention hall, trying unsuccessfully to get past the police line. Everything seemed to be noisy confusion, and Vidal quipped, "Ah, the beginning of the Kennedy Era."

———

THAT NIGHT, CONGRESSMAN Tip O'Neill found Jack Kennedy at eight o'clock at Chasen's Restaurant. " 'Jack,' I said, 'are you interested in Lyndon Johnson for the Vice Presidency?'

"He said, 'Of course I want Lyndon Johnson. The only thing is, I would never want to offer it and have him turn me down. . . . I would be terrifically embarrassed. He's a natural. If I could ever get him on the ticket, no way could we lose. We'd carry Texas.' "

The brothers had earlier talked it all out with the family. None of them liked Johnson. They particularly resented Johnson campaign statements that old Joe was a Nazi and that Jack was a sick man, physically unable to be President. What made it more interesting was that Joe himself earlier had called Johnson, urging him to run with Jack, but Johnson then felt he had more power as Majority Leader of the Senate.

Bob described their indecisive discussion on the vice presidency. "We changed our minds eight times during the course of it, Jack and myself."

Bob and Ken O'Donnell then had a meeting with representatives of organized labor. Only one of them approved Johnson. The rest reacted with blue language. Bob then reported the problems to Jack. Bobby's report on the strong labor opposition soured Jack on Johnson, but he still felt the need to offer the nomination to him.

Meanwhile Johnson called his friend Jim Rowe and said that he expected Kennedy to come down and offer him the vice presidency; what did Rowe think? Rowe mentioned the power he already had as Majority Leader, something Johnson himself had used as an argument, but now Johnson said, "Power goes where power is."

Rowe was surprised because the Kennedy-Johnson relationship always had assumed Johnson's primacy and Kennedy's acceptance of the junior role and now it was like the son telling the father to get out of the driver's seat so that he could drive.

"We never dreamt that there was a chance in the world that he would accept it," said Bob. "I was up in Jack's room when he came back, and he said, 'You just won't believe it.' I said, 'What?' and he said, 'He *wants* it,' and I said, 'Oh, my God!' He said, 'Now what do we do?' So the thing is that we spent the rest of the day—and we both promised each other that we'd never tell what happened—but we spent the rest of the day alternating between thinking it was good and thinking that it wasn't good that he'd offered him the Vice Presidency, and how could he get out of it. . . . So then we decided . . . I'd go down and see if I could talk him out of it. And I would say to him that there was going to be a floor fight, and there'd be unpleasantness, and he shouldn't do it . . . but that he could be head of the Democratic National Committee instead, or anything else he wanted."

Johnson was stunned. He now believed that Bobby Kennedy was unilaterally trying to ease him off the ticket after John Kennedy had put him on. Johnson refused to withdraw, and called Jack.

James Rowe, who worked closely with Johnson, later reported Johnson telling Kennedy: " 'We've got Bobby here . . . and he seems to think that you don't want me for the Vice Presidency.' "

Jack, meanwhile, had been persuaded by a group of Democratic leaders that he needed Johnson on the ticket to carry Texas to win the election. So now he told Johnson, " 'Well, Bobby doesn't know . . . he's not up to things yet—not on top of what we've already decided. I've already made my statement, and expect you to make yours.' "

"Johnson then called in Bobby," said Rowe, "and told him. Everybody left the room; there was just Bobby and me. Bobby said to me, 'Don't you think that Jack has done a terrible thing?' And I said, 'No, I don't. I think he's going to help Jack get some votes in the South . . . I think he'll do very well with Lyndon.' And Bobby was saying, 'Well, if he weren't so tired, this wouldn't have happened.' And Bobby walked out, with his head hung low—very depressed."

The Kennedy family were all at the Marion Davies villa during the Johnson nomination. "Bobby was directing it from there, staying in touch with Larry O'Brien," said Charles Bartlett. "Nobody was very cheerful, and Bobby was in near despair . . . The sun was going down and all of Bobby's children were sort of in a big fountain out in front. I remember Old Joe standing there in the doorway, in a very grand manner, in a velvet dressing-jacket, with his hands behind his back, saying, 'Don't worry, Jack. Within two weeks, they'll be saying it's the smartest thing you ever did.' "

Correspondent Peter Lisagor later told JFK, "Boy, that was either the most inspired choice for Vice President or the most cynical." Jack Kennedy bristled at the word "cynical." He said, "It's not cynical at all. Democrats have always done this—an eastern candidate and a southerner."

As for Bobby's adjustment to the decision, Dave Powers later said, "Even if Jack wanted to give the vice presidency to Eleanor Roosevelt, Bobby would have said all right."

————

A REPORTER ASKED family friend Morton Downey why Joe didn't wait for Jack's acceptance speech before heading back to New York. Downey shrugged. "It was all over. The job was done. Jack had won, and Joe did have an important business engagement back in New York."

"Just right after the nomination, I remember I went back to the house to see the father and congratulate him," said Charles Spalding. He expected Joseph Kennedy to be basking and beaming, surrounded by well-wishers. After all, he had put much of his own power and time and money behind that nomination. And pride. Instead Spalding found Joseph Kennedy busy packing. His plane was leaving within the hour, by midnight, and he was telling somebody, " 'Now here's what we have to do.' "

"You can't leave now," I told him. "Why don't you stick around for the speech. This means more to you than anybody."

" 'No, there's work to be done, and I've got to get out of here.' "

Behind his quick retreat were hurt feelings. Joe wanted his

candidate-son to come and thank him for making it all possible, thank him and persuade him that he must stay to share the finale. And his son had other things on his mind.

Joe later admitted, "If asked, I would have stayed."

After the nomination, Jack briefly disappeared. Some reporters caught him climbing over a backyard fence near his suburban Los Angeles hideaway. Kennedy shouted that he was going off "to meet my father." Reporters later learned that he was paying a quiet visit to the nearby home of a former diplomat's wife he had known intimately for a long time.

———

DURING THE DEMOCRATIC National Convention in Los Angeles, Henry Luce received a call from Joe Kennedy, saying he was en route to Europe and was stopping off in New York. Could he see Luce that Friday?

At dinner, Luce came right to the point: "Well, now, Joe, I suppose you are interested in the attitudes *Time* and *Life* and I might take about Jack's candidacy. And I think I can put it quite simply." Luce divided the matter into domestic affairs and foreign affairs. "As to domestic affairs," he told Joe, "of course Jack will have to be left of center."

"Old Joe broke in with blazing blue eyes: 'Harry, you know god-damn well no son of mine could be a goddamn liberal,' " Luce recalled.

Luce insisted Kennedy had to take a liberal position to win as a Democrat, but then added, "If Jack shows any sign of going soft on Communism [in foreign policy], then we would clobber him."

"Don't worry about him being a weak sister," Joe retorted.

During the evening, Joe Kennedy discussed Luce's son Hank. "Why don't you buy him a safe congressional seat?"

"What do you mean by that?"

"Come on, Harry, you and I both know how to do that. Of course it can be done."

Joe Kennedy and Luce watched the Democratic National Convention together on TV. As Adlai Stevenson and Hubert Humphrey preceded Jack to the rostrum, Joe made derogatory remarks. "There was no respect for any of these liberals," said Luce's son Hank. "He just thought they were all fools on whom he had played this giant trick."

"When Joe left," Luce remembered, "he said, 'I want to thank you for all that you've done for Jack.' I think this was said with great sincerity and, if I recall, he repeated it."

Luce privately wondered how much he had done and whether he had perhaps done too much.

––––––––

BRADLEE DESCRIBED THE scene the day after the convention: "The Kennedy campaign was officially launched at 9:30 this morning with a closed meeting of 25 state chairmen in the Kennedy headquarters on the Galleria floor of the Biltmore. Twenty-four hours earlier it had been the scene of wild celebration. The walls were still rank with the smoke and smells of victory, and the victory posters were torn and cock-eyed, but—half-dead with fatigue—the Kennedy pros were already working for November 8."

Lisagor was aboard the same plane with Bobby heading home after the convention, and Bobby pulled at his coat and said, "I hear that you have an interesting story to tell about how Lyndon Johnson feels about Jack." Lisagor answered, "Well, I do, Bob, but I don't see why I should tell that story now. You're all in bed together now. He's your vice presidential candidate." Bobby persisted.

What happened, said Lisagor, was that he was on a five-hour flight with Johnson and John Steele of *Time*, "and I began to question him about the Kennedys, and all the enmity and hostility that he held for the Kennedys came out. He called Kennedy a 'little scrawny fellow with rickets and God knows what other kind of diseases.' He said, 'Have you ever seen his ankles? They're about so round,' and he made a gesture with his fingers. And he said, 'If he ever got elected President of the United States, his father, Old Joe Kennedy, would run the country.' Well, he had a lot of things to say about it. Well, I told Bobby all these things. I don't think I left out a single four-letter word. . . . Bobby simply turned to the window after I was through and said, 'I knew he hated Jack, but I didn't think he hated him that much.' "

Bobby had never liked Johnson, and never would.

Jack went back to Hyannis, physically exhausted but ready to start all over again. He had earlier contacted his personal lawyer and former Truman adviser Clark Clifford: " 'I want you to spend this summer writing up a plan of takeover. I'm going to win this election, and I don't want to wake up in the morning, after being elected President, and ask my father, my brother Bobby and my staff, "Now, what do I do?" I want a book right there, in hand, telling me exactly what to do.' So I worked all summer on that book, seventy or eighty pages," said Clifford.

Clifford earlier had decided that there was more veneer than depth in Kennedy. "It was only later that I realized he was something special."

————

BOBBY CALLED HIS exhausted staff together the next morning and announced, "We can rest in November."

"He's living on nerves," said Jack. His father later added: "Jack could lie down almost any place and be asleep in thirty seconds. . . . He could disconnect completely and pick himself up refreshed. He could carry through without sleep for periods of time, but he could recharge by sleeping eleven straight hours. Not Bobby."

"The key to our whole campaign," Bobby announced, "is a national registration drive . . . six million Americans every year reach the age of twenty-one, and these are the people with whom Jack runs so strongly."

————

THE JOHNSONS ARRIVED soon afterward to visit with the Kennedys at Hyannis.

"It's a rather small house we have there, and we wanted them to be comfortable, so we gave them our bedroom," said Jacqueline. "But we didn't want them to know it was our bedroom, because we thought they might feel they were putting us to too much trouble. There was a lot of moving things out of closets, so there'd be no trace of anybody's toothbrush anywhere. I remember that evening how impressed I was with Mrs. Johnson. She and my sister and I were sitting in one part of the room, and Jack and Lyndon and some men were in some other part of the room. Mrs. Johnson had a little spiral pad, in which when she heard some name mentioned, she'd jot it down."

Jacqueline remembered that Mrs. Johnson was talking to her, "but she was kind of listening to Jack talking with her husband. Yet she would sit talking with us, looking so calm. I was very impressed by that."

Kennedy repaid the visit. He landed in a drizzle at the LBJ ranch, and was met by Lyndon Baines Johnson, outfitted in a Texas rancher's cream pants and cowboy boots. Johnson seemed crestfallen when his leader, in gray pinstripe Ivy League, politely but firmly declined to put on a five-gallon Stetson before photographers. Nor did Johnson like to hear Senator Hugh Scott call Kennedy "the Majority Leader's leader."

———

MEANWHILE, THE FAMILY began working on Kennedy's image, stressing his private life and values. Jacqueline gave interviews describing the peace and comfort she brought to her husband's life and how he appreciated the cozy home she had created "because he has been living this crazy campaigning life for the past 14 years. . . . Of course he could fix things around the house . . . but as he is home so little, and those hours are precious, I would consider I had failed running our house if I had to waste his time here fixing fuses. . . . He has never had to since we were married . . . so he can spend that time with Caroline and our friends. . . . Yes, he is thoughtful about buying presents— mostly to Caroline. . . . She is at the age now where she misses him— and he is terribly interested in her. I think he probably suffers as much as she does (though neither of them are probably as aware of it as I am) from his absence."

During this period, there was minimal time for other women, and an urgency to burnish the family image for political purposes. This change pleased Jacqueline.

———

KENNEDY'S REPUBLICAN OPPONENT for the presidency was Richard Milhous Nixon. The two men had come into Congress at the same time and almost had faced each other as vice-presidential nominees in 1956. Kennedy's special aide McGeorge Bundy felt that Kennedy had "a continuing contempt" for Nixon. This was only partly true. The two men had always been openly friendly. Nixon was also ambivalent about the Kennedys, because old Joe—and even Jack Kennedy—had given generously to some of his early campaigns.

Kennedy framed a cartoon for his office wall from Richard Nixon, showing him and Nixon peeking out at each other from their adjoining offices, with the Nixon inscription, *To my friend and neighbor Jack Kennedy, with best wishes for almost everything.*

Kennedy might have been surprised had he known that there were suggested plans by certain Republicans at the Chicago convention for a mass picketing demonstration at Joe Kennedy's Merchandise Mart. Joe had bought the huge Mart earlier at a bargain price and put his son-in-law Shriver in charge of it. The Nixon people now planned to protest that Negroes were not hired there except to clean toilets. Nixon rejected the proposal. "I was running against Jack Kennedy, not against his father and brother-in-law."

––––––––––

KENNEDY WAS SOON scheduled to make forty speeches in more than thirty cities in the West and Midwest in ten days. The three television networks then offered both candidates free television exposure in prime time for a series of four person-to-person debates.

One of his favorite Kennedy campaign lines was, "Do you realize the responsibility I carry? . . . I'm the only person standing between Nixon and the White House."

"On the October 13 afternoon of a crucial campaign debate with Richard Nixon, Kennedy was so tense that a friend arranged an interlude with a girl to relax him," reported Jack Anderson. "The candidate took off in the middle of a strategy session, explaining that he wanted to deliver some clothes to the dry cleaner. His friend, waiting downstairs in an automobile, drove him to New York City's Plaza Hotel for the tryst."

Meanwhile, a Nixon aide naively asked Robert Kennedy his opinion of Nixon's makeup. Bobby noted Nixon's paleness, his sunken cheeks, and shadowed eyes, and replied, "Terrific! Terrific! I wouldn't change a thing!"

The two men set a new style that would become part of the nomination process. They simply stood at lecterns several yards apart, in front of microphones, before an audience of almost 60 million people. There were those who said that if you had heard the debates on radio, you might have thought that Nixon got the best of it, but if you saw it on television, you knew that Kennedy had won.

Alice Roosevelt Longworth summed it up for her cousin Joe Alsop. "Well, Joe, your man's in, my man's finished. I don't see why they bother to go on with the election. Dick has finished himself off." The consensus was that Nixon "looked awful."

A British correspondent later described Kennedy: "The most striking thing . . . is something that comes neither from his physical appearance nor his clothing, but from his mind. He can think on his feet and find words to express his thoughts with the utmost precision. He's a man who instinctively knows how to use the English language."

Abe Fortas, who became a Supreme Court Justice, later noted that "Nixon and Kennedy had the same kind of dead eyes. And I think they're both the same in many other ways," and that both were similarly hard working, intelligent, "and I think neither has a core. I think there is nothing that either man wouldn't compromise on to get the job."

On the night after the first debate with Nixon, Jack called his father, who said that he not only had won the debate but won the election. Jack didn't believe it, but he expected that kind of statement from his father and he liked it. And he also liked kidding his father.

In a speech at the Alfred E. Smith Memorial Dinner, New York City, October 19, 1960, Kennedy said: "On this matter of experience, I had announced earlier this year that if successful, I would not consider campaign contributions as a substitute for experience in appointing ambassadors. Ever since I made that statement, I have not received one single cent from my father."

It's ironic that his father had been approached to do just that. Earlier in the campaign, someone wanted to contribute $100,000 if he could become an ambassador. The senior Kennedy's reply was quick: "Any man who is dumb enough to ask you to do that is too dumb to be an ambassador."

Joe no longer dropped in on Jack, but even from a distance he never let up. Jack telephoned his friend Charles Bartlett and said: "The old man just called me from Palm Beach and said if I keep talking the way I did today, they're going to bury me six feet under. You know, I'm not going to talk to Dad anymore about this campaign. The one thing he doesn't understand is that if the Democrats are to get elected, they've got to excite a lot of people to believe that if they win the election, then life is going to be a helluva lot better, and if they don't excite the people then they're not going to get in."

The time came, as Charles Spalding remembered: "I think Jack just decided it was time to have a fight with his father. The issue didn't matter. I don't even know what it was. But I know it happened. I think he just said of his father, 'He's never going to stop. I'll never get out from under. I'll just have to carry this thing around until I draw the line.' And then one day he just drew the line. It was as if Jack went down in the pit with his father and went to war with him. I know they didn't talk to each other for a long time."

It was now Bobby who was truly in command.

Bob's phone line to his father was still open and busy, but the younger son knew, much better than Jack, how to cope with his father, how to listen intently and respectfully, then sidestep him and do it the way he wanted.

After Teddy got his law degree in 1959, reporters joked that "Jack and Bobby run the show, while Ted's in charge of hiding Joe."

But Teddy had done an effective job in Wisconsin and West Virginia, and now the young brother was ready for more important things.

"When we divided up the country at Bobby's house, my job was to cover the western states," Ted Kennedy said. "But all they gave me was a two-page memorandum with about ten different names on it, plus a speech my brother made in Montana in 1957. The rest was up to me. Lucky I learned how to fly a plane when I went to law school."

Ted was made responsible for the delegations of eleven western states, plus Alaska and Hawaii. For Ted, this was hugely exciting and the responsibility was enormous. Only a year before, he had been a struggling law school student, overshadowed and overlooked by both brothers, and now he was directing JFK's presidential campaign in half the country.

"Ted does not show his aggressiveness the way Bobby did," said Dave Powers. "Yes, he's like Jack in that. But he's a great competitor. It's that love, and the courage, that they all have. But they'd do things for Jack. One time, I said to Kenny O'Donnell, 'You know, Jack's the kind of guy you'd do things for, you wouldn't do for your mother!'" And then Powers added, "What I loved about Bobby and Teddy was that in the history of American politics, I never saw brothers as dedicated to the success of Jack as Bobby and Teddy were."

Perhaps Ted started with more of a leg up than any of the other brothers because he didn't have to compete so much.

Teddy did have a quality that some found unique among the brothers. A friend observed it while they played tennis. "Teddy bends over backward to be fair, is scrupulous about the calls, always giving the advantage to his opponent—and I haven't seen that in any other Kennedy."

Ted kept up a stream of memos to Bob. One of them suggested that what he heard most about in a tour of North Dakota was Jack's approach to farm problems. Ted added: "Little talk about religion in this area." He also noted that much of the press seemed favorable to JFK. "I would suggest that we have a separate file of these people and send them various news clippings and announcements."

In one of his memos, he was very explicit about contacts:

> First of all, I recommend contact of the Anaconda Company in New York, possibly to see whether there is any influence by the Congressional delegation of Montana there and by their lobby-ists. . . . A memorandum should be prepared on water power, natural resources, mining, and freight rates. Jack's views should be included in newsletters distributed in the Rocky Mountain area.
>
> When Jack talks in Maine on November 15th, I suggest he talks on the Pemaquid project. Army engineers have given a favorable report on this. . . . I would suggest the sending out of Jack's labor record to all the labor people in my state.

Teddy was trying to prove he was becoming more mature and more responsible. He decided that instead of simply preaching to the converted it was more important to go where he was not wanted and fight for votes. He did this throughout Oregon. He also learned the political and psychological advantage of packing a crowd into a small auditorium, where they would overflow, rather than having them look sparse in a big ballroom. When Senator Kennedy and his entourage arrived for a speech, and saw the packed place, he told Ted, "You sure know how to turn out a crowd."

———

TED MADE SPEECHES, got movements started, and helped build an organization. "Brother Teddy has largely been the man who goes after the grass-roots vote, and has seen more factory gates at dawn than many factory workers," said his candidate brother. Teddy described it:

"In the pitch dark, it's sort of like a hold-up . . . but it's the only place to see voters at that hour."

His brother repeated often—but not to Teddy—that his brother had accomplished wonders.

Teddy, as always, was ready for any challenge. At Harvard, he bet a friend that he could drive a golf ball across the Charles, and did. In Europe, when he was in the Army, on a pass in Switzerland, he scored the fastest time in the one-man bobsled race. When he broke his shoulder in a skiing accident, he had a leather brace made, and in two weeks he was back on the slopes.

Now, in the campaign, he had been challenged to make his first Olympic ski jump in Wisconsin. He rode a bucking bronco at the Miles City rodeo, in Montana, and stayed on for five and one-half seconds. The only offer he failed to accept was that of an Indian who wanted to shoot a cigarette out of his mouth with a .22. "He would have done that," a friend said, "but Teddy doesn't smoke."

A Wyoming delegate told him, "I wish you were running."

At a family party for father Kennedy, somebody wrote a parody of "Santa Claus Is Coming to Town," which went, in part:

> He sees you when you're sleeping,
> He knows if you're awake;
> He knows if Ted's campaigning,
> For his own or for Jack's sake.

Ted did make mistakes.

Frank Thompson, a New Jersey Congressman and family friend, dropped in at Bobby's campaign headquarters later to tell him that he had heard that Teddy had either bought or rented a house in California in an area where a star black basketball player had recently been turned away.

"Bobby picked up the phone. It was then just before seven A.M. in California. When his younger brother sleepily answered, Bobby said, 'Teddy, you dumb son of a bitch, you get out of there before this day is over. If you've rented the house, make a deal with your landlord. If you've bought the goddamn thing, then sell it or give it away. Just get the hell out of the neighborhood!!!!' "

Ted later sent a telegram to Hyannis: CAN I COME BACK IF I PROMISE TO CARRY THE WESTERN STATES?

––––––––

BOBBY HAD BEEN exhausted right after Jack won the nomination, and he never really had caught up on his rest. Now he was slumped with fatigue, slept seldom, never relaxed. "Nobody's ever worked harder in history," said Lem Billings of Bobby.

Asked how much of a campaign is work, Bobby replied, "Ninety percent . . . maybe more."

"Jack works harder than any mortal man," said his father, then added: "Bobby goes a little further."

During the campaign, the two brothers unexpectedly ran into each other at a windswept airport.

"Hi, Johnny," said Bobby. "How are you?"

"Man, I'm tired," said the candidate.

"What the hell are you tired for?" said Bob. "I'm doing all the work."

––––––––

JACK'S FAITH IN Bobby's campaign judgment was almost absolute. He later admitted, "I don't have to do a thing about organization. . . . I just show up. Bobby's the hardest worker. He's the greatest organizer. . . . Bobby's easily the best man I've ever seen."

During Jack Kennedy's visit to California, political boss Jesse Unruh wanted Lyndon Johnson to introduce him; Bob wanted Stevenson. When candidate Kennedy arrived, and heard Stevenson was to introduce him, he cursed loudly and asked who made that decision.

"Bobby," said Unruh.

And without a minute's hesitation, John Kennedy said, "He must have had a good reason."

"That was the end of it," said Unruh.

Bobby did cause a flap among southern Democrats when he got angry on a radio show and accused them, naming names, of blocking progressive legislation. Southern groups then sharply complained to Senator Kennedy, who told them Robert was "young and very hotheaded." And he promised that it wouldn't happen again. That didn't satisfy them. They wanted a promise that Bobby would keep out of

Florida and South Carolina and stop publicly attacking state political leaders who might happen to disagree with him or with the Senator. It was the first time anybody remembered Jack publicly apologizing for Bobby, and it would not happen often.

At the suggestion of a staffer, Harris Wofford (who later became a Senator from Pennsylvania), John Kennedy called Coretta Scott King to say he would do all he could to help her husband, Dr. Martin Luther King, Jr., get out of jail. When Bob heard about it, he was bitterly angry with Wofford: "You bomb-throwers probably lost the election . . . you've probably lost three states." Three southern governors had told him earlier that a kind word for King would kill Kennedy's southern hopes.

"I remember going into a room and there were Jack and Bobby talking, talking, and talking," said Teddy.

In the course of conversation, Bobby's anger shifted. He couldn't do anything about the telephone call anymore, but there was a judge who refused to grant bail to King. Shouldn't he call the judge and complain? His campaign assistant John Seigenthaler said no, it would only make things worse. He thought he had convinced Kennedy. But Bobby now felt that the whole incident would stir up the South and cost votes—and it was the judge's fault for starting it.

"It just burned me up," said Bob afterward, "to think of that bastard sentencing a citizen to four months of hard labor for a minor traffic offense and screwing up my brother's campaign and making our country look ridiculous before the world. . . . I think I'll call that judge and give him a piece of my mind."

Bob called the judge from a phone booth. "I made it clear to him that it was not a political call, that I am a lawyer who believes in the right of all defendants to make bond. I said that if he was a decent American, he would let King out of jail by sundown." The judge did.

"You are now an Honorary Brother," a black leader told Bobby.

Both brothers had acted independently, and neither had acted with any strong feeling for civil rights on the premise that "there are moments when the politically expedient is the morally wise."

King's father promised to swing his whole "suitcase full of votes—my whole church" for Kennedy, even though he admitted that he had been anti-Kennedy because he was a Catholic.

Kennedy later remarked on King's father's statement, "That was a hell of a bigoted statement, wasn't it. Imagine Martin Luther King having a bigot for a father." Then he smiled and added, "Well, we all have fathers, don't we?"

With the presidential election two days away, the Kennedy head-quarters distributed 2 million pamphlets describing Kennedy's inter-vention in this matter. Some cynics think that was the original intent of the call, but the call was quick and impulsive, with little discussion. President Eisenhower later told some business leaders in the White House that Kennedy won his slim victory with "a couple of phone calls."

———

ON ELECTION DAY, Kennedy posed for photographers at Hyannis Port, then changed into slacks and a sport shirt and relaxed, even tossed a soccer ball around for a few minutes with brother Bob. Author Cornelius Ryan was at Hyannis that day and saw Kennedy on the terrace, his face drawn, looking strained and tired. "He sat down on a bamboo chaise longue, and pulled a blanket up around his chin. It was quite nippy. His father came across at that point wearing a gray flannel suit with a monogram on the left breast pocket. He seemed very fit. Instead of nervously awaiting every scrap of news, Jack launched into a big discussion with me about World War II and my books."

Bob, however, quickly returned to his own home across the lawn, where he had set up an election command post in the breakfast room. Ninety appointed assistants in key precincts all over the nation phoned in their findings directly to him. He also kept in touch with Democratic National Committee Chairman Henry "Scoop" Jackson, in Washing-ton, over direct telephone lines. He had another private line to Jack's house.

"Bobby was in total command of the situation," Ryan added. "He was very crisp. Curiously, one of the strange things I noticed was that there was very little communication between Jack and Bobby. Jack would come into the breakfast room and stand with his back against the wall, just listening. Bobby would be at the far end of the table, surrounded by telephones. There were calls from political leaders all over the country. Bobby would say, 'How are things going there?' He had that particular Massachusetts twang in his voice, which always seemed to me . . . when he got tensed up . . . terribly pronounced.

"From time to time, Bob would come out and walk along the lawn down by the sea, in deep concentration, and then he'd come back in again. When the message came in that said Hawaii had gone for Kennedy, there was a great hurrah, and Teddy stood up and said, 'And you fellows all thought I was doing nothing else in Hawaii but lying on the beach!' The news that Connecticut had gone to Jack, a real victory, brought a 'Fantastic!' from Jack. Then he lit a big black cigar, while his gleeful sister Eunice warbled 'When Irish Eyes Are Smiling.' "

The New York Times, predicting victory, was even printing and circulating part of an edition announcing Kennedy's election—before stopping the presses. They were afraid of being caught, as the Chicago *Tribune* was in falsely headlining Dewey's victory over Truman in 1948. Kennedy later told James Reston, "If you were scared at the *Times*, you should have seen *me*!"

By midnight the race was still undecided. Bobby stayed up, making telephone calls and checking the late returns. "When my wife and I were leaving," said O'Donnell, "I noticed that he seemed perturbed, and I asked him what was worrying him.

" 'I'm worrying about Teddy,' Bobby said. 'We've lost every state [except Hawaii] that he worked in out west. Jack will kid him, and that may hurt Teddy's feelings.' " He had remembered how Jack had razzed him at the convention about two Montana delegates who had failed to vote the way he had predicted.

One of the states lost was Colorado. The Denver *Post* blamed Ted Kennedy's "inexperience." Others blamed the religious issue. "Their bigots beat our bigots."

———

AT 2 A.M. there was a call from Boss Daley in Chicago. Daley was an old political crony of Joe's. Their friendship was important for Daley because the mayor reportedly had some thoughts of running for governor. Daley told him, "Mr. President, with the help of your friends here, we will carry Illinois for you." Kennedy said afterward that was the first time anyone called him Mr. President.

Kennedy captured Illinois by 8,858 votes. Mafia boss Sam Giancana later claimed that he had stolen enough votes for Kennedy on Chicago's West Side to ensure his victory. The political fact is that Boss Daley was more influential in manipulating the final vote in Chicago than

Giancana. Ironically, the decisive victory vote would not come from Illinois, but from Minnesota.

The results were still uncertain when Jack went to bed.

Teddy later remembered that their father was the last one to go to bed on election night because he wanted to make certain that the final victory was assured—even though he kept telling everyone that it was never in doubt.

Two generations later, Rose Kennedy told her grandson about the Ross Perot campaign for the presidency. "I read in the paper that he was going to spend $100 million to buy the election. Your grandfather only spent ten."

———

IT WAS A bright, sunny morning and Caroline and her nannie, Maude Shaw, were having cornflakes and eggs, wondering about the final election result, when Shaw looked out at the lawn in front of the house and noticed a man in a dark suit, just standing there. "He wasn't going anywhere," said Shaw. "He just kept looking round rather carefully, taking an occasional glance toward the house. Who could it possibly be? . . . And then I realized. He was a Secret Service man! The President's bodyguard. . . . I realized then that Senator Kennedy must have won." At the time, the law required immediate protection for the new President.

" 'May I go and see Daddy now?' Caroline asked.

" 'Yes, right away,' I said. 'But when you go and wake him up, I want you to . . . say, "Good morning, Mr. President." '

" 'Will he like that?' she asked.

" 'Yes, I think he'll be very pleased.' "

As Maude Shaw recalled the scene, "The new President was just a hump in the bedclothes, but Caroline shot across the room, jumped on the bed, and pulled the blankets from her father's tousled head. He grunted, opened his eyes, and smiled at his daughter. Caroline played her part perfectly and with good timing. She said nothing until he had given her a hug and kiss. 'Good morning, Mr. President,' she said, her eyes shining with delight. 'Well, now, is that right?' Caroline looked over to where I stood in the doorway, and her father's glance followed hers. 'Am I in, Miss Shaw?' he asked. 'Of course you are, Mr. President,' I said. He looked at his watch a bit doubtfully. 'Well, I wasn't in the White House for sure at 4:30 this morning.'

" 'Oh, I'm sure you've been elected, sir,' I said.

"He sat up in bed and looked almost sternly at me. 'Now, you just go back to the television set,' he said, 'and wait there until the result is confirmed, and then come back and tell me the final figures.'

" 'Yes, sir,' I said.

"He had gone to sleep out of sheer exhaustion, uncertain of victory or defeat.

"Within five minutes, the result was through, and the election of the President could be definitely confirmed. I jotted down the figures, and fairly skipped back to Mr. Kennedy's room. When I burst in, he was playing and talking to Caroline, apparently quite calm and unconcerned.

"I felt tears of happiness pricking my eyes as I stopped a few paces inside the room. 'Mr. President, you have been elected.' "

Kennedy was elected President by 115,000 votes—the smallest plurality since Benjamin Harrison defeated Grover Cleveland in 1888. "Kennedy lost 10 million votes because he's a Catholic," said O'Donnell. "I think John Kennedy, if he were Stu Symington, would've beaten Nixon by 20 million votes!"

A photographer watched the Senator duck into the Hyannis Port kitchen to stuff his shirttail into his trousers in preparation for his first formal picture as President-elect.

"I've photographed him doing that a hundred times," the photographer said, putting down his camera, "but now he's President and somehow I don't think it's right."

That day after he was elected, the new President-elect held a meeting at the Cape. Sargent Shriver recorded:

"He came in and said, 'Well, now, we've got to get going. Bobby, I want you to go on vacation; you've been killing yourself in the campaign.' . . . He turned to me and said, 'Sarge, I'd like you to take on the job of getting together the very best people, regardless of party, in the whole U.S., to be members of the Cabinet, to staff the administration. That means we must get a very crackerjack man, right away, to be Director of the Budget. I have to come in with my budget by January. That's absolutely crucial. . . . We'll have to announce the Cabinet within the next 60 days. . . . You'll have to work on the

Defense Dept., Treasury, State, and all the other jobs. . . . I don't want you to have any hesitation about proposing anybody. Just go out and scour the country for the best possible people we can get. . . .'

"I remember sitting there. And sure, I knew Jack Kennedy," said Shriver. "Yes, I'd participated in his campaign. But, with all due respect to myself, I don't think, if I'd been Jack Kennedy, I'd have turned to me, to that job. First, I had minimal experience in Washington. Number two, I'd never gone out to recruit people for top positions in industry; it wasn't my business, you might say. Three, I was not an experienced economist, who knew all the people you might consider to be Budget Director. Didn't know all the people in banking, for Secretary of Treasury, etc. . . . But he decided to entrust the job that he considered crucial, right then, to somebody he knew and liked."

The new President was in charge.

7

FANFARE AND FAILURE

"The American people have chosen adventure," wrote the London *Daily Telegraph*. For John Kennedy, it would soon begin with the quick shock of waking up in the White House and realizing that he was not only the most important man in this country, but the most important man in the world. He knew the job "will take more than a hundred days or a thousand days."

The world he inherited was a quiet one. No immediate crises loomed. The Korean War had ended six years before. The Eisenhower years had been peaceful, and the economic recession had eased. The only looming issue of danger was what Kennedy called "the goddamn civil rights mess."

Under Eisenhower, Washington had been a placid place, a relaxed company town with a strong southern flavor. Suddenly, the town was really jumping.

"America was ripe and ready for the Kennedys when they appeared," Daniel Boorstin wrote in *Image*. "We have become so accustomed to our illusions that we mistake them for reality. We demand them. . . . The less faith Americans had in themselves, the more irrational faith they invested in the Kennedys."

It has been said that the health of a country can be seen in the political heroes they pick. "Like Roosevelt," said correspondent Sander Vanocur, "he allowed you to dream . . . you felt better."

For John Kennedy, it was also a time of personal pride. In his father's eyes, he finally had become the first son. Gone were the long, bitter years when his father had thought less of him. Gone were the times when his father and brother were in the limelight and he stood in the shadow. Now he asked, and insisted, that the father stand with him in *his* limelight as he appeared on national television to acknowledge his election victory.

No longer would he be known as his father's son. And the elder Kennedy settled happily for his new status. He told Ira Henry Freeman of *The New York Times*, "Now I can appear with Jack any time I want to."

Ted had made a $500 bet with his friend Carey that brother Jack would become President, and now Carey arrived to pay up. Instead Ted said, "Let's make it double or nothing on Bobby."

———

THE VICTORY WAS so thin that a single vote in each precinct would have changed the result. Kennedy feared Nixon might contest the election because of the close vote count. Kennedy Sr. contacted his old boss, former President Herbert Hoover, about the danger of the country being torn apart if Nixon demanded a recount on the election. Hoover then arranged a meeting of Nixon and John Kennedy at the Jamaica Inn, at Biscayne Bay in Florida. When Kennedy came in the door, Nixon's first words were, "How are you, Mr. President?" This was a clear indication to Kennedy that Nixon would not contest the election.

Asking for a recount would give Nixon the image of a sore loser, and he was still young enough to try again.

———

TO THE NATION, John Kennedy said, "So now my wife and I prepare for a new administration and a new baby."

At her post-election press conference, Jacqueline Kennedy looked frightened, dazed by the flashbulbs. Her unpolished nails were bitten to the quick. If her self-confidence was small, she had good reason. Jack may well have been President of the United States, but he was still not the husband of her heart. The marriage was shaky because he confided little in her, relied on her for less. Nor could she be indifferent to her husband's other women, although she tried. She would later surprise

Jack, and make him proud, but she would never have family support from the Kennedy women. They were never at ease with her. She could count on the father and the sons, but seldom on her husband. Most of all, she now would have to rely on herself.

Asked earlier if she thought being the First Lady would change her, she said, "I wouldn't put on a mask and pretend to be anything that I wasn't."

As the third-youngest of thirty previous First Ladies, Jacqueline said, "I have every confidence that my husband will be absolutely magnificent and give himself completely. And I hope," she said, almost inaudibly, "I won't fail him in any way."

A late-arriving reporter apologized, explaining she had been delayed by the President-elect's press conference.

"I'm sure that was more interesting," said the new First Lady.

THERE IS LITTLE question that Jack wanted a son—all the brothers did. It was a question of the succession of the Kennedy name. John Fitzgerald Kennedy, Jr., soon known as John-John, arrived two days after Thanksgiving. Charles Bartlett was there for the baptism at the chapel. "In this lovely family atmosphere, I thought we were going to have a fistfight," Bartlett recalled, "because, at this point, Jack wanted to make Bill Fulbright Secretary of State and Bobby was indignant at the idea. He had known Fulbright on the McClellan Committee and was vehement about him. I was saying nice things about Fulbright, too, and I thought Bobby was going to slug me. It all started at the chapel and ended up later in Jackie's room at the hospital. It was a hot fight."

"I mentioned that I had been at a party where I had heard Fulbright make some racist remarks," Bill Walton added. " 'See?' said Bobby. 'That's what I told you. We can't possibly have anyone who's a racist as Secretary of State.' "

The hot fight over Fulbright ended later with the new President selecting Dean Rusk, then President of the Rockefeller Foundation. Rusk had lectured and written that the President was the real formulator of foreign policy. "He was chosen for that reason."

When O'Donnell told Bob about the President's decision, Bob protested, "But he didn't tell me."

"He's not supposed to be telling anybody anything who works for him," Bob said.

O'Donnell added that the President was unhappy because of Bobby's leak to the press about Fulbright.

"I only told a few guys," said Bobby.

"He said you can't tell *any* guys."

Jack asked his brother to notify Rusk of his decision. Accompanied by his big dog, Bobby told Rusk that they needed "somebody who could organize and pull the place together."

The incident put the Jack-Bob relationship in a fresh perspective. The power had shifted. During the campaign, Bob's word was generally decisive. And, now, even though Bob had prevailed on Fulbright, Jack's selection of Rusk, without Bob's input, was his way of showing that he was the President and Bob should start limiting his horizons. They had been the perfect campaign team, but now the relationship would take on different dimensions. In private, Jack would still be "Johnny" and Bob would be "Robbie." But in public, O'Donnell told Bob, "He'd like me to let you know that *he* is the President." Jack had put it more succinctly: "I'm the chief. . . . Ain't no other chief . . . and don't you ever forget it."

But Bob was not always so easily put in his place.

One day after the election, Jack was playing touch football with the family at Hyannis. Leaping to intercept a pass, he hit the ground seconds later and landed at the bottom of a tangled heap of Kennedys and Kennedy in-laws. Leaning out an upstairs window of the beach house, the senior Kennedy overheard Bob rebuke the very new President-elect: "Plenty of guts, but no brains." It had been said of Bob when he was a small boy.

————

FAMILY AND FRIENDS noted that Jack was tired and deflated after his victory. For him the chase and the challenge had always been more exciting than the actual conquest, whether it was a campaign or a woman. Now came the overwhelming work of the office.

"You know, it's two different ball games. Winning is one . . . and being President is the other. . . . I spent four years getting to know the type of person that could help me win this fight. Now, I have only a few weeks to get the people who will help me be a good President."

Soon after the election, Kennedy called Clark Clifford. "Do you have the book ready?"

Kennedy sent a Secret Service man to pick up twenty copies of Clifford's book detailing the immediate steps a President must take after election.

Some things had to be done quickly. People had resigned, and their gaps had to be filled. Friends started calling Bobby, wanting jobs. "Bob sat down with us," said O'Donnell. "He knew all the players—we knew all the players. We'd check their competency, get the FBI reports on them."

Larry O'Brien was having cocktails before dinner with Joe and his sons. "We were just standing in the foyer. The father said to Bobby, 'Bobby, what are you going to do now?' Bobby said, 'Gee, Dad, I don't know . . . I hadn't really thought about it.' He added he might practice law. The father said, 'Well, do you have any plans? You know, you've got to get moving. You know, Bobby, you've got to remember, *you* weren't elected.' "

What Bob now wanted, of course, was to emerge as his own man, not his father's son, or his brother's brother. There was John Kennedy's vacant Senate seat. But Bob wanted to be elected, not appointed.

His father was adamant. "Bobby's got nothing. The President wants him around—wants him here—but where the hell do you put him? Anywhere you put him, under somebody else, the other guy's job is in jeopardy, from the beginning . . . how can you have the President's brother going over to the White House every five minutes, when you're the boss? It's just untenable."

If Joe Kennedy wanted to give Bob a job in the White House, nobody else did, especially Bobby. "It would be impossible with the two of us sitting around an office looking at each other all day. You know, it was like the campaign . . . he had his role in the campaign and I had my role and we would meet and discuss when a crisis came up . . . but he never involved himself in what I was doing—the running of the campaign—and I was not directly associated with what he was doing . . . we had to have our own areas—I had to be apart from what he was doing so I wasn't working directly for him and getting orders from him as to what I should do that day. That wouldn't be possible. So I would never consider working over at the White House."

His brother agreed. Bobby in the White House would soon assume the duties of a Vice President, and he already had a Vice President. The State Department was another suggested area, and some felt "Bobby would've shook up the place." Bob had thought of being "assistant secretary or something for Latin America." Another job mentioned was Secretary of Defense, but Ted Clifton (who would become Kennedy's military aide) warned him against it. "There's so much in the job that can get a President in trouble."

It was suggested that he might become Deputy Secretary and get an education observing. His father said he was willing to let Bob be Deputy if it was understood that the person appointed would be out in a year.

When Senator Abraham Ribicoff was offered the Attorney General job, he turned it down and suggested Bobby. "Jack was taken aback," said Ribicoff, "and then said, 'I can't name my own brother.'"

"Why should the President appoint people whose qualifications he doesn't know firsthand," asked his father, "and not appoint people whose qualifications he does know at first hand—simply because they are relatives?"

Dave Powers recalled being with the family on their yacht. "Bobby was there—making time with all the Washington correspondents, the elite of the Washington Press Club. And he could be very charming. None of us ever dreamed he was gonna be the Attorney General. He was thought of as an eager young guy. . . . Most of them were seeing Bobby, and talking to him, for the first time. . . . Teddy was getting drinks for us . . . sort of the cabin-boy."

————

WITH BOB SHOPPING around for a job, it was his father who decided his son should be Attorney General. "He wouldn't hear of anything else," said Bobby, "because he felt that, if I was there, I should be involved in all the major decisions that were made . . . he felt that Jack should have somebody that . . . had been close for a long period of time, and he wanted me in this job. I was against it and we had some rather strong arguments out here, all the family—a couple of my sisters, Jack and Teddy and my father." Teddy was one of those against it. So was Ethel.

Concerned with Bobby's reluctance, the father noted, "I don't know what's wrong with him. Jack needs all the good men he can get around him down here. There's none better than Bobby."

————

THE PRESIDENT CALLED Senator George Smathers aside one day at Palm Beach. "I don't know what the hell to do with Bobby. . . . My old man now wants him to be Attorney General. I don't know if the public will accept it. What do you think?"

Smathers agreed that Bob had no legal experience and such an appointment would be "a little bit offensive." Kennedy asked him to talk to his father. When the Ambassador arrived for his sunbath, Smathers, feigning ignorance, posed the question: "What do you think oughta happen to Bobby?"

The answer came quickly. "What's going to happen is, he's gonna be Attorney General."

"I said, 'Mr. Ambassador, you know, I don't think Bobby's old enough, don't think he's experienced enough to be Attorney General.'

" 'Nope. Attorney General, that's what he ought to be. And that's what he's gonna be.' "

When Jack returned, his father added, "Jack, I want you to know that nobody has given you more of themselves, in your lifetime, than Bobby has given to you . . . and I want you to make him Attorney General."

President-elect Kennedy tried again, sent Clark Clifford to try to change his father's mind.

"Now, Bobby's going to get his chance," the Ambassador told Clifford. "Bobby's going to be Attorney General. And he's going to make a fine Attorney General, and it'll give him an understanding and an exposure that will be very valuable to him. . . . When you speak to Jack next, well, you just pass the word on to Jack that we had a very nice visit and I said to you, 'Bobby's going to be Attorney General.' "

"I would always remember the intense but matter-of-fact tone with which he had spoken," said Clifford. "There was no rancor, no anger, no challenge. He did not resent my presentation or my opposition to the appointment, he was simply telling me the facts. For a moment I had glimpsed the inner workings of that remarkable family, and, despite my admiration and affection for John F. Kennedy, I could not say I liked what I saw."

As the possibility looked more certain, Bartlett observed that Bobby seemed increasingly unhappy about the prospect of being Attorney General. Bob had said he had been "chasing bad guys" for three years and was tired of it.

When Shriver presented their list of candidates, Jack Kennedy said, "Why give me these? Bobby will be Attorney General."

It was still Bobby's decision.

For advice, he sought out Justice William O. Douglas. "He had quite a decision to make," said Douglas. "Would he make a good Attorney General? Would he hurt or help his brother? Would it hurt or help him in his future? and so on. . . . We talked about it at great length."

Douglas also talked long-term alternatives with Bobby: a college president, the head of a public service foundation, governor of Massachusetts, or the Senate or the House. One thing was clear: Bobby did not really want to practice law.

"I talked to a number of people," Bob told Seigenthaler, "and not one of them thinks that I should go into the Attorney General's office." They all thought he should get out of government, except, surprisingly, FBI Director J. Edgar Hoover. In all probability, Hoover still saw Bobby as his father's son, and as the young man who had worked for his friend Senator McCarthy, and whom he therefore thought he could influence and direct.

Bob finally made his decision against the position during dinner after a discussion with Ethel and Seigenthaler at Hickory Hill. He said, "This will kill my father."

It seemed remarkable that Bob had progressed so much on his own that he would defy his father on a major decision. Bob called the President to tell him why he had decided not to do it, reciting all the opinions of people he had talked to. His brother said, "Well, don't tell me now. I want to have breakfast with you in the morning. Come to the house on N Street."

The morning was cold, with four inches of snow on the ground. Breakfast was bacon and eggs. Bobby had brought Seigenthaler with him. The President-elect began talking about his other Cabinet appointments and Bob finally said, "Now, Johnny, can we talk about my situation?"

They talked about forty minutes. Jack explained that in the Cabinet

there really was no person with whom he had been intimately connected over the years. "I need to know that when problems arise, I'm
going to have someone who's going to tell me the unvarnished truth,
no matter what he thinks. . . . I don't want somebody who is going to
be fainthearted," said Jack. "I want somebody who is going to be
strong; who will join with me in taking risks . . . and who would deal
with the problem honestly. . . . We're going to have to change the
climate in this country. And if my administration does the things I want
it to do, I'm going to have to be able to have someone as Attorney
General to carry these things out, on whom I can rely completely."

Then he added, "If I can ask Dean Rusk to give up a career; if I can
ask Adlai Stevenson to make a sacrifice he does not want to make; if I
can ask Bob McNamara to give up a job as head of that company—
these people I don't even know . . . certainly I can expect my own
brother to give me that same sort of contribution. And I need you in
this government." As he later added, he needed someone who would
"never screw him."

"So I said, well, I thought I should think about it," Bob replied.

"And as Jack got to that point," said Seigenthaler, "he pushed back
his chair and got up and went in the kitchen. And we sat there. And I
didn't know whether he'd gone for more coffee or bacon and eggs or
what. But the fact of the matter was, he had terminated the conversation. So I said, 'Let's go, Bob.' He said, 'No, wait. I've got some
points I want to make.' I said, 'There's no point to make.' So he
walked back in and said, 'So that's it . . . General, let's go.' He sort of
laughed, and maybe cussed a little. That's it, and we went. We came
back that day sometime around noon.

"He said, 'Well, let's go out and announce it. . . . Let's grab our
balls and go.' Jack also told him to brush his hair and not smile too
much 'or they'll think we're happy about the appointment.' "

Bobby added one last thought. "On my announcement," he said,
"why don't you paraphrase another prominent American, Dwight
Eisenhower. You can say: 'I know he's my brother, but I need
him.' "

———

VICE PRESIDENT JOHNSON felt that it was "a disgrace for a kid
who's never practiced law to be appointed," but then added, "But I

don't think Jack Kennedy's gonna let a little fart like Bobby lead him around by the nose.''

The press comments on the new Attorney General were mixed: brazen, disgraceful, never been in a courtroom in his life. The positive remarks emphasized that he had done a creditable job as chief counsel on the McClellan Committee, and he should not be excluded now just because the President was his brother.

The deed done, the President now concentrated on the positives: Dave Powers recalled sitting with Jack near the small bar at their home in Palm Beach, ''And then he said, looking right at me: 'I want the best men I can get for my Cabinet—and they don't come any better than Bobby.' ''

Powers later reflected, ''You know, what a wonderful thing to say about a brother.''

TEDDY WAS THEN at loose ends. A law school graduate, a married man, a father, and temporarily unemployed, he was still far from the public eye. ''You had to stop and think, and say, 'Oh yeah, there's another brother,' '' said reporter Esther Tufty. As far as brothers were concerned, he was a shadow's shadow. His brothers loomed too large. He got along particularly well with both of them: Jack had taken over from young Joe as his much-needed surrogate father in his early years, and Bobby had befriended him all his life. But now both brothers were intensely busy. Teddy was old enough now to be envious and ambitious.

He had written a letter to Bob when Bob became Attorney General:

Any room in the Department for a guy who graduated in the top half of the bottom quarter of his Class   congratulations

Eddy Edward Kennedy

Senator Frank Church had asked Teddy to come along on a Senate Foreign Relations Subcommittee tour of African countries. Teddy went as an observer on the five-week, sixteen-nation fact-finding tour, while his wife looked for a house in Boston. En route to Africa, Ted told reporters in London that he planned to return to his practice now that the election was over. Back home, it caused a big family laugh. "What practice," one of them asked, "touch football?"

Others in Washington, like Senate aide Ralph Dungan, felt that Ted was so young and unaware that if you gave him a world map without names, he probably couldn't even pick out the African continent, and sending him there was like sending a child to a lions' den.

Still, on a side trip to Cairo, the American Ambassador to Egypt was impressed that Teddy talked constantly about his brother, but never once referred to him as Jack. It was always, "President Kennedy would have done it this way."

It proved, perhaps, that while Ted had much to learn, his political potential was there.

———

IN A LONG, private talk at Hyannis, *New York Times* correspondent James Reston had asked Jack Kennedy what he wanted to have achieved by the time he rode down Pennsylvania Avenue with his successor. "He looked at me as if I were a dreaming child. I tried again: did he not feel the need of some goal to help guide his day-to-day decisions and priorities? Again a ghastly pause. It was only when I turned the question to immediate, tangible problems that he seized the point and rolled off a torrent of statistics about the difficulty of organizing nations at different levels of economic development."

Kennedy then only saw the goal of the office, the pragmatic, political goal—nothing else. Asked elsewhere what kind of world he hoped to help create, he replied, "I haven't had time to think about that yet."

Jack and Bob were sitting in the Kennedy compound in Hyannis Port, discussing the need to overhaul the State Department and the Foreign Service. Eavesdropping nearby, their father then told them he had heard Franklin D. Roosevelt saying the same thing, and "he didn't do a damn thing about it, and neither are you."

"Jack was amused by his father, admired him, always interested in his ideas," recalled William Walton. "And this phased out—the longer and the higher the office, the less he saw of his father. But still his father kept throwing in words when the Cabinet was being selected. And ideas, some of them terribly good. He had a marvelous feeling of how a young President should behave."

Earlier, when the newly elected President offered Robert McNamara, President of Ford Motor Company, the job of Defense Secretary, McNamara had said he didn't know anything about government, and Kennedy replied, "I don't know how to be President either . . . we'll learn together."

McNamara had some conditions, including final approval of staff, and the President passed the paper to Robert, who was sitting next to him. "Looks okay," said his brother.

Later Kennedy complained aloud, "Jesus Christ, this one wants this, that one wants this. Goddamn it, you can't satisfy any of these people." His father turned to him and said, "Jack, if you don't want the job, you don't have to take it. They're still counting votes up in Cook County."

———

PALM BEACH WAS a kind of organized chaos. Milton Gwirtzman remembered the Inaugural Address being proofread at one desk, in a monotone that made it sound very uninspiring; in another room President Kennedy's father was deciding who would sit where at the inaugural gala.

The elder Kennedy also had a question about his son's inaugural speech:

"Do you really have something tomorrow that's going to awaken America?"

"I think so, Dad."

———

THERE WAS A blizzard the night before the Inauguration. The President's father and Teddy were in a car that got stuck in the snow. Teddy remembers the two of them pushing the car, with the father telling him, "Push harder . . ." He was always telling his sons to do that. Some things would never change.

Later, in one of the inaugural party buses, Clare Boothe Luce recalled Ted singing Irish ballads. Ambassador Hervé Alphand of France remembered that Ted "had drunk more than is customary" and was later "dancing madly on the platform."

Word later came to the new President that Clare Luce had said of

Teddy, "He looks like a Greek god!" And John Kennedy said, "Are you sure you didn't say, 'He looks like a goddamn Greek'?"

On the day of the Inauguration, Jacqueline went to Ted, bewildered, and said, "No one's told me what I'm supposed to do . . . I don't know . . . Jack's told me nothing."

Jacqueline was not on her husband's priority list. Besides, the other Kennedys were all busy with themselves, and Jacqueline looked so poised—as though she had been briefed—that everyone assumed she was. But the poise was still straight from Miss Porter's School.

Eunice and Lem Billings sneaked away to survey the White House on their own. They prowled quietly until they found the Lincoln bedroom "and took turns bouncing on the bed, giggling like children and photographing each other."

Years later, in a memorial volume about Billings, Jacqueline wrote the shortest eulogy: "So many grown-ups lose the sense of play; Lem never did. And how he loved his friends!"

―――――――

THERE HAD BEEN an urgent appeal from the head of the New York Liberal Party, who was also head of the hatters' union, requesting that Jack and Bobby *please please* wear the enclosed black homburgs at the Inauguration. Both brothers decided on silk toppers, which had to be made to order because of their large heads.

"I remember at our wedding," said Jacqueline, "he was going to rent a cutaway, and grandpa told him he was crazy, that he should get one made. He looked so shining in it and he wore it at his Inauguration. . . . My favorite (no, one of my favorite) pictures of him—is standing in the doorway at the White House that day—in his cutaway—holding his top hat—so happy."

In the official car, en route to the Inauguration, Jacqueline listened to Mrs. Eisenhower say that President Eisenhower looked like "Paddy the Irishman in his top hat." . . . Then she realized she had made a slight gaffe.

The Kennedy clan arrived at the reviewing stand in three buses marked *Kennedy Family*. All of them took turns sitting next to their presidential brother, watching the parade of eighty-six bands.

Beaming, laughing Joe Kennedy was telling his friends that "this is what I've been looking forward to for a long time. It's a great day."

It was not just a great day—it was his *greatest* day. His daughter Eunice quoted poet Laurie Lee: "Any man's child is his second chance."

Clark Clifford, sitting near Joseph Kennedy, recalled, "I talked to him about Jack and again got the impression that this was the beginning of a dream that Ambassador Kennedy had; and it was just the beginning. . . . I think it was the creation, possibly, of a dynasty."

Earlier in the ceremony, when John Kennedy passed the inaugural stand, Eunice saw her father doffing his high hat in deference to his son. It was his way of saying, "You have done it. You are now not only my son but my President. You have fulfilled my ultimate ambition."

And his son, the President, in turn doffed his hat for his father. It was his way of saying, "I would not be here except for you, for your power."

It was a moving moment for those who saw it.

The National Park Service sprayed fresh green dye on the lawns surrounding the Lincoln Memorial. They tried to discourage the starlings by coating the trees along the inaugural route with a compound called Roost-No-More. Secret Service agents organized a security guard of 5000 men, set up surveillance posts on rooftops, even sealed manhole covers on the parade streets to discourage any bomb-planting saboteur.

Watching the inaugural parade on television, General Howard Snyder, White House physician to President Eisenhower, observed Kennedy perspiring heavily despite the freezing weather and despite being without a coat or hat.

"He's all hopped up," he told Admiral Arthur Radford. Snyder told Radford that Kennedy's doctor had prescribed a shot of cortisone every morning "to keep him in good operating condition." It was obvious to Snyder that Kennedy's heavy beads of sweat were the result of getting an extra dose.

Snyder described the effect when the cortisone wore off, of going from a high to a low, and added, "I hate to think of what might happen to the country if Kennedy is required at 3 A.M. to make a decision affecting the national security."

John F. Kennedy became the thirty-fifth President of the United

States at the age of forty-three. Among the aging leaders of the world, Kennedy could have been the son of almost any of them. He was twenty-three years younger than Khrushchev, Mao, and Macmillan; twenty-six years younger than de Gaulle; and forty-one years younger than Adenauer.

———

THE PRESIDENT'S SPEECH was electrifying—the rallying cry to a new generation: "Let the word go forth from this time and place, to friend and foe alike, that the torch has been passed to a new generation of Americans." President Kennedy pledged to defend freedom: "We shall pay any price, bear any burden, meet any hardship, support any friend, oppose any foe, in order to assure the survival and success of liberty." And he concluded, "And so, my fellow Americans, ask not what your country can do for you. Ask what you can do for your country."

It was a speech of the spirit. It didn't simply stir people; it caught them, raised them, moved them. They wanted to do something; they wanted to help; they wanted to be part of it.

Reviewing her emotions of that day, Rose Kennedy said she recalled the words of St. Luke, "which I had recited to him so often. 'Those to whom much is given, much is expected.'" What impressed the President's mother even more—as she informed Robert Coughlan— was that "Jack went to Mass the morning of the inauguration."

The President did make a point of attending Mass at the Holy Trinity Church in Washington with his brother Ted on the first Sunday after his Inauguration, and he would occasionally go off to church by himself. "He was very conscious of being a Catholic, but his religion was on a low level of intensity," said William Walton.

The intensity was usually so low that when the Robert Kennedys gave each of their children religious pictures to hang on their bedroom walls, Jack and Jacqueline confided to friends that "they wouldn't be caught dead with those pictures in their house." Asked about JFK's attitude toward religion or toward the church or clergy, Charles Spalding said, "Skeptical."

And yet Teddy recalled that during his father's first visit to the White House after the Inauguration, he was just about to go to sleep and he remembered something he neglected to mention to the

President. He knocked on the President's door, opened it and found Jack kneeling, saying his prayers. "Dad was deeply touched."

———

MORE THAN FORTY floats passed by, with some 32,000 marchers. Massachusetts portrayed highlights of Kennedy's life. Hawaii had a star of orchids fitted with a device that pumped out scent along the way. But when the President saw his PT boat on a truck, filled with his wartime crew, he raised his hands and cheered.

The family had tea at the White House after the parade, then made the rounds of the inaugural balls. Appearing after midnight at one of Washington's five inaugural balls, the new youthful President told an exhausted crowd brightly: "I think this is an ideal way to spend an evening and I hope that we can all meet here again tomorrow at 1 o'clock to do it all over again."

For Jacqueline, the Inauguration was a triumph and an ordeal. Still recovering from her cesarean surgery, she was unable to be with her husband for the full day.

"I had been in bed all afternoon after the parade," said Jacqueline. "I went to the first ball with Jack and the Johnsons . . . but suddenly in the car—there just wasn't any strength left—so he dropped me back at the White House and he went to the other four balls alone."

After Jacqueline retired at eleven, the rest of the Kennedys assembled at an Italian restaurant. "It was kind of a family party," said Bill Walton. Frank Sinatra joined them to entertain. "Frank just sat back and sang," said Joan Braden. "It was a wonderful party. I cut off about two o'clock in the morning," added Walton. "I was exhausted, and went home. Jack went on to Joe Alsop's party."

Columnist Alsop would never forget the picture of the new President standing on his doorstep. "He looked as though he were still in his thirties, with snowflakes scattered about his thick reddish hair," said Alsop. "Exhilaration always rejuvenated him, and he had been greatly exhilarated by his inauguration . . . there was a bounce in his manner and a light in his eye that would not be so prominent later."

He told Alsop that Jackie had gone to bed, and he was hungry and could find no one in the White House who could give him anything to eat. Alsop offered him terrapin, which the President ignored, and a bottle of champagne. "It hardly mattered," said Alsop. "I soon observed that what he really wanted was one last cup of unadulterated admiration, and the people crowding my living room gave him that cup freely, filled to the brim.''

———

WHEN HE ARRIVED home as the new tenant of the White House, Jack knew enough history to feel the awe of it. As usual, he had his own bedroom. And there is no record whether he fell asleep quickly or whether he lay there awhile in wonder. Either would be understandable. The parties would continue. The next night, during a party in the White House for a few old friends, Bill Walton needed to go to the bathroom, and said he couldn't find one downstairs. The President asked Franklin D. Roosevelt, Jr., ''You've lived here before . . . where's the plumbing?'' They finally all trooped upstairs, and stayed awhile.

———

ON THE PRESIDENT'S desk in the White House, he would keep a plaque on which was written the message given to Polaris submarine commanders: *Oh God, Thy sea is so great and my boat is so small.*

The President's aides soon discovered that in the morning, their boss ''opens up newspapers, two or three at a time,'' and knew what was in them. ''We realized we had to get papers before we walked into his room. So we read four or five papers every morning.''

The early group of Kennedy loyalists quickly moved into position at the White House, O'Donnell with the assignment key to the Oval Office and O'Brien as the liaison with Congress. When the newly elected President offered his friend John Sharon a job on the White House staff, Sharon refused.

''Why?'' Kennedy asked.

''Because I wouldn't survive,'' said Sharon.

''What do you mean?''

''That Irish Mafia of yours is too tight a circle.''

Kennedy's eyes twinkled. ''That's why I want you there—to protect me against them.''

———

AUTHOR JIM BISHOP spent a full day with him, and described the daily routine. ''Kennedy's valet, George Thomas, leaves the little kitchen and walks into the private family quarters in the West Wing of the mansion. He walks softly into the bathroom, and taps lightly on another bedroom door at the far side.

" 'Mr. President,' he whispers hoarsely, 'it's close to 7:30.' . . . Mr. Thomas listens, and hears a clearing of the throat. The President of the United States is awake. Unlike some of his predecessors, he requires no time for collecting his wits, yawning, or a second rap of the door. He's out of bed at once, quickly and quietly. The metamorphosis from deep slumber to keen alertness is about ten seconds."

"There was a sense of wariness about him, a certain, you know, caution. And he lost that only momentarily right after the Inauguration," said Spalding. "I think this terrific sense of power descended; it was more than he had anticipated. Like a lot of things, you know, he didn't have the time to anticipate them."

Kennedy classified most people as either boring or not boring, but was seldom cruel about them. "I always saved my best jokes for the time I would see him," said Laura Bergquist, "because I knew he had a low threshold of boredom. He wanted to be amused, and entertained, and informed." "You could never relax with Jack, because he never relaxed," Nancy Dickerson said. "I remember Charlie Bartlett saying, 'You could kick him, you could rob him, but you must never bore him.' "

As for decisions on issues, Jack was sometimes almost surgical and invariably pragmatic.

When the President wanted to master an issue, like the balance of payments, he read everything, listened to all the experts, and really applied himself. This was not like his time in the Senate when he often did not do his homework—the stakes were higher.

The President was going to make other important changes, too. Hearst correspondent Marianne Means reported a lunch at Hyannis at which the Kennedy father suggested the family go sailing. "Usually that would have been the signal for everyone to make for the boats. But the new President said he didn't feel like it. Anyway, he had a few things to do. There was a sudden silence. Everyone waited for Father Joe's customary outburst. It never came. 'I don't think the President should have to go if he doesn't want to,' said Joseph P. Kennedy."

"I want to help," the former Ambassador told Stephen Smith, "but

I don't want to be a nuisance. Can you tell me: do they want me or don't they want me?" Smith repeated this to Bob. Shortly afterward the father left for Europe. The message was clear: they had needed him, but now they wanted him at a comfortable distance.

———

THE NEW ATTORNEY General was sworn into office in the family's private quarters on the second floor of the White House. After the ceremony, Bob made his appearance at the East Room reception "by sliding down the banister of the great curved staircase that led from the second floor. He was followed by a squealing Kathleen, who was ten years old, and Michael, almost four."

Keenly conscious of the nepotism charge, the President arrived at the first Cabinet meeting with his brother, and before they entered told Bob, "Why don't you go through the other door?"

"The President waited until the Attorney General entered the Cabinet room from the hall door," said his secretary Evelyn Lincoln, "and then he walked into the room from my office."

"I really deferred to him," said Bobby. "I mean, I made a real effort because I recognized the fact that I was young . . . and all the rest of the business. So, I'd always go to his office. . . . I'd never ask him to come to my office. . . . Then, I had to put a special phone in so that we would have direct contact. And I'd just have to pick up the receiver and talk to him. I don't know how much he liked that either."

When Bob Kennedy arrived at the Attorney General's Office, there was a big bottle of aspirin on his desk with a note from his predecessor, William Rogers, saying that this was the only thing he felt was important for this job. "Bob loved that," said Angie Novello.

At first, Bob seemed shaky about everything. Some said he was intellectually insecure, had few close intellectual friends.

His legislative assistant, Peter Edelman, recalled how he tried to hide his nervousness when he met with Supreme Court law clerks. "I sat next to him, and during the whole conversation with this guy who I thought was a real toughie, he sat there with his hands absolutely shaking underneath the table, obviously not at all comfortable in the company of these young smart alecks. But he was asked tough questions, and he answered them very well."

"I don't think you can judge a man by his intellectual capacity," said

Theodore White. "I think you judge a leader by his capacity to use intellectuals. . . . Bobby was a man who knew how to use other men."

Bob soon roamed the marble corridors of the Department, hand open and outstretched. "I'm Bob Kennedy, the Attorney General," he said, asking men twenty years his senior where they had gone to law school and what they were working on. "When he came down the hall, you'd know it," recalled one lawyer. "The buzz was all over the Division."

What most impressed a top aide, Harold Reis, was how hard Kennedy worked, how much he learned, how fast he grew. And how late he stayed. "Some of his staff felt that if they left the office at 8, they were working only a half day.

"Before long, Kennedy's approach helped boost the Department of Justice up by its own bootstraps . . . the people Bob Kennedy brought in really shook it up."

"I liked that Robert," said Washington correspondent Esther Tufty. "I liked his force. I liked the fact that he cluttered up his office with all these young people with long hair and jeans."

On George Washington's birthday he even had an aide copy down the license plates of cars parked in the Justice Department garage. He sent the owners letters of commendation for working on a holiday. "I cannot tell a lie," responded one recipient, "I was in town for the one cent sale and I needed a parking space."

———

DURING THE CAMPAIGN, like his father, Bob was powerful but unseen. Now he would have to prove himself to the world as well as to himself. And he would have to do it under a national searchlight of public scrutiny. Some of the issues he faced, such as prosecuting the Mafia and enforcing civil rights, were among the most explosive, vital issues in the country. It seemed an enormous challenge for a very young man.

Every morning, while shaving, Bob Kennedy would listen to recordings of Shakespeare's plays. He did his serious reading at night, "at least ten books on American history and world resources, between Christmas and Easter," his secretary Angie Novello reported.

Kennedy liked to work on twenty things in a matter of two hours—

big, important things. "Get it done. It was a constant movement," said his secretary.

"The Kennedy style was informal consultation, anti-bureaucratic, round-the-clock vigils, the crash program, the hasty decision, the quick telephone call. Kennedy valued action, energy, motion and speed almost as much as direction," observed Victor Navasky in *Kennedy Justice.*

"Think it over, take as long as you want," Robert Kennedy told Bill Orrick, who had to decide between job offers, "just so long as you let us know by tomorrow morning."

When Bob became intense, he focused on a problem like a laser beam. Political observer George Reedy noted that Bob lived in a heaven and hell world, without any real give in him. And if he was impatient with results, he would get up and slam his chair down and storm out. His father always had operated that way. Many resented that kind of treatment of people, but it worked. Kennedy got things done.

But if anyone outside his office picked on someone on his staff, Bob would say, "Don't you pick on him; this is my responsibility. If you have anything to say, you say it to me."

"We used to get a lot of groups, usually businessmen, who'd want to sit in with the Attorney General and discuss a situation, or just to see how an Attorney General operated," recalled Novello. "Bob had a special button that would connect with the White House . . . all the Cabinet officers had it. . . . He would chat with these men, twenty or thirty of them . . . they'd talk about President Kennedy, and Bob would say, 'Just a minute; I'll ask the President that.' He'd push the button; and by golly, the President would come on, and Bob would put it on the loudspeaker. And all these men—just couldn't believe it!

"Any other President would say, 'Sorry, Bobby, I can't talk to you now,' but John Kennedy was always there, and say, 'Oh, yes, Bobby, OK'—and make a few remarks to the group. They just couldn't get over that.

"The Attorney General particularly favored a group of children from a poor section of Washington . . . all little, all sizes—from about four to eight. He marshaled them all into his office and they jumped on top of this desk, pointing out everything that would be of interest to them, including all the children's paintings," said Novello. "He asked each child what school they were in, what grade. The kids were all awed by this wonderful man, explaining things to them like their own dad."

Bob was an enthusiastic father who gave his children the attention and affection he had missed as a child. And Ethel was his perfect counterpart. "Without her," a friend said, "Bobby might well have gone off the deep end."

In many ways, Bob had married a woman much like his mother—but warmer and much more vivacious. For Ethel, Bobby was everything. She adored him. "With Ethel and Bobby, everything just clicked all the way," said Eunice. "I can still hear him on the beach, in his home, on his boat, on the front lawn playing football, at the tennis court, always with the same question, 'Where's Ethel?' He personally supervised her annual birthday party. . . . On a trip abroad without her, he sent a love message each day in the language of the country he was in."

"They were both physical, and absolutely enjoyed their children, and liked to hug them and kiss them, and each other," said Laura Bergquist. "They would hold hands. And she was fun for Bobby."

Hickory Hill was a big three-story white Georgian house, built in 1810, with a bright red door, sitting on a six-acre hill in McLean, Virginia, about twenty minutes' drive from Washington. General McClellan used it as his headquarters during the Civil War. On the sloping grounds of the estate were three century-old hickory trees.

Jack and Jacqueline had bought the house in 1954 and had a new nursery installed. But after her miscarriage in 1956, she didn't want to go back there.

Joseph Kennedy Sr. had pushed Bobby to buy the house from Jack, telling him, "You look like the one who's going to have all the kids. . . . You may as well get a big place now and develop it into something that suits you and your needs."

It soon had a crescent-shaped driveway, two swimming pools, a tennis court, a trampoline, a sauna, a cabana with a jukebox, and an obstacle course that most guests were encouraged to try. The course involved jumping off a roof, wriggling under sawhorses, climbing ropes, and diving over a bale of hay that landed you facefirst in the mud.

Hickory Hill was definitely a place to visit at your own risk. For a St.

Patrick's Day dinner, Ethel reportedly used live bullfrogs as a center-piece.

It was also a zoo. At one count, the Hickory Hill animals included two geese, several iguanas, an enormous turtle that one of the boys brought home in a suitcase, a donkey, lots of lizards, a thirty-inch-high midget Argentine horse named Sugar Plum, two Labradors named Battlestar and Firecracker, an Irish setter called Rusty, and an enormous Newfoundland the size of a pony, named Brumus. There were also two pheasants, a seven-week-old heifer, a pet rooster, five ponies and a horse, three cockatoos, uncounted homing pigeons, and what Ethel called "two horrible little guinea pigs." One cage even held a boa constrictor.

In contrast, the only dogs and animals in Jack Kennedy's home were stuffed ones. Jack was seriously allergic to dogs.

All kinds of people were welcome at Hickory Hill—unless they were dull. It was a cluttered, rough-and-tumble house, decorated with "a funny kind of opulent simplicity." There was an Aubusson rug in front of the fireplace, and an ornate gold mirror with gold sconces, but you might see a bottle of baby lotion on a Louis XV chair and a large yellow stain on the rug in the drawing room. "Don't look at that, please," Ethel said, "we can't keep Brumus out of there."

"We just try to keep breakable things out of the way," said Ethel, "and even that doesn't always work. That Etruscan bird over there dates from the second century—Bobby gave it to me for Christmas—and after surviving all those years, it was in this house just ten minutes before it got broken."

———

AT THEIR MONTHLY seminars at Hickory Hill, they designated a certain subject and then invited prominent people to discuss it with them.

"I got invited to one," said Jim Deakin. "They had this British don, an academic, a modern religionist; one of these 'God is relative' types. His theory was, you create whatever kind of God you need. . . .

"Ethel started interrupting, asked over and over again, 'But where is God, in your theory?'

"The poor guy was making his spiel. . . . Finally, Bobby got so upset that he turned to her and said, 'Can it, Ethel!' She subsided; the guy finished his talk, and invited questions. The first one was from Bobby, who asked, 'And where is God, in your theory?' "

The so-called Hickory Hill Institute was Bob's attempt to catch up. But it was not simply that he was trying to fill another gap between him and Jack—he was now thinking more of the need to know more for his own political future. Ethel liked to say that Bobby was her model because "he is so determined, he hates to give up."

———

AND YET ACCORDING to Harold Reis, Bob and Ethel's social friends "were people of very little intellectual abilities. No, there was no difference at the parties between the people who worked for him and his social invitees. . . . I suspect that people became friends simply by helping Ethel with her mail. Or they just plain liked them."

"Unlike JFK, they would not be lords and serfs, but friends and equals," said Don Irwin.

Still, "Bob assumed that, if you worked for him, you worked for the whole Royal Family. In the middle of a big crisis, if Ethel left a bag on an airplane, the whole office was supposed to take care of that problem," said Harold Reis.

———

A WRITER REMEMBERED interviewing Robert Kennedy, who was walking on the lawn of Hickory Hill, carrying one of his children on his shoulders. "And another one of his kids asked if I'd carry him on my shoulders, and that's how the interview was done, each of us carrying a kid."

Another said, "Bob could be talking to Khrushchev, or somebody—and the phone would ring, and it would be one of his kids—and he'd take the call. Absolutely, his family came first. It was a miracle how he could be so devoted to them, and yet throw such a tremendous effort into everything he did."

With his children, he was gentle and strong. If one of his boys was having trouble catching a baseball, Bob got up fifteen minutes early every morning to practice with him before school. He taught them to trim their sails, disciplined them with a gentle firmness, generally let the youngest climb all over him.

Bob's eldest son, Joe, remembered when he was a small boy and had a fight with one of his brothers. "We always followed the same pattern. I would go and tell my father and he'd tell me to grab my brother. And I would say my side of the story and my brother would have to sit in silence. And then my brother would tell his side of the story and I would have to be silent. And in that, the truth would out and I realized that I wasn't all right and he wasn't all wrong. And my father would then make us kiss and make up and go to our rooms and read for an hour."

Daily newspapers arrived for everybody, and the older Kennedy children had to report on a current event each day. Robert Kennedy, Jr., recalled how his father told history stories at the dinner table and read from the Bible almost every night. "Our family prayed together. We said the rosary almost every night. And then we did sports together."

Young Bobby praised his father for putting his children's advancement ahead of his own and for not visualizing "himself as a sun around which satellites would circle, or in the role of a puppet-master. He wanted us, not himself, to be the focal points."

"Sometimes Bob would do a curious thing with the boys, although never with the girls," said editor and friend Warren Rogers. "In the midst of a tickle-tumble or other roughhousing, he would slap them in the face, rather smartly. If the little boy cried, Bob would hug him and coo to him, but not in a coddling way. He would say softly, 'Hush now, a Kennedy never cries.' And the game would go on. Once, a guest, watching such a scene, suggested to Bob that perhaps he was too rough on so small a child. He replied again in his soft way: 'No, they have to get used to getting hit. It's going to happen out there in the world. They have to learn to take it and go on, to get used to getting hit so it's no surprise, no shock they can't sustain.' "

The big thing was still to win. In a family softball game, the score was tied at the end of the ninth, with two on base and two out. Bob was pitching. At bat was his six-year-old daughter, Kerry. The good father might have thrown an easy pitch to his small child. Instead, he threw a hard, fast ball she never saw, and won the game. When his family berated him, he simply shrugged his shoulders. Winning was still everything.

He explained his need to be with his children as much as possible. "Most people with our resources would hire a lot of people to take care of the children while they went off and did something else. We do it the other way around. We hire people to do something else, and that frees us up for the time that we can spend with the children."

Kennedy always tried to come home for dinner, and sometimes return to the office. Every so often, when he couldn't go home, his kids would come down in the evening with Ethel and have hamburgers with their dad in his office.

Bob and Ethel had a code to inform their children that another baby was en route. At the dinner table, after saying grace, Bob or Ethel called down blessings on all present: "God bless Mommy and Daddy and Kathleen and Joseph and Bobby and David and Courtney"—and then tacked on, "and whatever God sends." That never failed to create an explosion of squeals and yells.

————

IT WAS PERHAPS inevitable that he would play the part of his own father with his own children—driving them to do more, to do better, to be the best. But there were some things his father would not have done.

One of his children remembered: "We were all sitting at the dinner table, and there were eleven kids, so you can imagine that's a big dining room table. And we were all sort of yelling and screaming, there was a lot of food and milk and everything. And all of a sudden the door opened, and my father was standing there . . . and there was dead silence. And he said, 'I've just come from a place in America where three families live in a room this size. I want you to do something to help those children. You've got to help those children. Please help those children.' "

————

"OF ALL THE people I've ever seen," said Dave Hackett, "Bob was the only one with the guts and the nerve to go and do something that we talk about, but never do. . . . I think he was exactly that way when he was seventeen years old. At the church, he'd get up as the altar-boy, be helpful. I mean, he'd do those embarrassing things that we all should do. He never changed."

Like Jack, Bob basically believed that all problems could be solved with energy, imagination, intellect, and judgment. This was something ingrained in all of them.

He had announced early in his tenure that "I'd like to be remembered as the guy who broke up the Mafia." At that point, Bob was not fully aware of the interlocking complications of the Mafia with both his father and the President. They would not tell him, as they did not tell him many other things.

Within weeks of taking office, the new Attorney General had arranged for the abrupt deportation of Mafia boss Santos Trafficante to Guatemala as an undesirable alien. Trafficante, however, quietly returned to the United States. Kennedy renewed efforts to ban him permanently.

Nor did he forget James Hoffa. In the fall of 1961, there were thirteen grand juries, sixteen attorneys, and perhaps thirty FBI agents concentrating on Hoffa. A former Teamster reported that Hoffa once had asked him if he knew how to handle plastic bombs, and added, "I've got to do something about that son of a bitch Bobby Kennedy. He's got to go."

Hoffa's lawyer Frank Ragano tells of the time Hoffa requested a meeting with the Attorney General. Kennedy arrived late because he was walking his dog, and Hoffa got so mad that he slammed Kennedy against the wall, saying, "I'll break your fucking neck! I'll kill you!" and tried to strangle him with his bare hands. "Goddamn it, Jim," Ragano remembers shouting, "this is the Attorney General!"

Hoffa managed to elude indictments and escape in trials with hung juries. After one such verdict, Bobby wrote a note to his father in France: "As they said at Harvard, 'we'll get him next Saturday.' " To his staff, he was more specific: "We'll get the son of a bitch yet." Kennedy then announced a new series of hearings and served subpoenas on officials in five Teamster locals. Some said the Hoffa fight was a grandstand for his growing ambitions, and this surely was true. Bob gloried in being in the national TV limelight. Court defeat only spurred him on.

The President signed three bills in one month on crime and racketeering requested by Attorney General Robert Kennedy.

"ROBERT KENNEDY WAS the most successful bureaucrat in Washington because he made his Department responsive to the President's will," said Nicholas Katzenbach, who served as Assistant Attorney

General and later Deputy Attorney General. "And, whenever it was important—and everybody knew this—Robert Kennedy had no qualms in calling on the President. This gave him a leverage beyond belief. And, so, if he was not always loved, Bob Kennedy was always feared. Machiavelli would have approved."

Part of his powerful leverage came from the wiretap, which he abused quite flagrantly at times. A technician later testified that Attorney General Kennedy had hired him to bug the telephones of White House reporters during a presidential visit to Newport because he could not entrust the job to the FBI. Robert Kennedy would have been flabbergasted to hear Vernon Walters, a deputy director of the CIA under Nixon, claim that President Kennedy not only wiretapped his wife, but also his brother Bob.

Bob's conviction that he was on the side of God made him ready to authorize wiretaps, among other things.

———

BOBBY FACED A traumatic early decision in the case of Judge J. Vincent Keogh of the New York State Supreme Court. Keogh was accused of taking a bribe to go easy on a fraud case. Keogh's Congressman brother played a large part in the Kennedy campaign and was an old friend of Bobby's father.

"You've got to prosecute this," his deputy Byron White said to Robert Kennedy. The Attorney General buried his face in his hands and said, "Goddamn it, I told my brother I didn't want this job."

Yet, four days before the indictment, the President and Congressman Keogh attended the Army-Navy game together. It was the President showing that whatever happened, it was his brother Bob's fault.

"Bob was the family son of a bitch," said correspondent Dave Richardson. "Any time there was anything tough or unpleasant, Bob had to do it. He understood the rule of the inculpability of the principal—'the leader never takes the rap.' "

Much more traumatic was the Justice Department prosecution of James Landis for unpaid back taxes, for which he was sentenced to thirty days in prison. "If any goddamn reporter wants to say that the Kennedy administration, having prosecuted one of the best friends they've ever had—somebody who's been practically a father to me," said Bob, "who helped me get through my law exams, and who's been close to Ted and close to my father—if they want to say that we are now soft on criminals by having him serve that stupid thirty days in some degree of comfort, they can go to hell!"

Surveying the Kennedy appointments, many of them young and eager and most of them of high caliber, Speaker of the House Sam Rayburn commented to his friend Vice President Lyndon Johnson that he was pleased with these young gung-ho types in contrast to what he called the bureaucratic Eisenhower years—but he had one complaint: "I wish just one of them had run for sheriff once."

One of the President's first decisions was to reappoint FBI Director J. Edgar Hoover. Hoover was neither young nor gung-ho. He was a survivor. As John Seigenthaler testified, the reason the President did this was that "Bob Kennedy advised him to."

The FBI was Hoover's fiefdom. His files contained damaging evidence on everybody who could help and hurt him, especially Presidents. This made him a government icon, an untouchable. His file on the sex life of President Kennedy was rich and detailed. His relationship with the Kennedys was complex. The senior Kennedy was his good friend and supporter. In October 1955, Joseph Kennedy had written Hoover:

> The only two men in public life for whose opinion I give one continental both happen to be named Hoover—one John Edgar and one Herbert—and I am proud to think that both of them hold me in some esteem. . . . I listened to Walter Winchell mention your name as a candidate for President. If that should come to pass, it would be the most wonderful thing for the United States, and whether you were on a Republican or Democratic ticket, I would guarantee you the largest contribution that you would ever get from anybody and the hardest work by either a Democrat or Republican. I think the United States deserves you. I only hope it gets you.

Hoover had that letter framed in his office.

Hoover was one of the few men to whom Robert Kennedy had gone to for counsel on whether or not to become Attorney General—and Hoover was one of the few who had approved.

One reason why John Kennedy was happy in having his brother as

Attorney General is that he trusted nobody else to deal with Hoover. Bob quickly arranged for the President to have periodic lunches with Hoover, to keep him happy. Hoover even sent Attorney General Kennedy a note complimenting him on working on George Washington's birthday, in the spirit of Valley Forge, and telling him to keep up the good work.

The euphoria didn't last long. As Hoover's boss, the Attorney General felt free to rush into Hoover's office without an appointment. This made Hoover steaming mad, according to witness Luther Huston. He became even more angry when the young Attorney General declared that he wanted more FBI men fighting crime instead of hunting Communists.

"It was soon hammer-and-tongs," said William Hundley, chief of the Organized Crime Section. "I heard a couple of hot arguments between them."

Years later it was suggested that perhaps the Mafia had found evidence that Hoover was a closet homosexual and had threatened him with blackmail.

Whatever he knew of all this, Robert Kennedy soon decided that Hoover was "a psycho," and asked his brother "to make Hoover Boxing Commissioner, or something like that. . . . Jack said, 'Yeah, but first I gotta get re-elected. Then I'll get rid of him.' "

Hoover let Robert Kennedy know that he was fully aware of the case of Barbara Maria Kopszynska, better known as artist Alicia Darr. On January 31, 1961, an article in an Italian magazine, *Le Ore*, detailed the story that, ten years earlier, she had been engaged to marry John F. Kennedy and that his father vetoed the wedding because of Alicia's Polish-Jewish descent. According to the article, she had entered the United States as a "displaced person" and lived with her mother in Boston. Amazingly, the Italian article had not been picked up by the American press, but FBI Director Hoover had received the report from his man in Rome. Darr had filed suit against John Kennedy for breach of promise, and, reportedly, Robert Kennedy had paid a $500,000 settlement for Jack and had court records sealed.

Also in the Hoover files was the Library of Congress record of the Blauvelt Family genealogy, which recorded that Durie Malcolm Deslodge had been married to John Fitzgerald Kennedy. Confronted by a *Look* correspondent, the President denied the story, insisted he had only taken Durie to a football game, but seemed edgy about it. "You print that story," he told the reporter, "and I may wind up owning *Look* magazine."

It might have been his father talking.

Bob Kennedy later told Seigenthaler that his father had offered Hoover $100,000 to get a position out of government, and that Hoover had declined.

———

BESIDES BEING HIS brother's sexual policeman, Bob often served as the brunt of Jack's sharp wit. Occasionally there was a streak of cruelty in it.

The President had joked in a speech at the Alfalfa Club, "I see nothing wrong with giving Robert some legal experience as Attorney General before he goes out to practice law."

Bob told his brother that he did not find it funny and Jack replied that other people did and that he had better get used to kidding himself.

"Yes, but you weren't kidding yourself," Robert said. "You were kidding *me!*"

Another time, on the presidential yacht, at a birthday party for Jack, Bobby seemed a little hesitant about what to say and Jack broke in, "Bobby's all choked up; he can't deal with this occasion."

For Jack, it was his way of asserting continued family dominance. All the Kennedy sons were thin-skinned when it came to criticism, especially from each other.

And yet if you asked the President why he thought Bobby was great—as Ben Bradlee asked, adding, "And never mind the brother bit"—the President would reply, "First, his high moral standards, strict personal ethics. He's a puritan, absolutely incorruptible. Then he has this terrific executive energy. We've got more guys around here with ideas. The problem is to get things done. Bobby's the best organizer I've ever seen. Even in touch football, four or five guys on a team, it was always Bobby's team that won, because he had it organized the best, the best plays. He's got compassion, a real sense of compassion. . . . His loyalty comes next. It wasn't the easiest thing for him to go to [Joe] McCarthy's funeral. And then when Jean McCarthy's new husband needed a job, Bobby got him appointed to something."

If Bobby wanted so much to be like Jack, it was also surely true that

Jack must have often wished to be more like Bobby. But not in all things.

Sometime after the election, David Ormsby-Gore, who would become British Ambassador, went with Jack and Jacqueline to Newport, one of the oldest summer playgrounds of the super-rich.

"Just the three of us," he said. "There was a pool near the beach . . . when we got out to go to lunch, a group of elderly men near the pool made their way to Kennedy, and shook his hand and slapped his back. Afterwards, as we were heading home, he said, 'I really enjoyed that. That small group of men must've spent a million dollars trying to defeat me.' And he said it without any grudge. But not the way Bobby would have reacted. Bobby would have been bitter."

On the other hand, when a former Harvard football team captain called and wanted to meet him for lunch, John Kennedy told Jim Reed, "That prick, he wouldn't let my brother Joe get his football letter! Tell him to go to hell!"

WHEN BOBBY ONCE invited the Ormsby-Gores to dinner, they told him that they couldn't come because the President had invited them to a reception that night. "I remember how piqued Bobby was because he had not been invited."

Politically, Bob was the closest person in the world to his brother Jack; socially, they still lived separate lives.

Friend Rowland Evans would say, "I never once saw the President and Jackie out at Hickory Hill, and I know I would have been there. I don't think they ever went out there. . . . I think Jackie always liked Bobby, but I don't think the relationship between Ethel and Jackie was all that close. It wasn't brittle, but it wasn't very close."

It wasn't only the wives. Bob had an intensity of work and purpose that Jack didn't share. Jack was always ready to relax, especially at a party, but not Bob.

All the brothers had minimum concern about food. "Bobby was the kind of a guy who would go into the Pavilion Restaurant, where they had *pâté de foie gras* and all kinds of things under glass plus exotic desserts, and ask for bacon and eggs, and vanilla ice cream and chocolate sauce," said Charles Spalding.

His father's favorite family joke about Bobby, according to Arthur

Krock, was that he was tight with his money. Krock recalled lunching several times with the senior Kennedy, both ordering the most expensive things on the menu, and then signing Bobby's name on the check.

Historian Arthur Schlesinger, Jr., who knew the Kennedys well, regarded Robert as desperately vulnerable. "Friends wanted to protect the younger brother; they never thought the older brother required protection. One felt liked by John Kennedy, needed by Robert Kennedy." Schlesinger summed them up: "John Kennedy was a realist brilliantly disguised as a romantic; Robert Kennedy, a romantic stubbornly disguised as a realist."

Reporters admitted contrasting the brothers to Bob's disadvantage, calling him the ruthless hatchet man while depicting the President as "nice and relaxed." Some admitted it wasn't fair or even accurate.

It was true that RFK was often brutally honest: he might say, "Oh, I think that's the most ridiculous idea I've heard all day." Or, if a reporter asked a question, he might even answer, "Why, you know that's a stupid question."

If somebody made a serious mistake which hurt his brother, he could be brutal. Reporter Jim Deakin was at a party when somebody came over to Bob to apologize for a policy mistake. "And Bobby turned on this guy—I've seldom seen a human being treat another human being like that! He just demolished this guy—with what you call 'cold fury' . . . in front of everybody. He just tore this guy to pieces."

The father said often that "Bobby is the one most like me," and meant it. But Jacqueline Kennedy, who adored both Robert and his father, once told Arthur Schlesinger that, of the brothers, Robert was "least like his father."

A friend of both Jack and Bobby told David Halberstam, "You know, everybody thinks that Bobby is ruthless, but I think Jack Kennedy is the coldest man I have ever seen and Bobby is one of the most passionate."

Shortly after Bobby and Ethel were married, Charles Spalding recalled that "I was driving back from the airport at night with them, and we ran into a dog and killed the dog. It was unavoidable; the dog raced across in front of the car, and there was no way of stopping. But we must have spent three hours going up and down the road, trying to find the person who was the owner. There was no thought of placing the dog on the side—the dog was dead—and leaving it and going on. We went into every house, every single house, for ten miles, I suppose, until we finally found the person who was the owner. And Bobby explained what had happened, and said how terribly sorry he was, and asked about the dog—could he replace it, or was there anything possible that could be done. It was so typical of him."

Neither Joe Jr. nor Jack nor their father would have done that.

————

BOB USUALLY TALKED to his brother several times a day, a conversation range that included everything. "He was in that office; my desk was right here," said his associate, John Nolan. "And ninety-nine percent of the time, the door was open. . . . Jack and Bobby were very, very close. It was almost like a single organism, or the two cylinders of a two-cylinder engine. A closeness that was stifling. If you ever heard the two of them on a phone conversation . . . there were no completed sentences . . . they'd pick up each other's thoughts—telepathic . . . the first four words of a sentence would come from one, and the other one would say, 'Yeah.' Then the first one would understand that to mean that the idea that he had had been transmitted and received. Then he'd go on to idea two."

It was quite a difference from those uncomfortable silences of their earlier days.

————

WHAT GRADUALLY BECAME obvious was that the two brothers became partners in the presidency. It was difficult to exaggerate the closeness and quality of their relationship. Personally, there was still the difference in lifestyle, in preferences for men and women, in personality. Politically, they were one person. They worked together, thought together, supplemented and complemented each other, blended perfectly. Bob was not only the President's confidant, but his eyes and ears, his private chief of staff, his conscience. They seemed more alert when they were together. They trusted each other totally. Even when they rubbed each other the wrong way, they usually kept it within themselves.

"Bob worked very closely with the President on some of the things that nobody ever knew about," said Seigenthaler. "If something controversial was coming up that Bob knew about, he would call the President and say, 'Look, Johnny, this is coming up, and you're going to get your head knocked off. Get ready.' "

Bob was most influential when the President was in the process of making up his mind.

"It's shocking," Bob told his brother. "Here we are, supposed to be this young, vibrant administration and all over the world the young people regard us as stodgy stand-fasts supporting status quo regimes. We've got to do something about that!"

"All right," said the President, "why don't you do it?"

Bob became deeply involved in trying to make certain that our country did not tie in with dictators, colonial rulers, or tyrannical regimes "that have no following and no future." Out of this came the Inter-Agency Youth Community, with representatives from State Department, USIA, Treasury, CIA, and Defense, among others. One of its early programs was to bring young Latin Americans here for seminars with all kinds of groups, from labor to minorities. Bob was there to ask questions, urge debates, suggest programs.

JFK liked to tell his staff: "Let Bobby do it his way and he'll always come out ahead."

The President's private secretary, Evelyn Lincoln, insisted that Bobby had White House appointments like anybody else, "maybe a few times a week."

But at the White House, Bobby would slip in the back door. "He didn't come through the front, where the press would spot him," remembered Washington correspondent Esther Tufty. "But he was there . . . we always knew. I don't know how we knew, but we did. He wasn't announced, at all, but we knew he was in with Jack. Sometimes we'd see the car come up to the south entrance. . . . We'd always try to catch him on the way out."

"It was obvious that JFK needed to have him around," said White House assistant Fred Holburn. "I think he did conceive of Bobby as a future President—possibly even his own successor."

If Holburn thought so, many others agreed.

Life featured an article on Bob, calling him the Second Most Important Man in Washington. The President would often tease his younger brother about this. "I went into the Oval Office, and the President was on the phone," recalled Hugh Sidey. "Putting his hand over the phone, he looked up with that wonderful twinkle, and said, 'I'm speaking to the second most powerful man in the world! Do you want to tell him anything?' And I said, 'No, Mr. President, nothing this morning.' There was a little more speaking; then he put his hand over the phone: 'Bobby wants to know who Number One is!' "

And when *Time* did a cover story on Bob, the President asked Hugh Sidey, "Why don't you do one like that on me? . . . You're always doing good things for Bobby, but never me."

———

BROTHER BOB FEATURED a photograph in his office showing two children peering from under the presidential desk. The President's inscription was: "Dear Bobby: They told me you had your people placed throughout the government."

Bob's mother sent him a note from Paris, where she went for her annual fashion show: "I think you should work hard: and become President after Jack—It will be good for the country. And for you. . . . and especially good for you know who, Ever your affectionate and peripatetic mother."

———

THE PRESIDENT HAD his own way of keeping his brother in place.

Bob was not an official member of the National Security Council, but he was a regular participant. Presidential military aide Ted Clifton recalled one meeting when Bobby kept passing notes to the President, who ignored them. "The meeting went on without a look or a nod toward the Attorney General. Finally, almost everybody else had been called except Bob. Then the President, with a dry chuckle, said, 'I've asked almost everybody's opinion. I have a feeling that there is a very restless Attorney General. We will now entertain his comments.' "

On most matters, Bobby was also still the President's liaison to his father. But, although their father was now ostensibly out of the power orbit, whenever he called, whatever it was, Jack always took the call immediately. "He never said, 'Wait, I'll call you back in forty-five minutes, or I'm just walking out.' If old Joe called, and Jack was on his way out to make a big speech before 25,000 people, they waited."

"I had a separate telephone for his father on my desk," said Evelyn Lincoln. "A direct line, so when he called, he would get right through . . . the father called often . . . sometimes once a day. When the father called, I'd go in and put on a little three-by-five card, 'Your Dad.' "

Just before he delivered his State of the Union message to a joint session of Congress, Kennedy, ever eager to impress his father, would call him in Palm Beach to make sure he would be watching him on TV.

An Air Force aide went to the airport to pick up Joe Sr., who had come to see his son and also discuss the defense budget with McGeorge Bundy.

"He started ranting right away," the aide recalled.

"I don't know what the President is doing," declared the father. "Damn it, I taught Jack better than that! Oh, we're going to go broke with this nonsense. I told him that I thought it was ridiculous."

Then he grinned. "The election is over, I can disagree with him anytime I want to now." He later added, "You know, when he visits me, he still borrows my socks, if I have some clean ones."

When his father was traveling, his letters to Jack would always have a political point, usually enclosing complimentary news clippings.

Rose said she never saw too much of her President son. "I never wanted to intrude on his time. I always thought they had a lot of responsibilities, a lot of things on their minds, and I would keep out of the way and leave them uninterrupted. I wouldn't think of going to talk to Jack; I think if he had something particular to say he'd come to me. . . . I would never think of being in a car with Jack and saying, 'What are you going to do about Cuba, what is Castro up to?' " And yet Rose "was great on notes," said Dave Powers. "One time he was sitting on a stage and she noticed a hole in his sock, so one of the notes to me once was, 'Make sure the socks Jack wears do not have holes in them.' Another note advised, 'Make sure that if he eats bacon, it's broiled and not fried . . . that the eggs are boiled four and a half minutes.' "

She once wrote Bob, "Is there a fire escape in your house?" When he forgot her birthday, she chided, "If you can find me, send large expensive present. No flowers." And in a later note she reminded him about his father's birthday, and where his father would be. In her longer letters from abroad she seemed to concentrate on naming all the celebrities she met with such details as their villa in Antibes being a "great success because it is only a three minute drive to the cabana and it is only about 12 to 15 minutes from golf" and how she met Onassis and his wife at Monte Carlo. Her family news was that Teddy was en route to Pamplona to chase the bulls, but "your Pa did receive a letter acquainting him with maneuvers one night in Paris." The maneuvers she referred to, which everybody understood, involved women.

Rose kept her own notebook full of quotes. One of her favorites was: "Face old age boldly. Do not be deceived. For although the outer man is being corrupted, the inner man grows stronger day by day."

As far as the presidency as a prison, she said, "We didn't feel that way at all. We loved it. I knew he loved it and I loved it."

John Kennedy was perhaps thinking of his mother when he told Powers, "According to a recent poll, 73 percent of the mothers in America would like their son to be President."

When Carol Channing and George Burns dined at the White House, the President afterward decided to show them Abraham Lincoln's historic eight-foot bed. After opening the door to the Lincoln Room, where the Emancipation Proclamation was signed, the President hastily backed out and said: "Sorry, the tour is off. Mother's in it."

Straight man Burns: "Mother's in what?"

JFK: "Mother's in Lincoln's bed."

Although she claimed that she kept her distance, Rose Kennedy played her role as First Mother to the hilt. When Jacqueline was away, she often became her son's hostess at diplomatic functions. Her relationship with Jacqueline was never ever warm. And if there was little real relationship with her son, that didn't matter either. She was his mother, and that did matter to everyone else in the world. Rose, typifying the attitude of her generation, had often said that she would rather be the mother of a great man than be a great novelist or painter herself.

However, she never stopped enjoying the spotlight. When she was selected as one of the Ten Best Dressed Women in the World, Rose called her friend Gloria Guinness, told her the news, and added, "They want my photograph! What do I do? . . . What do I wear?"

She was in the presidential helicopter, en route to meet Emperor Haile Selassie of Ethiopia, when she pointedly informed the President's Air Force aide: "I'm trying to bring up these children properly, and I can't get it through Jack's mind that a woman walks out first. I am a lady and I know what ladies should do and I want to walk out of this helicopter first!"

General Godfrey McHugh passed on this message to the President.

"Well, I don't want that," he said. "I love my mother, but as President of the United States, I will walk off first. I'm charging you with seeing to it that she doesn't get off first."

The President couldn't tell it to his mother himself, said McHugh, "because no Kennedy has ever told another Kennedy things they didn't want to hear."

As the helicopter landed and the door opened, McHugh so positioned himself behind the President that Mrs. Kennedy could not get past him. The President walked out very fast with McHugh very close behind him, and then came the President's mother, running to catch up. To the waiting crowd, she said, "I'm Rose Kennedy, mother of the President."

Much of the time, though, Rose lived in her own world, still walking and swimming alone, reading in her little private cottage on the beach. A reporter once found her with Ted, in an Irish pub in Hyannis Port, on the anniversary of her first son Joe's death; she asked the two-man band to play an old ballad about a mother sending her son off to death, to face execution "that old Ireland might be free."

––––––––

THE PRESIDENT SIGNED Executive Order 10924 in March 1961, directing the State Department to create a Peace Corps. He put his brother-in-law Robert Sargent Shriver in charge, partly because Shriver had been pushing the idea for years. But, before he had given the job to Shriver, he had offered it to his old friend Lem Billings— who had turned it down.

Shriver had submitted the original program of skilled volunteers ready to work anywhere in the world to teach languages, fight disease, improve farm methods, and serve in local governments as administrators and clerks.

"Jack always used to say that if you set Sarge down, he'd come up with ten ideas in one hour and eight would be good," said Eunice. "Most people can't dream up one good idea a week."

However, Jack bristled when Larry Newman reminded him of it.

"Don't tell me my brother-in-law's giving me any big ideas. Nobody's given me any ideas, for a long time, that I haven't had myself!"

"He told me," said Shriver, "that everyone in Washington seemed to think that the Peace Corps was going to be the biggest fiasco in history, and it would be much easier to fire a relative than a friend."

Shriver's deputy, Bill Haddad, recalled its uncertain start. "Do you know who financed the beginning of the Peace Corps? We were financed by old man Kennedy's credit card. We had no government funds at all at the beginning and so we all stayed at the Mayflower Hotel and charged everything to his father. That's exactly the way it was."

In Washington, Shriver worked a fifteen-hour day. On Peace Corps missions, he traveled more than 500,000 miles in Africa, Asia, and Latin America. He had done major jobs for John Kennedy before—at conventions, during the campaign, in recruiting government talent—but this position put his skills to a new test and tested his relationship with the President as well.

"Sarge was very scared of the President—very, very scared," said McHugh. "He'd come to me and say, 'Do you think he likes what I'm doing? Do you think he thinks I'm doing a good job?' I said, 'He's never talked to me about you. But I'm sure in the Peace Corps you're doing well; everybody says so.' "

Within a year after the first volunteers sailed, Washington reporters quipped, "Kennedy handed Sarge a lemon and he's making lemonade out of it."

When Eunice Shriver kept pressuring JFK for a domestic Peace Corps to fight youth unemployment, he said, "Why don't you call Bobby? See if Bobby can get it going."

———

THE PRESIDENT'S NEXT executive order established the Committee on Equal Employment Opportunity, ordering all government agencies to grant "equal access to employment" to all Americans regardless of color and belief. Vice President Johnson headed the committee and Bob Kennedy was a member.

"I know," said John Seigenthaler, "that Bob went out of his way to demonstrate to Lyndon Johnson that he was appreciative of Johnson's service, of his help to his brother, but beyond that, he went out of his way to defer to Lyndon Johnson."

––––––––

ATTORNEY GENERAL KENNEDY tested the problems firsthand, walking through some troubled New York City neighborhoods talking to local young people who couldn't get jobs. At Bobby's urging, the President signed another executive order establishing a Committee on Juvenile Delinquency and Youth Crime and appointing his brother the chairman. Bob's old school friend David Hackett became executive director of the committee. With $10 million a year, the committee sought to promote comprehensive community action to remove the causes of juvenile delinquency and crime. Like Shriver's, Hackett's background was diverse, and not typically suited for the job to which he was appointed. He had owned a publishing company, edited a magazine, campaigned for Kennedy before he became Bobby's special assistant.

Kennedy also announced a plan for an Alliance for Progress, a ten-year program to encourage freedom and raise the standard of living in nations south of the United States. He pledged more than a billion dollars in aid. Bob had been keenly interested in Latin America ever since his first trip there.

The President also sent his brother to represent him at the independence ceremonies at the Ivory Coast. Before he left, Bob wanted a proper briefing. He angrily returned the first three State Department briefing people as inadequate. The embassy there had scheduled formal meetings with government officials, but Bobby had other plans. He insisted on meeting ordinary people. Although the embassy resented the way he issued orders, and demanded all kinds of special treatment, he made many friends among the Ivory Coast citizens.

On his return, word went out that if you had an important unconventional idea, the best way to help it happen was to talk to Robert Kennedy.

Bob was always buoyant about the Kennedy accomplishments. Queried by an interviewer about any mistakes they might have made,

Kennedy replied, "Mistakes? It's a bad thing to say, but I don't think we made any."

———————

BOB KNEW, WITH a brother's instinct, just how far he could go in arguing against the President before running into a cold and final wall of disapproval. The President was tough enough and quick enough to pick out any flaws in Bobby's proposals. Bob once suggested at a Cabinet meeting that the quickest way to raise a patriotic feeling was to raise income taxes. None of the other Cabinet members disagreed. "I couldn't believe that they were serious," the President said to Ken O'Donnell afterward. Announcing a tax raise during that period seemed to him the worst possible political move, as well as a bad blow to the economy. "I'm not going to ask for a tax raise no matter what anybody says . . .

"I won't mention it now to Bobby, and don't you say anything to him," the President said. "We'll let him find out for himself how wrong he is . . . But we'll let Bobby listen to Heller talk about it." Walter Heller, the President's economic adviser, agreed completely with the President.

"Usually when I disagreed privately in a conversation with the President on something suggested by Bobby," O'Donnell said, "the President would call me later into his office and say to me, 'Tell Bobby why you think that idea of his is terrible.' Then the President would sit back and enjoy our argument. . . . As he frankly admitted, he found it comfortable to have me burdened with the task of saying no for him."

Bob was more of a worrier than Jack. He hated wasting time. In restraining his impatience with long-winded argument, he would "clasp his hands as if in prayer and regard his clenched knuckles with a cataleptic stare. If the ordeal continues he comes slowly upright again, pats the arms of his chair in slow and feverish rhythm and looks off into the beyond with . . . muted despair."

———————

FOR JOHN KENNEDY, it was the happiest time of his life. He always had defined happiness as the full use of ability along the lines of excellence. All his earlier concerns gradually seemed to disappear. He felt like the conductor of a big symphony orchestra who didn't know what music he was going to play, but he loved playing.

"About six months after he was elected, I asked Kennedy how things had changed for him," said Marianne Means. "He said, 'I can't remember what it was like, not to be President!' Yes, he loved it; all the trappings, the honors, everything."

And so did his wife.

But she also had plaintively pointed out to a friend: "I've hardly seen Jack in the last five years. Now that he's President, I suppose we won't see him at all."

It was Jacqueline who gave the administration a sense of elegance it had seldom had before. "And she got no help from anyone, none, zero," said Charles Spalding. "She was fighting for her life, her individuality. To everyone else, she looked just fine, but the tension inside of her was tremendous."

What she managed to do, which was extraordinary, was to retain a strong sense of herself, refuse to let herself be completely absorbed into either the powerful Kennedy family or the overwhelming demands of Jack's position. This caused friction in her marriage, but, secretly perhaps, Jack liked and respected her for it. She established clear boundaries and kept to them.

Correspondent Laura Bergquist once asked her which First Lady she admired most, and she named Mrs. Truman because "she kept a family together—under the bright hot heat of the limelight that suddenly hits a President . . . that is what I wanted to do more than anything . . . keep my family together in the White House—I didn't want to go into coal mines [Mrs. Roosevelt] or be a symbol of elegance [Dolley Madison]. . . . My first fight was to fight for a sane and normal life for my babies and their father."

———————

THE KENNEDYS NEVER had a taste for excellence or style. Jacqueline changed all that. "She brought taste in furniture, and food, and clothes, style, music and art," said Lord Harlech, their family friend. "Jack had none of that, before Jackie. Once, when they'd come back from a trip to Paris, while they lived in Georgetown, when he was still Senator, she showed him some chairs she'd bought in France. He asked her, 'How much did you pay for them?' She told him . . . and it was quite a lot of money. And he was obviously irritated, and said, 'But you've got plenty of chairs!' "

But he learned enough from her so that on the day of the Inaugural he walked into the empty White House with his brother Ted, turned over some of the chairs and examined them, and said, with some contempt: "Reproductions . . . Sears, Roebuck stuff."

Jacqueline agreed. When Mrs. Eisenhower first gave Jacqueline a tour, the new First Lady noticed how run-down the White House was. She decided to make it elegant and solicited gifts of historic American art and furniture. The following spring, 45 million Americans watched a sixty-minute taped TV program entitled "A Tour of the White House with Mrs. John F. Kennedy." The applause was loud and glowing.

Washington women were wriggling with envy. Critics said Jacqueline's look was too ethereal, her smile too fixed, her voice too whispery, and a Colorado minister complained that her bathing suit was too skimpy. A Boston dowager was even more horrified that Mrs. Kennedy wore slacks in public. There were those who criticized her for buying too many expensive clothes. In response to a query whether she spent $30,000 a year on clothes, Mrs. Kennedy quipped, "I couldn't spend that much unless I wore sable underwear."

Some felt it was overdone to have White House menus in French and intimate parties at which ten pounds of caviar was consumed from an enormous gold bucket, "as big as a milk pail."

"She is not as American as apple pie," wrote Dorothy Kilgallen, "she is as American as caviar."

"Many people did not like her," said Kennedy aide General McHugh. "It's strange. They were jealous of her. . . . I would get dresses, jewelry, flown in for her; and she was beautiful in those things. The girls would look and say, 'Hah! With that amount of money, no wonder she can.' It's not the money; it's the taste. She had it."

Few mentioned that she helped transform her husband "from a fumbling person with a long tie that he couldn't tie . . . looked like he'd just got out of bed—into an immaculate dresser."

She also showed her sensitivity, right at the beginning, in having a reception not only for the Cabinet members but for their children. Her mother-in-law had told her "how nice Mrs. Roosevelt was in managing to have all the children of the people who were in Roosevelt's administration to the White House. And how much that had meant to her children. . . . I remembered that . . . we also had the Johnson girls to a steak dinner, when Vice President and Mrs. Johnson weren't there. Anyone who had someone young, we'd try to have them."

Jacqueline was very jealous of her prerogative as the leading Kennedy woman. She seldom invited her sisters-in-law to any of her intimate parties. Nor did they ever drop by for lunch. There was simply a minimal relationship. The same was true of her mother and her mother-in-law. Only Joseph Kennedy Sr. was always welcome at any time. "When the President's father came to visit," recalled Chief Usher West, "she fairly danced down the halls, arm in arm with him, laughing uproariously at his teasing, her face animated and happy."

Despite the public image of a luminous First Lady reveling in all the adoration she received, Jacqueline wrote her mother-in-law that this "was not a happy time in my life . . . and I never let you know what was happening to me." She later wrote that she felt in the White House "like a moth banging on the windowpane."

Jacqueline was a wife to be proud of, but, still, not confided in. A feminine critic of the First Lady insisted she could have helped her marriage if she had learned about politics—even if he didn't tell her about it. "She could have surprised him with her knowledge. But she didn't." Friend Charles Spalding insisted she would have been destroyed if she had started dabbling in politics. "So she just resisted it. She thought, 'You're not going to colonize me.' If you get colonized, you get evaporated. She didn't want that to happen."

She and Jack were attracted to each other because each represented a kind of image and mystery, and now the image was no mystery, and the mystery was gone.

According to his friend Charles Bartlett, Jack was a lousy husband. "I can't think of any outlandish rumor I've heard about Jack that isn't true," said Spalding. "For a man who was very kind to people, and was very concerned about how he treated people, Jack was not very conscious about how much he hurt his wife. He wasn't trying to keep it [his women] too much of a secret. . . . it was all over Washington. . . . I think he wanted people to know that with women he was better than his father. I remember going to a party once, and the hostess saying to me, 'How could you be friends with that alley-cat?' . . . He certainly inspired a lot of passion, if he didn't evince it, himself."

Her unhappiness wasn't simply a matter of separate bedrooms or his other women. Her stepbrother, Gore Vidal, observed, "Jackie, you know, is ultrafastidious. . . . Therefore she never particularly concerned herself with sex. She finds it," he added, 'untidy.' "

Blair Clark tells the story of a party he attended at which Bob noticed Vidal putting his hand on Jacqueline's bottom. It was probably just a friendly gesture, since he was more interested in men. But Bobby saw it and was incensed and almost started a fistfight, with Lem Billings breaking it up. "Oh, Bobby," said Jacqueline. "You're so sweet to protect me, even when I don't really need it."

Charles Roberts, one of the most observant reporters on *Newsweek*'s Washington bureau, said of the marriage then: "He'd go his way, she the other—or she'd stay; he'd go. They were almost never, weekends anyway—or time off—under the same roof."

"Jackie could stand up to anybody, including her husband," said Laura Bergquist. "I heard her say, 'Where is this great Irish wit you're supposed to have, this celebrated wit?—you don't show much of it when you're home.' They played a lot of these psychological marriage games on each other. She was always trying to deflate his ego; and he was hitting at her core of self-contained privacy. She'd created this whole world for herself—of art, and redecorating the White House, and her children. She was a good mother, a devoted mother, even though it seems out of character with everything else about her, and even though she didn't get much love from her own mother."

Some psychologists assert that many people marry to resolve conflicts with their parents. Jack married a woman the opposite of his mother, but in certain emotional ways, quite similar. Both Rose and Jacqueline had husbands who resembled their fathers, who had many affairs with other women. Publicly, both maintained the same façade. To a reporter Jacqueline said, in the best private school tradition, that she was delighted that women responded to her husband so enthusiastically. Was she jealous? "Of course not!"

But she showed her insecurity when she asked Godfrey McHugh—a man she had dated before her marriage—to tell her about some of her husband's women.

For Jacqueline, however, her husband's sexual adventures caused obvious embarrassment, and she countered with her sharp satirical bite. When asked what she thought was the President's favorite piece of music, she thought a minute and said, "Well, I think it's 'Hail to the Chief.' "

In one of her frequent sparrings with her husband, there was this exchange:

"The trouble with you, Jackie," he said, "is that you don't care enough about what people think of you."

"The trouble with you, Jack," she said, "is that you care too much about what people think of you."

Yet he didn't seem to care what people knew—or said—about his women. Somehow he felt an increased invulnerability as President. It was a kind of sexual arrogance, the feeling "I can get away with this." It heightened the excitement that he was doing all this while he was President of the United States.

When James Reston suggested that a representative of the press be assigned to the Secret Service and accompany the President at all times, Salinger quickly rejected the idea. "The President will do what he damn well pleases."

"You can see it in a lot of the films and there's this slight little smile on his face and it's as if he's putting one over on people and very often, he was," said Judith Campbell. "He had a niche, a little niche for every single part of his life and they didn't overlap."

One of the unprinted press jokes was, "Let's sack with Jack." Another was, "His administration is going to do for sex what the last one did for golf." But what Kennedy felt—and he was right—was that the press would never print any of this in his lifetime. And, as he said, "After I'm dead, who cares?"

Of course, he did care greatly about his "thumbprint on history"; he wanted to achieve "greatness," and saw no real connection between his private and public life. He simply refused to derail his constant search for private pleasure. More often now, he said what he had said before: "You've got to live every day like it's your last day on earth."

"I heard him say that five or six times," said George Smathers. "Not a day went by that he didn't give it his hundred-percent shot."

———

TO LARRY NEWMAN, Jack often quoted a line he had learned in church: "Stay out of the occasion of sin." To him, the idea was to be careful enough so that you were never caught. But there was another axiom all the Kennedy boys got from their father: "What you want, you take."

Talking about Jack's women, his father wistfully told writer Joe McCarthy, "I wish I had his leavings."

"The President's taste in girls was not very good," said General Godfrey McHugh. "He looked at good-looking, cheap girls."

A young woman he knew, Chiquita Carcano, once asked him if he had ever even been in love. "No," he said simply, then smiled, and added, "though often *very* interested."

"Jack was a romantic in his reading choices, but not a romantic when it came to women, said Laura Berquist." "I don't think he could've been passionate with anybody," McHugh added. "He was too self-centered."

Lyndon Johnson reflected on family afflictions, saying that some ate too much or drank too much, but that with the Kennedys, it was women. He told one writer that the father had bought a townhouse for each son, equipped with a mistress, to acquaint them with the way of the world. Asked about it, Jack Kennedy said, "I wish my father had done that, but it's not true at all."

Robert Kennedy tried to downgrade the stories about his brother's women. "I remember on one occasion that somebody said that my brother and I had a group of girls on the twelfth floor of the La Salle Hotel [in Washington] and that, I think, the President used to go over there once a week and have the place surrounded by Secret Service people and then go up and have assignations. . . . A lot of it was so far-fetched that even on the face of it, it didn't make any sense. I mean, if you were going to do that kind of thing, you wouldn't go on over to the La Salle Hotel with the Secret Service surrounding the place."

Bob may have been right about the LaSalle Hotel, but according to McHugh, the President did maintain a duplex penthouse apartment at the Carlyle in New York. "No one got in that apartment, even with a government pouch. If there was something vital, he would come down to the lobby and get it. Rarely did even McHugh get into his apartment. It had a downstairs living room, bathroom, and kitchen; an upstairs bedroom and bathroom. Absolutely private. Whatever happened in there, few knew. The Carlyle basement also opened into the underground city system so that he and his Secret Service could walk underneath the streets to any other hotel or apartment in the area where the President wanted to meet someone, or take someone."

"Jackie knew about his women," said Kennedy's aide McHugh, "and it showed insecurity, her asking me about them."

Jacqueline made it easier for Jack when she insisted on renting a weekend retreat called Glen Ora, a beautiful 400-acre estate near Middleburg, in the Virginia hunt country, less than an hour by car from the White House.

Glen Ora was a peaceful, hideaway place where Jacqueline could ride her horses. The President would have preferred a house on the water, preferably on the eastern shore of Maryland. He found Glen Ora "deadly," boredom broken only by some golf.

"Can you imagine me ending up in a place like this?" he asked friends.

Besides, the President "was extraordinarily sensitive to horsehair and horse dander," said Dr. Travell. "He went to a horse show in Washington one night, only once, but he could not remain in the arena without developing acute symptoms. Foreign embassies with shaggy dogs were also instructed to keep them away when the President visited. He received weekly or biweekly injections of increasing doses of vaccine."

Jacqueline spent four days a week riding in Glen Ora.

"Why did she go to live in Glen Ora when he was in the White House?" asked McHugh. "I think it was a mistake on her part, under those conditions."

Without his wife at the White House, the president felt free for all sorts of diversions. "For here he was, night after night, all alone," said McHugh. "And he had a Senator from Florida . . . Smathers—who was a playboy, and quite often his guest. They'd talk and joke . . . bawdy things—he liked to do that, with a very intimate friend, all by himself, not openly. Which he wouldn't have done, if she was there."

One of his more frequent diversions was Judith Campbell, with whom he had kept a continuing relationship. Senator George Smathers saw her at the White House, in the President's private quarters. White House logs show that during a fifty-four-week period in 1961 and early 1962, she telephoned Kennedy seventy times.

Ted Kennedy's aide Richard Burke later revealed that during his involvement with preparing materials for the future Kennedy Library, he discovered staffers who had erased hours of White House tapes, primarily Kennedy conversations with his various women. Burke recalled one long Campbell tape that was "fairly erotic and steamy."

In her memoir, Campbell remembered that once when she and the President "walked into the [White House] dining room, he said, 'Have you heard from Teddy?'

"That stopped me. 'You mean your brother?'

" 'Yes. Has Teddy called you?'

" 'Of course not,' I said. 'You should know that.'

" 'Well, I just wondered.' "

Then, when she and the President were in bed together, he said, several times, "Boy, if Teddy only knew, he'd be eating his heart out."

"I think he got a big kick out of the fact that he had succeeded where Teddy had failed," said Campbell.

When FBI Special Agent Dodge questioned one of Giancana's girl-friends about Campbell, he was told, "If you want to know anything about Judy, I know she just got back from the White House. Why don't you go ask the President?"

Arthur Schlesinger, Jr., pointed out many years later: "Criticism of alleged personal conduct is nonsense. I'm told that Pol Pot was never once unfaithful to his wife, but murdered millions of his countrymen." Charles Spalding felt the same: "When you think about it, in terms of time, to get all excited about the sex thing and castigate him, like Victorian times—it doesn't make any sense. In the sense of history, it means nothing."

In terms of history, they were absolutely right. President Kennedy would be finally judged on his record, not on his convoluted sex life.

Gloria Steinem put it more simply: "I'd rather have him screw his women than screw the country."

Kennedy once startled two proper Britons, Prime Minister Harold Macmillan and Foreign Minister R. A. B. Butler, during a 1962 conference in Nassau by casually confiding that if he went too long without a woman, he suffered severe headaches.

————

THE REMARKABLE IRONY was that despite his freewheeling, pleasure-loving personal life, he was completely disciplined in his political life. And, suddenly, he needed that discipline more than ever.

An Eisenhower plan involved training Cuban exiles in Florida to invade the southern coast of Cuba and overthrow Castro. It sounded like a Hollywood script: invading under cover of darkness, setting up a stronghold in the mountains, then rallying the people to kick out the dictator. The CIA would be pulling the strings, giving the orders.

The President was not enthusiastic. He didn't bring in Bob at the beginning because he felt that foreign policy was his own area of expertise. Besides, this was a military matter about which Bob knew nothing.

Perhaps, too, on this particular project, there was a little bit of presidential arrogance in keeping it to himself.

But he did seek out his father, who knew all about movie scripts. He also knew international crises. In foreign policy, especially at the beginning, Jack was partly what his father was—a vigorous anti-Communist. But his father was also an isolationist. According to Schlesinger, before going to Palm Beach to see his father, the President seemed to be veering away from the project.

What was ironic and inexplicable was that his isolationist father was now a hawk on Cuba. Perhaps he was disturbed by a Secret Service report that some pro-Castro Cubans were planning to kidnap the President's daughter Caroline. Or perhaps he was simply changing his mind. The movie he showed that night was *Posse from Hell.*

"The old man wanted to go in on an air strike," said Senator Smathers, who was also there, "but Jack bucked him on that." He did listen hard to his father's other arguments to back the Cuban invasion.

On returning to Washington, Kennedy had made up his mind. "We're going ahead!"

"He *told* us," said McGeorge Bundy. "He didn't *ask* us." He and his father were then in telephone contact as often as six times a day. Asked afterward of the father's efforts to influence the President on foreign affairs, Bundy rolled his eyes. "There was this one meeting where everybody voted. And Bobby wasn't even there!"

Walking with Smathers on the South Lawn of the White House, the President told him, "There is a plot to murder Castro. Castro is to be dead at the time the thousand Cuban exiles trained by the CIA hit the beaches."

"Someone was supposed to have knocked him off and there was supposed to be absolute pandemonium," said Smathers.

It was only then that Kennedy brought in brother Bob to check the legality of the project. "Bobby was getting a tremendous input of legal advice from the Justice Department and feeding that into Jack, trying to tell him what he ought to do," said Sarah McLendon. "But Jack had a far better mind than Bobby, no doubt at all. Bobby was the lieutenant, the aide, trying to carry out orders."

The CIA had started to make military mistakes. Plans for a landing near a mountain redoubt now had been changed to put the invasion force closer to the areas where Castro's military forces could resist, and attack them. The judgment was made probably because they expected the President to come out openly with full support, including air strikes. They also expected a general uprising after Castro was assassinated.

The President had growing qualms, especially about air support. He kept getting complete assurance from the Chiefs of Staff that all would turn out well, even without the air strikes, and he finally agreed. Besides, he felt he had started something in motion he could no longer stop. He told his brother, "I'd rather be an aggressor than a bum."

The invasion was still supposedly so top secret that the Chiefs couldn't check the plans with their staffs.

Hugh Sidey of *Time* was at a Hickory Hill party on April 11, 1961, when he saw Bobby sitting in a corner, very quiet and reflective, and went over to talk to him. "And Bobby said, 'Have you got a man in Havana?' Hugh said he wasn't sure, but he certainly thought they could make contact with one. And Bobby said, 'Well, you better do it as soon as you can, and that's all I can tell you, because things are going to happen there.' "

At that same party, Bobby also approached Schlesinger. "I hear you don't think much of this business," he said. Schlesinger told him why. "You may be right and you may be wrong," Bob replied, "but the President has made up his mind. Don't push it further. Now is the time for everyone to help him all they can."

The President had an Abraham Lincoln statement he later quoted: "If the end brings me out all right, what is said against me won't amount to anything. If the end brings me out wrong, ten angels swearing I was right won't make any difference."

A Fort Lauderdale publisher later insisted that the President had told him that Bobby had made the final decision not to use American power in the Bay of Pigs. Marilyn Monroe also confided to a friend that Bobby had told her that he ran the country for one day during the Bay of Pigs crisis "because Jack had been taking medication for his back and wasn't feeling well."

On April 12, some 1200 anti-Castro Cubans invaded Cuba from Florida. They had been trained and were operating under the direction of the CIA and the American government. They had expected support from insurgents within Cuba and from American aircraft. They got neither. Nor was Castro assassinated.

Replying to reporters, the President said, "This government will do everything it possibly can . . . to make sure that there are no Americans involved in any action inside Cuba."

As the invasion was being battered, the most the President would concede was permission to move the Navy closer to Cuban shores. Robert Kennedy told his press aide, Edwin Guthman, "I think we've made a hell of a mistake. . . . You can start praying for those fellows on the beach."

There was another factor nobody had mentioned: the invasion was never a secret. Three months before the actual landing, *The New York Times* had reported that exiles were being trained in Guatemala to invade Cuba.

As the defeat became stark, an anguished Robert Kennedy grimly warned the presidential advisers that if they didn't come up with ideas for action, Moscow would judge them to be paper tigers. With all the famous talent around the table, he insisted that somebody ought to find something to do. Everybody stared. They were dumb and numb.

National Security Council member Walt Rostow took him aside and said quietly, "If you're in a fight and get knocked off your feet, the most dangerous thing is to come out swinging." This was a time "to pause and think," he said, and there was plenty of time to prove their strength.

"That's constructive," Bobby Kennedy answered.

Again and again, the invading exiles requested American air support, but the President refused. The decision was pivotal. Without air support, the invasion was quickly smashed, and the remaining force surrendered. One hundred and fourteen were killed, 1189 captured.

John Kennedy now felt he had erred about Bobby. "I should have had him involved from the very beginning. . . . He's the only one I can trust."

8

CRISES AND SWIMMING POOLS

The President was still wearing his white tie and tails after attending the annual congressional reception at the White House. He had come to the Cabinet Room for a postmidnight meeting on Tuesday, April 18, 1961, when the final sour details of the Bay of Pigs fiasco were spelled out for him. It was close to 4 A.M. when Kennedy opened the doors to the South Grounds, walked out onto the damp grass, hands in his pockets and head bent, to contemplate what would become his first major presidential failure and the single biggest defeat of his administration. For the country, it was a small historical embarrassment; for the President, it was major tragedy, a political blot on his foreign record that would be hard to erase and would always haunt him.

True, the original responsibility belonged to the Eisenhower administration, which had created the idea of overthrowing Castro by invading Cuba with Cuban exiles, trained, armed, and supervised by the CIA. But it was President Kennedy who had given the final orders to make it happen. History would fault him. His secretary Evelyn Lincoln remembered him berating himself, "How could I have been so stupid!"

Jacqueline had seen her husband suffer when the pain in his back grew so intense that the lines around his eyes would get whiter and the tears would roll down his cheeks. But when he came to her that night, he put his head on his hands and almost sobbed. She later said, "I felt so sorry for him."

There wasn't much they could do—the only thing left was damage control. The President was so incensed that he wanted to splinter the Central Intelligence Agency "into a thousand pieces and scatter it to the winds."

What he had to do now was to explain all this to the American people. Judge Louis Oberdorfer was with Robert Kennedy when the President publicly accepted responsibility on TV. Bob Kennedy put his fist in his palm and said, "That's right!" Oberdorfer felt then he was working for an Attorney General who understood the basic principle of leadership—for this man there would be no scapegoats.

That was a Robert Kennedy tenet: if you make mistakes, accept responsibility and admire the one who does. Jack felt that too, then, but not always. Jack was more grief-stricken; Bob was more bitter, more anxious to do something about it. Bob blasted the presidential advisers. "You people are so anxious to protect your own asses that you're afraid to do anything. All you want to do is dump the whole thing on the President. We'd be better off if you just quit and left foreign policy to someone else." The President sat there, quietly listening, tapping his teeth with his pencil. "I became suddenly aware," said White House aide Richard Goodwin, "that Bobby's harsh polemic reflected the President's own concealed emotions."

John Seigenthaler had said of Bobby that "he would have taken a bolt of lightning for Jack."

As a lightning bolt, Bob now defined his new role in a memo to the President: "You talk to McNamara but mostly on defense matters. . . . You talk to Dillon but primarily on financial questions, Dave Bell on AID. These men should be sitting down and thinking of some of the problems facing us in a broader context." In proposing that the President use the best minds in government in times other than deep crisis and emergencies, Bobby Kennedy put an asterisk after "best minds" and wrote in the margin—"ME."

Bobby was then kidding, but the truth was—about the Bay of Pigs and other crises—he was the only one who could look his brother in the eye and tell him that something was a lousy idea.

In a poll of the most effective members of the Cabinet, Bobby was given only eleven first mentions compared to 154 for Defense Secretary Robert McNamara. But one Congressman perceptively added about the President, "I do not think he can make a decision without his brother Bobby."

————

IN HANDLING HIS failure, President Kennedy talked openly to a chosen few. To General Maxwell Taylor he confided, "I'm in a situation here which I don't understand. You now see what the whole world knows, what a fiasco has taken place in Cuba. Yet, all my advisers were for this. . . . I thought it was going to be successful—that there was very little risk involved. And now, quite the contrary has been proved. . . . I must find out what has happened. . . . I want you to take charge, and have an investigation made. And, as soon as you can, lay it out in front of me."

Taylor afterward pointed out that the President barely knew the critical members of his Cabinet, or the military, or how the vast machinery of government operated, "where you put in gas, where you put in oil, where you turn on the throttle."

Kennedy also called in Clark Clifford to work with Taylor. "For two full days I haven't slept," he told Clifford. "This has been the most excruciating period of my life. This is such a tragedy. I don't know if I can survive another one like it. . . . I know you were the main draftsman in the CIA. . . . And I want to find out what's wrong with the intelligence operations."

————

ROBERT KENNEDY BECAME the driving force of that committee. Taylor was so impressed with him as a direct action man that he gave him his highest praise, told him he might have gotten into the 101st Airborne Division.

Jack hid his defeated feelings behind a cool public façade. During the Cabinet session when he detailed everything that had gone wrong, some members felt he was almost talking to himself. At the end of the meeting, the President got up and went alone out onto the terrace. A few minutes later, Bob joined him, and they walked along the White House grounds.

————

"I SHOWED THE whole world I'm weak," the President told George Ball.

He felt another such disaster would destroy him and his administration. The presidency was no longer a great and glorious adventure. He now saw it as "the most unpleasant job in the world." He told his friend Billings, "Lyndon can have it in 1964." And when Barry Goldwater paid a visit to the Oval Office, the President said unsmilingly, "So you want this fucking job, eh?"

Whatever he said then, he really was not interested in surrendering the presidency. When Ted made a speech in Detroit raking Goldwater at a Democratic political dinner, the President told Ted not to do it again because he wanted Goldwater to run against him the next time because he felt Goldwater was more beatable than any other Republican candidate.

But, at the same time, White House correspondents now saw a physical change in the President. He was heavier physically, looked older, and no longer seemed inclined toward small jokes and light banter.

He was also increasingly sensitive about any further discussion of Cuba. When Senator George Smathers inadvertently brought up the subject again at an informal White House dinner, the President, noted Smathers, angrily "took his fork and hit his plate so hard that it cracked."

————

ONLY HIS FATHER projected his usual optimism. "He's the luckiest kid in the world. . . . I always said, 'Fall in a pile of dung; you'll come up with a rose.'" The "rose," according to the elder Kennedy, was that "he's had the greatest lessons that a President could possibly have, and he's had 'em in his first year. He knows who he can trust, and who he can't."

Larry Newman recalled a meeting at Hyannis with the President and some of his staff to discuss how they could further protect the President. "We got to talking about how the President could be isolated, and things could be kept away from him. . . . The essence of what was said, basically, was, you know, if there's anything really that we want to keep away from the President, that it's a very simple matter. That if a letter comes in, it can just be diverted. If we think it's something for his eyes, even a top-secret message, we can divert it from him for a long enough time. . . . They were using rather hypothetical cases. But he was taking it in, all very seriously. . . . I could see him flush; and he put the beer down, and said, 'Listen, you sons of bitches, I want you to remember one thing,' and he was pointing to either Salinger or Sorensen. He said, 'You know there's a guy right behind you who's working for me. And there's a guy behind him that's working for me. So there's not a goddamn thing any one of you guys can do to keep things away from me. I also have fellows on the outside, like Larry Newman, and a lot of other civilian friends, who have friends in the CIA and in the State Department. So, if you try to pull any bullshit, the next thing you know, you'll be back hoeing corn in Nebraska!'

"There was a chill. But all of a sudden he said, 'How about another beer?' "

DURING THIS GRIM period, Lem Billings remained Jack's constant companion. They watched the weekly news shows together on Sunday, played backgammon together for ten dollars a point. White House usher Bernard West noted that Billings was there so often that he kept his clothes in one of the six guest bedrooms. And Dave Powers noted that "Lem was in and out of the White House almost as much as the White House usher, and some staff people saw him so often they thought he was with the Secret Service." Jacqueline summed it up: "He's been my houseguest since I was married."

Some of the President's friends who knew Billings—and knew he was gay—worried that the close alliance between Jack and Lem could prove politically dangerous, although none of them had the courage to say so. Jack, on the other hand, knew this was not a subject the press would broach, and continued to spend a great deal of time with his closest friend, on whom he so much relied.

Lem was with the President at Glen Ora and watched him throw a copy of *Time* into the fireplace so he wouldn't have to read the magazine's assessment of the Bay of Pigs. When Lem tried to switch the subject to talk about a presidential library, Kennedy openly doubted whether anyone would want to erect a monument to a tragic administration.

Jack knew that, to Lem, he could do no wrong. And that he could count on him for his optimism and adoration. Lem knew how to maneuver Jack out of his depression. "Lem was great around the President," said Kennedy's newspaper friend Charles Bartlett. "He supplied that solid link with past values and attitudes which a President needs in order to stay human and keep his perspective."

On his desk in the Oval Office, the President kept a special gift from Lem: a set of whale's tooth scrimshaw—it would be buried with him.

Lem had framed a note from Joseph Kennedy Sr., saying that "all the Kennedy children from young Joe down should be very proud to be your friend because year in and year out you have given them what few people ever really enjoy: true friendship. I am glad we all know you."

The senior Kennedy had once written a letter of recommendation for Billings referring to his "peculiar qualities." Jack had teased Lem on the word "peculiar."

"What could he possibly be referring to? . . . Your habit of picking your chin—your paranoiac desire for sunburn—or perhaps he means that rather 'peculiar' expression that comes over your face when you start inhaling your asthma medicine."

Despite his needling, Jack tried to keep Lem close by offering him a variety of jobs in Washington. Besides the Peace Corps, the President considered Lem for top positions in the Post Office and Commerce Departments, but Lem refused all of them.

"I wondered why Jack never made him an ambassador," said Huntington Hartford, a friend. "But then I remembered General Marshall's anxious desire to go overseas and FDR's reply that he would never have felt safe in Washington without him."

It wasn't that Lem made Jack feel safe; but he did make him happier.

———

INSTEAD OF LEAVING his position as Attorney General to supervise the CIA's clandestine operations, Bob simply added the CIA to his existing responsibilities. Senator Frank Church had called the CIA a rogue elephant rampaging out of control, but few people knew how true that was. Under Bobby, CIA covert action now received a new lease on life.

RFK had persuaded his brother to issue a top-secret order to "use all our available assets to help Cuba overthrow the Communist regime." Jack issued the order as top priority and urged that no time, money, effort, or manpower be spared.

The brothers were now obsessed with Cuba. At a White House gala, President Kennedy told publisher Gardner Cowles, "If a man stays in hot politics long enough, he acquires an albatross. . . . I've got Cuba." Thomas Powers remembers that Bob kept calling for larger and more destructive terrorist attacks against Cuba, and would check on the progress of operations almost hourly. Bobby's constant phrase was "Get going . . . get going!"

For his liaison, Bobby appointed General Edward Lansdale, the government's foremost expert on unconventional warfare. Lansdale said that Bobby felt his brother had been insulted at the Bay of Pigs fiasco and that the insult needed retribution—immediately.

Bobby and Lansdale started a secret war against Castro. It was called "Operation Mongoose," and its goal was to sabotage the Cuban economy. Tactics included polluting shipments of sugar and motor oil. The operation had not been cleared with President Kennedy, who didn't like it, and canceled it. One project that *was* approved involved embarrassing the Castro image by putting thallium salts in his shoes. This metallic poison presumably would cause Castro's beard to fall out. But Castro never went to the designated hotel where someone was ready to sprinkle the poison in his shoes.

———

THE PRESIDENT MAINTAINED his own Cuban contacts. Laura Bergquist had gone to Cuba to interview Castro for *Look*. "Bobby at that time was absolutely intolerant of any Cuban discussion," said Bergquist. "Anybody who'd met Castro or talked to him was on his black list, because he assumed the contact was sympathy. On the other hand, the President called me in and asked me to tell him about Fidel. But his first question was, 'Who is Fidel sleeping with?' Well, I didn't know who Fidel was sleeping with . . . and it didn't matter to me. But it did, to him.

" 'I hear he doesn't even take his boots off.'

"I said, 'I haven't a clue.'

"He said, 'He runs around making those long speeches, but where are the dames?' That was one of the things he wanted to know about. He was fascinated by people's love lives."

Kennedy was also fascinated with Che Guevara, and Bergquist recalled Guevara was equally curious about Kennedy. She regarded both men as cool, pragmatic, very smart characters. She was not prepared for Kennedy telling her, " 'Something gives me the feeling you've got the hots for Che.'

"That made me sore as hell. I felt put down. I protested. Hadn't he seen the photo of me and Che arguing during the interview? 'Yeah,' said the President, 'but that kind of hostility often leads to something else.'

"At the same time, I considered myself as the President's friend, and he treated me as a friend, and saw me often, I know that he had the CIA check on me. It simply showed the different levels on which he operated. There were so many sides to him. Personal friends Red Fay and Dave Powers saw one side. Arthur Schlesinger saw another. Joe Alsop saw another. His wife saw another. The women he slept with saw another. And he kept them all separate. And he was always on the sidelines, watching himself do all this."

The President could contain himself. It was his disposition. But not Bob. The intensity within him seemed to be growing. Counterinsurgency had a special appeal for his need for excitement and adventure. It was far away from the bureaucracy of the Attorney General's office. It was his own way of expressing his need for action. CIA Deputy Director Ray Cline remembered, "Bobby was so emotional [about Cuba], he always talked like he was the President, and he really was in a way."

"How would you feel if the U.S. assassinated Castro?" President Kennedy asked Tad Szulc of The New York Times. The journalist said he told the President it was a very poor idea. Kennedy replied that he was testing Szulc, and that he felt the same way because the U.S. morally must not be a party to assassinations. Kennedy told Szulc that he was under terrific pressure from advisers to okay a Castro murder. He said he was resisting the pressures. Then he added, "Look, I'd like you to talk to my brother." It was almost as if he was saying, "Look, this isn't my idea, it's Bobby's."

John Kennedy often got assorted opinions before he shaped his own. Two days after talking to Szulc, he discussed the subject with Richard Goodwin, from the point of view of danger: if they started killing people, he himself might be killed.

Goodwin was chairing a meeting of the White House task force on Cuba, in the State Department conference room, when Secretary of Defense Robert McNamara said forcefully, "The only way to get rid of Castro is to kill him . . . and I really mean it."

"I was surprised and appalled to hear McNamara propose this," said Goodwin. He believed then that Robert Kennedy might have stimulated such methods only indirectly . . . with McNamara trying to anticipate Bobby's every wish.

IT IS INCONCEIVABLE that the Central Intelligence Agency, so highly structured, would proceed on a major assassination without presidential approval. And it is highly doubtful whether Bob would have organized it.

The way it worked was to create as many layers as possible between the thought and the deed. In overall charge of the assassination was a stoop-shouldered Yale economist, the CIA's Deputy Director for Plans, Richard Mervin Bissell, Jr.

Bissell was the one who ordered the Technical Services to produce a deadly poison pill that would dissolve in a glass of water and never be detected in an autopsy of Castro. It was the CIA's Security Director, Colonel Sheffield Edwards, who suggested using the Mafia to pinpoint the hit men. Bissell liked the idea. Former FBI man Robert Maheu, who was on retainer with the CIA, became the contact man with the Mafia. Maheu approached mobster John Rosselli, who had once acted as bagman for the Kennedys in buying votes in the West Virginia primary. Rosselli was now the Mafia man in Hollywood, so elegant and dapper that he was even proposed for membership in the Friars Club.

Rosselli had good reason to cooperate. He had run a gambling casino in Cuba before the Castro regime and wanted to get back again. He also still faced deportation because he had entered the U.S. illegally.

Rosselli brought in two men with tight lips who were on the FBI's list of the ten most wanted criminals: Salvatore "Momo" Giancana, Chicago Mafia chief, and Santos Trafficante, former Mafia chief in

Havana. They agreed to arrange the gangland killing of Castro in Cuba. After discussion, Giancana and Trafficante persuaded Rosselli, who persuaded Maheu, who persuaded Edwards, who persuaded Bissell that it would be better to come up with a cleaner killing. Bissell then passed on the poison pills laced with botulism toxin.

Up to this point, only CIA director Allen Dulles knew of the plot, without knowing any of the details. Dulles soon resigned, to be replaced by Richard Helms. Bobby still did not know about the Mafia connection, even though Helms later revealed that he and Robert Kennedy conferred almost daily on the assassination.

The irony of it all was that Giancana had appeared earlier before the Senate Rackets Committee, faced Robert Kennedy, and pleaded the Fifth Amendment fifty-three times. An FBI-tapped phone overheard Rosselli saying, "Here I am, helping the government, helping the country . . . and that little son of a bitch is breaking my balls. . . . You fuck them," he said, "you pay them, and then they're through."

It was finally decided to brief Bobby on the Mafia connection because he might otherwise be embarrassed in his prosecution of the two men.

"Bobby Kennedy listened, as I outlined the case in detail," said Lawrence Houston, Information Officer of the Department of Justice. "You could see Bob's face getting grimmer and grimmer. . . . We told him the whole thing: the CIA had developed the idea that there could be an attempt on Castro's life, using the Mafia people who'd lost their gambling interest down in Havana, and would like a chance to get it back. . . . And some kind of poison pill had been developed and given to Rosselli, who'd called it off and given the poison back."

Houston added that he was told that the operation was now canceled because the Cuban scheduled to drop the pills in Castro's water had lost his access to the dictator.

The Attorney General's reaction, according to Houston, was, " 'This means, I suppose, we cannot go ahead with our intended indictments on these two fellas [John Rosselli and Sam Giancana].' . . . He never criticized, once, the assassination attempt. But, he said, 'Don't you ever again get in touch with any gangster-Mafia types again, without consulting me first!' Yes, sir. He was furious. I don't blame him."

In a letter to the editor of the *Atlantic Monthly*, two of Robert

Kennedy's top aides, Frank Mankiewicz and Adam Walinsky, years later wrote, "Attorney General Kennedy was briefed about the CIA-Mafia plot after the fact; he was told (falsely) that the plot had ceased; he ordered that no such further attempts be made; but attempts continued despite his orders that they cease."

Mankiewicz and Walinsky both insisted that the Bob Kennedy they knew was an intensely moral man who wouldn't have anything to do with an assassination. They had discussed the matter with him and felt that he believed that his opposition was largely responsible for the project's end.

As if to emphasize Bobby's morality, William G. Hundley, chief of the Organized Crime Section for the Attorney General, pointed out that despite the knowledge that Giancana could embarrass the Kennedy administration, "Bobby pushed to get Giancana at any cost." However, Giancana eventually decided on a confrontation, and brought a civil suit against the Federal Government. This left him open in court to cross-examination. Observers were confounded when the Assistant United States Attorney never questioned Giancana on the stand.

Somebody—possibly the President—obviously had second thoughts. The threat of a national scandal concerning the Judith Campbell affair would be too dangerous. While Robert Kennedy may not have known of the Mafia connection in the assassination, Judith Campbell, who first met JFK during the campaign, insists that the President did "because I carried the intelligence material between Jack and Sam, and I have to state that this was always at Jack's request."

"What would Kennedy give you to give to Sam?" Larry King asked Campbell in an interview years later. "He told me that it was intelligence material. He never used the word 'assassination.' He used the word 'elimination.'" Their discussion had concerned Cuba and Castro.

It seems hard to believe that President Kennedy would deal with the Mafia in killing Castro without first conferring with Bobby. It raises many questions. But then the President—as much as he used his brother on critical matters—still did not tell him everything. He didn't consult him on early key Cabinet selections; he didn't involve him in the early planning for Bay of Pigs; he didn't share the details of most of his sexual adventures until he needed help and cover-up. So it is not inconceivable that he kept these Mafia negotiations to himself—at the urging of the CIA—because Bobby had fought the Mafia so intensely and would disapprove.

Campbell told an interviewer that she not only acted as a courier but she also arranged ten meetings between Kennedy and Giancana.

Giancana's daughter Antoinette, interviewed by Larry King in February 1992, was asked whether her father had been asked by Kennedy to kill Castro. She replied, "Yes, he did."

———

ON FEBRUARY 27, 1962, Bob received a memo from FBI Director J. Edgar Hoover about a woman who had a relationship with Giancana and was repeatedly calling the President. It is conceivable that Bobby did not know until then that his brother had shared Campbell with the same Mafia mobster the CIA had hired to kill Castro.

Knowing the Hoover–Bobby relationship, it is easy to visualize J. Edgar gloating and Bobby squirming.

It is not difficult to imagine Bobby's anger at his meeting afterward with the President. He had been Jack's sexual policeman for a long time, but this was an affair beyond belief. It was not only morally wrong and politically stupid, but it put the office of the Presidency in jeopardy—in danger of blackmail and corruption.

Hoover detailed the dangers of the Campbell affair even more completely for the President the next month at a White House lunch. It must have been a pleasurable lunch for the Director. Hoover, who had his own problems as a homosexual, exulted in the exercise of power over presidents, particularly this one, whom he didn't especially like.

"According to White House logs," a Senate committee report later revealed, "the last telephone contact between the White House and the President's friend [Mrs. Campbell] occurred a few hours after the luncheon."

"Jack called me after meeting with Hoover," said Campbell, "and he told me my phone was probably not safe to use anymore." But she said that her relationship with the President continued for several months after that. While Judith Campbell was staying with Rosselli and Giancana at Miami Beach's Fontainebleau Hotel, she made a side trip to Palm Beach to spend time with President Kennedy.

When, years later, Campbell made some of this public in her memoirs, Jack Kennedy's close friend and editor, Ben Bradlee, said, "For the President of the United States to be involved with the mistress of a Mafia don is just not acceptable. . . . I have to think that if that kind of knowledge had come out, then he would have been impeached. . . . I just didn't want to believe it. . . . I felt . . . betrayed."

Bradlee believed it because he was one of the few friends who always had direct access to the President, through private White House phone numbers. The numbers changed every week, but Bradlee always had the new ones and kept the records. He later checked those numbers against ones Campbell listed in her memoirs. They were the same.

Several recommendations were made within the Justice Department in 1962 for a thorough investigation of Mrs. Campbell's Mafia ties, but no inquiry was ever conducted. When high Justice officials learned about her friendship with President Kennedy in early 1962, they looked on it as a "domestic matter," as one of them put it, and passed information on her to the White House.

For John Kennedy, this dancing with danger was part of his feeling of Kennedy invulnerability, absorbed from his father.

———

A GALLUP POLL indicated that President Kennedy's popularity had reached a new peak. "My God!" he exclaimed. "It's as bad as Eisenhower. The worse I do, the more popular I get."

James MacGregor Burns was concerned about the Kennedy buildup, concerned about overexposure. "The adjectives tumble over one another. He is not only the handsomest, the best-dressed, the most articulate, and graceful as a gazelle. He is omniscient; he swallows and digests whole books in minutes; he confounds experts with his superior knowledge of their field. He is omnipotent." Wrote Burns: "The buildup is too indiscriminate. The buildup will not last. The public can be cruel, and so can the press."

Congress, at that time, according to a *U.S. News & World Report* poll, regarded Kennedy as a strong President who believed in using his full powers. They considered him to be excellent at getting across to the country the image he sought to win support. Some 71 percent, however, said he was below average in effectiveness in getting the legislation he wanted from Congress.

Republicans—and some Democrats—had become quite open in their denunciations of the President and his programs. A veteran Democratic loyalist muttered, "The Republicans are determined now to kick Kennedy in the head every chance they get. Of all the Administration's major priority bills, only one—trade—has passed the House so far this year."

The President badly needed a success. "How safe is it to send a man into space now?" he asked Ed Welsh, director of the Space Project. It was only two weeks after the Bay of Pigs. Alan Shepard was primed to go on a ballistic shot, up into the stratosphere and down again. A failure, so soon after the Bay of Pigs, would have been a political catastrophe. A staff consensus counseled caution.

The Russians already had put a man in space, and the President felt a deep need to do the same, not just for the American image, but for his own.

"Well, Mr. President," Welsh said, "there's no more danger in this flight than in taking an airplane trip from here to Los Angeles and back in bad weather."

"There *isn't?*"

"No, sir," Welsh said.

Shepard's flight in space only lasted fifteen minutes, in a small cone on top of a missile that dropped him safely in the ocean, where he was picked up by a helicopter. The group with Kennedy watched it and cheered.

————

IF JACK KENNEDY was concerned about popularity, he and Bobby spent little political energy trying to deal with the erupting civil rights movement. President Kennedy supported peaceful change and gradualism in civil rights, and hoped changes would evolve without any help from him. He was not interested in a moral victory. And he felt the timing was wrong for a civil rights bill because there was little congressional concern for the issue—few Congressmen were dependent on the black vote.

A group of leaders from the National Association for the Advancement of Colored People came to the White House, asking for a

commitment on a civil rights bill. When asked by friend Charles Bartlett if he gave the commitment, Kennedy laughed. "No," he said, "I showed them Lincoln's bedroom instead."

The fact was that Jack had little personal contact with blacks, knew none at Hyannis or Palm Beach or Choate or Harvard, or even in the Navy. Kennedy once asked a close friend, "What are Negroes really like? I've never spent any time with them."

He also tended to distrust zealots, people with causes. He preferred rationalists like himself. When Undersecretary of State Chester Bowles prepared a strong civil rights speech for himself, saying the blacks had a right to be bitter, the President was negative about the speech, regarded it as "a call to rebellion."

Kennedy was reluctant to push anything that might not succeed. Even as a Senator, he hated to propose any amendment unless he was sure it would be passed. He was hesitant in facing confrontation. "People had JFK all wrong," said Kennedy economics adviser Paul Samuelson. "They thought of him as a dashing, deciding type. He was an extremely hesitant person who checked the ice in front of him all the time. He said it was vanity to use your political capital on lost causes." Generally, Jack chose the most moderate of available solutions and seemed willing to suspend his convictions and conciliate Congress.

During the presidential campaign, John Kennedy had promised that he would "end discrimination with a stroke of the pen on his first day in office."

One indignant citizen made photostat copies of the news report, underlining Kennedy's quote, rolled it around a ballpoint pen, and sent it to him for twelve consecutive months. Afterward, thousands of people sent him pens.

Thurgood Marshall remembered that it was not the President who slowed things down, but Bobby. Bobby later confessed that when he first became Attorney General, "I won't say I stayed awake nights worrying about civil rights." When hearings were scheduled on civil rights violations in Mississippi and Louisiana, Attorney General Kennedy contacted the Civil Rights Commission and had them called off. He also told them, "Remember, you never talked to me."

The United States Supreme Court had outlawed segregation in terminals as well as trains and buses used in interstate transportation, but the law was never enforced. Growing numbers of so-called

Freedom Riders, usually young volunteers, both black and white, now traveled through the South to test their constitutional rights. The result was confrontation and chaos—screaming mobs of white men beating and bloodying the young Riders with baseball bats and bicycle chains, then burning their buses.

Bob Kennedy told Harris Wofford, his civil rights adviser, how angry he was at the Riders for embarrassing the President just before he was going abroad. The President was even more direct with Wofford: "Stop them! Get your friends off those buses!"

Attorney General Kennedy sent Seigenthaler to Alabama for a firsthand report. In trying to help a young woman Freedom Rider who was being attacked, Seigenthaler was clubbed from behind. There were FBI men on the scene, taking notes, but they let Seigenthaler lie on the ground unconscious for half an hour without helping him. Robert Kennedy was incensed. Seigenthaler represented the Attorney General: now it was personal.

On May 21, 1961, the Attorney General ordered 500 marshals under Byron White sent to Alabama. Airborne troops in nearby Fort Benning, Georgia, were also alerted. "It's more important that these people survive," Robert Kennedy said, "than for us to survive politically." It is questionable how seriously he meant that then, although he surely meant it later.

The marshals formed a barrier around the First Baptist Church, in Montgomery, where 1500 blacks had come to hear Martin Luther King. Some observers thought that the white mob might break through into the church and burn it down. When King protested that Robert Kennedy's action was inadequate, Kennedy told him that if it hadn't been for U.S. marshals, "you'd be dead . . . right now." With a National Guard truce, the churchgoers were escorted home.

The issue of Freedom Riders was finally resolved when an ingenious Department of Justice lawyer petitioned the Interstate Commerce Commission to issue regulations ending segregation in interstate bus terminals. Thus, the buses would not be able to use stations where discrimination was allowed.

THE NEXT HURDLE for the President was overseas.

Just before his trip to see de Gaulle and Khrushchev, the President arrived at Hyannis Port with Lem Billings. Wrapped in a gray Navy blanket, on a cold foggy day, he sat in a lawn chair, studying background papers for his upcoming conference with Premier Khrushchev in Vienna. He told Billings, "I don't have any gift for Khrushchev." Instead of the usual silver-framed picture, he wanted to give something American and something historical. Lem had started him on collecting scrimshaw and now suggested a model of the USS *Constitution*. Months before, Jack had admired it, wanted to buy it but thought the price too high. He had wondered aloud to Lem whether his father would buy it for his birthday, knowing Lem would pass on the message. Lem did, and the father bought it. Now he had a gift for Khrushchev, "representing the United States as a young republic—strong, youthful, in love with freedom."

Kennedy's concern about Khrushchev centered on Berlin, which he saw as a conceivable trigger for an atomic war. Berlin was an island of freedom in Communist East Germany and Khrushchev wanted to swallow it whole. The United States was still committed to defend it.

Before Vienna, Kennedy went to Boston for a speech at a Harvard fund-raising dinner. As he left, the President sheepishly told his father that he didn't have "a cent of money." His father gave him a wad of bills and the President promised, "I'll get this back to you, Dad." As he walked away, his father remarked, "That'll be the day."

After his Harvard speech, poet Robert Frost advised Kennedy to be more Irish than Harvard when he saw Khrushchev.

The Bay of Pigs may have been only a historical blip, but it had considerable meaning in the Soviet Union with Nikita Khrushchev. Khrushchev was a rotund, forceful, energetic man, rude enough to bang his shoe on his desk at the United Nations to show his disapproval.

Along with the other older world leaders, Khrushchev was taking the measure of this young man and now saw him as someone who might be challenged. Because of his failure in Cuba, Kennedy was concerned and reluctant, but this was not a meeting he could postpone.

En route, the President had scheduled a stop at Paris, accompanied by Jacqueline and Billings. Billings usually joined the President on his official overseas trips, and the President introduced him to Germany's Chancellor Adenauer as "Congressman Billings." To astronaut Alan Shepard, JFK called him "General Billings of the Pentagon." But on the presidential yacht, the captain was introduced to "Lieutenant Junior Grade Billings."

Air Force One landed at Orly Field near Paris on May 31, greeted by Charles de Gaulle and a surprise guest. De Gaulle, one of the few political giants left in the postwar world, using his rare English, asked, "Have you made a good aerial voyage?"

The unexpected guest in the waiting room was the President's mother, then in Paris on her annual tour of the fashion shows. She later reported that she thought her son looked a little surprised when he saw her. She further decided that she was going to join the official party and not miss a thing. Billings said that Jack was a little embarrassed because he was "terribly sensitive" about his family being on these trips.

"Rose was a tough broad," said Laura Bergquist, "and she was very conscious of social status. I remember her telling me, 'How come the Rockefellers got away with all those things, and we couldn't?' "

Just at that time, there was a crisis in the Dominican Republic where dictator Rafael Trujillo was killed with American-supplied weapons. Trujillo's brother was in Paris and the Secret Service was concerned that he might want to take revenge by killing President Kennedy. The worry was that the violence might spill over into adjoining Haiti, and Kennedy wanted anything necessary done to prevent a Communist takeover in the Dominican Republic. The Secretary of State was en route to Paris and the President had asked him to "let Bobby play around . . . if he gets in your way, let me know."

Bobby did more than that. He felt that the Navy should send warships to the Dominican coast to scare the Communists against making any further moves. Undersecretary of State Bowles refused. Bowles finally called the President to explain the situation and ask, "Would you clarify who's in charge here?"

"You are," said the President.

"Good, would you mind explaining that to your brother."

Meanwhile, in Paris, at the state dinner, Jacqueline told the French President, "You know, Monsieur President, all my ancestors were French." And de Gaulle looked down at her from his lofty height, and said, "Really, Madame? So were mine."

But, by the evening's end, Jacqueline, who spoke French fluently, was dazzling, and had made a conquest of de Gaulle. "God, she's really laying it on, isn't she?" Kennedy observed. But later he would introduce himself to the French people as "the man who had accompanied Jacqueline Kennedy to Paris."

In his private moments, the President was quietly suffering. Before making the trip, his doctors had told him to use crutches to ease his pain, which was still acute. He refused, saying he would not meet Khrushchev "as a cripple." What he did do, several times a day, was soak in the oversize golden bathtub in his suite at the Quai d'Orsay Palace. Dr. Travell also injected him two or three times a day with an anesthetic to treat muscular disorders. He still wore his corset-like brace, and there was some discussion that he might be confined to a wheelchair for his second term. He once told Billings that he would trade all his political successes and all his money just to be out of pain.

As an extra insurance, he brought along "Dr. Feelgood," a German refugee named Max Jacobson whose celebrity clients also included writer Truman Capote, singer Eddie Fisher, and the President's brother-in-law Stanislas Radziwill.

Dr. Jacobson took on Kennedy as a patient in June 1961, about five months after he became President. Whenever Kennedy needed him, the doctor was there—Washington, Hyannis Port, New York City. Over an eighteen-month period Jacobson's assistant, Harvey Mann, accompanied Dr. Max at least six times to the swank Presidential Suite at the Carlyle Hotel. "Sometimes, before the treatment, Kennedy looked haggard. But after a visit from Dr. Max, the President was full of vim and vigor," reported Mann. Mann later revealed that he had mixed most of the ingredients in the doctor's famous shots, which contained vitamins, enzymes, steroids, hormones, animal organ cells, and amphetamines—at least 85 percent amphetamine.

Jacobson later recorded that shortly after they arrived in Vienna, Kennedy called him in and said, "Khrushchev is supposed to be on his way. You'd better give me something for my back."

Reporter Marianne Means later observed, "How much of JFK's personality was affected by the drugs he was taking, we don't know. Some felt it had put him in an unnatural high when he had talked to Khrushchev."

"No President with his finger on the red button has any business taking stuff like that," warned a staff doctor. Bobby had checked on the ingredients and advised his brother to stop taking the injections until he had them tested by the Food and Drug Administration.

Kennedy's reply: "I don't care if it's horse piss. It works."

Khrushchev had told a Westinghouse executive visiting Moscow that he expected to have great difficulty communicating with Kennedy because he was so young—younger than his own son. "Eisenhower I could deal with, because we're contemporaries."

Now, before leaving Moscow, Khrushchev told U.S. Ambassador Thompson that if he and Kennedy did not reach agreement on Berlin in Vienna, he would sign a separate peace treaty with Germany. Thompson warned Khrushchev that if the Soviets used force to block access to Berlin, it would be met with force.

"Only a madman would want war," warned Khrushchev, "but if the Americans want war, they'll get it."

Kennedy had small expectations. The most he expected, according to Robert Kennedy, was a nuclear-test-ban agreement, about which there was tentative approval.

————

KENNEDY KNEW THAT during Khrushchev's previous summit with Eisenhower in 1955, the Soviet leader had great contempt for Eisenhower because every time he asked him a tough question, the American President would turn to his Secretary of State for an answer. For this reason, Kennedy had asked for one-to-one meetings with Khrushchev, without advisers, only interpreters. Khrushchev had agreed.

Kennedy opened the conversation, recalling that he had met Khrushchev at a Foreign Relations Committee tea in 1959, when Kennedy was still a Senator. Kennedy now told Khrushchev, "I remember you said that I looked young to be a Senator, but I've aged a lot since then."

In the dining room, Kennedy asked Khrushchev about his medals. "This one is the Lenin Peace Prize," Khrushchev said.

"Tell him I hope they never take it away from him," Kennedy told the interpreter. Khrushchev laughed.

What followed was a long and heated conversation that afternoon while they walked in the garden behind the mansion. From an upstairs window, Ken O'Donnell saw Khrushchev shaking his finger and "snapping" at the President "like a terrier."

Jacqueline was getting a more friendly reception from Vienna crowds. They cheered her wherever she went and called her "the American Princess."

The President introduced his mother to Mrs. Khrushchev. This round, portly woman who wore no makeup, said Mrs. Kennedy, was the kind of woman who would make a perfect baby-sitter. Madame Khrushchev had confided to Rose, "I must learn your beauty secrets."

Khrushchev seemed enchanted with Jacqueline Kennedy at the banquet evening. She wore a long, pink-beaded white gown. When a photographer asked Khrushchev to pose shaking hands with President Kennedy, the Soviet leader nodded with a grin toward Mrs. Kennedy and said, "I'd like to shake her hand first."

Throughout the evening, Khrushchev sat beside her, complimented her gown, shifted his chair closer. But when he got too serious, she said, "Oh, Mr. Chairman, don't bore me with statistics." He laughed and then she found him "almost cozy."

Max Lerner wrote a column about her. "I am certain that right now there are lights burning in the Kremlin far into the night, while some commissars and their flunkies worry about exactly this impact of the Jackie image, and how to counteract it."

In the five hours of talks with Khrushchev, there was no agreement on Berlin. As they parted, Kennedy told him, "Well, Mr. Chairman, I see it's going to be a very cold winter."

There was indication among some that the President not only was disappointed, but caught off guard. Kennedy never had dealt with anyone like Khrushchev before. He had always thought he could charm anyone he wanted into doing anything. It worked with women, reporters, and even many politicians. But with Khrushchev, his charm hit a hard wall.

Lyndon Johnson later confided to cronies that "Khrushchev scared the poor little fellow dead." Johnson even dropped to his knees to dramatize Kennedy's begging Khrushchev for something. Georgi Bolshakov, a Soviet military intelligence colonel who posed as an embassy information officer, later revealed how surprised the Russians were that Kennedy seemed so "scared" of Khrushchev. "When you have your hand up a girl's dress, you expect her to scream," he said, "but you don't expect her to be scared."

It is unlikely that the President was "scared." But when Kennedy walked Khrushchev to his car, *Sunday Times* correspondent Henry

Brandon thought Kennedy looked "dazed." Elder statesman Averell Harriman later observed that the President was "shattered." At his hotel, when his secretary Evelyn Lincoln asked how the meetings had gone, Kennedy replied, "Not too well." "Talking to him then was like talking to a statue," she said.

President Kennedy later referred to his meeting with Khrushchev as part of "a very mean year."

Kennedy had scheduled an interview with *New York Times* correspondent James Reston at the American Embassy. He knew when he was talking to Reston that it would all become part of the historical record, and he had to explain himself to history.

Reston had been put in a darkened room, the blinds drawn. "I remember when he came in. He had his hat on. I remember that because it was one of two times I ever saw Kennedy with his hat on. As he came in, he looked around because he couldn't see me in the darkness. At last he saw me and I started to get up but he waved me back, came over and sat on the couch next to me, pushed his hat over his eyes like a beaten man, and breathed a great sigh.

" 'Pretty rough, was it?' I asked.

" 'The roughest thing in my life,' " Kennedy replied. 'I never heard anything like it.' "

The Khrushchev reaction was astonishing, Kennedy said. He had treated Kennedy with contempt, even challenged his courage. As Khrushchev had often said, the best way to get a capitalist's attention was to "pull his testicles." He made a violent attack on American activity everywhere in the world, attacked its presence in Berlin, and threatened war.

He had presented Kennedy with an ultimatum: if the United States did not agree to Communist control over access to Berlin in a peace treaty by the end of the year, he would seize control anyway. Kennedy replied that the U.S. would fight to maintain access.

"I have two problems," Kennedy told Reston. "First to figure out why he did it, and in such a hostile way. And the second is to figure out what we can do about it. I think he did it because of the Bay of Pigs. I think he thought that anyone who was so inexperienced as to get into that mess could be taken, and anyone who got into it and didn't see it through had no guts. So he beat the hell out of me.

"We've got a terrible problem," Kennedy told Reston. "Until we remove Khrushchev's ideas [about me] we won't get anywhere with him. And so we have to act. . . . The only place in the world where there is a challenge is Vietnam, and now we have the problem of making our power credible."

On the way home, Air Force aide Godfrey McHugh said, the mood "was like riding with the losing baseball team after the World Series."

Robert Kennedy observed that it was the first time his brother had met somebody "with whom he couldn't exchange ideas in a meaningful way." His brother had complained that dealing with Khrushchev "was like dealing with Dad. All give and no take."

If the trip was negative for the President, it was glowingly positive for the First Lady. They had cheered her even more loudly than they had cheered him. He now had to regard her as an increased asset in their marriage. For all her heightened celebrity, she still managed to maintain an untouchable aura, the ability to "drop this curtain in my mind."

"Just when you think you understand her, you're in trouble," said Dave Powers.

––––––––

BACK HOME, THE President and his wife did not attend Bobby and Ethel's backyard barbecue party for 300 people. They still rarely attended any of their parties.

French Ambassador Hervé Alphand, who was there, was struck by the general youth of the scene and especially the beauty of the young women. Alphand noted that "Ted Kennedy, of course, in a dinner jacket, fell into the pool with his dancing partner."

Everybody thought they understood young Teddy. "Teddy Kennedy was then a young man without a care in the world having the time of his life," said Jim Symington. "When Bob and Ethel gave a big party for astronaut John Glenn, Teddy was like a young colt full of high spirits, joshing and kidding, giving a shove to a woman in full evening dress kerplunk into the pool. Then he said, 'Gee, did I do that? My golly, then the least I can do is this.' And then he jumped in. That was the day almost everybody went into the swimming pool. Teddy dived in, not once, but nearly a dozen times."

"His father's last words to him were, don't go to the party, but if you do go, keep out of the swimming pool," recalled Rose Kennedy.

"He recalled his father's last words but it was too late to do anything about it."

Actress Shelley Winters recalled in her memoirs a conga line on a plank over the swimming pool, where she broke the heel of a sandal and limped away. Teddy followed. He helped her undo the strap, "and suddenly I was in his arms and he was kissing me. Although I was three champagne glasses into the party, I stopped the passionate kiss and stared at him." She claimed she was "terribly frightened." Teddy said, "For God's sake! I was only trying to kiss you. What did you think I was going to do?" As she hobbled back to the party, she grumbled, "Only God knows."

According to his mother, Jack exulted in Teddy's activities. "In fact," she said, "he used to rather egg him on to do stunts because he couldn't do them himself . . . his health wasn't good enough. Teddy had the strength and the vitality and Jack rather envied him."

"Teddy was the Prince Hal of his time when the King was Jack. And the minor Falstaffs were everywhere," said Charles Spalding. "I remember a time Ted came in to tell us how he'd had it with a Countess, gone right out from her apartment and had it with her daughter, and then downstairs with their mother . . . claimed he had sex some eleven times with the three of them, during that one day. And Jack was roaring with laughter at all this."

Friend James Symington also recalled Jack telling his brother, " 'Ted, for crying out loud! Here I am trying to run the country, and there you are in the pool. I mean, how can we handle this?' Partly good-natured, partly a small strain of 'You're letting the team down,' but nothing heavy. . . . I have a theory about youngest brothers; they get all the credit for growing up, and the older brothers do all the work."

Senator Barry Goldwater observed that the Kennedys' invitations to formal dinners ought to read: "Black tie and snorkel."

The swimming pool publicity caused enough national flak so that Ted Kennedy kept quiet and out of the limelight for the rest of 1961. He stayed in Massachusetts, seldom came to Washington, and saw his brother mostly on weekends at Hyannis.

Teddy had "liked the freedom" of working on his brother's presidential campaign in California, and considered staying out there. Symington remembered that Ted also had liked New Mexico, and two or three different states, and people there were saying, " 'Ted's going to come over here and live!' Ted was going to live everywhere."

A Harvard friend, Claude Hooten, later revealed that it was Joe Kennedy who kept Ted in groove, telling him how silly it was to live elsewhere. "Ted, you've got a base here, family, friends. Why go off somewhere and prove yourself for nothing?"

His wife, Joan, had been part of the family long enough to know some of what her husband was doing, and she loved him enough to accept it or was too insecure to demand anything else.

Now came the payoff time. He knew the unwritten Kennedy rule: every male Kennedy has to succeed. He also knew the arena already chosen for him.

Now, with Jack and Bobby out of his orbit, the father concentrated on Teddy. Teddy initially was none too eager to be launched into a political career. He was not a crusading liberal with a cause. He was not an intellectual or a man of driving ambition. He was a handsome, rich, friendly young man who enjoyed his easy pleasures of life. Ted's father had once said his youngest son had "the affability of an Irish cop."

It was the father, alone in the family, who insisted that Ted deserved his turn.

Ted, at twenty-nine, was working in the Boston area as the assistant district attorney for Suffolk County. It was an unpaid job, held by a young man obligated to the Kennedys, who was willing to surrender it to Ted.

"How's Ted getting along? Is he becoming a good lawyer?" the President asked Ted's boss, District Attorney Garret Byrne. "He loves it," replied Byrne.

Byrne remembered constant telephone calls from the White House to Ted. And whenever Byrne saw the Kennedy patriarch, he always gave him his standard report on Ted: "The hardest worker I've got."

There were increasing rumors that Teddy would soon be running for Massachusetts attorney general, lieutenant governor, or senator. "I was hearing too much of it," said Byrne, "so I called Teddy in, and I called up the father and I said, 'Look, I have Ted here with me now. Let's settle this once and for all. Just what have you and Jack decided? . . . What is he running for?' And he said, 'Lookit, get this straight, will you? He's running for the United State Senate. Now put him on the phone.' So Ted got on, and I think Mr. Kennedy must've done most of the conversation, and when he hung up, I said, 'Now do you know what you're running for?' "

The father wanted to see Teddy settled in a prestigious place while he was still alive. Joe Sr. had often predicted his own early death "because I have lived so hard." It also has been suggested that "the old man probably was trying to cut off the fall-back for Bobby so he would have to run for President."

"The person who was primarily interested in having him run was my father," said Robert Kennedy ". . . just as I would never have been Attorney General if it hadn't been for him, I don't think my younger brother would have been Senator, nor would my older brother have been President—but he just felt that Teddy had worked all this time during the campaign and sacrificed himself for the older brother and we had our positions and so that he should have the right to run, that it was a mistake to run for any position lower than that."

Jim Rowe quoted the father as telling Jack and Bobby, "You fellas got what you wanted . . . it's Teddy's turn." It was almost identical to what Joe had said to Jack about Bobby.

And the old man told a reporter, "If you want to make some money, bet all you can that Teddy will be the next Senator from Massachusetts." Asked what problems his youngest son might have if he ran for the Senate, Joe Kennedy put his fingertips together and said, "None."

"This wasn't a sudden decision," said Rose Kennedy. "It was all thought about and discussed, like the Presidency. Ted's father said he should run for the Senate, that he was up to it, and we must encourage him."

Robert Kennedy publicly insisted that he and the President were pleased that Ted was running.

None of this was really true. Teddy never sacrificed himself for his brother during the campaign—he was having fun. And neither brother was keen on Teddy making the race.

John Sharon recalled how unhappy Bobby was because he had his own ambitions of being the Senator from Massachusetts, and now Teddy was hurting those chances. But Bobby was not consulted; he was notified after the fact.

Godfrey McHugh was there when the call came from Bobby about Teddy's political decision. The President's reply was, "Your brother wants to announce that he's running for . . . what!?"

The President was most immediately concerned about his own reelection. Too many political Kennedys would be a campaign liability. "You can't have a whole mess of Kennedys asking for votes."

More pointedly, the President told Bartlett, "I don't know why the House isn't good enough for Teddy; it was good enough for me . . . and if the old man would leave Teddy alone, he would do what he likes to do, which is to chase broads in the south of France." Jack told his father, "Dad, don't be too hard on him; don't force him into politics. Let him be the playboy."

But, like Jack, Teddy quickly warmed to the idea. He had tasted the fun and the challenge and the excitement of a campaign, and he liked it. It suited him more than any of his brothers. Besides, it would give him a sudden prestige he now badly wanted—as much as anything, to put him on a better level with his brothers and gain him a new respect from his father.

Their father had told all his sons, "If you see blue sky, go for it."

Ted's mother put it more simply: "He naturally wants to do what the other boys did."

———

THE POLITICAL WHEELS moved quickly.

Massachusetts Democratic Party State Chairman Lester Hyman took a poll, which showed Teddy could win. So he took it to Teddy and said, "It's your turn to run; I want to run you. Teddy said OK."

"Nobody forced me to run. . . ." Ted Kennedy later told author Burton Hersh. "I wanted to."

Whether Ted had heard his father say it or not, his father had spoken; the die was cast.

"Teddy came bursting on the scene, eager to run for office," said his sister Eunice. "My father was then sixty-eight. He had to prove again to Ted . . . that his ideas and techniques still were modern and effective. Ted went to him for advice—not to be nice to his father, but because he knew he could help."

————

THE PRESIDENT ALSO still sought his father's advice, especially on the international issues.

"We always shuddered when he went to see his father for a weekend," Undersecretary of State George Ball said, "because we knew we were going to catch hell on the question of balance of payments when he came back. And we always did. I remember one long argument I had with him about it. 'George,' he said, 'I understand you and I agree with you, but how do I ever explain it to my father?' "

The last such visit was December 1961, in Palm Beach, and when he was leaving, old Joe said to Powers, "Take good care of the President, Dave."

Shortly after his son's departure, the senior Kennedy played golf. Just before teeing off on the par-three 16th hole at Palm Beach Country Club, Joseph Kennedy turned to his slender golfing companion, niece Ann Gargan, and, with a puzzled expression on his face, said, "We'd better go in." Miss Gargan and Kennedy walked slowly back to the clubhouse, where he slumped on a bench while she, alarmed, broke into a run for their car parked in the club lot. At the Kennedy oceanfront home in Palm Beach, they were met at the door by Jacqueline Kennedy. Joe gruffly brushed aside her concern and said, "I'm going up to take a rest, but don't call any doctors." A few minutes later Miss Gargan looked in on Kennedy and discovered he was not asleep, but unconscious. A private ambulance raced them at eighty miles an hour from Palm Beach, across the causeway to St. Mary's Hospital. Across the corridor from Joe's room was a plaque on the door: *In Memory of Joseph P. Kennedy Jr.*

As soon as the news of Joe Kennedy's illness reached the family, Steve Smith quietly disappeared from his government job in Washington, without saying goodbye, and went to New York to take care of the family finances. For many years he had been groomed for this job, and now the time had come.

Within six hours, Jack, who had left Palm Beach only that morning, was back at his father's bedside, taking up the watch against death that, three times, his father had done for him.

Jack had wanted so much for his father to share in the glory of his presidency. He wanted his father to pat him on the back and tell him, "You've done better than Joe would have done . . . you've done what I couldn't do." That would have been Jack's supreme moment—and now it would never happen.

But still there is no question, words or no words, that John Kennedy did feel the full force of his father's pride.

Joseph Kennedy was in a deep coma and received the Last Rites. The family took turns in an all-night vigil.

Ted was holding his hand late the next afternoon when he saw Joe's eyelids flicker. He called Jack. With barely a nod to Secretary of State Rusk and his party, who were climbing from their cars, the President dashed out the door, accompanied by Jacqueline and Pierre Salinger. After he visited his father at the hospital, Kennedy's face brightened. The elder Kennedy, still unable to speak, had shown recognition when his son bent over his bed.

The President would say of his father: "If my dad had only ten percent of his brain working, I'd still feel he had more sense than anyone else I know."

President Kennedy was able to spend twenty-five minutes with his father the next morning before taking off for Bermuda. The father could respond only by tightening his left hand when the President gripped it. He recognized his son and apparently understood most of what he said. When John Kennedy emerged from the elevator into the lobby of the hospital, he was accompanied by a coat-and-tieless Ted Kennedy, who had spent the night across the hall.

In the past, Jack occasionally mentioned in jest to his staffers that he wished his father would suddenly disappear in the middle of the ocean so he could be free of his constant advice, opinions, and demands. But now all that irritation was wiped out and all that was left was love.

"The love each child felt for Mr. Kennedy was always evident," said nurse Rita Dallas. "It was not easy for them to see him incapacitated, and time and again I would see them stand outside his door and actually seem to summon their courage before entering the sickroom. They went in with shoulders squared, but when they left him, they would often sag in despair."

James Symington, went with Bob. "He went in and saw his father and came back and didn't say a word. He just sat there, very solemn and almost on the verge of tears."

For the Kennedy brothers, it was almost as if the audience had left the theater. They were used to doing their best for their dad. They were always performing for him, waiting for his approval. Now they would have to internalize the applause, give it to themselves and each other.

Of the remaining brothers, the question was which of them needed that applause the most. Not Jack anymore, because he now had world approval. Not Bob, because, as soon as he was grown, he had the full measure of his father's respect and admiration. Teddy needed it the most. He was just starting to reach and grow.

Yet his father's stroke gave Teddy a freedom none of his brothers had. Teddy once quoted poet Kahlil Gibran, that parents may give their children "your love but not your thoughts, for they have their own thoughts." This was not true of his other three brothers—his father had given them the full force of his opinions, often insistently and incessantly. It was no longer true of Teddy. His brothers would be more instrumental in shaping his mind than his father, and now, more and more, he would shape his own.

———

TED SORENSEN DESCRIBED the bond between the father and sons now as both beautiful and sad. "The father so desperately wanted to speak, and he couldn't. Tears rolled out of his eyes. No one knows how much he understood; but he couldn't communicate in any way. . . . Kind of blue in the face. We could see emotion in the eyes, we thought, but we wanted to think so."

Lem Billings recalled lunching with the elder Kennedy, years before, at Pavilion. Elder statesman Bernard Baruch shuffled in, a mumbling old man, held up by a nurse. "I don't want to be like that—not ever," Kennedy said.

"Everyone thought he was a vegetable," a staff member told Coughlan about Old Joe. "But he'd hold a magazine in front of him and make a sign when he'd finished the page, and you'd turn it. He'd go right through the whole magazine." His niece Ann Gargan helped him move his legs in the water, and he could hop a little bit, holding on to the bars all around the pool. The doctors predicted he would die in a couple years, a prognosis typical of most stroke patients. Instead, he would live nine more years, mainly because of his fierce will to live.

When Rose came to visit at the rehabilitation center in New York, Dr. Henry Betts, Joe Kennedy's doctor, recalled how "they would sit around and watch television and she'd take her shoes off and they'd sit there just like any elderly couple you might see. . . . His children told me that he did not like having her around before his stroke—she made him nervous because she always was upset about something else. Well, she didn't make him nervous when I knew him. I mean, he loved having her around. . . . Mrs. Kennedy was not used to spending a lot of time with her husband but felt very obligated to him and, I think, loved him."

It is difficult to imagine how Rose really felt. She had married Joe out of love, and he had given her everything except love. He had dominated her, without her protest, and shamed her with other women. She was the one who kept the family together, but it was he who received the children's admiration. Now she was in control.

Jacqueline's warmth and tenderness was never more visible than when she was with her father-in-law at the rehabilitation clinic. She brought a sense of quiet with her. She sat on a footstool in front of him and said, "I'm praying for you every day, Grandpa, so you work hard while you're in here." She put her head in his lap, and when he placed his hand on her cheek in a caress, she kissed his hand, then stood up to kiss his cheek.

"One thing that I always admired about the First Lady," said nurse Dallas, "was that she completely accepted Mr. Kennedy's condition. While others pretended not to notice the side of his body that was affected by the paralysis, she always held his deformed hand and kissed the affected side of his face. She was trying to help Mr. Kennedy accept himself and not be ashamed."

"Next to my husband and my own father," Jacqueline had said of the elder Kennedy, "I love him more than anybody—more than anybody in the world." And then she made a surprising statement. "I'm more like Mr. Kennedy Senior," she claimed, "than any other members of his family." What she had admired and envied most about him was his sense of full freedom and independence. Independence she always had, but freedom was still elusive.

Dr. Betts was told "by a very good informant" who knew Gloria

Swanson that when told of Kennedy's stroke, Swanson said, "I hope he suffers."

When he was brought home from the clinic, secretary Evelyn Jones recalled that Rose Kennedy "went with me and ordered new linens— said, 'I want him to have the best.' One day, she said, 'I think the fact that Daddy still dresses and has his colors, just the same as if he were well, is important!' And he felt so, as he'd come down to the library and be so proud."

When his children came, Joe always dressed more carefully. When his sons came, he refused to wear his leg braces. "I couldn't understand what he was trying to tell me," said Evelyn Jones. "He got so furious! I was terribly upset. But they were trying so desperately to make him wear that brace, and he wasn't having any part of it."

"He was in a walker," said his wife. "He'd walk for Jack." And every time he took a single step, no matter how small, his family applauded.

"Here was a man who couldn't talk," said Dr. Betts, "and I'm sure he would have given up every arm and every leg to be able to talk. And so who was going to interpret what he meant, because he understood things he wanted to say and who was going to manage, who was going to make decisions and interpret his decisions, and who was going to decide what was going to be done for him when, and that sort of thing? So that there was, within the family, a lot of turmoil in determining who was going to be this interpreter and decision-maker for him. And for a group of people who don't want to face bad things, it was hard, it was harder than death because with death they always went on. . . . But how could you . . . he was around all the time, horror and death. So it was just terrible for all of them."

Former President Herbert Hoover invited former Ambassador Kennedy to dinner at the Waldorf-Astoria Towers. They sat in silence: Hoover could scarcely hear; Kennedy could not speak. "Throughout the meal, Kennedy wept." It was one of the few ways he could express emotion.

The grandchildren seemed to come in relays, always kissing their grandpa on the forehead. He was always the focal point, no matter who was there. Anybody talking to him had to look him in the eyes, and often you could tell what he was thinking by the slight smile or frown. "You talk about 'The Godfather'—he *was* 'The Godfather,' " a family member told Coughlan.

This would not be his last stroke. Recovery would get increasingly difficult.

————

THE PRESIDENT INSISTED that whenever he came home to Hyannis on weekends, his father should be waiting on the porch. Nobody else. Larry Newman observed that when he embraced his father, "it was a very moving thing."

Robert Kennedy later claimed that his brother Jack "was almost the best with my father because he said outrageous things to him and made him laugh. . . . At Hyannis, my father used to . . . just sit out there Friday afternoon waiting for the helicopter to arrive . . . it really made a big difference in his life. And then on Sunday afternoon, he'd take off and my father'd come out and see him leave in the helicopter."

Bob and Ted went to Hyannis every weekend, and once brought General Maxwell Taylor with them. Taylor was impressed by the way the two sons would report to their father on what they were doing and what they had done, and the most their father could do was to nod slightly or shake his head. But what impressed Taylor most was their feeling toward the old man.

Once, he suddenly started to get out of his wheelchair alone. He staggered. Bobby rushed over to help him, but the proud father screamed, swatted at him with his cane. Bobby ducked the blows, kissed his father. "That's what I'm here for, Dad. Just to give you a hand when you need it. You've done that for me all my life, so why can't I do the same for you now?"

"It was strange to me how so many people still talked about the father's influence over Jack even though it was after the father's stroke and the father couldn't even talk at the time," British Ambassador Ormsby-Gore said.

————

HE CONTINUED TO communicate with slight gestures, a lift of the eyebrow, and always managed to maintain his dignity in a roomful of strangers. His nurse read him *The New York Times.* He enjoyed "I Love Lucy" reruns on TV. When he saw some politician in the news whom he remembered, he once managed to say, loud and clear—to the laughing pleasure of his President son—"Son of a bitch."

When the stricken father visited the Oval Office, deeply moved, the President pushed his father's wheelchair over to his own rocker near the windows. "This is my rocker, Dad," he said, sitting opposite his father. "It looks as though we both need special chairs, doesn't it?" After the first few minutes, the father, in the wheelchair, indicated his displeasure. His sons finally got the message. He felt that they should be back in their offices working.

Arthur Goldberg, then Secretary of Labor, got a call from President Kennedy, saying his father was in the White House. "It would be great if you came over. I know my father likes you."

"I'd come and see the old man, for about an hour," said Goldberg. "The Old Man and I, for some reason, got along. . . . He couldn't talk—but he could communicate some . . . his father was exuberant—he was a smart old bastard."

Goldberg was not always that complimentary. Before Joe Kennedy's stroke, Goldberg was trying to settle a strike at United Airlines. "Jim Landis was the old man's lawyer, and his father and Landis got involved in the strike. I got furious; I had to settle. . . . So I called him at Middleburg, and I lost my temper, and said, 'Why don't you appoint your father Secretary of Labor?' . . . He said, 'My father won't appear anymore, nor will Jim Landis.' You could talk to him that way—that's what I think Presidents need."

John Nolan, a Justice Department aide, remembered a visit by Joseph Kennedy to the Attorney General's office. "Bob was pushing his Dad in the wheelchair, saying things like, 'Now, look, Dad, look at this. Did you ever have an office this big? Look at those pictures. Now, look at this view, out on Constitution Avenue. Did you ever have a view like that? Pretty good, huh?' "

It was a spontaneous monologue for a silent audience. The sons could not easily give up seeking their father's approval, even though they now had to imagine it.

On another Washington trip, Bob and Ethel were taking Joe to lunch on the *Honey Fitz*. "Mr. Kennedy was in a wheelchair," Angie Novello remembered. "Ann, the cousin, was there . . . we all sat around. . . . Bob sat next to his father, telling him funny stories about things that happened in the Justice Department, and discussing cases that had come up, that would be of interest to the father. . . . He'd just sit there and smile . . . and raising the one arm. . . . Just made me want to cry."

"I remember going to the White House for tea, when Jack's father was visiting there," said family friend Kay Halle. "And I said to him, 'I've never seen a handsomer dressing gown. It makes you look like a larkspur.' And Teddy, who was the actor in the family, did a funny imitation of his father in a robe, parading around, getting the attention of all the women."

That day, Halle said to the former Ambassador, "What other father, in all of American history, could ever say that, here's one son who's President of the United States; another who's Attorney General; and another, who's going to be a United States Senator?' And the old man started laughing, or doing the equivalent of a laugh."

This was exactly the remarkable prophecy Ambassador Joseph Kennedy made in the September 7, 1957, *Saturday Evening Post*. He said he expected his son Jack to be President, Bobby to be Attorney General, and Ted to become a United States Senator—all at the same time.

A later *Time* story about the three Kennedy brothers showed their portraits joined against a Washington, D.C., background. President Kennedy had the cover framed and hung in his father's bedroom at Palm Beach on the wall opposite his bed so that Joe Sr. could always see it.

––––––

ON HIS BIRTHDAY, all his seventeen grandchildren were there. "All the brothers picked up the wheelchair—picked up the old man and put him in it, then brought him into this huge gathering. How lovingly and affectionately they all treated him."

On Father's Day, the Kennedy children entertained him. Their spouses stayed on the sidelines while the President and his brothers and sisters put on a skit about their childhood memories—while their parents were weak with laughter.

Then the President applauded his father. He was joined by Bobby, then Eunice, then Teddy, then Pat, then Jean, then all of them applauding together. The boys bowed at the waist, and the girls curtsied, first to their father, then to their mother.

They were applauding the man who was always pushing them faster than they could walk.

9

MARILYN AND MISSILES

In February 1962, Attorney General Kennedy was leaving for a 26,880-mile month-long goodwill tour of a dozen countries, mostly in the Far East. Japan had invited him to visit, and Mayor Willy Brandt had asked him to give the Ernst Reuter Lecture at the Free University of Berlin.

Some columnists complained that it was a mistake for President Kennedy to take his brother away from his post as head of the Department of Justice, for which he was paid a salary, and to send him abroad to contact foreign government officials—a job that should be given to the Vice President. But an unconcerned JFK even had advice for his traveling brother. He was concerned that Bob would get sunburned on his trip because he was so pale, and suggested he get under the White House sunlamp before he left. "I wouldn't stay under there but 2 or 3 seconds. You've been staying indoors so much."

When Ted came to Washington, he explained he was in town to see his brother Bob before he left. But everyone knew that Ted was there "to put the arm on" Massachusetts Democrats and demand support in the Senate race. On Teddy Kennedy's schedule was Benjamin A. Smith II. Smith had been appointed as a "seat-warmer" to fill out two years of President Kennedy's senatorial term. There was the firm understanding, however, that Smith would retire whenever another Kennedy wanted the Senate seat. Teddy was there to tell him that the time was now.

Talking to the press, hands dipped in his pockets—a posture reminiscent of the President—Teddy Kennedy also announced "tentative plans" for a European junket the following week. All of his planned stops were countries with large ethnic groups in Massachusetts: Israel, Poland, and Greece. He said he would also rendezvous with Bob in Berlin and go to Brussels.

"Why Brussels?" asked one reporter.

"Well," replied Kennedy easily, "the Common Market." Then he added quickly, "To evaluate the effect of the Common Market on Massachusetts industry."

"The trip," he explained, would be "personal," although he would receive a briefing from the State Department that classified him as a distinguished private citizen on a fact-finding mission. Some hoped quietly that this would be more restrained than Teddy's previous world tour, on which he and a friend had some highly publicized wild nights on the town.

After paying respectful visits to various political leaders, Ted told the press that he still wasn't a candidate and therefore wasn't soliciting support. The press replies were cynical.

Then he added that he didn't think people would expect him to sit on his hands for the rest of his life because one brother was President and the other was Attorney General.

———

DURING THE DISCUSSIONS of the Common Market at the meetings abroad, Teddy seated himself inconspicuously in the background and took copious notes on everything that was said, never asking a question or making a comment.

In Berlin, too, it was clear the spotlight was primarily on Bobby. Mayor Brandt proposed a toast to "the President, government and people of the United States." The Attorney General, responding, said, "That's the three of us—the President, that's my brother; the government, that's me; and [looking hard at Teddy] you're the people." Brandt was not amused. He recorded in his memoirs that though he admired the Kennedys, this event made him "regard the family's political expansion with disquiet."

Not long after Bob and Teddy returned from their trip abroad, Teddy went into a higher gear on his Senate campaign.

Jack particularly was not happy. "The reason was simple," said Ted's assistant Milton Gwirtzman. "Whatever happened now, the President's prestige rode with his young brother. Every time he spoke, every time he appeared on TV, every blooper he might make would reflect somehow on the President."

Yet, once a thing was settled, the brothers all closed ranks to make it happen.

Jack told Charles Spalding that Teddy would win bigger than he had. At the same time, Jack directed Pierre Salinger: "I want you to wring him out. Get everything—every single thing that you know he has goofed off, that he's done wrong—and God knows he has done a lot of stupid things in his young life—they can all be put out, but it's got to be out now." The big thing was the cheating incident at Harvard and his expulsion. When Boston *Globe* reporter Robert Healy discovered the story, President Kennedy asked Healy to kill it. Healy refused.

"We're having more fucking trouble with this than we did with the Bay of Pigs," the President told his National Security Adviser. Bundy nodded. "Yes, and with about the same results."

John Sharon, an associate at Clark Clifford's law firm, suggested that Ted deal with the Harvard incident openly and directly, before anyone else hit him on it. Sharon even wrote the prearranged questions that were planted with friendly reporters.

Ted memorized his answers. Calling a press conference, Ted told the reporters, "What I did was wrong. The unhappiness I caused my family and friends, even though eleven years ago, has been a bitter experience for me, but it has also been a very valuable lesson."

Still worried about the voters' reaction, the President told his friend Ben Bradlee, "I just spoke to Ted on the phone. He feels like he's been kicked in the balls, really singing the blues. . . . It won't go over with you WASPs. They take a very dim view of looking over someone else's exam paper. They go in more for stealing from stockholders and banks."

In many respects Ted was a picturebook candidate: taller than his brothers, and more handsome, he had the infectious Kennedy smile, a backslapping instinct, and greater warmth than they did. He was not a man of too many ideas, and he was described by reporters as "helpless, hapless Ted" or "the finest political package

I've ever seen in Massachusetts.'' Nobody called him a man of destiny.

————

IN FEBRUARY 1962, Jacqueline was on a pleasure trip to India with her sister and was photographed riding horses and feeding a baby elephant. A reporter who followed her to a mosque, where visitors were required to leave their shoes outside, told the world that they were size ten.

At a Gridiron Club dinner, the annual Washington press affair at which reporters poke fun at political leaders, JFK had some fun of his own. Referring to his wife's trip to India, he said, ''I know my Republican friends were glad to see my wife feeding an elephant in India. She gave him sugar and nuts. But of course the elephant wasn't satisfied.''

The press loved him. It was once said of Kennedy that ''he worked the press like an entertainer works a room.''

Although the President was an intensely private person, he still hated to be alone in the evening. When his wife was away, he often asked Dave Powers to sit with him in the executive mansion's upstairs living quarters while he worked and listened to recordings of old dance tunes of the thirties and forties: ''The Very Thought of You,'' ''Beyond the Blue Horizon,'' ''Stardust,'' and ''Body and Soul.'' Dave would stay around, drinking the President's Heineken until Kennedy undressed and said, ''Good night, pal.'' Then Dave would turn off the lights and go off to his own home and family in McLean, Virginia.

''I used to call myself 'John's Other Wife,' '' Powers recalled years later. ''Those nights when Jackie was at the Cape, I sat with the President every night from Monday until Thursday, and, despite what you've been reading lately in the National Enquirer, I never saw anybody else in the house except the Secret Service on duty in the downstairs hall.''

''I was leaving the White House once, to get a cab after dinner,'' Charles Spalding recalled, ''and Jack went with me. We walked down the street, and came to that big fence, on Pennsylvania. He said, 'Charlie, what's out there, what's out there?' He's following me down the street—Secret Service all over. I said, 'There's people out there. People and places to go.' He'd often do that—like it was some scene from a play or movie we'd seen—building this up: 'Tell me, am I missing something? What am I missing?' "

His old friend Edward McLaughlin recalled one night when the Secret Service did lose the President. Jack later strolled in with Torby MacDonald—they had gone to the movies.

———

AFTER KENNEDY'S FIRST year, historian James MacGregor Burns wrote that there was not one President Kennedy, but four: "the rhetorical radical, the policy liberal, the economic moderate, and the institutional conservative." The four Kennedys, he argued, were incompatible, and the Kennedy presidency would not take on political momentum until these contending personalities were fused.

There was, of course, also a fifth Kennedy—the private one.

"I think Jack was vulnerable," said *Look* correspondent Laura Berg-quist. "I think he always felt an insecurity about himself. Not simply because he was part of the upward-mobile Irish, but because I think he recognized himself as an image that had been manufactured. And the questions came up: 'Who loves me and wants me for myself, and who loves me for what they think I am, and what I can do?' "

One of the women who loved him for herself was Mary Pinchot Meyer. Artist Mary Meyer, a longtime friend of Kennedy, was divorced from a CIA official in 1962. She kept a diary that detailed her relationship with John Kennedy. James Truitt, a former editor and executive assistant at the Washington *Post*, said he had been told of the affair by Mrs. Meyer at the time and that he kept notes on what he learned. Truitt said that Mrs. Meyer and Kennedy met about thirty times from January 1962 to the time of his death. Mrs. Meyer, then forty-two, was driven to the presidential mansion in a White House car and taken by private elevator to living quarters where Kennedy did not permit the Secret Service. The two would usually have drinks and dinner alone, or sometimes with one of the aides. Then the aides would excuse themselves and leave.

Detailed on the night of July 16, 1962, was their experiment smoking marijuana, when the President laughed and said, "We're

having a White House conference on narcotics here in two weeks."
They smoked three joints and then JFK told her, "No more. Suppose
the Russians did something now."

Harvard friend Blair Clark was invited to most of the White House
dances as an extra man. "I took Mary Meyer to one of them," he said.
"I was the 'beard.'. . .

"I found myself sitting at a table with Jack and others, on the edge of
this dance-floor, not far from where Lester Lanin's jazzy little group
was playing. Jack said, 'Blair, tell Lester to play the Twist and get
Teddy to do it.' Then Jack laughed like hell at Teddy doing the
Twist. . . . Jack couldn't do it, with his back."

Clark later learned that "this was the night that Jack broke with
Mary. . . . I noticed she was gone for quite a while. Then, after about
an hour, she turned up. It was wintertime; and I noticed the bottom of
her evening-dress was kinda wet and muddy. And I said, 'Mary! What
the hell! Where've you been?' And she said, 'Oh, I just got a little
upset and went out and walked around, outside the White House.' "

Mrs. Meyer was shot to death while strolling in a park on October
12, 1964, nearly a year after Kennedy's assassination. The crime was
never solved.

Mrs. Meyer's diary was found by her sister, Toni Bradlee, in Mary's
studio. She turned it over to a family friend, CIA counterintelligence
official James Jesus Angleton, who, "to protect the presidency," took
it to CIA headquarters and destroyed it.

"The whole dark side of John Kennedy wouldn't emerge until after
his death," reflected Hugh Sidey. "We had hints of it; we saw it
around the edges. . . . Then we began to see it. You just connected the
dots, and there was a picture there, that's all. . . . Bobby was the
cover-up man."

Walter Winchell privately described Bobby as the family's "sexual
policeman." When Bobby learned from the Secret Service that the
President also had asked for an introduction to a young German
socialite in Washington, he had the FBI investigate her and discovered
she had had an affair with a Soviet attaché. He had her quickly
deported.

"You know, in the end, Jackie knew everything," said Bill Walton.
"Every girl. She knew her rating, her accomplishments."

She knew everything, and of course she cared, but she had style.

When she found a pair of panties under her husband's pillow, Jacqueline held them daintily, with two fingers, and brought them to him, saying, "They're not my size."

———

"YOU KNOW, A President has complete protection—complete, because the Secret Service tells him, every moment, where his wife is. He knows, at every moment, where every member of the family is. So he can never be caught unawares," said society columnist Betty Beale.

With advance knowledge of exactly where Jacqueline was at all times, the President could plan his various liaisons with assorted willing women, as well as his naked swimming parties at the White House pool. He once called one of his close friends to confide, "There are two naked girls in the room but I'm sitting here reading *The Wall Street Journal*. Does that mean I'm getting old?"

Peter Lawford once won a JFK-inspired contest to be the first of the Kennedy brothers and brothers-in-law to sleep with a woman other than his wife in the Lincoln Bedroom of the White House. John Kennedy had privately won that contest much earlier, but wasn't saying so.

———

PRESIDENT KENNEDY TOLD his brother Bob that he missed his father's advice most of all during the steel crisis in April 1962.

The elder Kennedy once had said, "When you deal with a businessman, you screw him first or he'll screw you."

Roger Blough, head of United States Steel, had called on the President at the White House to give him a four-page press release declaring that U.S. Steel was raising steel prices six dollars a ton. A furious Kennedy told O'Donnell, "You know what those sons of bitches just did! They raised prices. We had an agreement. The workers wouldn't take a raise and the owners wouldn't raise their prices. Now this son of a bitch comes in and hands me a press release and says, 'It's all done.' He hands this press release to the President of the United States."

"They kicked us right in the balls," Kennedy continued. "The question really is, are we supposed to sit here and take a cold, deliberate fucking? Is this the way the private-enterprise system is really supposed to work? When U.S. Steel says 'go,' the boys go? How could they all raise their prices almost to a penny within six hours of each other? They've fucked us, and we've got to try to fuck them.''

Few on his staff had ever seen the President so angry for so long. ''My father once told me that all businessmen were sons of bitches,'' he told them. ''I never believed it until now.''

When the steel industry refused to cancel their increase, the Kennedy brothers quickly went into action. They felt the steel price rise could only hurt the economy.

Toasting Attorney General Robert Kennedy at a dinner party, the President described his ultimate victory. He referred to a telephone conversation with Tom Patton, president of Republic Steel: ''Patton asked me, 'Why is it that all the telephones of all the steel executives in the country are being tapped?' And I told him that I thought he was being wholly unfair to the Attorney General and that I was sure that it wasn't true. And he asked me, 'Why is it that all the income tax returns of all the steel executives in the country are being scrutinized?' And I told him that, too, was wholly unfair. . . . And then I called the Attorney General and asked him why he was tapping the telephones of all the steel executives and examining the tax returns of all the steel executives . . . and the Attorney General told me that was wholly untrue and unfair.'' After what Mr. Bradlee describes as ''another Stanislavsky pause,'' President Kennedy added, ''Of course, Patton was right.'' Bobby Kennedy interrupted, saying, ''They were mean to my brother. They can't do that to my brother.''

———

THE PRESIDENT AND Bob seldom talked trivia. Most often, the subjects were important events or issues. There is little question that President Kennedy was much more worldly and sophisticated than Bobby, but Bobby was growing in many ways. He no longer had doubts about his ability to hold his own with people of any rank. He was no longer shy about his role or his worth. He knew now how much his brother needed him. He had made himself a partner in the Presidency. He always had tried to measure up to his vision of Jack, and now this was becoming a reality.

The Bay of Pigs had been a defining time for Bobby. Ken O'Donnell, who claimed to be privy to the President's mind, insisted that JFK "didn't want Bobby to know everything." Perhaps this was because he sensed the growing force of his brother and wanted to keep it in its proper place. Perhaps this too was why the President had kept Bob out of the Bay of Pigs decision. But when defeat was certain, Jack confided to friends that he should have brought Bobby in at the beginning. Bob learned then how much his brother needed him. It was Bobby who picked up the pieces and ransomed the Cuban prisoners. From then on, he was involved in all major decision-making.

Arthur Schlesinger remembered the President making a crack at a Cabinet meeting: "The Attorney General has not yet spoken, but I can feel the hot breath of his disapproval on the back of my neck."

"Bobby was the stronger of the two when it came to policies," added columnist Robert S. Allen "He was the decisive force. . . . I don't mean he was leading Jack by the nose—Jack wasn't constituted that way. But Bobby was more aggressive and decisive." More than any of the other sons, Bobby adhered to the Kennedy credo of winning at any cost.

However closely they worked in the White House, their socializing together was still minimum. "Sometimes Jack and Jackie would have Charlie Bartlett and his wife over . . . and they'd invite Bob and Ethel," recalled Bobby's personal secretary, Angie Novello. But it wasn't often. And the President and his wife, even less often, came to Hickory Hill. "Only once do I remember John Kennedy being there," observed a close friend.

Bobby had reached the point where he could now entertain anybody, Spalding said, "but I don't think he ever learned how to entertain Jack."

The sharper fact was that Ethel and Jacqueline still did not like each other. In private, Jackie reportedly gave a devastatingly funny—and cruel—imitation of Ethel. It seemed easy to satirize Ethel and her favorite phrase, "Triffic!" and the way she separated the okay and non-okay types into "Goodies and Baddies." Jacqueline called Ethel "a baby-making machine—wind her up and she becomes pregnant." Ethel, in turn, did an exaggerated imitation of her sister-in-law's whispery voice and teased her sister-in-law's secret ambition to be a ballet dancer: "With those clodhoppers of yours? You'd be better off going in for soccer."

Reporter Fred Sparks, who was dining at La Caravelle in New York, overheard Ethel telling Jacqueline, "You've hurt the family a lot with all this publicity about your almost obscene big spending."

Jackie asked for the check and said, "I'm going to walk out on you. Every Kennedy thinks only of The Family! Has anybody ever thought about my happiness?"

There also seemed to be a keen competition between the two wives. Author Victor Navasky reported that when the papers said Jackie was buying new china for the White House, Ethel also bought new china, selecting a pattern of Lenox with the seal of the Justice Department on it.

Red Fay, a frequent visitor at the White House, remembered, "Whenever we came back from being with the President, Bob and Ethel always had this almost pathetic desire to know what had happened during the weekend. Who had been there? What was said? How were people dressed?" But regardless of her feelings for Ethel, Jacqueline still felt close to Bobby. She saw things in Bobby his own brother didn't. "She told a story about how Bobby had been the first one to come when she had lost her first baby," Bradlee recalled. "She stumbled, we thought quite uncomfortably, over JFK's absence, and said quickly, 'We couldn't get hold of Jack in time.'"

———

NOR DID JACQUELINE go to her husband's forty-fifth birthday party, which featured Marilyn Monroe, at Madison Square Garden.

When Jack was a Senator, hospitalized for his back surgery, he had a pinup poster of Marilyn near his bed. It showed her in tight blue shorts with her legs spread far apart. Jack had it hung upside down. Marilyn Monroe was to Jack what Gloria Swanson was to his father: the ultimate Hollywood sex symbol, the ultimate conquest.

Jack met Monroe in 1954 at a party given by Hollywood agent Charles Feldman. Marilyn was there with her husband, Joe DiMaggio, and Marilyn later told Robert Slatzer, who also briefly had been her husband, that Jack Kennedy "couldn't take his eyes off me." She and DiMaggio left early, but not before she gave Jack her private phone number.

Shortly after that, Jack had his back surgery. Marilyn divorced DiMaggio early in 1955 and spent much time in New York, where she had her own apartment. It was there and in his duplex penthouse suite at the Carlyle that Jack and Marilyn began their affair. The Carlyle has underground passageways to nearby areas that guarantee privacy. Whenever he came to California, their rendezvous was usually Lawford's beach house in Santa Monica, fronting the Pacific. The two would often be seen walking along the beach together, hand in hand.

After he became President, "Peter Lawford disguised her and took her to Washington on Air Force One as a secretary," said Lawford's wife, Patricia. "She hated it. She cursed him the whole way. And he'd make her take letters, to really play it out. And they went to the White House."

Marilyn confided to her friend Henry Rosenfeld that she considered Kennedy the most important person in the world. "She was so excited," said Rosenfeld, "you'd thought she was a teenager."

Later, when a friend asked her if she had ever slept with the President, she replied, "I'll never tell." But columnist Earl Wilson quoted her as saying, after a meeting with the President, "I think I made his back feel better." She also revealed to a friend that the reason the President didn't indulge in foreplay was that he was too busy and didn't have time.

She even asked her friend Jeanne Carmen, "Can't you just see me as First Lady?"

"The President always would use some excuse to go to the West Coast. . . . He'd always have to examine the naval facilities at San Diego, or something."

They were not the most discreet. Senior Kennedy aide Peter Summers said he personally saw the two emerging from the same shower. There had been stories about a pregnancy, an abortion at Cedars of Lebanon Hospital under an assumed name, and that the father had been Kennedy. She had told some of this to her hairdresser, Agnese Flanagan, and her publicist, Rupert Allan.

The President's Madison Square Garden birthday fund-raising party on May 19, 1962, was the highlight of his relationship with Monroe, an event the First Lady missed. She was riding horses in Virginia.

The party had the loose excitement of a revival meeting. Marilyn

Monroe arrived in an ermine wrap over a tight, glittering, almost transparent $12,000 Jean Louis dress of "skin and beads" and sang in a whispery voice, sensuously stretching out each word, as provocatively as it could be sung.

Hugh Sidey of *Time* was there, and remembered, "When she came down in that flesh-colored dress, without any underwear on . . . you could just smell lust. I mean, Kennedy went limp, or something. We all were just stunned, to see this woman."

"It was like mass seduction," said composer Richard Adler, producer of the show. For the American male, Marilyn Monroe was the blond, beautiful, sweet angel of sex.

The President quipped, "Now I can retire from politics." Writer Gene Schoor was with Jack Kennedy in the presidential box and Schoor heard the President comment, "What an ass, Gene. . . . *What* an ass!"

After Marilyn's seven-minute performance at the birthday party, she collapsed in her dressing room. "She was carefully snipped out of the designer dress, then bathed with cool hand towels in an attempt to lower her temperature." Two hours later, after resting, Monroe made her entrance at a party given by theater magnate Arthur Krim. Adlai Stevenson said of Monroe that night, "I do not think I have seen anyone so beautiful . . . my encounters, however, were only after breaking through the strong defenses established by Robert Kennedy, who was dodging around her like a moth around the flame." Dorothy Kilgallen noted in her column the next day that Bobby had danced with Marilyn at least five times. Ethel, who was also there, was reportedly furious.

After an hour, President Kennedy pulled the actress away from the other guests and into a corner, where they were soon joined by Robert Kennedy. The three stood talking for about fifteen minutes. When Bobby was informed by a Secret Service agent that a candid photo had been taken of all of them, his face grew stormy. The President and Marilyn then went to his suite at the Carlyle.

"I learned from an FBI agent that they remained in the suite for several hours," said Earl Wilson in an interview. "It was the last prolonged encounter between them."

What worried the President was that the affair was becoming too well known, and if anybody broke the story, the rest of the press would jump on it. He shared his concern with his friend Senator

George Smathers. Kennedy even sent William Haddad, a top New York *Post* reporter, then working for the Peace Corps, to visit the important editors, especially at *Time* and *Newsweek*, and tell them the Monroe story was not true.

"Marilyn realized the affair was over, but couldn't accept it," Peter Lawford told author C. David Heymann. "She began writing these rather pathetic letters to Jack and continued calling. She threatened to go to the press. She was bitter enough to tell Slatzer that the President made love like an adolescent. The President finally sent Bobby Kennedy to California to cool her off.

"She took it pretty hard. They met again the following day and passed the afternoon walking along the beach. It wasn't Bobby's intention, but that evening they became lovers and spent the night in our guest bedroom. Almost immediately the affair got very heavy, and they began seeing a lot of each other."

There was no competitive feeling about Marilyn as there had been between Jack and Ted about Judith Campbell. Jack and Ted both had met Campbell in Las Vegas at the same time. Ted had tried to date her "and became childishly temperamental" when she turned him down because she already had made arrangements to meet Jack. He kept calling her, urging her to change her plans, even sent her three dozen roses.

———

WHEN KENNEDY BIOGRAPHER Joe McCarthy interviewed Steve Smith, he said, "Everybody in New York is saying that Jack is friendly with Marilyn Monroe." Smith seemed surprised. "Jack?" he said. "I thought Bobby was the one who was friendly with Marilyn Monroe."

Bobby boasted to his brother-in-law, George Terrien, whom he had known since college, before he married Ethel's sister. Bob told Terrien that he had been "screwing the woman Jack used to jack off over, Marilyn Monroe." Terrien called him "the biggest bullshitter in the world," and added that Bobby "wouldn't have the balls to play around." But Bobby insisted that he not only "had Marilyn's pussy" but "I think she's in love with me."

———

NOT TOO MANY months before, Bob had been a single-minded moral married man. "I attended a Hollywood party once with

Bobby,'' said journalist Andrew Glass. "There were plenty of movie stars and starlets there, wildly attractive unattached women, some of whom made a play for him. I watched him carefully and I saw he wasn't the least bit interested in any of them, fantastically beautiful and shapely though they were. He wasn't just pretending, either . . . there was no covert interest. He was completely aloof from them.''

But it changed when he met Marilyn at another Lawford party in California. Lawford had urged Monroe to "fall all over Bobby" at the party, and she did. "I was sitting on the floor talking to Bobby when Marilyn Monroe came in,'' said Joan Braden. "Pat kicked him and said, 'Bobby, this is Marilyn Monroe.' '' Bobby did not rise, according to Braden, "but looked up and said 'Hi' and went on talking to me. I whispered, 'Bobby, this is *Marilyn Monroe*,' and it finally got through to him.'' Braden recalled that Monroe wore black lace and was braless. What Marilyn did to hold his attention was to use her lipstick to write questions for Bobby, such as 'What does an attorney general do?' He answered the questions, then talked to her.''

She then taught him how to do the twist and consumed most of a bottle of champagne. He drove her home.

Her masseur, Ralph Roberts, later recalled that she had said of the Attorney General, that there was no chance of an affair with him. "He's not my type.''

"I think the word she used was 'puny.' ''

All his life he had taken the tenets of his religion more seriously than his brothers, and it had reined him in on the morals of marriage. But he was privy to his brother's affairs, and now perhaps he began to feel that he was missing out on something exciting and perhaps the time had come for the Puritan to break loose.

Their affair lasted all summer.

———

BOBBY MADE FREQUENT trips to Los Angeles to check on the film being made of his book on organized crime, *The Enemy Within,* and neighbors later testified that he and Marilyn were often seen along the beach in front of Peter Lawford's oceanfront house. Marilyn's maid, Hazel Washington, described the calls between the pair as making love over the phone. "And I do mean love.'' Marilyn's stand-in for her films, Evelyn Moriarity, recalled that during this time

Marilyn was busy reading stacks of books about current events and politics.

A blond actress named Jeanne Carmen, a neighbor, was visiting Marilyn in her apartment when she answered the doorbell. "I went to the door," Miss Carmen said, "and I opened it up and there stands Bobby Kennedy. . . . Marilyn came rushing out of the bathroom all of a sudden. She jumped into his arms, and they started kissing madly." Carmen added that eventually "they settled down," and the three of them had a glass of wine together, after which Marilyn made a sign to her which she said meant, " 'Jeannie, go back to your apartment,' which I did."

"Now Marilyn was calling the Department of Justice instead of the White House," Lawford said. The calls would appear later in Justice Department telephone logs. "Marilyn called him a lot during the summer of 1962," Kennedy's press aide, Ed Guthman, said, "but then so did Judy Garland and other ladies in trouble."

Marilyn even invited Los Angeles hairstylist Mickey Song, a Kennedy favorite, to her house and asked, "What about Bobby and Ethel? I can't believe that's a happy marriage. What does he see in her?"

Responsible reporters like Dave Richardson refused to believe the Bob–Marilyn stories, and kept insisting, "With Bob Kennedy, it was *the* woman. The women in Bob's life were all of his daughters, and his wife and his mother. If there's any scandal in the life of Bob Kennedy, in my research I've uncovered no evidence of it . . . nobody else has, either."

Time White House correspondent Hugh Sidey had been similarly dubious. "I didn't believe, for a long time, those stories about Bobby and Marilyn Monroe. . . . I saw no chinks in that armor." But, as the evidence piled up, he changed his mind.

Bobby had been taped during his meetings with Marilyn, as his brother had been. Private detective Bernard Spindel, retained by Jimmy Hoffa to investigate the Kennedys, also mentioned taped intimate telephone conversations between Bobby and Marilyn Monroe. Marilyn even told her friend Slatzer that "Robert Kennedy promised to marry me. What do you think of that?"

Others who later confirmed this were Anne Karger, the mother of one of Marilyn's earlier lovers, and Joan Greenson, her psychiatrist's daughter. Years later Peter Lawford signed himself into an alcoholic and drug rehabilitation clinic—the Betty Ford Center in Rancho Mirage. As part of the therapy, patients wrote letters to people, dead or alive, whom they had hurt because of their addictions. In a letter to President Kennedy, Lawford wrote, "How are Marilyn and Bobby? Take care. Peter."

Bobby became similarly concerned with the relationship, and it began floundering. Marilyn was then finding it more difficult to cope with herself, couldn't sleep nights, and increased her drugs and drink. Twentieth Century–Fox finally fired her from the big-budgeted CinemaScope motion picture that was never completed—*Something's Got to Give*—because she was not only unreliable and unpredictable but too often slurred her lines during the shooting. Bobby was gradually retreating from her the same way Jack had retreated, and she bitterly told Lawford, "They treat everybody like that . . . they use you and then they dispose of you like so much rubbish."

When Marilyn heard that Bobby Kennedy and his family were staying near San Francisco, she got his phone number and called him. Bobby hesitated but then agreed to see her. He and Peter Lawford arrived at her Brentwood home the next afternoon. Lawford went out to the pool but soon heard them shouting. Marilyn insisted that he had promised to spend the afternoon alone with her. Bobby said he was going back to Lawford's house with or without her. "They argued back and forth for maybe ten minutes, Marilyn becoming more and more hysterical," said Lawford. "At the height of her anger she allowed how first thing Monday morning she was going to call a press conference and tell the world about the treatment she had suffered at the hands of the Kennedy brothers.

"Now Bobby became livid. In no uncertain terms he told her she was going to have to leave both Jack and him alone—no more telephone calls, no letters, nothing. They didn't want to hear from her anymore.

"Marilyn lost it at this point, screaming obscenities and flailing wildly away at Bobby with her fists. In her fury she picked up a small kitchen knife and lunged at him. I was with them at this point," said Lawford, "so I tried to grab Marilyn's arm. We finally knocked her down and managed to wrestle the knife away. Bobby thought we ought to call Dr. Ralph Greenson, her Beverly Hills psychiatrist, and tell him to come over. Dr. Greenson arrived at Marilyn's home within the hour.''

In a sworn deposition on the Monroe death, Robert Kennedy testified that he had gone to see her shortly before her death because she had been bothering his brother. He had taken a doctor with him and she had clawed at him when he held her so that the doctor could inject a tranquilizer. The final police report, condensing the 723 pages of original testimony to 53, made no reference to the Kennedy statement.

It was reportedly after that meeting that Monroe took the lethal dose of sleeping pills and sedatives that killed her. According to the police report, she had earlier called Peter Lawford again: "Her manner of speech was slurred. Her voice became less and less audible and Lawford began to yell at her in an attempt to revive her. Then she stated, 'Say good-bye to Jack [John Kennedy], and say good-bye to yourself, because you're a nice guy.'"

Private detective Fred Otash later told the BBC, "At two or three o'clock in the morning—on the tragic night that Monroe died—I got a panic phone call from Peter Lawford, and he said it was very important that we get together, and so I arranged to meet him at my office on Laurel Avenue. . . . Lawford showed up, completely disoriented and completely in a state of shock, saying that Marilyn Monroe was dead, Bobby Kennedy was there, that he was spirited out of town by some airplane back up north, that they [Marilyn and Bobby] had gotten into a big fight that evening and that he'd like to have me make arrangements to have someone go out to the house and pick up any and all information that was possible regarding any involvement between Marilyn Monroe and the Kennedys, whether it be diaries, notes, letters, et cetera."

Lawford's wife, Deborah, insists her husband told her that he was the first one to arrive at Marilyn's home that morning, and then went to see Otash. Lawford's last wife, Patricia, confirmed that he had gone to Otash after Marilyn's body was discovered.

Some felt Marilyn had been murdered. "Marilyn Monroe knew too much. . . . As she got more and more depressed and more and more concerned about her relationship with Bobby Kennedy, she became a loose cannon," said Sam Giancana, nephew of the Mafia boss. "And when she claimed to say, 'I'm going to blow the lid off this whole damn thing,' she presented a threat to everyone, and it was ultimately the CIA who said, 'We need to get rid of her. We need to have her eliminated.' "

There were the usual quick questions of conspiracy.

In the years since her death, more than a dozen witnesses have emerged, each with a different story about how she died. An ambulance driver insisted that he and his assistant were reviving her when her psychiatrist gave her an injection that killed her. The policeman who was the first to arrive at 4 A.M. claimed the housekeeper found her about midnight and called the psychiatrist. The psychiatrist said she committed suicide but gave no rational explanation for the four-hour delay in calling the police, saying only that the studio had to be notified first. An assistant district attorney sent police for evidence and they returned with her diary full of references to the Kennedys. The diary disappeared. He also said that the autopsy reports and other records were completely altered. The housekeeper, who at first said Bobby was not there that day, later claimed he was.

A supervisor at General Telephone was later approached by two federal agents and a Los Angeles police detective who took with them a sealed envelope with Marilyn Monroe's telephone records.

Afterward, family spokesmen denied that Bob had been with Monroe on the day of her death, insisted he had spent the whole weekend with his family at the home of a distinguished California attorney, John Bates, chairman of the Judiciary Committee of the San Francisco Bar Association. It was also pointed out that many of the dates mentioned of meetings with Monroe were ones when Bob was reported elsewhere.

If the affair with Monroe was real, as most evidence suggests, it was probably an exciting, transitory experience for Bobby. He had no compulsion to prove his sexuality. Unlike Jack, he had a strong marriage, with a large wonderful family, and was very committed to them.

The involvement of the CIA in a cover-up of the Kennedy involvement is not unlikely, but there is no hard evidence of their participation

in any murder. The evidence points to a drug overdose, either acciden-
tal or suicidal.

————————

DURING ALL THIS, Ted Kennedy's campaign for the Senate was
warming up.

Esquire reported that when asked about his qualifications, Teddy said,
"What are my qualifications? What were Jack's when he started?"

Ted said afterward, "There are both advantages and disadvantages to
being the President's brother. For the past four years, I've been on the
inside of great national and world decisions, and knowing how they
were reached. This is a unique advantage. The disadvantage of my
position is being constantly compared with two brothers of such
superior ability."

"Privately, I am informed JFK has made no decision about going to
Massachusetts," wrote Charles Roberts in *Newsweek*. "The best bet of
one of his closest advisers is that he won't raise a finger until after the
primary, then he'll go into Massachusetts for the Democratic nominee,
whoever he is."

Former Jack Kennedy campaign workers also kept clear of Ted's
campaign. Asked by the President what he was doing to help Ted, one
of them said, "Nothing." And there was no further discussion.

Publicly, the President was doing nothing; privately, he was deeply
involved. The White House could not afford to let Teddy lose.

A great number of pro-Kennedy people considered Ted's candidacy
ridiculous. After all, he was only three years out of law school.
"Despite a rugged, outgoing manner," wrote a *Village Voice* reporter,
"there is a certain air of First Communion perfection to his whole
appearance (dark suit, hair that wants to stay in place neatly). It is a
look that mothers cherish and other kids envy because they think it
allows them to get away with all the things they want to get away with,
but don't." Though he looked like a boy, full of niceness and naiveté,
this six-foot-two, broad-shouldered Ted also looked very much like a
boy who could take care of himself.

James Reston, in *The New York Times*, reported it as "widely regarded
as an affront and a presumption. And it is likely to cost the President
more votes in the Senate than Teddy will ever give him." And then he

added, "one Kennedy is a triumph, two Kennedys at the same time are a miracle, but three could easily be regarded by many voters as an invasion. . . . It's too much. A little nepotism is bad enough, but this is a dynasty."

A letter from Mark DeWolfe Howe, professor of law at Harvard, to all delegates to the Massachusetts Democratic Convention, pointed out that Teddy knew that if he wasn't a coattail candidate he would receive no political consideration at all, that his candidacy was both preposterous and insulting. Other reporters added that he had a mediocre academic record, only a year as an assistant district attorney, and was completely unqualified and inexperienced.

"Too much too soon" was the general consensus. But a similar consensus of the press agreed that there was no question that he would win. As one legislator told *The New Republic*, "He's an arrogant member of an arrogant family." The legislator grinned. "And I'm going to be with him." A convention delegate explained why he was going to vote for Kennedy: "The Kennedys will be around for a long time, and they have memories like elephants. What am I supposed to do, cut my throat?"

The President added that it didn't make any difference to him who or how many objected to Ted's candidacy. "He's going to run because I want him to run, and I want him to win. That's all that's important. I want him in the Senate of the United States because he'll work at the job better than the rest of us. He has a better political brain. And Teddy will be satisfied in there."

Ted worked the telephone hard in contacting delegates. One skeptical woman delegate asked, "If you're Ted Kennedy, tell me the date of the President's birthday." Ted wasn't sure whether it was the twenty-seventh or the twenty-ninth of May, finally guessed, "It's May twenty-seventh." "No it's not," said the delegate, "it's May twenty-ninth," and slammed down the receiver.

At the Massachusetts Democratic Convention, early in June 1962, Ted Kennedy won endorsements of the state delegates on the first ballot. After he called his father, Ted was on the phone with Jack during the actual convention balloting, telling him how it was going.

His Democratic opponent, Ed McCormack, indicated he would take his fight to the people, which was not unusual. That meant a final primary election in September. The winner would then face the incumbent, Republican Senator Henry Cabot Lodge.

————

SUCH POLITICAL SCUFFLES were of minimal interest to Jacqueline. If there was something magical in the Jacqueline Kennedy style of tasteful grace, it came to full flower during the state dinner in honor of President Mohammed Ayub Khan of Pakistan. Four yachts filled with 135 guests sailed down the Potomac to George Washington's historic home at Mt. Vernon. The tents were decorative, the orchestra impressive, the food gourmet, the service and setting elegant.

Later, in June, the presidential couple made a three-day diplomatic trip to Mexico. Like France, it was a social triumph for Jacqueline. With her fluency in Spanish, she also overheard a side remark of the Mexican President Mateos about the American President that was not very flattering.

"She had the ability to put on a presence as required, regardless of what the situation was," said Larry Newman. "At her absolutely magnificent best, she glowed with real beauty . . . a regal-type beauty. The great success of the two of them together was that they reached that zenith of royalty which we look for. We had such tremendous pride. And yet—we never had it again."

For all her trips abroad, the First Lady didn't want to travel with her husband around the United States. In Europe she was treated like a queen; in the United States she felt like a curiosity. In Europe she created her own aura; in the United States she was a campaign wife, shunted to the sidelines.

"I felt a little sorry for her," said longtime political observer Max Kampelman. "She was like a fish out of water."

Larry Newman recalled a time when Kennedy was returning to Hyannis from a trip "and some Boston pols were going to take her out. The airplane was coming in; the Secret Service were all ready for her to go. . . . I went upstairs, and she said, 'I'm not going.' I said, 'Well, you're gonna go.' And she said, 'Oh, no, I'm not.' I said, 'Well, why not?' She said, 'Well, I'll go out to the airport, and, as soon as I get there, some Democratic lady will give me some old, tired red roses and I'll be standing with these old, tired red roses, with a lot of people around me. And then the airplane will drop down, and he will get out . . . then everybody'll take off, and leave me standing in the middle of the airport, all by myself!'

"So I said, 'Jackie, I'll make you a promise. . . . You go to the airport . . . and everything you say is gonna happen, except one thing. They'll all be chasing him along the fence, as he shakes hands with the crowd, and all the politicians will be around him. But you and I will be standing in the middle of the airport, together, with your tired red roses. . .'

" 'All right,' she said, 'then I'll go.' "

————

IN AN ELOQUENT speech in San Antonio, the President repeated his intention to put a man on the moon before the end of the decade. The national pride had been dented four years earlier when the Soviets embarrassed the United States by being first in space.

Kennedy said, "Frank O'Connor, the Irish writer, tells in one of his books how, as a boy, he and his friends would make their way across the countryside. When they came to an orchard wall that seemed too high and too doubtful to try and too difficult to permit their voyage to continue, they took off their hats and tossed them over the wall—and then they had no choice but to follow them.

"This nation has tossed its cap over the wall of space, and we have no choice but to follow it. Whatever the difficulties, they will be over-come. Whatever the hazards, they must be guarded against . . . with the help and support of all Americans, we will climb this wall with safety and with speed—and we shall then explore the wonders of the other side."

Bob always had his own fascination with the exploration of space, and Ethel would talk of his secret ambition to be an astronaut. Jack Newfield once overheard a conversation between Bob Kennedy and astronaut John Glenn. Kennedy was not asking Glenn anything techni-cal about space travel, but rather what a sunset looked like from orbit.

————

NEITHER BROTHER WAS yet so eloquent about civil rights.

The President remarked to Lyndon Johnson's friend Abe Fortas that he did not understand the continued dissatisfaction of the Negroes, when he had appointed so many of them to positions in the federal government. He appeared, according to Fortas, "to be quite oblivious of the impending social revolution." He didn't understand that the plight of poor blacks in American ghettos had nothing to do with judicial appointments.

One of Kennedy's better appointments was Thurgood Marshall to the Circuit Court. Marshall, later appointed to the United States Supreme Court by President Johnson, recalled the story: "Bobby wanted me to go on the trial court in New York, and I told him no, and he says, 'Well, why?' I said, 'My boiling point is too low for the trial court. I'd blow my stack, and then get reversed. But I would go on the Court of Appeals.' He said, 'Well, you can't go on the Court of Appeals.' I said, 'There's an opening.' He said, 'But that's already been filled.' I said, 'So?' He said, 'You don't seem to understand, it's this or nothing.' I said, 'Well, I do understand. The trouble is that you are different from me. You don't know what it means, but all I've had in my life is nothing. It's not new to me, so, good-bye.' And walked out. That was about the second time I had a good run-in with him. . . .

"Maybe a week later, a fellow ran into me. He was a Negro who was the Vice-Chairman of the Democratic Party, Louis Martin, and he asked me, would I take the Court of Appeals job? I told him, sure. Then the next day I was appointed.

"Once my appointment was made by the President . . . Bobby was arranging for my hearings and all. You'd think he was the nicest guy in the world. Taking all the credit for it. . . . He took credit for all the civil rights stuff. . . . Bobby was like his father. He was a cold, calculating character. 'What's in it for me?' I mean, not like his brother. He had no warm feelings, none at all. That big old dog of his, walking around cocking his leg up on your leg. Bobby was awfully ruthless. Kennedy, the President, was a very sweet man."

In contrast, one of the Defense Department whiz kids, Adam Yarmolinsky, remembered a trip he and Bob took through Harlem. "For Bobby, that firsthand, quick exposure was an eye-opener. He'd never seen any of that before. Bobby pointed to the rat-trap slums and said, 'If only I could do something about *this*!' On another trip there, he found the stench of rats so overpowering that he never forgot it." And in Brooklyn, with columnist Pete Hamill, "there was a little girl with a mangled face all torn up. The Puerto Rican mother explained that the rats had bitten her face when she was a little baby."

His first real exposure to poverty had been during the West Virginia primary in 1960, and his further exposure had been incremental. Harlem was a hard hit.

His passion for the poor and powerless was real. "You could just tell. Very genuine. He was way ahead of his brother on it . . . It was as if God reached down and made his heart pure."

But yet he had not learned to express all this.

"There was a tentative quality about his body," said psychiatrist Dr. Robert Coles, a family adviser, "about the way he moved and the way he talked, which bespeaks a man who has a lot to say but isn't quite sure how to say it; who has a lot stirring in him but doesn't know how to put it into words; who has a lot of emotional things happening to him but isn't one of these glib, articulate, well-psychoanalyzed, well-intellectualized people."

Coles felt that Robert Kennedy had "a kind of groping quality . . . an urgent tension . . . this quality of the heart; this quality of emotion that sometimes is literally ineffable—that defies language, that defies formulation."

The President changed more slowly than Bob mainly because as President he now had a thousand constituencies, all of them with individual demands, all of them insistent. They were constituencies that Bob was simply not accountable to. Each group had its own conflicting tunnel vision, with little interest in the big picture. Only the President had to see the whole and consider carefully on whose toes he stepped, and he didn't like to be pressured by anyone—even Bobby.

For President Kennedy, civil rights was primarily a political issue; for Robert Kennedy, it was now a matter of right and wrong. Bobby always had approached politics passionately, but civil rights was one of the first issues that became personal to him. To him, now, it was about people and their lives. That opened a whole different dimension in Bobby that he didn't know existed.

Sorensen noted that Bobby's strong commitment to the substance of the civil rights issue caused Jack to subordinate his own political instincts and take positions and risks that politically he might not otherwise have done.

Spalding was with the two brothers one day. Bobby seemed moody and preoccupied. "Don't worry about Bobby," Jack said loudly, as he gestured at his brother. "He's probably all choked up over Martin Luther King and his Negroes today."

On a visit to the White House, a southern congressman said, "Mister President, I'm afraid I'm going to have to attack you in a speech for all this civil rights activity." The President laughed and said, "Why can't you just call Bobby a son of a bitch?"

———————

THE COUNTRY WAS boiling, and it even had the smell of revolution, with speeches of hate and anger on both sides, civil rights violations everywhere, people beaten and thrown in jail for little cause.

Integration also became a hot issue at some southern colleges. In September 1962 the Fifth Circuit Court ordered the University of Mississippi to admit James Meredith, a young Air Force veteran, thereby making him the first black student at the university. The United States Supreme Court upheld this decision. "We will not surrender," countered Mississippi Governor Ross Barnett. Barnett appointed himself temporarily as the registrar of the university so that he could personally block Meredith's entry. Attorney General Kennedy had been on the phone with Governor Barnett for hours in the previous ten days. "The orders of the Court are going to be upheld," Robert Kennedy insisted.

"Bob would call the Governor of Mississippi, then report to the President," recalled Angie Novello. "They would talk five or six times a day. Without any hesitation, Bob would push that red light, and right immediately we'd have the President on the line, through the operator." The Attorney General had the responsibility to assure the arrival of the troops. When John Kennedy called Barnett to step up the pressure, Bobby urged, "Go get him, Johnny boy!" And the President, getting in the mood before the call, rehearsed: "Governor, this is the President of the United States—not Bobby, not Teddy, not Princess Radziwill [Jacqueline's sister]." When the real call went through and Barnett finally agreed to cooperate, he was careful to thank the President for "your help on the poultry problem."

They finally arranged a deal in which Meredith would arrive with two dozen federal marshals, and Barnett would block their entry until forced to yield at gunpoint. The deal collapsed because Barnett insisted that all the marshals draw their guns against him at the same time. Television would cover it. Bob Kennedy refused.

The Fifth Circuit Court found the Governor guilty of contempt. Bob Kennedy also told Barnett that the President would make a speech and release tapes revealing how the Governor was making these deals with the White House. This would destroy Barnett politically. Bob now quickly suggested that while the Governor was at the football game, the federal agents would secretly take Meredith into the university. Three hundred federal marshals led by Assistant Attorney General Nicholas Katzenbach got Meredith into a dorm building. "Bobby's final words to me as I headed for Ole Miss," said Katzenbach, "were that 'if things get rough, don't worry about yourself; the President needs a moral issue.' "

Word traveled fast and soon there were 2000 citizens moving against the marshals with bricks and iron bars. One threw a Coke bottle filled with ignited gasoline. Bobby would never forget his phone conversations with his marshals. "Some of those guys outside have baseball bats with nails in them." He later stayed in his office, always in view, wearing a battered U.S. marshal's helmet.

The officers were under orders not to use live ammunition except to protect Meredith's life. They fired tear gas.

When the violence increased, the local police abandoned the scene. An angry, frustrated Attorney General blamed Barnett for breaking his promise to maintain order.

"We just didn't sit down, wring our hands, shake our heads, and have meetings about how awful it was about the Negro in Mississippi," said Bobby Kennedy. The most the President said about white rioters was, "Aren't they bastards?"

"Jack had something that would hold him back. . . ." said Charles Spalding. "He couldn't exhibit a kind of tattered emotionalism in front of people, the way Bobby could . . ." But it was more than that. Jack still carried some of his father's bigotry baggage. He saw the danger of losing southern support, but he also felt the greater danger of showing himself to the country as a weak President, afraid to act.

At his brother's urging, the President earlier spoke on radio and television, appealing to Mississippi residents not to disobey the federal integration order. "Americans are free to disagree with the law, but not to disobey it." The President had made his speech; he assumed that all had gone well.

It did not go well. The marshals of the Attorney General in Oxford, Mississippi, at the university, were under siege. Katzenbach requested soldiers. The Attorney General had persuaded the President to sign a proclamation putting the Mississippi National Guard under federal control. Troops were now called in. Time was critical.

Hours dragged on. No troops. John F. Kennedy was now in command. The Army kept saying that the troops were en route by helicopter and would be there within minutes, but they were obviously under orders to proceed very slowly. The National Guard still consisted of Mississippi men under Mississippi officers over whom the Governor's word had much weight—even if that word wasn't official. A bitter President cursed Governor Barnett for the delay. Robert Kennedy reported later that he had never heard his brother use worse language about anyone.

"People are dying in Oxford," Robert told the Army commanders. In the mob violence, shots were fired. Two people were killed. A marshal was shot in the leg. The rioters were moving closer, behind fire engines and stolen bulldozers. The marshals still had not fired a shot of live ammunition. "We could just visualize another great disaster, like the Bay of Pigs, and a lot of marshals being killed or James Meredith being strung up," said Robert Kennedy. The tear gas was gone when the troops finally arrived—five hours later. The Army then took more than a hour to move its troops the last half mile. But the wild night ended. The next morning, James Meredith registered at the University of Mississippi.

Bob tried to persuade the President to name an African-American as his first Supreme Court appointment: "We have one hundred ninety million Americans in this country, and ten percent of them are Negroes; therefore, we should have a Negro on the Court."

Instead, the President picked his old friend Byron "Whizzer" White, an all-American halfback and Rhodes Scholar who had gone to Europe with him before the war.

———

MEANWHILE, TEDDY'S POLITICAL voice was growing louder and reaching a wider audience. Campaigning in the Massachusetts primary,

Ted was what they call in Boston a "corner guy"—a man who enjoys standing around on the corner talking to people. He was the only Kennedy brother who could go into a bar, put his arm around a customer, and buy drinks for everybody in the house. Teddy still talked warmly of Grandpa Honey Fitz as the original corner guy. Politically, Ted was more like the Fitzgeralds than the Kennedys. Like Grandpa Honey Fitz, he could get on top of a sound truck in South Boston and sing the local Boston Irish song, "Southie Is My Home Town." None of his brothers could or would do that.

"If Teddy saw three people in a telephone booth, he'd have a rally," said Dave Powers. "He loved it."

Ted had none of Bob's shyness or Jack's phobia about being touched. He relished the physical contact of campaigning—putting his arms around voters, kissing women, rushing from one group to another group, shaking hands, milking the applause. It was no effort for him to smile. He loved to smile. It was as natural as breathing. He enjoyed the challenge, the excitement, the frenzy.

Even Jack Kennedy once admitted wistfully that he wished he were like Teddy. He once said to Philadelphia boss Bill Green, " 'I am very flattered at your saying you think that both Bob and I are excellent politicians. But,' he said, 'the member of our family who is the best politician, and likes it the most, and who I think is going a long, long way in politics, is our youngest brother, Ted.' "

Political adviser James Rowe spelled out the difference between the three brothers as politicians. "Once, at a fund-raising dinner, Jack Kennedy came in and he saw me, and he waved at me. Bobby came in and saw me, and sort of lifted his eyebrows in recognition. And Teddy came in . . . and he walked over the room to me to shake my hand. This was in 1959, and it showed the difference among the three. I think Teddy was the most natural politician of them all—because he liked being with people more than the other two did."

His brothers were still busy helping with his campaign.

With the press stirred up, the President told John Nolan, who worked for Bobby, "I don't know what everybody's so excited about, just because Teddy is running for the Senate. You've got to recognize that politics is just a question of alternatives. He's not running against Jesus Christ . . . it's only Eddie McCormack!"

"Eddie," Edward J. McCormack, Jr., his political opponent in the

Democratic primary and state Attorney General of Massachusetts, was the nephew of the Speaker of the House of Representatives.

President Kennedy sent Ted to Tip O'Neill to intercede with McCormack. O'Neill remembered Teddy had said, " 'Gee, I don't want to run against Eddie. . . . You know, it's not good for the party, it's not good for the relationships in Washington,' and Ted added, 'I'll pay—we understand Eddie owes $100,000. We'll take care of his expenses. . . . Anything that he's interested in . . . he can have. . . . My brother can make him an Ambassador.' " O'Neill relayed the message to McCormack. " 'And Eddie said no.' "

When the Kennedys couldn't buy him, they attacked: this was a basic Joe Kennedy principle. With Robert Kennedy's approval, Justice Department records were searched for anything detrimental about McCormack, and there was a similar search in the Pentagon files for anything useful in McCormack's service record.

Ted believed he had some personal material that might hurt his opponent, but the President warned him against any personal attack. "You're running for United States Senator. Stay on the issues . . . he'll be gone and forgotten when you are a United States Senator."

Ted had more softness in him than Jack or Bobby. Nor did he have the sharp mind of Jack or Bobby. He was bright and capable, but no deep thinker. As someone said, "He isn't very heavy mentally." He had the family conceit but not the self-discipline.

There was something else. "Bobby and I smile sardonically," Jack told Ben Bradlee. "Teddy will learn how to smile sardonically in two or three years, but he doesn't know how, yet."

————

TED'S CAMPAIGNING WAS done mostly from a Ford Falcon Station Bus, topped by a platform from which he often addressed street rallies. His organization was vintage Kennedy, highly professional, well financed, and smooth-working. No matter what else Ted lacked, his judgment was usually shrewd and sound.

Teddy had six secretaries and two part-time office assistants, working in various shifts on mail, and delegates to each of the 26 nationalities in Boston, and 345 Kennedy secretaries spread out in towns and villages across the state. His map of the state showed 204 red and black pins of incorporated communities, including one on the isle of Nantucket. In a random month, he made 108 speeches. "He's like one of those old Oklahoma football teams," said an admirer. "He's just going to run the Republicans to death.' "

"Saddle up, Joansie!" he would tell his wife. "We've got a two o'clock tea at Lowell, then another one at four. There's a banquet tonight in Boston, and after that a coffee in Lawrence. We should be back at Squaw Island tonight. Did I tell you six are coming for lunch tomorrow? Could you get lobster?"

Joan modeled herself after her sisters-in-law. She never forgot that Ethel always left their seven children at home and went whenever Bobby wanted to go anywhere in the world, even though she was terrified of flying because both her parents were killed in a plane crash.

Joan later told a reporter, "I lead an absolutely last-minute life. That's why I never put anything back in my closet that needs pressing or cleaning, and why I keep a cosmetic-bag always packed and ready. I like to look neat and well-groomed at these affairs. . . . I worry about looking too young. I don't want to look old, but, well, you know, mature."

Kennedy sister Jean called Joan "fantastically pretty." Joan was not gregarious, but she was always candid and uncomplaining. But, more than anything, she was fragile, vulnerable, and always on the edge. On the stump, when her husband was introduced, it was often as "Ted Kennedy, whose brother, incidentally, is President of the United States." *Newsweek* reported that at a Temple Israel breakfast in Natick, Massachusetts, Teddy leaped to his feet when the president of the brotherhood was introduced. His explanation was that he had responded when he misunderstood the phrase as "brother of the President."

Reporters at first criticized Ted Kennedy for his seeming inability to talk in direct sentences: he used a lot of ers, uhs, umms, and ahs. Ted told them that this was because he was the youngest of the Kennedy children and never had a chance to complete a sentence.

They also pointed out how much Ted soon copied his brother's speaking style—the way he chopped the air with his left hand and the stabbing gesture with the index finger, the same use of words, the same dying fall in his intonation, even the querulous inflection at the end of a sentence. His voice was remarkably the same. His speech had the same semi-broad "a," not quite Boston, not quite Harvard, but authentic

Kennedy. Peter Lisagor also observed that "Teddy also spoke at a rapid-fire clip . . . raced through everything . . . terribly fast."

His early speech trouble was with syntax, but Ted's speechmaking quickly improved. A director of a Boston lawyers' club said, "He's a whiz and a better speaker than Jack was at his age."

Author Joe McCarthy, who had written friendly books and articles about the Kennedys, was originally negative about Ted. "He was the type of guy that when you asked him a question, he'd start to answer and wouldn't finish a sentence. When I asked him, are you going to pay more attention to the Democratic Party in your state than your brothers did, he started to say, 'Yes I think so . . .' and never finished and simply wandered off. Jack and Bobby would always answer your question, honestly and frankly. Ted didn't strike me as the kind of a guy who thinks things through."

"I keep my speeches short," he said. "I don't present myself as an expert. I just give my views. If you give them too much, it goes over their heads. I talk on Latin America mostly, and Africa, and physical fitness. Later I'll move in on state problems. You have to know your audience. You can't give women too much. They get confused. Besides, if they've seen you on TV, they can't think anything bad about you. . . . And after ten at night, you don't read your whole speech. You tell some jokes and get it over. The main thing is to move around and meet people."

His condescending attitude toward women was typical of most of the male Kennedys. Nevertheless, his impact on them was immediate and obvious and seemed to be enhanced by his youth, his bubbling, superbly confident ebullience, and an almost overpowering vitality. When he toured a factory, a striking blond typist, Sandra Rubenstein, confessed to a reporter, "He's a doll. He made me make ten typing mistakes." At the National Casket factory, the women yelled, "We love you, Ted! Remember the girls of National Casket!"

"I'm not sure I ever realized what charisma was," said John Seigenthaler, "until I saw him operate." "Charisma, hell," said one woman reporter. "It's just plain old sex appeal."

———

THE PRESIDENT WENT to California to watch missile testing at an Army base and stayed with Pat and Peter Lawford. They had a campaign poster for Ted Kennedy over the mantel, with John Kennedy's old campaign slogan, "He can do more for Massachusetts." The President crossed out that phrase and wrote, "BULLSHIT."

"Ted debated whether to use that slogan for his campaign," said his staff man Milton Gwirtzman. "He realized it could be interpreted as if he would use his influence with his brother. But there was no other slogan which really projected what the people of the state needed and wanted."

As much as he loved Ted, it grated on Jack that his youngest brother was on such a swift springboard, a stronger, earlier beginning than his. It was like a foreshadowing of the new coming to replace the old.

Clearly, Jack had the tougher start. When you campaign for the Senate, you hit cities; when you run for Congress first, as Jack did, you concentrate on neighborhoods. That means climbing more stairs and fighting more primary opponents.

Whatever Jack's private feelings, he was still Ted's key adviser. "The President was always the first person Ted would call after anything important had happened," said Gwirtzman.

Before his stroke, his father was the first to hear from Ted.

"Ted had been so used to asking his brother's advice on day-to-day matters that he kept calling him," said Gwirtzman, ". . . and the two would see each other at the Hyannis family compound on weekends for longer sessions."

To the press, however, Ted denied any help from Jack. Of their future relationship, he said, "Personally, I anticipate continuing as his brother."

"The hot issue in Congress then was aid to education, and my brother was trying to work out a compromise and the discussions were very delicate," remembered Ted Kennedy after a "Meet the Press" interview. "So when they asked me that question, I had my answer. Afterwards my brother called up the moderator, Larry Spivak, and asked, 'How did Teddy do?' And Spivak said, 'Well, he did very well, but I couldn't figure out his answer on education.' And my brother said, 'Perfect.' "

A Teddy-watcher said that he regarded politics as a sort of a game to be won with minimal personal involvement with issues. "While he is well informed on most issues, Teddy reacts coolly and dispassionately to even the most emotionally laden ones." In this approach he was much like Jack.

"Teddy was not as cool as Jack, not as hot as Bobby," said Dave Powers. "He surely did not show his aggressiveness the way Bobby did. In that, he was closer to Jack. Teddy was very quiet, a listener, a good political quality because you never know what you can sop up and you don't commit yourself."

Bobby tried to explain that his brothers' style was different from his. "In politics I think there's a great advantage in remaining unemotional about issues. This doesn't mean that Jack or Ted feels less strongly about these issues. However, both feel that the American public is mature, and that issues should be discussed factually, not as though one were trying to stir up a revival meeting."

The political styles of all three brothers would continue to evolve, each at his own pace and in his own way. They had different qualities, different challenges, different contributions to make, and they were anxious to make their unique impact. Some would say of Teddy that, given all his advantages, they, too, could have accomplished what he had. They underestimated his own personal imprint that he added to his heritage. What he added was a greater gregariousness, an open warmth that immediately reached people, and he so obviously enjoyed campaigning much more than his brothers.

The President teased Ted when he saw him carrying his daughter Kara on his shoulders. "Relax, Ted, you can put her down now. There aren't any photographers around."

———

MRS. JOSEPH P. KENNEDY took up where her husband had left off. One of the things she did was to contact Lord Beaverbrook. "Now that Ted is a candidate for the United States Senate, I am asking you to help him as you helped Jack the last time. I believe that your papers in Canada were very influential. . . . Whatever you decide to do will be deeply appreciated."

Beaverbrook immediately replied that he would persuade *La Presse*—a newspaper that circulated widely among French Canadians in

Massachusetts—"to take an interest." As for the other papers, he added, "that is easy."

Ted Kennedy gratefully said of his mother, "My mother is the pol of all pols."

———

TED KENNEDY'S HIGH-POWERED campaign quickly eclipsed the rest of the state's Democratic ticket, so much so that one of them warned him, "Back off, Golden Boy."

The "Teddie-Eddie" televised debates on August 27 and September 5 stirred national attention. Ted's brothers, knowing that he was new to all of this, were uncertain how he would perform.

The President feared his inexperienced younger brother, when attacked, might give in to his emotions. Ted recalled "sitting in the Oval Office, being peppered by questions by my brother and by a couple of his aides, which was quite intimidating, certainly, to say the least—but I was being asked by the master."

"I was upstairs in the guest room at Hyannis," said Gwirtzman, "and suddenly I heard a door open and Robert Kennedy's voice saying, 'Have no feah. We are heah.'" Gwirtzman described the two brothers discussing the possible debate questions while they played football on the lawn. Bob suggested that one of the questions might concern Ted's reason for running. "If you get that question," said Bob, "tell them why you don't want to be sitting on your ass in some office in New York."

———

WHEN THE DAY of the first debate finally arrived, the nation was watching and wondered how the President's little brother would fare with the hot lights turned on him. They knew he had a formidable opponent.

McCormack had strong credentials: top of his class at Boston University Law School, president of the Boston City Council, and a strong record as the state Attorney General. And he was sharp. He attacked Teddy quickly, making the brutal point that if Teddy's name was Edward Moore "his candidacy would be a joke—but nobody's laughing." He had articulated what many had felt but few had said about Ted's campaign.

Teddy later said he had wanted to punch McCormack in the mouth because he felt he had slurred family friend Eddie Moore, after whom he had been named.

McCormack then launched in on his "inexperience, ineptness, lassitude, presumptuousness, political inbreeding," and Ted's voting record. "You didn't care very much, Ted, when you could have voted between 1953 and 1960, on sixteen occasions, and you only voted three times . . . three out of sixteen . . . and on those three occasions, your brother was a candidate."

Even though Ted had been a debater in law school, observers claimed that McCormack's assault clearly had a physical impact on Kennedy. Some say Ted's face became sallow. This attack was a new experience for Ted. Until then his life had been carefully cushioned, even during an occasional crisis. But there is no cushion in personal politics against a hungry opponent.

During the debate, Jack was in Palm Beach with Senator George Smathers. They had come in from a sail on Biscayne Bay to watch the action. Smathers noted how nervous Jack was—"more nervous than at any time since he debated Nixon"—because he loved Teddy and wanted Teddy to look good.

The President afterward asked Ted for his assessment of the debate result. Ted said he was too close to it to tell, and passed the phone over to Gwirtzman. Gwirtzman felt that some of McCormack's points had hurt, but that voters might be turned off by the crude tactics. The President listened, obviously annoyed by Gwirtzman's reply. He told him that the debate was over, and nothing could change it. There was only one thing to do: make Teddy feel good. It's what his father would have said.

Other Kennedy aides privately conceded that their candidate had been severely damaged, if not destroyed. Two campaign signs reflected a commonly held sentiment: MOMMY, CAN I RUN FOR THE SENATE? and WE BACK JACK BUT TEDDY ISN'T READY.

GWIRTZMAN WAS THERE on Labor Day weekend when the three brothers went sailing with their father on a family summit to discuss how to handle the second debate. They went over several questions and made suggestions. Joe sometimes managed a nodded assent when he agreed with something.

There was some public reaction in Ted's favor because of McCormack's bitter attacks, so in the second debate "Eddie McCormack was very gentlemanly and respectful to Ted."

On primary night, the President was at a small White House dinner, anxious to finish so he could go watch the returns. The staff was instructed to pick up the plates whenever the President finished a course. Kennedy's naval aide, Admiral Tazewell Shepherd, recalled that his wife was one of the last served, and by the time the food reached her, the President had raced through his meal. The servants would pick up her plate before she had a chance to eat. He disappeared immediately after dinner, and soon came back beaming, fairly exploding with the news, "Ted is winning *big*." He won the September primary by a margin of more than 300,000 votes.

At the celebration party that night, Teddy had invited Frank Sinatra and other kindred spirits, plus some friendly women. It was also the night his wife Joan gave birth to their second child, their first son, Teddy Jr.

Ted's victory revived a new era in Massachusetts: a powerful new Kennedy, now a proven vote-getter. Fearful critics saw that the Kennedy political dynasty was no longer in the making; it was here and now. They saw it as a danger, a danger they would find difficult to defeat.

The Berkshire *Eagle* commented, "There is a sort of 'princely' effect in the Ted Kennedy campaign. In any dynasty, the king is respected and obeyed, but everyone loves the prince, and Ted Kennedy seems to have that attraction, wherever he goes."

At a Democratic fund-raiser in Massachusetts, the President was ready with a quip. "I am Teddy Kennedy's brother and I am glad to be here tonight . . . I first of all want to express my appreciation to my brother Teddy, for his offering me his coattails. My last campaign, I suppose, may be coming up very shortly, but Teddy's around and, therefore, these dinners can go on indefinitely."

WITH TED'S STATUS settled, the President turned his focus to a fresh crisis.

At the end of August 1962, there had been CIA reports describing unusual Soviet construction in Cuba that resembled missile sites. Many earlier reports of missiles had proven bogus. But this time there were firsthand reports from twenty-five agents in Cuba that were impossible for Washington to ignore—eighty-foot-long objects on flatbed trucks were sighted that could not negotiate the turns on Cuban streets without removing mailboxes and lampposts. Normally, the U.S. had two U-2 reconnaissance flights a month over Cuba. They had been curtailed because of the fear of another diplomatic incident such as the one in which a U-2 was shot down over the Soviet Union in 1960. Now the reconnaissance flights resumed, and the missile sites were clearly revealed with the aid of high-altitude photography taken on October 14.

Robert Kennedy hurried to the White House basement to examine the most recent U-2 reconnaissance pictures. A magnifying glass revealed the missiles. His comment was explicit: "*Shit! Shit! Shit!*"

"When McGeorge Bundy broke the news to the President in his bedroom Tuesday morning at 8:30, I'd gone up there with the morning schedule," said Dave Powers, "and thought, 'God, he looks like someone had just told him the house is on fire.' "

The President told Bundy, "I'm going to call Bobby as soon as I get in the office."

Nikita Khrushchev later revealed how the Cuban missile base had been born. "[Defense Minister] Malinovsky and I happened to be walking along the Black Sea one day. Malinovsky said, pointing toward the sea, 'Over on the other shore, in Turkey, there is an American nuclear missile base. In a few minutes, rockets launched from that base can destroy Kiev, Odessa, Kharkov, and could even reach Moscow.' So I said to Malinovsky, 'Why is it that the Americans are allowed to have a base right under our noses? What if we set up a base in Cuba, right in America's back pocket? Let them see how they like it. What do you think? Will Fidel agree to it?' "

Fidel Castro had agreed.

The United States had missile sites in Turkey, on the Soviet border. We had lied to the Soviet Union about our U-2 spy flights from Turkey, and now the Soviets had lied to us about placing their missiles in Cuba, even though we had the photographs to prove it.

The Cubans now expected the United States to invade Cuba to destroy their missile sites. Their troops were pledged to fight to the death. Cuban authorities predicted 10,000 casualties. "If I had been a Cuban leader," said Defense Secretary Robert McNamara years afterward, "I might have expected a U.S. invasion. We had authorized the

Bay of Pigs invasion. . . . There were U.S. covert operations in Cuba extending over a long period of time. . . . There were important leaders in our Senate, our House, who were calling for the invasion . . . but we had absolutely no intention of invading Cuba."

The Soviet plan was to install nuclear missiles in Cuba, then negotiate on all future issues with the United States from a position of strength. "This was the stupidest part of the scheme," Soviet expert Fedor Burlatsky confessed years afterward. "The hope that U.S. intelligence wouldn't notice the movement of a hundred ships, and 42 bomber spy planes, nor the installation of 42 ICBM's and 144 anti-aircraft weapons. . . . But such is the logic of an authoritarian regime."

It was later revealed that there were 43,000 Soviet soldiers together with 270,000 well-armed Cubans, and 36 nuclear warheads. Soviet field commanders were free to use them at their discretion to repel a U.S. invasion.

"No one should believe," said McNamara later, "that U.S. troops could have been attacked by tactical nuclear weapons without the U.S. responding with nuclear warheads. And where would it have ended? In utter disaster."

Only Jack knew everything about Bob's secret meetings during the past year with Georgi Nikitovich Bolshakov in the Soviet Embassy. Bolshakov was a top KGB agent who described himself as "the only person in the embassy who can communicate directly with Khrushchev." He explained that Khrushchev didn't want to go through his Ambassador because he wasn't getting accurate reports and therefore the Chairman "didn't really understand the United States."

The reason Kennedy used Bobby with Anatoly Dobrynin, the Soviet Ambassador to the United States, explained Averell Harriman, "was that he didn't want to have it a matter of State Department record . . . when you get into a government agency, you can't avoid having a piece of paper seen by several hundred people. In addition to which, President Kennedy undoubtedly felt that Bobby would be far more impressive to Khrushchev—as coming directly from him—than even the Secretary of State."

The President was using his brother as his personal voice, which could have only an undiluted impact on the Russians.

"I saw Bolshakov on an average of once every couple of weeks," said Bobby. It was Bolshakov who had proposed a summit meeting between Khrushchev and the President.

The Attorney General and Bolshakov were on a first-name basis and usually met in Robert's office or occasionally in a doughnut shop next to the Mayflower Hotel. Bolshakov told Robert that his heroes were Khrushchev and John Kennedy, and that Khrushchev was trying to "Kennedyize" his government with younger people.

There were those like Justice Department deputy James Symington, who thought the Attorney General was playing "a dangerous game." Others also felt that it needed older, wiser heads than the young Bob Kennedy. But this group mostly wanted to please the President, tell him what he wanted to hear. The President listened harder to his brother because Bobby told it to him straight.

———

BURNED BY THE Bay of Pigs debacle, the President now understood the full ramifications of using force, and he was hesitant. The stakes were much higher now: the price of failure could be the death of a planet.

On October 17, John Kennedy maintained his announced traveling schedule of campaign commitments. Bobby was waiting for him at Andrews Air Force Base when he returned. The pictures were still inconclusive: there was still no final proof that the missiles were offensive. A U-2 pilot had gone back for more photographs.

Even in this time of world danger, the two brothers spent an hour with their father, who had spent the night in the White House. They tried to cheer him up, telling him funny stories, remembering a hundred family anecdotes, never once mentioning Cuba. Then they kissed him goodnight.

Bobby wanted the Russians to be aware that he knew what they were up to. Knowing that all calls to and from the Soviet Embassy were monitored by the Soviets, he called his aide, John Seigenthaler, after an embassy dinner and openly told of his knowledge of the missiles. He suggested that Seigenthaler warn any friends in Florida that they should leave before fighting began.

"Bobby was ringleader in the whole missile thing," said columnist Robert Allen. "Jack never did a thing without Bobby being right by his side."

————

WHILE THE PRESIDENT was still out of Washington, intent on giving the public impression that everything was normal, Bobby organized a small Executive Committee of military and diplomats, called Ex Comm, to handle the crisis.

The strong position being considered by Ex Comm was to destroy the missiles with an air strike. The pressing question was the accuracy of such an attack. Other questions concerned the size of an American invading force and how to neutralize any Russian submarines.

Agreeing with the President, Bobby argued against all of these actions because he saw them as a preliminary to global war. "I just didn't have the same confidence in Bobby that I did in Jack," said Ex Comm member Assistant Secretary of Defense Paul Nitze. "I got the feeling that Bobby was kind of an unhappy character. . . . Don't know why. Had the feeling he was being eaten by something—like a frustrated ambition. . . . I got that feeling that Bobby was trying to assert his individuality, apart from the President, and apart from Cuba. . . . He had an aura about himself which was not healthy. . . . But he did put energy and tension into things, where both were necessary."

As a first step in resolving the conflict, Robert Kennedy also agreed with his brother and favored a blockade.

Back in Washington, John F. Kennedy took time out to attend a small dinner party given by his friends Joe and Susan Mary Alsop. The President had gone to their private party right after the Inaugural, and now they often had small get-togethers with persons they thought would interest the President. Alsop reported that at the beginning of his administration, the President was always very witty, but later on he came less often and was not so witty. On this night, two of the guests were philosopher and historian Isaiah Berlin and Charles "Chip" Bohlen, former Ambassador to Russia, now on his way to France as U.S. Ambassador.

When Kennedy arrived, he took Bohlen out into the garden for a conversation. They were there for about twenty-five minutes, causing dinner to be late and overcooked. Later, during dinner, the President asked Bohlen and Berlin what the Russians had done in the past, in history, when they were backed into a corner. But he asked the question not just once but twice. Susan Alsop was the only one who noticed that it was the same question differently phrased. And she thought how unusual that was for Jack to repeat himself. After they'd gone to bed, she said to her husband, "Darling, there's something going on. I may be crazy, but I think something is going on." He said, "I think you're crazy. It was a delightful party, even though the President was late for dinner. Damn him, he really did ruin the lamb."

———————

MIDTERM ELECTIONS WERE two weeks away, and JFK went to Chicago for a scheduled political speech. Any schedule change would have raised national concern. Just before he left, he told Bobby, "I am depending on you to pull the group together." In Chicago the President told Pierre Salinger to tell the press he had a cold and was returning to Washington. Salinger confronted him with the fact that he had no cold and asked if something else was going on. "You bet something else is going on," Kennedy said, "and when you find out, grab your balls."

The President also asked Ted Sorensen to write two speeches, one announcing bombing, the other a blockade: nobody knew what unexpected incident might occur at any time.

Ted Kennedy called Sorensen that week. He didn't know what was happening but he had heard rumors. He was planning to make a speech on Cuba and wanted to clear the idea with Sorensen. "Get another topic," Sorensen said.

———————

WHENEVER THE PRESIDENT held any meeting in Hyannis, the President's flag was flown. His father pointed to that flag and indicated to his nurse that he wanted to see his son. John Kennedy was in a meeting with military advisers and replied, "Tell him I'll be right there." The father, not happy with the answer, pounded his fist on the chair. The nurse again interrupted the meeting. "Mr. President, your father wants you *now!*" The President, who had been in the midst of a heated discussion with the Secretary of Defense, now suddenly stopped, and, chuckling, said, "When Dad wants something, he wants it." He was not responding to his father simply out of compassion, although that was part of it. He was not going to him because he was still vulnerable to Joe's influence, although that was also true. He was going primarily because he was a son who really loved his father.

After embracing Joe Sr., Jack asked, "What's on your mind, Dad?"

He listened patiently to a long garble of indistinguishable syllables as if he understood everything. "Thanks, Dad, I'll take care of it. I'll do it your way. Right now I better get back to the boys." As the President left, his head sagged and his shoulders slumped. Just before he entered the meeting again, he straightened sharply and walked in briskly.

———

SOON AFTER, FRIEND and neighbor Larry Newman noted that the President took walks along the beach to Squaw Island. "His greatest relaxation—and the greatest decisions he made during his years in office—were made walking that beach," said Newman.

President Kennedy finally made his decision: a blockade. As a first measure he signed a proclamation ordering a search of all vessels proceeding toward Cuba. The Soviets rejected the American demand that ships bound for Cuba be inspected by the U.S. Navy and declared that America is taking a step toward unleashing a thermonuclear world war.

On TV, at 7 P.M. on Monday night, October 22, Kennedy explained the nature of the crisis and his decision on how to handle it. He seemed "the calmest man in the whole United States of America"—*New Republic* columnist Richard Strout later said of him that in a crisis "his blood pressure soars to normal."

"It shall be the policy of this nation to regard any nuclear missile launched from Cuba against any nation in the Western Hemisphere as an attack by the Soviet Union on the United States, requiring a full retaliatory response upon the Soviet Union." He announced his blockade of all ships bound for Cuba—those containing missiles would be turned back.

The President later told Sorensen that the odds the Soviets would go to war seemed to him to be "one out of three to even."

As in almost all national crises, most of the country rallied to support the President. But there was panic among some about the imminence of a Soviet nuclear attack. A reporter at a Vietnamese Embassy dinner party that night discussed with her husband whether or not they should go to the air raid shelter nearest their home. They decided not to because they couldn't take their dog with them.

Listening to her son's speech on TV, Rose Kennedy was quoted as saying, "My son, my poor son, so much to bear and there is no way now for his father to help him."

––––––

EIGHTEEN SOVIET SHIPS were heading for Cuba, and nineteen American ships were awaiting them in a picket line 500 miles off the island. The first U.S. Navy ship to arrive on the scene was a 2200-ton destroyer: the USS *Joseph P. Kennedy, Jr.* The President's brother would have been pleased.

The President had put the United States' military forces at Defense Condition Two, the highest state of alert short of nuclear war.

Meanwhile, within the blockade arc, a Soviet submarine was sighted. The quick question of this first encounter was whether or not to force it to the surface with small depth charges. If they did that, said the President, then they must expect retaliation from the Soviets.

Bob described his brother at that time: "His hand went up to his face and covered his mouth. He opened and closed his fist. His face seemed drawn, his eyes pained, almost gray." And then, Bob added, "we stared at each other across the table."

Bobby felt they were "on the edge of a precipice with no way off."

"Jack and Bobby communicated almost by instinct," said Defense Secretary Robert McNamara. "During the missile crisis, there was a kind of shorthand between them. It was a marvelous thing to see, how they completely understood each other." Sorensen commented that "they communicated instantly, almost telepathically."

That immediate crisis abated when the submarine disappeared, but the American response still needed to be determined.

This continuing crisis was changing Bobby. Remembered Harold Reis of the Justice Department: "He was becoming more and more thoughtful and less convinced there were any simple answers—you could see it all the time . . . more aware of the complexities of the world—more aware of people's motives. . . . There was a feeling of growth of character from someone who was an aggressive scrapper who believed in confrontation, into someone with the beginning of a kind of melancholy. . . . You could see this develop. . . . There was an appreciation of the intelligence of others. . . . And a willingness to listen."

"You could tell anytime you talked to him that he wasn't the same sort of flippant, perhaps overcocky, individual that he'd been in law school," said Gerald Tremblay, his classmate at the University of Virginia.

If Bobby had learned anything during these crises it was that tough talk and swaggering did not mean toughness. What mattered most was quiet inner conviction, and that never wavered.

Ex Comm was meeting daily, fourteen persons, all dedicated, all with great love for their country. But Bobby said later that if six among them had been President, the world would have been blown up: six were in favor of an air strike or an invasion.

Dean Acheson, who had sided with him on the Bay of Pigs, now differed. Acheson, once again the rigid, intemperate cold warrior, strongly urged that Khrushchev had presented the U.S. with a direct challenge, "a test of wills and the sooner we get to a showdown the better." He favored an air strike to clean out the missile bases.

Bob Kennedy was against a sneak attack: thousands of Cubans and Russians could be killed without warning. "I can't see letting my brother be a Tojo and make an unannounced Pearl Harbor attack on a little country. . . . My brother's got to be able to live with himself."

"This had, of course, a major effect," said the highly respected Undersecretary of State George Ball, who was against air strikes. "It was one thing for me to say . . . it was something else for the President's brother to say it."

Alexis Johnson of the State Department said he had seen Bobby express anger before, but had never heard him express his moral position very forcefully, against the air strike, almost with tears in his eyes.

Bobby's "intense but quiet passion" converted Treasury Secretary Douglas Dillon, who had favored an air strike. The Attorney General now made him feel that the Cuban situation was "a real turning point in history."

Bobby had used the phrase "Pearl Harbor in reverse," and Acheson was seriously concerned when he later saw the President alone and the President repeated that same phrase.

Besides being convinced by Robert Kennedy's eloquence, everybody there knew that he was the de facto leader of the group, speaking for the President. As one Ex Comm member said of another such meeting, "We all knew Little Brother was watching and keeping a little list of where everyone stood." Ex Comm now knew there would be no air strike without warning.

As the Soviet ships approached the blockade zone, they slowed, then stopped, then finally turned and went back. At the same time, work had speeded up on the four missile sites. They were almost operational, although the nuclear missiles had not yet been installed.

The President had promised the Joint Chiefs of Staff that if Khrushchev did not agree to withdraw the missiles, he would authorize an invasion within forty-eight hours.

"The noose was tightening on all of us," remembered Robert Kennedy.

The President was even more reflective than usual that evening when his brother returned to the White House. Jack talked about Abraham Lincoln and his crisis and his end. "This is the night I should go to the theater," he told Bobby. "If you go," said his brother, "I want to go with you."

The mood was typified by a salesman who came to the White House. He had strong Boston political recommendations. "He was with an outfit selling canned water—a can impossible to contaminate," recalled Dave Powers. "But the worst thing: they were selling something that, in case someone died in the room you were in, you put this thing over them, and there'd be no odor from the body!"

———

THE FINAL CRISIS began on Friday, October 26. Khrushchev had sent Kennedy a very conciliatory letter, long and rambling, saying, "We must not succumb to pressures." The letter outlined a reasonable settlement that he would withdraw the missiles, under UN inspection, if the United States agreed not to invade Cuba. The President then said, "We can sleep good tonight."

"Jackie had gone to Glen Ora and I had dinner with the President that night," said Dave Powers. "The last thing I remember, I'm leaving the White House; and he's reading the favorable letter. . . . Everything was fine. In fact, I found out afterwards that my neighbors used to wait until they saw the lights go out in my house to relax and go to sleep."

The next day—a day at first so disastrous that they later called it Black Saturday—as the President prepared to draft a reply to the Khrushchev letter, a second one arrived. It made no mention of the first letter, and, in hard language, demanded removal of American missile bases in Turkey and UN inspection of all nuclear bases in the United States.

There was more bad news. A reconnaissance pilot was shot down by a surface-to-air missile. His plane had crashed in Cuba, and he had been killed.

The Joint Chiefs of Staff now urgently recommended an air strike on Monday, October 29, followed shortly by an invasion.

It was the President's darkest hour. His dilemma was deep. He saw it as a start of a catastrophic war. And yet he could not forget that his reluctance to use air power during the Bay of Pigs was often given as a prime reason for its failure.

Powers remembered: "It was the strangest thing, because he was half talking to me, half talking to himself, how he felt—but he said, 'If it weren't for the children, it would be easy to press the button! . . . Not just John and Caroline, and not just the children in America, but children all over the world who will suffer and die for the decision I have to make.' "

Those closest to the President knew that he felt when he went to sleep those nights, he did not know whether he would ever wake up in the morning to anything left on earth.

When Powers later walked into Kennedy's bedroom, the President had Caroline on his lap, reading her a bedtime story. "I had the strangest feeling, like, 'Perhaps he's thinking this is the last one he'll ever read to her.' "

The meetings on Black Saturday were almost continuous, and then Bobby got a startling idea—so simple and so inspired that the President agreed immediately: forget Khrushchev's bellicose second letter and answer his first one. Bundy compared it to the Victorian maiden who construed the tiniest gesture as a marriage proposal that she could eagerly accept.

"I never thought much of Bobby at first," George Ball said. "I thought he was a man of very uncomplicated mind and I didn't like him very much. But then I went through the missile crisis with him, on an hourly basis, and there you saw the real depth and quality of the man."

Robert Kennedy felt that the Russians were probably open to sensible bargaining. UN Ambassador Adlai Stevenson had brought up the idea of trading our missiles in Turkey for the Cuban ones. Both Kennedy brothers felt that there could be no quid pro quo or any arrangement made under this kind of threat or pressure. Robert quietly assured Soviet Ambassador Anatoly Dobrynin that America did intend to remove the missiles from Turkey, but not as a trade for the removal of missiles from Cuba. In other words, the Russians could not claim credit for their removal. There could be no question of submitting to an ultimatum. For Kennedy, that would have been politically untenable.

This was not made public at the time because some senior Kennedy aides felt it would have been misunderstood and damaging to American security. Moscow, therefore, could also claim some victory.

Bobby told Dobrynin that the President was writing Khrushchev that we were willing to remove the blockade, and promised not to invade Cuba. Bobby said, "We're writing back to say we're in favor; we'll take off the blockade; we won't invade Cuba if the Soviets would dismantle and remove the missiles." Dobrynin was delighted.

But all was still uncertain. It was impossible to predict whether Khrushchev could or would forget the terms of his second letter. The expectation of a military confrontation was still stark and real.

"Bobby hasn't eaten," recalled Powers, "and now there's going to be one more meeting that night. We're sitting down, eating. . . . I have a big chicken breast and a glass of white wine. . . . Bobby's having a bottle of Heineken's and a chicken breast. The President, a glass of milk and a chicken breast . . . .

"To take off the pressure, the Kennedys would always direct attention to the other person. Bobby said, 'You're eatin' that chicken and drinkin' that wine as if it's your last meal!' And I said, 'After listenin' to you and the President, I'm not sure it isn't!' They both were laughin'."

WHAT THE SOVIETS did not say—but what was admitted years later by Fedor Burlatsky, an adviser to Nikita Khrushchev—was that Fidel

Castro had sent a telegram to Khrushchev stating: "I propose the immediate launching of a nuclear strike on the United States. The Cuban people are prepared to sacrifice themselves for the cause of the destruction of imperialism and the victory of world revolution."

Yuri Andropov, then in charge of the international division of the Communist Party Central Committee, quoted Khrushchev: "You see how far things can go. We've got to get these missiles out of there before a real fire starts."

It was then that Khrushchev announced that the Soviets would dismantle their missiles in Cuba and return them to Russia. He did this without consulting Castro. Castro heard the news over the radio and found it "deeply humiliating."

"For a moment the world had stood still," said Bobby, "and now it was going around again."

Pierre Salinger, who also served as an intermediary with Khrushchev, insisted that "the Soviets never put the nuclear warheads on the missiles during the entire crisis, although they were prepared to do it if they wanted to do it."

BOB'S IDEA OF answering the favorable letter of Friday and ignoring the Saturday, October 27, letter proved to be the superb solution.

"Thank God for Bobby," said the President.

He gave Bobby a framed sheet of yellow legal paper covered with hasty scrawl in ballpoint pen, accompanied by a black-bordered, hand-written card: "Notes made by President Kennedy at his last Cabinet meeting, October 29, 1963—For Robert Kennedy." It is signed simply "Jack." It was his way of saying thanks.

"Looking back on it," said British Prime Minister Harold Mac-Millan, "the way that Bobby and his brother played this hand was absolutely masterly. . . . What they did that week convinced me that they were both great men."

A later review of the Kennedy–Khrushchev correspondence showed that the Soviet Union evidently gave up on trying to get a written commitment from President Kennedy promising that the United States would not invade Cuba—the President refused to tie his hands in case of needed future action.

The Americans also did agree to lift the quarantine and promised not to make any invasion of Cuba as long as Cuba itself committed no aggressive action against any of the nations of the Western Hemisphere. It was a large loophole and it took a total exchange of fourteen Kennedy–Khrushchev letters before United States finally went off its highest state of alert on November 20.

––––––––––

AFTER IT WAS over, Ben Bradlee asked John Kennedy how he was sure the Russians weren't taking out old telephone poles instead of missiles under those canvas covers that appeared on the decks of the Soviet ships in the intelligence pictures. Kennedy admitted that nobody had ever seen the missiles without the covers on, and that the covered missiles looked the same leaving Cuba as they had en route there. But he emphasized that if the Soviets left missiles behind in Cuba, and we discovered it, there would be an immediate and massive invasion of Cuba by the United States.

In the past, John Kennedy first considered the political impact of any decision. This crisis had changed him. With the fate of the world in the balance, JFK was finally becoming a statesman.

10

DEATH AND MYTH

With the missile crisis resolved, the President could concentrate on family matters.

Just before the election, he sent Ted Sorensen to prepare Teddy for another appearance on "Meet the Press," this time with his Republican rival, Henry Cabot Lodge, just before the election. They knew then that Ted would win, but the President wanted him to win big, wanted him to have the latest information, and he wanted him to have the benefit of an expert like Sorensen.

In the general election, JFK came home to Boston to vote for his brother. If they were low-key at the start, the President's staff now felt that this was the time to pull out all the stops.

"The President's people wanted to make a big deal out of it," Ted's aide Eddie Martin said. "They wanted him to land in the Common in a helicopter, cast his vote on Beacon Hill, visit his brother's headquarters, then go to Locke-Ober's for a bowl of his favorite stew. We wanted him to land at the local airport, cast a vote and leave immediately." They didn't want it to look too much as if Ted was dependent on the President's coattails. The President later said, "I was allowed to come to Boston for twenty minutes." It is interesting that the youngest brother now felt strong enough to countermand the President.

On Election Day, Edward Kennedy won by 400,000 votes, beating a Lodge just as Jack had done. Ted Kennedy also became the first United States Senator elected while his brother was President.

There were some areas in Massachusetts in which Ted ran a little better than his brother had in his 1958 Senate race, and Ted made certain the President knew about it. Jack autographed a photograph for him saying, "To one coattail rider from another."

New York *Herald-Tribune* Washington correspondent Earl Mazo asked Ted Kennedy, "Was his ultimate goal in public life the Presidency?"

"Well, Mr. Mazo, I would say that having seen the problems of my brother, I just wonder whether that job is really worth it." His ambivalence about the highest office would persist throughout his life.

Accenting Teddy's youth, Johnny Carson, on the "Tonight" show, said, "He was the only candidate who made his acceptance speech while wearing Dr. Denton's."

THE WASHINGTON *POST* reported the election as "the transformation of Edward M. 'Ted' Kennedy into a national political figure. By a curious turn of fate, Robert Kennedy does not now have the firm political base that Ted Kennedy has. If the attorney general's political future is uncertain, Senator Kennedy is on a course that seems destined to carry him over the years to growing power in the Senate and growing influence in the Democratic Party."

The Kennedy dynasty never had looked so bright and shining.

Teddy's arrival in Washington was not wholeheartedly received: "Frankly, the Democratic party wasn't too thrilled to be getting Teddy down here," reported Robert Sherrill. "To tell the truth, three Kennedys in Washington seemed just a bit tasteless."

The day Bobby drove Ted to the Senate for the swearing-in ceremonies, he turned to his brother and asked, "Which way do I drive, Eddie? You know this routine better than I do."

On his first day in office, Ted Kennedy took the 7 A.M. shuttle from Boston to Washington. Wearing a dark-blue suit and dark-blue figured tie, Ted popped into a waiting car for the ten-minute ride to the Senate Office Building, and told his driver, "Well, we're here." Then he went to his new office, Room 432.

His Senate office, like his home in Hyannis, soon resembled a museum of Kennedy memorabilia, with photographs covering most of the walls, all of them featuring the famous Kennedy smile and reflecting the promise Ted considered his birthright.

Senators who had expected the worst from Ted Kennedy were very pleasantly surprised. Many of them were old enough to be his father, but Teddy, the youngest of nine children, had been dealing with older people all his life, and knew how. His respect was instinctive and proper and even deferential.

After dinner on his first day in Washington, Ted told some reporters that he planned to stay "out of the limelight, out of the headlines and out of the swimming pool." He added that there was no reason to think he was emphasizing his connection with his brother "just because I had a rocker installed in my Senate seat this afternoon."

––––––––––

TED WORKED HARD, tried not to be showy, and usually pushed other colleagues forward to garner the publicity.

He started each Senate day with two separate stacks of index cards, one stack with a detailed timetable schedule telling him whom he was supposed to see and when, the other stack telling him whom he was supposed to call and why.

Unlike Jack, who was bored most of the time in the Senate and used it simply for a political base, Teddy paid strict attention to senatorial chores. "Teddy was from the beginning a Senate man, more gregarious, more outgoing, more political in the clubhouse sense than his brothers," observed Milton Gwirtzman. "He immediately fitted in."

He didn't expect to shine—he had none of his brother's arrogance of expectancy. He seemed perfectly content to be part of the Senate system without making waves. He was there to learn. He was respectful and attentive. And, as part of the process, he hired some of the smartest staff available—and listened to them.

Once a Senator, Ted was careful not to step on any toes, not do anything that might embarrass the President. Said his aide, Milton Gwirtzman: "He did not let the fact that his brother was President interfere with discharging his duties as Senator from Massachusetts. But he could discharge them without any significant conflicts with the President because the interests of an urban industrial state like

Massachusetts, and the interests of a Democratic president are very similar.''

When he did vote against the President's position, it was on minor issues, and he not only told his brother but teased him about it.

Teddy learned fast. ''Some pipeline I have into the White House,'' he told Ben Bradlee. ''I tell him 1000 men out of work in Fall River, 400 men out of work in Fitchburg. And when the Army gets that new rifle, there's another 600 men out of work in Springfield. And you know what he says to me? 'Tough shit.' ''

The President joked about it. ''Teddy called me one day and said, 'You know, I think I'll hold a conference and invite those New York reporters. I could really tell them how ruthless you used to be to your younger brother.' ''

Congressman Tip O'Neill circulated the story that Ted Kennedy asked a judge to change his name. ''One Kennedy is President, the other a high-ranking cabinet member. . . . Your Honor, I want to become a success on my own.'' The judge, sympathetic, asked him what other name he would prefer. ''Well,'' Ted replied, ''I think Teddy is all right as a first name, but I'd like to change the last name.'' ''To what?'' asked the puzzled judge. ''How about Roosevelt?'' Ted replied.

————

THE PRESIDENT WANTED to minimize the public perception of too many Kennedys, and Jack and Teddy weren't seen together much publicly when Ted became Senator. In fact, Charles Spalding thought, ''Jack must've called Bobby and Teddy, and said, 'This is the way to do it.' . . . There must have been some understanding on how they were going to behave. Like his father said, 'When you become President, things are different.' . . . And I think Jack didn't want any mistakes made.'' But the fact was, as Ted later revealed, that he saw his brother often, simply coming in after a Senate session to the back door of the White House. And he and his brother would gossip and laugh and have a drink. His eldest brother was still his chief adviser, his model, his best friend, and now his surrogate father.

But Ted Kennedy insisted that his older brother did not offer him specific instruction on how to handle himself in the Senate. ''In our family, nobody briefed anyone on how to conduct himself in a job. We just picked things up by watching and absorbing. That's one advantage of being a Kennedy—there were so many of us, doing so much. You just soaked up things as you went along.''

Politics or no politics, the personal relationship between Ted and Jack was unchanged.

Lester David said, ''When Jack Kennedy gave a cocktail party, the invitations would set a time limit: 'From six to eight p.m.' And he meant it. Promptly at eight, the guests would be expected to pick themselves up and go, and the party would be over.

''After his election to the Senate, Ted gave a cocktail party at his red-brick Georgetown home. Ted's party invitations, as usual, read the same as Jack's—six to eight. When the guests rose to leave, Ted asked in astonishment: 'Where you fellows going?' He was told what the invitation said and that his brother had expected his guests to stick to it.

'' 'Well,' he answered, 'I'm not my brother! Take off your coats. Besides, we've got all that food.' And so we all stayed there, swapping stories until 3 A.M.''

ONLY OCCASIONALLY WERE the brothers at odds. Teddy and Bob conflicted on whether or not there were enough votes to restore funds for a mass transit bill. Bobby said no and Teddy said yes. The President sided with Teddy, and the bill passed. A Boston *Globe* article credited Teddy with maneuvering the victory, a clipping he proudly showed everybody, while the family kidded him about how lovingly he was already collecting clippings about himself.

Nobody in his family helped Ted decide on anything he said in the Senate, but they jumped in quickly with advice when he roughed up a photographer. The President told him, ''Sometimes you have to eat it, and this was one of them.'' Jack quickly appointed Ted Sorensen and Clark Clifford to draft Ted's public apology. Ben Bradlee added, ''If Teddy hadn't apologized, they would have tried to screw him when he runs again in 1964.''

Ted continued his swift assimilation to the Senate. Some Senators accepted him more readily than they had accepted Jack. The Kennedy name and the Kennedy money had opened the door to the Senate, but now Ted had to prove himself, and he soon did.

Ted Kennedy had come a long way. "I knew Teddy as a Senator," said Senator Claiborne Pell. "We both served on the Human Resources Committee. Now it's called Labor and Human Resources. He ranked next after me on the Education Committee. He was an enthusiastic . . . bright and able man. Much more than people gave him credit for . . . an excellent politician. I really liked Teddy, and respected him."

———

THE KENNEDY BROTHERS had matured remarkably: the pragmatic President had found compassion; Robert Kennedy, the ruthless McCarthy investigator, had become a man of passionate sensitivity— although some mean streaks remained. And now Teddy, one of the country's most publicized playboys, was finding something he enjoyed as much as women.

It was also challenging for the thirty-year-old Ted to combine his Senate responsibilities with family life. Remembers reporter Sarah McLendon: "The Senate was meeting late, one summer night; my sister and I were over at the Capitol. We saw this man there, just playing and playing with several children . . . on the grounds, with trees and grass. I said, 'That looks like Ted Kennedy, playing over there.' It was about 7:30 P.M. Then they rang the bell for the Senate vote, and he comes running over the balustrade, combing his hair as he ran. And it was Ted. He had some retainer bring the kids down there—and they had a little picnic there, on the lawn—the only time he could get to see his kids, at that time. I understand he's done that a lot."

———

THAT THANKSGIVING—the first since his father's stroke—the President assumed another responsibility: he became the acting head of the assembled Kennedy clan.

Anytime they were together, the teasing began. This time the President brought up the subject of what he planned to do after he finished the presidency. Ted rightly assumed this meant that Jack had his eye on running for the Senate from Massachusetts again. "And I would point out to him," said Ted, "that John Quincy Adams went from the Presidency to the House of Representatives and that the House was better suited for his experience."

The President also told friend Red Fay, "When a man comes from the White House to Congress, he could give a voice of judgment and authority." Then he added, "Of course, when Bobby or Teddy becomes President, then I'd probably be most useful as Secretary of State. . . . I'm not quite sure that I would ever get adjusted to addressing Bobby or Teddy as 'Mr. President.' Let's not dwell too long on the prospect of taking orders from Lovable Bob."

President Kennedy took considerable comfort in a Gallup poll at the start of 1963 that rated his national popularity at 76 percent.

The first two years in office had been rocky and eventful. The Cuban crisis had started as a high drama of disaster, and later became a crucial success. Relations with the Soviets were now on a more even keel. The civil rights situation was still explosive, but the Kennedys were beginning to earn the trust of black America with their action for student James Meredith. Congress had stubbornly resisted much of his proposed legislation, but this did not stop the young President and his wife from capturing the heart and spirit of the American people. And of the world.

———

IT WAS A debt paid when the government concluded final arrangements with Cuba on its release of its 1113 prisoners captured in the Bay of Pigs invasion. The terms for their freedom included $3 million in cash and $50 million of vital supplies raised by Robert Kennedy from private sources. But the chapter was far from closed. At a rally in Florida's Orange Bowl for the released prisoners, the President reassured his audience, "Cuba shall be free again."

Author Wilfrid Sheed made the point that "in joining his brother, Bobby had gone from being loose electricity in search of an outlet to perhaps his true destiny: being one half of a great President. . . . It would be too simple . . . to call Jack and Bobby respectively the head and heart, the intellect and will, of a great presidency, because each was more than a bit of both."

Ted Kennedy asked Milton Gwirtzman to list some suggestions as to what Robert Kennedy should do after the 1964 campaign. While Ted was surely concerned about his brother, he was also considering his own future options. There was much talk that Bob would resign as Attorney General to run either for Governor of Massachusetts or

Senator from New York. Two Kennedys in the Senate might be considered too much. Gwirtzman thought Bob would make a better governor, but either job would be a stepping-stone to the presidency. Ted passed the memo to Bob.

A *Newsweek* article quoted an unidentified family member that Bob would go for governor in 1966, run for reelection, then be ready to run for the presidency in 1972.

———

IN MAY 1963 the civil rights volcano erupted again.

The long-promised Civil Rights Bill had reached Congress at the end of February. In a special message, the President had promised that black Americans could freely exercise their voting rights, eliminating a variety of restrictions, including the poll tax. But Congress failed to act on it, and the President didn't push too hard.

Meanwhile, in Alabama, Governor George Wallace had refused state university admittance to two black students. Even though segregation was still widespread, Alabama was now the only state with a segregated state university. Wallace had pledged, "Segregation now! Segregation tomorrow! Segregation forever!" State police arrested many protesting black demonstrators, including Martin Luther King, Jr.

There were bombs, riots, police dogs, burning, looting in scattered cities. The rest of the country was torn with rumblings of conscience, hate, and fear.

Those close to him said that the President had never been emotionally caught by the civil rights protests until he saw television pictures of police dogs in Birmingham being set on black women. Then he acted. After signing a proclamation commanding the Governor of Alabama to stop obstructing enrollment of black students at the University of Alabama, he federalized the Alabama National Guard, taking the authority away from the Governor and giving it to the Attorney General.

Robert Kennedy expected to call out the Guard the next day. "Then I changed my mind," he said afterward. "I just never did do it."

The Attorney General was initially reluctant to call out the troops because of its obvious political impact on southern voters. But, like his brother, he was soon filled with such fury at the violence that he now took action.

RFK and his delegates, Burke Marshall and Joseph Dolan, finally arranged an uneasy settlement in Alabama. Birmingham's mayor was quoted as cursing Bob Kennedy: "I hope that every drop of blood that's spilled he tastes in his throat . . . and I hope he chokes to death."

During the first week of June, there were 161 civil rights incidents recorded in the United States. The situation seemed to be moving out of control, and Ted Sorensen suggested the President talk to the nation on national TV.

Bobby advised Jack, "I don't think you could get by without it."

The brothers seldom discussed such issues so directly in the presence of others. Those who were there also noted that the President seemed to be in physical pain, moving awkwardly, pressing his fist into his cheek, onto his teeth.

For the twenty minutes before airtime, the President sat alone with his brother in the Oval Office, still making notes. When he started speaking on TV, he had only part of the speech in front of him. For the first time, he was not reading a beautifully crafted set speech, he was not simply speaking from his head but from his heart. As he spoke, he was still seeing those pictures of police dogs tearing at black women in Birmingham. He spoke for eighteen minutes.

"For the first time, it was full of passion. It electrified us," said NAACP chairman Roy Wilkins.

Jacqueline had said of her husband in the past that his coolness was surface, but his passion was deep, and now the depth was showing.

The President had told the nation: "Today we are committed to a worldwide struggle to promote and protect the rights of all who wish to be free. . . . It ought to be possible . . . for every American to enjoy the privileges of being American without regards to his race or his color. . . . One hundred years of delay have passed since President Lincoln freed the slaves, yet their heirs, their grandsons, are not fully free. . . .

"If an American, because his skin is dark, cannot eat lunch in a restaurant open to the public, if he cannot send his children to the best public schools available, if he cannot vote for the public officials who represent him—then who among us would be content to have the color of his skin changed? Who among us would then be content with the counsels of patience and delay? . . .

"The fires of frustration and discord are burning in every city, North and South, where legal remedies are not at hand. . . . We face, therefore, a moral crisis as a country and as a people. It cannot be met by repressive police action. It cannot be left to increased demonstrations in the streets. . . . It is time to act in the Congress, in your state and local legislative body, and above all in our daily lives."

It was as if John Fitzgerald Kennedy had broken out of a cocoon, a cocoon of cautious pragmatism dictated by hard politics. He had emerged into the world of right and wrong. And he was following the precepts of Debs Myers, a twinkling man with wise eyes, whose plaque in City Hall Park in New York says, "Do the right thing, and nine times out of ten it will turn out to be the right thing politically."

———

ROBERT KENNEDY WAS now more ready to expand his racial education. He asked author James Baldwin to arrange a meeting with black intellectual leaders. He told the group that they must continue to be patient, that there would soon be a black American running for national office.

But Bobby still had much to learn. "You know, I have to tell you," said Baldwin, "your grandfather came over here from Ireland, just a generation or so ago, and your brother is President. My ancestors came over here a couple of hundred years ago on a slave ship, and you have no right . . . to tell me when I can participate in this government." The meeting became a noisy encounter that lasted several hours, with Bob exercising uncharacteristic control.

A dramatic climax was reached when a young man spoke about being beaten by southern police. He told Kennedy that it made him sick to beg for legal rights from the man supposed to enforce them, and he added, dramatically, "I want to vomit being in the same room with you."

Bobby left shocked and exhausted. He later told Arthur Schlesinger, "They don't know what the laws are—they don't know what the facts are—they don't know what we're doing or what we're trying to do." If he was bitter about what they had said, their torment had touched him deeply, and would make him feel even more urgent about the issue.

———

NOW THE PRESIDENT told his brother that he expected the poor to be a priority in his second term, and he expected it to cost billions of dollars. Jack explained his untouched isolation of the Depression. "We were one of the great fortunes of the world. Now and then, there'd be a new gardener that Dad or somebody had hired—who'd been out of work. But we had, relatively speaking, more money than ever. . . . We had bigger houses, more servants; we traveled more . . . absolutely untouched. I learned about the Depression at Harvard, reading about it. The first time I was fully aware of what it was. . . . The world began to intrude on everybody a good deal more in Bobby's generation. World War II, Vietnam, television. But he was susceptible to it, more vulnerable to it, it seems to me."

The brothers, after consulting economists, shaped major proposals that would later be incorporated into President Johnson's "War on Poverty." Ironically, Vice President Johnson, who knew so much more about this issue than the brothers, was not then consulted by them.

"Johnson was a fish out of water, at that point," said radio commentator Ed Morgan. "Had no leverage. . . . I think he could have had, if the President had just taken him up and said, 'Look, you're gonna be my lobbyist with Congress,' but he didn't do that."

Friend Charles Bartlett once passed on to the President that Johnson felt "awfully lonely, up there" and wondered whether the President could consult him more. "And he said, 'God I wish I could remember. . . . I feel so sorry for that guy. . . . You know, when you get into an exciting one . . . you just don't think to call the people who haven't read the cables.' "

Lyndon Johnson blamed much of his uncertain status on "that goddamn son of a bitch Bobby." What griped Johnson the most was that he wasn't the number-two man in government—Bobby was. Johnson said, "Bobby is first in, last out. And Bobby is the boy he listens to."

To friends, Johnson said he didn't really dislike Bob Kennedy—he just didn't trust him. Robert Kennedy said he didn't really dislike Lyndon Johnson—he just didn't respect him.

On the other hand, Bob insisted that the President always made it a point of asking Johnson at meetings to go on the record as to how he stood, but Johnson was always reluctant to state his position.

When Johnson did ask to speak near the end of a meeting, "Robert Kennedy would stand up to leave, and interrupt, 'Well this meeting has run much too long.' " Johnson even strongly suspected the Attorney General of wiretapping him while he was in office. It was no Washington secret that Johnson loathed Bobby.

Johnson once told his friend Senator Frank Church that he found the vice presidency a very trying relationship, with the President sometimes cold. Yet he regarded JFK as a man of justice, and for such a man Johnson said he could act as a good soldier.

The President never doubted Johnson's loyalty. "He's one guy that I knew wasn't gonna stab me in the back," he told Larry Newman. "And I can't say it for a lot of the guys who are around me." Kennedy told Arthur Krock, "I don't know what to do with Lyndon. I've got to keep him happy somehow. My big job is to keep Lyndon happy."

President Kennedy did call in his staff one day, and said, "Now, I understand that a lot of you guys have been bad-mouthing the Vice-President. Now I'm going to tell you this. If I ever catch anybody demeaning the Vice President, I'm going to fire him. I just want you guys to know how I feel about it."

The President enjoyed Lyndon on a personal level—especially his humor—but when Lyndon and Lady Bird were invited to White House social events, it was often at the last minute. Some faulted Jacqueline, who did a biting imitation of the Johnsons, referring to them as Mr. and Mrs. Cornpone.

Johnson was playing his cards carefully. He didn't want to antagonize the President, didn't want to give him any excuse for replacing him as Vice President for the second term. After Kennedy's second term, Johnson could run for President on his own.

Bobby Kennedy said he and the President had discussed Johnson as Vice President, but he insisted "there was never any thought of dropping him."

It was Eunice who asked a reporter what he thought of a Kennedy–Kennedy ticket in 1964. "You wouldn't dare!" said the startled reporter. "What's wrong with that?" asked the President's sister. "Nothing that I can think of."

On a plane with the President and Senator George Smathers, Ken O'Donnell heard Smathers say to the President, "Everybody on the Hill says Bobby is trying to knock Johnson off the ticket."

"George, you have some intelligence, I presume," Kennedy said. "And you're trying to say my brother is now going to put himself on the ticket? That would be a great ticket, wouldn't it? Now, that's not possible, correct? So why would he want to knock Lyndon Johnson off the ticket? Can you see me now in a terrible fight with Lyndon Johnson, which means I'll blow the South? I don't want to be elected, you mean? You know I love this job . . . I love every second of it."

Others recalled the Kennedy–Johnson relationship differently.

"Jack used to grumble about Johnson," said JFK's Secretary of Labor, Arthur Goldberg. "Johnson was threatening to quit all the time . . . and I'd say, 'He won't quit in a million years . . . this is his place in the sun.' "

Larry Newman remembered, "After a formal White House dinner was over, the President would say, 'Well, I'll go upstairs,' but then would give Lyndon the wink, and Lyndon would come up and they'd talk for an hour and he'd get Lyndon's viewpoint on things."

———

ONE OF THE terms of the World War II peace treaty was the four-power control of West Berlin, a city island inside the Soviet zone. The four powers—American, Soviet, French, and German—all patrolled and controlled the city together. They all had tanks and troops there, all had access to the city by road and train and plane. The physical contrast between West Berlin and East Berlin was stark. West Berlin was flourishing, with cabarets and packed stores; East Berlin, on the Soviet side, was still bleak and grim from the devastation of war. In the course of years, thousands of East Berliners escaped to West Berlin. To close this border to the West, in August 1961 East Berlin built a wall—concrete, barbed wire, minefields, dogs, searchlights, all backed up by troops ready to shoot and kill.

What few knew was that Kennedy had encouraged the Soviets to build the wall to stop the flow of refugees to the West—they had become an economic problem. Historian Michael Beschloss detailed the number of secret messages on this from Kennedy to Khrushchev, chiefly through Soviet agent Bolshakov.

When the East Germans actually started building the wall across Berlin in the middle of the night, President Kennedy's first reaction was, "Go get my brother!" What made the situation ominous was the fact that the Russians brought tanks near it. The Americans likewise had brought up their tanks on their side of the wall.

The President now told Bobby to contact Georgi Bolshakov to offer a deal to Khrushchev: if the Soviets withdrew their tanks, the Americans would do the same. The deed was done. Mutual consensus was that this was not worth a war.

The brothers agreed that it would not be politically wise to go public on their approval of the wall. The whole story was too difficult to explain. The American public might see it as an American surrender.

Then, when Carl Kaysen broke the news to Kennedy that the Soviets had resumed atomic testing, his reaction was, "Fucked again!"

———

IN VIEW OF all this, the President felt it important to visit Berlin and make a statement, confirm the American commitment to defend West Berlin's freedom against anyone.

Upon his arrival, Kennedy went first to look at the ugly barrier that now divided Berlin. "The Secret Service said, 'It's not a good idea,' " General Godfrey McHugh recalled. "He said, 'Yes, I want to see it.' And by God, when he wants to see it, he will do it. The President has the right to override his Secret Service, anytime he wants to."

The President had expected to look over the wall through the gate onto Unter den Linden, once the celebrated avenue of the German capital. But the five arches of the Brandenburg Gate had been covered by the Communists the night before with huge red banners to partially block his view of desolate East Berlin. As he stared at the gray, grim emptiness, "he looked like a young angry lion."

Conservative columnist Walter Lippmann had been wrong before, and was wrong again. He had said repeatedly that the world was not ready for a young President, with his lack of experience. But war-torn Europe, particularly, was hungry for a young hero to electrify it.

The motorcade arrived late at the Schoenberger Rathaus for a scheduled speech outside West Berlin's City Hall. The square was so packed that it seemed as if the whole city was there, a single mass with a single voice, chanting "*Kennedy . . . Kennedy . . . Kennedy.*" Placards were everywhere: JOHN, YOU ARE OUR BEST FRIEND. There was even a reference to the pregnant Jacqueline: WE HOPE TWINS.

Just before the trip, Bobby had talked to his brother informally about saying something in German while he was in Berlin. He thought of saying, "*Ich bin ein Berliner.*"

"I told him how to say it in German—in that marvelous Boston accent," said McGeorge Bundy. Kennedy had no feeling for language, no sense of music, no ear. "So there we were, in the goddamn airplane, coming down in Berlin, while he said it over and over. . . . He must have said it 5 or 10 times. . . . The particular idea of saying it, I'm pretty sure, was his. . . . That was another thing about him; he would have an impulsive idea, and then he'd be very careful how he said it."

When Kennedy shouted, in his speech to the crowd: "Today in the world of freedom, the proudest boast is *Ich bin ein Berliner!* the response was unimaginable, almost an animal roar, as if every person there were venting the frustration of a lifetime in a single exhilarating moment. He had touched the exact nerve with the exact phrase.

He intensified the hysteria when he added, "There are many people in the world who really don't understand, or say they don't, what is the great issue between the free world and the Communist world.

"Let them come to Berlin!

"And there are some who say in Europe and elsewhere that we can work with the Communists.

"Let them come to Berlin!

"And there are even a few who say that it is true that Communism is an evil system but it permits us to make economic progress . . .

"*Lass' sie nach Berlin kommen.* Let them come to Berlin!

"Freedom has many difficulties and democracy is not perfect, but we have never had to put up a wall to keep our people in. . . .'"

The roar was intense and so prolonged that Kennedy felt he could have asked them to march to the Berlin wall and tear it down and they would have done it.

"We'll never have another day like this as long as we live," he told Sorensen.

Before he left Germany, Kennedy quoted Abraham Lincoln to

another crowd: "I know there is a God. I see a storm coming. If He has a part and a place for me, then I am ready."

————

ON THAT TRIP to Europe, as a present to himself, the President included Ireland. If Berlin had stirred his blood, Ireland delighted his soul.

· For three days, the whole country stopped. "The pubs were open at five o'clock in the morning," said a man in New Ross, "and most of the town was drunk by eight, for days on end. They were dancing there on the quay. If the town wasn't burned down that night, it never will be!"

Children perched on their fathers' shoulders to see him, old women held up their rosary beads, and nuns danced in the streets. Eamon de Valera, the almost blind man from Brooklyn, who was then President of Ireland, was beaming as if his own son had come home. De Valera and Joseph Kennedy Sr. were longtime friends.

Kennedy once again visited New Ross, the birthplace of his great-grandfather Patrick Kennedy, where a Kennedy descendant was still living. The mayor had told his citizens not to clean up the manure from their front steps for the President's arrival. "If he wants chrome," said the mayor, "he can find it on Madison Avenue."

John Kennedy told a crowd, "There is an impression in Washington that there are no Kennedys left in Ireland, that they are all in Washington." He then asked for any Kennedys in the audience to raise their hands. A few did and he said, "Well, I am glad to see a few cousins who didn't catch the boat."

In Dublin, a newspaper reported that some 375 Irish women had confessed that they had intimate relations with President Kennedy during his three-day stay in Ireland.

The First Lady did not accompany her husband to Ireland, but her sister, Princess Lee Radziwill, did. President Kennedy also brought along some fifty members of the White House staff who were of Irish descent. One of them was his pastor at St. Edward's Church—where the last four rows were cordoned off for the Kennedy family and the Secret Service. The President introduced him as "the pastor of a poor humble flock in Palm Beach, Florida." Another was his sister Jean, who quoted her brother as saying that after he left the White House, he would like to be Ambassador to Ireland. Thirty years later, President Clinton would appoint her to that very position.

Included in the Kennedy entourage were Fiddle—of Fiddle and Faddle—who came to take his dictation and massage him—and Dr. Max Jacobson, popularly known as "Dr. Feelgood," with his painkilling shots. Fiddle and Faddle were the White House nicknames for two attractive young women, serving as secretarial assistants, whom Jacqueline once pointed out to a visiting French journalist as "my husband's lovers."

Items brought on the trip included bottled water and the presidential scales—so he could watch his weight.

The last time he had been there, he had come in a station wagon, searching for relatives and roots. Now he was celebrated as a national event and there was a choir, singing "Come back to Erin." As he boarded the plane to go home, someone said he had the sweetest and saddest look on his face.

"Those were the three happiest days of my life," he later told old Navy buddy James Reed. Reed was a guest at Hyannis Port the weekend of the President's return, and they saw a film of the tour earmarked for German-American groups around the country. Kennedy watched himself in Berlin making his *Ich bin ein Berliner* speech. At the end of it, automatically and enthusiastically, he applauded, almost as if he were applauding someone else.

His father would have applauded the Berlin speech too, if he could, but he might have been less sentimental about Ireland. All his life he had tried to take the Irish out of his sons' speech and souls. He saw it as a political handicap. He had neutralized his own speech at Harvard and elsewhere, and had sent his sons to private schools, where they met few, if any, children with Irish backgrounds.

———

BOBBY'S ADVICE IN the Cuban missile crisis had been pivotal, and the President had afterward consulted him on all the foreign problems. The President now seriously considered making Bobby Secretary of State, replacing Dean Rusk.

"I talked to Jack about it," Justice William Douglas said. "If Jack had lived, I think Bobby would have been Secretary of State."

Shifting Bob to the State Department might have blunted some of the southern anger against his Attorney General activities on equal rights. The White House was receiving a growing proportion of mail filled with hate and threats. President Kennedy's popularity plummeted in the polls, from 76 percent to 59 percent. "I was very concerned about it," said Robert Kennedy. He saw himself as a political albatross for his brother in the next election. What he overlooked was that the President's passionate speech on civil rights had bound the brothers tightly together in the southern mind.

It has been said that the reason Americans build triumphal arches out of brick is that the bricks can then be thrown at the fallen idols. But if there was dust from the broken brick, Jack would not have to eat it— his family would.

At one meeting, Jack teased Bob about his unpopularity, and suggested it might help his campaign if he and Bob got into a public fight.

"I spoke to my brother about resigning," Bob later told an interviewer. "The fact that I was Attorney General caused him many more problems than if I hadn't been his brother." His investigation of labor racketeering stirred up suspicion that he was antilabor, and it worried Bob that this rubbed off on the President. "Instead of talking about Robert Kennedy, they started talking about the Kennedy brothers, which he used to point out to me frequently." Jack refused to consider Bob's resignation, said it would seem that the Kennedys were running out on a commitment. But they both agreed to watch the political fallout most carefully and discuss it again.

At that time, Burke Marshall said with the certainty of someone who knew his friend, Bobby had no thought of the Presidency while his brother was President. "I don't think there was anything like that in his mind, ever. . . . He thought that by the time his brother had finished being President . . . that he would have made so many enemies that I don't think there was anything further from his mind."

But, however distant, the presidency could not have been too remote in Bob's mind. The father had planted the dynasty idea in all of them. The priority now, however, was his brother.

———

IN THE THREE years he was in office, the President's legislative program was still a shambles, one third of it still in subcommittee. Kennedy had never learned, either as a candidate or a Congressman, of the personal need to twist arms, promise patronage for votes, and say thank you. JFK, like his father, had a kind of arrogance, which included a sense of entitlement for anything he got. Said one observer, "Hell, Kennedy couldn't even get the best man at his wedding, George Smathers, to vote with him."

This was even more true of Bob.

Such was the legislative gridlock between Congress and the President that James Reston even wrote a column calling it a constitutional crisis. He pointed out the fact that while Kennedy was a great political campaigner, and a great inspirational leader, he was not a great political leader.

As a consequence, Kennedy took defeat after defeat. There seemed little likelihood that he would ever persuade Congress to enact any major legislation, especially his civil rights bills.

Reporter Jim Deakin of the St. Louis *Post-Dispatch* remembered Kennedy keeping tally on a Senate vote on a major bill he had proposed. "They beat him, and beat him bad. He took that pencil, just as hard as he could—and broke it. He was so angry—it was a hell of a sight."

"When I was in Congress, I thought all the power was down at the other end of Pennsylvania Avenue, at the White House," Kennedy told Deakin. "Now I'm down here, and am amazed at all the power those bastards have!"

The President was always vague when asked what kind of world he hoped to help create. But now he knew one certain fact about it— there must be no nuclear proliferation. "He felt stronger about that question than almost anything else," said his brother Bob.

Khrushchev seemed to share that concern. In the thirteen years of nuclear testing, there had been 336 nuclear explosions in the atmosphere. "But what the hell do we want with tests," Nikita Khrushchev told *New York Times* correspondent Cyrus Sulzberger. "You cannot put a bomb in soup. Or make an overcoat out of it."

One rainy day, the President asked his science adviser, Jerome Weisner of the Massachusetts Institute of Technology, whether the radioactivity was right there—in the rain. Yes, he was told, it was. He stood silent for several minutes, looking out the window in the White House at the rain.

He told the graduating students at American University in June

1963 that the "idle stockpiles" of nuclear weapons were not the true means of assuring peace, and that money spent on weapons should be used to fight poverty, disease, and illiteracy. "We all inhabit this small planet—we all breathe the same air, we all cherish our children's future, we are all mortal."

Khrushchev saw that speech as a signal, and the Soviet press reprinted it in full. A month later, the Nuclear Test Ban Treaty was signed. President Kennedy considered it a major accomplishment, the single issue closest to his mind and heart.

"It may sound corny," he said, "but I am not thinking so much of our world, but the world that Caroline will live in." It haunted him. "What kind of world am *I* going to leave behind?"

For most of his life, politics had been a game; now he understood the enormous power he held in his hands to change the world.

With the weight of the presidency, his exposure to fatherhood came in brief snatches. The First Lady had designed a play area for her two children near the President's office. If his son was out there playing, the President sometimes went out to hug him. John, not quite three, an uninhibited little boy with a chipped front tooth, loved the ceremonial parades for visiting dignitaries. Whenever he heard music, he would ask, "Where's the parade?" He liked to try on the hats of arriving generals, and was proud of his salute. He would also generously hand out chewing gum and greet all guests, "What's your name? My name is John Fitzgerald Kennedy Jr." When the president of the Socialist Federal Republic of Yugoslavia, Josip Broz Tito, walked out of the green helicopter onto the fifty-foot red carpet of the White House lawn, he was greeted by the shrill young voice of John Kennedy Jr., yelling from the White House balcony, "We want Kennedy . . . we want Kennedy . . ."

Of his memories of his father, the son later said, "I have a few. He had this desk in the Oval Office . . . which belonged to a sea captain . . . it was made from an American frigate. And I just remember the inside that you could climb around in, and there were kind of cavernous spaces in it . . . he used to give us chewing gum because my mother didn't like us to chew gum, so we used to go over to the Oval Office at night and he'd feed us gum under the desk."

With all the heavy emphasis on discipline and manners in his own childhood, with a largely absent father of his own, President Kennedy tried to give his son a freedom and a loving atmosphere that he himself had not had.

His daughter Caroline was only five when he invited her to witness the honorary citizenship ceremony for eighty-nine-year-old Winston Churchill. Her governess quietly suggested she watch her father.

Caroline quickly replied, "My father has told me to always watch the other people, because they're the important ones. My father says I can see him anytime, so today I think I'll watch Mr. Churchill." At the state dinner for the Grand Duchess of Luxembourg, Caroline watched the 170 guests from the stairs, wearing a robe over her pink pajamas, until she was finally whisked away by her nurse. Another time, when Caroline was asked by a guest where her father was, she answered that he was "upstairs with his socks and shoes off doing nothing."

Caroline had taken the White House in stride. "All she knows is that she lived in a red house and now she lives in a white house. The White House is bigger, that's all," Mrs. Kennedy said. But Caroline had grown more sophisticated than that. Shortly after she moved into the White House, she stepped out with her father, looked around, and inquired, "Where are the photographers?" And, another time, during her father's press conference, she made an unexpected appearance wearing high heels.

Jacqueline was a loving and attentive mother. She'd say, "If you bungle raising your children I don't think whatever else you do well matters very much." Knowing the Kennedy passion for sports, she taught her daughter how to water-ski at Hyannis. When Caroline whimpered before her first lesson, her mother raced to her and hugged her. "Darling, don't be afraid. You don't want others to think you're not brave, do you? . . . It will make Daddy so proud when he comes home this weekend."

Kennedy nurse Evelyn Jones remembered earlier, more difficult times. "They were conversing at the table one night—Mr. and Mrs. Jack, and Mr. and Mrs. Kennedy Sr. They'd gone there for dinner. They were discussing Caroline's education . . . and Mrs. [Rose] Kennedy was making suggestions . . . and suddenly Mrs. J. said, 'The trouble is, you want Caroline to be like you, and I want her to be like me!' "

When Jacqueline was in premature labor with her third child, and being rushed to the hospital, the President called his friend Larry

Newman, and asked him "to go over there and just sit in the lobby of the hospital until I get there."

"There's a small lobby-reception in this place," said Newman, "and I was sitting right where I could see him. He came in alone—this was the closest I ever saw him to a very highly emotional condition. He came over, and made a move as if he were going to put his arm on me. . . . Instead, he just put his arm out and shook hands with me, and said how grateful he was to have a close friend there in time of need. I was very close to tears," said Newman, "and I don't cry very easy— but he wanted this son so badly."

His wife later wrote in her notes, "He never wanted them all crowded together like Bobby and Ethel—so many small children in the middle were miserable and their parents harassed—but he always wanted a baby coming along when its predecessor was coming up— That was why he was so glad when he learned I was having Patrick."

This baby, born five weeks early by a cesarean, was a boy, four pounds ten ounces. They named him Patrick Bouvier.

"The first thing we've got to do is call Ted," Robert Kennedy said. Senator Edward Kennedy was presiding over the Senate when members broke into cheers at word that Joseph P. Kennedy's twenty-second grandchild had arrived.

Right from the beginning, the baby had breathing trouble. He was in a pressurized incubator when a Catholic chaplain baptized him. The baby was transferred to Children's Hospital Medical Center in Boston for special treatment, while Jacqueline remained at Otis Air Force Base hospital in Falmouth, recuperating from the surgery.

The President commuted by helicopter.

Wearing a white surgical gown and cap in the Boston hospital, he peered through a small porthole in the high-pressure submarine-like chamber to watch his boy fight for breath.

"I was with him in the hospital when he was holding Patrick's hand," said Evelyn Lincoln, his secretary, "and the nurse said, 'He's gone!' And tears came into his eyes. I had never seen tears in his eyes before." Neither had Dave Powers. "He just cried and cried and cried," said Powers.

Patrick Bouvier Kennedy had lived less than thirty-nine hours.

Kennedy was gone when Bobby arrived. "Bobby had his beads," said Powers, "and he said, 'Why don't we say a prayer? For the baby.' And so we did. He didn't talk too much. He just wondered how he was going to talk to his brother when he saw him."

They were not brothers who touched much, but Bob put his arm around him. At the funeral Mass, the weeping President grabbed the casket in such a disoriented way that Bob remembered Cardinal Cushing had to restrain him, saying, "Come on, Jack, let's go. God is good."

Jacqueline later wrote to Laura Bergquist, "Most men don't care about children as much as women do—but he does—and he felt this baby's loss as much as I did . . . basically I am a good Catholic—superficially I am not—and I have my little doubts or periods of laxity . . . and so I am not like Mrs. K or Ethel—who would run to church and thank God that their baby was in heaven . . . . I won't quite understand for a while why this baby so longed for was taken—to punish my sins is alright—but that is so unfair to Jack . . ."

Close friends said that their marriage improved after their shared pain. "You're not born full-blown, an ideal marvelous mate to a woman," Bill Walton observed. "You learn it very slowly, I would think, most people do. Maybe he was slower than most. But, in the end, I think they achieved a very terrific marriage."

———

ON THE DAY in August that Patrick was buried, the FBI was interviewing a young American named Lee Harvey Oswald. He had been arrested in New Orleans for handing out pro-Castro literature and getting into a fight with an anti-Castro group.

JFK posed a question to Lem Billings and Charles Bartlett: if he got killed, how did they think Lyndon Johnson would do as President?

"He talked about how Teddy Roosevelt was so far away, and almost fell down the mountainside because he was in such a hurry to take over the job," said Bartlett. Kennedy felt that Lyndon would also be running "like a son of a bitch" to get to the Oval Office. "I suppose I'd be the same way, if I was in the number two spot," Kennedy said. "If the President gets knocked off, he's got to have an immediate successor; it's the way our system works."

But JFK then also asked Bartlett, "Who do you think will be the nominee in '68 . . . Bobby?"

He afterward discussed with Bartlett what he might do after he left the presidency. He thought he'd like to be Ambassador to Italy "because he'd be out of the country . . . and the presidency wouldn't be in his way."

———

TWO WEEKS LATER, Martin Luther King, Jr., scheduled a march on Washington, to assemble in front of the Lincoln Memorial to support passage of legislation ending discrimination.

The President earlier had tried to persuade King to cancel or postpone his proposed demonstration. King refused. When the President realized he could not stop the march, he asked Bob to intervene. Bob channeled considerable funds into the six civil rights organizations sponsoring the march, so much so that Malcolm X announced that "The march has been taken over by the government."

The nation was anxious, even fearful. Polls of white America felt Kennedy was pushing too fast on civil rights. A California poll even showed outspoken liberals privately against integration in their neighborhoods and schools. King told Harris Wofford that he felt President Kennedy had the understanding of the civil rights problem, and the political skill to help solve it legally, "but the moral passion is missing."

The passion *was* there. The President confided to Wofford, "This issue could cost me the election, but we're not turning back."

Neither was Martin Luther King. The march was massive—some 250,000 people from all over the country, men and women of all ages and colors who came in peace. Young people eased their bare feet in the lily-pad pools, strangers happily talked to each other. They joined hands, shouted words of encouragement. Some played guitars, and the music gave the atmosphere a mood of a picnic combined with a revival meeting. There were no disturbances. It was a beautiful day.

Concerned that his presence at the demonstration might lose votes for the civil rights bill in Congress, the President refused an invitation to speak at the rally. Nor would he pose for pictures with King. He felt such photographs might make him look bad if, after the rally, there was trouble in the streets.

Ted was the only Kennedy scheduled to speak at the march, and he had a speech prepared, but the President vetoed it.

There could have been no other speech to match that of Martin Luther King. His message had the rhythm of a battle hymn and it caught the crowd and moved them memorably.

"I have a dream that one day on the red hills of Georgia, sons of former slaves and sons of former slave owners will be able to sit down together at a table of brotherhood. I have a dream . . ."

But there was one voice in the crowd from a black man: "Fuck that dream, Martin. Now, goddammit, *now!*"

ONE OF KING'S most bitter enemies was FBI Director J. Edgar Hoover. An assistant attorney general reported to Robert Kennedy on how Hoover had cursed King. "Oh sure," Kennedy replied, "that's the way it's been for a while." Another Justice aide told the Attorney General how Hoover had spent an hour discussing wiretapped bedroom conversations of King in sexual intimacy with various women, some of them white. The aide, James Symington, asked, "Bobby, what is this all about?" Bobby had no comment. "He would not say a word."

What few knew then was that the Attorney General had approved Hoover's wiretap of King, after three months of delay. He had done this, friends insisted, because he felt the tapes would prove King innocent of all charges of Communist connections. Wiretap permission technically was for thirty days, but "Hoover quietly ignored the condition Kennedy had set, and the King wiretapping went on and on." It was unclear whether or not RFK knew this and let it slide.

To get permission to wiretap King, Hoover had to pressure the Kennedys. As leverage, he used his file of revelations of the President's continuing extracurricular sexual life—with the implicit threat of exposure. And what was surely certain was that no matter how passionate Attorney General Robert Kennedy felt about the civil rights issue, he was even more passionate about protecting his brother.

AFTER THE DEATH of her child, Jacqueline needed space and change and went on a "strictly private" holiday in Greece.

"I don't think the marriage improved toward the end," said Evelyn Lincoln, "even if that's what she wanted people to think."

Aristotle Onassis sailed his 325-foot pleasure palace, the *Christina*, to Jackie's whitewashed villa and put the yacht at her disposal. "While the guests slept that night, the *Christina*, loaded with fresh peaches, black figs and pomegranates, and decorated from stem to stern with red roses and gladioli, weighed anchor and set sail through the Aegean for a visit to Istanbul."

The papers were full of stories about the "brilliantly-lit luxury yacht . . . gay with guests, good food and drinks . . . lavish shipboard dinners . . . dancing music . . . a crew of 60, two coiffeurs and a dance band." Questions were raised in Congress as to the propriety of the President's wife being the guest of a foreigner who had been under indictment. Toward the end of the cruise, Onassis presented Mrs. Kennedy with a diamond-and-ruby necklace.

She called that trip through the Greek islands "the dream of my life."

At one point the President sent his wife a teasing telegram: "What I'd like to see in the headlines is a little more about Caroline and a little less about Onassis."

The President had no cause to complain. While his wife was away, he toured some western states, urging new commitments to the nation's environment and natural resources. He spent a night at the home of Bing Crosby in Palm Desert. The public thought they were sharing the house. But Crosby told playwright Max Wilk that he had moved out and the President had moved in. Presumably the President was not alone. It was Peter Lawford's job to provide the female entertainment.

Physically the President was improving, his pain lessening, according to his secretary. "He wore that rubber athletic supporter for his back very little. . . . I used to go down to Coleman's and buy it. . . . A lot of people thought he had a steel brace . . . but the President never had a kind of heavy thing on his back."

However, he remained cautious. "Every spring before he went to throw out the baseball for the opening of the baseball season, he would come in and have me check his right shoulder," said Dr. Travell. An aide once walked briskly past the Rose Garden, suddenly noticed the President of the United States there alone. He was secretly practicing throws with a softball. "Obviously, he felt sheepish," she remembers. "He ducked his head and said, 'Hello.' "

Dr. Travell had said of him then: "His health improved steadily through the Presidency and I believe that . . . he was in the best health since the time that I first knew him in 1955."

———

BACK IN 1951, Jack and Robert Kennedy had visited Vietnam and were greatly impressed by the tough French paratroopers overseeing their colonial Indochinese empire. In India, Jahawarlal Nehru told both brothers that the French war in Vietnam was doomed and the French were "pouring money and arms down a bottomless hole." Robert Kennedy later noted that "my brother was determined early that we would never get in that position."

"I am frankly of the belief that no amount of American military assistance in Indochina can conquer an enemy which is everywhere and at the same time nowhere," Jack Kennedy later told Congress.

The defeated French left Vietnam in 1954, and Vietnam became two countries, a Communist north and an independent South. Congressman Kennedy, who had supported this independence, had said then in Congress, "This is our offspring . . . we cannot abandon it."

President Eisenhower had sent in the initial 685 American military advisers to South Vietnam to support the crumbling government, with a pledge to defend its integrity. He told Kennedy that no more troops needed to be sent in because most Vietnamese were pro-American. The Prime Minister, Ngo Dinh Diem, was a devout Catholic and an unpopular dictator with access to a force of more than 250,000 against an estimated 12,000 Viet Cong guerrillas. It seemed like a war the United States wouldn't have to fight. Even so, the Pentagon wanted to send in 3600 combat troops as military support insurance. Instead, Kennedy dispatched 100 military advisers and 400 Green Berets, and approved National Security Action Memorandum 52, which said that the objective of the United States was "to prevent Communist domination of South Vietnam."

Still, when correspondent Stanley Karnow returned from the Far East and warned the Attorney General of its growing danger, Bob had replied disparagingly, "Vietnam . . . we have thirty Vietnams a day."

———

IN APRIL 1961, General Douglas MacArthur came to lunch with the President. He had been the American hero of two world

wars until he was fired by President Truman for insubordina-
tion.

While waiting for his arrival, the President quoted aloud for Dave
Powers from MacArthur's Distinguished Service Cross Citation: "On
a field where courage was the rule, his courage was a dominant
feature." Then he turned to Powers and said, "Dave, how would you
like to have this said about you?" And before Powers had a chance to
answer, Bobby said, "I would love to have that said about me."

Alexis Johnson of the State Department recalled MacArthur's
hands shaking from palsy, "but his voice was just as strong as it ever
was." What he said was, "Never ever, ever put American soldiers on
the mainland of Asia."

"That made a hell of an impression on the President," said General
Maxwell Taylor, "so that whenever he'd get this military advice from
the Joint Chiefs or anyone else, he'd say, 'Well, now, you gentlemen,
you go back and convince General MacArthur, and then I'll be
convinced.' "

Kennedy had a lifelong hatred of Communism, bred into him by
his father, but also a personal knowledge of the human cost of war.
He sent Vice President Johnson to survey the scene, and Johnson
urged continued American strength and determination.

The President conferred with Secretary of Defense Robert
McNamara and General Taylor, who also had toured South Vietnam.
They recommended that the President commit 8000 combat troops
to Vietnam. The President refused. He told Schlesinger, "The troops
will march in; the bands will play; the crowds will cheer; and in four
days everyone will have forgotten. Then we will be told that we have
to send in more troops. It's like taking a drink. The effect wears off
and you have to take another."

Remembering his earlier visit to Vietnam, Kennedy said, "If we
converted it into a white man's war, we would lose just as the French
had lost a decade earlier."

But as the Vietnam War escalated, Kennedy told John Kenneth
Galbraith that there were limits to the number of defeats he could
justify in a twelve-month period. "I've had the Bay of Pigs, and
pulling out of Laos, and I can't accept a third." The U.S. was pledged
to maintain the government of South Vietnam. Any defeat would be
Kennedy's defeat. Besides proving himself to the nation he led, he

wanted Khrushchev to get the message about how far he was willing to go to keep Communism from approaching his shores.

The first combat troops sent in were two helicopter companies. Kennedy also "covertly" authorized American pilots to train Vietnamese to fly bombing missions. In doing this, he committed the power and prestige of the United States.

Undersecretary of State George Ball remembers being horrified, saying, "If we put ground troops in there, we'll have 300,000 in five years and you wouldn't even be able to find them."

"Kennedy was not really a conceptual thinker," said Ball. "He didn't have much patience with it. He would seize something and try to master it, but he would quickly spot the liabilities in something because he was a politician. Kennedy had a good sense of his own lack of experience, and said, 'All I've ever done is to be a politician.' "

There was little concern for Vietnam then, by either the public or the press. It was the time of the Berlin crisis and the Bay of Pigs. Robert Kennedy was busy with civil rights and other problems, and had little to do with Vietnam. In February 1962, Bob stopped over at Saigon, during a trip to the Far East, and declared, "We are going to win in Vietnam. We will remain here until we do win."

General Maxwell Taylor was one of Bob's heroes; Bob had named one of his sons after him. Taylor had worked with Bob on the Cuban counterinsurgency. Bob now adopted Taylor's judgment on Vietnam. Taylor felt we were winning the war in Vietnam and the Viet Cong would be wiped out in a few years. He was also highly impatient with President Diem's lack of progress.

Bob Kennedy told a British reporter, "I think the United States will do what is necessary to help a country that is trying to repel aggression with its own blood, tears and sweat." He also felt we had to follow through, not just to impress our Communist foes but so our allies could trust our word on Berlin.

Meanwhile, the President discussed plans for getting U.S. troops home. But critics loudly urged that such a withdrawal would give the wrong signal, perhaps result in the collapse of both South Vietnam and Southeast Asia. A national poll result of two-to-one showed the American public willing to send American troops "on a large scale" to South Vietnam if the Communist threat worsened.

It worsened. There was increased evidence of the growing corruption and unpopularity of the Diem government in South Vietnam. The Buddhists rose against the Catholic-dominated Diem regime, and some monks publicly burned themselves to death in protest. The reinforced Viet Cong were now shooting down American helicopters. Some Senators urged complete withdrawal of American troops.

In March 1963 the President told a press conference, "I don't agree with those who say we should withdraw."

Privately, he told friends such as Senator Mike Mansfield that he still believed in getting out of Vietnam, but he couldn't do it until after he was reelected, otherwise the Republicans would use it as a major campaign issue. And he confided to his friend Bartlett, "We've got to face the fact that the odds are about a hundred to one that we're going to get our asses thrown out of Vietnam."

Our allies were uneasy about being bogged down in Vietnam. The argument made was that once you get on a tiger's back, you can't pick the place to get off. The confusion of U.S. Vietnam policy was evident at a meeting in the Cabinet Room in September 1963.

Said the General: "The Diem government is strong, popular, and the war is going fine."

Said the State Department officer: "The Diem government is on the verge of collapse."

"Are you sure," asked President Kennedy, "that you two gentlemen are talking about the same government?"

Ted Sorensen recalled the conversation when Canada's Prime Minister Lester Pearson came to visit. "Kennedy asked Pearson's advice on Vietnam. 'Get out,' said Pearson. Kennedy stared at him and said softly, 'That's a stupid answer. The question is, *How* do we get out?' "

———

IT BECAME INCREASINGLY clear that President Ngo Dinh Diem was both inept and corrupt. The Pentagon still supported him, but Ambassador Henry Cabot Lodge, in Saigon, urged a military coup. Some anti-Diem generals were advised at the end of August 1963 that if they overthrew Diem, the Americans would recognize the new government. The generals not only replaced Diem, but they killed him. The CIA was later held responsible.

Killing was not part of the original Kennedy plan.

"I think Jack thought Bobby screwed up on Diem's assassination," said Smathers, ". . . that he knew something before Jack knew anything about it. But I think that had Jack known anything about it, that wouldn't have happened. I know Jack was very upset."

Jack had complained to Bartlett, "My God, my government's coming apart!"

But Robert Kennedy later insisted that he had been against the coup, feeling that if we replaced leaders, no matter how corrupt, it would make other countries nervous.

Meanwhile, the Viet Cong guerrillas were winning everywhere. The American press was demanding action and the Republicans were demanding victory. The battlefield situation at the time seemed critical, with South Vietnam's survival in the balance. At that time, we were still sending in "advisers," to reach a total of 16,500.

The President was pushing for a political solution. He repeatedly told Roger Hilsman, then Assistant Secretary of State for Far Eastern Affairs, that he was determined not to let Vietnam become an American war. And he confided to Richard Nixon, "The American people do not want to use troops to remove a Communist regime only 90 miles away; how can I ask them to use troops to remove one 9000 miles away?" And to Larry Newman he revealed that de Gaulle had warned him that Indochina was a quagmire and he should never get involved in it. "This war in Vietnam—it haunts me day and night," Kennedy told Newman. "It's never off my mind . . . and the first thing to do, when I'm re-elected, I'm going to get the hell out of there."

Robert McNamara insisted that President Kennedy, in an October Cabinet meeting, had authorized the withdrawal of a thousand troops by December 1963, "including the helicopter companies." McNamara added that he and Kennedy planned to withdraw all U.S. advisers by the end of 1965, "even if the South Vietnamese were going to be defeated."

Of course, no one knows if he could have maintained this resolve. "I think he would not have wanted to be the first American President to lose a war," said political adviser Jim Rowe. "So I think he'd have been sucked in."

The odds are good, though, that Bobby's later disaffection with the war would have had great impact on his decision. And it would have been easier for President Kennedy to pull out our troops without much public question because he himself was a war hero. And, as far as America was concerned, we were not yet in a war.

————

HIS FATHER WOULD have agreed. His father always believed in staying out of wars.

"The first thing he ever did when we reached the Cape would be to go over to his father," said Dave Powers. "And he'd always touch his hand and kiss his forehead. . . . The father would be waiting for him to come in—hear the plane landing—it was something for him to look forward to."

The President was no longer fidgety when the senior Kennedy was around. Now he showed the same kind of tender concern toward his father as he did toward his children. He would sit with Joe for long stretches, trying to understand his father's gibberish.

Dave Powers recalled the President's visit to his father in October 1963. It would be the last time Joe ever saw his son. They spent the entire day together. The father was still speechless, but as Powers put it, "Oh, that look . . ."

"You know, leaving him that day—maybe I'm putting something into it, knowing it was the last visit," said Powers, "but he left him— 'Goodbye, Dad'—and then he came back again, and held his hand on his shoulders. He had tears in his eyes, that day. The only two times I ever saw him cry in his life were over Patrick, and over his Dad." In the plane, he told Powers, "Look at him, Dave, and he made it all possible."

That was the sensitive side of Kennedy talking. And yet the voice of his harder mind once told his good friend John Sharon that if he had his life to live over again, he would have a different father, a different wife, and a different religion.

————

PRESIDENT KENNEDY HAD thought often of his mortality.

He talked about death with Larry Newman. "I have no fear of death. . . . You know, during my experience out in the Pacific, I really wasn't afraid to die. And I wasn't afraid of dying when I was in the hospital in New York. In fact, I almost welcomed it. Because I didn't want to live the rest of my life the way I was living. The pain was so bad.

I could stand the pain, but couldn't bear the thought of living the rest of my life with that kind of pain. . . . Maybe I'm not that religious. I feel that death is the end of a hell of a lot of things. But I've got too many things to do. And I just hope the Lord gives me the time to get all these things done!"

Newman recalled a Mass they were attending one Sunday morning along with some reporters sitting just behind him. Just as the Mass was starting, Kennedy turned to the reporters and said, "Did you ever stop and think, if anyone tried to take a shot at me, they'd get one of you guys first?"

Kennedy had a great sense of the theatrical. "I think it was Labor Day weekend," recalled reporter Frank Cormier. "Kennedy was up in Newport staying at Hammersmith Farm, the Auchincloss farm, with Jackie. The AP/UPI used to share the rental of a boat every afternoon wherever he was. . . .

"We followed him, this particular day. He had Red Fay with him, Secretary of the Navy, Jackie, and Countess Crespi. . . .

"The *Honey Fitz* docked at the end of this long pier that came out from Hammersmith Farm. There was a Navy photographer, assigned to the White House, right at the edge of the dock, on shore. So Merriman Smith and I were watching through binoculars, to see what transpires. Kennedy walks down this long pier—and suddenly clutches his chest, and falls over, flat on the ground, across the pier—blocking sideways, side to side. Then, Countess Crespi and her fat son came out, and just stepped over him, and went on walking to shore. Meanwhile, the Navy movie man kept grinding away. Then, Jackie came out—and very daintily stepped over him. Then, Ray Fay comes along—and he pretends to stumble over Kennedy. As he does so, falls on top of Kennedy, and all this red liquid gushes out of Kennedy's mouth and all over his T-shirt, or sport shirt.

"So I wrote a little piece saying that the Kennedys had starred in their own home movies. . . .

"Kennedy was absolutely furious. He liked to keep what he considered his private life separate from his official life. . . .

"I was in the doghouse. And Kennedy, who always addressed all reporters by their first name, never again addressed me by my first name. If he had occasion to say anything, it was always 'Mr. Cormier.' . . .

"I was in the Grand Teton Lodge a couple of months later, having dinner with Pierre and Kenny O'Donnell. Kennedy obviously had spoken to Pierre about it, for Pierre said to me, 'Cormier, you're nothing but a Peeping Tom reporter. It was in terrible taste to write about that thing up in Newport.' I said, 'Well, if it was in terrible taste for me to write about it, it was in terrible taste for the President to do it.' And Kenny O'Donnell says, 'I agree with you.' . . .

"I found out later . . . Kennedy was a James Bond fan. And they were making their own James Bond movie that weekend . . . he enacted his own assassination a couple of months before it happened."

Years before, walking along the beach at Hyannis with Ed Plaut, Jack had suddenly brought up the question of assassination and said, "The only way you can shoot a President is from a high window."

———

KENNEDY'S AIR FORCE aide, General Godfrey McHugh, once explained to him the need and cost of presidential safety on any trip. It was true, of course, for all Presidents. After a trip to Caracas, McHugh told him, "Mr. President, do you know that if ever the newspapers get hold of a story that we spend millions of dollars anytime you go anyplace—and particularly on a flight like this—it might be detrimental? We're doing everything we can not to talk about it. But it's bound to get out."

"I told you I didn't want to have a private escort going to South America," said the President.

"I know you said that, sir," McHugh replied, "but do you recall that the Joint Chiefs sent us a paper saying they won't be responsible for your safety? And I showed it to you, and you said, 'That's their business; let them do what they need to do.' "

McHugh explained to the President: "You have sixteen airplanes flying over your head—they keep renewing each other. We have an aircraft-carrier on three different positions. You have a squad of helicopters on the aircraft carrier, to rescue you . . . . They'll fly in, surround you, protect you and pick you up . . . . And, as you know, sir, we flew in nearly a hundred men from Communications, ahead of time. We flew in nearly 200 men for different weather and maintenance. We have a squadron of military people to defend them, in case they were attacked—or you were. It involves thousands and thousands of men, for a trip going from Washington to Caracas. We flew your car ahead; and that costs a lot of money. Because the Secret Service said they can only defend you in that car."

The Texas trip being planned required less security.

Representative Hale Boggs told the President that politics in Texas was so disturbed—at that time there was a terrible factional fight— "that it looked to me like he was apt to get into trouble. I didn't mean that somebody was going to try to shoot him. . . . I meant politically. And I remember he kind of laughed about that and said, 'Well, that makes it more interesting.' "

Bob Kennedy told his staff member Ramsey Clark that he thought the Texas trip was unnecessary, a useless strain on busy people.

———

"GOD, I HATE to go out to Texas," Jack told Senator George Smathers. "And I'm gonna make Jackie go with me. She hasn't been making trips. . . . But I hate to go. . . . I just hate to go," he said. "I have a terrible feeling about going. I wish I could get out of it."

"He really said that," recalled Smathers. "He kept saying, 'I wish this was a week from today; wish we had this thing over with.' "

Jacqueline Kennedy remembered the warnings by Bobby, Senator Fulbright, and Adlai Stevenson, urging the President not to go to Dallas. "I know he got really upset. Vice President Johnson came to our hotel room in Easton that night, before we went to Fort Worth. . . . They had a long talk. I know that was the point of the trip, to heal everything, to get everybody to ride in the same car or something. It was a long talk."

"I really don't think he thought, that day, he was going to die," said Newman. "You know, they talked for three weeks about him being shot in Texas! And they tried to talk him out of it, right to the last minute. But he just said, 'If this is the way life is, if this is the way it's going to end, this is the way it's going to end.'

"Connally was the pusher," Newman said. "Connally knew that Kennedy was coming in November; and Lyndon didn't know until two weeks before . . . but Kennedy and Johnson had talked about needing to win Texas in order to win the election."

"The day we went to Dallas, *Newsweek* had on its cover: 'Kennedy and His Critics.' . . . I think his popularity poll stood at forty-three percent—not good. He was in trouble . . . there were a lot of problems," said Marianne Means.

———

THE ATTORNEY GENERAL'S office staff had a party in November for his thirty-eighth birthday. It was a miserable party. Some forty employees formed a circle around Bob Kennedy as he stood beside his desk. They handed him his gifts, which included an Anti-Monopoly set, and he examined each one slowly, and said in a flat voice, "That's funny."

It was not funny. Bob was never a man who could talk trivia, and now he seemed strangely depressed. Some of the staff people cracked a joke, and some of the girls giggled, but basically it was a joyless party at which nobody came closer than six feet to the lonely guest of honor.

He stood in that circle for half an hour, everybody embarrassed, nobody knowing what to say. The only activity in the room came when the photographer arrived to record the event.

That was November 20, 1963.

The final date set for the Texas trip was November 22, with a motorcade planned through downtown to the Trade Mart. Local newspapers printed a map of the motorcade route. The President planned to spend four days in the city.

The President's secretary, Evelyn Lincoln, recalled that he and his wife had an earlier argument and he had to persuade her to forgive him and come to Dallas with him. She finally agreed, and Lincoln saw them walking together arm in arm. "You can't tell people these things," said Lincoln, "because they don't believe you."

The presidential plane landed at Love Field in Dallas at 11:39 in the morning. Ten minutes later, the motorcade left the airport for the forty-five-minute ride to downtown Dallas. President and Mrs. Kennedy sat in the backseat of an open limousine. Usually the Secret Service had him ride in a bubble-top.

"There's no way to get around it. They put me in a bubble-top thing, and I can't get to the people," Kennedy had told Larry

Newman. "I want them to feel that I am the President of the United States. . . . I belong to them and they belong to me."

———

THERE WAS A certain coolness in the crowds. There had been hostile ads against the President in the newspapers. The local Congressman, Representative Henry Gonzales, joked, "I haven't got my steel vest yet."

General McHugh remembered, "They'd asked me, for the first time, to please not ride in the President's car, because they want to give him full exposure. These are the words they used. Ken O'Donnell and the Secret Service said, 'The politicians here feel it's most important for the President to be given full exposure, to be seen coming and going. We already have Governor Connally in the car, and his wife— it'll be crowded. . . .' The President told me, 'Always be in the car,' because he gave me orders constantly. . . . I'd sit in the front, next to the driver, and would take notes. . . . So I was a little annoyed at that decision . . . but I went in the car behind.' "

Kennedy sat back and chatted with the Connallys.

"Well," said Mrs. Connally, "you can't say Dallas isn't friendly today."

Kenny O'Donnell was riding in a car right behind the President when the assassin's bullets struck. "I saw the third shot hit. It was such a perfect shot—I remember I blessed myself."

"We were in this car and heard these bullets—we heard three shots as clearly as you talk to me. . . . No questions about how many times they fired on him," said McHugh. "As we rode, bullets came over our head, one after the other, and I thought, 'My God, they're giving him a 21-gun salute!' Then he suddenly knew. 'Oh, my God, no. That's rifle bullets!' And we looked up, and saw the President, slumped."

Jean Hill was near the car, waving at the President, when she saw him grab his throat, and suddenly the blood and brains seemed to make a red cloud around his head, and the blood splattered her boyfriend, a motorcycle cop. "It was just horrible," she said. "I just saw this look in his eyes and then his head was gone."

The President's Secret Service driver raced toward Parkland Memorial Hospital, several miles away. The other agent urged him to slow down. "If he's not dead, we don't want to kill him now." In the backseat, an agent stood and pounded his fists against the back of the car in anger and frustration.

The President already was dying.

One bullet hit him at the base of the neck, a little to the right of the spine. Another hit Governor Connally in the back. He and his wife were seated in the front of the Kennedys. A third bullet entered the right rear of the President's head, splattering the brain tissue. The President fell onto his wife.

Dr. M. T. "Pepper" Jenkins, who had been at the President's side in Parkland Memorial Hospital's trauma room, remembered, "Jacqueline Kennedy was circling the room, walking behind my back. The Secret Service could not keep her out of the room. She looked shell-shocked. As she circled and circled, I noticed that her hands were cupped in front of her, as if she were cradling something. As she passed by, she nudged me with an elbow and handed me what she had been nursing in her hands—a large chunk of her husband's brain tissues. I quickly handed it to a nurse."

On the table in the hospital emergency room, the President drew one sharp breath and then his body lay still.

Some ten doctors still tried to revive him. They worked on him for fifteen minutes before pronouncing him dead.

Reporters clustered in a nurses' classroom to wait for official word. At 1:33 P.M., assistant White House press secretary Malcolm Kilduff pushed into the room, a piece of notepaper in one hand and an unlit cigarette in the other. Red-eyed and tremulous, he read: "President John F. Kennedy died at approximately 1 P.M., central standard time, today here in Dallas. He died of a gunshot wound in the brain."

"Oh, God!" someone choked. And then reporters dashed for the phones.

White House correspondent Tom Wicker of *The New York Times* recalled dictating the story over the phone and "I burst into tears. I had not expected to do that. I had not realized that I felt that way. I had not been a particularly deep, close friend or admirer. . . . It was just the absolute horrendous fact that this young leader had been cut down that way. . . . It was just an overpowering moment."

The Reverend Oscar L. Huber, who administered the Last Rites, later defended the "validity" of the sacraments he gave the President after his face had been covered with a white sheet: "It is my opinion that his soul had not left his body."

Somebody later noted that the President's great-grandfather had been killed by cholera when he was thirty-five on November 23, 105 years earlier.

———

THE ATTORNEY GENERAL was at a working lunch beside his back-yard pool at his house in Hickory Hill. Robert Morgenthau, the U.S. Attorney for southern New York, was there to discuss the organized crime conference that was to continue in the afternoon. Robert Kennedy took a swim, then joined the others and had a tuna sandwich.

Morgenthau noticed a workman, holding a transistor radio, running toward the pool, shouting. Nobody could hear him. Then the phone rang and Ethel answered it.

It was J. Edgar Hoover. Very abruptly he told the Attorney General, "I have news for you. The President's been shot." He would call later, he said, when there was further information.

For Hoover, it must have been a cold moment of triumph. Kennedy was a President he did not enjoy. He would not miss him. The next day, Hoover would be seen at Pimlico Race Track.

Morgenthau saw Robert Kennedy turn away and clap his hand to his mouth with a look of shock and horror. Ethel rushed to his side, and he finally managed to blurt out, "Jack's been shot. It may be fatal." Ethel put her arms around him and they went into the house.

In Dallas, all was massive confusion. Robert finally managed to contact a Secret Service man in the hospital in Dallas and they said the President was not conscious and it was critical. "I asked if they had gotten a priest and they said they had."

The Secret Service man soon called back with the news. "The President's dead."

Forty minutes later, Hoover called again, talking coldly of "critical wounds." Kennedy told author William Manchester that Hoover sounded "not quite as excited as if he was reporting the fact that he had found a Communist on the faculty of Howard University."

The Attorney General replied sharply, "You may be interested to know that my brother is dead."

For Robert Kennedy, the loss of this brother was the loss of himself.

All his life, his brother was his hero, his model, the one person in the world he wanted most to please. He had sacrificed all his personal plans and ambitions to serve him, help him. They had reached a point at which they no longer even needed words to communicate with each other—they seemed to sense what the other was thinking. It was true that Bobby loved Jack more than Jack loved Bobby. But that perhaps was partly because Jack was the king and Bobby was the prince. And now the king was dead, and the prince felt alone and deserted and empty.

A friend said of him later, "Bob would gladly have taken that bullet for his brother."

"There's so much bitterness," Bob later said. "I thought they would get one of us. But Jack, after all he'd been through, never worried about it." His voice was strained and expressionless. "I'd received a letter from someone in Texas last week warning me not to let the President go to Dallas because they would kill him. I sent it to Kenny O'Donnell, but I never thought it would happen. I thought it would be me."

JOHN MCCONE OF the CIA had rushed over to Hickory Hill. Mc-Cone saw Robert Kennedy adjust his PT-109 tie clip when the phone rang. He heard Bobby say, "God, it's so awful. Everything was really beginning to run so well."

Soon after, Robert Kennedy called McGeorge Bundy with a question: did the private papers of the President belong to his relatives? Bundy checked with the State Department. The answer was yes, and Bundy had all the combinations changed on the safes containing the President's private files. Bobby, who had protected his brother from so many scandals when he was alive, continued to protect him in death.

It was the chauffeur in Hyannis, Frank Saunders, who told Rose Kennedy that her son had been shot. She then seemed to hold on to the wall for support, her eyes closed, steadying herself. Then she asked Frank if her son had been killed. When he said no, she retired to her room to watch television. At 4:15 P.M., Admiral George Burkley, President Kennedy's personal physician, his shirt cuffs still blood-stained, called Rose Kennedy to tell her: "I wish to God that there was something I could do. I just wanted you to know that." He passed the phone to Lady Bird Johnson. "We feel like the heart has been cut out of us," she said, sobbing. "Our love and our prayers are with you."

"Even when I heard Jack was shot, I thought, those things happened," said Rose afterward. "I never thought, the first moment, that it was going to be serious. I never think the worst."

Almost nobody ever saw Rose Kennedy cry. She was a stoic who taught all her young children and grandchildren that Kennedys don't cry. Her friend Gloria Guinness said that the first and only time she saw tears in Rose's eyes was when young Jack Kennedy was close to death during surgery. "She recovered immediately, said, 'I am terribly sorry,' dried her tears, changed the conversation."

When Joseph Kennedy's private secretary, Diane Winter D'Alemberta, heard the news from Dallas, "the thing which ultimately brought me to grips with the incomprehensible reality was a hand-clapped cadence and the dear, familiar voice repeating over and over again, 'No-crying-in-this-house! No-crying-in-this-house!' "

Lem Billings did not share the Kennedy stoicism. Nobody cried longer or louder than Lem Billings. He wept inconsolably. He had given the full of his life to Jack Kennedy. He loved this man as he loved nobody else.

Senator Stuart Symington was making a speech in the Senate on the balance of payments. Only eight Senators were present. Press liaison officer William Langham Riedel suddenly rushed out onto the floor. "I looked around . . . and I saw it was Ted Kennedy presiding. He was looking down at the desk, busy with a portfolio filled with correspondence. I ran up to the rostrum and leaned over the desk. 'Senator Kennedy,' I said, 'your brother the President has been shot!'

"He looked stunned. Then he asked me how I knew and I told him."

Symington now had heard it too. "I was staring at Teddy," said Symington. "He sat back suddenly in his chair as if he had been hit by whiplash. With typical Kennedy guts, he very slowly assembled his papers, picked them up, and walked out."

In the lobby, he picked up a telephone just outside the Vice President's office to call the White House.

"His first thought was to get home to his wife and make sure that she was all right," said Milton Gwirtzman. "For some reason his car was not available. So I took him in my car to his house . . . . I remember we had the radio on . . . saying that the President was still alive—which, of course, was not the case . . . . I remember I tried going fast, going through red lights. Ted cautioned me to watch out. We got to his house. His wife wasn't there. She had gone to Elizabeth Arden's salon on Connecticut Avenue." Ted's wife was at her beauty parlor preparing for their fifth anniversary party that night. The caterers had started to arrive with food and drink. "There was a crowd gathering around the White House as we drove in. The police, on seeing who it was, waved us right in the entrance on East Executive Avenue. No one had to tell Ted. Just from the look of the people's faces—the women sobbing."

Ted finally got Bob on the phone. "He's dead," said Bob. "You better call your mother and our sisters." It was strange that he had said "your mother" and "our sisters" in that moment of tragic sorrow.

Rose went walking along the beach, her way of coping with her grief. She had not told her husband.

Eunice was soon with Ted, and they conferred with Bobby. Ted never had heard his brother sound so empty and flat. They divided assignments. Bobby would take care of Jackie; Ted and Eunice would go to Hyannis to be with their mother and break the news to their father. Sargent Shriver would help with the funeral arrangements.

Dr. Travell asked Ted if he wanted a sedative. He refused it. After the call, Ted suddenly thought of Caroline and John-John and ran up to the nursery. Their governess, Luella Hennessey, also had been Ted's governess. He had called her "Lulu," and now he kissed her. "His face was so white and drawn," she said afterward. "He was so shocked he could barely speak. . . . I got the feeling that if he said any more he would break down and cry." He hugged the children without saying anything and left the room.

Then he and Eunice got into a helicopter and left for Hyannis. Arriving at the airport, he found the usual throng of reporters, but this time one of them stepped forward to say, "Senator, we apologize for being here at this time of tragedy." The surprised Senator nodded. "I understand, gentlemen. I understand."

At Hyannis, his mother was telling her niece Ann Gargan, "I've got to keep moving." She told Ted that he should break the news to their father. She did not go with them.

His father was impatient and irritable because he wanted to watch the evening news. Those near him were certain he was aware of the heightened tension in the house. Secret Service agent Ham Brown, assigned to the house, had ripped the wires out of the set.

Ted decided to wait for his father's doctor before breaking the news. When the doctor arrived, he agreed to wait in the hall in case he was needed. Eunice and Ted climbed the stairs to their father's bedroom. Teddy's shoulders sagged when he entered, then, tears streaming from his eyes, he told his father that Jack had been shot and killed. Ted dropped to his knees and buried his face in his hands, nurse Rita Dallas recalled. And Eunice said, "He's dead, Daddy, he's dead."

———

EVERYBODY AFTERWARD REMARKED how steady Jacqueline was the night after the assassination. "It's extraordinary, the way she composed herself . . . and yet you could see that emotionally she was totally torn up," commented General McHugh. "She was as logical, as strong, as I've ever seen a person.

"I looked at her dress—at the soft, soft cashmere thing—mohair," added McHugh, remembering the blood on it. "She realized I was looking, and she said, 'I do not want to remove this. I want them to see what they've done to him.' And she was very bitter . . . but she never cried."

———

JOHNSON CALLED ATTORNEY General Kennedy, still concerned about the possibility of a worldwide plot. LBJ was extremely nervous. Earlier, the Secret Service had locked him up in a room because he kept saying, "They're going to kill us all. . . . They're going to kill us all."

"A lot of people down here think I should be sworn in right away," Johnson told Bobby. "Do you have any objections?" He also wanted to know who could swear him in. RFK called back to say that anybody could. LBJ was already convinced in his own mind that the oath-taking must be held before Air Force One could be airborne for Washington. The new President feared a Soviet attack and wanted to reassure the American people, but the stunned Kennedys apparently interpreted his actions as an impatient desire to seize power.

Judge Sarah Hughes of Dallas, a Johnson friend, was there on the plane back to Washington to give Lyndon Johnson the oath of presidency. She had told Johnson, "We ought to proceed." Johnson said, "No, let's see if Mrs. Kennedy can stand this."

Johnson told O'Donnell to ask her.

O'Donnell told him, "You can't do that! The poor little kid has had enough for one day . . . you just can't do that." Johnson replied that Jackie said she wanted to do it.

"So they went back to her compartment," said *Newsweek* correspondent Charles Roberts, "and she said she'd like to come out. She told O'Donnell, 'At least I owe that much to the country.' We waited five minutes until Mrs. Kennedy came out. She seemed composed, ashen, and quivering—almost as though she were in a trance."

Later she told Theodore White, "Everybody kept saying to me to put a cold towel around my head and wipe the blood off. . . . I saw myself in the mirror, my whole face splattered with blood and hair. I wiped it off with Kleenex. History! I thought, no one really wants me there. Then one second later I thought, why did I wash the blood off? I should have left it there, let them see what they've done. If I'd just had the blood and caked hair when they took the picture. . . . Then later I said to Bobby, 'What's the line between history and drama?' "

ON AIR FORCE One, flying back to Washington with the body, Jacqueline sat dry-eyed while others cried. Beside her were presidential assistants Lawrence O'Brien, Kenneth O'Donnell, and David Powers, men who had devoted their lives to her husband. "It was amazing, all the things she talked about in that seven-hour flight—the things the President had talked to her about—the President's trip to Ireland and how impressed he was with the Irish guard," said Powers. Then she looked at them and said, "What's to become of you all? . . . What are you going to do?"

"We were supposed to be tough pols," O'Brien said later, "but this frail girl turned out to have more strength than any of us."

Jacqueline no longer looked or acted like Limoges china, and her strength helped the whole Kennedy clan.

"I was watching the plane land at Andrews," said Kennedy friend Congressman Hale Boggs, "seeing that beautiful girl, the blood-splattered dress; a moonlit night, and the battered ambulance from Bethesda Naval Hospital. There was a man that I'd seen two days before, vibrant and full of life! That was one of his real qualities. He always gave you the impression of being totally alive, and then to see a casket moved out . . ."

"When we landed at Andrews, Evelyn and I were asked to escort Jackie from the plane after the lowering of the coffin," said her personal secretary, Mary Gallagher. "However, in the next instant, there came from behind us a startling voice: 'Jackie . . .' The voice and the accent were so much like those of the late President, I quivered. Then I suddenly realized that it was his brother, the Attorney General. He had boarded the plane at the other end as it touched ground. Quickly he made his way toward us and Jackie cried out, 'Oh, Bobby . . .' Evelyn and I stepped backward as he took her arm."

Bobby said later he had only one thing in his mind when he was running through the plane from the front door—he was trying to get to Jackie as fast as possible. Johnson later told Jim Bishop that when Bobby was dashing through the President's stateroom, Johnson stuck out his hand to shake Bobby's hand, and Bobby deliberately ignored him. "Knowing how emotionally upset Bobby was at that moment, and how anxious he was to get to Jackie, I doubt that he even saw the outstretched hand or Johnson. If the Pope had tried to stop him to offer condolences, Bobby, a devout Catholic, would have brushed past the pontiff."

"I watched Jackie open the door to that ambulance," said Congressman Hale Boggs. "She opened it herself. The casket went in there. I didn't have to take notes on that. . . . I remember every bit of it so vividly. So very vividly."

Instead of getting in the car behind, Jacqueline climbed up in the front seat with the driver.

When they brought the casket back to the White House, Mrs. Kennedy asked them to open it. Bobby collapsed when he saw his brother.

"The night Jack was killed, I went upstairs in the White House . . . and Bobby was going to bed," said Charles Spalding. . . . "I found a sleeping pill. . . . I closed the door . . . and Bobby just kept saying over and over, 'Why, God, why?' "

———

FAMILY FRIEND JOAN Braden was with Jacqueline when she said, "There'll never be another Jack." And then she added that she now understood so well "why Jack lived every minute of every day of his life, and I'm glad he did."

"I was there the next morning," said Dave Powers. "We had a Mass the first thing in the morning, about 10 o'clock. There was Jackie, Bobby, and the family—some relatives and friends. . . . Now we come out, and I'm standing there. Bobby said, 'Dave, come on with me; maybe we'll be able to help Jackie. I know you can help with John.' So we get on this elevator, the one that takes you from the ground floor up to the mansion. He's just standing there, and he said, 'You and the President had some wonderful times together,' and I said, 'He was the greatest man I ever met—the best friend I ever had.' And Bobby, with tears in his eyes, repeated what he had said several times before: 'He had a wonderful life.' "

Jackie supervised every small detail of the vast state funeral. "I want everything done by the Navy," she said. She sent people to the Library of Congress, which was closed, and they used flashlights to check all the details of Abraham Lincoln's funeral. She duplicated that funeral as much as she could, including a riderless horse with a horse-drawn caisson.

Cardinal Cushing had suggested that John Kennedy be buried in Boston, and the family fully approved. "We're all going to be buried around Daddy in Boston," said Eunice. But Jacqueline was firm: her husband would be buried in Arlington National Cemetery. He no longer belonged to Boston; he belonged to the nation. And she wanted an eternal flame.

Sargent Shriver softly suggested that some people might consider it pretentious. "Let them," she said. Not only that, but she wanted to light the flame herself.

Bobby was there always, to implement everything. Secret Service Chief James Rowley remembered the intensity with which Bobby insisted that his brother's burial plot be exactly where the Attorney General wanted it, looking down over Washington. Bobby had an engineer work all night to design the eternal flame, and Rowley thought, "This fellow has got his eye on history."

White House assistant Joseph Califano was also there at the cemetery with RFK. "In pouring rain, we walked the perimeter of a 3.2-acre site on the rolling hill." Califano was then asked "to tie up that land so that no one can ever take any of it away for any other purpose."

And Cyrus Vance, General Counsel of the Defense Department, added, "And I want to be damn sure we own it."

————

BOBBY'S PRIVATE TORMENT was that he himself bore some responsibility for his brother's death by pushing the assassination attempts against Castro—and that Castro might have, in revenge, engineered the death of the President. Or that his prosecution of the Mafia and corrupt labor leaders like Jimmy Hoffa might somehow have involved them in the murder plot.

Bobby's pain was visible, tangible, almost unbearable. It was easier for him to be angry than sad—anger gave him some opposing emotion to focus on. "The amazing thing was that he was still functional," said John Seigenthaler. Bob wore dark glasses to hide his red-rimmed eyes. He did most of his crying on his walks alone at home.

Bobby was incredulous about Jack Ruby's killing of Oswald: "Do you think the fellow was crazy?" he asked Seigenthaler. "No," Seigenthaler said, "all the reports I get are that he just blew sky-high." Bobby said, "It's terrible."

————

THE BODY LAY in state in the Rotunda of the nation's Capitol. Two hundred and fifty thousand people lined up to see Kennedy's body. The line stretched for three miles, moving slowly past the coffin. The crowd parted when they saw Jacqueline and Bobby coming in. Jacqueline put a letter in the coffin—a letter she had written her husband the night before. There was no copy. She took away a lock of his hair. Robert put his PT-boat tie clip, a silver rosary Ethel had given him, and a cutting of his hair into the coffin. Bob wanted a part of himself to be with his brother's body. They both knelt and silently prayed. And then the coffin was closed.

Governess Maude Shaw had put gloves on John-John for the memorial services at the Rotunda. Robert Kennedy told the boy to take them off: his father would not have approved. When Jacqueline asked about John's gloves, in the limousine, Robert replied that boys didn't wear gloves to a funeral.

At the funeral, John-John made the world cry as he saluted his father's body. He was clutching two small flags in his right hand. He had been given one, in the Speaker's office, to entertain him, and he had asked for the other one "for my daddy."

———

TED, ASSIGNED TO stay with his parents, watched the ceremony on television from Hyannis. His physical absence from that scene remained for him a thing of quiet hurt, about which he occasionally complained to his cousin Joey Gargan. Gargan, two years older than Ted, served almost as an extra brother—absolutely loyal, always available.

Watching the procession from the White House to the Rotunda on TV, father Kennedy remained composed, but the Secret Service man with him broke down and wept.

With her own eye on history, Jacqueline wanted Bobby and Teddy to read some most-remembered selections from Jack's speeches at the gravesite. Teddy and his parents arrived the night before the funeral.

Gwirtzman was at the White House when Ted arrived. "He looked as if he had not slept since Friday. He said, 'Let's go up.' He meant up to the Capitol, where the President's body was lying on the Lincoln catafalque in the Rotunda. No other words were said. As the car neared Capitol Hill, we began to see the enormous line of people waiting in the cold and the dark to pay their respects. The car dropped us off at the new East Front, and we went up to the Rotunda in an elevator. When the guards saw who it was, they quickly let him through the line; and when the people at the catafalque saw who it was, they stood aside. The slow, shuffling line halted for a few minutes, while Ted went right up to the casket, kneeled, and prayed."

Gargan had worried that Ted might collapse in sobbing. His tears were there but so was the Kennedy control. Then they left, and Gargan recalled the utter silence in the eerie night light.

The line behind them kept moving all night long until the early morning, when the casket was readied for its final journey.

When Rose Kennedy came to the White House after the assassination, Sargent Shriver, Eunice's husband, was escorting her. Suddenly, Shriver recalled, "tears streamed down her face. She fell into my arms." This tragedy required more self-control than even Rose was able to muster. But Rose was still concerned about Jackie: "She's so young and now she doesn't have even a home!"

———————

IT WAS BOBBY who decided that he and Ted and Jacqueline would say their final private goodbye at the casket before it was taken by the honor guard. There would be no television, no photographers. One thing John Fitzgerald Kennedy would have smiled at: his youngest brother was wearing the formal pants Jack had worn at his Inaugural— Jacqueline's maid Provy had let them out, but they were still too tight. Nor did he wear a top hat, because Jack's hat was not big enough—but Jack would have appreciated that too, because he never liked hats. Ted's decision to be hatless was quickly matched by the hatless procession of the world leaders.

For the watching world, the highly formal historical pageant helped ease the pain. The caravan of cars, hundreds of them, carried the leaders of the world, a six-mile drive past a watching crowd of more than a million.

"It was a mass movement," said Larry O'Brien, "it was not a very orderly procession. There was dead silence, just the beat of drums. To go up to that cathedral to the beat of drums, to see people like de Gaulle and Haile Selassie and Prince Philip walk along the street and into the church, to look around and see these world leaders in every direction you looked, then through the ceremony in Arlington, was overwhelming."

At St. Matthew's Cathedral for the Mass before the cemetery, Jacqueline started sobbing uncontrollably. Cardinal Cushing had performed her wedding ceremony, had baptized Caroline—and he himself was now dying. He circled the casket three times, chanting his Latin verses, sprinkling the incense and holy water, then said spontaneously, "May the angels, dear Jack, lead you into Paradise." Then the Cardinal himself began to cry.

At the grave, a squadron of cadets from Ireland, whom the President had so admired, marched in drill formation. The Cardinal made his blessing. The final twenty-one-gun salute was fired. Taps were played. But Ted found himself unable to read excerpts from his brother's speeches, despite Jacqueline's insistence. The flag was taken from the coffin and given to Jacqueline. She was given the burning taper to light the eternal flame. She then gave it to Bobby, who put the end of it into the flame and passed it to Teddy. Teddy seemed unsure what to do. He waved the taper slowly in the direction of the flame until an Army officer took it from his hand. But the torch had been passed.

JOHN SEIGENTHALER WAS INVITED to Bobby's house after the funeral. "He answered the door, and I think that you could say that the mood of depression was beginning to set in by that time. Still obviously in pain, Bob opened the door and said something like this, 'Come on in, somebody shot my brother and we're watching his funeral on television.'. . . I said, sort of with a half-laugh, 'Bob, that's not funny.' And he looked me dead in the eye and said, 'Don't you think I know that?' We walked into the little hall. Ethel and some of the children were in the room to the left. I remember they were watching. Ethel said she thought it was important for them to remember all about it they could."

AFTER THE FUNERAL, there was a buffet at the White House for some 200 dignitaries.

"Jackie called me," recalled General McHugh, "and said, 'I want to see two people: General de Gaulle and Haile Selassie. Want you to bring them to my apartment.' . . . I realized that those two had impressed her with their extraordinary strength and regal manner. They both were delighted to go."

Teddy was upstairs, watching on television what he had been experiencing all day. Jacqueline finally came to remind him of all the guests downstairs and the need for his presence. Bobby had been too restless to stay with the guests and kept roaming through the White House.

The Onassis presence at the funeral was noted by William Manchester in *Death of a President*: "Rose Kennedy dined upstairs with Stash Radziwill; Jacqueline Kennedy, her sister, and Robert Kennedy were served in the sitting room. The rest of the Kennedys ate in the family dining room with their house guests, Robert McNamara, Dave Powers and Aristotle Socrates Onassis, the ship owner, who provided comic relief of sorts. They badgered him mercilessly about his yacht and his Man of Mystery aura. During coffee, the Attorney General came down and drew up a formal document stipulating that Onassis give half his wealth to help the poor in Latin America. It was preposterous (and obviously unenforceable), and the Greek millionaire signed it in Greek."

That night, after all the visitors had gone, the family gathered upstairs. It was John-John's birthday party. He was three years old. He wore a party hat and carried a toy rifle and there was ice cream and cake and presents. After some stiff drinks, Jacqueline suggested they sing some of Jack's favorite songs. Teddy started singing, in his strong baritone, "Heart of My Heart," a song the three brothers had sung joyously on top of a table at the G and G Delicatessen on Blue Hill Avenue in Boston on the last night of Jack's campaign for the Senate.

> We were rough and ready guys,
> But oh, how we could harmonize. . . .

This time Bobby did not join in. Quietly, he left the room.

When Jacqueline's cousin John Davis sought out Rose Kennedy to pay his respects before he left, "she surprised me by responding in a cool, utterly controlled voice." She said, "Oh, thank you, Mr. Davis, but don't worry. Everything will be all right. You'll see. Now it's Bobby's turn."

"The night of the funeral, there was an Irish wake at Ted Kennedy's house," said Milton Gwirtzman. "It wasn't supposed to be a wake. Just a lot of Ted Kennedy's friends, and people who had been in the administration dropping by to be with one another. But it had the atmosphere, the sad yet boisterous atmosphere, of an Irish wake in which some people were crying and some were laughing and most were drinking."

Ted sang Irish songs, imitated prominent politicians, had great fun with one of Ethel Kennedy's wigs. He later returned to his brother's grave at Arlington cemetery.

A boyhood friend afterward commented, "It's just that Irish thing. When you want to cry, you laugh. . . . There were times when there were tears in his eyes or he was a little hysterical in response to sorrow . . . but Kennedys never cry."

———————

"SOMEONE," SAID MILTON Gwirtzman, "I forget who, told me that Robert Kennedy had said to them, 'You'd better get what you can out of the administration soon, because in two months the Kennedys will be forgotten in this country.' "

"We owe to William V. Shannon the first notice that the proper parallel for the Kennedys is not the Adamses," wrote reporter Murray Kempton, "two Presidents followed by admired generations of ambassadors, historians and railroad managers, but rather the Bonapartes, one Emperor followed by thirty-seven years of plotting first in palaces and then in garrets, and then another Emperor, followed by nothing."

———————

CIA DEPUTY DIRECTOR Ray Cline remembered feeling somehow that the grief he felt most was not really for John Kennedy but "for Bobby's future. I'm reading a lot into it, but it was focusing on the fate of the Kennedys—not on Jack himself; and that gave me a wrench. I thought, 'God, this great guy has just been shot down—and we're worrying about whether the Kennedys will be in power or not.' I've never quite gotten that out of my mind; it still haunts me a little bit when I hear Teddy running around, making an ass out of himself, because he feels he has an obligation to keep this Kennedy power. . . . Bobby was the author of this Kennedy myth, more than Jack. Jack was the actor, and Bobby was the playwright."

White House staffer Mike Feldman said, "I think the distinction between the Kennedy White House and every other White House I know is that—I'm not trying to indulge in hyperbole or be overly dramatic—but I believe in that White House of John Kennedy's . . . every person on that staff would rather have died, than John Kennedy."

Family friend Kay Halle told of the time, "One terribly cold and bitter night, a Secret Service man was guarding the President outside and President Kennedy came to the French doors, opened them and walked out, saying, 'I don't want you out there in this terrible cold. Come in here and get warm.' The Secret Service guard then recounted how he told the President that it was his beat to remain outside and he must stay there and could not come in. He saw him return to his desk and go on signing papers. About ten minutes later the President reappeared at the French doors coatless himself but carrying a fleece-lined coat, saying, 'I want you to put this on, you're not warm enough, I can tell.' So to appease the President the guard put on the coat. In about ten minutes, he told us the President reappeared at the door with a cup of hot chocolate for each of them. He opened the French doors and sat down on the icy steps, coatless, while he and the guard drank hot chocolate together. The guard then added, 'That's the kind of a President I've been serving.' Thereupon his voice broke and he wept unashamedly."

"In the very early hours after JFK was killed, when someone wondered out loud if Oswald was the man, Jacqueline said, 'Who cares.' When Oswald was captured in a movie theater, the arresting officers pummeled him, blacked an eye, bloodied his mouth. When they led him handcuffed out of the theater, some of the crowd yelled, "Kill him . . . kill him . . ."

Years later, shortly before his death, President Johnson told his former aide, Leo Janos of *Time*, that he had never believed Oswald acted alone. Johnson speculated that Dallas had been a retaliation for his thwarted attempt "to kill Cuban Premier Fidel Castro. He told Howard K. Smith, 'President Kennedy was trying to get Castro, but Castro got to him first.' " His staff member Marvin Watson also said that Johnson felt the CIA was involved somehow. As part of the still-untold story of the Kennedy assassination, KGB files revealed that they had rejected Oswald as a recruit because they found him mentally unstable. The Cubans also had refused to give him a visa in September 1963, when he had applied from Mexico. Back in Dallas, Oswald had applied for a job at four places, and he got the job at the Texas School Book Depository only because a friend interceded for him. That was a month before he could have known about Kennedy's parade route. It all seemed an accident of history and gave stronger weight for the theory that he did it alone. In thirty years, there has never been any hard evidence to prove otherwise.

But, as Gerald Posner, author of *Case Closed*, put it: "It is hard for many to swallow the notion that a misguided loser with a $12 rifle could end Camelot."

———

FIVE DAYS AFTER the assassination, Jacqueline Kennedy summoned Theodore H. White to the Hyannis family compound. She wanted White to know about Camelot.

"At night, before we'd go to sleep, Jack liked to play some records, and the song he loved most came at the very end of this record. The lines he loved to hear were: 'Don't let it be forgot, that once there was a spot, for one brief shining moment that was known as Camelot.' "

"Camelot, heroes, fairy tales, legends, were what history was all about," wrote White.

"That story of hers about listening to the music of *Camelot*," commented his secretary Evelyn Lincoln derisively, "he never listened to *Camelot* in his whole life! His favorite song was 'Bill Bailey, Won't You Please Come Home?' "

———

THE MURDER HAD a dimming effect on the dynamics of the Kennedy family. In some ways it changed their relationships with each other.

"What is meant to be will be," said Rose Kennedy, "and there is no use looking back."

She drove her own small car to 7:30 A.M. Mass several mornings a week. With her head tied up in a scarf, she knelt alone at the back of the large church, devoted the first half hour to prayers for those she had lost. The phrase she repeated most often was "I must never be vanquished."

What she had drummed into her children and grandchildren was the well-worn quote, "God grant me the serenity to accept the things I cannot change, the courage to change the things I can, and the wisdom to know the difference." "That has been her life," said her grandson Joseph Kennedy III. "She's accepted things, and it was really because of her faith in God."

"Rose bought a black mourning dress for his funeral which she would in the future pack and take with them when they traveled between Hyannis and Palm Beach." She was expecting her husband to die next.

Bobby said of her, "I was thinking. If mother only had three children, she would have none of them now." But when somebody said, "Is it ever going to end for you people?" Teddy replied, "There are still more of us than there is trouble."

For Ted, the loss was almost intolerable. "I miss him every time I see his children. I miss him every time I see the places, like Cape Cod, which had such meaning for him and still have for all of us. I miss him at the times our family used to get together, such as his birthday and Thanksgiving. I miss the chance to tell him about things I've done which I feel proud of, and I miss his encouragement and advice at times of difficulty. I miss him as you'd miss your best friend. . . . He was great fun to be with."

For Ted, these were not just words. Jack had not only been his brother, but his surrogate father, his friend, his anchor. With his brother Joe, Jack had made the mold for Ted. Jack and Ted had chased women together and shared the same ambitions. Bobby could never be to Ted what Jack had been. Bobby would care, but he and Bobby were of different cuts of the same cloth, while Ted and Jack had been part of the same weave.

The day after Jack was buried, Ted Kennedy came to the Senate to vote for a bill to expand federal aid to public school libraries. He then flew to Hyannis Port for Thanksgiving. The next time he came to the Senate, he could not go in.

———

ACCORDING TO AN NBC News/*Wall Street Journal* poll, Kennedy is still the face most Americans want to see added on Mount Rushmore. In one Gallup poll, he is the President most Americans regard as greatest, and by substantial margins. In that poll, he outranked Abraham Lincoln by four percentage points.

"When the Kennedy memorabilia toured the country by train, people would genuflect when they saw the rocking chair," said Dave Powers, "or make a sign of the cross if they touched his picture." In the years after the assassination, 1141 painted portraits of the President, and 289 sculptured busts, arrived at the Kennedy Library, and more were always coming.

It seemed incredible that this was the same President whose national popularity, just before his death, was lower than it had ever been.

Jack's old friend William Walton summed up much: "He wasn't the father of great legislation, he didn't make an opening to China or anything like this. . . . He made a new mold for the Presidency that no one has yet fitted into. And we do search for such a person."

After Kennedy's death, noted columnist Mary McGrory said to Daniel Moynihan, "We will never laugh again."

"Oh Mary, we'll laugh again," Moynihan replied. "But we'll never be young again."

James Reston wrote in *The New York Times* that Kennedy had put a sheen on American life that made it seem more youthful than it is. He had done this even though he often confused the national interest with his own political interest; even though he made morality a relative thing and often compromised his leadership by staying away from issues that were desirable but not popular; even though he sometimes seemed more obsessed with image and style than with substance.

But, somehow, in the final year of his life, he became more sensitive to the needs of people, more concerned with principle, more deeply aware of the fate of the world. The most terrible part of his brutal murder was the death of his political promise and potential. That's why the American people wept—not just for him but for them- selves. Watching the TV in Winthrop, Massachusetts, Robert Nisen- son slammed his fist on the table and told his wife, Pearlie, "Goddamn, there goes history!" It was the history of what might have been, the death of a "brilliant maybe."

And that would be the heritage of burden for his brothers.

Much later, after a speech somewhere, a six-year-old boy said to Bobby, "Your brother's dead . . . your brother's dead. . . ." Bobby picked up the boy and held him close. "That's all right . . . I have another brother."

11

OUT OF THE SHADOW

The death of a Kennedy brother always meant the growth of another brother. At thirty-eight, Bobby had spent his life submerging himself in his brother. For him, the loss of his primary peer model and competitor caused a powerful mixture of guilt and grief. But it opened the road to growth, and Bobby became his own man on the day Jack died.

Some Kennedy intimates felt that Bobby was overly ambitious and had his eye on the Oval Office even earlier—and that Jack was keenly conscious of it.

"The only thing I did feel towards the end of Jack's life," said Charles Bartlett, "was a feeling that clouded his last days in office, the apprehension over the implication of the fact that Bobby had decided to run for president. I think that bothered Jack. The last few times I saw him, Jack talked about how 1968 was going to be a contest between Bobby and Lyndon Johnson, and I don't think he took cordially to it at all."

Charles Spalding, who knew Jack so well, saw some envy in Jack when Bobby began to develop as rapidly as he did. Jack told him he felt Bobby was overly ambitious, was "hard-nosing it." This was a far cry from the self-effacing Bobby who thought primarily of his brother's political future.

It wasn't that Jack saw Bob as a political threat. But there was too much talk of Bobby brilliantly engineering his election victory, Bobby resolving the missile crisis, Bobby being the passionate defender of civil rights, Bobby sharing the presidency . . .

Jack didn't want anyone sharing his place in history. If Bobby succeeded him as President, he might eclipse him in greatness, overshadow him. He had gone through too much to beat back the overwhelming memory of young Joe; he now didn't want his younger brother to do the same to him. Similarly, Bob was resentful of Teddy's running for Senator too soon, hurting the progression of his political plans.

They were all seeds of destruction.

There were those who could hardly wait for these seeds to flower. Clyde Tolson, FBI Director Hoover's closest friend and associate, startled colleagues at an executive meeting after the assassination by saying, "God damn the Kennedys! . . . We'll have them on our backs until the year 2000." And then, in a discussion of Robert Kennedy, he added, "I hope someone shoots and kills the son of a bitch."

FOR BOBBY, THIS was a time of depression and darkness in his life.

His filial love was deeper than his envy, stronger than his ambition. Bobby's closest friend, David Hackett, described Bob and Jack as "almost both parts of the same human being." And Jack's closest friend, Lem Billings, added, "When they buried Jack Kennedy in that grave at Arlington, they buried much of Bobby, too."

A friend found Bob staring at his brother's photograph on the wall. Nobody else was there. His eyes were wet with tears. "I loved him," he said softly, then brushed past her.

Columnist Mary McGrory saw Bobby on St. Patrick's Day, four months after the death. He looked terrible, and she said, "Well, you're young and you're going to be productive and successful. . . . But before I could finish he just let out a yelp of pain and buried his head in my shoulder."

"Oh, how he suffered!" said his secretary Angie Novello. "He fell into a depression that I thought he would never come out of. . . . He would sit and stare. His hands would tremble. It would be hard to get his attention."

John Seigenthaler recalled that Bobby's grief was physically painful for him, "almost as if he were on the rack or had a heart attack. . . . When I say that he was not functional, I don't mean he was not able to do what he had to do . . . it was more that he did what he did through a haze of pain." Bobby was then having a hard time sleeping even three, four hours a night, and would sometimes get up at four in the morning and ride his horse.

––––––––

ABOUT THAT TIME, an interviewer asked Rose Kennedy if she had talked to Bobby to try to reconcile him to his brother's death. "No," she replied.

In the coming months, others did talk with him. "Bobby talked to me about his brother all the time," said Charles Spalding. "It's hard to fake something with somebody you see over a period of years. And I don't find Bobby's attitude toward Jack changing in the slightest. . . . He might have felt regret there wasn't more response from Jack, for the tremendous things that he did. . . . But the habit was ingrained: the brother below was expected to do all that sort of stuff."

––––––––

BOBBY WAS AT his best, almost normal, when he was with Jacqueline and his brother's children, when he knew he was helping. It was Caroline, at an age to remember, who was most deeply hurt by her father's death. She became a "changed child," observed reporter Laura Bergquist, "withdrawn at times, shy, quiet, moody. Only Uncle Bobby could coax her out of her shell. She would whisper to him the confidences she had once poured into the ear of her father. Robert Kennedy treated the children with infinite tenderness."

Wherever Jacqueline went now, she was seen leaning on Bob.

Two weeks almost to the hour, Jacqueline Kennedy, clasping the hands of her children, quietly left the White House. Somehow that was the bleakest day of all. A little truck passed through the gate bearing the birdcage, a model ship, the last of the family belongings.

On that day, Bob was there to help her, and he stayed long enough to write his final notes on White House stationery to the staff, thanking them "on behalf of the President and myself for all that you have done over the past three years."

After she moved out, the Johnsons automatically invited Jacqueline to every State dinner. "But I explained . . . that it was really difficult for me, and I really didn't ever want to go back. . . . I just couldn't go back to that place. Even driving around Washington, I'd try to drive a way where I wouldn't see the White House," she later said.

Jacqueline moved to Georgetown. "Bobby would drop in on Jackie some part of every day and ask how she was doing," said Dave Powers. "Some days, she'd be great; and others, she'd be terribly weepy."

Because the relationship between Jacqueline and Ethel was not friendly, Bobby almost always arrived without Ethel. En route to a party one evening, with Ethel, Bobby suddenly decided to spend the evening comforting his widowed sister-in-law. He persuaded his protesting wife to go to the party without him.

This happened repeatedly, and Ethel rationalized to a guest, "He's got to comfort Jackie." But later, she added that Bobby being with Jackie too much only deepened his sense of tragedy. On the other hand, Jacqueline's relationship with her mother-in-law grew warmer. Rose Kennedy would call Jacqueline "and ask would I like to take a little walk, because she didn't want me to be here alone, and be sad. . . . Then she called me the next day. Said would I come at such-and-such a time. You know, just taking care of me. Thinks that I'm in this house by myself, with my memories. . . . But that's what she's like, really. I call her *Belle-mère* . . . I've always called her that."

———————

"TIME HEALS THINGS, and you forget things," Jacqueline later told an interviewer. "I can't remember Jack's voice, exactly, anymore. But I still have pictures, all around the children's room. . . . This is the house where we were happy, where we had children. . . . And all your memories come before your eyes. Nothing's changed since we were here."

In the coming months, Bobby accompanied Jacqueline from a ski vacation in Stowe, Vermont, to Antigua. Ethel didn't go.

But being with Jacqueline allowed RFK the space in his busy life to grieve. She was not a born Kennedy, and so, with her, he didn't have to mask his feelings of sadness, as Kennedys were taught to do. The brothers closed in around Jacqueline and with each other. "They became even closer," said Novello, "they were their own best friends. Really stuck together. And their relationship with their sisters was extremely affectionate.''

Bob and Ted had reacted differently to Jack's death. Bob worked out the alienation and bitterness philosophically. He questioned everything, asked, ''Why, God?'' and often talked wildly. Ted coped more in action than in brooding.

Ted had been a boy with too many heroes. His father, his oldest brother Joe, and Jack had been so central in his life that, as a man, it was harder for Ted to emerge.

There was, too, in the youngest Kennedy, few of the qualities of his family heroes. He shared many similarities with brother Joe, but he was not pushy or compulsive. Some said he might have been more successful if he had these qualities. Nor did he have Joe's killer instinct. There was little greed in him. And he showed a constant compassion toward his adversaries that was not typical of the Kennedys.

Yet Jack, more than any of them, was Ted's model. He epitomized everything Ted might have wanted—the power, without sacrificing his lifestyle, the sharp intelligence, the easy wit. Ted's pain of his loss was deep and damaging.

Yet, when the deepest of his mourning subsided, Ted came out of it and regained himself. David Brinkley recalled when his buoyancy had bounced back. ''It was the first time Bob had been out after his brother's death. Teddy brought along a recorded tape—and it was of some New England character, some nice, likable, Irish storyteller in Boston . . . this New England raconteur talking about Jack Kennedy. They thought maybe Bobby and Ethel would enjoy hearing it. So they took it and put it on the tape recorder, started playing it, and they listened for just a few minutes. Then Bob and Ethel left—they went home.''

It was Ethel who pulled him out of it. She felt the prime purpose of her life was to make him happy. Everything else for her was secondary. She knew the depth of his melancholia, the deadness of his mind and soul, and she concentrated all her bubbly, restless energy into pulling him out of himself. And she did.

Bobby was at his best when others needed him.

''The whole family was like a bunch of shipwrecked survivors,'' said Lem Billings. ''I don't think they would have made it at all without Bobby. . . . He seemed to be everywhere. He always had an arm around a friend and was telling them that it was okay . . . he was the one who told them to set a term to their mourning and get on with their lives.''

Billings was one of the worst shipwrecks. Jack had been the best part of his life. He clung to the Kennedys with his own desperation. Jacqueline let him stay with her children several times, take them to the movies, and send them presents, but then she gently veered away from him. Lem then zeroed in on Bobby's family. "Lem used to say he loved Bobby from the first day he set eyes on him—when Bobby was eight years old," recalled Ted Kennedy.

Bobby saw his brother's friend as "a displaced person" and adopted him. To spend time with Bobby and Ethel, you had to like children. Lem became a wholesale godfather and a family cheerleader. For Bobby's family, Uncle Lem was a large, friendly man with thick glasses who was a master storyteller about their family. He described each family member so vividly "that you might have expected Kick and Jack to come walking in the front door, arm in arm, talking and laughing." While making these tales come alive, he accented them with his own high-pitched laughter.

"Lem told me about my father, too, the first time anybody really had," said Robert Kennedy Jr. "We'd be walking along and talking about something and he'd say, 'Oh that reminds me of something Jack and I did with your father when we were seventeen and he was ten.' '' Lem gave him and the other Kennedy children a continuous course in Legacy. For the myth to be successful, the Kennedys had to believe in it. That had been Joe Sr.'s job; now it was Lem's.

———

ONCE AGAIN THE Kennedy compound at Hyannis came alive with fun and football. "I don't mean they're laughing when they shouldn't be," said Jacqueline, "but in times of sadness, to make a real effort with this light touch, I think is wonderful . . . their gaiety, the way they all bounce off each other . . . they're a great help to me, because I'm more solitary, more introverted."

As the time passed, Jacqueline had to think about what she'd be doing. "I'm never going to live in Europe," she told a reporter, "I'm not going to travel extensively abroad. That's a desecration. I'm going to live in the places I lived with Jack."

Many thought she seemed lost without Jack; Evelyn Lincoln said, "I think if he'd had another term, she'd have left him at the end of the term, I'm sure. I'm sorry to say that, but I don't think they were compatible. And neither one wanted to give in. . . . Both very independent."

————

WITHIN HOURS OF John Kennedy's death, Robert Kennedy got a call from Hoover. Bob remembered the Director's "unpleasant voice" when he clearly indicated he would no longer deal through the Attorney General, but instead directly with President Johnson. "Then, I knew that within a few days, he was over to the White House giving dossiers on everyone that President Kennedy had appointed, in the White House . . . with the idea that President Kennedy had appointed a lot of people that were rather questionable figures.

"Those people," said Robert Kennedy, "don't work for us anymore."

If Bob Kennedy instinctively wanted to quit, President Johnson persuasively urged him to stay, with the appeal that he needed Bob more than ever to help complete John F. Kennedy's program.

"But the minute that bullet hit Jack Kennedy's head, it was all over," observed William Hundley, head of the Crime Section. "Right then. The organized crime program just stopped, and Hoover took control back."

"At the end of the Kennedy administration, members of the Justice Department's Organized Crime Section were working 6699 man-days in the field each year. Three years later the figure had dropped by half. Days spent prosecuting mobsters before grand juries dropped 72 percent, days in court 56 percent, court briefs prepared 82 percent."

Hoover kept the Kennedy autopsy pictures in his confidential files. They were the only autopsy pictures he ever kept.

Soon after Johnson became President, an aide strongly recommended that Johnson fire Hoover. Johnson may well have known that Hoover had his own personal Johnson file, which might prove embarrassing. Hugh Sidey recalled the Johnson reply: "No, son, if you've got a skunk around, it's better to have him inside the tent pissing out, than outside the tent pissing in."

LBJ was not so concerned about FBI dossiers on other people.

Columnist Murray Kempton told the story about Johnson lounging on a White House bed, watching the 1964 Republican Convention and reading Hoover's notes on the private sins of the speaker on the platform.

————

DESPITE ALL THE negative Kennedy feelings about Johnson, Jacqueline was grateful to him. In an oral history interview for the Johnson Library, she said, "I tell you, they were wonderful to me. Lyndon Johnson was extraordinary; he did everything he could to be magnanimous. . . .

"The man had incredible warmth. Didn't he? I really felt they were warm. I almost felt sorry for him because I knew he felt sorry for me. . . .

"It's funny what you do in a state of shock. I remember going over to the Oval Office to ask him . . . to name the Space Center in Florida 'Cape Kennedy.' Now that I think back on it, it's so wrong . . . it would have been the last thing Jack would have wanted. The reason I asked was that I had this terrible fear then that he'd be forgotten, and I thought, 'Well, maybe they'll remember some day that this man did dream.'. . .

"I think that's a wish that he could've easily said, 'Look, my dear, that's impossible.' But he didn't. He called Governor Collins on the phone right away."

Johnson's chief counsel, Henry McPherson, commented, "I suppose if they would want to re-name the United States of America 'the United States of Kennedy,' that would practically have been done at the time. Johnson did not want to be in the position of opposing anything like that."

Yet, on Air Force One, some of his long-suffering envy oozed out. LBJ held public monologues for reporters. "They were stream-of-consciousness. . . ." said Jim Deakin. "He'd vilify and run down Jack Kennedy's little spindly legs, that he had better-looking legs than Jack Kennedy. . . . I heard this man say this dozens of times."

————

CHARLES DE GAULLE once said that Jack Kennedy was a mask on the face of America, while Lyndon Johnson *was* America.

Poverty and civil rights were vividly real to LBJ because he had lived close to them. But when he talked to the joint session of Congress, a watching Congressman observed that Robert Kennedy "seldom clapped; he just seemed to smolder."

The contrast between Bobby Kennedy and Johnson was almost absolute. Robert Kennedy was innately shy and private, observed Johnson biographer Merle Miller, while Johnson "had this habit of coming very close to you, of drawing in very close, and putting his arm around your shoulder, and sort of hugging you and bringing you in close. In American society, we don't do that as often as we should. I think in European society, they do that much more. Also, you don't expect that to happen to you when you're dealing with the President of the United States. So the combination is sort of unnerving, a mixture of pleasantness and unpleasantness."

It was not only intimidating, but there was also the psychological suggestion that the person who touches the other one first in a conversation establishes a dominance.

"Bobby scorned Lyndon Johnson's character," said RFK's friend Rowland Evans. "He'd fill me in with all kinds of fascinating tidbits . . . he'd find out from his spies in the White House. . . . He said the last conversation they ever had about Johnson before his brother was shot, Jack Kennedy said, 'Don't ever forget that Lyndon Johnson is a congenital liar.' " After his speech to Congress, Johnson asked Kennedy to come and see him. He explained that he had moved so quickly into the Oval Office only at the insistence of Secretary of State Rusk and Defense Secretary McNamara. Then he said, "People around you are saying things about me. . . . You can't let your people talk about me and I won't talk about you."

Even Bobby Baker, a close associate of Johnson's, admitted that his friend's complaints against Robert Kennedy "may have bordered on the paranoiac."

Despite this, LBJ knew he needed the political backing of Kennedy supporters. When Lyndon Johnson dominated the Senate, he considered Jack Kennedy "a kid." Yet this kid had beat him out of the presidency. His only explanation, according to Larry O'Brien, was that these people had some special kind of magic, so he wanted them to work for him so he would obtain it.

As Merle Miller pointed out, "He didn't like them but he was awed by them.'' And, to keep the Kennedy crowd on his side, he needed to keep Bobby in the Cabinet, as much as he hated him. And that's why he told Bobby that he needed him more than his brother did.

"I didn't get into an argument about it. . . ." said Robert Kennedy later. "I don't know quite what I did say."

But the deep hate was always there. When his White House aide Bill Moyers asked Johnson, "How do you get to where you've gotten?" he replied, "You outlive the bastards." To Johnson, Bobby was one of the "bastards."

"Everybody was trying to probe and analyze their relationship," said Gerald Siegel, a Johnson aide. "And I said, 'You're all nutty. It's a very simple one. They didn't like each other.' "

The tone was set at the first Cabinet meeting. Robert Kennedy was late, and when he entered, some of the members rose to their feet. Johnson sat and stared. It was his way of declaring his status and his strength. As for Bob, his soul was squirming. Secretary of Agriculture Orville Freeman, who was there, recalled, "His general demeanor as he came into the room and as he sat down, was . . . that he could hardly countenance Lyndon Johnson sitting in his brother's seat."

"Three or four months after the assassination, Johnson saw one of the Secret Service men wearing a PT-boat tie clip, and he took it off him and threw it away," recalled Milton Gwirtzman. "And as I heard the story, this particular Secret Service man walked over, retrieved it, and put it back on—and he was reassigned. Now, you know, there may be nothing at all in that story, but Robert Kennedy heard it. He believed it, and he didn't like it, because it was disrespectful towards his brother."

What Robert Kennedy could not forget or forgive was Johnson telling Pierre Salinger that "what happened to Kennedy may have been divine retribution."

———

"THE FIRST TIME I ever saw Bobby, I was picketing him," remembered Jack Newfield. "I was a civil rights activist in the South, and he was Attorney General. That was in 1963. Then I saw how he was beginning to change, how his hair was getting longer until he started looking like the fifth Beatle. I sensed something was going on with this guy. What I realized when I got to know him was that he had never thought about what he believed until his brother was murdered . . . then he stayed home reading Camus and Emerson."

"Before John Kennedy was shot, Bobby was cold and tough," said Larry Newman. "He was always like that, from a kid, all the way up. It wasn't something he inherited with the White House. . . . But when John was shot, you could almost see the compassion that had been missing from Bobby's life just sort of begin to move out of him. He walked these streets for days and nights, for months . . . alone—because it was a terrible, terrible blow. . . . It was watching a featherweight become a man. The little kid on the block who'd fight every other feisty little kid . . . all of a sudden, you could almost see him just grow up. He didn't take much fun in playing touch football any longer. Got closer and closer to the family. Got friendlier and friendlier with his neighbors, whom he never looked at . . . you could just see the guy growing in stature. And I thought he would've made a great President."

After the assassination, Bobby didn't come to his office for almost a month. An associate commented that for the rest of the year, he didn't think Bobby was in the Department for a full week at any time.

Bob was in the process of trying to define his life. He was no longer his brother's keeper. In a way, it was almost like starting from scratch. For so many of President Kennedy's inner circle, their lives had stopped. It was "as if somebody did a lobotomy on them," said Adam Walinsky.

OTHERS WERE NOT so convinced about the emergence of the new Bobby.

"What are my credentials for saying that I have doubts about the conversion of Bobby from the calculated little operator into a saintly figure? I don't know. . . ." said Blair Clark. "But I never could believe in the instant conversion of Bobby to the great liberal humanitarian. . . . It was pure hagiography . . . when he talks about 'My favorite poet, Aeschylus.' I mean, that's not real. Know what I mean? I don't care how learned you are, in a classical way, you'd never say, 'Aeschylus, my favorite poet.' It rings wrong. And a lot of his hot-button statements about issues, etc. didn't ring right to me. I'm not saying that the death of Jack, and the whole very odd business of his relations with LBJ, didn't make him think about life and politics in a

different way. But he had a long way to come back, to be the hero. . . .
I believe he was visibly moved by Harlem, etc., but no, I didn't think
the conversion was immediate and complete. Oh, I think there was a
real change. But the Jack Newfield attitude, it goes too far.''

Another old friend, David Hackett, was more mixed: "I never saw
any real change in Bobby, over the years. He may have become more
tolerant towards imperfection, as time went on . . . became less
abrasive, over the years. I think he'd become more philosophical . . .
more fatalistic, perhaps. It was sort of subtle—not black and white.
He had this quality of compassion, and tried to act on injustice. . . . He
was a very complex person in 1942 and I think he was a very complex
person in 1968.''

————

NO ONE QUITE understood why Robert Kennedy showed a strange
passivity in the investigation. None of his close associates in the
Attorney General's Office ever heard him discuss the case, certainly
never saw him bang his fist in anguish or anger, vowing revenge. On
the contrary, he took steps to squash conspiracy rumors. He supported
the Warren Commission without even reading its report. He even
limited the commission access to autopsy photographs, keeping them,
and his brother's brain, in his personal custody.

"I had one conspiracy theorist who claimed to have all kinds of
evidence, and insisted on seeing me. . . .'' said Ted Sorensen. "When
I spoke about it to Bobby, he said, 'I don't want to hear it. I just can't
be involved in that.' ''

"Sitting next to him in an airplane,'' said Jack Newfield, "I would
see his eyes avoid any newspaper article about the assassination. He
could only speak around the event, or in euphemisms. . . . He spent
each anniversary of Dallas in prayer and brooding seclusion.''

His deputy Nicholas Katzenbach said that Robert Kennedy "never
really wanted any investigation.'' In a memo to Bill Moyers at the
White House, Katzenbach stressed that "the public must be satisfied
that Oswald was the assassin.''

Bob's reluctance to dig too deeply into the assassination was because
he was fearful of all the sexual dirt that would be uncovered blemishing
his brother. Then, too, there were all the convoluted relations with the
Mafia that would be so difficult for the public to understand. It would

not only hurt his brother's image, but it might destroy any political future for himself and Ted.

––––––––

THE WARREN COMMISSION ruled in 1964 that Oswald had acted alone, killed the President with two shots from a cheap mail-order rifle. A House Select Committee on Assassinations later said there was evidence to support a theory that another shot may have come from a grassy knoll across the plaza.

Hoover told Johnson that the President "was hit by the first and the third shots, the second shot hit the governor. The third shot . . . tore a large part of the President's head off and . . . and a complete bullet . . . rolled out of the President's head when they massaged his heart." Hoover said he had looked through the telescopic lens "and it brings a person as close to you as if they were sitting right beside you. They also tested the gun and you could fire those three shots in three seconds."

Arthur Schlesinger recorded a long session with Robert Kennedy. "As we talked till two-thirty in the morning in P. J. Clarke's saloon in New York City, RFK wondered how long he could continue to avoid comment on the report. It is evident that he believes that it was a poor job and will not endorse it, but that he is unwilling to criticize it and thereby reopen the whole tragic business."

At the Polish Student Union in Cracow in 1964, Bobby was asked for his version of the assassination. For the first time in public, he said, "It is a proper question and deserves an answer." He described Oswald as a misfit in society, dissatisfied with the American way of life, who took up Communism and went to the Soviet Union. "He was dissatisfied there. He came back to the United States and was anti-social and felt the only way to take out his strong feelings was by killing the President of the United States."

Former FBI agent Walter Sheridan, who had worked for Bob, revealed years later that RFK had told him that he asked the head of the CIA if the CIA "had killed my brother, and I asked him in a way that he couldn't lie to me—and they hadn't."

––––––––

THE WARREN COMMISSION had left many unanswered questions. Even Supreme Court Chief Justice Warren made the cryptic remark that there were aspects of the Kennedy assassination that could never be known in our lifetime.

After reading all the reports, Senator Ted Kennedy had his own team of investigators check the various stories. He was not privy to all the damaging connections that Bob knew of, and felt the need to know more. Appearing before a closed session of the Senate Select Committee on Intelligence Activities, the Senator said that he had seen no new evidence to cast doubt on the Warren Commission's conclusion that his brother was assassinated by one man, acting on his own.

There is no record of Bob and Ted discussing this. It is doubtful that they did. It would have been too painful.

In a bitter comment, historian H. A. Fairlie noted that the Lincoln assassination industry had remained viable for more than fifty years, and he recommended the Kennedy assassination industry as "one of the most promising fields for the young to enter."

———

IN A STRANGE way, Bobby seemed to assume Jack's identity: his expressions, quoting so many things he said, even his cigar smoking. He frequently wore, or carried, his brother's old tweed jacket. Whenever he left it somewhere, as he often did, he always managed to retrieve it. A psychologist analyzed it as a deep inner conflict to cling to the past or leave it behind him.

"He was sailing, with a bunch of people, in Maine—in the Portland area," said Dave Richardson. "He always wore or carried his brother's presidential jacket. He was lazing on the deck of the boat, as it putted along. A breeze suddenly came up . . . a gust of wind blew the jacket overboard, quite far away from the shore. He dove in. The water was so cold, icy-cold that you could last about four minutes. When they pulled him out, he was blue. But he had the jacket."

In his first speech since the assassination, Bob spoke before the Friendly Sons of St. Patrick of Lackawanna County, Pennsylvania, on St. Patrick's Day, 1964. He had included a ballad by a seventeenth-century champion of Irish independence. His press secretary, Ed Guthman, cut out the ballad from the final draft. When Bob asked why, Guthman told him, "You'll never get through it . . . you don't have to put yourself through that." But Bob said he had been practicing in front of a mirror. "I can't get through it yet, but I will."

not only hurt his brother's image, but it might destroy any political future for himself and Ted.

––––––

THE WARREN COMMISSION ruled in 1964 that Oswald had acted alone, killed the President with two shots from a cheap mail-order rifle. A House Select Committee on Assassinations later said there was evidence to support a theory that another shot may have come from a grassy knoll across the plaza.

Hoover told Johnson that the President "was hit by the first and the third shots, the second shot hit the governor. The third shot . . . tore a large part of the President's head off and . . . and a complete bullet . . . rolled out of the President's head when they massaged his heart." Hoover said he had looked through the telescopic lens "and it brings a person as close to you as if they were sitting right beside you. They also tested the gun and you could fire those three shots in three seconds."

Arthur Schlesinger recorded a long session with Robert Kennedy. "As we talked till two-thirty in the morning in P. J. Clarke's saloon in New York City, RFK wondered how long he could continue to avoid comment on the report. It is evident that he believes that it was a poor job and will not endorse it, but that he is unwilling to criticize it and thereby reopen the whole tragic business."

At the Polish Student Union in Cracow in 1964, Bobby was asked for his version of the assassination. For the first time in public, he said, "It is a proper question and deserves an answer." He described Oswald as a misfit in society, dissatisfied with the American way of life, who took up Communism and went to the Soviet Union. "He was dissatisfied there. He came back to the United States and was anti-social and felt the only way to take out his strong feelings was by killing the President of the United States."

Former FBI agent Walter Sheridan, who had worked for Bob, revealed years later that RFK had told him that he asked the head of the CIA if the CIA "had killed my brother, and I asked him in a way that he couldn't lie to me—and they hadn't."

––––––

THE WARREN COMMISSION had left many unanswered questions. Even Supreme Court Chief Justice Warren made the cryptic remark that there were aspects of the Kennedy assassination that could never be known in our lifetime.

After reading all the reports, Senator Ted Kennedy had his own team of investigators check the various stories. He was not privy to all the damaging connections that Bob knew of, and felt the need to know more. Appearing before a closed session of the Senate Select Committee on Intelligence Activities, the Senator said that he had seen no new evidence to cast doubt on the Warren Commission's conclusion that his brother was assassinated by one man, acting on his own.

There is no record of Bob and Ted discussing this. It is doubtful that they did. It would have been too painful.

In a bitter comment, historian H. A. Fairlie noted that the Lincoln assassination industry had remained viable for more than fifty years, and he recommended the Kennedy assassination industry as "one of the most promising fields for the young to enter."

———

IN A STRANGE way, Bobby seemed to assume Jack's identity: his expressions, quoting so many things he said, even his cigar smoking. He frequently wore, or carried, his brother's old tweed jacket. Whenever he left it somewhere, as he often did, he always managed to retrieve it. A psychologist analyzed it as a deep inner conflict to cling to the past or leave it behind him.

"He was sailing, with a bunch of people, in Maine—in the Portland area," said Dave Richardson. "He always wore or carried his brother's presidential jacket. He was lazing on the deck of the boat, as it putted along. A breeze suddenly came up . . . a gust of wind blew the jacket overboard, quite far away from the shore. He dove in. The water was so cold, icy-cold that you could last about four minutes. When they pulled him out, he was blue. But he had the jacket."

In his first speech since the assassination, Bob spoke before the Friendly Sons of St. Patrick of Lackawanna County, Pennsylvania, on St. Patrick's Day, 1964. He had included a ballad by a seventeenth-century champion of Irish independence. His press secretary, Ed Guthman, cut out the ballad from the final draft. When Bob asked why, Guthman told him, "You'll never get through it . . . you don't have to put yourself through that." But Bob said he had been practicing in front of a mirror. "I can't get through it yet, but I will."

And he did.

A stanza read:

> We're sheep without a shepherd,
> When the snow shuts out the sky;
> Oh! Why did you leave us, Owen?
> Why did you die?

When Lord Beaverbrook wrote his letter of sympathy to Rose Kennedy after the assassination, he noted, "May Joe find solace in the unexampled triumphs of his son and in the assurance that Bobby will repeat Jack's career." Earlier, Beaverbrook had written, "I find Bobby a most lively character with an exceedingly aggressive mind, well-balanced, clear in statement, powerful in argument, well-read and bound to do a great deal in life. Possibly much mischief if he becomes President. For my part, I expect the Kennedys to equal the record of the Adams family."

The Adams family had father and son as Presidents, the Roosevelts had cousins in the Oval Office, but never before had there been the possibility of a dynasty of brothers.

Author Joe McCarthy, who had the confidence of Joe Sr., heard him say with a laugh that the three Kennedys beat two Adamses. His son Jack was then still alive. McCarthy told author Lester David that the old man had said, "Each of those kids is going to be President of the United States. There would have been four if Joe had lived. Hell, that's three Presidents named Kennedy going down in the history books, one after another."

Joe Sr. was once asked to pick his favorite son. He replied with the cliché that he had five fingers on his hand, and each was equally important. "Each one of them is equally important to me." But, after more discussion, he finally named Bobby "because he resembles me much more than any of the others."

———

ROBERT KENNEDY WAS now prepared to take his political future in his own hands. What he had going for him was the Kennedy name, public sympathy, and a familiarity with the process. On the negative side was his difficult personality, the enormous shadow of his brother, the persistence of his grief—and his hatred of Lyndon Johnson.

For politics, the personality is primary. His was a strange mixture of bashfulness and distrust. He was also a "shrewd nonconformist who knows exactly what he wants and doesn't mind going outside established channels to get it," Gore Vidal said. "It will take a public-relations genius to make Bobby appear lovable. . . . He has none of his brother's human ease, or charity."

This was a man easier to respect than to like, a man of many burning fires. He was not a man for half measures. Life to him was a series of challenges. He was not an intellectual, but he knew how to listen to them and how to use them—with a quick grasp of other people's ideas. He had intuition but little imagination. What was surprising about him was his unpredictability. His most obvious fault was still his rudeness. It was not in his nature to put people at ease. "His face, when it lacks that boyish, photogenic grin, is not a pleasant sight," said Vidal. "It has a certain bony harshness and those ice-blue eyes are not the smiling ones that Irishmen sing songs about. At best, he recalls Fitzgerald's description of Gatsby: 'an elegant young roughneck.' He is too preoccupied with the salvation of humanity to be polite to individuals."

Commentator Edward Morgan observed, "Bobby didn't transmit that dignity, that upright electricity of leadership. He was one of the boys . . . the fellow that just came out of the football game, after having his head bashed—and was still a hero . . . a gut fighter."

Ted Sorensen noticed something interesting: President Kennedy always had called his brother "Bobby" and Sorensen thought that the brother bristled at it. In his first note from Robert Kennedy after Jack's death, it began "Teddy old pal" and was signed "Bob."

———

IT WAS VERY difficult to talk to Bob. You'd have to start the conversation. And he wasn't interested in small talk. "If you just sat down with Bob for an evening," said friend Gerald Tremblay, "to keep a conversation going that had enough scintillation in it to keep Bob interested, you really had to keep your brain working. . . . He didn't like to hear people's individual problems but he was great on the problems of a group, like Indians, colored people, the people that were being unjustly oppressed, or the poor. But his flair for one-on-one . . . that wasn't his cup of tea at all.''

Hugh Sidey recalled interviewing Bob Kennedy while striding up and down the side of the swimming pool, shouting his questions as Bob swam. ''When one question offended Bob, he simply submerged, swam underwater to the other side of the pool, crawled out and stalked off up the hill, leaving the perplexed newsman standing.''

According to Dave Powers, because Bobby felt so strongly about things, people felt strongly about him. ''The President never had that. I never met anyone that really hated the President. They either loved him, or liked him. With Bobby, they loved him or they hated him.''

But the national guilt and sympathy for his dead brother was now washing Bobby clean, giving him a warmer image.

After the President was killed, Rose Kennedy spoke at a party for friends in Boston. ''There wasn't a dry eye in the place,'' said Jim Smith, who was there. ''And she said that her favorite son was Bobby. . . . 'Because he was a good boy . . . a moral man and, yes, more sensitive . . . the most religious of the three.' ''

It was revealing that Bob was the favorite of both parents. Maybe it accounted for some of his arrogance, the knowledge that he had the complete approval of his parents. It was something neither Jack nor Ted ever had.

His mother was right in saying that Bob was the most religious of her sons, but the strength of her faith was not his. After his brother's murder, Bobby reexamined his belief in God as he was reexamining everything else. He had written the line: ''The innocent suffer—how can that be possible and God be just?''

Kay Halle was with Bobby at Hickory Hill, at a discussion group with a very prominent Catholic theologian, Father Darcy. Bobby started the discussion by saying, ''Father, why is it, of all the sermons I've ever heard in church, ever since I was a child, I've never heard one that really stirred my mind. How is it, Father, that I've never yet gone to church where I've heard a sermon that has either enlightened me or uplifted me?''

Although his doubts were intellectual, they were temporary,

directed more at the priests than at the institution, and his deep faith was basic and remained.

———

THE GET-HOFFA SQUAD, headed by Walter Sheridan, had presented evidence to thirteen grand juries by October 1961 and involved sixteen attorneys and some thirty FBI agents. Some of Hoffa's underlings had been sent to prison, but the harassed Hoffa still managed to stay free. Hoffa had the best lawyers money could buy. A Teamster dissident, E. G. Partin, told Sheridan that Hoffa had asked him what he knew about plastic bombs, adding, "I've got to do something about that son of a bitch Bobby Kennedy . . . he's got to go."

Frank Ragano, a lawyer for Santo Trafficante and Jimmy Hoffa, quoted Hoffa as saying after the President's death, "Did you hear the good news? They killed the son of a bitch."

A year before, Trafficante, a friend of Jimmy Hoffa's, had said that John Kennedy was in trouble, "and he will get what is coming to him. . . . He is going to be hit."

In Miami, Hoffa, hearing that Harold Gibbons and top Teamsters in Washington had lowered the flag over the union headquarters to half-mast after the assassination, "flew into a rage." He yelled at his secretary for crying. A reporter asked him about the Attorney General. Hoffa spat out: "Bobby Kennedy is just another lawyer now."

Years later, on his deathbed, Trafficante told Ragano, "Carlos fucked up. . . . We should have killed Bobby." Ragano originally had understood that the reason for killing John Kennedy instead of Bobby was that "if you cut off the head, the tail is dead." Carlos was Carlos Marcello, the head of New Orleans rackets, who had been taped by the FBI discussing the projected assassination of John Kennedy.

Tapes also quoted a Mafia member Stefano Megaddino: "We should kill the whole family, the mother and father, too."

Malcolm X made an unforgettable public taunt after the assassination: "The chickens have come home to roost."

For Bobby, and for many Americans, this tore at a raw nerve. Most Americans felt subtly guilty because they had never acknowledged the undercurrent of violence in our society. Chief Justice Warren later said in his eulogy how hate and malevolence "have eaten into the blood-stream of American life."

———

KENNEDY FINALLY BROUGHT Jimmy Hoffa to trial in January 1964, on charges of bribing jurors in an earlier trial. Hoffa was sentenced to eight years. The following month, at another trial, he was found guilty of diverting Teamster pension funds to his private use, and received another five-year sentence. A Teamster historian, Nicholas Kisburg, discussing the Kennedy-Hoffa vendetta, recalled, "Their ego was so great that it overpowered the cause. They deserved one another."

But Kennedy's associate William Hundley recalled his surprise when Robert Kennedy asked, "How's Hoffa doing, in jail? How do you think he's doing? . . . I hope he gets out." Hundley believed that if Bobby ever became President, he would have pardoned Hoffa.

"You have to understand Bobby," said Hundley. "He just wanted to win. Yeah, all the Kennedys did." For the Kennedys, whether it was politics, or women, or anything else, it was the chase and the challenge rather than the prize.

Columnist Murray Kempton observed, "His biographies . . . all feed off the same ration of anecdotes about his compassion. These instances run to compassion toward dying old ladies and politicians whom he has just beaten, two categories in nature remarkably similar for having not the slightest threat left in them. . . . This compassion for enemies who can no longer hurt him is quite royal: it is how kings talked in the eighteenth century."

There was even a seeming change in his relationship with Lyndon Johnson.

When Johnson picked his Cabinet, Bobby held a press conference, denouncing Lyndon's choices. It was a political declaration of war by someone who still felt that the White House was his domain, that he was a government in exile. In the later months, he felt strongly that Johnson was taking credit "for an awful lot of things" that President Kennedy had started.

Johnson awarded the late President the Posthumous Presidential Medal of Freedom, which Robert Kennedy accepted.

And he continued to court Bobby.

"He used to tell Kenny and Larry and all the others that he thought I hated him," said Robert Kennedy, "and what could he do to get me to like him, and whether he would have me over for a drink or have some conversation with me."

They finally met after a White House dance for General James Gavin. They were in an upstairs kitchen scrambling eggs when Johnson said, "Bobby, you do not like me. Your brother likes me. Your sisters-in-law like me. Your daddy likes me. But you don't like me. Now, why? Why don't you like me?"

"This went on and on for hours," said Charles Spalding, who was there, "like two kids in the sixth form. . . . Johnson kept pursuing him. . . . It was rather persistent questioning and a little difficult for everybody. . . ."

Stewart Alsop once said that when Johnson poured on the full treatment, "it would be like standing under Niagara Falls."

Bob afterward told John Seigenthaler that Johnson had said, "I know why you don't like me. You think I attacked your father, but I never said that. Those reports were false, all false. They were in error. I never did attack your father and I wouldn't, and I always liked you and admired you. But you're angry with me, and you've always been upset with me."

Seigenthaler checked *The New York Times*, found the story of the Johnson attack on the Kennedy father, and forwarded it to Bobby.

Generally, President Johnson played it cool with Bobby, kept clear of the Department of Justice, letting the Attorney General do what he wanted. However, Johnson later sent RFK on a special peace mission to mediate a cease-fire between Indonesia and Malaysia. The Malaysian mission had a double purpose. It pulled Kennedy out of the country while Johnson sent his friend Abe Fortas to houseclean some of the Justice files that might be potentially embarrassing to Johnson.

Sarah McLendon remembered, "Bobby didn't realize what would happen . . . when he found out, he had fits—just furious."

———

IN THE SPRING of 1964, the Attorney General still believed, as he told journalist John Bartlow Martin, that we had to win the war in Vietnam or else we would lose Southeast Asia. That summer he even scrawled a note to President Johnson, volunteering to replace the retiring Henry Cabot Lodge as the American Ambassador in Saigon. Some felt it was a political ploy. Robert Kennedy insisted it was simply because Vietnam was "obviously the most important problem facing the United States."

"I told him I didn't think Lyndon Johnson would name him Ambassador to anywhere except Greenland or Iceland," said Seigenthaler.

Johnson officially rejected that offer because he said the Kennedy family already had lost two sons and he did not want to put another son in a position of danger. But he also knew it would put Bob Kennedy in a national publicity spotlight, possibly in direct confrontation with him. Johnson, feeling Bobby breathing down his neck, repeatedly told associates that he fully expected that one day Robert Kennedy would run against him.

———

JOHNSON HAD ESCALATED the Kennedy beginnings in Vietnam of 16,000 troops to a full-scale war with several hundred thousand troops. It was said of Johnson that he was initially reluctant on Vietnam, but was highly sensitive that he had been described as "a phony veteran" who did not deserve the Silver Star—which he reportedly always wore even on his pajamas.

"Bob did a nice thing," recalled his secretary Angie Novello. "When Johnson was agonizing over the Vietnamese war, whether to escalate it, Bob wrote him a long letter by hand, and sent him a copy of one of Bruce Catton's books and marked a passage of Lincoln, agonizing over the Civil War. He wrote this beautiful letter, telling Johnson how he felt for him, what a hard decision it was to make—that another President went through the same thing. Johnson acknowledged it with a 'Thank you very much for your thought'—something short like that."

The timing was wrong for the overtures by both men: Johnson could not penetrate Robert Kennedy's grief; Kennedy was suspected of currying favor with a President who still had to select his Vice President. But there were others who felt part of Bob's compassion for Johnson on this issue may have come from his still-fresh memory of the intense trauma he and Jack shared during the Cuban missile crisis.

Senator Kennedy still agreed with the President in supporting the South Vietnamese government with American troops to keep the

Communists out of their country, "but not a minute more than necessary."

Then the Senator added, "We are going to win and we are going to stay here until we win."

———

IN THE COMING months, Robert Kennedy would break ground for the first elementary school in the country to be named after his brother, and the Treasury Department would put 26 million Kennedy half-dollars into circulation. This currency was a remarkable honor, given to only a few previous Presidents, such as Lincoln and Washington.

John F. Kennedy had sent a special message to Congress in June 1963, declaring the civil rights bill's passage "imperative." Edward Kennedy also passionately urged the Senate to pass the bill. "I want to see an America where everybody can make his contribution. Where a man will be measured not by the color of his skin but by the content of his character." He then paused and looked off to one side. When he resumed, his voice was less strong, less clear than before. "I remember," he said, "the words of President Johnson last November twenty-seventh." He paused again, clearly faltering. Then he quoted: " 'No memorial oration or eulogy could more eloquently honor President Kennedy's memory than the earliest possible passage of the civil rights bill for which he fought so long.' "

And suddenly, he had to stop. His voice had broken. His last sentence had ended in an audible sob. In the family gallery, his wife dabbed at her eyes with a handkerchief. In the spectators' gallery, tears began to flow freely as Teddy struggled for the control necessary to continue. No, he had not spoken at the grave. But he was speaking now, and he would finish. "My brother," he said, "was the first President of the United States to state publicly that segregation was morally wrong. His heart and soul are in this bill."

Momentarily, Teddy had to stop again. His own eyes were wet; his pain seemed not only emotional but physical. "If his life and death had a meaning," Teddy said, his voice so low now, so strained, "it was that we should not hate but love one another. We should use our powers not to create conditions of oppression that lead to violence, but conditions of freedom that lead to peace. It is in that spirit," he concluded, "that I hope the Senate will pass this bill." As Joan wept openly in the gallery and other onlookers continued to cry, he took his seat, his face as pale as it had been during the debate with Eddie McCormack.

Congress passed the bill and President Johnson signed it in July 1964.

It took considerable heavy pressure from President Johnson, using the political carrot and stick, of patronage and political threats, to persuade a reluctant Congress to pass the backlog of Kennedy legislation. Congressman Richard Bolling recalled that LBJ even felt it necessary to lobby for a bill, saying repeatedly, "Why don't you get aboard and help pass this for Jackie, Caroline and little John-John." Commented Hugh Sidey, "I didn't understand why the Kennedys so ridiculed Johnson in the White House. . . . My God, he got everything through . . . the whole Kennedy program."

———————

AT NO TIME in her life had Ethel been put to a greater test. It was the challenge of pulling her husband away from his grief and giving his life an increased normalcy. It took time. She acted as the buffer to ward off all those who wanted to intrude on her husband's time and his grief. If Bob took a trip anywhere, particularly a long one, she had no hesitation in leaving all her children to be with him. He was her absolute priority.

John Seigenthaler was with Bobby at Hickory Hill on the first anniversary of Jack's assassination. "Somber and preoccupied, Bobby finally put on Jack's aviator jacket with the presidential seal and said, 'Let's go for a ride. I want to go to Confession.' En route to the church, he suddenly said, 'Let's stop at Arlington and look at Johnny's grave.' The cemetery gate was locked, and they climbed over it. As a military guard approached them, Robert Kennedy yelled, 'I'm Mr. Kennedy!' At the grave, he knelt and prayed. Walking back to the car, Robert said, 'You know, I had a conversation with him a couple of days before it happened. He had called to wish me a happy birthday. The thing is I can't remember what he said. I've tried and tried and I can't remember. I've searched my mind over and over. I should have had somebody on the line taking down what he said.' "

———

IT WAS NO Washington secret that the Kennedy family continued to exert considerable pressure on Johnson to select Bobby as his vice-presidential nominee.

"If one looks back in the newspaper files on the day that the President made his now-famous purge of vice-presidential candidates," said journalist William Shannon, "one sees an item where Mrs. John F. Kennedy was 'understood' to be most interested in the fact 'her brother-in-law was being considered for the Vice Presidency.' Mrs. John F. Kennedy was thinking of attending the Democratic National Convention. She had not quite made up her mind yet whether to go and take part in the events or not. It was clear that if Jackie went there and gave Bobby her blessing, President Johnson would find it difficult to reject the Attorney General. Later, Bob told columnist Rowland Evans that it all depended on whether Johnson would follow through on the Kennedy program."

When asked if he would accept a vice-presidential nomination on a Johnson ticket, Bob replied, "The question reminds me of my brother. When he was posed with such a question, he used to say that is like asking a girl if she would marry that man if he proposed."

"Every day as I opened the papers or turned on the television," President Johnson told author Doris Kearns Goodwin, "there was something about Bobby Kennedy; there was some person or group talking about what a great Vice President he'd make. . . . Somehow it just didn't seem fair. I'd given three years of loyal service to Jack Kennedy. During all that time I'd willingly stayed in the background; I knew that it was his Presidency, not mine. If I disagreed with him, I did it in private, not public. And then Kennedy was killed and I became the custodian of his will, I became the President. But none of this seemed to register with Bobby Kennedy, who acted like he was the custodian of the Kennedy dream, some kind of rightful heir to the throne. It just didn't seem fair. I'd waited for my turn. Bobby should've waited for his. But he and the Kennedy people wanted it now."

Johnson made it clear to mutual friends like Larry O'Brien that he wanted no part of Kennedy for Vice President, that he much preferred

Sarge Shriver. But word soon came from the Kennedys: "If you're going to take a Kennedy, it's got to be the real thing; it's got to be Bobby . . . not a half-Kennedy."

The powerful political boss of Chicago, Mayor Daley, made it clear that he also wanted Kennedy on the ticket. But LBJ stood firm. He told Clark Clifford that if he picked Kennedy on the ticket, "he would forever be sandwiched between the two Kennedy brothers, unable to govern or command public support for his programs . . . and would be treated as a lame duck for the entire four years of his elected presidency."

Later he backtracked. "Look, if I need Robert Kennedy, I'll take him," he told Ken O'Donnell. "I'll take anybody. I want to get elected. . . . If I don't need him, I'm not going to take him."

Clifford prepared a political memorandum for Johnson detailing why Robert Kennedy would not be the right running mate in 1964. It also provided Johnson with his political solution: he would eliminate all Cabinet members from vice-presidential consideration.

Privately, and with great delight, the President called Kennedy into the Oval Office and read him the statement. Johnson described Bobby as stunned, with his mouth hanging open, not knowing what to say, gulping, "his Adam's apple going up and down like a yo-yo."

For his friends and associates, Bobby put on a brave front. "Aw, what the hell," he laughingly told some of his staff, "let's go form our own country." And when he lunched with Ted and Larry O'Brien afterward, O'Brien insisted that Bob did not evidence any degree of disappointment, "unless he was putting on a performance."

He probably was. Of course it was a disappointment. Bob didn't like to lose in anything. He wouldn't have tried for it if he didn't want it. And he must have thought, often, how differently Johnson might have felt about him if there had been no bitterness about Johnson becoming Vice President for Jack.

––––––––

TEDDY SOON STOLE the headlines. He was scheduled to go to Springfield, Massachusetts, to the Democratic State Convention in June 1964 to be nominated for a full Senate term. Visibility was zero, "like flying through a black void." Ted pressured the pilot of their small private twin-engine plane not to divert to another airport: "Damn it, we're late already." With him was Senator Birch Bayh, who was to nominate him. To show how safe he felt, Teddy had unfastened his seat belt and was half-standing. The pilot finally found a hole in the fog and zoomed down to find himself on the top of an orchard, three miles from the airport. It was too late to start climbing. The plane crashed into a hillside and killed the pilot and a passenger. Bayh and his wife were uninjured. Senator Edward Kennedy fractured several vertebrae, but fortunately the spine was not severed. A difference of a quarter of an inch in the fracture would have left him permanently paralyzed. His blood pressure was also dangerously low and he was placed in an oxygen tent because he had a punctured lung.

"Jean heard the news on the 11:00 P.M. radio," recalled Rose Kennedy. "She crossed the street and told Bobby, who was at home in bed, and they left immediately for Ted—without disturbing their parents. So the seventh and eighth child were a great blessing for the ninth."

Ted was given several transfusions and antishock treatment. None of his internal organs were ruptured, otherwise surgery would have been critical.

Bobby was there when his brother became conscious. Ted looked at him, smiled, and said, "Is it true that you are ruthless?"

Looking at his brother, recalling the early death of young Joe in the war, and the crippling illnesses, and the murder of Jack, Bob felt fatalistic—that the family was doomed, and none of them would live long.

After leaving the hospital, Robert Kennedy went for a walk with his friend Walter Sheridan. "We just lay down in the grass," Sheridan said later, "and he said, 'Somebody up there doesn't like us.' "

Three weeks later, Ted was transferred to the New England Hospital, in Boston, where he was strapped into an orthopedic frame and told he could not move until his spine healed—which would take months. He was forced to eat facedown and was rotated "like a human rotisserie" several times a day. The doctors told him that he would have back pain for the rest of his life. All his life, Ted had tried to model himself after Jack; now he even had Jack's constant pain.

The senior Kennedy, in his wheelchair, was taken to the hospital to see his youngest son. He sat intently, his eyes looking first at the feet, then slowly at the face. And then even more slowly, he surveyed the entire length of his son's body—to convince himself that everything was okay.

"You should've seen his face," said Clayton Reed, on staff at the hospital. "His eyes were wet and pained."

After examining Ted's jagged spinal fractures, doctors recommended surgery. Ted was willing, but his father "stormed at the doctors" in such a way that it was clear that no operation was to be permitted. His father could not speak then, but he could understand, and he could react. Two spinal operations had nearly killed Jack. "Dad doesn't like doctors and doesn't believe half what they say," Ted remarked afterward.

Coming so close to death didn't seem to change Ted's personality. He was still outgoing, determinedly good-humored, brave. Dave Powers, after visiting, said, "He cheered *me* up."

Now sharing Bobby's fatalism and Jack's determination after three Last Rites to milk every moment, Ted's accident only intensified his pleasure-seeking. It also encouraged him to consider his political future. He was not an intellectual, but he realized more than ever that if he were to prepare himself for any political potential, he had to expand his knowledge and capabilities. He was only thirty-two, and although the presidency was still something remote, the glow of it was surely in his mind.

Teddy invited professors from Harvard and MIT to come and brief him on economics. Afterward the professors reported to the press Teddy's "astonishing depth and maturity." They were also impressed that he was busy reading biographies of Roosevelt and the Adams family, and the history of World War II, by Winston Churchill. Ted probably didn't mention his passion for the spy novels of Ian Fleming.

His brother Jack had written a book while he was recuperating from surgery, and Ted also busied himself editing reminiscences about his father in a privately printed book, *The Fruitful Bough*. In the book, Bobby had written, "When we grew a little older, we realized he wasn't perfect, that he made mistakes, but by that time, we realized everyone did. I remember listening to him talk with an important figure in business, the theater, or politics, and always observing that he was the dominant figure—that he knew more—that he expressed it better. . . . If he was more clever or wiser than others, he would be unusual. But then, perhaps everyone's father is cleverer and wiser than anyone else."

This private awareness of their father's faults, as well as his gifts, came separately to each of his sons, at different times of their lives. It never really tempered their admiration or lessened their love.

Like Jack, Ted, too, turned to painting landscapes during his recovery. He completed seven oil paintings, working when he couldn't sleep. Bobby compared him to Michelangelo, but only because both of them had painted on their backs.

Ted received some 80,000 letters and visitors, even including President Lyndon Johnson, with whom he had retained a friendly relationship.

Meanwhile, he was still running for reelection, and his wife, Joan, filled in for him at political rallies. It was less than a month after her second miscarriage. Campaign staff statistics indicated that Joan visited thirty-nine cities and 312 towns in Massachusetts, making an average of more than eight appearances per day.

She started out nervous and awkward, but the band, where there was one, played "A Pretty Girl Is Like a Melody," and the crowds were always on her side, often gave her standing ovations.

Ted won that election, getting 74 percent of the vote. And Bob would needle him: "Joan won it for you."

————

EVEN THEN THERE had been some press speculation on whether Ted might be the presidential candidate before Bob. It was a question that reporter Marvin Sleeper had been instructed not to ask. But, after he completed the interview, just as he was ready to leave, he did so.

Teddy glared at him, then softened and said quietly, "The older brother is always first."

"I used to fly up to the Cape with Bobby and Ted in the *Caroline*," said old friend Dun Gifford. "We'd leave right after the Friday voting in the Senate ended. . . . There was a seat in the plane towards the middle just off the aisle everybody called the 'President's Chair.' Nobody ever mentioned it, but I noticed that whenever Bobby was along he sat in that seat, and whenever he wasn't, Ted sat there. It was the clearest example of . . . primogeniture—anybody could ever want." Even more clear, and more personal, was that this epitomized the envy and competition between the brothers. There was no question about that. Ted would never step out in front of Bobby. That's simply the way it was.

———

A WEEK AFTER his brother's air crash, Bobby and Ethel and several of their children were touring Germany, making many of the same stops where he and President Kennedy had gone. He unveiled a plaque in his brother's honor in West Berlin and even made a speech to some 250,000 people, repeating his brother's words: *Ich bin ein Berliner.* He made that speech in the freezing cold, wearing a thin coat, shaking so hard that he could hardly speak. Ethel came quickly to his side, slid her hand under his coat, and massaged his back until he finished his remarks. Asked later what was his greatest achievement, he answered quickly and simply, "Marrying Ethel."

Later, receiving an honorary degree from the Free University of Berlin, he told them that even though his brother was dead, the hope he offered for a better world lives on. "The torch still burns."

In Poland, Bob ignored State Department protocol and barnstormed the country, speaking to huge, enthusiastic crowds, sometimes standing on top of his car. Polish officials were furious with his conduct. "Do you know who you shook hands with this morning in the market?" asked an indignant deputy minister of foreign affairs. "My maid." Bobby could not have been more delighted.

And, in London, waiting for the Prime Minister at Ten Downing Street, Robert wrote his father a letter recalling the family's stay in London nearly thirty years before.

Mobbed by cheering students in Manila, Bob said, "It wasn't really for me. . . . It was for him."

A friend seated beside him quietly replied, "You've got to do it for him now." For perhaps thirty seconds Bob sat there lost in thought. Then he slowly nodded his head. It was time to step out of his brother's shoes and into his own.

———

HOW BIG A step should it be?

The vice presidency was no longer feasible. He couldn't run for anything in Massachusetts when Ted was Senator. His staff urged him to run in New York for the U.S. Senate.

"He didn't really want to run for the Senate," said Angie Novello. "He was so destroyed by the death of his brother. But I think he felt that he had to carry on his brother's ideals, and programs. So many people said, 'Oh, he was ambitious.' Well, listen, you have to be ambitious to be a politician!"

The appeal was strong. It was time to open a fresh chapter in his life, a new direction. He always had felt that being appointed to office wasn't enough, that he had to be elected to something, even if it was only Mayor of Hyannis Port.

"Edward Kennedy told me his brother was going to run for the Senate, and asked me to go over to the Justice Department and begin to assemble some material on New York and New York's problems," said Milton Gwirtzman. When Bob went on a sailing trip, he took with him a series of reports about the major New York problems as well as a standard New York State high school text about history and government. And, before he left, he resigned as Attorney General.

Mayor Robert F. Wagner of New York City endorsed him for the Senate on August 21, 1964, and, promising to devote all his efforts and talents to the State of New York, Kennedy announced his candidacy on the front lawn of the Mayor's Gracie Mansion.

Although his family had lived in New York for many years, that had been a long time ago. When Bobby flew to New York with Ben Bradlee, he asked, "Is the East River on this side, and the Hudson on the other; or is it the other way around?" He wasn't joking.

For Bob, it was a new beginning. As he told a New York *Post* reporter at the start of the campaign, with a small-boy pride, "This is *my* first political campaign."

Polls showed he would win over Republican incumbent Senator Kenneth Keating, by a healthy margin. New Yorkers loved the idea of having their own Kennedy. Bob's strongest asset was the country's guilt. It had washed him clean and now it was setting him on a new path. As somebody said, "If Abraham Lincoln had a younger brother, he might have gone far in national politics."

Advisers who had served his brother Jack did not feel bound to Bobby. "JFK was the catalyst who kept them all together," said Ted Sorensen. "After his death, they separated and didn't even come together for Bobby's campaign." Sorensen was one of the few who did.

While Bobby was busy in New York, the Democratic National

Convention nominated Lyndon Johnson and Hubert H. Humphrey to head their ticket.

"Johnson was frightened stiff that Bobby was gonna come in and make a speech and be nominated for President. Just unbelievable," said Ken O'Donnell. "Johnson just had something in his mind, that the Kennedys had some insurmountable power, a call from heaven, and he, Johnson, was gonna be obliterated."

Johnson realized that he could not prevent Robert Kennedy's presence at the convention. The compromise was to let him make a speech of introduction for a short film called *A Thousand Days,* on the life of President Kennedy. President Johnson not only had carefully censored the film to eliminate any mention of Robert Kennedy, but made certain that it was not to be shown until the vice-presidential nomination had been safely made, on the last day of the convention.

When Bobby appeared, there was an emotional explosion. Applauding, waving, cheers and tears—a touching, memorable eulogy to a dead hero. In the nine months since his murder, the legacy of JFK had grown into a legend.

For twenty-two long minutes, Robert Kennedy stood there, unable to speak above the great roar of applause. "It hit. I mean, it really hit," said John Seigenthaler. . . . "It just went on and on. I had to leave. I walked away . . . and I just fell apart because I knew that he should have been a much bigger part of it. And that was the true indication that he was better than anyone that Lyndon decided to go with. . . . I think all of us felt some of that, too. But it just wouldn't stop, went on and on."

Speaking briefly and emotionally, with eyes wet, Robert Kennedy used a quote Jacqueline had given him from act 3 of *Romeo and Juliet:* "When he shall die, take him and cut him out into stars and he shall make the face of heaven so fine that all the world will be in love with night and pay no worship to the garish sun." When he read it, the convention audience listened in utter silence.

"It was a moment I will never forget," said Angie Novello. "The tears were just running down his face. I was in Washington, having dinner with some friends. We watched that, and we all wept with Bob. Yes, I'd seen him cry before, but he'd only do it in front of someone he knew."

Standing under the platform at the convention, Wilson Wyatt, highly respected liberal Mayor of Louisville, Kentucky, recalled how

President Harry Truman had planned to offer him the vice-presidential nomination until he heard Senator Alben Barkley's fiery keynote speech, and then selected Barkley. But there was nothing that could persuade Lyndon Johnson to pick Bobby. The hate was too deep.

———

ROBERT KENNEDY TOOK temporary residence in New York City at the United Nations Plaza, and rented a home in Glen Cove, Long Island, but he was still quickly attacked for being a carpetbagger—running for office in one state while living and voting in another. Senators all over the country thought, "This could happen to me, too—that a glamorous type could move into my state, and oppose me, as Bobby did."

Bob named his brother-in-law, Stephen Smith, as his campaign manager. It was Smith, a New Yorker, who had helped persuade him to run.

"Do what you have to do," Smith told campaign workers, "but if it doesn't work out, we'll come looking for you the day after the election."

R. Sargent Shriver was clearly not part of Bobby's inner circle. Turned down by Johnson as Vice President, he had become a firmer part of the Johnson administration, as the head of the Office of Economic Opportunity, an agency set up to relieve poverty in the distressed areas of the country.

Lem Billings, as usual, was available. Ted Kennedy later said that "Lem's genius and good sense in his chosen profession of advertising made him a key architect of the successful strategy in the difficult days of Bobby's first 1964 campaign for the Senate. Lem knew my brother's true humanity, and it was Lem who helped New York to see it."

The key influence on his campaign was all the memories and all the conversations, and all the advice Bob got from his father on a daily basis when he managed his brother's campaigns.

Ted's aides played a strong support role.

Once they became involved in politics, the brothers attracted different kinds of people. "Bob was more apt to attract people who were 100 percent, more interested in issues," said Hackett, "and more interested in work and, I think, less interested in themselves." But some of Ted's staff, according to Barbara Coleman, who worked

for Bob's campaign, never stopped serving Ted's interests and ambitions as well as their own.

At first it was very difficult for Bob, and even embarrassing. This was the first time he was selling himself and not Jack. He had learned to speak forcefully for an issue, or a cause, but not for himself. He was awkward. For himself, he was a dull speaker, a terrible campaigner. His tight smile looked phony. He had a massive case of shyness. When he spoke, often in a flat monotone, his arm jerked up and down like a spring. His voice was too high and too nasal, and he read most of his early speeches.

"So he had to be self-trained," said Billings. "He had to stand in front of a mirror—do all the terrible things. . . . I admire Bobby . . . he had to work for everything."

It took a lot of hard work and determination to become a decent speaker—never as good as his older brother—but a speaker that sounded sincere and honest. He created his own style, using the audience. "He'd say, 'How many here believe that we should be in Vietnam?' This was on a college campus, for example. And three quarters of the hands would go up. He'd say, 'All right, now, how many here believe in student deferment from the draft?' And the same hands would go up. He'd say, 'Aahh, you believe in the war, as long as somebody else fights it, is that what you're telling me?' Now there's nervous laughter from the audience."

Despite his substantial efforts, Bob felt the polls were slipping and so he went to see Hubert Humphrey.

"Well, I insisted on staying in the room with them," said Humphrey aide Bill Connell. "I frankly didn't trust him, so I wanted to be a witness there. Sure enough, Bobby said, 'Senator, I want you to attack Jimmy Hoffa up here . . . that Hoffa is spending money against me, and has got his organization going against me, and is saying untrue things about me. I want you to attack him, call him a liar, and say that Jimmy Hoffa's out to get Bob Kennedy.'

"I didn't even let Humphrey open his mouth before I jumped in and said, 'Mr. Kennedy, have you any evidence on this, or is it just something you understand is taking place?' He wouldn't answer . . . just looked right past me and said, 'Senator Humphrey, I need you to do this.'

" 'I don't know,' said Humphrey."

Connell again broke in asking for hard evidence, "and wow, you could see the steam coming out of Bobby's ears. . . . I remember how cold Bobby was; just like a glacier, and furious."

During an early meeting to organize the campaign, noted public relations adviser Fred Papert, who planned the television advertising for Bob, said, "The basic aim of all our commercials, Bob, will be to present you as a warm, sincere individual." Deadpan, Kennedy asked: "You going to use a double?"

He worried about his public image of a tough and ruthless prosecutor. "Why do you think so many people dislike me?" he once asked. Because of this image, aides felt he must be photographed as often as possible with children, smiling and happy and athletic, in every way a boy's ideal man.

He tried to lace his speeches with more humor, but it was often misdirected. One day in the campaign, it started to rain while he was speaking from the back of an open truck. He didn't have a coat or a hat, and a middle-aged man tossed him a raincoat.

"Can I keep it?" asked Kennedy with a laugh. "In memory of your brother," the man replied.

Kennedy blinked. "Thank you."

Another time, on Fordham Road in the Bronx, somebody in the crowd reached in his car to grab his PT-boat tie pin. Bob grabbed his hand and said quietly, "Don't take that, my brother gave it to me."

———————

KENNEDY MONEY AGAIN made a difference. Two planes criss-crossed the state every day, delivering news film about Bobby Kennedy to TV studios in different cities.

As she had recently done for Teddy, his mother again came out on the campaign trail. He joked that none of her children liked to get on the same platform with her because none of them could compete with her.

While the Kennedy family rallied around another campaigning brother, Jacqueline Kennedy still had not found her way.

A magazine editor recalls meeting her fourteen months after Dallas. He proposed that she write a monthly column about anything that interested her.

She said, "What I really would like to do is keep President Kennedy's ideas alive. But"—and she hesitated—"the only way I know is to work through some man. Maybe I could do it somehow through Robert Kennedy . . ." And her voice trailed off.

However, friends reported that she used fewer sleeping pills, and although she looked thinner, her appetite was back. John-John still liked to tell everybody that his daddy had gone to heaven.

Bob was the person Jacqueline saw most often. She knew she could always count on him. There were even those who said, "Jackie was in love with Bobby. Everybody knew it. If you could have seen the way she clung to him, put her head on his shoulder, and looked up into his eyes."

But a close friend told Lester David, "I am certain that this rumor wounded Kennedy more than any other story spread about him in his life. He could accept philosophically almost any other kind of personal attack against him, his beliefs, his religion, his character, but this was too much."

A laundress at Hyannis, Mary DeGrace, who worked for Ethel Kennedy at Hyannis Port for seventeen years, recalled the Jackie–Bobby rumors among the staff. "One time, Jackie walked in for dinner and Ethel just rose from the table and went to her room. There was a strain between the two women . . . something was going on. It seemed as though Bobby and Jackie were working up to something, and while nothing happened, Ethel worried that something might happen."

———

DURING BOBBY'S CAMPAIGN, he asked two interviewing women reporters, "Do you like my brother Teddy better than me?" One of the women recalled, "We both said 'oh no,' and then he seemed to relax."

Envy existed among the brothers as long as they lived. It was part of their training as well as their heritage. It merged with their competitiveness. It spurred them on. And, finally, it killed them.

"He lacked Jack Kennedy's absolute confidence in himself and his charm, and most important, his confidence that he could project that charm. . . ." reported author David Halberstam. "The people around Robert Kennedy were regularly telling him to loosen up, but it did not come easily: his knuckles would be cracking away, his hands wrestling with each other—he was not a loose man. He was less graceful and more committed than his brother."

Lyndon Johnson also spent a day campaigning with Kennedy, and Bobby needed his help. Johnson's support for Bob Kennedy was political, not personal. Kennedy was another Senate vote he wanted.

After a brutal battle, Robert Kennedy was elected with a plurality of over a half million votes. Johnson made much of the fact that his own victory margin in the state was considerably larger. Robert afterward sent Ted a print of the Justice Department's main entrance. Across it he scrawled:

> For Eddie
>
> It's out of this building into yours
> move over!!
>
> Robbie

As a freshman Senator, Kennedy sat in one of the so-called rumble seats added to the back of the Democratic side of the Senate floor. He observed tartly, "I had better seats for *Hello, Dolly!*" At his press conference, an attractive blonde asked, " 'If elected President, would you appoint your brother as Attorney General?'

" 'No, we tried that once,' " he replied, and then asked her whom she represented.

The blonde was Ted's wife, Joan.

Despite her incredible campaign success for her husband, Joan could never become a Kennedy. Whenever she was with them, the Kennedy women shattered her self-confidence. They mocked her leopard bathing suit, her see-through blouse, and when she seriously sprained an ankle, they insisted she could keep playing. She had been the college beauty queen, and compared with her they were all plain Janes, but at Hyannis they made her feel incapable and insignificant. She had tried to emerge on her own by parading her beauty in short skirts and low-cut dresses, but the Kennedy women only mocked her more. She was increasingly vulnerable.

Looking gaunt after months in the hospital, leaning heavily on a cane, his smashed back enclosed in a steel brace, Edward Kennedy took the oath with Bobby. Not since 1803 had two brothers served together in the Senate.

"I recall the first day that Edward Kennedy came back from his

airplane crash . . . the first day of Congress. It was the first day that
Senator Robert Kennedy entered Congress. I had to do a double
profile," said John Lindsay of *Newsweek*. "The contrast between the two
men at that time was just beyond belief. I went in to see Robert,
prepared for fifteen minutes of questions and possibly fifteen minutes
of answers. . . . I asked rather lengthy questions, and he would say,
'No.' Or he would say, 'Yes.' Or he would say, 'Well, I don't think it's
wise to go into that right now.' So I came out without a line, really, and
I was mopping my brow when I came out. . . . Some potentate in
Indonesia had given him a giant stuffed tiger, and it was sitting in the
middle of the floor. Halfway through my interview a large group of
youngsters from New York came in, twenty or so children, and one of
them cringed at the sight of the tiger. Bob pressed the button on his
desk and Angie, his secretary, came in, and he said, 'Angie, get this
tiger out of here. It's scaring my constituents.' That's the only thing I
got out of the interview.

"Then I went down to Ted's office, and there was a real old Irish
gathering going on down there, including all the Kennedy sisters, and
they were having sandwiches and a few drinks, coffee, tea . . . this kind
of thing. The place was totally jammed with well-wishers, mostly from
Boston, and . . . he gave me a very interesting and lovely interview,
mostly anecdotes of his days as a boy with Honey Fitzgerald in Boston. I
got a great deal."

Newsweek also wanted a cover picture of the first brother team in the
Senate in a hundred years.

When the magazine's Washington bureau asked the Kennedys to
pose together for a cover picture on the steps of the Capitol, Bobby
sent Ted out to meet the photographer, explaining haughtily that he did
not have time for such trivia, and that a stock photograph of him could
be mechanically pasted in beside Ted: it must, he insisted, show him
standing slightly higher than Ted. *Newsweek* agreed. So did Ted, who had
learned to accept this sort of treatment from his brother.

When both brothers did pose for pictures, a photographer asked
Robert to "step back a little, you're casting a shadow on Ted." Edward
smiled and said, "It'll be the same in Washington."

The country was still ravaged by race riots and student demonstrations against the war in Vietnam. General MacArthur died,
soon to be followed by Winston Churchill. The Medicare bill, first

proposed by Kennedy, would soon be signed into law by President Johnson.

Shortly after he was sworn in on January 4, 1965, Bob was asked how he felt being a member of the U.S. Senate. He suddenly seemed sad, more like a man who had lost rather than won. "I regret the circumstances that led to my being here," he replied.

But when somebody asked whether he would have run for office if his brother were still alive, he answered, "I suppose I would have eventually. Otherwise I'd have been sitting around waiting for a place in the Administration. But after it was finished . . . with the President . . . I just wanted to keep myself busy and have something to occupy my mind. But I might have run even if he had lived. I didn't really want to be a Senator, but I like it more than I expected to."

―――――――

WHEN PRESIDENT LYNDON Johnson was inaugurated, a film clip showed Bobby as grim and unsmiling. The interdependence of the brothers became quickly obvious when Ted's aide prepared a memo for the new Senator on how to set up his office. It included a specific recommendation that he hire Adam Walinsky, a bright young lawyer in the Justice Department. Walinsky would become a pivotal influence, unafraid to push his own ideas, especially on social issues.

Walinsky used to wince when Robert would introduce an amendment about which he was unfamiliar and stumble through his explanations. And, when asked what it really meant, Bob might say, "I haven't the slightest idea, but I know it's a good idea, so let's do it anyway."

In the 89th Congress, the two brothers were on the same Committee of Labor and Public Welfare, and also on a subcommittee on Health. The Republicans wanted to know Bob's explanation of a certain paragraph of a health bill. "With his eyes he implored his brother for help. Ted didn't move a muscle. His brother finally scribbled him a note, saying, 'Goddamn it, why don't you help me out?' And Ted scratched on the bottom, 'You're not in real trouble yet.' "

He was saying, you're just passing through; I'm the senior Senator here.

Ted was thirty-two; Bob thirty-nine. But it was clear that the younger Senator was guiding and protecting his older brother. It was a unique situation for Ted, and he loved it.

Bob would ask Ted, when pushing a bill, "You know how to handle these fellows. . . . You're the likable one. . . . What should I do now?"

During some Labor Committee hearings, Robert asked Ted if he should cancel some New York appointments and stay for the afternoon hearings. Ted said yes, certainly. All afternoon Robert fumed at the utter dullness of the hearings and leaned over and asked his brother, "Is this how you became a good Senator?" Ted answered, "Yes. You just sit there and wait your turn now, Bobby, and you'll be all right. I'll take care of you."

Whenever Bob made a move, he would always call Ted first. They would talk every morning and every night, wherever they were. If Bob had a statement to make, he'd want Ted to read it first, and approve it. More and more, Ted had become to Bob what Bob was to Jack.

Another friend of both noted, "Bobby and Teddy had a closeness that came from the genes, not really the heart. . . . They were terribly close but not instinctively close, if that makes sense."

It did make sense. Bob was Ted's best friend, and Bob was the man Ted most admired, most respected, most loved. But the fact that Bob needed Ted at all was high reward for Ted. And, still, Ted was always ready to defer to him.

But there was a high point for Ted when he took Jack's old sailboat and beat Bobby in a race at Hyannis—when Bobby had a new boat with the latest equipment.

The two brothers seldom differed on a roll-call vote. During the committee sessions they followed the same lines of questioning.

If Robert spoke too long, Ted passed him a note saying he had just lost a Senator's vote. "Stop talking and let's vote or you'll lose all the others too."

Ted would twit his brother whenever he could.

When Bob was speaking on some complex amendment, Ted would break him up by passing a note to him saying, "I don't care about the other fellows. I understand it, Bobby."

Ted, a consummate Senate man, understood the need for compromise and persuasion. He knew how to sidle up to some Senator with quiet reason instead of hammering him with hot argument. Ted found all this fun; Robert was restless and bored. Bob felt there was so much to do that he never saw any good reason for just not going ahead and doing it.

John Kennedy had waited five months to deliver his maiden speech; Teddy had waited sixteen; but restless Robert waited only three weeks. Rose Kennedy remarked "how eery it was" when Teddy and Bobby spoke in the Senate "just like Jack."

"You see, in terms of our general philosophy, my brother and I started off the same," said Ted. "Much of the input from the family was the same. Our exposure and development as human beings was very similar. And so we moved in similar, or maybe parallel, directions. Bob was interested in education; I got interested in health. He got involved in the problems of the Middle East; I spent more time on the problems of the Far East. But we had the same general parameters of interest and concern."

Still, when Robert Kennedy moved in on an issue, Ted kept clear. "But Robert felt no such qualm if Ted was centered on an issue," said Ted's aide David Burke. "On some issues, however, such as immigration or the outlawing of the poll tax that Ted has made his own, Robert was careful not to upstage him. But there was no doubt that the older brother was the star."

The easy, affable Ted was far more popular with the Senators, yet there was little question that Bob's views carried far more weight. "Whatever Bobby says tends to become the 'Kennedy position' in the public mind."

Washington observers noted quick differences between the brothers. A friend of both then said, "Ted was always big trying to be little; Bobby was always little trying to be big." Bob was more interested in Vietnam than he was in New York; Ted was more interested in Massachusetts than he was in Vietnam.

Reporter Hobart Rowen recalled how forcefully Ted talked about the dire straits of the unemployed shoe and textile workers in Massachusetts. He kept saying, "You know, we've got to do something!"

"I think you're giving Kennedy preferential treatment," a Senator told a committee chairman about Robert Kennedy.

"Oh no," the committee chairman replied. "I treat him the same way I'd treat any future President."

One Senator remarked with amiable envy, "How can you compete? He has 'future' written all over him."

Bob Kennedy was highly conscious of this, too. A fellow Senator said, "He understands very well the limitations of achieving a national identity if you keep your nose close to the legislative grindstone. I would call Bobby a hit-and-run senator. He'll come into a committee room where the TV cameras are, take a slug at General Motors, and leave. The drudgery of writing and shepherding a bill is left to someone else." Almost everything Bob Kennedy said or did was front page. For example, when he made a speech about China, the press gave it major notice; when Ted had made an earlier speech on China, he got little mention.

Because of this, Bob was able to attract the best and the brightest for his staff. Jack's staff had been mainly political pros who knew where the votes were and how to get them. Teddy's staff was the same—and he listened to them.

There was obviously a quiet competition between the staffs. "When Bobby began to surround himself with people of his own," said journalist Hayes Gorey, "he was thinking in terms of a White House staff. . . . Bobby needed people who were attuned to what was happening with the young, the New Left, the Old Right, the poor, the black, business, and labor. His staff, rather than being tailored to win elections, was to serve as a source of continuing education." His staff was a bubbling caldron of very good, very bright, very aggressive people. As a boss, he expected much and was not easy with his compliments.

Bob's learning technique involved peppering people he met with innumerable questions. With his retentive memory, he learned more from briefings than from reading. But he got quickly impatient with long replies. His staff soon learned to give him short explanations. Remarked observer William Shannon, "He seemed just as satisfied with the short, superficial answers as the long, complete ones. So you figure it out. Does he really want to know or does he just like to ask questions?"

"Teddy takes in everything you tell him," commented author Burton Hersh, "and gives it back exactly as you told it to him. Bobby takes it in, and you get that and something more back. With John Kennedy, of course, you had a discussion."

Those who knew both Jack and Bob said that Bob was the harder to work for but that he dealt with more substance than style. Some, like Laura Bergquist, who also knew Ted, felt there was then not all that much to him except that he usually voted on the right side.

It was true that Ted seemed to lack his brother's passion for causes.

His speeches were carefully crafted by staff, cautiously worked out in accord with party principles, and he read them as written.

When Defense Secretary McNamara gave the government position on Vietnam, it was Teddy who spoke against it in the Senate. "Robert Kennedy had put Teddy up to that," said Ted staff man Peter Edelman, "because he didn't want to do it himself. Because he thought that would be taken as too personal between him and Johnson, and that again, there's a sort of credibility problem."

Discussing Teddy's apparent lack of emotional involvement in issues, his brother Robert said, "In politics, I think, there's a great advantage in remaining unemotional about issues. This doesn't mean that Ted feels less strongly about these issues." He had said the same thing about Jack. He went on to say that it wasn't necessary to treat an issue as if you were stirring up a revival meeting, that it was far more effective to be emotionally detached and see both sides. "In choosing between the politician who becomes emotional on certain issues and the one who is able to discuss questions judiciously and factually, I'd choose the latter every time."

Bobby could preach this, but not practice it.

————

A FRIEND OF both Jack and Bobby remarked that each differed in his choice of daytime associates in part because of whom they could expect to find at home at night. "Jack would go home to dinner and find that Jackie had invited Truman Capote and Leonard Bernstein. Bobby could expect Andy Williams and Carol Channing." In contrast, Ethel and Bob preferred the more casual "down-home" music surrounded by family values.

During Robert's tenure in the Senate, his family was rapidly growing. Ethel gave birth to her ninth child, and sixth son. His children were still his prime concern. He was out sailing at the Cape once when he received a radio report that his daughter Kathleen had been hurt in a fall in a horse show. "Told that the weather was too rough to take the boat in, he dove over the side and began to swim to shore."

As a father, Ted was just as loving as Bobby, but less like a camp counselor. Ted was a storyteller, enthralling his four-year-old Kara, and Ted Jr., a year younger, with stories and animal imitations. Occasionally, Ted broke loose. He gave a fortieth birthday party for Robert at his rented Washington home on 28th Street. "This was a party that had long been scheduled," said Milton Gwirtzman. "Most of the Democratic members of the Senate, and others who'd been friendly with Robert Kennedy and who worked for the media, in law firms, and in other walks of life in Washington were invited, along with several former members of the Kennedy Administration.

"It lasted quite late, into the wee hours. Toward the end of it, the band was still playing outside. It was a lovely spring night. The air was very still, and the music carried through it. Evidently some of the neighbors, at about two o'clock, got upset by the music and noise, and called the police. A couple of policemen dropped by, just to see what was going on and to urge a little quiet. They were not about to make a bust, in view of who the host and guests were. But as soon as Robert Kennedy saw a policeman walk in, he left, and didn't come back. He might have just been looking for an excuse to leave, because he was tired; on the other hand, he might have felt that, if anyone was going to tangle with the police over keeping the neighbors up for the party, it should be his brother, and not he. Anyway, he said, 'Good night, Teddy,' just as the police made their appearance."

Ted was satisfied to be a good Senator because the presidency was still too remote to think about. He allowed himself more leeway for extramarital pleasures. After all, the presidency had never stopped his brother's private pleasures.

"The demands to live up to the President's memory make Edward's alternate exaggerated efforts at seriousness with collapses into rowdy relaxation . . . one minute Peck's Bad Boy, the next an Elder States-man. His name and his past imprison him. It is hard to cross every stage escorting History on your arm," said Gwirtzman.

One of his Senate friends warned Ted about his indiscretions: "I have told him ten times, 'Ted, you're acting like a fool. Everybody knows you wherever you go. . . . Jack could smuggle girls up the back way of the Carlyle Hotel. But you're not nearly as discreet as you should be.' He looks down with a faint smile and says: 'Yeah, I guess you're right.' But he never listens."

When Bob wrote a note to Lord and Lady Harlech, old friends of the family, he added a postscript: "It's eleven o'clock at night and I just saw Teddy putting on his coat and starting out for the night. . . . He is a rascal—I'll go after him and see if I can teach him how to behave."

"There's a pattern that we have to think about," said RFK speechwriter Richard Goodwin on the "Geraldo" show. "The womanizing is there, no question, but would you rather have Richard Nixon in his striped pajamas talking to Bebe Rebozo at night and doing things to the country you don't like or poor Jimmy Carter lusting after women that he never gets or do you want a senator who may do things at night that you don't like, but is a good senator during the day? As a citizen, that's what you have to think about."

Johnson would often invite Teddy to the White House just to chat. "Teddy had to be a little uncomfortable with his brother's dislike of Lyndon Johnson." Yet, Kennedy adviser Larry O'Brien continued, "it was clear to me that he preferred having a comfortable relationship with the President, not an adversarial situation."

"I really like Teddy," Johnson told O'Brien. "We get along. We had a great conversation last night." And then, once again, he wondered aloud why it was that Bobby disliked him so much and yet he got along so well with Teddy.

"It just didn't make any sense to him," said O'Brien.

———

HIS WIFE HAD said that Ted "was born knowing how to get close to people."

Yet some felt his extroversion was a cover, that Ted was basically a quiet person who didn't let people get too close to him. He also wasn't willing to plumb the depths of his own feelings. He was shrewd, incisive, sensitive and retentive, and his instincts were "awful damn good." Other side notes included his sharp temper, which all the brothers had, and a disposition to do good for a lot of people without talking about it.

"Ted doesn't have exactly the quickness of John Kennedy or Robert Kennedy," Richard Goodwin confided to a friend. "But he has a shrewdness about human motivation."

Robert took very strong stands, very often unyielding, unbending, and he still liked to say that "political matters are negotiable; matters of principle were not."

———

BOBBY GRADUALLY FOUND ways to soften his approach in the Senate. There is the story told by Senator Hugh Scott of Bob's conversion of Senator Joe Clark, who was very anti-Kennedy. Bob Kennedy sat next to him during a committee hearing and said, "I hope you'll get to know this ruthless Bobby Kennedy a little better." It wasn't long before Clark became a strong admirer.

He won over another liberal Senator, Phil Hart, by sending him a note saying, "Thanks for helping me on the floor; and the next time you see the Bishop, tell him to pray for my black heart."

He even sent President Johnson a handwritten note thanking him for his very moving tribute to his brother Jack at a dedication of a shrine in Runnymede, England, the site where King John signed the Magna Carta in 1215.

The whole country continued to name things and places after the late President. In front of an audience of Kennedys, President Johnson lifted the first shovelful of dirt, breaking ground for the John F. Kennedy Center for the Performing Arts, in Washington D.C. John Kennedy was being honored everywhere—an elementary school was named after him in Scranton, Pennsylvania; a housing project in Mexico City; an airport in New York City; a command headquarters for Special Warfare at Fort Bragg, North Carolina; and even a five-cent stamp. In the Judean hills of Israel, a few miles west of Jerusalem, the government dedicated a John F. Kennedy memorial. The house where he was born, on Beals Street, in Brookline, Massachusetts, was now a National Historic Landmark.

When the Yukon Territory in Canada named a mountain after John Kennedy, Robert saw it as a personal challenge, a mountain he must climb. It never had been climbed before, and Bob was asked how he was practicing for it. "I'm practicing running up and down the stairs and yelling 'Help.' "

"Bobby followed that older brother thing to the hilt," said author William Honan. "Ted wanted to climb Mount Kennedy, too. He was willing to let Bobby carry the flag, but he felt he should be able to make the climb. He had to wait six or eight months, however, for his back to mend. Bobby said, 'Hell, I'm not waiting for him.' "

He had joked about it first, saying, "My younger brother suggested that we both do it, but where is he?"

Just before he left, his mother told him—seriously, "Don't slip, dear." Starting at a base camp of 9000 feet, where they were dropped by a Royal Canadian Air Force helicopter, Robert Kennedy, with a party of seven, started their climb. The mountain peak was 13,880 feet.

"Bob didn't like the whole experience; he hated it," said reporter Martin Arnold. "He suffered from acrophobia . . . and he told me later if he had known what it involved, he would never have done it. But once he was there, he was very gung-ho to get started. He wanted to get it over with. While he was climbing, what he was doing the whole time was repeating to himself the words of every popular song he knew . . . so he wouldn't be thinking about what the hell he was doing."

When he was thirty feet from the summit, the others told him, "This is your brother's mountain. You should go alone." He planted a flag with the family crest, and a Canadian flag, buried a copy of the 1961 inaugural address of his late brother plus a PT-109 tie clip.

12

A DREAM DIES

Bobby had his own sense of destiny. Like General MacArthur, he felt that he could stand up in front of a trench and the bullet wouldn't hit him.

This fatalism, this reckless defiance, created concern about what kind of President he might be. But some saw it as a man-of-action image, a need to get things done.

Lem Billings felt that Bobby was often searching for danger, especially when they went on a family raft trip in the rapids of the Salmon River. Bobby went off by himself for seven miles alone in a kayak—his first time down the rough swirling white water. "It was like he was thumping his chest," said Billings, "like he was saying, 'Okay, Death, you just try it, I dare you!' "

Bob wanted to define himself in action. He would never drive as dangerously as Jack, never ski as recklessly as Ted, but his daring could never be doubted.

If John Kennedy was sometimes willing to challenge institutions, Bob was ready to change them.

The public now saw him differently. He was no longer the young roughneck with a sandy forelock jutting over his left eyebrow, but a Senator with a growing voice, and now, more than ever, a potential President.

During a question period after a speech at the Orpheum Theater in Sioux City, Iowa, someone asked, "Do you ever think about running for President?'' Senator Kennedy repeated the question, paused, and then answered, "Yes!" There was a pandemonium of approval. "What year are you going to run?" someone shouted. "That's a ringer of a question," the Senator grinned and again there was a thunder of applause."

In 1964, Lyndon Johnson was running for his first full term. Bob felt he had to prepare himself for what he knew to be his future. He not only had to expand his knowledge of issues and his exposure to the world, but he also had to court the press—as his brother Jack had done so skillfully. What he wanted from reporters was what all his brothers wanted—100 percent loyalty. But no matter how hard he tried, he got less than his brothers did.

One example of this came during the brouhaha over William Manchester's book on John Kennedy's death. Manchester earlier had written admiringly of President Kennedy. The family had agreed to provide complete cooperation and access to Manchester in return for final approval of the manuscript. Manchester remembered his first meeting with Senator Robert Kennedy, who told him, "I don't want anyone to make a killing out of my brother's death." Most of the money was to go to the Kennedy Library. Robert Kennedy and Mrs. Kennedy found it too painful to read the book, but their trusted advisers did. Manchester later described Jacqueline:

> Her fragile manner had always been deceptive, and since his death, she had grown increasingly strong-minded. Nothing in her new life discouraged this tendency; the homage of the press and the deference of those around her had strengthened an imperious air. . . .
>
> Isolated by her great wealth, revered by the New Frontiersmen who had transferred their fealty from the martyred President to his young widow . . . she presided over the elegant world around her as a lovely, graceful, ineffably tragic queen regent.

When it was announced that *Look* would serialize the book, Mrs. Kennedy denounced it as commercialization.

Bobby was soon in tune with Jacqueline. "Like her, he appeared to be wholly irrational. He accused me of raising my voice," said Manchester. "He pretended to leave the room, hid in an alcove, and leapt out, pointing an accusing finger at me." Manchester saw him hold a whispered conversation with Harper editor Evan Thomas, "glaring meantime at me." Robert Kennedy then told Manchester that he was acting on the advice of lawyers "because of his own political future." In his book, Manchester had detailed the conflict between Kennedy and Johnson.

"How much do you want?" Robert Kennedy briskly asked Manchester, in trying to stop the book. "Three hundred thousand? Four hundred thousand?" They were arrogant words his father would have used. The quiet payoff was not unfamiliar to Robert in covering up for his older brother.

Kennedy then wrote to Thomas that under the circumstances he felt that the Manchester book should neither be published nor serialized. Ironically, Thomas had been the editor of Jack Kennedy's *Profiles in Courage*.

Jacqueline Kennedy filed suit against *Look*, the book publisher, and the author. It was considered a most revealing slip of the tongue when she remarked, "Anyone who gets in a fight with me will look like a rat unless I run off with Eddie Fisher." Bob was "appalled" by the lawsuit and did not join Jacqueline as co-plaintiff.

Robert Kennedy then admitted to Frank Mankiewicz that it was "a terrible mistake but nothing can be done about it." The case was scheduled for court, and Jacqueline was due to testify. It was only then that she read the book, with what one of her friends called "growing surprise and fascination." Some editorial changes were made and the case was dropped and the book was published.

The Manchester affair hurt Bob's political future because it again revived his public image as "an arrogant, unattractive bully."

———

SENATOR ROBERT KENNEDY had earlier faced another public controversy in the nomination of Francis Xavier Morrissey for a federal judgeship.

Morrissey had been their father's crony. Father Joe had promised the judgeship to Morrissey and asked his sons to honor that promise. President Kennedy had nominated him in 1961. "Look, my father has come to me and said that he has never asked me for anything," said the President, "that he wants to ask me only this one thing—to make Frank Morrissey a federal judge. What can I do?"

Francis X. Morrissey, long regarded as Joe Sr.'s spy during Jack Kennedy's campaign, was classified by the American Bar Association as being totally incompetent. "We are going to appoint Frank Morrissey just to show that *The New York Times* isn't making the judicial appointments around here," insisted the President. But public and political pressure finally persuaded him not to make the appointment.

"What shall I tell Dad?" the President asked.

"Tell him he's not the President," said Robert.

Charles Roberts of *Newsweek* described Morrissey as "a guy who wouldn't even qualify to be an alderman in Boston."

But Morrissey was not easily discouraged, and, as Ted later added, "his wife was very insistent."

Bob Kennedy saw it as a dirty political job, and steered clear, but promised to help behind the scenes. Ted liked Morrissey, who had helped him in a variety of ways during his campaign, and Ted was willing to make the nomination. "I simply felt it was something that had to be put forward . . . so I asked the President to support Frank."

President Johnson not only approved the nomination but even called a press conference to announce it. Johnson's motives were muddy. The Morrissey issue would not only prove bad public relations for the Kennedys but it would obligate them to him. Still, both Johnson and Ted miscalculated the storm it would create.

Teddy fought hard. He used all his charm and persuasion working on individual Senators for commitments. Finally, Bobby, most reluctantly, joined him.

"I recall one day in Edward Kennedy's office," said his aide Richard Burke, "when Robert Kennedy spent the whole day trying to work out the question as to whether or not we had these votes or not, and whether it was worth it or not. . . . He was very angry and very unhappy."

Bob told Ted that he would be speaking in front of ladies' teas for the rest of his life as the price of some of these promised votes.

A powerful Senator Everett Dirksen quickly admitted to Bob that JFK "was one of the best friends I ever had," but then added that "I'm out to get Morrissey.'' And he did, destroying him with his delicately prodding questions on his background.

Finally, Ted saved the Senate the embarrassment of voting on the nomination by asking the White House to shelve it.

AS A SENATOR, Ted made courtesy calls even on those with whom he completely disagreed. During an early-morning interview with Mississippi's James Eastland, chairman of the Judiciary Committee, of which Kennedy was a member, Eastland offered him a stiff shot of bourbon. Teddy smiled and accepted, and soon afterward became a subcommittee chairman. Although he would always be known as ''Teddy'' to some, it gradually gave way to ''Ted.''

His self-confidence was growing.

Senator Barry Goldwater was haranguing the Senate on a labor bill late one night. Ted had taken the presiding officer's chair on the promise that he would be relieved at six o'clock because he had a dinner date. ''Well, six o'clock came and nobody was around, just Goldwater and Kennedy and one other senator who wouldn't take the chair. And Goldwater kept rambling on, and finally Kennedy picked up a piece of paper and wrote Goldwater a note which said, 'Do you always have to be such a shit?' Goldwater got a good laugh out of it.''

Ted was slowly emerging on his own, and he had developed his own areas of expertise. As chairman of the Senate Judiciary Subcommittee on Refugees, he became a leader in liberalizing the basic U.S. immigration law. He became a strong voice at the International Red Cross meeting in Geneva urging an exchange of American prisoners of war in Vietnam for Viet Cong captives held in South Vietnam. He also worked hard and effectively to increase aid to South Vietnamese refugees.

Ted liked Washington, liked the Senate, and was determined to cut his own swath. On major issues he would follow Robert's lead and do what his brother asked him to do. But he knew how much Bob still depended on him for maneuvers in the Senate. And, while he would always help his brother, this did not apply to his brother's friends when it conflicted with his own interest. He now considered Massachusetts his own turf, and when Bob's close friend Ken O'Donnell decided to run in the primary for governor, Ted refused to endorse him. He didn't want O'Donnell moving in on him.

———

LATIN AMERICA HAD been a special interest for Bob. Fresh out of the Navy, he had gone on a trip there with Lem Billings. His brother Jack had initiated the Alliance for Progress for economic development in Latin America. Bob now saw a more dramatic potential for the area as well as a demonstration of his own foreign policy initiative.

In November 1965 the Senator took his wife and staff members on a three-week fact-finding tour of Latin America. What RFK found was that the middle class had made progress, but the poor were poorer. The rich controlled ninety percent of the land.

With the usual Kennedy quota of stubborn persistence, he sought out student groups, urging them to communicate with African and Asian groups with whom they shared many problems. Some militant students threw eggs and garbage at Kennedy because of the American support of a military junta in the Dominican Republic.

On his return, he told the Senate that we must reshape our Latin American policy to support those forces working for peaceful change. He felt the key to that future meant maintaining more communication with the students of the region. Not only should we increase our aid to the area, he said, but we must support social reform "to build a better life for its people." But, for all his effort, the Senate rejected his request for an increase in funds for the Alliance for Progress to help the Latin American economy.

Bob also initiated a controversial campaign in South Africa and accepted an invitation to speak to the National Union of South African Students. He condemned apartheid and praised the champions of civil rights. "Each time a man stands up for an ideal or acts to improve the lot of others, or strikes out against injustice, he sends forth a tiny ripple of hope, and crossing each other from a million different centers of energy and daring, those ripples can build a current which can sweep down the mightiest walls of oppression and resistance."

He toured Africa with Ethel for two weeks. They also expanded their trip to visit the Pope in Rome, with whom Bob discussed Vietnam.

Back in Congress, Bobby then did something that would have caused his father to curse.

American Communist Party leader Robert Thompson died, and his family requested his burial in Arlington National Cemetery. He had been decorated for heroism during World War II. The Pentagon, which had jurisdiction over the cemetery, shuddered and refused.

Senator Robert Kennedy, who had served alongside Senator Joseph McCarthy in fighting all Communists, seen and unseen, now stood alone in the United States Senate and said that this was wrong. "I don't think anyone now buried in Arlington would object to having Thompson there, so I don't see why all these living people are objecting." For Kennedy, a paramount factor was that Thompson had won the Distinguished Service Cross, and so had paid his dues as a sinner and should not be harried to his grave.

This was a Bobby few knew.

———

SENATOR ROBERT KENNEDY stirred up more controversy when he joined Martin Luther King, Jr., in addressing the Southern Christian Leadership Council, urging stronger federal measures to help poor black families, calling for a "major upgrading" of opportunities in education, housing, and unemployment. The conference was held in the wake of several race riots.

In his increasing paranoia, Lyndon Johnson blamed RFK for "stirring up the blacks," and even privately accused him of putting Martin Luther King on his payroll.

Kennedy also testified before the Executive Reorganization Subcommittee of the Senate Government Operation Committee, discussing the demoralizing condition of the blacks in city ghettos and calling for federally funded employment programs. Shortly after that, he condemned those black leaders urging violence to combat racial prejudice.

As a member of the Subcommittee on Employment, Manpower and Poverty of the Senate Welfare and Labor Committee, Robert Kennedy visited a number of poor black communities in the Mississippi Delta.

"He went into a foul windowless shack and found a starving child with a distended stomach," observed columnist Russell Baker. "He held the child, talked to him, tried to arouse a response. Rats and roaches were on the floor. Kennedy just sat there, tears running down his cheeks.''

''In this country with a 700 billion dollar gross national product,'' Bob said, ''where we spend 75 billion dollars on armaments and three billion dollars on dogs, it seems we could do more for our starving children.''

In Chicago, at a YMCA halfway house for federal prisoners, reporter Ed Rooney sat close to him while he talked to a few prisoners. ''I had the impression, and always will have, that he wasn't 'on-stage' . . . he was genuinely concerned, and the fact that we were around didn't mean anything to him.''

Bob Kennedy would never forget the words of the young offender who had asked him, ''What would happen to you if you grew up where I grew up?''

He began to think more deeply about these inequities and was now reshaping his views.

That summer of 1967 also saw in Detroit the most violent race riots thus far. Forty-three people were killed in one week. There were 7200 arrests and $22 million in damages. After riots in several other cities, accompanied by fires and looting, a week that left twenty-three dead, Kennedy proposed legislation for industrial development in urban poverty areas. He also testified on the urgent need for gun control.

Bobby was soon making speeches advocating the redistribution of wealth. He also announced a program to form two companies in the economically depressed ghetto of New York's Bedford-Stuyvesant, to renew and rehabilitate the area.

He was further involved in Senate hearings on migratory labor, bills for collective bargaining, and regulating child labor. He introduced legislation for increasing welfare and social security benefits. Another bill he cosponsored required cigarette manufacturers to put a warning in all their ads that cigarettes might be harmful to the health.

Humphrey complained that if he and Bob Kennedy both made speeches on urban problems and said the same thing, he would wind up with one paragraph in the paper, but: ''Bobby says it and *The New York Times* runs the text.''

Some felt that this feeling for the poor minorities was a political ploy for Bob Kennedy. But the fact was that the poor seldom voted, and middle-class whites were not enamored of the new Kennedy direction.

Minorities now sensed in Bob a champion who felt their suffering. "It was like he was ours," said sharecropper organizer Cesar Chavez.

————

IN THE MIDST of all this, in the summer of 1967, Bob and Ted took their father to the first game of the World Series between the Boston Red Sox and the St. Louis Cardinals. The father collapsed in his seat and had to be given oxygen and taken from the stadium.

————

THE VIETNAM WAR was worsening, casualties were high, and the war was becoming increasingly unpopular when for the first time TV brought the ugly reality of combat death into the nation's living rooms.

Both public and press had at first supported President Johnson's huge increase in troops to win the war. It was the cumulative effect of seeing body bags on TV that changed public opinion—and started to change the Kennedys.

Bob Kennedy had difficulty remembering remedial statistics, but his aide, Frank Mankiewicz, noted that "he never forgot 'victim statistics,' like the unemployment percentage in Northeast Brazil, or the suicide rate on Indian reservations . . . or the number of casualties for a given week in Vietnam."

Protesters were already holding signs and chanting, "Hey, hey, LBJ, how many kids did you kill today?"

Johnson was reported to be "hunkering down like a jackrabbit in a rainstorm." Johnson later confessed ruefully to the author Doris Goodwin, "I knew from the start that if I left the woman I really loved—the Great Society—in order to fight that bitch of a war . . . then I would lose everything at home. All my hopes . . . my dreams."

Bob warned the Senate against any American escalation in Vietnam until the Saigon government became more stable. To Lyndon Baines Johnson he said nothing.

RFK's growing involvement in the issue gave him a place and a voice in the center of action. Discussing his brother's responsibility for the Vietnam War with a friend, he thought a minute and said, "I don't know which would be best: to say that he didn't spend much time thinking about Vietnam; or, to say that he did and messed it up."

Bobby then thrust his hand to the sky and said, "Which, brother, which?"

Senator Kennedy admitted publicly that he had been one of the formulators of his brother's Vietnam policy, but now he declared that bombing would not win the war and that if we thought it would, we were "heading straight for disaster." He urged a negotiated peace, bringing both Communist and non-Communist elements into a coalition government.

There is strong question whether his change in attitude on Vietnam was a matter of passion and principle, whether he was moved by seeing body bags, or whether it was the changing political wind.

The issue was splitting the party and the country, and in June 1967, Robert Kennedy introduced President Johnson at a fund-raising dinner, saying that in 1964 Johnson had won the greatest popular victory in modern times, "and with our help, he will do so again in 1968."

Friends asked how he could say that, knowing how he really felt. Bob's reply was that if he hadn't said it, Johnson would blame everything bad "on that son of a bitch Bobby Kennedy."

Critics called it hypocrisy coupled with ambition. But Arthur Schlesinger saw his despair when Bob later confided, "How can we possibly survive five more years of Lyndon Johnson? Five more years of a crazy man?"

———

TED AUTOMATICALLY SIDED with Bob on any major issue. It would never have occurred to him to differ. On Vietnam, he was simply echoing his brother's views. In a speech at Yale, Ted said, "I am an authority on violence—all it brings is pain and suffering, and there's no place for that in our society. . . . If you want to bring an end to war—then work to elect men who agree with you."

Ted soon became a strong spokesman against the Vietnam War. When Vietnam veterans marched on Washington to protest the war, Ted spent several hours talking with them. Later, after a dinner party, Ted could not get the veterans out of his mind. He changed into old clothes, including an Air Force flight jacket that used to belong to Jack, and returned to the Mall to talk with them some more and share their cheap wine. Ted even carried an antiwar poster in a parade.

Johnson saw this as a Kennedy plot: the Kennedys had got him into this war, now they would tell him to get out—and he would look the fool either way.

With the escalated bombing and higher casualties, public opposition intensified. Robert McNamara even told a radio interviewer—the day after Jacqueline Kennedy's death—how she came to him during the Vietnam bombing, "pounding my chest with her hands, saying over and over again, 'You've got to stop the killing! . . . You've got to stop the killing!' " For her, it was completely uncharacteristic.

McNamara later spoke against the proposal to increase the Army in Vietnam by another 205,000 men. He also opposed the accelerated bombing—we already had dropped more bombs on Vietnam than we had dropped on Germany during the entire Second World War.

LBJ blamed Bob Kennedy for McNamara's new opposition to the war.

"When he came to work for me," Johnson said of McNamara, "I believed he developed a deep affection for me as well, not so deep as the one he held for the Kennedys but deep enough . . . to keep him completely loyal for three long years. Then the Kennedys began pushing him harder and harder. Every day Bobby would call up McNamara, telling him that the war was terrible and immoral and that he had to leave."

Passion was now merging with Bob's political pragmatism.

McNamara finally resigned. His successor was another former Kennedy stalwart, Clark Clifford.

Bobby, meanwhile, went on an eight-day trip to Europe to discuss the Vietnam War with political leaders in four countries.

When he asked de Gaulle for his judgment, "there was a long silence for the translation, and then de Gaulle said, 'You are a young man and you have a great political future. I am an old one and I have known many battles and carry many scars. I will give you my advice: avoid the problem.' "

In Paris, Bob reportedly received a "peace signal" from the North Vietnamese government. The signal supposedly said that North Vietnam would negotiate peace if Americans stopped bombing their country.

The President confronted Kennedy on his return, accused him of leaking the peace offer to the press, just as America seemed to be winning the war. Kennedy denied receiving any specific peace signal, and told the President, "I think the leak came from someone in your State Department."

"It's not *my* State Department," Johnson angrily replied. "Goddamn it, it's *your* State Department."

Johnson later confided to Doris Kearns Goodwin, "It would have been hard on me to watch Bobby march to 'Hail to the Chief,' but I almost wish he had become President so the country could finally see a flesh-and-blood Kennedy grappling with the daily work of the Presidency and all the inevitable disappointments, instead of their storybook image of great heroes who, because they were dead, could make anything anyone wanted to happen."

Speaking to the Senate, Kennedy proposed a three-step plan to bring peace to Vietnam: stop bombing to see if the North Vietnamese really would negotiate, agree that neither side expand the war by infiltration or reinforcement, and gradually reduce American forces to be replaced by an international peacekeeping force.

As he put it, he was trying to save thousands of lives "with little risk to ourselves."

"When he [Kennedy] was intense about something," said Johnson special assistant George Reedy, "it was almost like a laser beam. He lived in a heaven or hell world. You were either on the side of God or with the devil."

On "Face the Nation," Senator Robert Kennedy staked out some political ground for a national election issue. When his brother was President, he said, his administration was trying to let the people of South Vietnam choose their own form of government. Now we were fighting a war that perhaps even the South Vietnamese did not want. "We're killing South Vietnamese, we're killing women, we're killing innocent people because we don't want the war fought on American soil."

Making his own fact-finding tour of South Vietnam, Kennedy reported that the South Vietnamese were not devoted to the war and that corruption was rampant among them.

Johnson planned to add more than 200,000 service personnel to the 500,000 already committed. Senator George McGovern felt strongly that once the country understood the Johnson Vietnam policy, they would not tolerate it, "and that an articulate, forceful figure who could attract nationwide press, like Bobby, could explode the policy

. . . if he challenged the President directly. This was the course that I urged."

A confrontation between the President and the Senator was coming closer. So far neither had directly attacked the other. RFK rationalized that he hoped to have greater impact on Johnson behind the scenes; Johnson could claim that he was merely carrying out John F. Kennedy programs—as he largely was.

Privately, an angry Johnson told Robert Kennedy, "We are going to win this war, and in six months all of you doves will be politically dead." North Vietnam, he said, was on the verge of losing the war, but Senator Kennedy and his doves were encouraging Hanoi to prolong it. Johnson told Kennedy, "If you persist, the blood of American boys will be on your hands." He looked at Kennedy and told him, "I could attack you in exactly those words and if I do, you will be finished."

"I don't have to sit here and listen to this kind of talk," Kennedy said, and left. Afterward, Bob told Sorensen, "I can't just stand on the sidelines. . . . I've been a leader against all this and I'm not in it when it counts."

The boyish-looking Senator Kennedy not only had talked with world leaders, but he was beginning to sound like one.

———

TED KENNEDY WAS also proving his mettle on other things. When Senator Thomas J. Dodd of Connecticut faced censure on charges of appropriating campaign funds for his own use, Ted was the only Senator to pay his respects and tell Dodd how much he regretted his need to vote for the resolution. A political observer told author Lester David, "Jack Kennedy would have ignored the likes of Dodd. Bobby Kennedy would have threatened to punch him in the mouth. Ted Kennedy paid a social call on him." When Dodd's son later became a Senator from Connecticut, he and Ted Kennedy became close friends.

———

IT WAS ALMOST four years since Jack's death, and Bobby's social life was becoming more extensive, with more parties at Hickory Hill. At their yearly anniversary party, in June 1967, Ethel, as always, tried to outdo herself. "And this was the best," said Angie Novello. "They had cameras going, with old family pictures, old films projected on the

walls. Two or three of them going constantly. This year was marvelous, a summing-up. Showing Bob and his brothers and sisters
growing up. Just a wonderful evening.''

Reporter Esther Tufty noted that all over Bob's house were pictures
of Jack when the two of them were young. ''The place is full of
memories. . . . Jack was part of that house.''

It was strange that Bobby, the shy one, would blossom socially like
this. It was perhaps more Ethel than Bobby, just as the President's
elegant parties in the White House were more Jackie than Jack. In
contrast, Ted and Joan's social life was still quiet, even though Ted was
the most ebullient of the brothers, because, most of all, the quiet life
suited Joan.

———

DESPITE THEIR OBVIOUS dislike of each other, and constant friction, Senator Robert Kennedy told reporters that Lyndon Johnson
''has been an outstanding president'' and that he would support him
for reelection in 1968.

Correspondent Sander Vanocur put it to him on ''Face the Nation.''
''You say these things about Vietnam and then you say that you'll
support Lyndon Johnson. How can you reconcile these two things?''
He hit a very sensitive nerve. Cartoonist Jules Feiffer highlighted the
inner debate between the Good Bobby and the Bad Bobby and called it
''the Bobby Twins.''

What he referred to was the Good Bobby complaining about our
killing innocent women and children and the Bad Bobby saying that he
expected to back Johnson for President and then the Good Bobby
saying, ''I think we're going to have a difficult time explaining this to
ourselves.''

RFK had tried to explain: ''I must examine the issue in relation to
my concern about my own future, to my own conscience and my
judgment on what can be.'' It was a very fuzzy statement of an
undecided mind.

During that time, there was a growing group that wanted Bob to run
for President against Johnson. Ted opposed it, not only because
Johnson was a sitting President of his own party, but because he had
been their brother's Vice President. Ted's case was simple: why rush?
If Bob waited until 1972, he was certain of nomination. To try it now

would hurt, maybe kill Bob's future because it might divide and destroy the Democratic Party.

It is highly questionable how much Bob relied on Ted for any final judgment on this. He and Jack had been partners for a long time; he and Ted had been best friends, but not really partners.

Bob had confided to Milton Gwirtzman that "nobody in my family wants me to run. No one whose political judgment I respect wants me to run. And not a single leader in the country wants me to run."

In a letter to his friend Anthony Lewis of *The New York Times,* Robert Kennedy wrote, "I don't know quite what to write to you. The country is in much difficulty . . . that it almost fills one with despair. I just don't know what Johnson is thinking. But then when I realize all that I wonder what I should be doing. Just everyone who I respect with the exception of Dick Goodwin and Arthur Schlesinger have been against my running. My basic inclination and reaction was to try and let the future take care of itself. . . . So once again—what should I do? By the time you receive this letter, both of us will know."

Bob wanted to be President not simply because he was ambitious but because he felt his heritage demanded it. It was as if it were ordained. He had been part of critical presidential decisions; he had created national and international programs; he had met other world leaders and felt himself a match for them in mind and spirit. More than all that, he wanted to continue Jack's dramatic life and make it part of his own—and he felt qualified and ready to do it.

The only other serious candidate in the primaries was Senator Eugene McCarthy of Minnesota, who had become the strongest voice in the Senate against the Vietnam War. A poll in November 1967 showed Bob Kennedy leading McCarthy, but well behind Johnson.

Antiwar protesters pleaded with Kennedy to get into the presidential race against Johnson. The temptation was strong and his ambition was gnawing at him. When he ran for the Senate in New York, the public adulation had stirred him. He always sensed the hovering of his brother's ghost, and there was this constant restlessness and the enormous need to discover the extent of his own reach, to prove his own worth, his own leadership, his own place in history. Bob had been at the heart of power during his brother's presidency and it was not something he could forget.

But, finally, he allowed himself to be persuaded by those he trusted most, and he replied, "Philosophically, I wish I could do it; realistically I know I should not do it."

Bobby had his name removed from the New Hampshire primary. Ted Sorensen urged his supporters there to dissolve their effort, and said that the Senator "would regard one vote for him as too many."

The anti-Vietnam leaders, mostly younger people, then turned to Eugene McCarthy.

At this point, Johnson wanted Ted Kennedy to be a stand-in for him at the Massachusetts primary. Ted had a pleasant relationship with the President, but refused. Even though Bobby had presumably edged himself out of the race, Ted still felt he might change his mind.

He knew his brother well. Robert Kennedy was still seesawing on his decision. He asked his speechwriter Richard Goodwin, "Why don't you give me the best case for my running."

"Which I did," said Goodwin. "Then he asked me to get together with Teddy. Teddy and I had dinner down at the Charles Restaurant for three hours. Teddy was always against it, but he knew Bob's instincts were to go."

If Bob didn't run, he felt he would lose credibility with the young people who were now turning away from him and might never come back. The young people were involved in an unprecedented rebellion, a social revolution. Mixed in with this was a feminist revolution and a bitter fight for civil rights. Bob must have felt that to be President at such a time would be a thrilling and frightening challenge.

But, more than that, more than almost everybody else, he could visualize himself as President because he had been so close to it.

Ted later told Goodwin that he wasn't so sure what his brother Jack would have said about Bobby's decision to run for President, "but I know what Dad would have advised . . . 'Don't do it.' "

His father would have told him to wait for the same reasons Ted gave: you don't run against the President of your own party, and, if he waited, he would be the unbeatable candidate in 1972.

Several weeks before the New Hampshire primary, Ted stopped pressuring Bob against running. Although he still thought it politically inadvisable, he felt it was more important for his brother's peace of mind to let things take their course; let Bob run and get it out of his system, even if he lost.

As always, Ethel was Bob's biggest confidence builder. During a staff discussion meeting, where she was listening, "Robert Kennedy shouted across the room to Ethel, who was sitting up against the wall, 'Well, what do you think?' Ethel said, 'Run. You'll beat him. Run and do it.' "

She had told him, "You are never going to be happy with yourself unless you do."

She was right and he felt it.

"You've got to run," Ken O'Donnell told him. "This war is a terrible thing. Kids are dying who shouldn't be dying, and you have to run, not for the country, not for yourself and not for anyone here in this room. You have to run to help end that war. Maybe you'll lose. But you've got to run."

Ted Kennedy had sidled up to McGovern in the Senate gym and suggested that Bob would move toward the Presidency if McGovern and others urged him. "If just one or two people push him, he'll go."

Never had he been more tortured by any decision. He knew the consequences of splitting the party—it could ruin his political future.

Shortly before the New Hampshire primary, Bob went to California to offer moral support to union leader Cesar Chavez in his hunger strike in protest against the violence caused by the union's struggle for survival. Chavez, the founder of the United Farm Workers, had spent his life fighting for the migrant Latino workers who worked in the dusty vineyards and lettuce fields of California. Kennedy saw Chavez as a Spanish-speaking Gandhi consumed by a cause. It was this kind of understated passion, more than anything, that drew them together.

Chavez was too weak from fasting to speak, but his speech was read for him. It contained the lines: "So it is how we use our lives that determines what kind of men we are . . . only by giving our lives do we find life."

If his brother Jack had viewed people from a historic or political stance, Bobby now saw them mainly in personal terms. Jack would have stayed away from Chavez and his migrant workers—too few votes and too many political risks.

"Do you know why we loved Robert Kennedy so?" Dolores Huerta, United Farm Workers organizer, told a legislator. "Do you know why the poor loved those millionaires John Kennedy and Robert Kennedy? It was their attitude. I think Ted has it, too. Robert didn't come to us and tell us what was good for us. . . . All he said was, 'What do you want? And how can I help?' That's why we loved him.''

En route home from California, Kennedy told John Seigenthaler that he now had made up his mind to run. ''What have I got to lose besides Dad's money?''

Bob would have to act fast. Two days before the New Hampshire primary, he asked McCarthy to withdraw from the race after that primary and leave the field clear to him. The McCarthy response was that Bob should support *him*. ''I only want one term as President. After that, he can take it over.''

There was no deal.

At the annual 1967 Gridiron Dinner for the Washington press, Robert Kennedy joked, ''All those stories about President Johnson and me not getting along during my brother's years do not square with the facts. We started out during the Kennedy administration on the best of terms—friendly, close, cordial—but then, as we were leaving the inaugural stands . . .''

Kennedy had said with a grin, ''I have no designs on the Presidency, and neither does my wife, Ethel Bird. . . . I'd like to settle any disputes I have with the President by making it clear that I am willing to go more than halfway to the White House.''

''In a sense,'' David Halberstam pointed out, ''there were not just two political parties in America in the sixties, but really three—the Democrats, headed by Johnson, the Republicans, and the Kennedys. . . . With their power and their ability to attract intellectuals the Kennedys so dominated the young leadership of the party that anyone else virtually had to fall into their orbit.''

On March 12, in New Hampshire, President Johnson barely defeated Eugene McCarthy, 49 percent to 42. Write-in votes in the Republican primary put McCarthy within a few hundred votes of topping Johnson's total vote. It was a sharp defeat for the President.

''How do you think I could have done?'' Bob Kennedy asked Richard Goodwin, who had worked hard for McCarthy. Goodwin told him he could have polled at least 60 percent. Kennedy seemed depressed. ''I think I blew it.''

The American youth had been the Kennedy bulwark. They were now positioning themselves behind McCarthy for his firm stand against the war. Bob realized that if he didn't try to regain their support now, it would be gone forever.

Bobby asked one of his earliest and most fervent campaign workers, Polly Fitzgerald, a question he had asked her eight years earlier: "If you had a choice of dying and going straight to heaven, or of living and taking your chances, which would you choose?" Polly replied that she would live and take her chances. "Not me," Bob said. "I'd still take the other."

Polly would later comment, "It comforts me now to know this and to remember his simple faith in God's promises."

Bob had questioned that faith after his brother's death, but now his world was back on its axis. Also restored was his faith in his own abilities, and his faith in public service.

———

THE CORE OF Kennedy advisers collected at Stephen Smith's New York apartment to discuss Bob's candidacy. Arthur Schlesinger, Jr. who was there, described Ted Kennedy, looking a bit unhappy, crisply setting forth various alternatives—from total inaction to total participation.

While awaiting Bobby, they turned on the evening news, knowing that he had taped an interview earlier that day with Walter Cronkite. Discussing his reasons for reassessment, he stopped only a hairline short of declaration. "I don't know what we are meeting about," Ted Kennedy said. "He has made all the decisions already and we're learning about them on television. What the hell's the point of holding this meeting when he's already made up his mind."

Bob clearly had made his decision earlier that day. He was going to run.

Afterward, when Robert Kennedy arrived at the Smith apartment, "there was a lot of jocularity and a great deal of relief . . . all the tensions were off. . . . After dinner, which was a lot of fun . . . we broke into groups, and I think by regions," said Ted's aide David Burke. . . . "I remember Robert Kennedy was sort of pacing around the room. When I opened the book to 'A,' Alabama, and the page was blank, I shouted out that perhaps we should reconsider. . . . That was the last bit of lightness that we had. . . . Clearly, the word was Go."

Ted already had moved into action. He was sitting in a room with a secretary, working from a list. She would place a call and hand him the phone. He talked to whoever it was, put the phone down, and then turned to something else. He managed, in a few hours, to call scores of people.

———

BOB ASKED TED to fly to Wisconsin with Richard Goodwin and Blair Clark to discuss a new proposal with McCarthy: Bob and McCarthy would divide up all the primaries and battle it out only in California and New York. Bobby hoped that this would help force Johnson to retire. McCarthy insisted that his wife, Abigail, listen to their proposal too. He relied much on her judgment. When they returned to Hickory Hill that night, Ted told Schlesinger, "Abigail turned it down."

The next morning, Schlesinger proposed that Bob delay formally announcing his decision to run, thus avoiding charges of opportunism. The opportunism was clear. Bob had stayed out of the race until McCarthy had proved that Johnson was highly vulnerable.

But this time Ted reacted. "No, Bob's mind is made up. Let's have no more discussion. Let's not weaken his confidence."

Ted was right about Bob. That night Ted Kennedy "took a long walk around Robert's house, and he was very, very, very concerned," said David Burke. "I think the basis of his concern was what he felt was Bob's lack of preparation. . . . He felt at that point in time that the chances for success weren't good." Ted later would say, "Bobby's therapy is going to cost the family eight million dollars."

———

HE ALREADY HAD decided to run, but the surprise of McCarthy's showing against Johnson now spurred him into quicker action.

"Do you think I'm crazy, running?" Bobby asked *Life* writer Sylvia Wright. "My brother thinks I'm crazy . . . you know, Teddy and I are such different people. We don't hear the same music. Everyone's got to march to his own music."

The next day, St. Patrick's Day, Bobby and Teddy marched together in Boston. "I was in the car with Bobby going back to the airport," said Wright. "I said, 'It looks to me, Senator, that you were marching to the same music.' Bobby looked at me mischievously and said, 'My brother learns fast.' ''

Several days later, at a New York dinner party, Jacqueline Kennedy took Arthur Schlesinger aside and said, "Do you know what I think will happen to Bobby? . . . The same thing that happened to Jack. . . . There is so much hatred in this country, and more people hate Bobby than hated Jack. . . . I've told Bobby this, but he isn't fatalistic, like me.''

———

BOB FLEW TO Hyannis to tell his parents. Nurse Rita Dallas noted how tired and worn he was when he got out of the plane, "but then he ran to his father, kissed him, then drove him to the compound, laughing, talking, elaborately emphatic in his gestures. Mr. Kennedy never took his eyes off his son. He was completely absorbed by every move, every word.'' Then Bob told them, "I'm going to run for the Presidency.''

The elder Kennedy dropped his head to his chest in obvious sorrow. Bob said, "Dad, I'm doing it just the way you would want me to—and I'm going to win.'' He stayed on till his father's nap. They said goodbye, the old man holding his son's hand with a tight, lingering grip.

The father was no longer a man of arrogant ambition. One of his sons had become President, and he knew there was nothing more he needed to prove. Now the only thing that really mattered was their safety and survival. Two of his sons had been killed, and he feared for the remaining two, especially his favorite, Bobby. He had been a ruthless, bigoted man, overwhelmed by personal ambition and pride, but he also had been a loving, loyal father. As for Rose Kennedy, she would believe, as she always did, that it was in the hands of God.

"It's going to be all right," Bobby told them. "It's going to be all right.''

Lem Billings confided to authors Peter Collier and David Horowitz, in *The Kennedys*: "Bobby didn't know that his father was trying to stop this thing that had gotten started—this Kennedy thing of daring the gods. The two of them never understood each other on this.''

Two days later, on March 16, 1968, Senator Robert F. Kennedy stood in the crowded Senate caucus room, where his older brother had stood for the same reason eight years earlier, and formally announced he would run for President. He used the same opening line as his brother did, that the reason he was running was "because the country is on a perilous course."

The same site, the same phrase—Jack was obviously their talisman for success.

He was trying to plant his own political flag, but millions saw him and heard him and visualized Jack—as he knew they would, especially when he repeated his brother's phrase, "I think this country can do better."

————

PRESIDENT JOHNSON TOLD Doris Kearns Goodwin: "The thing I feared from the first day of my Presidency was actually coming true. Robert Kennedy had openly announced his intention to reclaim the throne in memory of his brother."

Two days after the announcement, Ted Kennedy visited Larry O'Brien, who was now Postmaster General. After a bottle of wine and a leisurely steak, Ted asked Larry if he would direct his brother's campaign. The next day, Bobby called to put on some personal pressure.

But O'Brien already had signed on with President Johnson, who had sent telegrams to hundreds of Democrats around the country: "Please state your loyalty to the President immediately."

The Johnson people had a caustic comment: "It took sixteen years for Bobby Kennedy to come out against McCarthy and then he came out against the wrong one."

"Well, by the time he got there, Gene McCarthy had already been knocking on the door, and many people in the liberal community had both arms and both legs around Gene McCarthy and were kissing him on the neck and biting on the ear," said John Seigenthaler. "And so, we came into that campaign behind."

The McCarthy people soon had radio ads saying, "I used to be for Robert Kennedy, but then I learned about how he bugged my brother Martin Luther King's phone."

A surprisingly biting criticism of Bobby came later from his father's friend Arthur Krock in his memoirs: "Both the timing of his candidacy to supplant President Johnson as the nominee of the Democratic

National Convention of 1968, and his decision to contest with McCarthy in carefully chosen state primaries, were so baldly expedient as to diminish his claim that a 'moral issue,' and not the attainment of a driving personal ambition, had impelled him to advance his Presidential target date by four years." Decrying Kennedy's reported shyness and diffidence, Krock now emphasized Kennedy's reputation as a gut fighter and added, "There is great arrogance implicit in laying claim to the presidency, and I do not think Bob Kennedy had any difficulty in summoning it."

Perhaps what motivated Krock to explode was the built-in frustration of being a hired flack for the Kennedy father for so many years, and the uncomfortable knowledge that he had been used. Joe Kennedy Sr. could no longer hurt Krock, or berate him, or reward him with money or cars. Krock could now speak for himself.

Columnist Murray Kempton, Bob's strong early supporter, now saw his announcement as opportunism and called him a coward for coming in after McCarthy had made his grand gesture. "In one day, he managed to confirm the worst things his enemies have ever said about him."

Eunice joined in the defense of Bob's motives. "What difference does it make? Why waste time arguing about that? What counts is all that energy, all that power, all that ability is being used for peace and for civil rights and for the poor."

Eunice and Bobby remained close. However, her husband had his own political ambitions. There was family friction when Sargent Shriver accepted a new Johnson appointment as the Ambassador to France. Bobby, particularly, was not happy.

KHRUSHCHEV SAW KENNEDY as an unpredictable adventurer, too volatile to become President. A *New Yorker* cartoon, which President Kennedy had kept, showed Khrushchev having a nightmare, with the caption, "I dreamt we got the first man on the moon, and it turned out to be Bobby Kennedy."

Some believed Bobby's militancy would make him either a great President or a disaster, that he was a zealot who might be too apt to push the atomic button, that he was more ready to destroy people he didn't like, that he was caught in a national revolution he still didn't understand.

"I think he would've made a very interesting President," said Ben Bradlee. "He gave the feeling, at the end, that he was a very gut liberal—the only one with the courage to say the things nobody else would say."

————

HIS SUDDEN DECISION to run made it difficult to put together a cohesive campaign. When it came to presidential campaigns, Bob had a basis for comparison. He said wistfully to a reporter, "I wish there was somebody who could do for me what I did for my brother."

Bob listened hard to Teddy, but he picked brother-in-law Steve Smith, the first-rate organizer, to get things started. Ted and Smith were given matching corner offices in the headquarters.

Ted was a working Senator and couldn't really devote one hundred percent of his time to the campaign. Besides, Ted was not yet qualified to mastermind a campaign. Some suggested that he asked all the correct questions but didn't know what to do with the answers. Nor did Ted have Bobby's aggressive assurance and fierce leadership qualities. But, as always, he was ready to work. In an early discussion of campaign strategy, he said jokingly, "Let's see, there's California over there, there's New York over there. That leaves forty-eight for me."

"There was no great triumvirate sitting around plotting this and that," Burton Hersh reported, "and that can be seen, because I guess there were a lot of mistakes made."

It didn't matter, because the entire campaign for the presidency lasted only eleven weeks.

"From the first day he ran for the presidency when he went to Kansas by plane to start his first great rush, everybody with him talked only of one thing," said columnist Jimmy Breslin. This was the one thing his staff never dared to discuss, even at the beginning of the campaign.

"He's going to be shot," said *Newsweek* correspondent John Lindsay. "He's going to be shot as sure as we're here." His aides had pressed Bob to get more security guards. "That's not the way I want to run a campaign," Bobby replied. "That's not the United States of America. In some other kind of country a candidate may have to talk through some kind of shield, but not here."

A police chief in one town pointed out one of his men on the nearby roof with a telescopic rifle and explained, "We want this man to leave our town the same way he entered it."

"When we got on the plane back in Kansas," said reporter James Tolan, "Bob was smiling, and he said, 'Listen, I haven't felt this good. . . . This is what I should be doing.' Having made the decision to run, and running, to know he was doing what he was supposed to be doing made him feel alive again. . . . He had arrived at a crux. He had to put certain priorities ahead of party loyalty and just do what he thought he had to do. He was a free guy coming back on the plane from Kansas. . . . You could just see him growing, emerging from the shell of the President's death into his own."

There would also be criticism about Robert Kennedy's invoking the President's name too frequently and playing on nostalgia.

The nostalgia was always there. There would always be giant pictures of President Kennedy at every Democratic dinner.

While campaigning for Bobby in Iowa, Ted told a crowd, "Eight years ago, I was introduced as a brother of a President. Today, I'm introduced as brother of a Presidential candidate. If about eight years from now you see me coming back to this picnic . . ." A long pause, a wide grin, and, playing his audience like a seasoned stand-up comedian, a lift of the eyebrows and a drawn-out, "Well-l-l-l . . ." The crowd roared.

———

INDIANA BECAME A critical battleground, looming as the West Virginia primary had during Jack's campaign. Bob needed an Indiana victory to prove that his appeal was national and deep, but Indiana was conservative country. Robert Kennedy knew he was in trouble. Time was tight, and he was surely the underdog. His self-assurance, never very solid, was already thinning. In poured the Kennedy money. The Kennedys spent an estimated $3 million and hired hundreds of staff for Indiana.

Adlai Stevenson, fighting an uphill political battle against Eisenhower in 1952, still had the fresh honesty to tell audiences what he wanted to say rather than what they wanted to hear, speaking the same hard truths about civil rights in the North as he did in the South. Robert Kennedy now seemed to have the same kind of style.

He talked to a large audience in an Indiana medical school and presented an indictment of American medical programs—we were lagging behind other countries.

Applause was polite, and then the floor was open to questions. The students attacked any government participation in health care. Kennedy replied: "The fact is that there are people who suffer and we have a responsibility. I look around and I don't see many black faces here. Frankly, the poor have difficulty in entering your profession . . . the poor are the ones who are doing most of the fighting in Vietnam, while white students sit here in medical school. . . . The dying is going on now." He was against college deferment, he said. "I don't want to break my record today and say something you approve of."

————

ROSE KENNEDY AGREED to tape a Walter Cronkite interview, along with her two surviving sons. Fred Dutton was with Bobby when he got in the elevator and went down a floor to pick up Ted and then down another floor to wait, as always, for Rose. "When she got in and the elevator began to descend, Bobby began to plan the appearance: 'Well, I guess I'll start out by saying . . .' Rose cut him off coldly. 'Listen, I'm the one being interviewed.'

"They asked me if I'd like to be a senator's mother or a senator," recalled Rose Kennedy to Robert Coughlan, "and I said I would rather be a senator's mother. And one of the girls [Eunice] said, 'Oh, she would rather be a senator.' "

She still had an easy ability to communicate with an audience, but her political sense occasionally wandered. Reacting to a question about the Kennedy wealth used for the campaign, she replied, "It's our money and we're free to spend it any way we please."

Rose campaigned for Bobby, as she had for both Jack and Ted. She told a crowded room, "I used to spank him with a ruler."

Bobby Kennedy replied, "That's what we've gotten down to, in this campaign. . . . After some of these polls came out that we were not doing too well, we took mother." Then he kidded her, saying, "The reason . . . we never go on the same platform with her . . . we couldn't possibly compete."

BOBBY WAS MORE excited about campaigning for his brothers; campaigning for himself was still painful. He simply did not have Jack's detachment and charm.

Television had become a necessary campaign tool, yet Bobby was at his worst in a sterile television studio without an audience. The one phrase that did come easily to him belonged to his brother: "We can do bettah." But the comparison was constant: BOBBY AIN'T JACK. When Bob saw that sign, he quietly told an aide, "I'm not trying to be."

The most frequent public reaction: "He looks like a little kid."

To lighten his somber image, his speechwriters put in such jokes as Bobby asking Teddy to order campaign buttons, and they all arrived with Ted's picture on them. But Bob had his own sense of humor. He liked to recite to reporters a litany of clichés from his standard speeches.

RFK managed to maintain a stream of letters to his own children during his travels. He told them he hoped they were reading the news each day, "and not just the funnies." He looked forward to taking them to football games, wondered whether the tree had been fixed so they could play in it, and, again and again, how much he missed them. His secretary and friend Angie Novello made it a ritual to forward all kinds of clippings about their father to his children.

Unlike Jacqueline and Joan, Ethel took campaigning in good grace—the crush of crowds, the pulling and hauling, the long motorcades. At the end of an eighteen-hour day she seemed as fresh as at the start.

Ethel could be a tiger in her husband's defense. When a reporter wrote a story about her husband that she didn't like, she saved the paper and threw it in the reporter's face when she saw him.

Because her parents were killed in a plane crash, she had a real fear of flying, especially the landing. When the plane was ready to reach ground, she would say, "Would you mind getting my husband back here. He always holds my hand when we land."

In the public eye, the image of the brothers had blurred. They saw only the sameness, not the differences. Even as Jack's myth still seemed to smother Bob, he and Ted became increasingly interchangeable. The emotional balance between them was changing. The older Bobby, who constantly kidded and teased his younger brother, now increasingly needed his support—not just the political support, but psychological. In a presidential campaign, the brothers supplied the traditional Kennedy balance. If Bob didn't always rely on Ted's advice, he needed his brother's optimism and Ted was there to give it to him.

The biggest encouragement came from a surprising quarter—President Johnson.

Returning to New York from an Indian subcommittee meeting in Arizona, Robert Kennedy was met by an aide with a news item: "The President is not going to run." "You're kidding," said Kennedy.

Bobby understood Johnson's reasoning, and admitted to a reporter, "I wonder if he'd have done this if I hadn't come in."

The Johnson presidency reached a dramatic climax in a March Gallup poll that showed that Democrats preferred Kennedy to Johnson by 44 to 41. On top of that, Johnson heard the news that McCarthy would beat Johnson in the Wisconsin primary by two to one. The President saw himself being dumped by his own party.

It was a degrading, lonely moment for the President. But he was a wise enough politician to know when to quit, and he announced his decision not to run for reelection.

Johnson told Democratic congressional leaders at their weekly breakfast that he was "tired of begging anyone for anything."

"I had a partnership with Jack Kennedy," Johnson told them, "and when he died I felt it was my duty to look after the family and stockholders and employees of my partner. I did not fire anyone. The divisions are so deep within the Party that I could not reconcile them. I'm not going to influence the Convention . . . probably won't even go. Much to everyone's disbelief, I never wanted to be President to begin with. I'm leaving without any bitterness."

He had desperately wanted to be President and he was leaving with a great deal of anger. It came from the fact that he never had achieved the public admiration and affection that the Kennedys always had. Unlike Kennedy, "Johnson was never that happy, sparkling, sense-of-destiny man, with a morning quip," said General Maxwell Taylor. "His White House was never scintillating. It was, in fact, a rather gloomy place." He would always be known as the man who lost the Vietnam War. And now it was a Kennedy who had helped destroy him, and would probably succeed him.

He was tired, his health was poor, and he was bitter and stunned by the intensity of the antiwar hate poured on him. The realization that he never could be the great President he so much wanted to be was devastating. He would die of a broken heart.

Ethel Kennedy reacted by bringing out a bottle of Scotch and saying, "Well, he never deserved to be President anyway." She was wrong. His initial record of passing more important legislation in the first hundred days was greater than almost any President's except Roosevelt.

Robert Kennedy sensed early that the President's withdrawal hurt his campaign because it took away the moral issue—a key to the campaign. Johnson was no longer a target; Vietnam no longer the focus. Johnson had ordered a halt to the bombing of North Vietnam and invited North Vietnamese leaders to a peace conference.

Locked-in Johnson delegates were now invitingly available. Although the outcome was still uncertain, the Kennedy–Johnson conflict appeared to be over.

President Johnson at first refused a Kennedy request for a meeting, saying, "I won't bother answering that grandstanding little runt."

When they did meet on April 3, Johnson delivered a monologue on foreign affairs. Kennedy asked whether he intended to participate in the Democratic campaign, but Johnson declined to reply. The President then talked about how well he and John Kennedy had worked together. He had tried to continue the Kennedy policies, he said, but had failed with the young people, no matter how much he had done for education; and he had failed with the blacks, no matter how much he had done for civil rights. Ted Sorensen recalled that Johnson's voice "grew a little tremulous" when he said that as President Kennedy looked down at him every day from then until now, he would agree that he kept the faith. Bob Kennedy finally said, "You are a brave and dedicated man."

"I don't know," recalled Sorensen, "whether it was because he found it difficult to say or whether the emotion of the situation had overcome him, but it sort of stuck in his throat, and Johnson asked him to repeat it."

It was a time of fast-changing history and monumental events. In

April 1968, the Reverend Martin Luther King, Jr., was assassinated by a sniper in Memphis.

Earlier that day, a young black student at Ball State University in Muncie, Indiana, asked Kennedy, "You are placing great faith in white America. Is this faith justified?"

"Yes," said Kennedy, and then he added, "I think the vast majority of white people want to do the decent thing."

An aide told him about King just as Kennedy boarded the plane for Indianapolis. He seemed staggered, and finally said, "To think that I just finished saying that white America wants to do the right thing, and even while I was talking this happened. . . . It gets worse and worse . . . all this divisiveness, all this hate. We have to do something about the divisions and the hate."

Big cities all over the country were burning that night. The rally at which Robert Kennedy was scheduled to speak was in a black ghetto in Indianapolis. Advisers were warning him not to go, that it was too dangerous. The mayor pleaded with him to cancel his speech, and he was told that if he went, his police escort would turn back when his car reached the slum. He sent Ethel to the hotel and went on alone.

Bob reacted well to tension. He saw it as a challenge.

It was said of him: "It was his vulnerability as a person, the nakedness of his being, that moved us. This he could not hide; nor, for that matter, did he try to."

It was a bitter, cold night and he stood on a flatbed truck on a street corner. He was wearing a long, black overcoat that seemed two sizes too large.

The tension was palpable when he started speaking. He spoke hesitantly. But, as John Lewis said, "He spoke from the depths of his soul." He spoke extemporaneously, a speech many said was "the best speech he ever gave in his life . . . absolutely beautiful." "I know in my heart what you must be feeling. I had a member of my family killed. For those of you who are black, and who feel hate for all white people, I want to say that my brother was also killed by a white man."

It was the first time he had publicly referred to his brother's assassination.

He quoted Aeschylus: "Even in our sleep, pain that cannot forget falls drop by drop upon the heart, and in our own despair, against our will, comes wisdom through the awful grace of God."

He went on to say: "What we need in the United States is not violence and lawlessness, but love and wisdom and compassion toward one another, a feeling of justice toward those who still suffer within our country, whether they be white or whether they be black. And to dedicate ourselves to what the Greeks wrote so many years ago, to tame the savageness of man and make gentle the life of this world.

"So I ask you tonight to return home, to say a prayer for the family of Martin Luther King, that's true, but more importantly to say a prayer for our own country, which all of us love."

"And then he started to leave," said James Tolan, an advance man in RFK's presidential campaign, "and a very funny thing, a very eerie thing happened. . . . Some of the people close to the platform . . . started grabbing for him, like they usually did—to try to touch him . . . and you could see the awful magnetic power that he had—the charismatic power . . . it was like, you know, 'Well, you're our last hope.' "

Almost alone in the big cities, there was no violence in Indianapolis that week: "Not a match was struck."

Afterward Bobby went back to his hotel—opened his collar, put his head back. He said, "I've never been afraid before . . . and it reminds me of Jack."

Later that night, restlessly roaming the hotel's corridors, Bob came upon a member of his senatorial staff, sleeping in his clothes on a bedspread. Bob put a blanket over him. Wakening, the aide said, "You aren't so ruthless after all." Bob said: "Don't tell anybody."

Roy Jenkins, who would become Britain's Chancellor of the Exchequer, joined Bobby on the Rockefeller plane going to the King funeral procession in Atlanta, "and then joined him on the platform, singing 'We Shall Overcome.' "

At the funeral, "when Kennedy came along, slight, almost hard to find in the crowd, they began to clap, 'Yes, Bobby, Bobby,' and more clapping." Said David Halberstam: "It's as if they're anointing him."

Spiritually, almost chemically, RFK and King had become merged in the public imagination of blacks throughout America. It changed the RFK image forever. It was ironic, because it had been only five years since RFK had given the FBI permission to wiretap King.

"For the nation, it was the time of a lightning rod, a frenzy, with revolution around the corner," said King aide John Lewis, "and we felt only Bobby could heal the nation. When Martin Luther King died, we were in shock, but then we felt, 'Well, we still have Bobby Kennedy.' "

"If I could have sung one song to them," said Lena Horne, celebrated singer and civil rights activist, "it would be 'Stormy Weather,' because that's what it's been. Lord, have mercy."

Race riots throughout the nation continued for a full week. Robert Kennedy chartered a plane to bring King's body back to Atlanta. Kennedy said that legislation alone would not end the division between blacks and whites in America. He declared that the survival of America is much more threatened by injustice and violence than by a foreign enemy.

It was an appropriate time for President Johnson to sign the Civil Rights Act, ending discrimination in housing in the United States.

"The 1968 campaign was full of frenzy: people clawing at Bobby; long, long days," recorded Associated Press reporter Saul Pett. "And then he'd come back on the plane and maybe one or two aides would discuss something with him, and then he'd wave them away. And there would come a look in his eyes of the deepest kind of hurt a human can project. He was still feeling the loss of his brother. When he was away from the crowds and the noise and so forth, this look of what must have been eternal sadness came over him. It was remarkable. You couldn't fail to see it."

But he also felt a sense of himself growing.

There was the time in an Indiana hotel when Kennedy was called from the shower to take a telephone call. Soap in his eyes, towel around his waist, he walked through the room where some aides were working: "Make way for the future leader of the free world," he said.

The Indiana primary was on May 7. In a highly conservative state, the political tactic for Kennedy was to preach against violence as well as injustice. McCarthy still had strong support among students; labor was holding itself in readiness for Humphrey, who still had not declared himself.

———

IF BOBBY WAS coming strongly into his own, so was Teddy. Kennedy aide Gerald Doherty observed, "I don't know how, exactly, but he *senses* things like the right room to use with people he wants to influence, which of the approaches, how long to talk. If there was one single guy who understood it best, it was Ted."

Ted became a buffer for Bob, trying to keep him from being tense and abrasive, helping him lighten his approach.

Ted put Bob on the five-car train, the Wabash Cannonball, for a slow, ten-day whistle-stop tour cutting through the small towns of Indiana. And he made certain his brother had a proper haircut and a shoeshine.

Besides McCarthy, Bob had to contend with Vice President Hubert Humphrey, who had rushed into the campaign after Johnson's withdrawal.

Bob still seemed to be groping for a speaking style of his own, and a warm personality he could project. Years earlier, Eugene McCarthy had said of him, "Bobby Kennedy holds his head down and looks up through his eyebrows like a coon peering out of a henhouse. . . . Throw an arm around those shoulders and the big white teeth might snap at you."

Ted tried to keep Bob to the political center, but "Bob went into that thing in Indiana way over to the left on race and poverty issues," said Fred Dutton.

"You never saw anything like it," said reporter Jim Deakin. "People were just pouring out of the buildings to see Bobby. I remember women coming out of beauty parlors with their hair in curlers. A few months later, I came up that same street, at literally the same time of day—noon—with Barry Goldwater, and it was a ghost city. Nobody on the streets . . ." Robert Kennedy won the Indiana primary over McCarthy with 42 percent to 30.

That same day, he also won the District of Columbia primary, beating Humphrey almost two to one.

Moving into action during the month of May, the hustling Hubert picked up delegations from Maine to New Jersey. He had certain strengths Bobby couldn't compete with. During a Nebraska speech, in Tecumseh, the wind blew away a tiny piece of paper from the lectern and Bob showed his own kind of humor, "That's my farm program . . . give it back quickly!"

In Omaha, at a Jefferson–Jackson Day dinner, Kennedy preceded Humphrey as a speaker. Playing the underdog, he said, "You have put me ahead of Vice President Humphrey, something I haven't been able to achieve in six weeks of campaigning."

In talking to college students, outlining the social programs he wanted to put into force, Bob asked for questions. "Who's going to pay for all this?" a student asked. "Bob Kennedy looked the student straight in the eye and answered, 'You are!' "

Bob won the Nebraska primary.

There was still hatred for Bobby, though, and violence still seemed to follow him. In Lansing, Michigan, police spotted a sniper where Kennedy was to deliver a campaign speech and caught him before Kennedy arrived.

Being closer to Jacqueline, having her so dependent on him, Bob sent her clippings that might interest her. He even wrote a note to a reporter thanking him for an article on Jacqueline:

It has been a difficult time and particularly for someone who has already had difficult times and doesn't deserve another one—
And it seems to me that you recognized this and perhaps more as a human being than a journalist you put out a helping hand
And for that she was grateful
And so am I—
And so my thanks to you.

There was little question that Ethel was still jealous of this relationship. When the two were together, Jacqueline said to Ethel, "Won't it be wonderful when we get back in the White House?"

"What do you mean *we*?" Ethel asked sharply.

Jacqueline looked as if she had been hit, then gave an embarrassed smile and left.

Author C. David Heymann would later claim, mainly from accounts of former Kennedy servants, that Bobby and Jacqueline had maintained a long affair that ended only with his death. There was indeed a warm and deep bond between them, and it is true that the only framed photograph in her living room was of Bobby. They did take trips together, and it is conceivable that there might have been a brief romantic encounter between them, but the evidence for an extended affair seems thin. After her husband's death, Jacqueline had numerous beaus, some of them serious and long-lasting.

At this point in his life, Ethel regarded herself as Bob's strongest ally and deepest love. If she had any knowledge of her husband's alleged affairs, she did not let on. Bob's relationship with Marilyn Monroe would never see print until after his death, and neither would his efforts to bed Joan Braden, wife of his friend Tom Braden. Years later, the Washington *Post* would print Joan's description of her encounter with Robert. "My heart wrenched from complicated tugs of emotion. . . . He never seemed more vulnerable. When he asked me to go upstairs, I went. On the bed, we kissed. Then he got up to take off his tie. But I could not go through with it. He was hurt, silent and angry. I watched his straight back under the street lights as he walked toward the car. Why hadn't I done it? . . . Tom [Braden] would have understood, even if Ethel would not have."

For Robert, it was not so much a needed fulfillment—he had the richest family life. It was more a kind of challenge. He could be as great as any of his brothers—in anything.

Like his brothers, Bobby sought out married women for his occasional sexual encounters. Some of them were even in his social circle. Singer Dean Martin's former wife Jeanne described Bobby as "a grabber" and said he would flirt with a woman while his wife was in another room. She told of her friend who went with him into a room, and before she knew it he had locked the door and thrown her onto the couch.

Ross Traphagen, a prominent Washington attorney who had once dated Ethel as well as Jean Kennedy, told of Bobby at a party asking Mrs. Traphagen, "Why don't you come home with me. I have my car outside, Ethel's away." And Peter Lawford told friends that Bobby had a brief but intense affair with singer Andy Williams's wife, Claudine Longet, who played sex-kitten roles on television and film. The two couples had been close friends, sailing and skiing together. Claudine was a Parisian, pretty and petite, and fifteen years younger than Bob. Her favorite photograph of Bobby was of him holding an umbrella in the rain, with the inscription, "If you ever need to share a raincoat. . . ."

"I remember walking with Bobby," said Charles Spalding. "We walked past a very pretty girl . . . and I said to him, 'What if she loved us? Would it be wrong to have a relationship with her?' Bobby's eyes just twinkled, as if he was thinking about it."

Even years later, his children refused to believe the stories about their father's possible romantic adventures. "He was never with another woman before he was married or afterward," said Robert Jr. "He was completely moral."

Rose Kennedy had fewer illusions about her husband or her sons. "She read the papers," said her secretary Barbara Gibson. "She read three or four papers a day. She knew everything. . . . She told me once she couldn't believe that Bobby was having an affair with Marilyn Monroe because he was always so sanctimonious. She just couldn't believe it. . . . On the other hand, she knew about Teddy's philandering, she knew it was going on, but she was indifferent towards it."

———

OREGON WAS SUPPOSED to be a cakewalk, a state that completely agreed with Kennedy on the Vietnam issue, a big winner for JFK in 1960. Furthermore, Congresswoman Edith Green, who ran the JFK campaign then, volunteered to run it again now for Bobby.

An Oregon poll had shown him barely leading McCarthy, but there was a large undecided vote. The state seemed cold for him, "a great white suburb with no problems—he knew he frightened Oregon by what he spoke of and his visions," reported Theodore White. McCarthy told one crowd that surveys showed Kennedy strongest "among the less intelligent and less educated . . . bear that in mind as you go to the polls."

McCarthy kept his campaign on a quiet, low key, whereas most news clips showed Kennedy in a noisy, frantic crowd. "I think what a lot of the people were in the market for in 1968 was a little peace and quiet," said Steve Smith. "And that was hurting Kennedy."

Kennedy's staff had underestimated McCarthy, and they had erred in refusing to debate him there.

Bob told *Time* writer Gorey, "I just don't feel I ever got a handle on Oregon. The people don't really cheer you. Sometimes I wish they'd boo me or kick me or do something. I just couldn't get much response. . . . I would be happy to win it by one vote. I just want to stay alive."

When McCarthy beat him in the Oregon primary, Kennedy was furious. The shock was strong, the first time in twenty-eight political

Having suffered from back injuries during the campaign, Jack nevertheless won his first election.
A beaming Rose looks on. (JOHN F. KENNEDY LIBRARY)

Jack's next goal was the U.S. Senate. Bobby, whose wife, Ethel, is seated here in the center, was his campaign manager. (© YALE JOEL/LIFE MAGAZINE)

One of America's most eligible bachelors married Jacqueline Bouvier in Rhode Island, 1953. (UPI/BETTMANN)

At the start, their marriage was happy.

(© HY PESKIN/FPG INTERNATIONAL)

When Jack traveled to Palm Beach to recuperate from back surgery in 1954, Jackie was at his side. (UPI/BETTMANN)

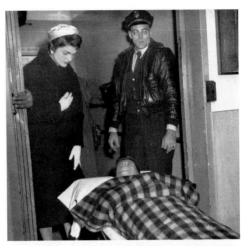

Painting became a special pastime for Jack during his recovery. (© MARK SHAW)

Jack and Bobby were side by side in Washington: (top) during the McCarthy hearings and (left) in front of the Capitol.

The campaign for Jack's presidency was a family effort . . . and the brothers shared the victory.

*Jackie and former President
Eisenhower listen to JFK usher in
a new era.* (UPI/BETTMANN)

*At their son's inauguration,
Joe and Rose realized a dream.*
(PHOTOGRAPH © 1995 JACQUES LOWE)

For Jack, and Bob, whom the new President appointed his Attorney General, the work had just begun. (TOP: UPI/BETTMANN; BOTTOM: JOHN F. KENNEDY LIBRARY)

Two new Kennedys had arrived:
Caroline and John.

The founding father at this point
was ebbing away.

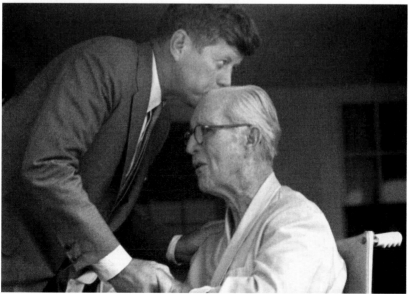

Jack supported Ted's decision to run for the U.S. Senate. (JOHN F. KENNEDY LIBRARY)

Father and son heading home in the summer of 1963.

(JOHN F. KENNEDY LIBRARY)

That November, the pain for the family—and for the nation— would be deep and lasting.

(UPI/BETTMANN)

For months after JFK's death, Bobby retreated from the world. (UPI/BETTMANN)

*By 1968, supported by his wife and ten children, Bobby had recovered sufficiently
to run for the presidency.* (UPI/BETTMANN)

During the campaign, Ted was always at Bobby's side.

Once again, the Kennedy magic captured the country.

And once again, Kennedy children mourned a dead father.

In 1969, Chappaquiddick cast a
shadow over Ted's career.

(UPI/BETTMANN)

Joan stood by his side, as she did
the next year, when he grimly
ran for reelection and won.
Ted and Joan's children
(left to right), Kara, Ted Jr.,
and Patrick, with their parents.

(ARCHIVE PHOTOS)

Ted on the campaign trail with Joan in 1976. He made a halfhearted run for the presidency and lost.

(© GEORGE TAMES/
NEW YORK TIMES PICTURES)

With his wife, Victoria Reggie, at his side, Ted beat back a major challenge to his career in the 1994 Senate race.

(UPI/WORLD WIDE PHOTOS)

The seeds of hope: Bobby's son Joseph P. Kennedy, here campaigning for Congress, was the first of the new generation of Kennedys to carry on the dynastic dream of the patriarch, Joseph P. Sr.

campaigns that any Kennedy brother had been defeated. He had confided to a friend, "I don't know what I'll do if I'm not elected."

When the results came in, Ethel held his hand and Robert smiled, trying to hide his hurt, trying to raise the spirits of his depressed friends. His son, Robert Kennedy Jr., would later say of him, "My father was not the kind of a person who spent a lot of time looking backward."

He had not helped himself by telling Oregon crowds that if he lost in their state primary, "I would not be a very viable candidate for President." The Los Angeles *Herald Examiner* now headlined, "Bobby to Quit—If." Bobby now had learned that hard work could not manipulate demographics. He also learned of the ever-present power of fate. He had told Jack Newfield earlier, "I can't plan. Living every day is like Russian roulette."

Bobby was careful to keep his criticism of Johnson very quiet. He worried that the President might well blacken the Kennedy name by publicly releasing everything Hoover knew about Marilyn Monroe. Johnson also had already told a *Time* reporter, Leo Janos, that the Kennedys "had been operating a damned Murder Incorporated in the Caribbean." Now that Johnson no longer had a political future, he had no constraints.

––––––––––

THE GALLUP POLLS were zigzagging again. Humphrey was starting to soar, and many who had been leaning toward Kennedy were switching to him. Ted was circulating everywhere, asking delegates not to commit themselves yet. After Oregon, Kennedy verified that California was the key. If he lost it, he would urge all his supporters to back Humphrey before the convention.

But, internally, Kennedy was optimistic. One day, before California, after making appearances in New York, New Jersey, and Nebraska, Bob insisted on flying to Hyannis to have lunch with his father. A jet was unavailable, so he hitched a ride on a corporate plane that made a detour to drop him off. Since his father couldn't speak, one wondered now how much he understood, but Bob talked to him about all his plans and hopes, and told him, "Dad, I'm going to California for a few days and I'm going to fight hard. I'm going to win one for you."

Steve Smith had moved the full force of Kennedy staff and money into California early in May. O'Brien saw the state as critical and doubtful. "We were greatly dependent upon longtime Jack Kennedy supporters, in turn, to support Bobby."

Coming into California, Robert Kennedy had a deep tan, and his hair was bleached blond from campaigning in an open car. He showed his weariness only in private. The California campaign quickly climbed into high gear. Kennedy needed to restore his soul and made intensive tours among "my people"—the blacks and Chicanos. He would tell them, "America can do better!" . . . and they would roar back, "Bobby, Bobby, Bobby!" It frightened one to drive in the open car with him—the screaming, the ecstasy, the hands grabbing, pulling, tearing, snatching him apart. To them he was The Liberator.

"For every man working for John Kennedy," said union leader Cesar Chavez, "we must have had about 50 men working for Bobby." "If I don't win," Bob told an aide, "these people are not going to trust another white politician for a long time."

His image had changed for good. "Kennedy stood for giving yourself to a noble purpose," said Jimmy Breslin. "All that energy and emotion and passion for people who've been denied—I haven't seen anything like this ever since."

Posters with his likeness had begun to sell as well as many posters of Hollywood celebrities; he was a myth, a folk hero, a public fantasy. Jack Newfield told how "the young especially saw in him . . . the qualities they most easily identified with—youth, dissent, authenticity, aliena- tion, action, even inarticulateness. They saw in him the same incon- gruous combination of toughness, humor, and sensitivity they saw in other generational cult figures."

JFK also had his cult of the young, but for different reasons. JFK was a model for them; RFK was a part of them.

But if one half the nation was intensely for Bobby, the other half was intensely against him. His political danger was that he had polarized the country into a place that was filled either with loyalty toward him or with hate. It had been that way most of his life: the true believers and the haters. It was almost as if there was no large area of people still willing to be convinced or swayed.

When critics pointed out that the country was too turbulent and fragmented, the races splitting it apart, and that, if elected, he would be beaten by the system, Bob replied, "I think the country wants to be led and needs to be led. I think it wants to do the right thing." There was something else that he left implicit: that if he was elected, the people would know that they had a President who cared for them. And then he could put the pieces back together again.

Like his brother Jack, he started each political speech with self-mocking wit. His favorite quip was to greet the large crowd, then quote Churchill, saying that the crowd would have been twice as large for a hanging. He also seemed more adept at using humor to squash hostile questions.

MCCARTHY'S AND KENNEDY'S views were so similar on most issues that even when they debated there seemed to be no obvious winner. One critic remarked that they "exchanged powder puff punches."

Bob's popularity soared in the polls in the final weekend. His pace never slowed, campaigning until one or two every morning, then starting all over again after five hours' sleep.

In twelve hours on Monday, June 3, one day before the polls would open, Robert Kennedy traveled 1200 miles through the cities and towns of California.

A string of firecrackers in San Francisco's Chinatown terrified Ethel and she crouched down in the open car. But Robert Kennedy didn't flinch, observed Jack Newfield. He did ask a reporter to climb into the car and hold Ethel's trembling hand while he kept his face calm and cool.

Perhaps he was challenging fate—more than he ever did when he climbed mountains or raced the rapids. His brother had been killed in a convertible, so now he felt he had to ride in a convertible, almost inviting the assassin's bullet. Some even wondered whether he had a peculiar psychological death-wish.

Reporter Jack Newfield remembered "how John Lindsay of *Newsweek* had warned us that first wild weekend in California, that 'this country is going to kill another Kennedy. And then we won't have a country.' "

THE NIGHT BEFORE the primary vote, Bob finally collapsed, unable to finish his last speech.

Kennedy took Ethel and six children that evening to a Malibu beach house. When his aide Richard Goodwin arrived, he found Kennedy by the pool, "stretched out across two chairs, his lips slightly parted, motionless." Goodwin's stomach contracted with a spasm of fear. But Bob was sleeping, only sleeping. "God," Goodwin thought, "I suppose none of us will ever get over John Kennedy."

AS CALIFORNIA VOTERS went to the polls on June 4, Robert and Ethel Kennedy and six of their children had their picnic on the beach. He let his children roughhouse him. The day's most dramatic incident was when twelve-year-old son David was caught in a dangerous undertow before his father rescued him.

Ted had been scouting the western states for second-ballot strength among committed delegates. He also supervised an unexpected victory in South Dakota, Humphrey's birthplace, where Kennedy cornered a sweep of the delegates.

Elsewhere, the Humphrey strength was growing, with increasing momentum. It was generally agreed that Bobby had an uphill battle going into the convention, and even Larry O'Brien analyzed afterward that "Hubert had it."

The night the returns were coming in, Bob was late for his speech at the Ambassador Hotel. Hollywood producer John Frankenheimer raced him there in his Rolls Royce Silver Cloud, "and I really hit it— about 120 miles an hour—going across Malibu Canyon and down the Ventura Freeway. . . . Bobby kept saying, 'Go through the red light, go through the red light.' He liked going fast."

That night he found out California was his. He won California with 50 percent of the vote.

He was met by cheering campaign workers in the Embassy Room of the Ambassador.

"I remember watching him on television that night," said Richard Goodwin, "and there was a kind of an ease and a grace that he had that really had been missing. You know, I mean, he always had the passion and he had the ideas. The substance didn't change, but he was at ease with himself. This was his victory. This was not a Kennedy victory; it was *Bobby* Kennedy's victory. And I looked at him and I said, 'My God, the guy looks like a President.' " Correspondent

Sander Vanocur recalled that the last line in his speech was "And on
to Chicago!"

Bob had the reputation for fierce hate when he campaigned for Jack.
But, campaigning for himself, it was gone. An observer noted, "Joe
hated; Bob loved." He had been softened by his exposure to the hurt
and poverty of so many people. He had been made more vulnerable by
his own tragedy and grief. He had simply become a more compassionate human being, and this flowed out of him to people.

After the results came in, talking to his friend Ken O'Donnell,
Robert Kennedy said, "You know, Ken, finally I feel that I'm out from
under the shadow of my brother. Now at last I feel that I've made it on
my own. All these years I never really believed it was me that did it, but
Jack." He paused, then continued: "But I believe it now, and I also
believe I can go on and be elected President—on my own." He had
told his friend Frank Mankiewicz, "Free at last!"

"In a sense, Bobby became his own man on the day Jack died," said
Ted Sorensen. "But he still lived under the haunting effects of that
tragedy." But now they had voted for him, not his brother. This was his
own, without his father directing behind the scenes. Robert Kennedy
was now going to make his own history.

He was exuberant. "It was a madhouse," columnist Jimmy Breslin
said. "The only way Bobby could have a private conference was to lock
himself in the toilet with somebody."

In the bathroom of his Ambassador Hotel suite, he talked to aides
about a hard campaign in New York for next month's primary—if
McCarthy stayed in the race. He also planned visits to many other
states, a trip to Europe, and a meeting at Hyannis with convention
delegates from eastern states. He left his suite to go to the hotel
ballroom to thank all his supporters. He was "full of hope, energy and
enthusiasm," said Ted Sorensen. "I stayed in his bedroom to watch it on
TV until he returned. But he never returned."

————

BOBBY'S SPEECH WAS full of shining optimism. He left the stage to
hold a press conference in the Colonial Room and took the back exit as
a shortcut through the hotel kitchen, through an entanglement of
television cables. His entourage included Ethel, campaign workers,

and security guards. He told one of his security men, Bill Barry, "Take care of Ethel."

"Bill hesitated," said *Look* correspondent Warren Rogers. "He felt his place was directly in front of Bob, where he had been throughout the eighty days of the campaign. He was worried about possible injury among the squirming, shoving, shouting celebrants despite all their good wishes. But he knew, as few others did, that Ethel was pregnant again."

Bill found another Kennedy staffer to help Ethel through the crowd and began pushing his way back toward Bob.

As Bob passed through the swinging doors of the kitchen, he turned to shake hands with a busboy.

"I was waiting in the pantry," said Juan Romero. "I was hoping he'd remember me from the night before, when I cleaned the dinner table in his room. There were only two busboys that night and I gave the other all my tips so he would let me go. He just reached out and shook my hand. He wasn't very tall or very big, but his hand—which had calluses all over it from handshaking—felt so strong. Then he just let go, and I thought he had tripped or something. But when I tried to pick him up by one arm, he was limp. Then I put my hand under his head and felt the warm blood. I could see his lips moving, and I put my ear down, and I could have sworn he said, 'Is everyone all right?' . . . As people were loosening his shirt, I gave him my rosary, a crucifix with black beads. He didn't clutch it. It kind of hung on one finger. . . . People kept telling me how I'd been at the right place. No, the right place would have been in front of him."

The shots came from a short, dark-haired, twenty-four-year-old man named Sirhan Bishara Sirhan, who fired a .22-caliber Iver-Johnson eight-shot revolver at the Senator at a distance of less than four feet. He had shouted, "Kennedy, you son of a bitch."

There were yells: "Get the gun! Get the gun! Kill him! No, don't hurt him! Kill him! Break his thumb! No! No! We don't want another Dallas here!"

Back at the ballroom, where some of the reporters had lingered, Jack Newfield reported "an awful sound that rolled across the packed ballroom that was like a moan. . . . And the moan became a wail until the ballroom sounded like a hospital that has been bombed. . . . A college kid with an RFK peace button was screaming, 'Fuck this country, fuck this country!' "

ONE BULLET HAD penetrated Robert Kennedy's head behind the right ear. Another had entered the mastoid bone and lodged in the midline of the brain; a third had lodged in the back of the neck. Still another had grazed his forehead. Sirhan was wrestled to the ground, yelling, "I did it for my country," and taken away. Five other people were also wounded.

"I happened to be next to Mrs. Kennedy," said Roger Mudd, "and I remember she was standing there all alone—alone as you can be in a crowd. When it was obvious that the Senator was down, she was shaking—her shoulders, arms, hands. So I tried to break through and open up a crack for her so she could get to the spot where he was."

"He was lying with his head at the ballroom end of the kitchen when Ethel came over," observed columnist Pete Hamill. "She was behind him to his left, and she cradled his head in her lap and began talking softly to him. She began rubbing his chest and opening his shirt, all the while talking to him."

Ethel asked people to move back, give him room. She seemed, somehow, to keep control. "Bobby's open eye now focused on his wife, and he recognized her. 'Ethel, Ethel,' he said, and she leaned closer, whispering, 'It's O.K.' He lifted his right hand toward her and she took it, and they held hands there as he lay on the concrete floor—all four hands clasped around the crucifix."

If Ethel's voice was controlled, her eyes were fearful, and she asked *Look* correspondent Warren Rogers, who knelt beside her, "Help me."

Nobody could help much. A staff man put his blue blazer under Bobby's head. When the ambulance arrived, and they lifted him onto the gurney, Bob's jaw was working, and he finally said, "Please don't." Jimmy Breslin remembered that Bob seemed to have a look of total understanding.

Ethel saw her friend Father James Mundell, not wearing his clerical clothes, trying to convince a policeman to let him by. Ethel ran to the officer, identified herself, but the stubborn cop still refused. Ethel pushed him and he pushed back, and she fell to the ground. A crowd surrounded the cop, and the priest joined Ethel in the ambulance, made the sign of the cross, and granted absolution to Robert Francis Kennedy.

"I STAYED AT the hotel awhile until they took Sirhan away," said former pro football lineman Roosevelt Grier. Grier was a friend who tried to keep Bob from falling off the open cars when people pulled at him. "I was crying," said Grier. "I just couldn't stop crying."

At Yale, days before his graduation, William Jefferson Clinton remembered, "my roommates and I went to sleep full of hope—then woke to despair."

TED KENNEDY WAS with his aide David Burke at a San Francisco rally. "That was a rough affair, that rally," said Burke. "There were a lot of unfamiliar faces, a lot of people who were pushing and shoving. . . . There was no sense of control. And people kept yelling and screaming things that had nothing to do with Robert Kennedy's victory, and I felt frankly uncomfortable for Edward Kennedy. I told him we ought to get out of there, and we did as soon as possible.

"We drove back to the Fairmount and went to our suite up there on the fourth floor, and of course the first thing we did was turn on the television set in the living room to get the latest results and see what was happening down there in L.A. The instant the set lit up we heard someone say there's been a shooting at the rally. I assumed, and I think Edward Kennedy assumed, that the rally they were talking about was the one we had just left. . . .

"As we were listening we saw Steve Smith on the screen asking people, over and over, to be calm and be quiet and leave the auditorium. We knew, of course, that he hadn't been at our rally. This was Los Angeles and there had been a shooting down there.

"And then there was the sudden, horrible dawning realization that Robert Kennedy had been shot.

"The Senator didn't say anything," his aide remembered. "There was no outcry. The one reaction I remember most vividly was that there was no reaction at all.

"Ted Kennedy stood in the middle of the living room, staring at the screen. I stood beside him, unable to say anything. I heard him say: 'We have to get down there.' That was all. We just stood there, the two of us, staring at the screen, watching this thing unfold. I don't know how long we stood there; it may have been thirty seconds or it could have been three to ten minutes. We were just frozen there, because we were learning things that were more horrible all the time.

"Finally, the Senator spoke. 'I want to go to Los Angeles.' "

At the airport, a call came from Pierre Salinger in Los Angeles to tell Ted the latest medical report. A distraught aide asked for the news and Ted said grimly, "It's going to be all right." Pierre had told him how hopeless it was, but Ted simply refused to accept it. On the plane, in the course of the trip, nobody spoke.

———

DR. VICTOR F. BAZILAUSKAS, on duty at the emergency room at Central Receiving Hospital, heard the sirens. The back door pushed open and there was Ethel Kennedy saying, "Please help him! Please help him!"

The doctor checked Kennedy's vital signs and immediately ordered him transferred to the better-equipped Good Samaritan Hospital, where he was connected to a heart-lung machine. Neurosurgeons operated for more than three and a half hours to remove lead fragments from his brain.

Eugene McCarthy joined Ted Kennedy at the hospital. McCarthy kept repeating that the name of the assassin, Sirhan Sirhan, was also the name of a character in Albert Camus's *The Stranger*, "a man who comes out of nowhere and kills."

Astronaut John Glenn and his wife were also there at the hospital, and Ethel asked that they go back to her kids, who were staying with friends, and fly them home to Hickory Hill. "Next morning," said Glenn, "my wife Annie and I had to tell the kids their dad was dead. We were just sitting on the edge of the bed. That was about as tough as anything I've had to do. The little kids were just three or four. You just had to tell them that he wasn't going to be coming home."

Poet Robert Lowell said afterward, "One of his possibilities was that he was always doomed. . . . It's very strange when you sort of antici-pate something; then, when it happens, you're almost more astonished than if you hadn't anticipated it. He felt he was doomed, and you knew that he felt that. . . . The ambition was a burden . . . that he had to run for President, that he was doomed with that possibility and duty, and it's rather an awful thing. He knew that, and he had no middle course possible to him."

When the doctors told Steve Smith that Bob would die, that it was only a matter of time, Smith began planning the funeral. Rose and Joe Kennedy had watched their son's California campaigning until shortly after midnight, when they went to bed. Rose awoke shortly before six o'clock, as usual, to attend early Mass. Her niece Ann Gargan then told her what had happened. "But I didn't think it was a serious accident. I kept praying like I do. Lord, have mercy. I couldn't believe it."

At 6:40, Rose emerged in a blue spring coat and gray-blue scarf, entered St. Francis Xavier Church, unseen through a side entrance. She listened to several priests offer Mass for the recovery of her son, later received holy communion, and made the fourteen stations of the cross.

Photographer Ted Polumbaum, who had managed to scale the back fence, saw Rose Kennedy "just walking and bouncing, walking and bouncing a tennis ball, just like a little girl, really—missing it and kneeling down to get it." It was her way, in her loneliness, of dealing with the incomprehensible. She later went to the Hyannis Port Club golf course to play several holes of golf; starting on the fifteenth tee and carrying her own clubs.

———

MORE THAN TWENTY-FIVE hours later, at 1:44 A.M., Senator Robert Francis Kennedy was pronounced dead. Frank Mankiewicz, who read the announcement to the press, added, "He was forty-two years old." Then he wept.

The irony was that Congress passed a bill—that same day—providing Secret Service protection for major presidential candidates. President Johnson had signed it.

When John Kennedy was assassinated, Larry O'Brien and Ken O'Donnell were in such disbelief that they had refused to allow the public announcement of his death for at least half an hour after they had been told he was dead. And they still signed letters with his name for a week after he was dead. "In Los Angeles, I reacted the opposite," said O'Brien. "I felt immediately it was all over."

At Mass the next morning, Rose's head rocked from side to side, and she stopped twice to ask reporters to lower their voices. At the end of the service, when she was alone in the quiet church, she continued praying. Those who saw her when she left by a side exit said she was extremely pale, her jaw set, her head bowed.

Judging Rose's reaction to disaster and death on the question of "sheer guts or sheer faith," Ethel commented, "It probably doesn't matter whether any of the faith comes first."

When she was shopping for a mourning dress at Bergdorf Goodman, a salesgirl reported Rose saying, in despair, "Oh, why did it have to be Bobby? Why couldn't it have been Joe?" She knew that her husband was "eager to go."

"She never wanted anyone to see her cry," said Jacqueline Kennedy. "But I did. Once in her room at the Cape after Bobby died."

"When the President was assassinated, the family became very stoic," said Joe Kennedy's nurse, Rita Dallas. "When Bobby was shot, the whole house fell apart. Mrs. Kennedy kept saying, 'My son, my son.' And Mr. Kennedy cried, I cried. It was too much!"

"Having had two sons assassinated, and one killed in the war, and Kathleen dying in a plane crash. . . . And going on to say that God never gives you a cross that you cannot bear. See, that's what makes her great!" said Dave Powers, ". . . tragedy after tragedy . . . and they seem to make her stronger! I think she's the nearest to a saint—that if you're looking for a Saint Rose, you have it."

"Rose concentrates on what's left to her—the living," said her friend Gloria Guinness, ". . . she's made that way. She's the only woman I know in the world who loves life. Ironic, as life has been taken away from her, over and over again."

AN AIDE DESCRIBED Ted Kennedy in Bobby's hospital bathroom: "Ted leaning over the washbasin, his hands clutching the sides, his head bowed. . . . I never expect, for the rest of my life, to see more agony on anyone's face. There are no English words to describe it."

Afterward Ted rode the elevator down to the Good Samaritan Hospital's autopsy room with his brother's corpse strapped to a gurney beside him. Allard Lowenstein had pushed the elevator button and when it stopped, he got in. "I felt I shouldn't be there," Lowenstein recalled, "but there was no way I could get off, nothing I could do." In the basement, the body was wheeled off and the passengers followed.

Lowenstein recalls being "emotionally out of control" and saying "a lot of presumptuous things." One of the things he said to Kennedy was, "Now that Bobby's gone, you're all we've got." Then Lowenstein beseeched Kennedy to "take the leadership."

Kennedy thanked him "with great politeness," embraced him, and stated, according to Lowenstein, that he would "carry on." This seems to have been the moment at which the "draft Kennedy" movement was born, for it was Lowenstein who was to become the unsanctioned, undercover organizer of the effort to induce Kennedy to lend his name to the ticket at the nomination convention in Chicago three months later. Hearing about it, civil rights leader Charles Evers angrily told Lowenstein, "You're not going to do it to that family a third time."

The autopsy took six hours. An attending surgeon stated that if a bullet had struck one centimeter farther to the rear, the Senator would have lived. As with JFK's assassination, there were many dubious details, including the matter of "the girl in the polka-dot dress." Several people remembered seeing her with Sirhan and another man at the hotel before the shooting. She disappeared. There was also the fact that the Los Angeles police had destroyed three rolls of film confiscated from an eyewitness who took pictures at the very moment shots were being fired. Of 3470 police interviews on tape, only 301 were kept. Also, the tapes of fifty-one significant witnesses seem to be missing, along with five pantry ceiling tiles, two of which contained bullet holes. The door frame containing two bullet holes was also missing.

The morning after the murder, reporters Jack Newfield and Robert Scheer went back to the exact place in the serving pantry where the body had been. "There was one red rose now on the dirty floor to mark the spot. On the wall above the rose was a neatly lettered cardboard sign that read 'The Once and Future King.' A kitchen employee explained to us that the sign had been up there for a few weeks."

In Sirhan's room, a notebook was discovered in which he wrote that Robert Kennedy must be killed by June 5, the first anniversary of the six-day Arab-Israeli war. On Sirhan's person, police found four one-hundred-dollar bills and a newspaper article describing Kennedy's sympathy with Israel's cause.

A witness insisted that he stopped Sirhan from firing his gun after the second shot. Besides, the number of people wounded and the number of bullet holes indicate that more than a dozen shots were fired.

Sirhan's pistol contained only eight bullets. The autopsy determined that the shot that killed Kennedy came from behind his right ear, indicating that it came from another gun.

When California released its voluminous files on the assassination, it included a certificate showing that 2410 police photographs in the assassination case were burned on August 21, 1968.

One of the many unanswered questions about the assassination concerns the involvement of the man who hated him most: Jimmy Hoffa. During the campaign, a representative of the International Brotherhood of Teamsters came to Ted and asked him what they could expect for Jimmy Hoffa if Robert Kennedy were elected President of the United States. Specifically, there was the immediate question about the possibility of Hoffa's being transferred from the mattress factory in the prison to the farm, so he could be outdoors. "A day or two later, Robert Kennedy arrived in Indianapolis. I remember he was taking a bath. Edward Kennedy went into the bathroom, and I went in with him, and related to him this conversation. Robert Kennedy said, 'Well, I'll tell you. . . . As far as I'm concerned, Jimmy Hoffa can stay in the mattress factory forever. And if I'm ever elected President of the United States, he has a darn slim chance of ever getting out of jail.' "

Whether or not Hoffa was involved in the murder, the hate was there.

———

PRESIDENT JOHNSON HAD sent an Air Force 707 to bring back the body, and it was waiting at Los Angeles International airport. Ethel and Teddy arrived with the hearse at the West Imperial Terminal. Ted had picked the coffin, made of African mahogany, and it was wedged into the narrow area between the forward compartment and the cockpit. Jacqueline had come immediately. Bob had been her anchor in almost every crisis. Now she had a question: to her the blue-and-silvery-white plane looked like the one that had carried her husband's body from Dallas. If it was, she could not get on it. They assured her it was not.

On the flight home, Ethel fell asleep against the coffin. A friend put a pillow under her head and her rosary next to her. Later, during the flight, she talked to each of the seventy passengers, asking if she could get them anything. She and Ted and Jacqueline went down with the casket on the plane's hydraulic lift when the plane landed at La Guardia Airport.

On the plane, Ted was heard to say, "I'm going to show them what they've done, what Bobby meant to this country, what they lost."

The news of the assassination reached Joan Kennedy in Paris, where she was staying with the Shrivers after dedicating a John F. Kennedy Memorial Forest in Ireland. Joan flew to New York to join Ted, who was helping Ethel arrange the funeral services at St. Patrick's Cathedral.

Ethel wanted her friend Andy Williams to sing "Ave Maria" at the cathedral service, but the monsignors flatly refused because Williams wasn't an operatic singer. They relented reluctantly only when Ethel personally threatened to pull the funeral from St. Patrick's. The compromise was that Williams would sing "The Battle Hymn of the Republic."

"Ethel Kennedy, incredibly composed, told me to come to the United Nations Plaza apartment," said Arthur Schlesinger, Jr. "When I arrived, she was terrifyingly solicitous of stricken friends. Her first words to me were, 'You were in Chicago for a meeting, weren't you? Wasn't it on Vietnam? How did it go?' Rose Kennedy was there, still stoic. Jean Smith and Eunice Shriver said good night to their mother. She said, 'I'm so glad all you children are home again.' "

At the hospital in Los Angeles, Jacqueline Kennedy had told Mankiewicz: "The Church is . . . at its best only at the time of death. The rest of the time it's often rather silly little men running around in their black suits. But the Catholic Church understands death."

Ted didn't sleep for two whole days and nights, said his wife. "I worried about what the strain and pressure would do to him. There were so many decisions only he could make. He was being bombarded by them. . . . The second night, Ted went into a room in our brother-in-law Steve Smith's apartment and wrote Bob's eulogy. I kept bringing him coffee and trying to do what I could. I don't think I have ever seen Ted work harder at anything."

Others later revealed that the eulogy was really written by his speechwriters. "We felt pretty funny about it," said one of the writers, "because how could we know what he felt about his brother? He just said write something on the theme of love. . . . I wrote what turned out to be the start and finish of the speech he finally delivered, but I've always felt odd about it. I thought maybe that was the one speech he shouldn't have asked us to write." Ted himself was too torn to put such a speech together. Besides, he was not a writer and he wanted this eulogy written superbly well, and it was.

Ted Kennedy was twelve years old when his eldest brother, Joe, was killed on a bombing mission, he was thirty-one when his brother Jack was assassinated, and he was thirty-six when his brother Robert was murdered.

Despite the advice of friends who feared he might be overpowered by emotion, Ted insisted on delivering the eulogy at St. Patrick's. He told a friend, "I've got to gut this thing through." In a breaking, tremulous voice, the remaining Kennedy brother delivered his feelings, full of dignity and defiance. "My brother need not be idealized, nor enlarged beyond what he was in life. He should be remembered simply as a good and decent man, who saw wrong and tried to heal it, saw war and tried to stop it. Those of us who loved him and who take him to his rest today pray that what he was to us, and what he wished for others, will someday come to pass for all the world."

He quoted a favorite poetic passage of both his brothers:

> Some men see things and say,
> "Why?"
> I dream of things that never were and say,
> "Why not?"

The body lay in state at St. Patrick's. Rose Kennedy was there to see the casket placed in the nave of the church, in the center aisle, just beyond the apse. She would come twice to visit the casket. So would Jacqueline Kennedy. The former First Lady, who had borne the loss of her husband with such quiet dignity, now broke down and wept as she knelt beside the coffin. But after she was helped to her feet and went out to face the waiting crowd, her eyes were dry. On her second visit, a child in line popped a paper bag and Jacqueline reacted, according to an observer, "with frenzy like a rearing horse."

Mourners lined up for a mile and a half outside the church, some waiting for seven hours before they entered to pay their respects to the closed coffin. Over one hundred thousand people were estimated to have done this. In a wide-ranging *New York* magazine poll, 52 percent of the blacks interviewed said they visited his coffin in St. Patrick's, compared to 8 percent of the middle-class whites polled. Another survey, in that same magazine, noted that 92 percent of Harlem residents said Robert Kennedy's assassination affected them as much or more than the assassination of John Kennedy.

———

AFTER THEIR INITIAL outpouring of grief, the Kennedys regained their control. Ethel, then pregnant with her eleventh child, never again publicly lost her composure. It was because she was absolutely certain, with all her heart and soul, that Bobby was in heaven, where she would join him.

The coffin was taken down Fifth Avenue past thousands of weeping mourners and put on a twenty-one-car train to Washington, D.C. It was said that more than a million additional mourners lined the tracks, silently watching the train go by.

On the funeral train, Ethel Kennedy and her oldest son, Joe—who was wearing one of his father's pinstripe suits—walked down the aisles, shaking hands, with the fourteen-year-old son saying, "I'm Joe Kennedy, thank you for coming." Of her husband, years later, Ethel would simply say, "I had the best. And I was so lucky."

Actress Shirley MacLaine, a friend of the family, marveled at Ethel and Jacqueline Kennedy on the train. "Jackie first, very regal, as only she can be, with this marvelous sense of sort of anticipatory dignity. She was always able, somehow, to anticipate when the train was going to lurch or when it would bump, and queen-like, take hold of something so that when the bump came, she wasn't disturbed or dislodged. Ethel, standing right beside her, was so unaware, with a complete lack of self-consciousness about herself, that she got bumped every single time. She lurched and fell against a chair or against somebody, always recovering and doing it with humor; but it was so poignant that she allowed herself to be exposed that much."

"Nobody collapses," said Rose Kennedy. "That's what is so wonderful about the children . . . that they rise to the occasion, they always have since they were young even if they didn't want to do it. . . . We sat in the car with Bobby, different times, sometimes together, sometimes we would replace one another. . . . I do think of course I'm a good example because if I collapse it would be more difficult for them."

A high school band at New Brunswick played "Holy God, We Praise Thy Name" and "The Battle Hymn of the Republic" over and over again until the train passed—then it played "Taps." Little Leaguers saluted with their caps over their hearts. One sign read, WE LOVES YOU BOBBY.

When Schlesinger commented on the "marvelous crowds" along the tracks, Ken O'Donnell replied, "Yes. But what are they good for now?"

———

"ETHEL ASKED ANDY Williams to go see Rose Kennedy," recalled Art Buchwald. "So Andy did. . . . in the car where Bobby lay, and where his sisters and Teddy were. She was waving from the window. She looked at Andy and she told Andy to wave too. She said, 'After all, the people came to see. I think they'd like us to wave.'

"Andy was amazed because he was almost afraid to go sit beside her. He thought she would be so silent and uncommunicative and depressed. He sat down beside her, and she was just like a mother.

" 'Start to wave . . . wave,' she repeated."

The source of her strength, Rose told Robert Coughlan, was her devotion to the Stations of the Cross. "As we know," she told Coughlan, "the fourteen pictures represent events in the last three hours of our Lord's life just before his death. I follow this journey often, in church, kneeling before each one as I knelt in Jerusalem on the Via Dolorosa. . . . I recall His words in the Garden of Gethsemane to His Heavenly Father, 'Not my will but thy will be done.' I repeat His words again and again. Finally, the Twelfth Station when he died and I think of my three sons in their last moments—on their final missions, undertaken for the benefit of humanity, I bow my head in silent resignation to God's Holy Will. I think of my eldest son Joe when his airplane was torpedoed over the English Channel. I recall kneeling heartbroken at Jack's catafalque in the Rotunda at Washington and I weep again at the remembrance of Bobby's funeral cortege, in New York, led by Ethel and his ten children. . . .

"At the fourteenth station I see the Blessed Mother view, for the last time, her Son placed in the tomb and I think again of my beloved ones and I take renewed strength and courage in the thought that as Jesus Christ rose from the dead, that my husband and sons will one day rise again and we shall all be happy together, never more to be separated.

My spirits are lightened and my heart rejoices and I thank God for my belief in the Resurrection as I valiantly try to wipe away my tears."

———

AN OBSERVER REMEMBERED Ted Kennedy standing on the back platform. "The crowd reacted frightfully; they were just in complete shock. No one expected him. There were two smaller Kennedy children standing with him . . . and you could see the flag. You could see Ted sort of standing there with his hand slightly raised . . . and nodding. It was just very shocking and kind of frightening. The crowd gasped. He wasn't really waving . . . he was more acknowledging. Then the singing began again. After the train went through, people stood there transfixed for maybe five or six minutes. It was difficult to leave . . . so people mainly stood there."

Ted told his aide Dun Gifford, "I can't let go. If I let go, Ethel will let go, and my mother will let go, and all my sisters will let go."

———

THE FUNERAL TRAIN slowed down at every hamlet on the way to Washington, and always there were throngs of people. As the train slowly passed, Ted Sorensen saw somebody hold up a hand-lettered sign that read: "PRAY FOR US BOBBY."

"You know how you say someone would've loved a certain funeral? He would've loved that train ride from New York to Washington, and seen the people and all," said Dave Powers. "These are the people he inherited from Jack . . . the people that will make Teddy President."

It seemed likely at the time.

Ted remembered the unloading of the casket at Union Station and the drive to Arlington Cemetery, passing through the Mall, where the homeless men of the Poor People's Campaign were waiting silently on the side of the road, holding their hats. Ted sat in front of the hearse.

If the nation was stunned into silence, it was symbolized by Sander Vanocur's coverage of the ceremony on NBC: "I said nothing for seventeen minutes."

It was Teddy who had decided that it shouldn't be a military funeral, because his brother was not really a military man "and it just wouldn't have been right." He was buried in lot 45-A, section 30, close to his brother John, in the shade of a Japanese magnolia tree, high on a hillside.

At the graveside, in Arlington, President Johnson offered words of consolation to Ethel and tried to kiss her, but she averted her cheek. She could not forget or forgive his hate, and she would not be hypocritical.

"We had a reception at our house afterwards," Robert Kennedy, Jr., recalled. "And I went up to my father's room, and I lay on my father's bed. He had pictures on his wall of my aunt Kick [Kathleen] in her nurse's uniform during the war, and pictures of my uncle Joe and Jack.

"And I remember sitting there thinking, 'They all looked so young and they were all dead. . . .' And I lay there and wept for probably an hour or more, and then my father's best friend, Dave Hackett, came in and sat with me. He just sat there silently for I don't know how long, maybe forty minutes or something. Then he said to me: 'He was the best man I ever knew.'

"That's the only thing that I remember," young Kennedy said. "I don't remember after that."

————

AFTER THE FUNERAL, editor Ben Bradlee said, "When Bobby was killed, after checking out the paper and coming home for breakfast, I sobbed uncontrollably all during breakfast." His wife, Toni, was worried because she knew her husband and Bobby weren't that close. But afterward they decided that his grief was cumulative, and included all the crying for Jack that he had not done.

It was that way for many others. They were not simply crying for Bobby; they were still crying for Jack, too. They were crying for the tragedy of a family. They were crying for our country and the violence that had taken hold.

————

AT A FUND-RAISER to pay off Bob's campaign debts, Rose Kennedy reminisced: "Bobby, to me he was always Bobby. When I think of him, I think of children—his personal life was filled with children. I used to tell him, take Ethel and go away for a quiet vacation . . . just the two of you. But they'd go, and the children would always be right behind them." She would tell as many as would listen that Bobby was always the most softhearted of her children.

THERE IS SMALL question that Robert Kennedy's potential was bright. If he had not been elected that year, it would have been in the next election, or the one after that. He had expanded his ideas to an extent his father might not have believed and his older brother would have envied. David Hackett, who knew him best, felt that if both Kennedys had lived another four years "there might have been no more riots . . . because this grass-roots organization in the Harlems of the country, in the ghettos of the country, was beginning to take hold." Hackett pointed to the creation of small-business activity in the Brownsville section of Brooklyn with corporate, public, and private backing as something seldom tried before.

It would be said of Robert Kennedy that he was the last white politician to be trusted by blacks, that he was the kind of man other men might follow into combat, feeling they could not die, that he was one of the few men you could love and hate at the same time.

The residue of hate and bitterness and envy of Bob Kennedy remained deep in Lyndon Johnson. He earlier had called in Clark Clifford to discuss whether or not Bobby Kennedy had the right to be buried in Arlington. Clifford persuaded him that he did. Johnson later refused to agree to an appropriation of federal funds to create a permanent gravesite for Bobby. Only after Richard Nixon became President was the appropriation made.

THE LOSS OF BOBBY was like the loss of Jack—the disappearance of a potential. "He didn't necessarily believe that we were going to cure those things as a nation or as individuals," said his son Robert Jr., "but he believed that if we stopped trying to, if we began accepting those things, that we diminished ourselves as a nation and we diminished ourselves as individuals."

On Pasadena's radio station KRLA, the "staff poet-singer," Len Chandler, recited a poem about the circle dance of hate and death, asking where it would end.

After Bobby's murder, *The New York Times* set into type the advance obituary of Edward Moore Kennedy.

13

THE LAST TORCH

Senator Edward Kennedy, who had replaced Bob on the Special Subcommittee on Indian Education, sat in a plane alongside writer Brock Brower, drinking from a silver hip flask of whiskey that had belonged to his brother. It was April 1969, and a group of senators from the committee had hedgehopped with their three small C-30s over 3600 miles of Alaskan tundra. They had sloshed through deep snow to see impoverished Indians and Eskimos. Now they were en route back to Washington.

Ted insisted to Brower that this was the first time he had used his brother's silver flask. One of his aides recalled that Ted had had nothing much to eat for several days, "and since then it was drink drink drink *drink*, no sleep at all." Ted suddenly burst out, with a fierce insistence, loud enough to be heard throughout the plane, "They killed Jack and they killed Bobby and now they're trying to kill me . . . they're trying to kill *me* . . . !"

It wasn't just fear of being next. Much deeper was the loss, the incredible, unforgettable loss. He saw it constantly on the flat ground outside their house at Hyannis, where the brothers had played touch football. He saw it in the vision of the boat his oldest brother had named after him. He saw it in the framed letter from Jack to their mother asking her if he could be the new baby's godfather. He saw it in Jack's leather jacket, which he now wore. Bobby had worn it before him. He saw it on all their pictures on his walls. They were all so alive, so vital, so happy. It was the pain of the loss, the horrible pain, and there was no way to grapple with it.

The four of them had been part of a great dynastic design, and he had watched it be removed piece by piece, until he could no longer see the pattern. And somehow it didn't seem to make sense anymore.

Dave Powers verbalized it: "Jack always had his Dad, and Bobby and Teddy; and Bobby had Teddy but now Teddy is all alone."

But, in a sense, Teddy would never be all alone. The force of his father, like the shadows of his brothers, had merged with him. He said their causes were now his. But, beyond that, he had absorbed everything from the cut of their hair to the style of their speech; their principles, their attitudes, their loyalties, their tastes in women. Their children were now his children. Their wives were now part of him, too. It was not simply the full stamp of a heritage, it was a blended soul.

"Can you imagine what's been going on inside him?" asked Ted's friend Senator John Tunney. "Can you imagine? Someday his autopsy is going to show some scars that no one—not even us—realized were there."

Ted couldn't cope because he couldn't communicate. He acted lifeless, doomed. For a long time he seemed even oblivious of his wife and children. "I couldn't talk to him," Joan said. And when she did, he didn't reply. Their children were still young: Kara, seven; Teddy Jr., six; and Patrick, only fifteen months old.

But Joan was best when she was needed, and never before had he needed her so much. "I began to realize," she told her biographer, Lester David, "that I, Joan Kennedy, had something important to contribute." When Ted reached for her, she was there.

"Maybe the country lost a lot from the death of Bobby and Jack," said Charles Spalding, "but Teddy suffered more than anybody. I don't think Bobby would have been the same restraint that Jack would've been on Teddy. I think Jack would've saved Teddy. . . . In the presence of Jack, Ted was best, because Jack could cover up for his bad decisions. If he made a political mistake, or something, Jack could correct it. Maybe in some cases, not even let it happen."

"I remember walking with Teddy, after Bobby died," said Tunney, "and saying to him, 'You know, you've just got to get away. You can't think about this. You can't think about it. You must not allow yourself, ever, to think about you being next in line for this terrible treat-ment.' "

"Once Ted told me that if he could do what he wants, what he really wants, he might take his uncommonly beautiful wife and their daughter and two sons and set sail for the Caribbean, to hobo around among the islands," said friend and reporter Warren Rogers. "He would idle and explore and read and just plain live. He would set the pace, one day at a time. There would be no exigencies of public office, no inner voice goading him on schedules set by others, no self-reminders that, with his background, training and experience, he owes something to the country."

His brother Jack had had an identical fantasy.

For the next two months, Ted did a lot of sailing, usually alone, along Nantucket Sound, sometimes along the coast of Maine. On his return, he checked in with his parents at Hyannis.

"Dad rose up in his chair, his eyes wide, pointing a finger at me. . . . I didn't know what was wrong—the old sweater I was wearing, or something. I went over to kiss him, and he held up his hand and put it on my chin. It wasn't much of a beard, a couple of weeks or so. But I hadn't had a haircut the whole time. My mother threatened to shave off the beard herself right there, but I did it. We all had a good laugh afterward, and, seeing my father laugh like that at last, my mother said, 'I wish we could do this every day.' "

———

TED WAS THIRTY-SIX. He was no longer the comic brother doing imitations, no longer the spoiled kid brother from whom nobody expected much. He was now the surrogate father of Bobby's ten—soon to be eleven—children and Jack's two. His was an enormous burden, and there was serious question as to whether he could manage it.

The temptation of many would be to run away and hide. But the imprint of legacy was strong. In him was young Joe's sense of duty, Jack's pragmatism, and some of Bob's passion. Ted Kennedy still treasured a small cigarette box Jack had given him, engraved with the words "And the Last Shall Be First."

"It's altogether different to think what any one of them would've done. . . ." said Jack's old friend Blair Clark. "In subtracting pieces, you get a different person."

———

THE DIFFERENT PERSON that was Ted had no real options. He knew nothing else but public service. And, though he had loved Jack the most, and absorbed everything his father had said, it was Bob who had the greatest political impact on him. Not just because they were closer in age and had served together in the Senate, being intimately part of the same issues, but because Bob, in the end, had been driven by a passion for causes such as civil rights and poverty—and, for Ted, those causes were contagious, contagious because he had come of age during the period when these issues came into center stage.

All his life Ted had been in the public eye, and he had learned to revel in it. The intoxicating cheers of crowds, the waves of adulation, all of it giving him a sense of meaning beyond himself.

He was an ebullient man, and sorrow did not come as easily to him as it had to Bob—and he felt guilty about it. But when he saw Bob's good friend Ken O'Donnell, friend Dun Gifford remembered, "they suddenly put their arms around each other and didn't say a word. You know, it really hurt. You could see it in both faces. They couldn't say anything; neither one could say anything to the other; and they didn't try." Ted could only say what Bob had said when Jack was killed: "I'm just feeling my way, day by day."

To those who knew him, Ted Kennedy seemed visibly older, somewhat slower of step. His waist had begun to thicken. Close friends feared for his emotional stability, watching his inexplicable shift in moods, the tendency to stop in midsentence, and how he would break into unexpected tears with a sudden intensity of desperation. Even his driving became frightening. At times he would lose himself in conversation, look back over his shoulder while at the wheel, paying little attention to where he was going.

The first time he drove to the Senate Office Building, to do some work, he couldn't get out of the car—and drove home.

Home was on the Potomac, on six and a half acres, unpretentious enough to be described as "throwaway architecture," even though it was large and elegant. The living room had a fireplace with an old English mantel, a huge Turkish rug, and sliding glass doors leading out to a balcony overlooking the hills. Every surface of the living room was covered with family photographs. A large master bedroom with an attached private office featured a deck with a spectacular view of the Potomac. The bedrooms for Kara, Teddy, and Patrick were in a separate wing on the main floor. There were also rooms there for several live-in servants, a guest room, a library with a massive stone fireplace. Taped onto the white phone was a list of the extended family's telephone numbers.

The stone stairs went down the slopes, filled with dogwood trees. The swimming pool was enclosed by a boarded fence, the tennis court on a high terrace, the children's play area with swings and trampoline on another nearby terrace. It was a perfect place for privacy and peace.

Joan was there to help, and so were the children. There were some who urged him to quit, and enjoy the peace for the rest of his life. He had the money. Why not?

But Ted couldn't enjoy the peace because there was none. Peace meant time to brood and remember, and he knew that the only thing that would save him was his work. He needed to be consumed by a cause, as Bob was. If he had the training for public service, he saw it as a sin not to pursue it. He talked to his friend Stewart Alsop about all the things still so wrong with the world, so many suffering people, and how he felt that if he could help, he had to try.

Privately, Ted told a friend, "Both of my brothers, in addition to my parents, were the most important influences in my life, certainly in my public life. I relied on them perhaps more than I understood before their loss, not only as brothers but as friends. . . . The causes with which they were so closely identified have, to a great extent, become my causes, and I am attempting to carry on as best I can."

But what did it mean to "carry on"? Did it mean that he had to finish what his brothers had started? Or could he still be his own man, shape his own legislative philosophy, his own political future? Was their record a firm, fixed fact that he had to keep intact or was it mainly a direction?

———

WHEN HE FINALLY did return to the United States Senate, he said at a press conference, "Some have suggested that for safety's sake I retire. But now I must put up a fallen standard of justice, excellence and courage that typified their lives."

Ethel was listening over the radio at Hickory Hill. As he spoke that moving passage, Lester David reported, "she collapsed in sobs, her face in her hands . . . wept convulsively."

In its report on the speech the next day, the Boston *Globe* said, "It may be painful to recall but it is a fact that Ted Kennedy was a more popular figure than his brother Robert in Democratic circles prior to the New York Senator's assassination."

Gradually Ted's humor and sprightliness returned.

"He loves politics and is good at it," wrote Meg Greenfield in the Washington *Post*. "And I am referring here to politics in its very best sense: as a skill requiring generosity, compassion, sensitivity, a sense of fun and an ability to enjoy combat without getting uptight or nasty about it."

There was no question then about his ability, as there had been earlier.

"I served in many conferences with him," said James Symington. "I was on the Health Sub-Committee . . . and we had many head-to-head conferences with the Senate. Anyone who had any questions about his competency, or his homework, should just have attended those things! Because he was in control . . . on top of it . . . he was a serious Senator . . . he came a long way from Ethel's swimming pool party."

As chairman of the Judiciary Subcommittee on Administrative Practices, he attempted to explore job discrimination by the Pentagon and the Department of Transportation in federal contracts.

He also started a foundation with a goal of $10 million in the name of Robert Kennedy to further his charities and goals, such as aid for the starving people in Biafra. He pushed the suggestion that the District of Columbia Stadium be renamed Robert F. Kennedy Memorial Stadium.

During a civil rights demonstration, Ted stepped forward to take the heat and responsibility when others would not.

Comparing Bobby and Teddy, a state president of the NAACP, Aaron Henry, who knew all the Kennedys in terms of their civil rights activities, commented, "Bobby believed in schooling you to what he wanted you to do. And once he felt that he had done his part of teaching you, then he expected you to carry through. And when you messed up, he was gone. . . .

"Now, with Teddy," Henry added, ". . . you're much more likely to get a second or third chance to mess up. Teddy's not a perfectionist, shall we say, and does not demand perfection of every man. I've always felt freer around Teddy in dealing with him than Bobby.''

Bobby, he was saying, was the man of ideas and principles, but Teddy was the man who stayed around to put them in practice.

In his office, Ted used the same desk his father had used when he was Ambassador, and both brothers had when they were senators. There was also a fireplace, reportedly the same fireplace the British used to light their torches when they burned the building in 1814. Elsewhere was a copy of his brother's presidential flag and a duplicate of his rocking chair. On the walls were Jack's dog tags from PT-109 and a letter from him congratulating Ted on becoming a senator. Also framed were a letter from his mother, complaining about his spelling; his own report card from Milton Academy; school papers from the Senator's children. And there was a mobile from Teddy Jr., made out of Popsicle sticks. The tall windows revealed the broad sweep of Pennsylvania Avenue and the White House, which Ted knew so well, but would probably never know well enough.

''THE SOURCE OF Ted's troubles is that all his life people have expected him to be somebody else,'' wrote the Boston *Globe,* ''. . . an ideal, a mantle, a torch, a ghost. But not Teddy.''

''We all felt a lot of bitterness toward him. . . .'' said his nephew Chris Lawford. ''It was probably unfair. There was no real reason for it except that he couldn't fill Uncle Bobby's shoes and didn't try.'' For most of the nieces and nephews, some of their resentment was understandable—their fathers were dead and their uncle was alive, and they saw their fathers as better men.

Comedian Mort Sahl told the story of a Democratic fund-raiser at which every candidate was said to be ''just like Kennedy. Finally, in exasperation, I turned to a waiter and asked, 'Is there anyone in the Democratic Party who isn't like Kennedy?' And he said, 'Yeah. Ted.' ''

Ted's press secretary recalled how uncomfortable Ted felt when people would want to talk about the Kennedy mystique or the myth of the Kennedys. ''That's just something he doesn't like to deal with. I've seen it happen so many times in the past: Things are going fine, he's very loose and relaxed, and then somebody brings up the Kennedy legend stuff, or asks him something about Camelot or carrying the torch, and he freezes. He absolutely freezes. His eyes glaze over and that muscle on the right side of his face starts to twitch and then it's all over, buddy. He pulls back into his shell and you've had it.''

At a dinner of 2500 paying tribute to Bobby, the perceptive columnist Mary McGrory observed, ''It was obvious that the participants had come as much to cheer Edward as to mourn Robert. There is little quibbling about Teddy's qualities. If he is not as brainy as John, or as committed as Robert, he enjoys the political process. . . . If it seems early to be running, to the Kennedys it has never been too early.'' The plain fact was, McGrory stated, ''nobody can stand for long in Teddy's way.'' She quoted one leading Democrat as saying, ''Teddy is ready— that's all there is to it.'' And another is suggesting that ''he has none of Bobby's problems with labor. The kids like him because he's young and the blacks like him because of Bobby. The bosses will go for reform if it's the only way to get Teddy.'' Summing it up, a party leader told McGrory, ''Let's face it: Teddy is a Kennedy without problems.''

President Johnson sensed in him a compatible Populist streak and told Joseph Califano, his chief aide on domestic affairs, ''Teddy has the potential to be the greatest of the three.''

Ted still appeared distant when somebody started discussing his future. He would only repeat, ''I have no timetable.''

The political pressure soon started mounting. Bill vanden Heuvel, an aide and friend of the Kennedys, told Ted that a lot of people had started thinking of him for the Democratic ticket. The two later went sailing along the Maine coast, and were anchored on a foggy night. Ted got the signal of an important phone call and so they rowed ashore and found a pay phone. It turned out to be Mayor Richard Daley of Chicago, one of the Democratic kingmakers. They wanted Ted on the ticket—''either the bottom or the top of the ticket.''

Biographer Robert Coughlan referred to a note Rose Kennedy had written about Teddy becoming President. Rose had written ''Never!'' Coughlan asked her why. She replied that she felt that way at the moment. Then she reflected, ''You see, we had a monopoly. . . . We had money, we had talents, we had relationships with one another, boast of good looks, we had so much that those things . . . Something breaks . . . and it just couldn't continue.''

She later told Charles Van Rensselaer, who used to write for the

Hearst newspapers under the name Cholly Knickerbocker, "He prom-ised me . . . he promised me faithfully that he would not run," she said. "I told him I did not want to see him die, too, that I could not stand another tragedy like the deaths of his brothers John and Bobby."

But she also had insisted that the accumulation of tragedies had not affected her a great deal. "I just think that it's selfish to be concerned with one's self about tragedies . . . It would be very selfish, and very demoralizing. When the children come home . . . we try not to talk about the dreadful things that have come to our family."

She felt that the situation might change for Ted, that he might feel it is something he has to do, "and if that's his decision, I would support him. I'll campaign for him, anywhere he wants me to. You know, I'm quite a campaigner."

The fact was that she was ambivalent. "He shouldn't run, though. Oh, no. No. We've had so many tragedies already." And then she recalled that there had been women who had been the mother of one President, "but there never has been a mother of two Presidents," and told Ted jokingly, "so get busy."

Ted Kennedy supporters did get busy. Articles pressing the issue of a Kennedy dynasty began to appear. "Will Edward Kennedy Now Move Up?" The answer seemed to be "Maybe."

At the Democratic National Convention in Chicago in 1968, the Robert Kennedy delegates had switched to George McGovern. Word spread throughout the hall that Ted Kennedy's brother-in-law, Steve Smith, was in a Chicago hotel to scout the political terrain for Teddy. Steve was one of the few in the family to whom Ted could go for guidance.

Everything seemed possible for Teddy—a draft nomination for President included. Mayor Daley said that the project of drafting Senator Edward M. Kennedy for President is "still up in the air."

For two days Daley watched what he considered the amateurishness in the Kennedy camp. "Your young man had better make up his mind," he told Smith. Daley said that Jack and Bobby both knew how to count delegates, "and your young man had better learn quick."

Smith told McCarthy that Senator Kennedy was not a candidate, and that neither he nor anyone else had lifted a finger on his behalf. Said Richard Goodwin, a special assistant to JFK and LBJ, "Nor would they do so. His only role was to listen and observe, making sure that no one did anything that might be misinterpreted as a Kennedy desire for nomination.''

McCarthy listened, then said, ''I can't make it. . . . Teddy and I have the same views and I'm willing to ask all my delegates to vote for him. I'd like to have my name placed in nomination, and even have a run on the first ballot. But if that's not possible, I'll act as soon as it's necessary to be effective.''

''McCarthy had not been asked for support, and he had asked nothing in return. Both Smith and I walked from the room, deeply moved,'' said Goodwin.

Smith later quoted McCarthy in *New York* magazine as adding, ''While I'm doing this for Teddy, I never could have done it for Bobby.''

Teddy himself stayed in touch by phone from Hyannis Port, a thousand miles away, now saying no, now demanding, ''Is it a genuine draft?''

Some would say of Ted Kennedy afterward that he seemed to lack the Kennedy aggressiveness.

''There's a big movement on,'' enthused California political boss Jesse Unruh in one phone call to Hyannis. ''I don't care about a big movement,'' Teddy replied impatiently. ''What are the facts?''

Nobody discussed his qualifications, only his availability. He had the charm and the money and it was assumed he could pick up the pieces—pick up the mantle.

''I was here, with just two people, my sisters Jean and Pat. . . .'' Senator Kennedy reminisced. ''The three of us talked among ourselves, and on the phone with Steve, and more and more, I felt confirmed in my original decision not to accept a draft. You can't imagine what pressure there was. We sat here, the three of us, with those phone calls coming in from Steve, and we made decisions as they were required.''

One of the drafts of a proposed Kennedy statement had the sentence ''I will never follow the path of my brothers, I will never seek the presidency.'' The Kennedy sisters objected so strenuously that it was taken out.

Steve Smith later reported, ''We had it. . . . There was no question but that the Senator could have had the nomination. All he had to say was yes. But the way we saw it, he could win the nomination but not the election.''

"Basically, I just didn't have the feeling at that time for politics and campaigning,'' said Ted Kennedy. ''And beyond that, I was too vulnerable. . . . After all, how could I conscientiously combat allegations by Nixon—and we had to anticipate he would make them—that I was too young, that I had no record in public life strong enough to recommend me for the high office of President, that perhaps I was trying to trade on my brothers' names.'' Then he added, ''Even if I were willing to reach out for this opportunity, personal pressures are overriding—subjecting my family to fears over my safety . . . the tensions on my mother.''

It was also reported that the Nixon people had hired a private investigator, Tony Ulasewicz, to dig deep into Senator Kennedy's personal life, particularly past affairs with women, for possible political blackmail. In the diaries of H. R. Haldeman, President Nixon's chief of staff, in an entry dated June 23, 1971, Haldeman suggests how to make political use of Ted Kennedy's sexual excapades ''and get him in a compromising situation if we can.''

Nixon felt strongly that he would soon face Ted in a presidential election, and he didn't want to lose to another Kennedy.

Daley finally announced that he didn't expect Kennedy to run in 1968. But nobody doubted he would ultimately make the race.

His cousin Joe Gargan emphasized to Ted that there was no political need for him to hurry. If he waited until 1980, he would still only be forty-eight—the same age Jack would have been during the first year of his second term.

''Forget about 1980,'' Ted replied, ''because by that time I'll probably be dead.''

''You mean—''

''Shot? Maybe, or more likely an airplane or an automobile accident.''

Hubert H. Humphrey was nominated for President, and there was talk of offering Senator Edward Kennedy the nomination for Vice President. He refused to accept it under any circumstances.

In a filmed introduction at the convention, Senator Kennedy appeared on a huge screen at the amphitheater. The men who weren't there—the dead Kennedy brothers—dominated the imagination of the delegates.

"He has no one but ghosts at his side and they count more against than for him, eclipse him with bright images from the past," wrote Joe McGinniss.

Observing Ted, Senators reported on "the way he tightened his jaw and gritted his teeth . . . moments when shadows fall across his face."

———

TED STILL TOOK his role seriously as the husband to his brothers' widows and father to their children. As Bob had found solace in giving comfort, so did Ted. Because of complication with her pregnancy, Ethel was soon ordered to bed. The baby was born six months after her father's assassination. Ted Kennedy was with Ethel when she went to the delivery room, holding her hand throughout her cesarean section. "Watch him!" doctors warned as he blanched. He slipped the gauze mask over his eyes awhile, then, recovering, started giving suggestions until shushed.

After the birth, Ted put a notice outside his Senate office which read: IT'S A GIRL! She was named Rory, a combination of Robert and Bobby. After leaving the hospital and before going home, Ethel took her new baby to her husband's grave at Arlington and knelt in prayer.

Reporters who had traveled with Bobby during the campaign showed up on Christmas eve, in a driving cold rain, to sing Christmas carols under Ethel's window. "Every one of them fell in love with her during the campaign," said Art Buchwald. "I think what shook all of us was her amazing ability to cheer everybody else up. It was almost as though she drew her strength from giving pleasure to those most concerned about her."

It was a marvel, too, that Bobby, the least charming of the brothers, the one apt to be most direct and most hurtful, had captured the traveling press. He could credit this to both his passion and his artlessness, and to Ethel. Close friends noted some signs of Ethel's inner turmoil; a rapid tremor of the hands when she lit a cigarette and her heavy smoking. Ethel had surfaced only infrequently, and usually very informally, in the months since Los Angeles. Her only public appearance was an invitation-only dedication of a bust of her late husband on a gray afternoon in the courtyard of the Justice Department.

When Jacqueline learned that Bobby, shortly before his death, had selected a sixteenth-century gold annunciation scene as Ethel's Christmas present, she bought it and gave it to Ethel as her own present that December. The friend, who knew that Jacqueline saw Ethel on her customarily infrequent basis, commented tersely, "Jackie's better at bestowing presents than presence."

"It is thought by some that Jackie's giving of gifts, instead of giving of herself, reflects the same distrust of people." Friends said she now detested the world's devouring and often cruel interest in her.

In October 1968, Jacqueline Kennedy married shipping multi-millionaire Aristotle Onassis, sending shock waves through America. They had met periodically since 1963, and he had made his yacht available to her and courted her intensively with calls and lavish gifts.

"I knew Onassis pretty damn well," said family friend Larry Newman. "In fact, I met him through Big Joe. I figured he was the kind of guy who'd take Jackie right off her feet, because he riveted all his attention right on her—with any woman he was with. In my opinion, she was really in love with the guy."

The previous May, Jackie had called her brother-in-law Bobby away from his primary campaign duties to tell him that Ari Onassis had proposed to her. He was appalled and could only reply with a weak joke. "For God's sake, Jackie, this could cost me five states." She agreed to postpone the wedding until after the presidential election.

All through the summer before Bobby's death, Onassis called Jacqueline almost daily, flooding her with flowers, talking endlessly about her need to get away from it all and of the kind of life the two would live together. He spent several weekends visiting Hyannis, getting to know Caroline and John better. An observer recalled the children introduced him to the game of musical chairs, but noted that they ran around the chairs while he controlled the phonograph needle.

"After the President was killed, I used to date her a lot," said Roswell Gilpatric, JFK's Undersecretary of Defense. "We took a trip to Mexico, and Latin America; and she was very interested in the Mayan culture and learned a lot about it. She was very, very bright, very astute, very learned. . . .

"She did not reminisce about Jack, or the White House. . . . We never talked about it. It was as if it was a curtain over her mind. She did not want to talk about the past—the White House, or about him. But she was always talking about Bobby. Bobby was her anchor of strength and security. . . ." She needed his sense of security, and she needed his strength.

She had never been interested in politics before, but she was now. She wanted to know from Gilpatric about all the people who had political influence and what she could do with them to help Bobby.

Gilpatric was with her when the news came of Bob Kennedy's death. After Jack died, she had no relationship with any of the Kennedy sisters, or the mother, and not very much with Teddy. The father had had a stroke, so she could no longer count on his support. So it was Bobby. She absolutely depended on Bobby, and when he was killed, she was shattered.

"She was wiped out," observed writer Fred Sparks. "It was as if she didn't care anymore, and that's why she married Onassis. She just didn't care." Friends felt she needed someone quickly to fill the new vacuum in her life.

The only Kennedy whose approval of the marriage she wanted was her surrogate father, Joseph Kennedy, who was wheeled into Jacqueline's presence one day in her Fifth Avenue apartment. Before he left, Jacqueline felt he had communicated his blessing.

His Eminence Richard Cardinal Cushing, Archbishop of Boston, later disclosed that some members of the Kennedy family had sought his aid in their efforts to dissuade Jackie from the match—and that Jackie herself had visited with him for about two hours just four days before the wedding. He hinted that the consultation had been highly emotional and deeply personal. "Few people understand Jacqueline Kennedy," he said.

At the time of their wedding, Onassis was sixty-two, and Jacqueline was thirty-nine. She once had quipped that the public would always approve of her as long as she didn't marry Eddie Fisher, but this was worse.

JACKIE, HOW COULD YOU? headlined Stockholm's *Expressen*. Said a former Kennedy aide, "She's gone from Prince Charming to Caliban." Paris news vendors hawked: "The latest Kennedy tragedy."

"Jackie was the one I never really completely understood. . . ." said family friend Ben Bradlee. "It was always hard to know what she was thinking and feeling. She was very self-contained. And while she was so zealous about protecting the Camelot image, how can you explain her marrying Onassis? The answer, I guess, is money. She'd never had much money when she was young; I guess she wanted and needed the security.''

"Money is security to a lot of people,'' said columnist Betty Beale, with an added explanation. "I think lacking it, and not having seen an ideal marriage . . . that money became absolutely necessary for her inner security. . . . And then, she was a big spender.''

Onassis's former steward Christian Cafarakis reported that there was a 173-page prenuptial agreement guaranteeing Jacqueline $10 million for every year they were married and specifying separate bedrooms and scheduled conjugal visits.

Jacqueline denied it. Author Truman Capote told of her strolling with him in New York when she spied *The $20,000,000 Honeymoon* in a bookstore window. "Those are lies, all lies,'' said the former First Lady. "I don't have any money. When I married Ari, my income from the Kennedy estate stopped. I didn't make any premarital financial arrangements with Ari. I know it's an old Greek custom, but I couldn't. I didn't want to barter myself. Except for my personal possessions, I have exactly $5,200 in a bank account.'' Asked, "How do you live?'' Jackie replied, "I just charge everything to Olympic Airways.''

Senator Edward Kennedy's statement wishing the couple well was chilling in its formality and brevity. Teddy afterward remarked bitterly to Lem Billings that on top of everything else he now had to carry what should have been Jackie's load as well.

———

NEITHER OF TED'S brothers had tried for a legislative leadership post. They were too impatient with Senate protocol, and their restless ambition was on a fast track. Ted would change that tradition. He decided to try to be Senate Majority Whip.

After a tough race against veteran Senator Russell Long in January 1969, Kennedy became Majority Whip, the second-most-important position in the Senate. The post offered a strong political sounding board and gave him a major role in formulating party policy. His victory had all the organized planning of a Machiavellian coup, a very personal triumph that clearly enhanced his presidential prospects.

He became increasingly adept in Senate maneuvers. He now spoke up on foreign issues as well as domestic and felt obligated to be well informed on everything from refugee problems to our missile defense system.

Once, Senator Strom Thurmond fell into a heated Labor Committee argument over additional federal aid to education. After several barbed exchanges, Kennedy cut off the discussion and gaveled the session to a close. But as the two senators left the room for a meeting of the Judiciary Committee, Kennedy threw an arm around his colleague's shoulder. "C'mon, Strom," he urged, "let's go upstairs and I'll give you a few judges."

Reporters were already pressing him about the 1972 election. Kennedy replied in mock anger: "This goddamned— Always trying to shove me out in front where I can get shot."

"Okay, I'll go out and look for somebody else," said the reporter.

"Well-l-l-l, check with me before you do *that,*" said Kennedy.

The prize was too rich. It was obviously on his mind.

But surely also in the back of his mind was the knowledge that he would not only be the repository of the memories and magic of his brothers, but also of the simmering skepticism, resentment, and hatred directed at them.

Despite her ambivalence, Rose Kennedy privately expected Teddy to be President. She sent him a newspaper story saying that the newly elected President, Richard Nixon, did not plan to use a certain room in the White House. Ted told an audience that his mother had said, "Teddy, I see where the President isn't going to use that room. . . . I think *somebody* ought to use it." After a pause for laughter, Kennedy added, "We are looking into that."

Somebody asked whether 1972 was really the best time for Ted's presidential run or whether it would be best for him to wait awhile. Aboard a small plane with a reporter, Ted answered the question. "The thing about being a Kennedy is that you come to know there's a time for Kennedys. And it's hard to know when that time is, or if it will ever come again. . . . I mean, is the country going to be receptive? Will it be the time? And if it is, is it really the best thing for me to do? And how much of a contribution could I make, even if . . . ?"

———

THERE WAS INCREASED Washington talk about Ted's drinking.

"Does he drink? Sure. Teddy obviously drinks," said Richard Goodwin. "Does he drink too much? For what? To keep himself from functioning? Well, he's functioning. To keep himself from being effective? Well, he seems to be as effective as can be in the Senate."

If he drank too much, he never forgot to turn up at Hickory Hill on most nights, just to check in. But reporters dwelled more on the delinquent husband rather than the surrogate father. Reporter Richard Harwood, who wrote much about the Kennedys in Washington, voiced the views of many when he said that Ted Kennedy drove too fast, drank too much, and chased too many women.

"He is the least discreet guy on the Hill," said an old congressional friend. "I have told him ten times, 'Ted, you're acting like a fool. Everybody knows you wherever you go.' " Other senators could get away with it, the friend said. "Jack could smuggle girls up the back way. . . . But you're not nearly as discreet as you should be. He looks down with a faint smile and says, 'Yeah, I guess you're right.' But he never listens."

Life reporter Sylvia Wright sent a memo to her editors: "He's living by his gut; something bad is going to happen."

———

IN MID-JULY 1969, there was a party at Lawrence Cottage on Chappaquiddick Island near Martha's Vineyard following the annual Edgartown Regatta. Ted was there along with friends and staff people. The party was later described as "a group of middle-aged married men entertaining a group of young unmarried girls." The women were later described as campaign "boiler-room girls," picked for their brains and discretion, and accorded wide freedom to act, negotiate, close deals in the name of the candidate. "People brought *them* coffee," described a staffer.

Esther Newburg, who was at Chappaquiddick that night, insisted, "It was a steak cookout, not a Roman orgy. No one was drinking heavily." Kennedy later said he drank only two rum-and-Cokes that evening. The Senator left the party later that night with twenty-eight-year-old Mary Jo Kopechne, a former secretary to his brother Robert. A witness said that the two took a bottle with them as they left the party.

Ted's chauffeur was available, and invariably did the driving, but this time Ted asked for the keys. Kopechne told no one she was leaving and did not ask her roommate for their room key. Crossing the narrow wooden Dyke bridge, the car went off the side of the bridge into a tidal pond. Kennedy claimed that he had been going 20 mph. There were no skid marks to indicate that he had braked. Kennedy's car got only eighteen feet onto the bridge before plunging into the water. Locals recommend stopping altogether before leaving the road, then inching forward onto the bridge at 5 mph. Kennedy had had four traffic convictions in the 1950s, two for speeding and two for reckless driving.

New York Times correspondent James Reston, who was visiting his family newspaper on the Vineyard that weekend, recalled the scene. "I know the old wooden bridge very well, and whatever his condition or intentions, it's easy to imagine how a sober man could drive off in the dark into the water. The first part of the bridge—no more than a few yards—rises steeply, so that the lights of a car at night are tilted toward the sky, leaving the bridge in darkness. Then the bridge veers sharply to the left and levels off. . . . Kennedy didn't turn but plunged straight ahead into the deep and swirling channel."

Ted's father's nurse, Rita Dallas, contributed the fact that Ted once took his father for a drive and got lost. "His sense of direction was always so bad . . . there was a family joke about his never knowing what turn to take." A friend had commented, "I'm not nearly so worried about another assassination as I am about his crazy driving." Ted himself once had predicted he might get killed in a car crash.

In his statement to the police, Kennedy claimed to have taken a wrong turn onto the bridge. When the car fell into the water, he said he had no recollection how he got out. "I came to the surface and then repeatedly dove down to the car to see if the passenger was still in the car. I was unsuccessful in the attempt. I was exhausted and in a state of shock. I recall walking back to where my friends were eating. There was a car parked in front of the cottage, and I climbed into the backseat. I then asked for someone to bring me back to Edgartown. I remember walking around for a period of time and then going back to my hotel room. When I fully realized what had happened this morning, I immediately contacted the police.''

Yet Ted Kennedy had waited ten hours before reporting to the police. He claimed to be in ''a state of shock.'' But, during that state of shock, he managed to make seventeen phone calls.

It said much for Ted's state of mind, his panic, lack of decisiveness, and immaturity that he needed the advice of so many people to help him decide how to respond publicly. The large brain trust soon started arriving at the Vineyard. They included the senior Kennedy circle of Steve Smith, Theodore Sorensen, Robert McNamara, Richard Goodwin, Kenneth O'Donnell, Burke Marshall, and others. There were also his close friends John Tunney and Charles Hooten. Many of them were soon busy writing his speech for TV.

Ted's own doctor diagnosed the damage as a ''slight'' concussion. Those who saw him later in the morning, eight hours after the accident, said he seemed in a pleasant mood, showed no ''grief, fear, doubt, exhaustion, panic, confusion and shock.''

Ted later said, ''I do not seek to escape responsibility.''

But when he made his first call to the Kopechne parents to tell them of the accident and their daughter's death, he had not even told them he had been the driver of the car.

Columnist Jack Anderson, citing sources close to Kennedy, said the Senator appeared calm and natural to those who saw him at the breakfast hour ''because he had arranged for his cousin Gargan to take the rap and admit driving the car. At the last minute, according to Anderson, Kennedy decided to put aside this sleazy plot.''

Family friend Larry Newman tried to reach him before he made any statement. Newman felt he could have saved him ''if Ted had admitted that he was drunk and she was driving. . . . He had a hairline fracture on the right ear . . . that means he was sitting on the right side . . . he *wasn't* driving the automobile.''

''I called out there,'' said Newman, ''and got Joan. I said, 'Joan, will you get a message to Teddy?' She said, 'Larry, how can I get a message to him when they won't let me talk to him?' ''

''No one told me anything,'' Joan said later. ''Probably because I was pregnant, I was told to stay upstairs in my bedroom. Downstairs, the house was full of people, aides, friends, lawyers. And when I picked up the extension phone I could hear Ted talking to Helga. Ted called his girlfriend Helga before he or anyone told me what was going on. It was the worst experience of my life. I couldn't talk to anyone about it.'' She shook her head and looked away. ''Nothing ever seemed the same after that.''

It typified again the unhappy status of their marriage as well as Joan's serious passivity. Joan afterward tried to explain it. ''Ted is the last of the Irishmen who revere their mothers and put their wives on a pedestal but don't talk to them.'' It was true of the father and his sons, except for Bobby.

Rose later commented to Robert Coughlan, ''Teddy had everything. . . . He goes out one night in an accident and everything is smashed. As I say, it just seems as though, I realize that from Shakespeare, how much destiny decides, really.''

''I do not understand why Joe Gargan or Markham did not report the matter to the police even if Ted did not have sense enough or control enough to do so—especially when the body of the girl was in the car,'' said Rose Kennedy. ''That is what seems so unforgivable and brutal to me. . . . Some newspapers were rough on Ted. . . . The criticism put in a question is, What would he do under stress as President, when he was so unstable in this predicament? . . . I felt very badly, to think he was responsible. The girl was a wonderful girl.

''No, I've never discussed it with him. . . .'' Rose added. ''What's the use in discussing it? It's all over—for the girl, for him and for me.''

Rose Kennedy wrote a note to the Kopechne parents and later dined with them in New York.

''Aunt Nan'' Coleman believed that Jack would never have gotten himself into a situation where anything like that could happen.

''Jack would never have gotten caught . . . it wouldn't have happened,'' said Charles Spalding. ''But Bobby would have called the cops, right off the bat. Just said he'd had too much to drink, and the car slipped. He would have gone off to jail.'' (In view of the Bobby–Marilyn stories, this may be questionable.) ''I don't think that even Jack could have protected Teddy once it happened. Who could protect him?''

One man who might well have protected him, somehow, was another Kennedy who was not there—Old Joe. Had he been alert and available, he would have somehow covered up Chappaquiddick.

Rita Dallas recalled the day Teddy came to tell his father, "I was in an accident, Dad, and a girl was drowned. That's all there was to it but you're going to be hearing a lot about it on TV." Then he covered his face with his hands and added, "I don't know, Dad. I don't know." His father simply dropped his head to his chest. Here was the horror of his final impotence.

Few had ever questioned the courage of any of the Kennedy brothers, but many now saw in Ted Kennedy a tendency to panic. The Kopechne drowning now helped stir up anti-Kennedy feeling. And the ferocity of the attacks indicated, too, that America's formal period of guilt and mourning for JFK had ended.

Many never forgave him for leaving the girl's body in the car. "We don't know what he was doing, but you never leave a body in the water," they said. "I think Teddy, not unlike John and Robert, struggles with bad tendencies in himself," another islander said. "And I don't think I will ever be able to discount his flight from the accident—not that he could have saved anyone submerged like that when he himself was drunk."

John Farrar, the expert diver on the Edgartown Search and Rescue Squad, brought Mary Jo Kopechne's body out of the car as it lay submerged in Poucha Pond. "She didn't drown," he said later. "She died of suffocation in her own air void. It took her at least three or four hours to die. I could have had her out of that car twenty-five minutes after I got the call. But he didn't call." Farrar has been the only person connected with the incident who has loudly and publicly accused Ted Kennedy of manslaughter.

The alcohol content of her blood was put at .09 percent. Massachusetts police consider a level of 1.0 percent as evidence of drunken driving.

It was said of Police Chief Dominick Arena that he had never investigated anything more serious than complaints of "snapping turtles or snakes in people's yards." Arena never thought to question Kennedy. "After all," he told reporters, "when you have a U.S. Senator, you have to give him some credibility." There would be no official autopsy.

Watching the news on his ranch in Texas, ex-President Johnson was certain that because he was a Kennedy, Ted would not go to jail.

Johnson became almost bitter about the double standard. "But if I had been with a girl and she had been stung by a bumblebee, then they would put me in Sing Sing."

Judge Boyle's twelve-page summation reached two conclusions: Kennedy was not telling the truth when he said he was taking Mary Jo to Edgartown and Kennedy's "negligent" driving "appears to have contributed to the death of Mary Jo Kopechne."

Ted Kennedy received a two months' suspended jail sentence.

There were many who felt that the case left a very bad taste because of the slipshod—even mystifying—way in which so many questions had been permitted to remain unanswered.

Ted's carefully crafted speech on TV was aimed at turning the watching audience from curiosity to sympathy, without giving too many details of the accident. Many compared it to the "Checkers" speech by Richard Nixon, in which Nixon tried to explain and apologize for what he called his indefensible conduct. Kennedy's seventeen-minute speech was even described by one sympathetic politician as "a Checkers speech with class." The class came from Ted Sorensen, who remained loyal to Ted after many other "honorary Kennedys" had deserted him.

All three networks broadcast the speech live at prime time. More Americans watched than had seen Neil Armstrong take his first step on the moon. Rita Dallas later revealed that the TV set had been disconnected in Joe's room so he would not see his son that night.

What struck one critic as odd about Ted's speech was the eloquent passage on courage from his brother Jack's book, which he recited "as though oblivious to the way its meaning rebuked him." And author Garry Wills added, "Each time he evokes his brothers, he seems to dwindle beside the shadowy evocations. Yet he must go on evoking them. He is a prisoner of his brothers' charm, which he must trade in even as he seems to cheapen it. He was using the Kennedy name, but using it up."

For the first time ever, many Americans felt embarrassed for a Kennedy. William F. Buckley was even more specific: "What Chappaquiddick did was to shatter the dynastic claims of Edward Kennedy. . . . He will now have to make it more or less on his own, Chappaquiddick having apparently broken the natural line of succession."

In his speech, Ted asked Massachusetts voters if he should resign.

"They're calling by the millions," said an editor at the Boston *Globe* after the speech—mostly urging Teddy to stay. Boston radio stations logged keep-Kennedy majorities ranging from 3 to 2 to 4 to 1. Western Union offices in Boston and Springfield were swamped with telegrams to Hyannis Port, heavily for keeping Kennedy on. A Western Union man delivered 10,000 of them in one batch to the Compound the morning after the speech. Massachusetts would always want him.

"For now, I think he's done it—he's off the hook," said one public opinion analyst. "But Mary Jo Kopechne will cast a long political shadow over tomorrow."

In the weeks that followed, Teddy called Mary Jo's parents and told them that he wished it had been him and not Mary Jo. Then came the funeral.

Joan came with him. "There was a gasp in the crowd as the Kennedys slipped into their pew, across from the Kopechnes. Mrs. Kopechne wept into her black-gloved hands. The 'boiler-room girls' cried. Teddy, in plain torment, glanced once at the coffin, then looked away. Then, at the hillside cemetery, Kennedy stood under an open tent behind the Kopechnes, with head bowed, through a brief last prayer commending Mary Jo's soul to God. When Ted looked up, his eyes were wet."

A month later Joan suffered her third miscarriage.

———

YEARS LATER, STANDING at the rear terrace of his house on Squaw Island, Ted Kennedy pointed out to author Lester David, "Over there, at the foot of the breakwater, is Dad's house." He turned his head. "Just at the horizon is Martha's Vineyard. You can just barely make out the outlines of the shore. It's about twenty miles, a nice sail."

Ted then stared in the direction of the unseen Chappaquiddick, and his eyes brimmed with tears. "It's with me," he said, "and always will be with me."

"His voice dropped," said David, "and he spoke almost to himself. Moving closer, I caught his words. 'I'll never forget that,' he was whispering. 'I'll never forget that.' Quickly he turned, sat on a metal chair, and changed the subject. As he spoke of other matters, his eyes were still wet."

Chappaquiddick would have a long fuse. A year later, tourists ripped up the bridge for souvenirs so badly that it had to be rebuilt. Twenty years later, Senator Alan K. Simpson was on a train with Ted when a woman came over to him and said, "What do you think of what you did to that woman on Chappaquiddick?" Ted turned pale, then replied, "Ma'am, that's with me every day of my life."

A sign on the office wall in the Shiretown Inn on Martha's Vineyard, where Kennedy had been staying the weekend of the accident, read: PLEASE DO NOT ASK US TO ANSWER QUESTIONS CONCERNING THE KENNEDY INCIDENT. THANK YOU. THE MANAGEMENT. Some Republican Party handbills at the next election featured a picture of Ted Kennedy: WANTED—EDWARD MOORE KENNEDY, FOR MURDER OR PRESIDENT?

It would crop again and again in every campaign: how could he save a nation when he couldn't save Mary Jo Kopechne? He had shown the inner workings of his mind under grave stress and it wasn't good enough for a potential President. His speech had come across phony, leaving more questions than answers and revealing little sense of responsibility. It was not the end of the House of Kennedy, not the death of a dynasty—because there would be another generation—but it was the death of a legend, the death of a myth.

However, it was not the death of a career.

———

TED RECEIVED A PRIVATE NOTE from a surprising quarter: Richard Nixon, who had lived through his own political trauma, wrote him, "A man's not finished when he's defeated; he's finished when he quits."

Political cartoonist Oliphant showed a caricature of Nixon looking at Senator Kennedy and commenting, "So once upon a time he went on TV and lied to the people; so what's wrong with that?"

Years later, in a TV interview, Ted was asked, "Senator, when you gave your televised speech after Chappaquiddick, you mentioned thinking that there was some awful curse that was hanging over the Kennedy family. Do you still think that?"

In front of the vast TV world, Ted said he no longer felt that way. But the obvious torment in him made him stammer and stumble in the worst possible performance.

Of the blighted Kennedy career, a friendly Senator said, "It's my feeling that he'll stay in the Senate—it's a club and they'll rally around him—and I think he'll come back less as the guy on the white horse and more of a human being. He'll never be the same again. He'll go through life haunted by the ghost of that girl. Every morning he'll have to face himself in the mirror, and it won't be easy. But once this presidential thing is eradicated, he will live better with himself."

In the immediate aftermath of Chappaquiddick, the Kennedy women quickly collected from all over the world to form a protective support for their remaining brother. They spent most of their days with him, dined together every night, sailed with him.

"After Chappaquiddick, Teddy spent days, weeks, even months with his father," said author Richard Whelan. Perhaps he was looking for absolution he would never receive.

Soon afterward, his father began refusing nourishment and started slowly wasting away. Before long, even his few intelligible sounds ceased. He also had stopped wanting to get out of bed.

"Mort Downey was probably the last of the old friends that went to see Joe," said Larry Newman. . . . "Buckley from New York, and a lot of those guys came up here, and they just stopped because they couldn't stand to see Joe disintegrating before their eyes—we just couldn't take it any longer. Because I don't think he even knew who in the hell we were."

"His father looks so helpless, bereft of even that minimal spark which used to light up when Ted approached," said Rose Kennedy at the time. "Now he is plagued by new ailments—inability to swallow, so he eats only ice cream, baby food or finely minced food which has been put through the blender. His cheeks are sunburned and when I feel his arms and legs I feel only bones. He goes seldom downstairs or on the boat. July has been unusually sunless, clouded—the worst season in years."

Shortly before the sixth anniversary of John Kennedy's death, the Kennedys started collecting. Jacqueline flew in from Greece and spent several hours alone with Joe. When the Shrivers came from France, son-in-law Sargent fell on his knees at the bedside and cried. "Oh, Grandpa, I want to tell you how much I love you, and I want to thank you for everything you have done for me. Without you none of us would be anything."

The death watch had begun. Ted slept in a sleeping bag on the floor in his father's room; Jacqueline stretched out in a chair, a blanket over her legs. The next morning, his last surviving children—Eunice, Pat, Jean, and Teddy—surrounded his bed. Rose was brought in at the last minute. She knelt beside him with a rosary, put it to his lips, and then draped the beads over his fingers. She and the children had almost finished the Our Father when he died.

Jacqueline would later tell Laura Bergquist, "If God does not take him straight to heaven I will be really mad at God—for look how valiant and loving he is in all this sickness."

Joseph Patrick Kennedy died in 1969 of cerebrovascular thrombosis. He was eighty-one. President Richard Nixon said of him that he left "a genuinely unique record that involved his entire family in the making of American history. Surely, he felt great satisfaction in his own and in his family's service and accomplishments."

Ted Kennedy was "almost white with anger" when he read a newsmagazine account of his father's death. It was an article that seemed to accentuate all the many negatives in Joe's life.

Ted wrote to the magazine, "I wish you could have devoted at least a line to the generosity, humor and heart my father had in such abundance, but nowhere were these qualities indicated. I could not recognize my father from your portrayal of him. . . . We who are in public life must learn to live with petty gossip and baseless slander. My mother, however, is not in public life, nor are her grandchildren—and they will want to know in later years what kind of man their grandfather was. So I must protest for their sake when my father is maligned at the last moment by those who never knew him and made no effort to find out."

To Ted, his father would always remain a giant figure. Cousin Joey Gargan had confided, "You'll see a tremendous change in Teddy when his father dies."

A change, surely, but not tremendous. For Ted, the force of his father had died with Joe's stroke, with his loss of speech. Before then, the force was absolute. It was true that Ted found it difficult, even afterward, to confront even this shadow of a father. But it was the death of his brothers that released Ted—not the death of his father.

"Joe Kennedy put the first Catholic in the White House," said family friend Eddie Dowling. "In my book, this would make him the greatest man of accomplishment in all history. . . . Here is a man who didn't understand failure. It doesn't make any difference what it is. If it's a train you've gotta catch, catch it. . . . If you're sent out to get a loaf of bread, come back with a loaf of bread. . . . If he said to you, '. . . at one o'clock tomorrow, Wednesday, the 13th of November, I'm going to be at the South Pole,' he'd be there, at the South Pole . . . he'd find a way to get there. This is the kind of training these boys have had."

Somebody else said that Joe was willing to pay any price for power. He never could have imagined how high that price would be. He never could have imagined such a price because one of the most destructive seeds he had planted in his sons was the feeling of invulnerability. They had the money, they had the power, and the gods were smiling on them. They could have their wives and their mistresses, and the American people were with them partly because they liked the easy confidence with which the Kennedys walked the line between morality and power, making their own rules and going beyond them, always living on the edge. They represented everything most people wanted and lived lives that they could never have.

"You want kings, but on the other hand, you want to destroy the king," said author Doris Kearns Goodwin. "When they seem to be doing too well, we want to pull them down. That's what that whole royalty myth is about."

They seemed invulnerable because they looked like heroes and acted like heroes and the country was hungry for heroes. The father knew this better than most and he drove his sons with the same intensity that he always had driven himself. However, after all, they had shown themselves vulnerable. Vulnerable to death, to tragedy, and to disgrace. Many wondered what Joe would have said near the end if he could have talked.

Perhaps he would have agreed that the price of his ambition was too high—especially for his youngest son. His other sons had indelibly stamped the Kennedy name into American history. How many American families could say the same?

Despite his ruthlessness, his bigotry, his amorality, his evil deeds— this was still a father who passionately loved his children and would do anything for them. His children never doubted the depth of his feelings and of his commitment to them. And so, in turn, at the end, despite everything, his children loved him.

TED'S TWO YEARS as Minority Whip were a disaster, and he lost the post in January 1971 to southern conservative Senator Robert Byrd. He said gracefully, "Unless you know how to lose, you don't deserve to win." More privately, he confided, "I can't be hurt anymore. After what's happened to me, things like that just don't touch me, they don't get to me."

He tried to make a joke of it. Trying to smile, he thanked "the 28 Democratic Senators who pledged to vote for me . . . and especially the 24 who actually did. . . . The Secret Service says I receive more anonymous threatening letters than anyone else on Capitol Hill. It wasn't until January that I realized most of them came from my colleagues in the Senate." Privately, he philosophized, "It hurts like hell to lose, but now I can get around the country more, and it frees me to spend more time on issues I'm interested in."

REGARDLESS OF EVERYTHING that had happened, there were still those urging him to run for President in 1972. Kennedy friends such as Cesar Chavez had mixed feelings. "Our people . . . they'd be afraid to have Teddy Kennedy run for President. Not that they don't want him, they love him so much they don't want to see him killed. It's more important for him to live than for him to be President. This would be the feeling of all of us. We already tried it with the membership, and they say, 'Oh, God, no, no. We don't want any more of that.' "

He still hadn't said a flat no. Speaking with much feeling, Joan Kennedy said bitterly, "And all this you hear about the Kennedy family pressuring Ted to run for President. . . . What family? What's left of the Kennedys? Besides Ted, only women and children! You don't seriously think we want Ted to be President, do you? To have the one Kennedy man left risk having happen to him what happened to his brothers? . . . Ted knows the Kennedys are not pushing him toward it. He is quite aware of how we feel." And then she added, "I worry all the time about whether Ted will be shot like Jack and Bobby. I try not to, but I can't help myself. Ted tries to keep things from me—serious threats against his life, that kind of news—but I know what's going on. . . . A few months ago we were in a plane and a child exploded a balloon right behind us. It sounded just like a gunshot. Ted jumped so. What a terrible thing! A balloon pops and my husband thinks he's being shot. I could read his mind—and I could have cried for him."

Close friend Varick Tunney said, "I'll make bets that the word 'fear' has not been spoken aloud between Ted and his wife since Bob's death."

Whether or not fear was a spoken word, it was always there.

A reporter quoted another Kennedy veteran. "If he doesn't become President, he's a failure; but if we win, we're going to put together the best goddamn government you ever saw." He slumped. His voice sagged. "Sure as hell, somebody will try to kill him."

Once Ted reportedly said, "I know that I'm going to get my ass shot off one day, and I don't want to." His mother saw him quoted using the word "ass" and she sent him a note: "I do not think you should use that word." He had it framed for his office.

———

WHAT TED KENNEDY did not know then was that a pudgy young man had waited for him in his outer office with a loaded pistol in his pocket more than three hours before finally leaving. His name was John Hinckley, Jr., and he would later try to assassinate President Reagan.

Around this time, police picked up a disoriented woman in Ted's empty house who said she was stalking the Senator.

Senator Kennedy ignored a telephoned death threat to attend a Justice Department ceremony for his dead brother. It once took a flying wedge of police to help escape from an ugly crowd. At a centennial celebration of the birth of John Greenleaf Whittier in Haverhill, Massachusetts, someone fired a signal cannon a few dozen feet away as Ted was getting out of his car. Stunned, Ted grabbed his stomach as if he had been shot, and his face turned white.

As the 1972 election came closer and the presidential pressures came alive again, Ted told Warren Rogers of *Look*, "I try not to think about the presidency, but people like you keep bringing it up. I don't discuss it with my family. We just don't talk about it. That business about promising my mother not to run, well, that's just not true." And later he added to an intimate "How can I run for the presidency, for God's sake? . . . I'd have to do it with my back to the wall, and these days, there isn't even a wall behind me anymore."

Many believed that only Senator Kennedy could have bridged the divided party regulars with the antiwar insurgents. "Kennedy was uniquely situated to make peace between the two warring factions," said William Schneider, a political analyst at the American Enterprise Institute.

They also felt he could heal the continued conflict on civil rights. "It is eerie, Kennedy's appeal in the black community," said Clarence Mitchell, Jr., chief Washington lobbyist of the National Association for the Advancement of Colored People. "When he speaks to a black audience, people stand on chairs, the help comes out of the kitchen to listen, everybody wants to be in his presence, to touch him. It isn't due to his work. They don't know about that. It is a mystique."

Publicly, the Senator repeated, "I have said I am not a candidate, and I don't believe in drafts. I can't see myself reconsidering under any circumstances." Nevertheless, in ten months, he made twenty-five trips around the country, traveled to India, Israel, and Sweden. Reflecting on Kennedy's hectic noncandidacy, Art Buchwald fantasized his riding up Fifth Avenue "in an open convertible, with his wife Joan, hoping to discourage New Yorkers from considering him as a Democratic hopeful."

Kennedy took an entourage to five midwestern states, making a dozen public appearances, always wearing his gold JFK cuff links. "If he isn't a candidate," asked a North Dakota committeeman, "why did he bring his wife way the hell up here?"

Joan Kennedy maintained the public image. She told one interviewer, "I am more in love with him than ever, and we will be married fourteen years on November 29."

She had her fill of heartache: the horror of Chappaquiddick, her third miscarriage, her serious drinking problem. And, rising above everything, she had made her concert debut as a pianist at the Academy of Music in Philadelphia, where she got a standing ovation. The most her husband could say was a condescending, "Well done, mommy!"

Despite Chappaquiddick, a Gallup poll ranked Ted Kennedy as one of the most admired men in America. Politically, he edged out Ed Muskie as the front-runner for the presidency. He joked about it. He had heard a lot about a Muskie-Kennedy ticket, he said, but he understood that Muskie had not yet selected his Vice President. Then he paused, and added, "Neither have I."

Ed Muskie, speaking off the record, conceded the '72 nomination to

Kennedy, "except that"—shaking his head gravely—"the way Ted had recently been drinking at times, and driving at times. . . ."

"How long can he evade the issue, or can we?" asked Williams College political science professor James MacGregor Burns in *The New York Times.* "For the irony is that the more firmly he pursues his non-candidacy the more likely he is to end up in the grip of forces and events he cannot control—crises abroad, a deadlocked convention and the failure of a strong candidate to emerge on the Democratic left. . . . Edward Kennedy must be reckoned with in 1972."

"He may not be running," said one Washington Democrat, "but if I were running I'd do it precisely the way he is doing it."

Ted had gone to China and had proposals for improving United States relations with the Communist regime. Before his formal speech he told a New York audience that he had briefed President Nixon on his proposals, especially one calling for diplomatic recognition. He said the President had agreed with him on one condition: that Senator Kennedy agree to serve as United States Ambassador to Peking for the next eight years.

Nixon still saw Teddy as his obvious opponent in 1972 for the presidency. His aide Charles Colson had a private detective follow Kennedy in Paris and photograph him with various women, including the daughter of the former King of Italy, with whom he danced until dawn. Colson then circulated these pictures to the press and to members of Congress.

————

MEMPHIS MARKED THE anniversary of the death of the Reverend Martin Luther King, Jr., with a peaceful march of more than 15,000. Senator Kennedy was invited to speak. The Reverend Ralph D. Abernathy announced that he wanted the Senator to speak first so that he wouldn't have to sit and be exposed to any assassin's bullet, "because one day he will be the President of the U.S." Kennedy replied that he planned to "stay right here and listen," that if the lives and deaths of his brothers had a meaning, "it was that we should not hate but love one another."

A review of Secret Service intelligence contacts with U.S. senators since 1964 revealed that Ted Kennedy has received more than three times as many threats as any other senator. Some criminologists believed that Kennedy's life was endangered by the "symmetry proposition"—the desire of psychotic persons to commit acts that will complete cycles. And killing the last of the Kennedy brothers would be such an act.

"Never, never did Teddy want the job, no matter what he said publicly," said Senator Smathers. "Some politicians need recognition, some thrive on being in a more important and powerful position. It's food for them. Ted Kennedy grew up with power all around him. . . . He didn't need more power. He didn't need to be a bigger shot than what he already was."

————

HE WANTED THE power but he was not yet ready for it. His final decision was not to run. The Democratic candidate, George McGovern, introduced Ted to a campaign crowd as "not the next President but the President after the next President."

For Ted, the private pressures were still too great. "I don't believe you can do one job well while thinking of another. I have important work to do in the Senate. . . . With my brothers, I've seen the frustrations that go along with the Presidency, the logjam that can develop with Congress, and things like that. Sure, I know the Presidency is the real power for bringing about change. But that isn't the whole story. A lifetime in the Senate can be damned fruitful, in the sense of accomplishing things."

Moreover, Ted was still strapped in a brace, and the physical pain was often intense. He confided to a friend, "I am in agony."

This was reportedly the reason he started experimenting with drugs and drinking more heavily. Some on his staff believed that Ted was developing a psychological dependency on drink, sometimes consuming a bottle and a half of wine in about a quarter of an hour, followed by large glasses of scotch. He gained an enormous amount of weight, looked glassy-eyed and sleep-deprived. He neglected his appearance and personal hygiene. He was observed by his worried staff, sitting at his desk, staring at nothing, barely responding to their questions. Staff members told author Lester David that Ted "had started to suffer periodic blackouts, unable to remember in the morning what he did or where he was the night before."

The persistence with which he chased women became notorious.

Reporters joked about his "Blonde of the Week Club." Columnist Marquis Childs quoted a Senator friend of his who occasionally traveled abroad with Teddy Kennedy: "It was just like traveling with a bull. . . . He'd see a woman down there, and he'd say, 'I want her, tonight.' "

A column in the Boston *Globe* by Mike Barnicle declared, "Surrounded by sycophants, Edward Kennedy thinks his name and title are license to do whatever he wants, and apparently the only voice he hears in that dark lonely time before danger calls is the drink saying, 'Go ahead, you can get away with anything.' "

———

BRITISH AUTHOR HENRY Fairlie told *Time* about a Washington dinner party at which "for a full hour and a half, fourteen talented and interesting men and women talked of nothing but the sexual activities of Edward Kennedy."

Joan had found her own way to survive. She told an interviewer, "Rather than get mad or ask questions concerning the rumors about Ted and his girlfriends, it was easier for me to just go and have a few drinks and calm myself down, as if I weren't hurt or angry."

For ten years she had tried to talk about it with her husband, and couldn't. "I was embarrassed about it and Ted was embarrassed about it. Everybody was embarrassed, but nobody would really talk about it. Even my best friends would tiptoe around it."

In July 1973, tragedy again hit the Kennedys. Edward Jr., the Kennedys' thirteen-year-old son, was diagnosed as having bone cancer. Every three weeks in Boston, and later in Washington, father and son spent a weekend alone together while the son suffered intense nausea from a powerful drug that offered minimal hope. The Senator explained that the treatment was like picking up coffee grounds with a sponge. "Unless you get every last cell, there's no point."

The father learned to give his son the needed injections at home, showed him movies, and kept talking to him. "It formed a bond between them that has been just extraordinary."

Telling young Teddy that his lower right leg would have to be amputated was "the hardest thing I ever had to do in my life," Ted said. "You know, I really believe that we are not given more than we can effectively endure or cope with. I make no judgment on others who have suffered pain and illness and responded differently. But honestly, I don't want to have to endure much more."

When Ted told his son about the amputation, the night before the surgery, Teddy cried and his father cried with him, and they hugged each other. Joan, in the other room with the family nurse, was unable to confront the situation.

Joan and Ted both helped their son adjust to his artificial leg until he could ride a bicycle and even ski. After Teddy recovered, Joan's drinking got worse. She was now thirty-six. One day she showed up on the arm of a state trooper in Quincy District Court and surrendered her license. The next week the judge imposed sentence, which was that she sign herself into an alcoholic clinic and stay there for at least fourteen days, then follow an intense regimen of rehabilitation. Otherwise he would give her ninety days in jail. When she was arrested, she had been weaving over several lanes with an open bottle of vodka beside her on the seat.

"By sheer coincidence," said John Lindsay of *Newsweek*, "I was on an airplane with Joan. She had been in a drying-out tank in Point David, which was just four or five miles up the coast from San Clemente. She was coming back and was in a really awful condition. Whatever she'd been out there to have done had not been done. She was vague and she was on tranquilizers. We got down to Dulles terminal that Saturday night. It was raining and miserable. All the kids were there. But Ted wasn't. I went home and said to my wife, if this guy takes this family through a presidential campaign, there is no pain in hell that is enough for him."

In September 1974, citing family responsibilities, Ted Kennedy announced that he would definitely not be a candidate for President in 1976. He had repeated several times, "What no one can seem to understand is that I don't *ever* want to be President!"

Lindsay thought, "This is the best thing this man has ever done in his life, as a human being."

In the early polls, Kennedy led all Democratic and Republican candidates for President in 1976—including President Ford. Ford had succeeded Nixon, after Nixon's resignation when he was faced with impeachment for the crime and corruption of Watergate.

One of the decisive factors in Ted's decision was an appeal from his son not to run. When he was younger, his son often asked his mother,

"If Uncle John was shot and Uncle Bobby was shot, will Daddy be shot?"

Perhaps Ted's old friend Senator John Culver of Iowa best summed up Ted's decision: "Teddy doesn't want to be President . . . he just doesn't want anyone else to be President."

If he had felt destroyed at Chappaquiddick, if he had felt the full weight of the Kennedy curse, with only sudden death in his future, Ted must have been surprised at his daily survival. Out of some hidden reserve, out of his stubborn determination, he had created a new self filled with purpose. Perhaps, too, he knew his important position as the family role model for so many children of his brothers.

Surprisingly, through all the tragedy and scandal, Ted Kennedy's career in the Senate remained viable. His legislative record became increasingly impressive. He sponsored almost two hundred bills and amendments of his own, and cosponsored twice that many. He started a personal crusade for national health insurance, and confidently took over responsibilities on the Judiciary Committee. He intensified his stand on tax reform, gun control, and campaign financing reform. And, as a Catholic Senator from a Catholic state, personally opposed to abortion, he still beat back attempts to cut off federal aid for abortions for poor people.

"If John F. Kennedy were alive today to write another book about courageous Senators, he just might have to profile his brother Ted," wrote columnist Carl Rowan.

Most of the young Kennedys campaigned for Kennedy's Senate reelection campaign, with his twenty-four-year-old nephew, Joseph Kennedy III, as campaign manager. It had been a Kennedy blitz against a relatively obscure Republican selectman running his first statewide campaign. Kennedy won overwhelmingly.

Ted Kennedy found little pleasure in campaigning for Jimmy Carter. A *Wall Street Journal* reporter wrote that for Senator Kennedy it was "a little like swallowing castor oil."

After Carter was elected President of the United States, it seemed inevitable that one day Ted Kennedy would have to face the challenge himself. It was not something he could turn his back on. It was not that he wanted it anymore, but the world expected it; family tradition demanded it. As somebody said, "He wouldn't be a Kennedy if his goal were not the White House."

Besides, he told friends, too many things were just no longer fun for him. As a family friend observed, "Boredom was a very powerful dynamic." Perhaps upping the ante was the only thing that could keep him feeling alive. Smathers remembered Jack telling him that he was bored with being in Congress and so "I might as well go for the big ring."

In 1977, after nineteen years of marriage, the delicate balance Ted and Joan had maintained finally collapsed. Joan finally made the break. She moved to Boston, publicly acknowledged herself an alcoholic, and enrolled at a small teachers' college, Lesley College Graduate School of Education. Her objective was to get a master's in music education. She wanted to work on children's television programs. She stayed sober and maintained a strict daily schedule. Her children chose to stay in Washington with their father. The youngest, Patrick, was then twelve, Kara almost nineteen, and Ted Jr. a year younger.

Asked to describe her condition then, Joan replied, "Vulnerable. I guess that's it."

She said she saw her husband once or twice a month and they often talked on the telephone. "I ask Ted to call me," she says. "This is my pad and I just like him to call me first and say 'Can I come up?' I may be having some friends and relatives of my own here. Besides, Ted never comes alone; he's always with some aides."

Senator Kennedy became chairman of the Senate Judiciary Committee in January 1978, and his personal life seemed under greater control. He attended fewer parties, jogged every morning, arrived at his office early. Rumors about him seemed to stop. If there were other women now, he saw them more discreetly.

The newly completed John F. Kennedy Library, on twelve acres of Columbia Point overlooking Dorchester Bay in Boston, was dedicated on October 1979 by the Kennedy family. The speakers included President Carter, Senator Edward Kennedy, and Robert Kennedy's eldest son, twenty-seven-year-old Joseph Kennedy III.

On the night before the library opening, there was a private dinner party in the pavilion of architect I. M. Pei's stark white-and-black house. Some 150 invited guests of the Kennedy network included a Who's Who of the New Frontier and subsequent Kennedy campaigns. These included Edward Kennedy's people as well as all the Kennedy children, shepherded by Joe III. Inevitably the band played the theme from *Camelot.*

Joe III had to be persuaded to speak as scheduled because he had discovered that the ceremony included only a fifteen-minute film about his father compared to a forty-five-minute film about Uncle Jack. He recalled his father's attempt to improve the circumstances of blacks, tenant farmers, Indians, Chicanos, and migrant farm workers besides ordinary working families, and he added the hope that the new generation would summon "the moral courage . . . to bring about the decent and just world he so much wanted to see in his lifetime."

Then his speech became bitter: "As I stand here and think about my father and what his life was all about . . ." he began. Then he denounced the power of Big Coal, Big Oil, and Big Money, and the lack of moral courage in government, pointing an accusing finger at President Carter. While Uncle Ted hid his head in his hands, the other Kennedy grandchildren shouted their approval.

Young John Kennedy afterward confided to his cousins that he wasn't certain what he wanted to do in the future, "but I think whatever I do will probably involve working with blacks." Bobby Junior listened, smiled, and said, "My father was more concerned with blacks than yours was."

———————

TED'S LIFE SEEMED to run in four-year cycles, and the 1980 race had begun. He had finally decided to make his run for the Presidency. He was forty-five.

It was his solitary decision. "Because of what happened to my brothers," Ted said, "nobody close to you will advise you."

Campaigning had been fun once, Kennedy said. It had been fun when he was younger. It had been fun to see the country and meet the people, but it was, by and large, fun no more: "The basic joy of it went out with my brothers."

But even though the Senator did not mesmerize audiences the way his brothers had, people were always waiting in line afterward to shake his hand and touch history.

Those who watched him campaign saw a man whose voice was strained, eyes glazed with tiredness, timing off. Ellen Goodman of the Boston *Globe* described him as "a great athlete striving for a comeback with bad knees." And she added, "One sentence keeps recurring in my brain: The guy doesn't want it."

He was tired of the probing press asking again and again about Chappaquiddick, always more interested in his sex life than in his Senate record. He felt that if he walked on water, the headlines would report only that he couldn't swim.

There seemed to be a general sense of public disappointment in his presidential bid. Many Americans hated all the Kennedys, who, they felt, had had it so good and so easy for so long. The family had seemed to move too fast on the horizon; it was high time for a fall.

"They hounded the poor guy into running for President," complained Geraldine Tirella, a Boston North End housewife, to *New York Times* reporter Steven Roberts, "and when he does, they wash his clothes for him. I suppose that's politics—but it's dirty politics."

The Secret Service provided the Senator with a Kevlar bulletproof vest. He wore one under his shirt and it was so heavy that it aggravated his back pain. Another protector was built into his trench coat.

When Ted Kennedy went anywhere, it was in an armored limousine, followed by a station wagon full of Secret Service men carrying Uzi submachine guns. Part of the entourage consisted of sharpshooters and antisniper teams. "He had more security than the President: three shifts of Secret Service men with fifty-four on each shift, 162 in all. In a sense the campaign had begun with the working press wondering: would the last Kennedy be killed too?"

Columnist James Reston called Ted's presidential bid that year a calamity. "But his assumption that he could defeat a President and then win with a divided and embittered party was preposterous. His organization for the campaign was as poor as his judgment, and while he made the best convention speech I had heard since Adlai Stevenson in 1952, he was soundly defeated."

Afterward, Kennedy replied quietly when asked what he had learned during the campaign: "Well, I learned to lose, and for a Kennedy that's hard."

Kennedy staff member Melody Miller expressed the thought of many when she said, "It's sad that he lost, but thank God he's alive."

Despite their estrangement, Ted had asked Joan to be with him at the convention, and she had agreed to come. Interviewed on television long afterward, a friend told how Joan flew home with him after the convention. "She thought they were going to have a lovely reconcilia-tion on the Cape and instead, the plane dropped him off at Montauk, Long Island, and he went off to meet some girlfriend and the pilot flew her home to Massachusetts."

"Oh, I know what people are saying about me," Joan said later. "Sometimes, at functions, I stay in the john and listen." She rolled her eyes heavenward and clasped her hands in imitation. " 'Oh, that poor woman. She's been through so much.' "

Not long afterward, Joan filed for divorce. "I spent four hours talking to Jackie," Joan confided to author Lester David. "She said she's crazy about Ted, but she's known for years that I should have done it fifteen years ago. She was so supportive. Jackie said not to worry about Ted, that he'll be fine. She said I should look out for myself."

ON THE TWENTIETH anniversary of John Kennedy's assassination, in November 1983, the night before a memorial Mass at Holy Trinity Church in Georgetown, Ted stopped abruptly while rehearsing his remarks and walked out of the church.

In a speech before the John F. Kennedy School of Government, at Harvard Uiniversity, Ted said, "I recognize my own shortcomings— the faults in the conduct of my private life. I realize that I alone am responsible for them, and I am the one who must confront them." He added, "I believe that each of us as individuals must not only struggle to make a better world, but to make ourselves better, too. . . . Unlike my brothers, I have been given length of years and time, and as I approach my sixtieth birthday, I am determined to give all that I have to advance the causes for which I have stood for almost a quarter of a century."

He had given much. Fifth in seniority in the Senate, he would become one of the longest-serving senators in U.S. history, and the longest-serving U.S. Senator in the Commonwealth's history. Creating a shadow government as chairman of the Labor and Human Resources Committee and head of Judiciary and Armed Services subcommittees, he dominated the domestic agenda as few legislators have in the 200-year history of Congress. In the 100th Congress, he maneuvered thirty-nine bills through his committee and into law.

"He's becoming the statesman that we all hoped he would be," said Senator Orrin Hatch of Utah, the ranking Republican on Labor.

"Whether you agree with him or not, he's become one of the all-time great senators."

"I don't think anyone could look at his record of public achievement and personal adversity—personal sorrow—without coming away with great respect for his character," said former senator John Culver of Iowa, a close Kennedy confidant since Harvard. "He has pursued some of these causes for 25 years or more—isn't that character? The integrity and perseverance of his positions—isn't that character?"

———

WHEN, IN 1962, at the age of sixty, he married an attractive thirty-eight-year-old lawyer, Victoria Reggie, more of his hair was turning white and his waistline long ago had thickened. Interviewed at the home of his 102-year-old mother, bedridden upstairs, he commented, "I had not ever really intended to get married again. The people who had been closest to me over the course of my life had disappeared, with that enormous amount of emotion and feeling and love. . . . I thought I probably wouldn't want to go through that kind of experience again."

"What kind of woman would marry Ted, 'midnight romp,' Kennedy?" queried Laura Blumenfeld in the Washington *Post*. "A direct, funny, slightly lonely divorced mother of two . . . ripe with childhood memories of good, brave Kennedys."

"Vicki is hilarious, and he wants to laugh," said longtime Kennedy aide Peter Edelman. He had proposed to her at a performance of *La Bohème*.

Victoria Reggie was a summa cum laude from Tulane Law School, editor of the *Law Review,* and Phi Beta Kappa. A corporate lawyer specializing in bad loans at big banks, she has been called "a bold personality, strong-minded and direct." She also was the one who helped Ted write his "mea culpa" speech at Harvard.

Vicki told Ted bluntly that he had to curb his use of alcohol and set a limit of two drinks a day, plus a small quantity of wine. "Your life is going down the tubes and you have no one to blame but yourself," she told him in the spring of 1992. "If you don't straighten up, you'll end up in the gutter dead because of liver failure." And she said that, while she loved him, it was up to him to decide to turn his life around.

MOST OF THE younger Kennedys were involved in good causes and led almost normal lives; some were confirmed alcoholics seeking help. A few had serious drug problems. One, Bobby's son David, died of a drug overdose. The relentless publicity was deeply destructive. John Kennedy, Jr., ruefully recalled that when he failed the bar exam, the New York *Post* headlined THE HUNK FLUNKS. (He would later pass it.)

Many believe that the Kennedy vision was too overwhelming for the coming generation and hurt more than it helped them. Chris Lawford observed that the Kennedy story has continued to be about people who broke the rules and were ultimately broken by them.

Many of the children rebelled by making the Lem Billings apartment on Fifth Avenue their social center, often for drink and drugs, in the 1970s and 1980s, with Lem joining them. The impeccable Lem had let himself go: his hair was uncut; his clothes disheveled. "His home was an incredible kind of sanctuary where people came in order to laugh in the same way they go to church to pray."

After a bitter argument with one of the Kennedys, Lem called a friend, Harvey Fleetwood, and asked, "Do you think I've wasted my life on the Kennedys? Do you think they appreciate me?" Then he sobbed over the phone, "I'm taking all my Kennedy pictures off the wall. I don't want to see them anymore." That night he died in his sleep.

ON THE TWENTIETH anniversary of Bobby's death, his widow, Ethel, and their children arranged for a small graveside memorial Mass for family and friends. The area had been roped off. Ethel announced that the public was welcome, but few were expected. "We were vaguely aware of increasing commotion in the general area, but we were too involved in reminiscence to glance around," said author William Manchester. "Then we looked up. And we caught our breath. As far as you could see, the slopes around us were dense with people who had been undiscouraged by the long hike to the gravesite. There were over 10,000 of them. It was what newspapermen used to call mute testimony."

When Jacqueline Kennedy Onassis died, America mourned, not

only for her and her husband, but for themselves and the Kennedy dream they shared when they were young. Author Norman Mailer said of the legend that the Kennedys had seemed magical "because they were a little better than they should have been, and so gave promise of making America a little better than it ought to be."

IN THE 1994 election, Senator Ted Kennedy fought the fight of his life to win his sixth term, telling the voters, "The dream will never die."

In that same election, Ted's twenty-seven-year-old son Patrick was elected in Rhode Island as the youngest member of the House of Representatives, Kathleen Kennedy Townsend became Lieutenant Governor of Maryland, and Congressman Joseph Patrick Kennedy II won his fourth term.

It was their grandfather, Joseph Patrick Kennedy, who had wanted to see each of his four sons elected President of the United States. The dream died because he had planted too many seeds of destruction.

It was Joseph Patrick Kennedy II who first gave the Kennedys a fresh vision of public service in 1986 when he stood up in Cambridge, Massachusetts, and said, "I've come to the city of my ancestors, and the district of my birth, to run for Congress of the United States."

This seat in the Eighth Congressional District had been held by his great-grandfather John "Honey Fitz" Fitzgerald and by his uncle John F. Kennedy.

It was time to plant seeds of hope.

SOURCE NOTES

FOR FULL CITATIONS OF BOOKS, REFER TO THE BIBLIOGRAPHY.

—

PROLOGUE

xvii *"What are you doing"*: Interview with Mary Bailley Gimbel, Feb. 19, 1975, by Arthur Schlesinger, Jr., *Robert Kennedy and His Times*, vol. 1, p. 13.

xvii *"I'd just come out"*: Gore Vidal, "The Holy Family," *Esquire*, April 1967, p. 106.

xviii *"Where else but"*: Robert Coughlan Papers.

xix *Then he gloated:* Interview with Joseph Kennedy by author Joseph McCarthy, quoted to Lester David and told to author.

xx *"Isn't the most"*: Interview with Pat Gardner Jackson by Ed Plaut for Ralph G. Martin and Ed Plaut, *Front Runner, Dark Horse*.

xx *"he had inherited"*: David E. Koskoff, *Joseph P. Kennedy*, p. 6.

xx *"He'd call everybody"*: Interview with Henry Luce by Robert Whalen, Oct. 1, 1962, Richard Whalen Papers. Box F-1: Friends, Ex-Assoc. JFK Library.

xx *Joe felt democracy:* Interview with Arthur Goldsmith, ibid.

xxi *"It's not what you are"*: "The American Experience," WGBH-TV, Sept. 20, 1992.

xxi *"A day without"*: JFK quoted by Clare Boothe Luce to Paul and Shirley Green, Interview with author.

1

THE YOUNG YEARS

1 *"Well, of course"*: Doris Kearns Goodwin, *The Fitzgeralds and the Kennedys*, p. 261; Boston *Post*, July 26, 1915, p. 12.

1 *"When you hold"*: Herbert Parmet, *Jack, the Struggles of John F. Kennedy*, pp. 13–14.

2 *"always did have"*: Coughlan Papers.

3 *"dependent enough"*: Ed Plaut interview with Wilton Vaugh, former press secretary to Governor Furcolo.

3 *Rose felt:* Hersh, pp. 14–15, Mrs. George Connelly, letters to Burton Hersh, Nov. 3, Oct. 25, 1969.

3 *"because she couldn't"*: Oral history interview with John Seigenthaler by William Geoghegan, July 22, 1964, JFK Library.

4 *"What is past"*: Goodwin, p. 307.

4 *"It's easy"*: Hank Searls, *Young Joe, the Forgotten Kennedy*, p. 42.

5 *"The children came"*: Coughlan Papers.

5 *"the children met"*: Ibid.

5 *"the Grand Duchess"*: Ibid.

6 *"You stand up"*: Interview with Kathleen Kennedy by Robert Coughlan, Coughlan Papers.

6 *"Suit-sleeves"*: Interview with Joe Gargan by Robert Coughlan, Coughlan Papers.

7 *"Mother was"*: Author interview with Ted Kennedy.

7 *"because when they're"*: John H. Davis, *The Kennedys*, pp. 52–53.

7 *"I always spanked"*: Coughlan Papers.

7 *If a child:* Ibid.

7 *"I think they said"*: Interview with Rose Kennedy by Robert Coughlan, Coughlan Papers.

7 *"institutionalized living"*: Interview with Paul Morgan by Collier and Horowitz, *The Kennedys*, p. 61.

7 *"My mother never"*: Author interview with William Walton.

7 *"I don't know"*: Private interview.

8 *Young Joe:* James MacGregor Burns, *John F. Kennedy: A Political Profile*, p. 19.

8 *"One day"*: Edward Kennedy, *The Fruitful Bough*," p. 22.

8 *"As a little boy"*: Interview with Eddie Moore by Robert Coughlan, Coughlan Papers.

9 *"You didn't talk"*: Whalen Papers, box F-1: JPK, JFK, and Politics. Wash/NYK—June 6, 1960. To: Johnston from Sidey (Washington). *Time* magazine staff, pp. 12–13, JFK Library.

9 *"This is a shrine!"*: Searls, p. 44.

9 *"it was a wonder"*: Leo Damore, *The Cape Cod Years of John Fitzgerald Kennedy*," p. 26.

9 *"Joe had"*: Author interview with Eunice Shriver, Interview with Rose Kennedy by Robert Coughlan, Jan. 6, 1972, Coughlan Papers.

10 *"Miss Cahill don't"*: *Fruitful Bough*, p. 194.

10 *"He was shrewd"*: Interview with Arthur Goldsmith by Richard Whalen, Whalen Papers, box 1, page 2, JFK Library.

10 *"The first time"*: Theodore Sorensen, *Kennedy*, p. 34.
11 *Rose drilled them:* Ibid.
11 *"Bobby wanted"*: Interview with Pat Lawford by Robert Coughlan interview, Coughlan Papers.
11 *"If father gave"*: Interview with Eunice Shriver by Ed Plaut, Martin and Plaut, *Front Runner, Dark Horse.*
11 *"She made American history"*: Author interview with Eunice Shriver. Also letter to the editor of *The New York Times* by Jean Kennedy Smith, Eunice Kennedy Shriver, Patricia Kennedy Lawford, and Edward M. Kennedy.
11 *"she was either"*: Author interview with William Walton.
12 *They often heard:* *Esquire*, April 1962.
12 *"his eyes would"*: Interview with Joe Gargan by Jean Stein, Stein and Plimpton, *American Journey*, p. 35.
12 *"I grew up"*: Interview with Walter Cronkite, Schlesinger, *Robert Kennedy*, p. 16.
12 *"Even when"*: Interview with Eunice Shriver by Ed Plaut for FRDH.
12 *Once the young Kennedys:* Ralph G. Martin, *A Hero for Our Time*, p. 26.
12 *"What was wrong?"*: Author interview with Sargent Shriver.
12 *"He could be"*: Martin, *Hero*, p. 121.
12 *"He scared"*: Whalen Papers. Box F-1: JPK, JFK, and politics. Wash/NYK—June 6, 1960. To Johnston from Sidey (Washington) (FG) Roy Larsen. 1960. *Time* Magazine Staff, p. 4, JFK Library.
13 *"He wanted"*: Ibid.
13 *"the savage domination"*: Interview with Gardner Jackson by Ed Plaut for FRDH.
13 *"We don't want"*: Rose Kennedy, *Times to Remember*, pp. 142–44.
13 *"One of the kids"*: Oral history interview with John Hersey by Herbert Parmet, Dec. 18, 1976. #1141, PRCQ. Columbia University.
13 *"For almost an hour"*: *The New York Times*, Aug. 18, 1992, C1.
13 *"They almost didn't"*: Author interview with Dave Powers.
13 *"You hear a lot"*: Interview with Joseph Kennedy, by Ed Plaut for FRDH.
14 *"The origin"*: Gore Vidal, "The Holy Family," *Esquire*, April 1967.
14 *"They use such people"*: Interview with Norman MacDonald by Ed Plaut for FRDH.
14 *"Children in a large family"*: *McCall's*, June 1965, p. 89.
14 *"I've been thinking"*: Searls, p. 57.
15 *"Even when still"*: Arthur M. Schlesinger, Jr., *A Thousand Days*, p. 672.
16 *"I felt it"*: Joseph McCarthy, *The Remarkable

Kennedys* (New York: Popular Library, 1960), p. 27.
16 *"show those bastards"*: Author interview with Betty Beale.
17 *They were accompanied:* Coughlan Papers.
17 *Joe Sr. was the first:* Interview with Rose Kennedy by Robert Coughlan, Coughlan Papers.
17 *"We never grew"*: Ibid.
18 *"How unchic"*: John Corry, *The New York Times Magazine*, March 13, 1977, p. 19.
18 *"My husband had"*: Ibid.
18 *In the ten years:* Author interview with Sargent Shriver.
18 *"I never traveled"*: Coughlan Papers.
18 *"Joe knew"*: Interview with Henry R. Luce by Richard Whalen, June 11, 1962, Whelan Papers, p. 3, JFK Library; Tommy Corcoran on JPK—highlights, Whalen Papers, Box F-1: Friends, Ex-Assoc., p. 1, JFK Library.
19 *Swanson soon became:* Author interview with Frank Waldrop, who had seen the letter.
20 *"I think only"*: Blair, Joan and Clay Jr., *The Search for JFK*, p. 16.
21 *"I stepped aside"*: Interview with Rose Kennedy by Robert Coughlan, Coughlan Papers.
21 *"It must have been"*: Victor Lasky, *JFK, The Man and the Myth*, p. 41; Hedda Hopper, *Under My Hat* (Garden City, NY: Doubleday, 1952).
21 *"This is absurd"*: Coughlan Papers.
21 *"We never had"*: Ibid.
21 *"He was wonderful"*: Ibid.
22 *"Haven't you showed"*: Author interview with Nancy Coleman.
22 *"some of the ecstasies"*: Ibid.
22 *Just being together:* Coughlan Papers.
22 *"I think it's very selfish"*: "Rose Kennedy Memories," *Washington Star*, Oct. 4, 1977.
22 *"I was always calm"*: Interview with Rose Kennedy by Robert Coughlan, Coughlan Papers.
23 *"Almost to the second"*: Author interview with Nancy Coleman.
23 *A Kennedy neighbor:* Axel Madsen, *Gloria and Joe*, pp. 240–41.
24 *"Well, if they do"*: *Newsweek*, Sept. 1960.
24 *"as long as the fame"*: Quoted in *People*, May 27, 1991.
24 *One young woman:* Private interview.
24 *His niece remembered:* Lawrence Leamer, *The Kennedy Women*, p. 193.
24 *"Joe was not"*: Coughlan Papers.
25 *"You wonder"*: James MacGregor Burns, *Edward Kennedy*, p. 40.
25 *"It was like"*: Nancy Gager Clinch, *The Kennedy Neurosis*, p. 325.
26 *"The minute we got out"*: Interview with Tom Bilodeau by Collier and Horowitz, *The Kennedys*, p. 60.

26 *"I was scared"*: As We Remember Joe, p. 59.
26 *"A quiet maid"*: Private interview.
26 *"When he was there"*: Rose Kennedy, Times to Remember, p. 148.
26 *"Jack loved"*: Interview with Billings, by Collier and Horowitz, p. 174.
26 *"My mother"*: Interview with Mary Gimbel, ibid.
27 *"because all my life"*: Interview with Rose Kennedy by Robert Coughlan, Coughlan Papers.

27 *His Sunday afternoon ritual*: Fruitful Bough, p. 216.
28 *"Mr. Kennedy used to"*: Interview with Rose Kennedy by Robert Coughlan, Coughlan Papers.
28 *"If I wanted"*: Ibid.
29 *But Rose became*: Coughlan Papers.
29 *"His friends thought"*: Collier and Horowitz, p. 59.
29 *"Jack always lost"*: Ibid., pp. 60–61.
29 *"especially Bobby"*: Ibid.
30 *"Joe's appetite"*: Searls, p. 60.

2
SCHOOL AND SEX

32 *"a hell of a guy!"*: Oral history interview with Arthur Houghton by Clay Blair, Jr., Blair Papers, pp. 3–4, American Heritage, University of Wyoming.
32 *"Joe was the golden guy"*: Oral history Interview with Seymour St. John by Herbert Parmet, June 22, 1978, p. 49, #1141, PRCQ, Columbia University.
32 *"it's a pretty place"*: JFK Personal Papers, Correspondence, 1933–1940, Box 4B, JFK Library.
33 *"He did the things"*: Interview with Rose Kennedy by Robert Coughlan, Coughlan Papers.
33 *"He couldn't have"*: Oral history Interview with Kay Halle by William M. McHugh, JFK Oral History, JFK Library.
33 *"It reminds me"*: Oral history interview with Seymour St. John by Herbert Parmet, pp. 49–50, Columbia University.
33 *"and here was this"*: Unpublished Coughlan manuscript, Coughlan Papers.
33 *"I never had"*: Author interview with John Kennedy, 1959.
34 *"I regard"*: Coughlan Papers, JFK Papers, personal correspondence, 1933–1950, box 4B, JFK Library.
34 *"My brother"*: Author interview with John Kennedy, 1959.
34 *"Everybody admired him"*: Oral history interview with Seymour St. John, by Prof. Herbert Parmet, pp. 49–51, 1141, PRCQ, Columbia University.
34 *"My studies"*: JFK Personal Papers, Correspondence, 1933–1935, Box 4B. Gene Schoor, Young John Kennedy, JFK Library.
36 *"his eyes filled"*: Billings Collection, Mrs. Robert Kennedy, p. 31, JFK Library.
36 *Lem designed*: Kerry Kennedy Cuomo, Billings Papers, JFK Library.

36 *"Lem was clearly"*: Private interview.
36 *"everybody knew"*: Jerry Oppenheimer, The Other Mrs. Kennedy, p. 463.
36 *"a toady"*: Private interview.
37 *"Actually, I was"*: The Billings Collection, Senator Edward M. Kennedy, p. 67, JFK Library.
37 *"Getting Lem"*: Ibid.
38 *"Many times"*: Robert Coughlan, unpublished manuscript, p. 231.
38 *"Joe just kind of"*: Interview with Betty Young by Collier and Horowitz, p. 62.
39 *"Joe set"*: JFK Personal Papers, Correspondence, 1933–1950, box 4A, Jos. P. Kennedy Condolence Mail, folder 2, JFK Library.
39 *"underneath it"*: Goodwin, The Fitzgeralds and the Kennedys, pp. 465–66.
39 *"that he valued"*: Author interview with James Rousmaniere.
40 *"Now, Jack,"*: Coughlan Papers.
40 *"Jack and I"*: Interview with Billings by Collier and Horowitz, p. 65.
41 *"Well, I have"*: Searls, The Lost Prince, p. 67.
41 *"you can be sure"*: Nigel Hamilton, J.F.K., p. 127.
41 *"When the air"*: Ibid.
41 *"Only the boys"*: Whalen Papers. Box 1. F: JPK, JFK, and Politics. Wash/NYK—June 6, 1960 (requested) To Johnston from Sidey (Washington) (FG). Roy Larsen. 1960. Time Magazine Staff. pp. 4–5, JFK Library.
42 *"He'd look at you"*: Author interview with Dave Richardson.
42 *"We didn't have"*: Author interview with John Kennedy, 1959.
42 *"No, I never"*: Interview with JPK Sr. by Ed Plaut for FRDH.
42 *"I was always"*: Interview with Rose Kennedy by Robert Coughlan, Coughlan Papers.

42 "a rather high level": Interview with Ted Kennedy by Robert Coughlan, Coughlan Papers.

42 "However, if an outsider": Oral history interview with Ralph Horton by Joseph Dolan, June 1, 1964, JFK Library.

42 He would ask: Author interview with Sancy Newman.

43 "That is what's": Oral history interview with Kay Halle, Feb. 7, 1967, p. 12, JFK Library.

43 Frankfurter later wrote: Goodwin, p. 469; F. Frankfurter to JPK, Oct. 24, 1933, JP Kennedy Papers.

44 "Joe wanted the Treasury": Boston Post, July 1, 1934, p. 12.

44 "I feel definitely": Goodwin, p. 469; JPK to JPK Jr., Nov. 21, 1933, Rose Kennedy Papers.

44 "My husband": Oral history interview with Mrs. Frida Laski, London, Aug. 5, 1966, JFK Library.

45 "I don't know the answers": Memo to Robert Coughlan from Rose Kennedy, June 8, 1973, Robert Coughlan Papers.

46 Joe had letters: Searls, p. 73.

46 "see the Pope": Ibid., p. 71.

46 "It was excellent": Goodwin, pp. 471–74.

47 "Well, they only have": Author interview with Harvey Klemmer.

47 "he was just like me": Searls, p. 123.

47 "I always thought": Coughlan Papers.

47 "In Munich": Searls, p. 80.

47 "You cannot imagine": David Koskoff, Joseph P. Kennedy, p. 378; Jan Wscelaki. Memorandum of conversation with Kennedy, June 16, 1939. From Polish Documents Relative to the Origin of the War, First Series (Berlin: Auswärtiges Amt, 1940), no. 3, pp. 42–43.

48 Afterward, concerned: Interview with Lem Billings by Collier and Horowitz, p. 65.

48 "Joe came back": Hamilton, p. 114.

48 "My husband": "Rose Kennedy Memories," Washington Star, Oct. 4, 1977.

49 "I made my choice": Joseph Dineen, The Kennedy Family," p. 110.

49 "I don't want": Oral history interview with John Seigenthaler, by W. A. Geoghegan (July, 1964), p. 94, JFK Library.

49 "I find myself": "The American Experience: The Kennedys," WGBH-TV. Sept. 20, 1992.

49 "How can one guy": As We Remember Joe, pp. 17–18.

49 "because I wanted": Coughlan Papers.

50 "my old buddy Billings": Whalen Papers. Box 1. F: JPK, JFK, and Politics. Wash/NYK— June 6, 1960 (requested) to Johnston from Sidey (Washington) (FG) Roy Larsen. 1960. Time Magazine Staff, p. 6.

50 "There is a fat Frenchie": Hamilton, p. 140.

50 "because I want you to see": Essay by James Fayne, The Fruitful Bough, pp. 84–85.

51 "I know he went": Author interview with James Rousmaniere.

51 "B.D. came to see me": Hamilton, p. 152; Billings Papers, Feb. 13, 1936, JFK Library.

51 Jack's footnote: Ibid.

52 "Got a fuck": Ibid., p. 156.

52 Neighbor Pat Gardner Jackson: Interview with Pat Gardner Jackson by Ed Plaut for Martin and Plaut, Front Runner.

52 "Jack gunned": Hamilton, p. 162.

52 "but he worked hard": Oral history interview with James Farrell by Bud Collins, May 11, 1964, JFK Library.

52 "being out for the team": Goodwin, p. 478.

53 "certainly put an end": Ibid., p. 480.

53 "By the way, Barbara Cushing": Ibid., pp. 479–80.

53 According to Rousmaniere: Author interview with James Rousmaniere.

54 "Jack, if you want": Goodwin, p. 505; Boston Globe, Nov. 19, 1964, Harvard University Archives.

54 "His brother was six-two": Interview with Torbert MacDonald by Ed Plaut for Martin and Plaut, Front Runner.

54 "Coach, what about": Oral history interview with Thomas Bilodeau, Kennedy and Sports, p. 1, JFK Library.

54 "I was fascinated": Author interview with Sen. George Smathers; private interview quoted in Martin, Hero, 56.

54 "I thought his reputation": Author interview with Betty Beale.

54 Another friend: Author interview with Charles Spalding.

55 Jack's Harvard friend: Hamilton, p. 172.

55 Once he saw Jack: Interview with Timothy Reardon by Collier and Horowitz, p. 91.

55 Another time, Joe cut: Goodwin, p. 355.

55 "Joe had no sense of humor": Author interview with Rousmaniere.

55 "Very aggressive": Oral history interview with Charles B. Garabedian by Ed Martin, June 19, 1964, JFK Library.

55 "I'd find it hard": Author interview with Arthur Schlesinger, Jr.

56 "I don't remember": Author interview with Blair Clark.

56 "You know, when I": Author interview with Stephen Smith.

57 "Joe really took": Author interview with James Rousmaniere.

57 "a unique girl": Whalen Papers. Box 1. F: JPK, JFK, and Politics. Wash/NYK—June 6, 1960 (requested) to Johnston from Sidey

(Washington) (FG) Roy Larsen. 1960. *Time Magazine* Staff, p. 5.

57 *"I've always known":* Goodwin, p. 90; Billings Collection, JFK Library.

58 *"He had the idea":* Interview with Arthur Krock by Clay Blair, Jr., Clay Blair Papers, American Heritage Center, University of Wyoming, box 43, file 23, pp. 2–3.

58 *Jack Kennedy later told:* Hamilton, p. 212; interview with Houghton, Blair Papers, University of Wyoming.

58 *Richard Harwood. Washington Post,* April 24, 1993.

58 *"no political ambitions":* Beschloss, p. 270; *The New York Times,* Nov. 6, 1936.

59 *"I remember it":* Oral history interview with William Randolph Hearst, Jr., by James A. Oesterley, New York, March 25, 1971, JFK Library.

59 *Returning home: Kennedy Women,* p. 234.

59 *Once when someone:* Collier and Horowitz, p. 71; *Fruitful Bough,* p. 216, Mary Gimbel, July 11, 1980.

59 *Bobby* was *awkward:* Allen Roberts, *Robert F. Kennedy: Biography of a Compulsive Politician,* p. 21.

60 *"What I remember":* Jack Newfield, *Robert Kennedy: A Memoir,* pp. 41–42.

60 *"more anxious":* Schlesinger, *Robert Kennedy,* p. 93.

60 *"the most thoughtful":* Ibid., p. 22; Billings interview July 8, 1975; Margaret Laing, *The Next Kennedy,* pp. 64–65.

60 *"If he saw":* Author interview with David Hackett.

60 *"the dirtiest fighter":* "The American Experience: The Kennedys," WGBH-TV, Sept. 20, 1992.

60 *"I think he was a misfit":* Oral history interview with David Hackett by John W. Douglas, July 22, 1970, Washington, D.C.: RFK Oral History Program, pp. 2, 4, 6, 8, 9, JFK Library.

61 *After three months:* Interviews with Father Damian Kearney, Rose Kennedy, and Ted Kennedy by James MacGregor Burns; Burns, *Edward Kennedy,* pp. 36–37.

61 *"They would be swimming":* Interview with Ted Kennedy by Robert Coughlan, Coughlan Papers.

62 *"I was terribly sorry":* Ibid.

62 *"Dad wanted":* Fruitful Bough, p. 203.

63 *"The way it worked":* Garry Wills, *The Kennedy Imprisonment,* p. 10.

3

WAR AND DEATH

65 *When her husband:* Interview with Rose Kennedy by Robert Coughlan, Coughlan Papers.

65 *When Kennedy came:* Martin, *Hero,* p. 37.

66 *"The job of Ambassador":* "The American Experience," Sept. 20, 1992, WGBH-TV.

66 *"Well, not wishing":* Collier and Horowitz, p. 82.

66 *"When will the nice people":* Author interview with Blair Clark.

66 *"It's my first trip":* "The American Experience."

66 *"I want to go":* Lester David, *Ted Kennedy,* p. 40.

66 *"countless footmen":* JFK Personal Papers, Correspondence, 1930–1950, Box 4A, F. Kennedy Eunice, JFK Library.

66 *"The Queen asked":* Interview with Rose Kennedy by Robert Coughlan, Coughlan Papers.

67 *"I would remind":* Ibid.

67 *"Joe was away":* Coughlan Papers.

67 *"You don't expect":* Martin and Plaut, *Front Runner,* p. 120.

68 *"He was then in his fiftieth":* James Reston, *Deadline: A Memoir,* pp. 68–69.

68 *"When Kennedy paid":* Private interview.

68 *"kind of the last gasp":* The Kennedy Women, p. 351.

69 *"When a classmate told Teddy":* Interview with Luella Hennessey by Lester David, in *Good Ted, Bad Ted,"* pp. 13–14.

69 *"I hope the house":* James Seymour Papers, Seymour Correspondence, 1919–1939, box 2, JFK Library.

69 *Teddy would often:* Interview with Ted Kennedy by Robert Coughlan, Coughlan Papers.

69 *There was a big park:* David, p. 44.

70 *"When Teddy's turn came":* Lynne McTaggart, *Kathleen,* p. 36.

70 *"big, square-shouldered":* Joe Dineen of the Boston *Globe,* quoted in Hamilton, p. 793.

70 *Arthur Krock remembered:* Oral history interview with Arthur Krock by Charles Bartlett, p. 10, JFK Library.

71 *"magnificent":* Interview with Pamela Harriman by Clay Blair, Jr., Blair Papers, box 40, p. 5, University of Wyoming.

71 *"The lights were dim":* Searls, 121.

72 *Aide Klemmer recalled: Kennedy Women*, pp. 248–49.

73 *He confided that:* Author interview with Ed Plaut.

74 *"I remember thinking":* Searls, p. 142.

74 *"Every house":* As We Remember Joe, Joe's letter in the *Atlantic* from Valencia, Spain, Feb. 15, 1939, p. 61.

74 *"Good night, Dad":* Goodwin, p. 578; JFK letter to father, Feb. 19, 1939, JFK Papers.

75 *"He not only thought":* Reston, *Deadline*, p. 68.

75 *"I have four boys":* Whelan, *Founding Father*, p. 234.

76 *Max Aitkin:* Author interview with Ed Plaut.

76 *Roosevelt ordered him:* Interview for Martin and Plaut, *Front Runner*.

76 *"Buster, you publish":* Ed Plaut interview with Mike Ward for Martin and Plaut, *Front Runner*.

77 *"But the main point":* Robert Coughlan, "The Kennedys, for Better or Worse: The First 101 Years" (unpublished manuscript), pp. 363–64.

77 *From Palestine, Jack wrote:* JFK Personal Papers: correspondence, 1933–1950, box 4A, letters from JFK, 1939–1942, undated, JFK Library.

77 *Another ambassador, George Kennan:* George Kennan, *Memoir: 1925–50*, quoted by Robert Coughlan in unpublished manuscript.

78 *"Of this you may rest":* Letter to King and Queen from JPK, Sept. 14, 1939, Coughlan Papers.

79 *"There's a big":* Boston *Globe*, Aug. 15, 1944.

79 *"it was time":* Interview with Rose Kennedy by Robert Coughlan, Coughlan Papers.

79 *"Mr. Kennedy is a very foul":* Harvey Rachlin, *The Kennedys*, Dec. 31, 1970, p. 334.

79 *"Dad cannot be blamed":* Letter from JPK Jr. to JPK Sr., undated, Coughlan Papers.

79 *"unguessable potential dangers":* James Seymour Papers, box 2, pp. 13–14, JFK Library.

80 *"for how long":* Hamilton, p. 239; Sept. 26, 1938, Arthur Krock Papers.

80 *"God, I'd give anything":* Kennedy Women, p. 296.

81 *"Churchill phoned":* Rose Kennedy to Coughlan, Coughlan Papers.

81 *"He drinks too much":* Reston, *Deadline*, p. 70.

81 *The Ambassador, who didn't:* "The American Experience," Sept. 20, 1992, WGBH-TV.

81 *"it would be tough":* As We Remember Joe, p. 49.

81 *"It was a terribly tough":* Goodwin, p. 602;

JPK to JPK Jr., June 6, 1940, Rose Kennedy Papers.

82 *One of his professors:* Interview with Bruce Hopper by Ed Plaut for FRDH.

82 *"You know, my brother Joe":* Author interview with James Rousmaniere.

82 *"That never came out":* Oral history interview with James Rousmaniere by Neil Gold, Columbia University.

82 *"Six or seven times":* Martin, *Hero*, p. 30.

83 *"Kennedy knew the human race":* Interview with Arthur Krock by Joan and Clay Blair, Jr., in *The Search for JFK*, p. 16.

83 *"I simply made":* Martin, *Hero*, p. 41

83 *According to Jack Kennedy:* Stuart Alsop, the *Saturday Evening Post*, Aug. 13, 1960, p. 59.

84 *"The Easter vacation":* Letter from JFK to JPK, undated, Coughlan Papers; Searls, p. 156.

84 *"Bobby has increased":* Robert Coughlan, "The Kennedys, for Better or Worse: The First 101 Years" (unpublished manuscript), p. 376, Coughlan Papers.

84 *"Whether you make":* Ibid., p. 377

85 *"I should get it":* JFK Personal Papers, Correspondence, 1930–1955, box 4B, F: Gene Schoor, *Young John Kennedy*, 1940, JFK Library.

85 *"I had to rewrite":* Author interview with Harvey Klemmer.

85 *"Two things I always knew":* Coughlan, "Kennedys," pp. 379–80.

86 *"stolen, quite innocently":* Searls, p. 82.

86 *"Once I said":* Author interview with Harvey Klemmer.

86 *"You are a great":* Coughlan, "Kennedys," pp. 384–385.

86 *"I'll bet you":* Interview with Harvey Klemmer in "The American Experience."

87 *the jig was up:* Richard Whalen Papers, box 1.F: Friends, Ex-Assoc. Conversation with H. R. Luce re Joe Kennedy, June 11, 1962, JFK Library.

87 *"Joe has . . . been giving":* Rose Kennedy, *Times to Remember*, p. 259.

87 *"Even before the delegation":* Ibid., p. 266.

88 *"After all, if he's going":* Ibid., p. 268.

88 *"My wife and I":* Collier and Horowitz, *The Kennedys*, p. 109; *The New York Times*, Oct. 30, 1940.

88 *"For Joe, . . . Harvard was":* Goodwin, p. 178.

89 *Susan Imhoff . . . Harriet Price:* Hamilton, p. 351.

90 *"When I hear these mental midgets":* JFK Personal Papers, Correspondence, 1933–1950, box 4A, F: Kennedy, Jos P. Sr. Letter to JFK, 1940–1945, JFK Library.

90 *"if both of us":* To Mr. Robert Coughlan, Mr. S. Richardson, from Mrs. Joseph P. Kennedy, July 21, 1973, Coughlan Papers.

90 *"The job is terribly boring"*: Coughlan, "Kennedys," p. 370.

90 *"Continuous London air"*: James Seymour Papers, Seymour Correspondence, 1940, Oct. 9, 1940, JFK Library.

91 *"I've got nine children"*: Coughlan Papers.

91 *"He was embarked"*: Whelan, *The Founding Father*, p. 203.

91 *"I never felt it!"*: Coughlan Papers.

91 *"Of course I do not"*: JFK Personal Papers, Correspondence, 1933–1950, box 4A, JFK Library.

92 *"Rumours have sprung"*: Ibid.

93 *"On the way home"*: Author interview with Charles Spalding.

94 *"They took great care"*: Joan and Clay Blair, Jr., *The Search for JFK*, p. 111.

94 *"Jack had a high regard"*: Oral history interview with Charles Spalding, JFK Library.

95 *"Kathleen got all"*: Interview with Rose Kennedy by Robert Coughlan, Coughlan Papers, pp. 15–16, Jan. 27, 1972.

95 *"a shot of lead"*: Hamilton, p. 508; Box 4A, JFK Private Papers, JFK Library.

96 *"Try and make"*: JFK Personal Papers, Correspondence, 1930–1950. Box 4A, Correspondence with friends, 1933–1947. File—Billings, Lemoyne K., 2/17/42, JFK Library.

96 *"Eunice is the most"*: Searls, p. 118.

97 *"a roll in bed"*: Interview with Veronica Fraser in Lynne McTaggart, *Kathleen Kennedy*, p. 33.

97 *"With you, popular"*: JFK Personal Papers, Correspondence, 1933–1950. Box 4A, F: Kennedy, Jos P. Sr., Letter to Kathleen Kennedy, JFK Library.

97 *"As for your words"*: Ibid., Kennedy, Kathleen, Correspondence, 1942–1947, undated.

97 *"the big Romance"*: Ibid., Correspondence, 1930–1950. Box 4A, Correspondence with friends, 1933–1947. File—Billings, Lemoyne, 101 East Preston Street, Baltimore, MD, Monday. JFK Library.

98 *On December 7, 1941*: Ibid.

98 *"big Joe has"*: JFK Personal Papers, Correspondence, 1933–1950. Box 4A, Correspondence with friends, 1933–1947. F: Arvad, Inga, JFK Library, undated, JFK Papers, Correspondence, 1930–1935. Box 4A, JFK Library.

99 *"I've returned"*: Beschloss, p. 615, March 11, 1942.

99 *"full of enthusiasm"*: JFK Personal Papers, Correspondence, 1933–1950. Box 4A, Correspondence with friends, 1933–1947. F: Arvad, Inga. JFK Library.

99 *"Maybe your gravest mistake"*: Ibid.

100 *"Please tell big Joe"*: Ibid.

100 *It was Kick*: Beschloss, *The Crisis Years*, p. 613; Waldrop interview.

100 *Before Jack left*: JFK Personal Papers, Correspondence, 1933–1950. Box 4A, Correspondence with friends, 1933–1947. F: Arvad, Inga. JFK Library.

100 *"men have to get rid"*: Interview with Betty Coxe in Hamilton, pp. 637–38.

101 *Jack loved as a boy*: Interview with Arthur Krock by Clay Blair, Jr. Papers, American Heritage Center, University of Wyoming.

101 *"I don't think"*: Interview with Charles Houghton, ibid., p. 18.

101 *"He wasn't in it"*: Ibid.

101 *"I mean he admitted"*: Interview with Henry James in Hamilton, p. 358.

101 *"the most memorable"*: The Nation, Dec. 28, 1992.

101 *"Tell young Kennedy"*: JFK Personal Papers, Box 4A, Correspondence with friends, 1933–1947.

102 *"They certainly are wows"*: RFK Papers, Pre-Administration Personal Files Correspondence Files: Letters from Kennedy Family, 1942–1949, Box 1, JFK Library.

102 *"I don't know"*: Schlesinger, p. 44; RFK to JPK, Dec. 13, 1942.

102 *"I think everything"*: Interview with David Hackett by Jean Stein, Stein and Plimpton, in *American Journey*, pp. 36–37.

103 *"He talked differently"*: Author interview with David Hackett.

103 *"I think, if you talked"*: Rogers, pp. 8–9.

103 *"truly his best friend"*: Author interview with Warren Rogers.

104 *"That was hard"*: *Kennedy Women*, p. 325.

104 *"My brothers and sisters"*: David, *Ted Kennedy*, p. 177.

104 *"He'd try to bring"*: "The Kennedy Mystique," *The New York Times Magazine*, June 17, 1979.

104 *"I did more things"*: Interview with Ted Kennedy by Robert Coughlan, Coughlan Papers, Nov. 13, 1972.

105 *"I remember Teddy"*: Interview with Lemoyne Billings by Burton Hersh, Hersh, p. 46; Notebook 13, June 3, 1969.

105 *"I daresay"*: Rose Kennedy, p. 285.

106 *Honey Fitz once*: Robert Coughlan, "The Kennedys," p. 472, footnote, Coughlan papers.

106 *"The message came"*: Collier and Horowitz, p. 117.

108 *"almost depicts"*: "What JFK Told a PT Boat Buddy," New York *Post*, Jan. 13, 1976.

108 *Another report*: Blairs, *Search for JFK*, quoted in *Time*, Jan. 19, 1976, p. 31.

108 *"He was very skinny"*: Author interview with Edward McLaughlin.

108 *"Sure I remember"*: Interview with Joseph Alecks by Ed Plaut for FRDH.

108 *"Ted and I"*: *Fruitful Bough*, p. 173, essay by Joseph F. Gargan.

108 *"One of the common"*: Oral history interview with Dr. Janet Travell by Theodore Sorensen, JFK Library.

109 *"considerably upset"*: Goodwin, p. 662; JPK to JPK Jr., Aug. 31, 1943, Rose Kennedy papers.

109 *"When news came"*: Searls, p. 201.

109 *"By God"*: Collier and Horowitz, p. 131.

109 *"I understand"*: Searls, p. 204.

110 *"The folks sent"*: Nov. 14, 1943, quoted in Robert J. Donovan, *PT 109*, p. 216.

111 *"You better not"*: Searls, p. 202.

111 *"We were away"*: *As We Remember Joe*, pp. 53–54.

111 *"One feels"*: Collier and Horowitz, p. 132.

112 *Angela Laycock*: McTaggart, p. 146.

113 *"Tell the family"*: Letter from Joe Kennedy to JFK, Aug. 10, 1944, England, JFK Library.

114 *"at this point"*: Schlesinger, p. 55; RFK to JPK Jr., undated, (spring 1944) JPK Papers.

114 *"It would be"*: Hamilton, p. 646, May 3, 1944, Billings Papers.

114 *"I got scarlet fever"*: Interview with Lemoyne Billings, Clay Blair Papers, p. 11. American Heritage Center, University of Wyoming.

115 *"and he knows"*: McTaggart, p. 138.

115 *"It's a horrible"*: Hamilton, p. 652; Eunice quoted by Jack in letter to Billings, May 19, 1944, Billings Papers.

115 *"Billy is crazy"*: Goodwin, p. 678.

116 *"Your plaintive howl"*: Collier and Horowitz, p. 135; JFK to LB, May 19, 1944, Billings Papers, JFK Library.

117 *"Although he's had"*: JPK letter to Beaverbrook, May 24, 1944, Beaverbrook Papers, House of Lords Library, London.

117 *"I think I was"*: Oral history interview with Frank O'Ferrall by O'Connor, Aug. 5, 1966, JFK Library.

118 *"I just wonder"*: Searls, p. 261.

118 *"I think I'm gonna"*: Collier and Horowitz, p. 136.

118 *"was a gambler"*: Rose Kennedy to Robert Coughlan, Coughlan Papers.

118 *"You take this"*: Searls, p. 264.

118 *"about to go"*: Ibid., pp. 270–71.

118 *"I was in the plane"*: Undated letter by Ensign Simpson, JFK Library.

120 *"There were no tears"*: Rose Kennedy, *Times to Remember*, p. 300.

120 *Then Joe went*: Private interview by Ed Plaut for Martin and Plaut.

120 *"and she could never"*: Author interview with Robert Coughlan.

120 *"Nobody's ever"*: *The New York Times*, Feb. 15, 1965, page 1, comment to Jacqueline Kennedy.

120 *"We both decided"*: Rose Kennedy to Robert Coughlan, Coughlan Papers.

120 *"Let's go"*: *The New York Times Magazine*, June 17, 1979, p. 16.

120 *"For an hour and a half"*: *The Kennedy Women*, p. 372.

121 *"He's in heaven"*: Oral history interview with John Hooker, Jr., by Geoghegan, Nashville, Tenn., JFK Library.

121 *"You know, the waste"*: Author interview with James Reed.

121 *"we both sat down"*: Oral history interview with George Taylor by Sal Micciche, May 7, 1964, JFK Library.

121 *"or in fact done anything"*: Goodwin, p. 355.

121 *"But don't you dare"*: Boston *Globe*, August 15, 1944, quoted in Hamilton, p. 662.

122 *"One morning"*: *Fruitful Bough*, Jack Dowd essay, p. 102.

122 *"For a long time"*: Collier and Horowitz, p. 143.

122 *"Joe simply"*: Goodwin, p. 692.

122 *"One of the top"*: Blair, p. 343.

123 *"Bobby wasn't allowed"*: Author interview with David Hackett.

124 *Joseph Kennedy, Sr., sent*: Goodwin, p. 689; Rose Kennedy Papers, Aug. 14, 1944.

124 *"Jack, don't you"*: McTaggart, p. 179.

4

EARLY POLITICS

127 *"all my plans"*: Goodwin, p. 693; JPK to Arthur Houghton, Sept. 11, 1944, Joseph P. Kennedy Papers.

127 *"You never really"*: Goodwin, p. 792; JPK to Jack Knight, March 11, 1958, JPK Papers.

127 *"I feel bad"*: Interview with Robert Downes by Collier and Horowitz, p. 144.

128 *"This war makes"*: Letter to Harold Tinker from JFK, Feb. 9, 1945, in Harold Tinker Papers, Brown University Library.

128 *"Of course, he was"*: Author interview with Edward McLaughlin.

128 *"I've never read"*: Private source.

129 *"Joe was the heart"*: Letter to JFK from

Michael Grace, JFK Personal Papers, Correspondence, 1933–1950. Box 4A, F: Kennedy, Jos P. Jr., Condolence Mail, folder 2. JFK Library.

129 *"I don't know what"*: Author interview with John Kennedy.

130 *"was apt to goof"*: Laura Bergquist Interview with Rose Kennedy, Laura Bergquist Papers, Boston University Library.

130 *"I would like to offer"*: Interview with Mark Dalton by Collier and Horowitz, *The Kennedys*, p. 164.

130 *"Jack and Teddy put"*: Ibid. pp. 292–93.

130 *"hour after hour"*: Burton Hersh, *The Education of Edward Kennedy: A Family Biography*, pp. 42–43.

131 *"where self-panickers come"*: Paul B. Fay, Jr., *Pleasure of His Company*, pp. 146–47.

131 *"Haven't you found"*: Letter to JFK from LeMoyne Billings, JFK Personal Papers, Correspondence, 1933–1950. Box 4A, Correspondence with friends, 1933–1947. F: Billings, LeMoyne. JFK Library.

132 *"I was not present"*: Oral history interview with Edward M. Gallagher by Ed Martin, Jan. 8, 1965, p. 8, JFK Library.

132 *"Was it a conscious"*: Kenneth P. O'Donnell and David F. Powers, with Joe McCarthy, *Johnny We Hardly Knew Ye: Memories of John Fitzgerald Kennedy*, p. 44.

132 *"Sometimes we all"*: Victor Lasky, *JFK, the Man and the Myth: A Critical Portrait*, p. 92.

132 *"I was drafted"*: Whalen, p. 392.

132 *"I got Jack"*: Ibid.

132 *"I'm certain"*: Herbert S. Parmet, *Jack: The Struggles of John F. Kennedy*, p. 136; Letter to Rose Kennedy from George St. John, August 22, 1945. JFK file, "Choate, Rosemary Hall," JFK Library.

132 *"When we lost"*: Interview with Rose Kennedy by Robert Coughlan, Jan. 6, 1972, Coughlan Papers.

133 *"Daddy, do you really"*: Collier and Horowitz, p. 150.

133 *Kennedy Sr. put up:* Interview with Joe Kane by Ed Plaut for FRDH.

133 *"he was having much more"*: Oral history interview with Arthur Krock by Charles Bartlett, JFK Library; author interview with Charles Spalding.

134 *"Bobby tells me"*: Letter to JFK from LeMoyne Billings, JFK Personal Papers, Correspondence, 1933–1950. Box 4A, F: Correspondence with friends, 1933–1944. JFK Library.

134 *"I'm going into politics"*: Author interview with Charles Spalding.

134 *"I can feel Pappy's eyes"*: Robert Coughlan,

"The Kennedys, for Better or Worse: The First 101 Years" (unpublished manuscript), p. 463, Coughlan Papers.

136 *Kennedy wrote Beaverbrook:* Letter to Max Beaverbrook, from Joe Kennedy, Sr., June 22, 1945, Max Beaverbrook Papers, House of Lords Library, London.

136 *"We went for a walk"*: Author interview with Blair Clark.

136 *"To be perfectly truthful"*: Thomas "Tip" O'Neill, "The American Experience," WGBH-TV, Sept. 20, 1992.

137 *"Why didn't you stay"*: Author interview with Ed Rooney.

137 *"Suddenly, the time"*: Author interview with Dave Powers.

137 *"Jack hustled"*: Interview with Rose Kennedy by Robert Coughlan, Robert Coughlan Papers.

137 *Ed Plaut, who was:* Author interview with Ed Plaut.

138 *Campaign worker Anthony Gallucio:* Interview with Anthony Gallucio by Ed Plaut for Martin and Plaut, FRDH.

138 *"You know, you can be"*: Author interview with Tip O'Neill.

138 *For all these reasons:* Interview with Joe Kane by Ed Plaut for Martin and Plaut, FRDH.

138 *"I wish Joe"*: Ibid.

138 *"You can trample"*: Thomas "Tip" O'Neill, *Man of the House*, p. 83.

139 *"It's the old bullshit"*: Hamilton, p. 729; Letter to Patrick Lannan from JFK, Sept. 23, 1946. J. Patrick Lannan Papers, Lannan Foundation, Los Angeles.

139 *"One of them said"*: Interview with James Reed by Clay Blair, Clay Blair Papers, box 53, file 15, American Heritage Center, University of Wyoming,

139 *"everyone there thought"*: Oral history interview with James Reed by Robert Donovan, June 16, 1964, JFK Library.

140 *"It cost Old Joe"*: Author interview with Robert S. Allen.

140 *"The more excited"*: Oral history interview with Charles Spalding by Bartlett, JFK Library.

140 *"My first tip-off"*: Interview with Dave Powers by Robert Coughlan, Robert Coughlan Papers.

141 *"We'd start Jack out"*: Interview with Patsy Mulkern by Ed Plaut for Martin and Plaut.

141 *"And they'd feel"*: Oral history interview with Wilton Vaugh by John Bartlow Martin, JFK Library.

142 *"The American people"*: Interview with Arthur Krock by Clay Blair, Clay Blair Papers, box 43, file 23, University of Wyoming.

143 " 'Gene,' he said": Gene Tierney with Mickey Herskowitz, *Self-Portrait* p. 13.

143 "*I remember showing up*": Coughlan papers.

144 "*my usual moody self*": Robert Coughlan, unpublished manuscript, Coughlan Papers.

145 "*Whatever you do, Lem*": The Billings Collection, Privately printed memorial book.

145 "*You could disagree*": Interview with Charles Houghton by Clay Blair, Blair Papers, American Heritage Center, University of Wyoming.

145 "*I'm sitting in Jack's*": Author interview with Dave Powers.

145 *But Jack's early supporter*: Interview with Joe De Gulielmo for FRDH.

145 "*If I had this fellow's*": Author interview with Dave Powers.

146 "*a very good-humored*": Interview with Arthur Hall by Lester David in *Ted Kennedy, Triumphs and Tragedies*, pp. 53–54.

146 "*When I was going*": Interview with Ted Kennedy by Robert Coughlan, Nov. 13, 1972, Coughlan Papers.

147 *In another election*: *Parade*, April 28, 1957, p. 10.

147 *The one thing*: *Harvard Crimson*, Oct. 19, 1946.

147 "*He was running*": Interview with Lemoyne Billings by Collier and Horowitz, *The Kennedys*, p. 153.

148 *On the first day*: Robert Coughlan, unpublished manuscript, Coughlan Papers.

148 "*so whenever you want*": Interview with Ted Reardon by Ed Plaut for Martin and Plaut.

148 "*extremely appealing*": Interview with Robert Shriver by Clay Blair, Blair Papers, box 54, file 18, University of Wyoming.

149 "*seeing all four of the Kennedy*": Interview with Robert Sargent Shriver by Clay Blair, Blair Papers, box 54, file 18, University of Wyoming.

149 *Shriver recalled*: Author interview with William McCormick Blair, Jr.

151 "*We could be sitting*": Interview with Ted Reardon by Ed Plaut for FRDH.

151 "*I didn't go*": William V. Shannon, *The Heir Apparent: Robert Kennedy and the Struggle for Power*, pp. 58–59.

151 "*I'm certainly not hitting*": Arthur M. Schlesinger, Jr., *Robert Kennedy and His Times*, p. 55; RFK oral history project, JFK Library.

152 "*Bobby's great second effort*": Author interview with Dave Powers.

152 "*Nothing came easily*": Author interview with David Hackett; Schlesinger, *Robert Kennedy*, p. 47.

152 "*a good metaphor*": Oral history interview with Harold Ulen by Ed Martin, JFK Library.

152 "*He is just starting off*": Letter to Max Beaverbrook from JPK Sr., March 23, 1948, Max Beaverbrook Papers, House of Lords Library, London.

153 "*I wined and dined*": Letter to JPK Sr. from Max Beaverbrook, March 12, 1948, ibid.

153 "*Bobby was very capable*": Jerry Oppenheimer, *The Other Mrs. Kennedy*, p. 119.

153 "*I just wish*": Schlesinger, *Robert Kennedy*, p. 76.

153 "*it was not so much*": Harvey Rachlin, *The Kennedys*, p. 109.

154 "*With Kick, of course*": Alsop, p. 409.

154 "*When I awakened him*": Rachlin, p. 107.

155 *The thing about Kathleen*: James MacGregor Burns, *John F. Kennedy: A Political Profile*, p. 54.

155 *She was reportedly pregnant*: Interview with Charles Houghton by Clay Blair, Blair Papers, University of Wyoming.

155 "*a horrible mess*": Letter to Max Beaverbrook from JPK, July 27, 1948, Beaverbrook Papers, House of Lords Library, London.

156 "*the only one of her nice children*": Lynne McTaggart, *Kathleen Kennedy: Her Life and Times*," p. 25.

156 "*Between you and me*": Schlesinger, *Robert Kennedy and His Times*, vol. 1, p. 82; Letter to Patricia Lawford from RFK, June 5, 1948.

156 "*if I was to have*": Oppenheimer, p. 120.

156 *After six months abroad*: Schlesinger, p. 79.

157 *His friend Gerald Tremblay*: Oral history interview with Gerald Tremblay by Roberta Greene, Jan. 8, 1970, p. 1, RFK Oral History Project, JFK Library.

158 "*To my knowledge*": Ibid.

158 "*At law school*": Lester David and Irene David, *Bobby Kennedy*, p. 55; oral history interview with Endicott Peabody Davis, p. 116.

158 "*Ethel was really*": Author interview with Stanton Gilderhorn.

158 "*Prepare yourself*": Joe McCarthy, *The Remarkable Kennedys*, pp. 39–40.

159 "*I got that idea*": Interview with Rose Kennedy by Robert Coughlan, Coughlan Papers.

159 "*I didn't really care*": Author interview with Joe McCarthy.

159 "*I went to his funeral*": David E. Koskoff, *Joseph P. Kennedy*, p. 5.

159 "*We had a party*": Jean Stein and George Plimpton, *American Journey*, pp. 38–40.

160 "*I like marriage*": Margaret Laing, *The Next Kennedy*, p. 43.

160 "*was in the same class*": Interview with Dr. Arthur Holcombe by Lester David in *Good Ted, Bad Ted*, pp. 35–36.

161 *"College girls"*: Garry Wills, *The Kennedy Imprisonment: A Meditation on Power*, p. 24.
161 *"I heard in my"*: Edward Kennedy, *The Fruitful Bough*, pp. 204–05.
161 *"while Ted was not"*: William Peters, *Redbook*, June 1962.
161 *Other coaches*: Oral history interview with James Farrell by Bud Collins, JFK Library.
162 *"I thought he was"*: Author interview with Richard Bolling.
162 *"Of course Jack"*: Oral history interview with Arthur Krock by Charles Bartlett, JFK Library.
162 *The Ambassador was*: Interview with Ralph Coughlan for FRDH.
162 *"I disagree"*: Interview with Ed Michelson for FRDH.
162 *"one very vivid instance"*: Author interview with Kay Halle.
163 *"I was at some posh"*: Ibid.
163 *"I'm sure glad"*: Ibid.
164 *Rose Kennedy recalled*: Coughlan Papers.
164 *"When a man"*: Letter to EMK from Max Beaverbrook, April 14, 1962, Beaverbrook Papers.
164 *He now hired*: Wills, p. 129.
164 *"quietly aided"*: Lasky, p. 28.
164 *"I was told"*: Interview with Senator Edward Kennedy by Robert Coughlan, Nov. 13, 1971, Coughlan Papers.
164 *Fearful that Teddy*: Hersh, p. 82
164 *"your ninth"*: Interview with Edward Kennedy by Coughlan, Nov. 13, 1971.
165 *"I hope, if you run"*: Author interview with George Smathers.
165 *"Everyone thought"*: Coughlan Papers.
165 *"The guy who really"*: Interview with Sargent Shriver, Clay Blair Papers, American Heritage Center, University of Wyoming.
165 *"When you've beaten him"*: Martin, *Hero*, p. 57.
165 *"I will work out"*: Gore Vidal, "The Holy Family," *Esquire*, April 1967; *The Fruitful Bough*, p. 106.
166 *"You cannot live"*: Interview with Dr. Henry Betts by Robert Coughlan, July 6, 1972, Coughlan Papers.
166 *"I am finding"*: Letter to Max Beaverbrook from JPK Sr., Feb. 19, 1952, Beaverbrook Papers, London.
166 *"for Jack to make"*: Interview with Ralph Coughlan for FRDH.
166 *"The Kennedys leave"*: Interview with Abe Michelson by Ed Plaut for FRDH.
167 *"disciplined Jack"*: Interview with Norman McDonald for FRDH.
167 *"Probably not a guy"*: Ibid.
167 *"As far as the running"*: Interview with

O'Neill, Clay Blair Papers, American Heritage Center, University of Wyoming.
168 *He also had his star*: Interview with Joe Timilty, ibid.
169 *"The sheer animal vitality"*: Tom Corcoran quoted in Richard Whalen Papers, box 1, JFK Library.
169 *When Ken O'Donnell*: Wills, pp. 153–54.
169 *"I have heard so much"*: Interview with Rose Kennedy by Laura Bergquist, Laura Bergquist Papers, Mugar Memorial Library, Special Collections, Boston University,
169 *"Jack and I spent"*: Interview with Charles Spalding by Clay Blair, Blair Papers.
170 *"My father's one motive"*: Interview with Pat Gardner Jackson for FRDH.
170 *"I'll screw it up"*: Jean Stein and George Plimpton, eds., *American Journey: The Times of Robert Kennedy*, p. 41.
171 *"If you hand"*: Author interview with Dave Powers.
171 *"We worked from eight"*: Interview with Mary Jo Clasby by Robert Coughlan, Feb. 18, 1972, Coughlan Papers.
171 *"too sensitive"*: O'Donnell and Powers, p. 241.
171 *"Bobby could handle"*: Ibid., p. 83.
171 *"suddenly found"*: Schlesinger, p. 101.
172 *"sweet-and-sour"*: Stewart Alsop, "Kennedy's Magic Formula," *Saturday Evening Post*, Aug. 13, 1960.
172 *"a virgin"*: Interview with John Powers by Collier and Horowitz, *The Kennedys*, p. 185.
172 *"had a hell of a brother"*: Author interview with Warren Rogers.
172 *"Every politician"*: Interview with John Kennedy by Hugh Sidey in *The Kennedy Circle*, ed. Lester Tanzer, p. 207.
173 *If they were meeting*: Interview with Rose Kennedy by Robert Coughlan, Coughlan Papers.
173 *"Eunice was really"*: Author interview with Charles Spalding.
173 *"When she speaks"*: Interview with John Fenton for FRDH.
174 *During one event*: Martin and Plaut, *Front Runner, Dark Horse*, p. 164.
174 *Even their father*: Interview with Joe Healy for FRDH.
174 *"Let's watch"*: Interview with Willie Sutton by Burton Hersh; Burton Hersh, *The Education of Edward Kennedy*, p. 56.
174 *"I'm Ted Kennedy"*: Theo Lippmann, Jr., *Senator Ted Kennedy: The Career Behind the Image* (New York: Norton, 1976), p. 12.
174 *"When Ted came"*: Interview with James King by Burton Hersh, *Education of Edward Kennedy*, p. 108.

175 *Joe Kennedy reportedly pulled:* Interview with Norman MacDonald for FRDH.

175 *"We didn't have a single":* Laura Bergquist and Stanley Tetrick, *A Very Special President*, p. 30.

175 *"You know, we had":* Martin, *Hero*, p. 58.

175 *"That's the way":* Interview with John Seigenthaler in Stein and Plimpton, *American Journey*, pp. 44–45.

5

SENATE SPOTLIGHT

180 *"My pleasure":* Author interview with Richard Whelan.

180 *"Hey, Frip":* Interview with Ted Reardon by Collier and Horowitz, *The Kennedys*, p. 202.

181 *"intolerant, opinionated":* Sorensen, *Kennedy Legacy*, p. 36.

181 *"Bobby would call":* Author interview with Earl Mazo.

181 *"headed for disaster":* Schlesinger, *Robert Kennedy and His Times*, p. 106; Robert Kennedy, *The Enemy Within*, pp. 170, 291.

181 *"It was so exciting":* David Halberstam, *The Unfinished Odyssey of Robert Kennedy*, p. 134.

182 *"Remind me":* Roy Cohn, *McCarthy*, pp. 47, 66.

182 *one of his staff members:* Interview with Mary Davis for Martin and Plaut, FRDH.

183 *"Besides being assistant manager":* Letter to Max Beaverbrook from JPK Sr., Jan. 30, 1956, Max Beaverbrook Papers, House of Lords Library, London.

183 *"the old man . . . still":* Schlesinger, p. 108; interview with Lemoyne Billings by Stein in Stein and Plimpton, *American Journey*.

184 *"This would be":* Author interview with Larry Newman.

185 *"I sat next to":* Author interview with William McCormick Blair, Jr.

185 *"Oh, Ted is coming":* Author interview with Marquis Childs.

185 *"Not more than ten":* Author interview with Helen Fuller.

185 *"He never talked very much":* Interview with Eunice Kennedy by Clay Blair, Blair Papers, box 42, file 12, American Heritage Center, University of Wyoming.

185 *"Do you really want":* Interview with Priscilla McMillan in Collier and Horowitz, *The Kennedys*, p. 174.

186 *"No, I don't think":* Author interview with John Kennedy.

186 *"Perhaps, but over time":* Harris Wofford, *Of Kennedys and Kings: Making Sense of the Sixties*, p. 176.

186 *"But I never had":* Author interview with Jim Sundquist.

187 *"I think she was":* Interview with Eunice Shriver, Clay Blair Papers, University of Wyoming.

187 *"Fasten your eyes":* Doris Lily, *Family Circle*, July 10, 1978.

188 *"Actually, it wasn't":* Selma Roosevelt, "Mrs. John Kennedy Is a 'Thrilled' Listener," *Sunday Star*, March 14, 1954, p. D-6. Box 11, JFK Library.

188 *"He and Jackie":* Author interview with William Walton.

188 *"I used to think":* *Fruitful Bough*, p. 233.

189 *"Jackie was really":* "A New Kind of First Lady," *Look*, "Kennedy and His Family in Pictures," undated.

189 *His longtime friend:* Author interview with John Sharon.

189 *"There was a Senator Kluger":* Author interview with Joel Fisher.

190 *"You might even call":* Bergquist and Tetrick, p. 179.

190 *Frank Waldrop called in:* Laurence Leamer, *The Kennedy Women*, p. 429.

190 *"I don't think":* Kitty Kelley, *Jackie Oh!*, p. 67.

190 *"I couldn't visualize":* Interview with Lemoyne Billings in Collier and Horowitz, *The Kennedys*, pp. 193–94.

190 *"full of love":* Author interview with Lindy Boggs.

190 *"Maybe it's just":* Author interview with Marquis Childs.

191 *"even made a play":* *Newsweek*, Sept. 1960.

191 *"Let's say that":* Author interview with Nina Straight.

191 *"Jack and I both":* Stan Opotowsky, *New York Post Magazine*, March 24, 1961, p. 6.

192 *"I only got married":* Interview with Priscilla McMillan, "The American Experience," Sept. 20, 1992, WGBH-TV.

192 *The great difficulty:* Author interview with Lindy Boggs.

192 *"the public life":* Interview with Jacqueline Kennedy by Fletcher Knebel, p. 4, Mugar Memorial Library, Special Collections, Boston University.

192 *"What are you":* Author interview with Marianne Means.

192 *"You see, I never"*: Oral history interview with Jacqueline Kennedy, p. 2, LBJ Library.

193 *"She wasn't really interested"*: Author interview with Evelyn Lincoln.

193 *"Being married"*: "Fresh Approach, Confidence," undated clipping, Sunday *Standard Times*, p. 16, JFK Library.

193 *"See that smile"*: Author interview with Charles Spalding.

194 *"When I first met"*: Author interview with Angie Novello.

194 *"The staff thought"*: Author interview with Ralph Dungan.

194 They were very much alike: Author interview with Angie Novello.

195 *"At the wedding"*: Author interview with Larry Newman.

195 Correspondent Phil Potter: Author interview with Phil Potter.

195 *"You know, when I get"*: Author interview with Charles Spalding.

195 *"What was I to do"*: Irwin Ross, New York *Post*, July 30, 1956.

196 *"Is it still open?"*: Interview with Lemoyne Billings by Collier and Horowitz in *The Kennedys*, p. 205.

196 *"and he wept"*: Oral history interview with Arthur Krock by Charles Bartlett, JFK Library.

197 *"He was thin"*: Oral history interview with Dr. Janet Travell by Theodore Sorensen, JFK Library.

197 *"All the Kennedys"*: Coughlan Papers.

198 *"It was really Mr. Kennedy"*: Interview with Jacqueline Kennedy, Coughlan Papers.

198 *"Oh, please"*: Bergquist, *Very Special President*, p. 18.

198 *"Bobby never"*: Author interview with Benjamin Bradlee.

198 *"Some people"*: Author interview with John F. Kennedy for FRDH.

199 *"Bob and Ethel would"*: Author interview with Angie Novello.

199 *"I was at Harvard"*: Author interview with Senator Edward Kennedy.

199 *"He really had a second-"*: Oral history interview with Justice William Douglas, by Stewart, p. 9, JFK Library.

200 *"Bobby didn't want"*: Laura Bergquist Papers, Special Collections, Mugar Memorial Library, Boston University.

200 *"It can only be"*: Sarasota *Herald Tribune*, Oct. 18, 1955. "U.S. Official Says Reds Spied on Him In Russia."

201 When family friend Arthur Krock: Oral history interview with Louis A. Starr by Evan Thomas III, June 1974, #1177, PRCQ, 52-43, Columbia University.

201 Jack then went to see: Clark Clifford, *Counsel to the President*, p. 307.

201 Even after the book: Bergquist, p. 17.

202 *"Listening to them talk"*: Oral history interview with Charles Spalding by L. J. Hackman, March 22, 1969, p. 70. RFK Oral History Program, JFK Library.

202 *"because I want them"*: Newsweek, Jan. 24, 1962.

202 *"and his health was"*: Interview with John Kennedy by Ed Plaut for FRDH.

202 *"I never could get"*: Author interview with Senator George Smathers.

203 *"As I told you"*: Larry Newman Papers.

203 *"No question"*: Author interview with Sam Zagoria.

204 *"Why is Bill trying"*: Author interview with Kenneth Crawford.

204 *"in case lightning"*: Interview with Abe Michelson by Ed Plaut for FRDH.

204 *"Where will Teddy go"*: "What Makes the Kennedy Family Tick?" Boston *Daily Globe*, March 20, 1957.

204 *"I am afraid"*: RFK Papers, Pre-Administration Working Files, Personal Correspondence, 1954–1959. Files: 1956, Kennedy Family and NY Office 6/56–8/56, box 20, JFK Library.

204 *"considering everything"*: Ibid.

205 *"I'd come down"*: William Honan, "Can Teddy Kennedy Survive His Reputation?" *The New York Times Magazine*, n.d., p. 80.

205 *"Yes, that's the way"*: Author interview with Carl Marcy.

206 *"The Ambassador's language"*: Author interview with Kenneth O'Donnell.

206 *"The only advice"*: Interview with Joseph P. Kennedy, Sr., by Ed Plaut for FRDH.

206 *"Jack's campaign"*: Author interview with Abe Michelson.

207 *"I'll never forget"*: Interview with Congressman Quentin Burdick for FRDH.

207 Stevenson uttered: Overheard by author.

207 *"Something I'll never"*: Author interview with Mrs. Dixon.

208 *"After Jack lost"*: Author interview with Senator George Smathers.

208 Bob said to him: Martin, *Hero*, pp. 120–21.

208 *"Coming back"*: Interview with Dave Talbot by Ed Plaut for FRDH.

208 *"If I had been there"*: Interview with Joseph Kennedy Sr. by Ed Plaut for FRDH.

208 Afterward, Jack reflected: Collier and Horowitz, *The Kennedys*, p. 210.

209 *"One of the things"*: Author interview with Marquis Childs.

209 *"If you are ever planning"*: Author interview with Senator George Smathers.

210 *"Joe Kennedy told me"*: Author interview with Igor Cassini.

210 *"A million?"*: Interview with Norma Nathan, "The Kennedy Women," "Geraldo," ABC-TV, July 17, 1991.

210 *"would come in at eight"*: Interview with Frances Farmer, Lester David, *Good Ted*, p. 42.

211 *"would come into the room"*: Interviews with Charles Spalding and Mary McCarthy in Collier and Horowitz, *The Kennedys*, p. 285.

211 *Joe and Jack*: Interview with Peter Lawford, ibid., p. 216.

211 *"My mother"*: David, *Ted Kennedy*, p. 80.

212 *"Anybody else"*: Thomas Morgan, *Esquire*, April 1962.

212 *"was asking all"*: Oral history interview with Laura Bergquist by Sheldon Stern, Aug. 1, 1977, JFK Library.

212 *"Joe thought Jack"*: Interview with Rose Kennedy, Coughlan Papers.

213 *"I used to thank"*: Martin, *Hero*, p. 130.

213 *"You know, Jack"*: Oral history interview with Hale Boggs, JFK Library.

213 *"Kennedy is"*: *Time*, Feb. 24, 1961.

214 *"Jack and Jackie and I"*: Author interview with William Walton.

214 *"You're not to speak"*: Interview with Lemoyne Billings in *The Kennedys*.

214 *"One day, Fulbright"*: Author interview with Carl Marcy.

214 *"Bobby was pretty green"*: Author interview with Arthur Goldberg.

215 *"I said, 'You're out' "*: Ibid.

215 *"The big burden"*: Undated International News Service story.

215 *Reporters, however*: Jack Anderson and Fred Blumenthal, *Parade*, April 28, 1957, p. 9.

215 *"For the first time"*: Interview with Lemoyne Billings in *The Kennedys*, p. 225.

216 *"Your name"*: RFK Papers, Pre-Administration Working Files, Personal Correspondence, 1954–1959. File: 1957 Kennedy Family, 1/57–4/57, box 42, JFK Library.

216 *"too great"*: Interview with Mercedes (Douglas) Eicholz by Arthur Schlesinger, p. 155.

216 *"I think I'm gonna"*: Author interview with Arthur Goldberg.

216 *"Joe McCarthy"*: Interview with Clark Mollenhoff, Sept. 9, 1982, in *The Kennedys*, p. 218.

217 *"We think"*: "People in the News," *Seattle Times*, Oct. 3, 1957.

217 *"We didn't think"*: RFK Papers, box 42, JFK Library.

217 *"Tell them"*: Oral history interview with John Seigenthaler by Bill Singer, pp. 6–7,

University of North Carolina, Chapel Hill, Southern Intellectual Leaders Project, Part II, #1197 PRCQ.

218 *"My biggest problem"*: Arthur M. Schlesinger, Jr., *Robert Kennedy and His Times*, p. 156; Paul Healy, "Investigator in a Hurry," *Sign*, Aug. 1957.

218 *"I doubt if Jack"*: *Newsweek*, April 1, 1957.

219 *"Let Bobby"*: Author interview with Ralph Dungan.

219 *"He turned"*: Author interview with Carroll Kilpatrick.

219 *"I don't think"*: Author interview with Esther Tufty.

220 *"I recall driving"*: Oral history interview with Laura Bergquist by Nelson Aldrich, Dec. 8, 1965, JFK Library.

220 *"and stood in front"*: Author interview with Angie Novello.

220 *"I remember later"*: Author interview with Laura Bergquist.

220 *"They would talk"*: Author interview with William Walton.

221 *"People will come"*: Interview with Congressman Gerald T. Flynn for FRDH.

221 *"Weren't you surprised"*: Letter to Max Beaverbrook from JPK Sr., Dec. 9, 1957, Beaverbrook Papers, House of Lords Library, London.

221 *"Yes, I am getting"*: Author interview with Rowland Evans.

222 *"There is no"*: Interview with Joseph Kennedy Sr. by Ed Plaut for Martin and Plaut.

222 *"he was running"*: London *Observer*, March 2, 1980, p. 35

222 *"feverish schedule"*: Author interview with Kenneth O'Donnell.

222 *"I accepted that"*: Oral history interview with Lawrence O'Brien by Michael L. Gillette, p. 97, LBJ Library.

222 *"I had to live"*: Martin, *Hero*, p. 125.

223 *"Jack's name"*: Author interview with Jim Rowe.

223 *"Joe sent"*: Richard Whalen, *The Founding Father*, p. 496.

223 *"He was tall"*: Haynes Johnson, "Why Camelot Lives," Washington *Post*, n.d.

223 *"It was almost"*: Author interview with Jack Raymond.

224 *"If he thought"*: Author interview with Laura Bergquist.

224 *"But unlike"*: Reston, *Deadline*, p. 287.

224 *"Joseph Kennedy said"*: *Fruitful Bough*, p. 253.

224 *"He won't have"*: Author interview with Charles Bartlett.

224 *"Oh no. None"*: Interview with Joseph P. Kennedy Sr. by Ed Plaut for FRDH.

225 *"Jack does have"*: Ibid.

226 *"Joe pointed up"*: Author interview with Sarah McLendon.
226 *"I just can't understand"*: Author interview with Charles Spalding.
226 *"I don't want to be"*: Whalen, p. 457.
226 *"If I need"*: Ibid., p. 177.

6

THE BIG PRIZE

227 *"But you have to"*: Joseph Alsop, *I've Seen the Best of It*, p. 406.
227 *"Otherwise I'd rather"*: Author interview with John Kennedy.
227 *"What you need"*: Interview with Joseph P. Kennedy Sr. by Joe McCarthy, Joe McCarthy Papers.
228 *"You know, if I"*: Author interview with Arthur Schlesinger, Jr.
228 *"Piecing it all"*: Interview with Anthony Gallucio by Ed Plaut for FRDH.
228 *Jack told author*: Joseph McCarthy Papers.
228 *"This country"*: U.S. News & World Report, Nov. 15, 1993, p. 40.
229 *Jack also fired*: Author interview with Ed Plaut.
229 *"Well, Mike"*: Author interview with Myer Feldman.
229 *"If Jack had"*: Author interview with Kenneth O'Donnell.
229 *"What do you want"*: Ibid.
229 *"I have just"*: Author interview with Porter McKeever.
230 *Steve Smith said*: Author interview with Stephen Smith.
230 *"You keep"*: Interview with Jimmy Breslin by Merle Miller, Merle Miller Papers.
230 *One of the reasons*: Richard E. Burke, *The Senator: My Ten Years with Ted Kennedy*, pp. 101–102.
231 *Kennedy could never*: Interview with Abraham Ribicoff by Ed Plaut.
231 *"He was on crutches"*: Author interview with Larry Newman.
231 *"Teddy Kennedy was better"*: Interview with Edward McCormack by Burton Hersh, *Education of Edward Kennedy*, p. 110.
232 *"I want you to meet"*: Interview with Joan Kennedy, Coughlan Papers.
232 *Rose later called*: Ibid.
232 *"I'd heard terrifying"*: Ibid.
233 *"If you don't marry"*: Marcia Chellis, *The Joan Kennedy Story: Living with the Kennedys*, pp. 33–34.
233 *"Joe Sr. was furious"*: Laurence Leamer, *The Kennedy Women*, p. 474.
234 *"Later, when Ted"*: Ibid.
234 *"I told my daughters-in-law"*: Interview with Rose Kennedy, Coughlan Papers.
234 *"I suppose"*: Joan Kennedy, "The Truth About My Marriage," *Sunday Herald Traveler and Sunday Advertiser*, Oct. 15, 1972, Box 12, JFK Library.
234 *"Jackie could"*: Author interview with Larry Newman.
235 *"I not only want"*: Author interview with Nancy Coleman.
235 *"his whole face"*: Author interview with John Sharon.
235 *"All right, Jack"*: Interview with Paul Fay, "The American Experience," WGBH-TV, Sept. 20, 1992.
236 *"I'm going to see"*: Author interview with Evelyn Lincoln.
236 *"Anybody who'd"*: Author interview with Kenneth Crawford.
236 *"smooth as silk"*: Author interview with General Godfrey McHugh.
237 *"Has your brother"*: Interview with John Kennedy by Ed Plaut for FRDH.
237 *"Check those things"*: Author interview with Pierre Salinger.
237 *"I know Bobby"*: JFK to Ralph Martin.
237 *"For a fee"*: Author interview with Charles Bartlett.
237 *"the reward"*: Letter to JPK Sr. from Max Beaverbrook, Sept. 3, 1960, Beaverbrook Papers, House of Lords Library, London.
238 *"He can't run"*: Oral history interview with John Kennedy by Joseph Alsop, JFK Library.
238 *"God, if I hadn't"*: Paul B. Fay, Jr., *The Pleasure of His Company*, p. 33.
238 *"The Ambassador"*: Author interview with Theodore Sorensen.
238 *"Joe Kennedy"*: Author interview with Marquis Childs.
238 *"I'm beginning"*: Author interview with Helen Fuller.
238 *The pressure to support*: Interviews by Ed Plaut for FRDH.
239 *"I understand"*: Ralph G. Martin, *A Hero for Our Time*, prologue.
239 *"I think if you'll"*: Author interview with Charles Roberts.

240 *"Jack, when you're"*: Interview with Priscilla McMillan, "The American Experience," WGBH-TV, Sept. 20, 1992.

240 *"the old man"*: Interview with Frank Riley for FRDH.

240 *"It's strange"*: Author interview with Marquis Childs.

240 *"Teddy wanted"*: Author interview with Theodore Sorensen.

241 *"It's so boring"*: Author interview with Jacqueline Kennedy.

242 *"For once I'd like"*: Author interview with Oscar Chapman.

242 *"Isn't it possible"*: Interview with Mark Dalton for FRDH.

242 *"Let's get back"*: Ibid.

242 *"Nobody enjoyed"*: Author interview with Dave Powers.

242 *"Landing in Jackson"*: "Democrats: Through the Roadblock," *Time*, Oct. 28, 1957, p. 23.

243 *"We met a publisher"*: Author interview with Laura Bergquist.

244 *"We all looked"*: Author interview with James Symington.

244 *"Acapulco"*: Andrew Tully, New York *World Telegram*, March 18, 1960.

244 *"Jack wouldn't"*: *Time*, Jan. 20, 1961.

244 *"I put my finger"*: Oral history interview with John Seigenthaler by Larry Hackman, June 5, 1970, p. 57. RFK Oral History Program, JFK Library.

245 *"You know something"*: Sorensen, *Legacy*, p. 44.

245 *"I wanted to get"*: James MacGregor Burns, *Edward Kennedy and the Camelot Legacy*, pp. 66, 68.

245 *"I felt totally"*: William Peters, *Redbook*, June 1962.

245 *"Ethel, what"*: Martin, *Hero*, p. 195.

246 *"One Kennedy employee"*: Paul Healy and Tom Allen, *Sunday Daily News*, July 10, 1960, p. 4.

246 *"Eunice was"*: Interview with Robert Ajemian, Collier and Horowitz, *The Kennedys*, p. 248.

246 *"I think Jackie"*: Author interview with Joan Braden.

246 *"My sister Eunice"*: Author interview with John Kennedy.

247 *"Muriel and I"*: "JFK & the '60 Campaign," New York *Post* Magazine, Jan. 19, 1978, p. 21; Hubert H. Humphrey, *The Education of a Public Man*.

247 *"Little girls"*: Bergquist and Tetrick, *A Very Special President*, p. 60.

247 *"I can literally"*: Author interview with Jim Deakin.

248 *"Bobby must be"*: Sorensen, *Legacy*, p. 64.

248 *"Come back"*: O'Donnell, Powers, and McCarthy, *Johnny We Hardly Knew Ye*, p. 161.

248 *"Me an issue?"*: Paul Healy and Tom Allen, *Sunday Daily News*, July 10, 1960, p. 64.

248 *"They were unanimous"*: *The New York Times*, Oct. 31, 1992, p. 10.

249 *"anywhere from two"*: Margaret Laing, *The Next Kennedy*, pp. 174–75.

249 *"And they passed"*: Interview with Thomas O'Neill, "The American Experience: The Kennedys," WGBH-TV, Sept. 20, 1992.

250 *"I took the reservations"*: Anthony Summers, *Official and Confidential: The Secret Life of J. Edgar Hoover*, pp. 269–70.

250 Sam Giancana and Mafia: Robert Blakey and Richard Billings, *The Plot to Kill the President*, p. 376, footnote citing December 1961 wiretap seen in original by author; Summers, pp. 269–70.

250 One thing they did: Beschloss, pp. 140–41.

250 Judith Campbell: Interview in *People*, Feb. 29, 1988; Beschloss, p. 142.

251 *"It's a great deal"*: Interview with Judith Campbell Exner on "Larry King Live," Cable News Network, Nov. 20, 1992.

251 *"spoke terribly fast"*: Oral history interview with Peter Lisagor by Ronald J. Grele, Columbia University.

251 *"I'd just like"*: Author interview with Dave Powers.

251 *"Damn that Hubert"*: O'Donnell et al., p. 171.

252 *"It was Bobby"*: Author interview with Benjamin C. Bradlee.

252 The old man: Bradlee, *Newsweek*, Dec. 20, 1961.

252 *"The door opened"*: Oral history interview with Joseph Rauh by Charles Morrissey, JFK Library.

252 *"Muriel stiffened"*: Hubert H. Humphrey, *Education of a Public Man*, p. 221.

253 *"I keep reading"*: Author interview with Bill Connell; also Humphrey, *Education*.

253 *"licked the Catholic"*: Author interview with Kenneth O'Donnell.

253 *"I remember his father"*: Author interview with Charles Spalding.

254 *"We were interested"*: Richard Whalen, *The Founding Father*, p. 491.

254 *"someone with the greatest"*: July 2, 1960, Independence, Missouri.

254 *"I'm not against"*: O'Donnell, Powers, and McCarthy, p. 151.

255 *"They knew all"*: Summers, *Official and Confidential*, p. 264; Summers' interview with Cartha DeLoach, 1988, also her letter to author, Dec. 28, 1988.

255 "offered to get": Edward Thompson, ed., Theodore H. White at Large, p. 550.

255 "If you don't": Oral history interview with John Seigenthaler by William Geoghegan, July 22, 1964, pp. 92–93, JFK Library.

255 "What shall I": Oral history interview with Akers by Moss, p. 15, JFK Library.

255 "And I remember": Author interview with Hugh Sidey.

256 "I sat down": Oral history interview with Dr. Janet Travell by Theodore Sorensen, Jan. 20, 1966, JFK Library.

256 "They wouldn't": Ibid.

256 After his death: Dr. Robert F. Karnei and Dr. J. Thornton Boswell, The New York Times, Oct. 6, 1992.

257 "In the art of": David, Ethel, p. 36.

257 "That young man": Interview with Eugene Keogh by Collier and Horowitz, p. 240.

257 "Hubert, we want": Halberstam, p. 139.

257 "Dad, Adlai": Author interview with Kenneth O'Donnell.

257 "I remember": Oral history interview with Hugh Sidey, JFK Library.

258 "You son of a bitch": Author interview with Arthur Goldberg.

258 "Some people": Author interview with Evelyn Lincoln.

258 "Ah, the beginning": Interview with Peter Lisagor by Ronald J. Grele, April 22, 1966, pp. 23–24, JFK Library.

258 "'Jack,' I said": Oral history interview with Congressman Tip O'Neill, JFK Library.

259 "Power goes": Oral history interview with James Rowe by Michael Gillette, p. 17, Sept. 9, 1969, LBJ Library.

259 "Johnson then called": Author interview with James Rowe.

260 "Bobby was directing": Author interview with Charles Bartlett.

260 "Boy, that was": Interview with Peter Lisagor by Ronald Grele, April 22, 1966, pp. 23–24, JFK Library.

260 "Even if Jack": O'Donnell, Powers, and McCarthy, p. 191.

260 "It was all over": Newsweek, Sept. 1960.

260 "Just right after": Author's interview with Charles Spalding.

261 "Well, now, Joe": Richard Whalen Papers, box 1. F: Friends, Ex-Assoc., Interview with H. R. Luce, 10/1/62, JFK Library.

261 "There was no": Ralph G. Martin, Henry and Clare, pp. 359–60.

262 Luce privately: Oral history interview with Henry Luce by John Steele, pp. 10–12, Columbia University.

262 Lisagor was aboard: Oral history interview with Peter Lisagor by Ronald J. Grele, April 22, 1966, pp. 23–24, JFK Library.

262 "I want you": Author interview with Clark Clifford.

263 "It was only later": Ibid.

263 "The key": Newsweek, July 15, 1960.

263 "but she was kind of": Interview with Jacqueline Kennedy, LBJ Library.

264 "the Majority Leader's": Author interview with Senator Hugh Scott.

264 "because he has been": Interview with Jacqueline Kennedy by Fletcher Knebel, Special Collections, Mugar Memorial Library, Boston University.

264 "a continuing contempt": Author interview with McGeorge Bundy.

265 "I was running": Richard Nixon, Six Crises (Garden City, NY: Doubleday, 1962), p. 421.

265 On the October 13: Jack Anderson with Les Whitten, "Hoover, JFK and Sex," New York Post, Jan. 13, 1976.

265 "Terrific!": Martin, Hero, p. 122.

265 "Well, Joe": Joseph Alsop and Adam Pilatt, I've Seen the Best of It All, p. 430.

266 "The most striking": "Mr. Kennedy's Language Key to His Power," London Telegraph, April 10, 1961.

266 "And I think": Author interview with Abe Fortas.

266 "Any man who": Author interview with William Walton.

266 "The old man": Author interview with Charles Bartlett.

266 "I think Jack": Author interview with Charles Spalding.

267 "When we divided": Martin, Hero, p. 160.

267 "Ted does not": Author interview with Dave Powers.

267 "Teddy bends over": Time, Nov. 29, 1971, p. 18.

268 "Little talk": RFK Papers, Pre-Administration Political Files, 1960 Cam + Trans Gen Subject 1959–60, File: Memos Edward Kennedy, 11/2/59–1/5/60, undated, box 39, JFK Library.

268 "First of all": Ibid.

269 Teddy, as always: Esquire, April 1962.

269 "Bobby picked up": Author interview with Frank Thompson.

270 "Jack works harder": Boston Globe, Oct. 20, 1979, p. 38.

270 "I don't have to do": Schlesinger, Robert Kennedy and His Times, vol. 1, p. 229; Arthur Edson, "Bobby—Washington No. 2 Man," AP feature for release April 14, 1963.

270 During Jack Kennedy's visit: Interview with Jesse Unruh by Jean Stein in Stein and Plimpton, American Journey, pp. 72–73.

270 *Bobby did cause:* Barry Gray, WMCA Radio, Aug. 24, 1960.

271 *"You bomb-throwers":* Oral history interview with Harris Wofford, JFK Library.

271 *"I made it clear":* Martin, *Hero*, p. 229.

271 *"That was a hell":* Schlesinger, vol. 1, p. 228.

272 *"a couple of phone calls":* Martin, *Hero* notes, Mugar Memorial Library, Special Collections, Boston University.

272 *"Bobby was in total":* Time, Nov. 16, 1960, p. 5, box 12, JFK Library.

273 *" 'I'm worrying' ":* O'Donnell, Powers, and McCarthy, p. 225.

274 *Teddy later remembered:* Letter from Edward Kennedy to Max Beaverbrook, Dec. 17, 1963, Beaverbrook Papers, House of Lords Library, London.

274 *"I read in the paper":* The New York Times, Aug. 16, 1992.

274 *" 'May I go' ":* "The White House Nannies," from *The Kennedy Reader*, Maude Shaw and Jay Davis eds., p. 334.

275 *"I've photographed":* William Haddad, On the Road with Kennedy, New York Post, Nov. 27, 1960.

275 *"He came in":* Interview with Sargent Shriver by Clay Blair, pp. 11–13, Blair Papers, University of Wyoming.

7

FANFARE AND FAILURE

277 *"Like Roosevelt":* Author interview with Sander Vanocur.

278 *"Now I can appear":* Ira Henry Freeman, "Joseph Kennedy Is Back on Scene after Seclusion in the Campaign," *The New York Times*, Jan. 8, 1961.

278 *"How are you":* Time, Nov. 28, 1960.

279 *"I wouldn't put on":* "Broadcasts Set by Mrs. Kennedy," *The New York Times*, Sept. 20, 1960.

279 *"In this lovely":* Author interview with Charles Bartlett.

279 *"I mentioned":* Author interview with William Walton.

279 *"He was chosen":* Interview with Abram Chayes, David Halberstam Papers, Mugar Memorial Library, Special Collections, Boston University.

279 *"When O'Donnell told":* Author interview with Kenneth O'Donnell.

280 *Leaping to intercept:* Marguerite Higgins, "Rose Fitzgerald Kennedy," *McCall's*, May 1961.

281 *"Bob sat down":* Author interview with Kenneth O'Donnell.

281 *"We were just":* Author interview with Lawrence O'Brien.

281 *"It would be impossible":* Oral history interview with John F. Kennedy by John Bartlow Martin, JFK Library.

282 *"Bobby would've":* Author interview with Dave Powers.

282 *"Jack was taken":* Woody Klein, Interview with Abraham Ribicoff, *The New York Times*, April 4, 1993.

282 *"Why should the President":* Cannon, *Newsweek*, Dec. 20, 1961.

282 *"Bobby was there":* Author interview with Dave Powers.

282 *"He wouldn't hear":* Oral history interview with Robert Kennedy by John Bartlow Martin, JFK Library.

282 *"I don't know what's wrong":* Author interview with Hugh Sidey.

283 *"Jack, I want":* Author interview with Senator George Smathers.

283 *"Now, Bobby's going":* Author interview with Clark Clifford.

283 *"I would always remember":* Clifford, *Counsel to the President*, p. 337.

284 *"Why give me":* Wofford, pp. 90–91.

284 *Douglas also talked:* Oral history interview with William O. Douglas by Stewart, JFK Library.

284 *"This will kill":* Oral history interview with John Seigenthaler by Ronald Grele, Feb. 22, 1966, pp. 305–07, JFK Library.

284 *"Now, Johnny":* Third Interview with John Seigenthaler by Grele, pp. 307, 309, 321, 322, JFK Library.

285 *"I need to know":* Ibid., pp. 323–26, Feb. 22, 1966, JFK Library.

285 *"If I can ask":* Ibid.

285 *"On my announcement":* Hugh Sidey quoted in Lester Tanzer, ed., *The Kennedy Circle*, pp. 187–88.

285 *"a disgrace":* Bobby Baker with Larry King, *Wheeling and Dealing: Confessions of a Capitol Hill Operator*, pp. 120–21.

286 *"You know, what":* Author interview with Dave Powers.

286 *"Any room":* RFK Papers, Pre-Administration Political Files, 1960 Campaign + Transition Corresp., 1959–1960. File: Kennedy, A-M, box 16, JFK Library.

287 *"He looked at me":* Bruce Miroff, *Pragmatic*

Illusions, the Presidential Politics of John F. Kennedy, p. 8.

287 *"he didn't do a damn thing"*: Peter Lisagor interview with Grele, Columbia University Oral History.

287 *"Jack was amused"*: Interview with William Walton by Clay Blair, Jr., Blair Papers, box 56, file 4, p. 1, American Heritage Center, University of Wyoming.

288 *"I don't know how"*: Reeves, p. 25; Oral History interview with Bell, pp. 1–3; *Time*, April 7, 1961.

288 *"Jack, if you don't"*: Interview with Daniel Patrick Moynihan by Richard Reeves, Reeves, p. 25.

288 *Palm Beach was*: Oral history interview with Milton Gwirtzman by Ronald J. Grele, Jan. 19, 1966, JFK Oral History, JFK Library.

288 *The elder Kennedy*: Interview with Senator Edward Kennedy, "The American Experience: The Kennedys," WGBH-TV, Sept. 20, 1992.

288 *"had drunk more"*: Hervé Alphand, *L'Étonnement d'être: Journal, 1939–1973* (Paris: Fayard), translated for the author by Doris Cramer.

289 *"He looks like a Greek god!"*: Author interview with Hugh Sidey.

289 *"No one's told me"*: Author interview with Marquis Childs.

289 *"and took turns"*: Martin, *Hero*, notes, Mugar Memorial Library, Special Collections, Boston University.

289 *There had been an urgent*: In Search of History, p. 514.

289 *"I remember at our wedding"*: Coughlan papers.

289 *In the official car*: Ibid.

290 *"this is what"*: *Time*, Jan. 27, 1961.

290 *"I talked to him"*: Author interview with Clark Clifford.

290 *"I hate to think"*: Beschloss, p. 187.

291 *"Jack went to Mass"*: Interview with Rose Kennedy by Robert Coughlan, Coughlan Papers.

291 *"He was very conscious"*: Author interview with William Walton.

291 *"they wouldn't be caught"*: Martin, *Hero*, pp. 186–87.

292 *"Dad was deeply"*: Fruitful Bough, p. 207.

292 *"I think this is"*: Jack Anderson, "What Makes Kennedy Laugh?" *Parade*, Feb. 26, 1961, p. 22, box 11, JFK Library; Alsop, pp. 434–35.

292 *"I had been in bed"*: Coughlan Papers.

292 *"It was kind of"*: Author interview with Joan Braden.

292 *"I cut off"*: Author interview with William Walton.

293 *"You've lived here"*: Ibid.

293 *"opens up newspapers"*: Author interview with General Godfrey McHugh.

293 *"Why?" Kennedy asked*: Author interview with John Sharon.

294 *" 'Mr. President' "*: "An Intelligent, Courageous Presidency," editorial, *Life*, Nov. 29, 1963, from Jay Davis, ed., *The Kennedy Reader* (New York: Bobbs-Merrill, 1967), p. 228; Jim Bishop, *A Day in the Life of President Kennedy*.

294 *"There was a sense"*: Author interview with Charles Spalding.

294 *"I always saved"*: Author interview with Laura Bergquist.

294 *"You could never relax"*: Author interview with Nancy Dickerson.

294 *"Usually that would"*: Victor Lasky, *J.F.K. The Man and the Myth*, pp. 539–40; Marianne Means, New York *Journal-American*, Dec. 20, 1961.

294 *"I want to help"*: Interview with Stephen Smith by Arthur Schlesinger, Jr., *Robert Kennedy*, vol. 2, p. 613.

295 *"by sliding down"*: David and David, *Bobby*, pp. 124–25.

295 *"The President waited"*: Evelyn Lincoln, *My Twelve Years with John Kennedy*; Gore Vidal, "The Holy Family," *Esquire*, April 1967, p. 103.

295 *"Bob loved that"*: Author interview with Angie Novello.

295 *"I sat next"*: Interview with Peter Edelman by Jean Stein, Stein and Plimpton, *American Journey*, pp. 83–84.

295 *"I don't think"*: Interview with Theodore White by Jean Stein, ibid.

296 *"When he came down"*: Navasky, p. 25.

296 *"Some of his staff"*: Author interview with Harold Reis.

296 *"Before long, Kennedy's"*: Author interview with Lawrence Houston.

296 *"I liked that Robert"*: Author interview with Esther Tufty.

296 *"I cannot tell"*: Navasky, p. 348.

297 *"Get it done"*: Author interview with Angie Novello.

297 *"The Kennedy style"*: Navasky, p. 331.

297 *Political observer George Reedy*: Interview with George Reedy, "The American Experience: The Kennedys," WGBH-TV. Sept. 21, 1992.

297 *"We used to get"*: Author interview with Angie Novello.

298 *"Without her, Bobby"*: Vivian Cadden, "Jacqueline: Behind the Myths," *McCall's*, July 1975.

298 *"With Ethel and Bobby"*: Author interview with Eunice Shriver.

298 *"They were both"*: Author interview with Laura Bergquist.

298 *"You look like"*: Rogers, p. 11.

298 *For a St. Patrick's Day:* Author interview with Angie Novello.

299 *"We just try"*: Interview with Ethel Kennedy by Gail Cameron, *Ladies' Home Journal*, Feb. 1967, p. 143.

299 *"I got invited"*: Author interview with Jim Deakin.

300 *"Unlike JFK"*: Halberstam Papers, Mugar Memorial Library, Special Collections, Boston University.

300 *"Bob assumed"*: Author interview with Harold Reis.

300 *"And another one"*: Interview with Robert Kennedy by Ed Plaut, FRDH.

300 *"Bob could be"*: Author interview with James Symington.

301 *"We always followed"*: "Larry King Live," CNN, June 4, 1993.

301 *"Our family prayed"*: "Sonya Live," CNN, June 4, 1993.

301 *"Sometimes Bob"*: Rogers, *When I Think of Bobby*, pp. 25–26.

301 *The big thing:* David, *Good Ted, Bad Ted*, p. 29.

301 *"Most people"*: Rogers, p. 7.

302 *"God bless"*: Ibid., p. 14.

302 *"We were all sitting"*: Interview with Kerry Kennedy Cuomo, "Good Morning America," July 15, 1992; Robert F. Kennedy, *Legacy*, p. 8.

303 *"I've got to do something"*: Schlesinger, p. 280; Sheridan, *Fall and Rise of Hoffa*, p. 193.

303 *"I'll break"*: Frank Ragano and Selwyn Rabb, *Mob Lawyer*, p. 142.

303 *"As they said"*: RFK to JPK, RFK Papers, Pre-Administration Working Files, Pers. Corresp., 1954–1957. Files: 1957 Kennedy Family, 5/57–9/57, box 42, RFK Papers, JFK Library.

303 *"Robert Kennedy was the most"*: Author interview with William Hundley.

304 *A technician:* Beschloss, p. 347.

304 *Robert Kennedy would have been:* Ibid.

304 *"You've got to prosecute"*: Navasky, pp. 368–89; Schlesinger, p. 398.

304 *"Bobby was the family"*: Author interview with Dave Richardson.

304 *"If any goddamn"*: Oral history interview with Justin Feldman, JFK Library.

305 *"Bobby Kennedy advised"*: Interview with John Seigenthaler by Ronald J. Grele, p. 483, JFK Library.

305 *"The only two men"*: Summers, pp. 260–61; *The FBI Pyramid*, p. 195.

306 *Bob quickly arranged:* Oral history with Robert Kennedy by John Bartlow Martin, JFK Library.

306 *Hoover even sent:* Oral history interview with Robert Kennedy, p. 191, JFK Library.

306 *"It was soon"*: Author interview with William Hundley.

306 *Years later it was suggested:* Ibid.

306 *"a psycho"*: Ibid.

306 *On January 31, 1961:* Washington *Post*, Jan. 13, 1978, quoted in Summers, p. 280; letter Rome to Hoover, Jan. 30, 1961.

307 *"You print that story"*: Author interview with Laura Bergquist.

307 *Bob Kennedy later told:* Letter: Rome to Hoover, Jan. 30, 1961, Official and Confidential files, vol. 13; Washington *Post*, Jan. 13, 1978; Summers, p. 280.

307 *The President had joked:* Schlesinger, p. 247.

307 *"Bobby's all choked"*: Author interview with Charles Spalding.

307 *And yet if you asked:* Bradlee, pp. 142–43.

308 *"Just the three"*: Author interview with Lord Harlech.

308 *"I never once"*: Interview with Rowland Evans by Roberta Greene, July 3, 1970, p. 48, RFK Oral History, JFK Library.

308 *"Bobby was the kind"*: Oral history interview with Charles Spalding, JFK Library.

309 *"Friends wanted"*: Schlesinger, p. 627.

309 *"nice and relaxed"*: Jerry Bruno and Jeff Greenfield, *The Advance Man*, p. 40.

309 *Some admitted:* Author interview with Esther Tufty.

309 *"And Bobby turned"*: Author interview with Jim Deakin.

309 *"least like his father"*: Schlesinger, p. 102.

309 *"You know everybody"*: Halberstam Papers, Mugar Memorial Library, Special Collections, Boston University.

309 *"I was driving"*: Author interview with Charles Spalding; Oral history interview with Spalding, JFK Library.

310 *"He was in that office"*: Author interview with John Nolan.

310 *It was quite:* Interview with Lem Billings by Collier and Horowitz, *The Kennedys*, p. 23.

311 *"It's shocking"*: Author interview with Adam Yarmolinsky.

311 *"maybe a few times"*: Author interview with Evelyn Lincoln.

311 *"It was obvious"*: Author interview with Fred Holburn.

311 *"I went into"*: Author interview with Hugh Sidey.

312 *"Why don't you"*: Ibid.

312 *"Dear Bobby"*: Ibid.

312 *"I think you"*: Rose Kennedy to RFK, Oct. 4, 1961, RFK Papers, JFK Library.

312 *"He never said"*: Author interview with Senator George Smathers.

312 *"I had a separate"*: Author interview with Evelyn Lincoln.

313 *An Air Force aide*: Martin, *Hero*, pp. 321–22.

313 *"was great on notes"*: Interview with Dave Powers by Robert Coughlan, Coughlan Papers.

313 *"Is there a fire"*: RFK Papers, box 16, JFK Library.

313 *And in a later note*: May 9, 1957, Rose Kennedy to RFK, Pre-Administration Working Files, Pers. Corresp. 1954–1957. File: 1957 Kennedy Family, 5/57–9/57, box 42, RFK Papers, JFK Library.

314 *"We didn't feel"*: Rose Kennedy interviewed by Robert Coughlan, Jan. 28, 1972, Coughlan Papers.

314 *When Carol Channing*: Martin, *Hero*, p. 431; *Newsweek*, Feb. 4, 1963.

314 *Rose, typifying*: Gloria Emerson, "How Rose Kennedy Survived," *McCall's*, Aug. 1975.

314 *"They want my"*: Gloria Guinness interviewed by Robert Coughlan, Coughlan Papers.

315 *"I'm Rose Kennedy"*: Author interview with General Godfrey McHugh.

315 *"that old Ireland"*: Harris Wofford, *Of Kennedys and Kings*, pp. 453–54.

315 *"Jack always used"*: Author interview with Eunice Shriver.

316 *"Don't tell me"*: Author interview with Larry Newman.

316 *"He told me"*: Author interview with Sargent Shriver.

316 *"Do you know"*: Author interview with Bill Haddad.

316 *"Sarge was very"*: Author interview with General Godfrey McHugh.

316 *"Why don't you"*: Author interview with Eunice Kennedy Shriver.

316 *"I know that Bob"*: Interview with John Seigenthaler by Larry Hackman, June 5, 1970, p. 8, JFK Library.

318 *"Mistakes?"*: T. George Harris, "Eight Views of JFK," *Look*, Nov. 17, 1964.

318 *Bob knew*: Joe McCarthy Papers; O'Donnell, Powers, and Joe McCarthy, p. 278.

318 *"Usually when I"*: Ibid., pp. 278–80.

318 *"clasp his hands"*: Paul O'Neill, "The Number Two Man in Washington," *Life*, Jan. 26, 1962.

319 *"I've hardly seen"*: Martin, *Hero*, p. 236.

319 *"And she got"*: Author interview with Charles Spalding.

319 *"she kept a family"*: Interview with Jacqueline Kennedy by Laura Bergquist, Bergquist Papers, Mugar Memorial Library, Special Collections, Boston University.

319 *"She brought taste"*: Author interview with Lord Harlech.

320 *"as big as a milk pail"*: Joseph Alsop and Adam Platt, *I've Seen the Best of It*.

320 *"She is not as American"*: New York *Journal-American*, Jan. 19, 1961.

320 *"Many people"*: Author interview with General Godfrey McHugh.

320 *"from a fumbling person"*: Author interview with Evelyn Lincoln.

320 *"how nice Mrs. Roosevelt"*: Interview with Jacqueline Kennedy by Robert Coughlan, Coughlan Papers.

321 *"When the President's"*: Martin, *Hero*, p. 321.

321 *"was not a happy"*: Letter from Mrs. Onassis to Mrs. Rose Kennedy, June 1973, Coughlan Papers.

321 *"She could have"*: Author interview with Jill Cowan.

321 *"So she just resisted"*: Author interview with Charles Spalding.

321 *According to his friend*: Author interview with Charles Bartlett.

321 *"I can't think"*: Author interview with Charles Spalding.

322 *"Jackie, you know"*: *Family Circle*, July 10, 1978.

322 *Blair Clark tells*: Author interview with Blair Clark.

322 *"He'd go his way"*: Author interview with Charles Roberts.

322 *"Jackie could stand"*: Author interview with Laura Bergquist.

322 *But she showed*: Author interview with General McHugh.

323 *"Well, I think"*: Author interview with Charles Roberts.

323 *In one of her frequent*: Author interview with Joseph McCarthy.

323 *"The President will"*: Worth Bingham and Ward S. Just, "The President and the Press," *The Reporter*, April 12, 1962, p. 18, box 12, JFK Library.

323 *"You can see"*: Interview with Judith Campbell, "The American Experience: The Kennedys," WGBH-TV, Sept. 20, 1992.

323 *"thumbprint"*: Interview with Billings by Collier and Horowitz, *The Kennedys*, p. 263.

323 *"I heard him"*: Author interview with Senator George Smathers.

323 *To Larry Newman*: Author interview with Larry Newman.

324 *"I wish I had"*: Author interview with Joe McCarthy.

324 *"The President's taste"*: Author interview with General Godfrey McHugh.

324 *"Jack was a romantic"*: Author interview with Laura Bergquist.

324 *"I don't think"*: Author interview with McHugh.

324 *"I wish my father"*: Interview with Doris Kearns Goodwin, "Geraldo: 'The Kennedys: The Dark Side of the Dynasty,'" Feb. 20, 1990.

324 *"I remember"*: Oral history interview with Robert Kennedy by John Bartlow Martin, p. 644, JFK Library.

324 *"No one got in"*: Author interview with General Godfrey McHugh.

325 *"Jackie knew"*: Ibid.

325 *"was extraordinarily"*: Interview with Dr. Jane Travell by Theodore Sorensen, Jan. 20, 1966, p. 7, JFK Library.

325 *White House logs*: Nicholas Cage, "Link of Kennedy Friend to Mafia Is Still a Puzzle," *The New York Times*, April 12, 1976; *Time*, Dec. 29, 1975.

326 *"fairly erotic"*: Richard E. Burke, with William and Marilyn Hoffer, *The Senator: My Ten Years with Ted Kennedy*, p. 108.

326 *In her memoir*: Garry Wills, *The Kennedy Imprisonment: A Meditation on Power*, p. 23.

326 *"Criticism of alleged"*: Author interview with Arthur Schlesinger, Jr.

326 *"When you think"*: Author interview with Charles Spalding.

326 *Kennedy once startled*: "Jack Kennedy's Other Women," *Time*, Dec. 29, 1975, p. 11.

327 *"The old man"*: Author interview with Senator George Smathers.

327 *"He told us"*: Author interview with Smathers; Beschloss, p. 107.

327 *"There is a plot"*: "JFK, Questioning the Myth," interview with Michael Beschloss, "Larry King Live," June 21, 1991.

327 *"Someone was"*: Author interview with George Smathers.

328 *"Bobby was getting"*: Author interview with Sarah McLendon.

328 *"And Bobby said"*: Author interview with Hugh Sidey.

329 *"because Jack"*: Martin, *Hero*, p. 335.

329 *"I think we've"*: Beschloss, *The Crisis Years*, p. 119.

329 *Three months*: Obituary of Richard Bissell, *The New York Times*, Feb. 8, 1994.

329 *As the defeat*: Wills, p. 248.

329 *"If you're in a fight"*: Martin, *Hero*, p. 330.

329 *"I should have"*: Joseph McCarthy papers; *Johnny We Hardly Knew Ye*, p. 278.

8

CRISES AND SWIMMING POOLS

331 *"How could I"*: Author interview with Evelyn Lincoln.

332 *"I felt so sorry"*: Coughlan Papers, Rose Kennedy.

332 *What he had to do*: Author interview with Judge Louis Oberdorfer.

332 *"You people"*: Richard Goodwin, *Remembering America*, p. 400.

333 *"I'm in a situation"*: Author interview with General Maxwell Taylor.

333 *"For two full days"*: Author interview with Clark Clifford.

333 *Robert Kennedy became*: Author interview with General Maxwell Taylor.

334 *"the most unpleasant"*: Beschloss, *The Crisis Years*, p. 143; Billings diary, May 7, 1971.

334 *"So you want"*: Barry Goldwater, pp. 136–38.

334 *"took his fork"*: Author interview with Senator George Smathers.

334 *"He's the luckiest"*: Author interview with Hugh Sidey.

335 *"We got to talking"*: Author interview with Larry Newman.

335 *"Lem was in"*: Oral history interview with J. B. West, JFK Library.

336 *"Lem was great"*: Oral history interview with Charles Bartlett, p. 105, Billings Collection, JFK Library.

336 *"What could he"*: Collier and Horowitz, *The Kennedys*, p. 120; JFK to LB, Feb. 12, 1942, Billings Papers, JFK Library.

338 *Kennedy was also fascinated*: Interview with Laura Bergquist by Nelson Aldrich, JFK Library.

338 *At the same time*: Author interview with Laura Bergquist.

338 *"How would you"*: George Lardner, Jr., "Aide Tells JFK's View on Killings," *New York Post*, July 21, 1975.

338 *"Look, I'd like"*: Martin, *Hero*, p. 508.

239 *"The only way"*: Taylor Branch and George Crile III, *The Kennedy Vendetta*, p. 16; *New York Post*, July 21, 1975; Beschloss p. 411.

239 *"I was surprised"*: Ibid.

340 *Bobby still did*: Reeves, footnotes p. 714.

340 *"Here I am"*: Beschloss, pp. 140, 142, Giancana file, FBI, Stephen Fox, *Blood and Power*:

Organized Crime in Twentieth Century America, p. 341.

341 *"Bobby pushed"*: Author interview with William G. Hundley.

342 *Campbell told*: James Spada, *Peter Lawford, the Man Who Kept the Secrets*, p. 285.

342 *"Yes, he did"*: Interview with Antoinette Giancana, "Larry King Live," CNN, Feb. 24, 1992.

342 *Hoover detailed . . . "Jack called me"*: Nicholas Cage, "Link of Kennedy Friend to Mafia Is Still a Puzzle," *The New York Times*, April 12, 1976.

343 *"For the President"*: Author interview with Benjamin C. Bradlee.

343 *Bradlee believed*: Ibid.

343 *"The adjectives"*: *Time*, April 21, 1961, "The Presidency," quoting article in *The New Republic* by James MacGregor Burns.

344 *"Well, Mr. President"*: Author interview with Ed Welsh.

345 *"No, I showed"*: Author interview with Charles Bartlett.

345 *"What are Negroes"*: Author interview with Charles Roberts.

345 *"People had JFK"*: Paul Samuelson, "Conversations," *The New York Times*, Oct. 31, 1993, p. 7.

345 *"Remember, you never"*: Garry Wills, pp. 208–9.

346 *"It's more important"*: Oral history interview with Nicholas Katzenbach by Larry Hackman, JFK Library.

346 *"you'd be dead"*: Schlesinger, p. 298; Victor Lasky, *Robert Kennedy*, p. 428.

346 *The issue of Freedom Riders*: Author interview with Kenneth O'Donnell.

347 *"a cent of money"*: Diane Winter D'Alemberta essay, in *Fruitful Bough*, pp. 264–65.

347 *Billings usually joined*: Interview with Billings by Collier and Horowitz, *The Kennedys*, p. 275.

348 *"Have you made"*: Sidey, pp. 175–76.

348 *She later reported*: Rose Kennedy, p. 492.

348 *"terribly sensitive"*: Oral history interview with Lemoyne Billings, JFK Library.

348 *"Rose was a tough"*: Author interview with Laura Bergquist.

348 *"Would you clarify"*: Halberstam, *The Best and Brightest*, p. 89; Reeves, p. 152.

348 *"You know, Monsieur"*: Author interview with Jim Deakin.

349 *"as a cripple"*: He said this to his aide, General Chester Clifton.

349 *"Khrushchev is supposed"*: Heymann, p. 305; Beschloss, *The Crisis Years*, p. 193.

349 *"How much of JFK's"*: Author interview with Marianne Means.

349 *"No President"*: *The New York Times*, Dec. 4, 1972.

350 *"I don't care"*: Heymann, p. 313.

350 *"Eisenhower I could"*: Author interview with Ben Loeb.

351 *"I must learn"*: Rose Kennedy, pp. 404–05.

351 *"I am certain"*: Max Lerner, New York *Post*, June 6, 1961.

351 *"Khrushchev scared"*: Martin, *Hero*, p. 351.

351 *Johnson even dropped*: Kern, p. 263.

351 *"When you have"*: Beschloss, *The Crisis Years*, p. 234.

351 *But . . . Sunday Times*: Henry Brandon, *Special Relationships*, p. 169.

352 *"Not too well"*: Evelyn Lincoln, *My Twelve Years with John Kennedy*, pp. 268–75.

352 *"Talking to him"*: Collier and Horowitz, pp. 277–78.

352 *"I remember"*: Interview with James Reston by David Halberstam, Halberstam Papers, Mugar Memorial Library, Special Collections, Boston University.

352 *"I have two problems"*: Ibid.

353 *"with whom"*: Oral history interview with Robert Kennedy by John Bartlow Martin, JFK Library.

353 *"was like dealing"*: Beschloss, *The Crisis Years*, p. 234; Collier and Horowitz, pp. 277–78.

353 *"Just when you think"*: Author interview with Dave Powers.

353 *"Ted Kennedy, of course"*: Hervé Alphand, *L'Étonnement d'être: Journal 1939–73*.

353 *"Teddy Kennedy was then"*: *Newsweek*, Aug. 7, 1961, p. 72.

354 *"and suddenly I was"*: Shelley Winters, *The Middle of My Century*, p. 381.

354 *"In fact, he used"*: Interview with Rose Kennedy by Robert Coughlan, Coughlan Papers.

354 *" 'Ted, for crying' "*: Author interview with James Symington.

355 *"Ted's going to"*: David, *Ethel*, p. 77.

355 *"Ted, you've got"*: Author interview with James Symington.

355 *It was an unpaid*: Author interview with David Acheson.

355 *"the hardest worker"*: Thomas Morgan, "Teddy," *Esquire*, April 1962, box 12, JFK Library.

355 *"I was hearing"*: Oral history interview with Garret Byrne by John Steward, p. 27, JFK Library.

356 *"the old man"*: Author interview with Charles Bartlett.

356 *"You fellas"*: Author interview with Jim Rowe.

356 *"This wasn't"*: Interview with Rose Kennedy by Robert Coughlan, Coughlan Papers.

356 *John Sharon recalled:* Author interview with John Sharon.

357 *"You can't have":* Fletcher Knebel, "Jack Kennedy: First Catholic in the White House?" Detroit *News*, Nov. 1, 1959, page 4G. Box 12, JFK Library.

357 *"I don't know":* Author interview with Charles Bartlett.

357 *"Dad, don't be":* Author interview with Charles Spalding.

357 *"It's your turn":* Author interview with Marianne Means.

357 *"Nobody forced me":* Burton Hersh, *The Education of Edward Kennedy*, p. 147.

357 *"Teddy came":* Eunice Kennedy Shriver, *McCall's*, June 1965.

358 *"We always shuddered":* Author interview with George Ball.

358 *"Take good care":* Author interview with Dave Powers.

359 *"If my Dad":* Martin, *Hero*, p. 435.

359 *"The love each":* Rita Dallas, R.N., with Jeanira Ratcliffe, "The Kennedy Case," *McCall's*, 1973, p. 134.

359 *"He went in":* Author interview with James Symington.

360 *"The father so":* Author interview with Ted Sorensen.

360 *"Everyone thought":* Interview with J.R.C.S. (staff member), Coughlan Papers.

361 *"they would sit":* Interview with Dr. Henry Betts by Robert Coughlan, Coughlan Papers, July 6, 1972, p. 6.

361 *"One thing":* Dallas with Ratcliffe, "Kennedy Case."

361 *"Next to my husband":* Martin, p. 95.

362 *"I hope he suffers":* Interview with Dr. Henry Betts by Robert Coughlan, Coughlan Papers, July 6, 1972, p. 6.

362 *"went with me":* Interview with Evelyn Jones by Robert Coughlan, Coughlan Papers.

362 *"He was in a walker":* Ibid.

362 *"Throughout the meal":* Richard Whelan Papers, box 1, JFK Library.

362 *"You talk about":* Interview with JCRS by Robert Coughlan, Sept. 3, 1972, Coughlan Papers.

363 *"it was a very moving":* Author interview with Larry Newman.

363 *"was almost the best":* Oral history Interview with Robert F. Kennedy by John Bartlow Martin, pp. 243–44, JFK Library.

363 *Bob and Ted went:* Author interview with General Maxwell Taylor.

363 *"It was strange":* Author interview with Lord Harlech (David Ormsby-Gore).

364 *"This is my rocker":* Ibid.

364 *"It would be great":* Author interview with Arthur Goldberg.

364 *"Jim Landis was":* Ibid.

364 *"Bob was pushing":* Author interview with John Nolan.

364 *"Mr. Kennedy was in":* Author interview with Angie Novello.

365 *"What other father":* Author interview with Kay Halle.

365 *"All the brothers":* Author interview with Rowland Evans.

9
MARILYN AND MISSILES

367 *"I wouldn't stay":* Fourth Interview with John Seigenthaler, Feb. 23, 1966, by Ronald J. Grele, Nashville, TN, for the JFK Library.

368 *"regard the family's":* Schlesinger, p. 600; *The New York Times*, Aug. 18, 1976; Willy Brandt, *Begegnungen und Einsichten* (1976).

369 *Jack told:* Author interview with Charles Spalding.

369 *"I want you":* Author interview with Pierre Salinger.

369 *"We're having more":* Warren Rogers, "Ted Kennedy: Talks About the Past, and His Future," *Look*, March 4, 1969, p. 45.

369 *John Sharon, an associate:* Author interview with John Sharon.

369 *"I just spoke":* Author interview with Benjamin C. Bradlee.

370 *"I know my Republican":* *Life*, John F. Kennedy Memorial Issue, 1963.

370 *"I used to call":* Author interview with Dave Powers.

371 *His old friend Edward:* Author interview with Edward McLaughlin.

371 *After Kennedy's first year:* Undated clipping, *The New York Times*.

371 *"I think Jack":* Author interview with Laura Bergquist.

371 *Detailed on the night:* Don Oberdorfer, "JFK, Sex, Marijuana," New York *Post*, Feb. 23, 1976, p. 2.

372 *"this was the night"*: Author interview with Blair Clark.

372 *"to protect"*: Ibid.

372 *"The whole dark side"*: Author interview with Hugh Sidey.

372 *"You know, in the end"*: Author interview with William Walton.

373 *"You know, a President"*: Author interview with Betty Beale.

373 *"There are two"*: Private interview by Collier and Horowitz, *The Kennedys*, p. 310.

373 *"When you deal"*: Martin, *Hero*, pp. 412–15, based on author's interviews with James Symington and Benjamin C. Bradlee, as well as RFK interviews for oral history, JFK Library. William Safire, "The Kennedy Transcripts," *The New York Times*, March 22, 1975.

374 *"didn't want Bobby"*: Author interview with Kenneth O'Donnell, Sept. 24, 1970.

375 *"The Attorney General"*: Author interview with Arthur Schlesinger, Jr.

375 *"Sometimes Jack and Jackie"*: Author interview with Angie Novello.

375 *"Only once"*: Private interview.

375 *"but I don't"*: Author interview with Charles Spalding.

375 *The sharper fact*: Author interview with Laura Bergquist.

376 *Reporter Fred Sparks*: *Family Circle*, July 10, 1970.

376 *"Whenever we came"*: Interview with Paul "Red" Fay by Collier and Horowitz, *The Kennedys*, p. 288.

376 *"She told a story"*: Author interview with Benjamin C. Bradlee.

376 *"couldn't take his eyes"*: James Spada, Peter Lawford, *The Man Who Kept the Secrets*, p. 189.

377 *"Peter Lawford disguised"*: Patricia Seaton Lawford quoted on "Geraldo," Dec. 7, 1998; also in *The Dark Side of Camelot: The Peter Lawford Story*.

377 *"I'll never . . . I think I made"*: *Time*, Dec. 29, 1975, pp. 10–12; Earl Wilson, *Show Business Laid Bare*, p. 11.

377 *"The President always"*: Author interview with Patricia Lasky.

377 *They were not the most discreet*: Brown and Barham, "Dangerous Liaisons," *People*, Aug. 10, 1992, p. 67.

378 *"When she came down"*: Author interview with Hugh Sidey.

378 *"What an ass"*: Patte B. Barham and Peter Harry Brown, *Marilyn: The Last Take*, p. 149.

378 *"She was carefully"*: Ibid.

378 *"I learned from an FBI"*: Interview with Earl Wilson, Brown and Barham, *Dangerous Liaisons*.

379 *"Marilyn realized"*: Interview with Peter Lawford by C. David Heymann in *A Woman Named Jackie*, pp. 366–67.

379 *"She took it"*: Ibid.

379 *Jack and Ted both*: Margaret Montagno, *Newsweek*, Jan. 26, 1976.

379 *"Everybody in New York"*: Author interview with Joe McCarthy.

379 *Bobby boasted*: Jerry Oppenheimer, *The Other Mrs. Kennedy*, p. 237.

379 *"I attended"*: Lester David, *Ethel*, pp. 132–33.

380 *"I was sitting"*: Author interview with Joan Braden.

380 *Her masseur*: Brown and Barham, "Dangerous Liaisons," *People*, Aug. 10, 1992, p. 63; Barham and Brown, *Marilyn*.

381 *A blond actress*: Lester David and Irene David, *Bobby Kennedy*, pp. 175, 177; "The Last Days of Marilyn Monroe," BBC documentary.

381 *"What about Bobby"*: Oppenheimer, p. 241.

381 *"With Bob Kennedy"*: Author interview with Dave Richardson.

381 *"I didn't believe"*: Author interview with Hugh Sidey.

381 *Bobby had been taped*: Jack Anderson, with Les Whitten, New York *Post*, Jan. 13, 1976.

381 *"Robert Kennedy promised"*: "Dangerous Liaisons."

382 *"How are Marilyn"*: *The Dark Side of Camelot*, p. 464.

382 *"They argued"*: Ibid.

383 *"Marilyn Monroe knew"*: Interview with Sam Giancana, "Larry King Live," CNN, Feb. 24, 1992.

385 *"widely regarded"*: Reston, *Deadline*, p. 297.

386 *"He's an arrogant"*: Robert Sherrill, *The Last Kennedy*, pp. 38–39, quoting undated *New Republic* article.

386 *"The Kennedys will be"*: Victor Lasky, *J.F.K.: The Man and the Myth*, p. 62.

386 *"He's going to run"*: Author interview with Larry Newman.

386 *One skeptical woman delegate*: David, *Good Ted, Bad Ted*, p. 75; *Time*, June 15, 1962.

387 *"I felt a little"*: Author interview with Max Kampelman.

387 *Larry Newman recalled*: Author interview with Larry Newman.

388 *"This nation"*: Remarks at dedication of Aerospace Medical Health Center, San Antonio, Texas, Nov. 21, 1963, in *Public Papers of the President*, vol. 3, pp. 471–72.

388 *Jack Newfield once*: Jack Newfield, *Robert Kennedy: A Memoir*, p. 46.

389 *"Bobby wanted me"*: Oral history interview with Thurgood Marshall by Ed Edwin, Co-

lumbia University, pp. 8–9, #1595, Session 3.

389 *"For Bobby, that firsthand"*: Author interview with Adam Yarmolinsky.

389 *"there was a little girl"*: Interview with Pete Hamill in *American Journey*, p. 89.

390 *"You could just tell"*: Author interview with William Hundley.

390 *"a kind of groping"*: Interviews by Jean Stein, in Stein and Plimpton, *American Journey*, pp. 278–79.

390 *Sorensen noted:* Author interview with Theodore Sorensen.

390 *"Don't worry"*: Interview with Charles Spalding by Collier and Horowitz, p. 289.

391 *"Mister President"*: Halberstam, *Bobby*, p. 140.

391 *"Bob would call"*: Author interview with Angie Novello.

391 *The Attorney General:* Author interview with William Hundley; oral history interview with Hundley, JFK Library; Schlesinger, p. 324.

392 *"Bobby's final words"*: Interview with Nicholas Katzenbach by Jean Stein, *American Journey*, p. 104.

392 *"Jack had something"*: Author interview with Charles Spalding.

393 *"We could just visualize"*: Oral history interview with RFK, JFK Library.

394 *Even Jack Kennedy:* Oral history interview with Tobridy, box 5, JFK Library.

394 *" 'I am very flattered' "*: Oral history interview with Richardson Dilworth, pp. 22–23, JFK Library.

394 *"Once, at a fund-raising"*: Author interview with Jim Rowe.

394 *"I don't know"*: Author interview with John Nolan.

395 *" 'Gee, I don't want' "*: Thomas P. O'Neill, "The American Experience: The Kennedys," WGBH-TV, Sept. 21, 1992.

395 *"You're running"*: Richard Reeves, p. 324.

395 *"Bobby and I"*: Author interview with Benjamin C. Bradlee.

395 *"Teddy had six"*: Thomas Morgan, *Esquire*, April 1962.

396 *"I lead"*: *Ladies' Home Journal*, October 1962, box 5, JFK Library.

396 *Newsweek reported: Newsweek* quoted in William Peters, *Redbook*, June 1962, p. 68.

396 *Ted told them:* Richard E. Burke, with William and Marilyn Hoffer, *The Senator: My Ten Years With Ted Kennedy*, p. 11.

397 *"Teddy also spoke"*: Oral history interview with Peter Lisagor, by Ronald Grele, p. 20, Columbia University.

397 *"He was the type"*: Author interview with Lester David.

397 *"I keep my speeches"*: *Esquire*, April 1962, box 5, JFK Library.

397 *"Charisma, hell"*: Stewart Alsop, *Saturday Evening Post*, Oct. 27, 1962.

398 *"He can do more"*: Beschloss, p. 367.

398 *"Ted debated"*: Interview with Milton Gwirtzman by Ronald Grele, JFK Library.

398 *"Personally"*: James MacGregor Burns, *Edward Kennedy and the Camelot Legacy*, p. 80.

399 *"Teddy was not"*: Author interview with Dave Powers.

399 *"Relax, Ted"*: "The Kennedy Mystique," *The New York Times Magazine*, June 17, 1979.

399 *"Now that Ted"*: Aug. 1, 1962, Beaverbrook Papers, Beaverbrook Library, House of Lords Library, London.

399 *"to take an interest"*: Ibid., Aug. 12, 1962.

400 *"My mother"*: *Esquire*, April 1962, typed excerpt, box 5, JFK Library.

400 *"sitting in the Oval"*: "The American Experience: The Kennedys."

400 *"If you get"*: Oral history Interview with Milton Gwirtzman by Roberta W. Greene, RFK Oral History, pp. 16–17, JFK Library.

402 *"Eddie McCormack was very"*: Ibid.

402 *"Ted is winning"*: Author interview with Admiral Tazewell Shepherd.

402 *"There is a sort"*: Murray B. Levin, *Kennedy Campaigning*, p. 26; *The Kennedy Neurosis*, p. 340.

402 *"I am Teddy"*: "The American Experience: The Kennedys."

403 "Shit!": Beschloss, p. 5.

403 *"[Defense Minister] Malinovsky"*: Fedor Burlatsky, *The New York Times*, Oct. 23, 1992, Op-Ed page.

403 *"If I had been"*: Robert S. McNamara, *The New York Times*, Oct. 21, 1991.

404 *"This was the stupidest"*: Burlatsky, *The New York Times*, Oct. 23, 1992.

404 *It was later revealed: The New York Times*, Op-Ed page article by J. Anthony Lukas, Jan. 20, 1992. Code name was "Anadyr." General Staff Archives, file 6, volume 2, p. 144.

404 *"No one should believe"*: *The New York Times*, Nov. 2, 1992, letter to the editor.

404 *"the only person"*: Oral history interview with Robert Kennedy, JFK on the Presidency, JFK Library, p. 1.

404 *The reason why:* Oral history interview with W. Averell Harriman by Edward W. Barrett, p. 40, Columbia Oral History.

405 *"I saw Bolshakov"*: Oral history interview with Robert Kennedy, JFK on the Presidency, JFK Library, p. 1.

405 *Even in this time:* Martin, *Hero*, p. 459.

405 *Bobby wanted the Russians:* Interview with John Seigenthaler by Bill Singer, Southern

Intellectual Leaders Project, Part II 31197 PRCQ, University of North Carolina, Chapel Hill.

406 "*Bobby was ringleader*": Author interview with Robert Allen.

406 "*I just didn't have*": Author interview with Paul Nitze.

407 "*Darling, there's*": Author interview with Susan Mary Alsop.

407 *Whenever the President held*: *Hero*, pp. 463–64.

408 "*His greatest relaxation*": Author interview with Larry Newman.

409 "*My son, my poor*": Martin, *Hero*, p. 467.

409 "*His hand went*": Ibid. pp. 466–67.

409 "*on the edge*": Ibid.

409 "*Jack and Bobby*": Author interview with Robert McNamara.

409 "*they communicated*": Sorensen, *Kennedy*, p. 268.

409 "*He was becoming*": Author interview with Harold Reis.

410 "*You could tell*": Oral history interview with Gerald Tremblay by Roberta Greene, Jan. 8, 1970, p. 5, RFK Oral History, JFK Library.

410 "*I can't see*": Author interview with George Ball.

410 "*This had, of course*": Interview with George Ball by Jean Stein, *American Journey*, pp. 131–32.

410 *Alexis Johnson*: Author interview with Alexis Johnson.

410 "*a real turning*": Martin, *Hero*, p. 461.

410 *Acheson was seriously*: Author interview with Ray Cline, Dec. 6, 1979.

411 "*We all knew*": Ibid.

411 *The President had promised*: William Safire, *The New York Times*, Jan. 20, 1992.

411 "*He was with*": Author interview with Dave Powers.

411 "*Jackie had gone*": Ibid.

412 "*I had the strangest*": Ibid.

412 "*I never thought*": Author interview with George Ball.

413 "*Bobby hasn't eaten*": Author interview with Dave Powers.

413 *What the Soviets*: Fedor Burlatsky, *The New York Times*, Oct. 23, 1992, Op-Ed page.

414 "*deeply humiliating*": *The New York Times*, Jan. 20, 1992, A-19, article by J. Anthony Lukas.

414 "*the Soviets never*": Pierre Salinger, "Good Morning America," Jan. 7, 1992.

414 "*Thank God*": Author interview with Dave Powers.

414 "*Looking back*": Schlesinger, *Robert Kennedy and His Times*, p. 555; Robert McNamara, April 14, 1968, RFK Papers, JFK library; Harold Macmillan and Lord Harlech discuss missile crisis with Robert MacNeil, "Listener," Jan. 30, 1969.

414 *A later review*: Raymond L. Garthoff, a senior fellow at the Brookings Institution who had worked at the State Department in 1962, quoted by Robert Pear, "The Cuban Missile Crisis," *The New York Times*, Jan. 7, 1992.

415 *After it was over*: Author interview with Benjamin C. Bradlee.

10

DEATH AND MYTH

418 "*Was his ultimate*": Author interview with Earl Mazo.

418 "*Frankly, the Democratic*": Sherrill, p. 45.

418 "*Which way*": Lester David, *Ted Kennedy: Triumphs and Tragedies*, p. 160.

419 "*Teddy was from*": "Now It's Ted's Turn," Dallas *Morning News*, Nov. 7, 1979, page 23A, box 11, JFK Library.

419 "*He did not let*": Oral history interview with Milton Gwirtzman, Jan. 19, 1966, p. 35, JFK Library.

420 "*Some pipeline*": Author interview with Benjamin C. Bradlee.

420 "*Teddy called*": Martin, *Hero*, p. 409.

420 *Congressman Tip O'Neill*: David, p. 122.

420 "*Jack must've*": Author interview with Charles Spalding.

420 *But the fact was*: Author interview with Ted Kennedy.

420 "*In our family*": David, p. 119.

421 "*When Jack Kennedy*": Ibid., p. 240.

421 "*Sometimes you have*": Author interview with Benjamin Bradlee.

422 "*I knew Teddy*": Author interview with Senator Claiborne Pell.

422 "*The Senate was meeting*": Author interview with Sarah McLendon.

422 "*And I would point*": Theodore Sorensen, "Ted Kennedy's Memories of JFK," *McCall's*, Nov. 1973.

423 "*When a man*": Reeves, p. 654.

423 "in joining his brother": Wilfrid Sheed, *The Kennedy Legacy*, p. 170.

424 *A* Newsweek *article:* Newsweek, March 18, 1963, p. 26.

424 "Then I changed": Oral history interview with Robert Kennedy by John Bartlow Martin, Bobby & JFK, p. 1, JFK Library.

425 "I hope that": Navasky, p. 32; Schlesinger, p. 330.

426 "You know, I have": Oral history interview with Kenneth Clark by Ed Edwin, p. 40, Columbia University.

427 "Johnson was a fish": Author interview with Ed Morgan.

427 "awfully lonely": Interview with Charles Bartlett by Fred Holborn, Jan. 6, 1965, p. 157, JFK Library.

427 "that goddamn": Author interview with Robert S. Allen.

427 "Bobby is first": Author notes for Martin, *Hero*, Mugar Memorial Library, Special Collections, Boston University; Merle Miller Papers (interview Bell).

428 "Robert Kennedy would stand": Califano, p. 64; oral history interview with Victoria McCannon, LBJ Library.

428 *Johnson once told:* Interview with Senator Frank Church by Merle Miller, Merle Miller Papers.

428 "He's one guy": Author interview with Larry Newman.

428 "Now, I understand": Interview with Jack Valenti by Merle Miller, Merle Miller Papers.

428 "there was never": Oral history interview with Robert Kennedy by John Bartlow Martin, p. 308, JFK Library.

428 *It was Eunice:* Margaret Laing, *The Next Kennedy*, p. 247.

429 *On a plane:* Oral history interview with Kenneth O'Donnell by Paige E. Mulhollan, June 23, 1969, LBJ Library.

429 "Jack used to grumble": Author interview with Arthur Goldberg.

429 "After a formal": Author interview with Larry Newman.

430 "Go get": Collier and Horowitz, *The Kennedys*, p. 278; Time, Feb. 16, 1962.

430 "Fucked again!": Interview with James Greenfield by Halberstam. Halberstam Papers.

430 "The Secret Service": Author interview with General Godfrey McHugh.

431 "I told him how": Author interview with McGeorge Bundy.

433 "I talked to Jack": Oral history interview with Justice William Douglas by Greene, p. 7, JFK Library.

434 *At one meeting:* Warren Rogers, *When I Think of Bobby*, pp. 118–19.

434 "I spoke to my brother": Oral history interview with Robert F. Kennedy by John Bartlow Martin, pp. 521–22, JFK Library.

434 "I don't think": Oral history interview with Burke Marshall by T. H. Baker, Oct. 28, 1968, LBJ Oral History, AC74-215, pp. 14–15, LBJ Library.

435 "Hell, Kennedy": Author interview with Ed Plaut.

435 "They beat him": Author interview with Jim Deakin.

435 "When I was": Ibid.

436 "I have a few": "Primetime Live: Profile in Courage," ABC News, Dec. 31, 1992.

437 "They were conversing": Interview with Evelyn Jones by Robert Coughlan, Coughlan Papers.

438 "to go over there": Author interview with Larry Newman.

438 "He never wanted": Beschloss, p. 631.

438 "I was with him": Author interview with Evelyn Lincoln.

438 "He just cried": Author interview with Dave Powers.

438 "Bobby had": Ibid.

439 "Come on, Jack": Oral history interview, Richard Cardinal Cushing, JFK Library.

439 "Most men": Laura Bergquist Papers. Special Collections, Mugar Memorial Library, Boston University.

439 "You're not born": Author interview with William Walton.

439 "He talked about": Laura Bergquist papers.

439 "Who do you think": Oral history interview with Charles Bartlett by Fred Holborn, JFK Library, Jan. 6, 1965, p. 156.

440 "because he'd be": Ibid.

440 "The march": Reeves, p. 580.

440 *A California poll:* Sorensen, *Kennedy*, p. 504.

440 "but the moral": Oral interview with Harris Wofford, March 29, 1965, JFK Library.

440 "This issue": Ibid, p. 506.

441 "Fuck that": Schlesinger, *Robert Kennedy*, p. 351.

441 "Bobby, what": Author interview with James Symington.

441 "Hoover quietly": Anthony Summers, *Official and Confidential*, p. 450; Athan Theoharis, *Secret Files*, p. 99.

441 "I don't think": Author interview with Evelyn Lincoln.

442 "While the guests": Time, Oct. 11, 1963.

442 "He wore": Author interview with Lincoln.

442 "Every spring": Oral history interview with Dr. Janet Travell by Theodore Sorensen, Jan. 20, 1966, p. 19, JFK Library.

442 "Obviously, he felt": T. George Harris, "Eight Views of JFK" Look, Nov. 17, 1964.

442 *"His health"*: Interview with Travell.

443 *"my brother was determined"*: Schlesinger, *Robert Kennedy*, p. 701.

443 *"Vietnam . . . we have"*: David Halberstam, *The Best and the Brightest*, p. 77.

444 *"On a field"*: Author interview with Dave Powers.

444 *"but his voice"*: Author interview with Alexis Johnson.

444 *"That made"*: Author interview with General Maxwell Taylor.

444 *"If we converted"*: Arthur Schlesinger, Jr., *A Thousand Days*; "JFK and Vietnam," *The New York Times Book Review*, March 29, 1992, p. 3.

444 *"I've had the Bay"*: Schlesinger, *Robert Kennedy*, p. 705.

445 *"Kennedy was not"*: Interview with George Ball by David Halberstam, Halberstam Papers, Mugar Memorial Library, Special Collections, Boston University.

445 *"I think the United States"*: Schlesinger, p. 713; *The New York Times*, Feb. 19, 1962.

446 *The confusion of U.S.*: Sorensen, *The Kennedy Legacy*, p. 206.

447 *"I think Jack"*: Author interview with Senator George Smathers.

447 *"The American people"*: Roger Hilsman, *The New York Times*, letter to the editor, Jan. 20, 1992.

447 *"including the helicopter"*: Author interview with Robert McNamara.

447 *"even if the South Vietnamese"*: Herbert Mitgang review of *Promise and Power: the Life and Times of Robert McNamara*, by Deborah Shapley, in *The New York Times*, Feb. 3, 1993.

447 *"I think he would"*: Author interview with James Rowe.

448 *"Oh, that look"*: Author interview with Dave Powers.

448 *"Look at him"*: Ibid.

448 *And yet the voice*: Author interview with John Sharon.

448 *"I have no fear"*: Author interview with Larry Newman.

449 *"Did you ever"*: Ibid.

449 *"I think it was Labor Day"*: Memorandum to author from Andrea Cormier.

450 *"The only way"*: Interview with John Kennedy by Ed Plaut for FRDH.

450 *"Mr. President, do you"*: Author interview with General Godfrey McHugh.

451 *Representative Hale Boggs*: Oral history interview with Hale Boggs by T. H. Baker, March 13, 1969, pp. 20–21, LBJ Library.

451 *Bob Kennedy told*: Oral history interview with Ramsey Clark, Feb. 11, 1969, p. 18, National Archives.

451 *"God, I hate"*: Author interview with George Smathers.

451 *"I know he got"*: Interview with Jacqueline Kennedy Onassis by Joe Franz, Jan. 11, 1974, AC78-32, p. 5, LBJ Library.

451 *"I really don't think"*: Author interview with Larry Newman.

451 *"The day we went"*: Author interview with Marianne Means.

452 *He stood in that circle*: "Robert's Character," *Esquire*, April 1975.

452 *The President's secretary*: Author interview with Evelyn Lincoln.

452 *"There's no way"*: Author interview with Larry Newman.

453 *"It was just horrible"*: Interview with Jean Hill, "The Maury Povich Show," Nov. 22, 1991.

454 *"Jacqueline Kennedy"*: Dennis L. Breo, "Examining JFK," *People*, June 8, 1992.

454 *"Oh, God!"*: "The Day Kennedy Died," *Newsweek*, Dec. 2, 1963, p. 23.

454 *"I burst into tears"*: Interview with Tom Wicker on National Public Radio, Nov. 20, 1993.

455 *"Jack's been shot"*: Schlesinger, *Robert Kennedy and His Times*, pp. 635–36; Interview with Robert Morgenthau by Jean Stein, *American Journey*.

455 *Forty minutes later*: Summers, p. 315.

456 *"Bob would gladly"*: William Shannon, *The Heir Apparent*, p. 69.

456 *"There's so much"*: Rogers, p. 121.

456 *John McCone*: Beschloss, p. 672.

457 *"Even when I heard"*: Interview with Rose Kennedy by Robert Coughlan, Coughlan Papers.

457 *"She recovered"*: Interview with Gloria Guinness by Robert Coughlan, Coughlan Papers.

457 *"the thing which"*: *Fruitful Bough*, p. 265.

457 *"I was staring"*: Author interview with Stuart Symington.

457 *In the lobby*: David, *Ted Kennedy*, pp. 128–30.

457 *"His first thought"*: Oral history interview with Milton S. Gwirtzman by Ronald J. Grele, Jan. 19, 1966, pp. 42–43, JFK Library.

458 *"There was a crowd"*: Ibid.

458 *"His face was"*: McGinniss, p. 63.

459 *"It's extraordinary"*: Author interview with General Godfrey McHugh.

459 *"They're going to"*: Ibid.

460 *"You can't do"*: Oral history interview with Kenneth O'Donnell, LBJ Library.

460 *"So they went"*: Author interview with Charles Roberts.

460 *"Everybody kept"*: Theodore White, *In Search of History*, p. 544.

460 *"It was amazing"*: Author interview with Dave Powers.

460 *"We were supposed"*: Author interview with Lawrence O'Brien.

460 *"I was watching"*: Oral history interview with Hale Boggs by Morrissey, p. 35, JFK Library.

461 *"When we landed"*: Mary Berelli Gallagher, *My Life with Jacqueline Kennedy*, pp. 327–28.

461 *"The night Jack"*: Author interview with Charles Spalding.

461 *"There'll never"*: Author interview with Joan Braden.

462 *"I was there"*: Author interview with Dave Powers.

462 *"In pouring"*: Joseph Califano Jr., *The Triumph and Tragedy of Lyndon Johnson*, p. 14.

463 *Governess Maude Shaw*: Oral history interview with Robert Kennedy by William Manchester, pp. 63–65, JFK Library.

463 *At the funeral*: Dora Jane Hamblin, "Mrs. Kennedy's Decisions Shaped All the Solemn Pageantry," *Life* Magazine: John F. Kennedy Memorial Issue, 1963.

464 *Watching the procession*: Whelan Papers; Report from Ruth Mehrtens, *Time* Boston bureau, from Hyannis, Nov. 29, 1963, JFK Library.

464 *"He looked as if"*: Oral history interview with Milton Gwirtzman by Ronald J. Grele, Jan. 19, 1966, JFK Library.

464 *"tears streamed"*: Coughlan papers, Unpublished manuscript, p. 489.

465 *"It was a mass"*: Oral history interview with Lawrence F. O'Brien, #7, by Michael L. Gillette, Feb. 12, 1986, p. 8, LBJ Library.

466 *"He answered"*: Oral history interview with John Seigenthaler by Larry Hackman, June 5, 1970, p. 7, RFK Oral History, JFK Library.

466 *"Jackie called me"*: Author interview with General McHugh.

467 *"It's just that Irish"*: *The New York Times Magazine*, June 17, 1979, "The Kennedy Mystique," p. 18.

468 *"Someone, I forget"*: Oral history interview with Milton Gwirtzman by Roberta Greene, p. 19, RFK Oral History, JFK Library.

468 *"We owe"*: *Esquire*, July 1968, p. 90.

468 *"for Bobby's future"*: Author interview with Ray Cline.

468 *"I think the distinction"*: Author interview with Mike Feldman.

468 *"One terribly"*: Author interview with Kay Halle; also oral history interview Kay Halle with McHugh, JFK Library.

469 *"to kill Cuban"*: Wofford, p. 418.

469 *His staff member*: Cartha DeLoach, FBI, in Washington *Post*, Dec. 13, 1977.

470 *"That story"*: Author interview with Evelyn Lincoln.

470 *"What is meant"*: Interview with Rose Kennedy, Los Angeles Times, April 20, 1969.

470 *"That has been"*: Joseph Kennedy III interview on "Good Morning America," July 13, 1990.

470 *"Rose bought"*: Collier and Horowitz, *The Kennedys*, p. 287.

471 *"I miss him"*: Theodore Sorensen, "Ted Kennedy's Memories of JFK," *McCall's*, Nov. 1973.

471 *"When the Kennedy"*: Author interview with Dave Powers.

472 *"He wasn't the father"*: Interview with William Walton in Clay Blair, Jr., Papers, box 56, file 4, p. 7.

472 *Much later, after*: Martin, *Hero*, p. 561.

11

OUT OF THE SHADOW

473 *"The only thing"*: Author interview with Charles Bartlett.

474 *"God damn the Kennedys!"*: Summers, *Official and Confidential*, p. 365; William Sullivan, *The Bureau*, pp. 48, 56.

474 *"almost both parts"*: Author interview with David Hackett.

474 *"When they buried"*: Interview with Lemoyne Billings by David and David, *Bobby Kennedy*, pp. 221–22.

474 *Nobody else*: Ibid., p. 270.

474 *" 'Well, you're young' "*: Interview with Mary McGrory by Collier and Horowitz, pp. 315–16.

474 *"Oh, how"*: Rogers, p. 172.

475 *"almost as if"*: Oral history interview with John Seigenthaler by Larry J. Hackman, p. 13, RFK Oral History, JFK Library.

475 *About that time*: Interview with Rose Kennedy by Robert Coughlan, Coughlan Papers.

475 *"Bobby talked"*: Author interview with Charles Spalding.

475 *"changed child"*: Bergquist and Tretick, p. 199.
475 *Two weeks*: Ibid., p. 198.
475 *"on behalf of"*: Rogers, p. 124.
476 *"But I explained"*: Interview with Jacqueline Kennedy Onassis by Joe B Frantz, Jan. 11, 1974, AC-70-32, pp. 13–16, LBJ Library.
476 *"Bobby would drop"*: Author interview with Dave Powers.
476 *"He's got to"*: David, *Ethel*, p. 126.
476 *"They became"*: Author interview with Angie Novello.
477 *"It was the first"*: Interview with David Brinkley by Jean Stein, Stein and Plimpton, *American Journey*, p. 146.
478 *"Lem used to say"*: Interview with Senator Edward M. Kennedy, Billings Collection, p. 67, JFK Library.
478 *"Lem told me"*: Interview with Robert Kennedy Jr. by Collier and Horowitz, p. 381.
478 *"I don't mean"*: Interview with Jacqueline Kennedy by Robert Coughlan, Coughlan Papers.
479 *"I think if he'd"*: Author interview with Evelyn Lincoln.
479 *"Then, I knew"*: Oral history interview with RFK by John Bartlow Martin, p. 639, JFK Library.
479 *"Those people"*: Interview with Joseph Dolan by Summers, Summers, p. 332.
479 *"But the minute"*: Interview with William Hundley by Summers, ibid.
479 *"At the end"*: Summers. p. 332; Navasky, p. 49.
479 *"No, son"*: Author interview with Hugh Sidey.
480 Columnist Murray Kempton: Murray Kempton, *Esquire*, July 1968, p. 90.
480 *"I tell you"*: Interview with Jacqueline Kennedy Onassis by Joe B. Frantz, Jan. 11, 1974, AC-70-32, pp. 13–16, LBJ Library.
480 *"It's funny"*: Ibid. pp. 6–8.
480 *"I suppose"*: Oral history interview with Henry McPherson by T. H. Baker, Dec. 5, 1968, p. 23, LBJ Library.
480 *"They were stream-"*: Author interview with Jim Deakin.
481 *"seldom clapped"*: Schlesinger, *Robert Kennedy*, p. 719; Congressman Donald Riegle of Michigan, Donald Riegle with Trevor Armbruster, *O Congress* (New York: Popular Library, 1972), p. 144.
481 *"had this habit"*: Oral history interview with Charles McNair by Joe B. Frantz, June 14, 1971, p. 8, LBJ Library.
481 *"Bobby scorned"*: Interview with Rowland Evans by Roberta Greene, July 30, 1970, pp. 16, 18, RFK Oral History, JFK Library.

481 *"may have bordered"*: Bobby Baker with Larry King, *Wheeling and Dealing*, p. 126.
481 *His only explanation*: Interview with Lawrence J. O'Brien by David Halberstam, Halberstam Papers.
481 *"He didn't like"*: Merle Miller Papers.
482 *"I didn't get"*: Oral history interview with RFK by William Manchester, pp. 71–72, JFK Library.
482 *"His general demeanor"*: Oral history interview with Orville Freeman by T. H. Baker, Feb. 14, 1969, p. 26, Accession Record No. 74-18, LBJ Library, University of Texas.
482 *"Three or four months"*: Oral history interview with Milton Gwirtzman by Roberta Greene, p. 20, RFK Oral History, JFK Library.
482 *"what happened"*: Harris Wofford, *Of Kennedys and Kings*, p. 417.
482 *"The first time"*: *Life*, April 1993, p. 65.
483 *"Before John Kennedy"*: Author interview with Larry Newman.
483 *An associate commented*: Oral history interview with Ramsey Clark by H. Baker, Oct. 30, 1968, LBJ Library.
483 *"What are my credentials"*: Author interview with Blair Clark.
484 *"I never saw"*: Author interview with David Hackett.
484 *"Sitting next to him"*: Jack Newfield, *Robert Kennedy*, p. 30.
484 *"never really wanted"*: Wofford, p. 415.
485 *"was hit"*: "Inside Politics," CNN, Nov. 30, 1993.
485 *"As we talked"*: Schlesinger, *Robert Kennedy*, p. 644; from Schlesinger journal, Oct. 30, 1966.
485 *"It is a proper"*: Lester David, *Jacqueline Kennedy Onassis*, p. 73.
485 *"had killed my brother"*: Oral history interview with Walter Sheridan by Roberta Greene, RFK Oral History, JFK Library.
485 *The Warren Commission*: Jack Ludwig, "Who Killed Kennedy?" *Partisan Review*, Winter 1965, p. 65.
486 *"one of the most promising"*: H. D. Fairlie, "Kennedy Assassination," *The New York Times*, Dec. 16, 1977.
486 *A psychologist*: *The Kennedy Neurosis*, pp. 293, 295.
486 *"He was sailing"*: Author interview with Dave Richardson.
486 *"You'll never get"*: Rogers, p. 128.
487 *"May Joe"*: Letter to Rose Kennedy, Nov. 24, 1963, Beaverbrook Papers.
487 *"I find Bobby"*: Ibid., Dec. 11, 1957.
487 *"Each of those kids"*: David, *Good Ted, Bad Ted*, p. 26.

487 *"Each one":* Author interview with Edward McLaughlin.

488 *"shrewd nonconformist":* William V. Shannon, *The Heir Apparent*, p. 253; Trevor Armbruster, "A Loser Makes It Big," *Saturday Evening Post*, Jan. 14, 1967.

488 *"It will take":* Gore Vidal, "Bobby Kennedy Buildup," *U.S. News & World Report*, March 4, 1963.

488 *"His face":* Pat Anderson, "Robert's Character," *Esquire*, April 1975, p. 142.

488 *"Bobby didn't":* Author interview with Edward Morgan.

488 *"Teddy old pal":* Garry Wills, *The Kennedy Imprisonment: A Meditation on Power*, p. 113.

488 *"If you just sat":* Oral history interview with Gerald Tremblay by Roberta Greene, Jan. 8, 1970, p. 13, RFK Oral History, JFK Library.

489 *"When one question":* Hugh Sidey, "John F. Kennedy, President," in Jay Davis, ed., *Kennedy Reader*, p. 248.

489 *"The President never":* Author interview with Dave Powers.

489 *"There wasn't a dry":* Author interview with Jim Smith.

489 *"Father, why":* Author interview with Kay Halle.

490 *"I've got to":* Schlesinger, *Robert Kennedy*, p. 292.

490 *"and he will get":* George Crile II, "The Mafia, The CIA, and Castro," *Washington Post*, May 16, 1976.

490 *"Bobby Kennedy is just":* Oral history interview with Walter Sheridan by Roberta Greer, pp. 3–4; JFK Library.

490 *"Carlos fucked up":* Frank Ragano and Selwyn Raab, *Mob Lawyer*, p. 356.

490 *"We should kill":* Wofford, p. 413.

491 *"Their ego":* A. H. Raskin, *The New York Times*, Dec. 20, 1992, p. 18.

491 *"You have to":* Author interview with William Hundley.

491 *"His biographies":* Murray Kempton, "The Emperor's Kid Brother," *Esquire*, July 1968, p. 92.

491 *"for an awful lot":* Oral history interview with RFK by John Bartlow Martin, p. 470, JFK Library.

492 *"He used to tell":* Ibid.

492 *"Bobby, you do not":* Interview with Charles Spalding by Jean Stein, *American Journey*, pp. 13–14.

492 *"it would be like":* Oral history interview with George Reedy, by Michael Gillette, Dec. 20, 1983, LBJ Library.

492 *"I know why":* Oral history interview with John Seigenthaler by William Geoghegan,

July 22, 1965, pp. 100–03, RFK Oral History, JFK Library.

492 *"Bobby didn't realize":* Author interview with Sarah McLendon.

493 *"Bob did a nice":* Author interview with Angie Novello.

494 *"I want to see":* Joe McGinniss, *The Last Brother*, p. 361.

495 *"I didn't understand":* Author interview with Hugh Sidey.

495 *"Somber and preoccupied":* Interview with John Seigenthaler by Collier and Horowitz, pp. 324–25.

496 *Later, Bob told:* Author interview with Rowland Evans.

497 *"If you're going":* Interview with Bill Moyers by Merle Miller, Miller Papers.

497 *"he would forever":* Clifford, p. 396.

497 *"Look, if I":* O'Donnell, Powers, and McCarthy, p. 391.

497 *"his Adam's apple":* Martin Papers, *Hero*.

497 *"unless he was":* Oral history interview with Lawrence O'Brien by Michael Gillette, Feb. 12, 1986, pp. 19–22, LBJ Library.

498 *"Jean heard":* Interview with Rose Kennedy by Robert Coughlan, p. 3, Coughlan Papers.

498 *"Is it true":* Burns, p. 69; Interview with RFK by John Bartlow Martin, JFK Library.

498 *"We just lay":* Oral history interview of Walter Sheridan by Roberta Greene, JFK Library; Margaret Laing, *The Next Kennedy*, p. 13.

499 *"You should've seen":* Bethlehem *Globe Times*, Dec. 9, 1964, UPI.

499 *"Dad doesn't like":* Interview with David Burke by Burton Hersh, Hersh, *The Education of Edward Kennedy*, p. 205.

499 *"When we grew":* Martin, *Hero*, p. 216.

500 *"The older brother":* Author interview with Marvin Sleeper.

500 *"I used to fly":* Interview with Dun Gifford by Hersh, Notebook 21, June 12, 1970, Hersh, *Education*, pp. 210–11.

501 *"Do you know":* David Halberstam, *The Unfinished Odyssey of Robert Kennedy*, pp. 151–52.

501 *And in London:* Schlesinger, p. 799; William vanden Heuvel and Milton Gwirtzman, *On His Own*, pp. 228–30.

501 *"It wasn't really":* William V. Shannon, *The Heir Apparent*, p. 8; Peter Maas, "What Will RFK Do Next?" *Saturday Evening Post*, March 28, 1964.

502 *"He didn't really":* Author interview with Angie Novello.

502 *"Is the East River":* Author interview with Benjamin C. Bradlee.

502 *"If Abraham Lincoln":* Shannon, p. 293.

502 *"JFK was the catalyst":* Author interview with Theodore Sorensen.

503 *"It hit"*: Oral history interview with John Seigenthaler by Larry Hackman, June 5, 1970, p. 47, RFK Oral History, JFK Library.

503 *"It was a moment"*: Author interview with Angie Novello.

504 *"This could happen"*: Author interview with Senator Hugh Scott.

504 *"Lem's genius"*: Interview with Senator Edward M. Kennedy, Billings Collection, p. 67, JFK Library.

504 *"Bob was more apt"*: Oral history interview with David Hackett by John Douglas, RFK Oral History, July 22, 1970, pp. 46–47, JFK Library.

505 *"So he had"*: Interview with Lemoyne Billings by Clay Blair, Jr., Blair Papers, p. 17.

505 *"He'd say"*: Author interview with Dave Richardson.

505 *"Well, I insisted"*: Author interview with Bill Connell.

506 *"The basic aim"*: Shannon, p. 254.

506 *"Why do you"*: Gore Vidal, "The Holy Family," *Esquire*, April 1967, p. 104.

506 *One day in the campaign:* Author interview with Debs Myers.

506 *"Don't take that"*: Oral history interview with James E. Tolan, by Roberta Greene, June 27, 1969, pp. 32–33, RFK Oral History, JFK Library.

506 *"What I really"*: Vivian Cadden, "Jacqueline: Behind the Myths," *McCall's*, July 1975.

507 *"Jackie was in love"*: Doris Lily, *Family Circle*, July 10, 1978, p. 54.

507 *"I am certain"*: David, *Ethel*, p. 128.

507 *"Do you like"*: Laing, pp. 40, 41.

507 *"He lacked"*: David Halberstam, *The Unfinished Odyssey of Robert Kennedy*, pp. 272–73.

508 *"I had better"*: Theo Lippman, Jr., *Senator Ted Kennedy*, pp. 29–30.

508 *"If elected President"*: Jules Witcover, *The Last Campaign of Robert Kennedy*, p. 180.

508 *Not since 1803:* Dwight Foster of Massachusetts and Theodore Foster of Rhode Island.

508 *"I recall the first"*: Interview with John J. Lindsay by Jean Stein, Stein and Plimpton, *American Journey*, p. 317.

509 *When the magazine's:* William Honan, *Ted Kennedy*, pp. 132–33.

509 *"step back"*: Shannon, *The Heir Apparent*, p. 75; "Topics," *The New York Times*, Jan. 4, 1964.

510 *"I regret"*: Shannon, *The Heir Apparent*, p. 70.

510 *"I suppose"*: Laing, p. 31.

510 *Walinsky would become:* Newfield, p. 52.

510 *"I haven't the slightest"*: David, *Good Ted*, p. 116.

510 *"With his eyes"*: Hayes Gorey, "The Kennedy Mystique," *The New York Times Magazine*, June 17, 1979.

511 *"You know how"*: Oral interview with Joseph Dolan by Hackman, RFK Papers, JFK Library.

511 *"Bobby and Teddy"*: Oral history interview with Peter Edelman by Larry J. Hackman, July 15, 1969, p. 117, RFK Oral History, JFK Library.

511 *But there was:* Honan, p. 132.

511 *"Stop talking"*: Interview with Dun Gifford, *American Journey*, p. 183.

512 *"how eery"*: Coughlan Papers.

512 *"You see"*: Honan, *Ted Kennedy*, p. 33.

512 *"Whatever Bobby"*: Laing, pp. 272–73.

512 *"Ted was always"*: Gorey, "The Kennedy Mystique," p. 15.

512 *"You know, we've"*: Author interview with Hobart Rowan.

512 *"Oh no, I treat"*: Richard Reeves, *The New York Times*, Nov. 14, 1966.

512 *"How can you"*: Shannon, p. 74.

512 *"He understands"*: Nancy Gager Clinch, *The Kennedy Neurosis*, p. 300; Dick Schaap, *RFK*, pp. 116–17.

513 *"When Bobby"*: Gorey, "The Kennedy Mystique."

513 *"He seemed"*: Shannon, pp. 59–60.

513 *"Teddy takes"*: Hersh, p. 102.

513 *Some, like Laura Bergquist:* Author interview with Laura Bergquist.

514 *"Robert Kennedy had put"*: Oral history interview with Peter Edelman by Larry J. Hackman, July 15, 1969, p. 80, JFK Library.

514 *"In politics"*: William Peters, *Redbook*, June 1962, p. 73.

514 *"Told that the weather"*: Interview with Mary Gimbel by Collier and Horowitz, *The Kennedys*, p. 331.

514 *"This was a party"*: Oral history interview with Milton Gwirtzman by Roberta Greene, pp. 22–23, RFK Oral History, JFK Library.

515 *"The demands"*: Ibid., pp. 287–78.

515 *"I have told him"*: Wills, p. 24, quoting James MacGregor Burns.

515 *"It's eleven o'clock"*: RFK Papers, Sen. Corresp. Pers. File, 1964–1968, 5/20/65, box 20, JFK Library.

515 *"There's a pattern"*: Interview with Richard Goodwin, "Geraldo: The Kennedys: The Dark Side of the Dynasty," Feb. 20, 1990.

516 *"Teddy had to be"*: Oral history interview with Lawrence J. O'Brien by Michael Gillette, April 23, 1987, p. 21, LBJ Library.

516 *"I really like"*: Ibid., Feb. 12, 1986, pp. 12–14.

516 *"was born knowing"*: *Ladies' Home Journal*, Oct. 1962, box 5, JFK Library.

516 *"Ted doesn't have"*: Interview with William Honan by Burton Hersh, Hersh, pp. 128–29, Notebook 16.

516 *"political matters"*: Pat Anderson, "Robert's Character," *Esquire*, April 1965.

517 *"I hope you'll"*: Author interview with Senator Hugh Scott.

517 *"Thanks for"*: Author interview with Bill Welsh.

517 *"I'm practicing"*: Honan, p. 132.

517 *"Don't slip"*: Gloria Emerson, "How Rose Kennedy Survived," *McCall's*, Aug. 1975.

518 *"Bob didn't like"*: Interview with Martin Arnold by Jean Stein, Stein and Plimpton, *American Journey*, p. 170.

12

A DREAM DIES

519 *"It was like"*: Interview with Lemoyne Billings by Collier and Horowitz, *The Kennedys*, p. 332.

519 *If John Kennedy*: James MacGregor Burns, *Edward Kennedy and the Camelot Legacy*, p. 15.

519 *"Do you ever"*: "Edward P. Morgan and the News," ABC Radio, Oct. 10, 1966.

520 *"Her fragile manner"*: "William Manchester's Own Story," *Look*, April 4, 1967, p. 71, box 12, JFK Library.

521 *"Anyone who gets"*: *The New York Times Magazine*, May 31, 1970, p. 37.

521 *"an arrogant"*: Shannon, p. 256.

521 *"Look, my father"*: Schlesinger, p. 376.

522 *"We are going"*: Oral history interview with Anthony Lewis, JFK Library.

522 *"What shall I"*: Navasky, p. 362.

522 *"a guy who"*: Author interview with Charles Roberts.

523 *"Well, six o'clock"*: Jack Bell, "The Private Kennedy," Associated Press, Boston *Globe*, Oct. 20, 1979, p. 8, Box 12, JFK Library.

525 *In his increasing paranoia*: Reston, *Deadline*, pp. 309–10.

525 *"He went into"*: The New York Times, May 31, 1993, p. 23.

526 *"I had the impression"*: Author interview with Ed Rooney.

527 *"he never forgot"*: Newfield, p. 56.

527 *"I don't know"*: Martin, *Hero*, p. 498.

528 *"and with our help"*: Schlesinger, p. 776; June 3, 1967, RFK Papers, JFK Library.

528 *"How can we"*: Schlesinger, p. 777

529 *"pounding my chest"*: Radio interview with McNamara, National Public Radio.

529 *"there was a long"*: Murray Kempton, *Esquire*, July 1968, p. 93.

531 *"We are going to win"*: Halberstam, *Unfinished Odyssey*, p. 36.

531 *"I can't just stand"*: Sorensen, *Legacy*, p. 132.

531 *"Jack Kennedy"*: David, p. 163.

531 *"And this was the best"*: Author interview with Angie Novello.

532 *"The place is full"*: Author interview with Esther Tufty.

533 *"I don't know quite"*: RFK Papers, Sen. Corresp. Pers. File, 1964–1968, Files: Kennedy, Robert F.: handwritten notes and letters, box 20, 3/13/68, JFK Library.

534 *"Why don't you"*: Interview with Richard Goodwin by Jean Stein, *American Journey*, p. 224.

535 *"Robert Kennedy shouted"*: Halberstam Papers.

535 *"You've got to run"*: Author interview with Kenneth O'Donnell.

535 *"If just one"*: Interview with Senator George McGovern, *American Journey*, pp. 21–22.

535 *"So it is how"*: Schlesinger, p. 884; Peter Matthiessen, *Sal Si Puedes*, p. 176.

535 *"Do you know"*: Burns, p. 207; Jacques Levy, *Cesar Chavez*, p. 449.

536 *"What have I got"*: Interview with John Seigenthaler by Collier and Horowitz, *The Kennedys*, p. 345.

536 *"I have no designs"*: Sorensen, *Legacy*, 117.

536 *"In a sense"*: Halberstam, *Unfinished Odyssey*, quoted by Elizabeth Drew, *Atlantic Monthly*, July 1969.

536 *"How do you think"*: Hersh, pp. 296, 314.

537 *"If you had a choice"*: Rogers, p. 187.

537 *"I don't know what"*: Schlesinger, *Robert Kennedy and His Times*, vol. 2, pp. 887–88.

537 *"What the hell's"*: Hersh, p. 297.

537 *"there was a lot"*: Oral history interview with David Burke by Larry Hackman, Dec. 8, 1971, pp. 35–36, JFK Library.

538 *"Abigail turned"*: Ibid.

538 *"No, Bob's"*: Hersh, p. 298.

538 *"I think the basis"*: Oral history interview with David Burke.

538 *"Bobby's therapy"*: Hersh, p. 290, Collier and Horowitz, p. 346.

538 *"I was in the car"*: Interview with Sylvia Wright, *American Journey*, p. 232.

539 *"Do you know"*: Schlesinger, vol. 2, p. 895.

539 *"Dad, I'm doing"*: Ibid., pp. 908–09; Rita Dallas, *The Kennedy Case*, pp. 301–04.

539 *"It's going"*: Coughlan Papers.

539 *"Bobby didn't know"*: Interview with Lemoyne Billings by Collier and Horowitz, p. 340.

540 *"Well, by the time"*: Interview with John Seigenthaler, "The American Experience: The Kennedys," WGBH-TV, Sept. 21, 1992.

540 *"I used to be"*: Halberstam, p. 200.

540 *"Both the timing"*: Arthur Krock, Memoirs, pp. 344–45.

541 *There was family friction*: Author interview with Max Kampelman.

542 *"I think he would've"*: Author interview with Benjamin C. Bradlee.

542 *"I wish there was"*: Hersh, p. 296.

542 *"Let's see"*: Ibid.

542 *"There was no great"*: Ibid.

542 *"He's going to be"*: David, *Ethel*, pp. 192–93.

543 *"We want this man"*: Halberstam, p. 70.

543 *"When we got"*: Oral history interview with James E. Tolan by Roberta Greene, Nov. 3, 1969, p. 214, RFK Oral History, JFK Library.

543 *"Eight years ago"*: David and David, *Bobby*, p. 281.

544 *"The fact is"*: Halberstam Papers.

544 *Fred Dutton was*: Interview with Fred Dutton by Collier and Horowitz, pp. 347–48.

544 *"They asked me"*: Interview with Rose Kennedy by Robert Coughlan. Coughlan Papers.

544 *"That's what we've"*: Interview with Robert Kennedy, Jr., "The American Experience."

545 *"We can do"*: Jules Witcover, *85 Days: The Last Campaign of Robert Kennedy*, p. 21.

546 *"I wonder"*: RFK to Richard Dougherty of the Los Angeles *Times*, quoted in Witcover, pp. 126–27.

546 *"I had a partnership"*: Califano 271; James Jones memo for the record, Congressional Leadership breakfast, April 2, 1968, LBJ Library.

547 *"Well, he never"*: Newfield, p. 244.

547 *"I won't bother"*: Sam Howard Johnson, *My Brother Lyndon*, pp. 251–52.

547 *"I don't know"*: Sorensen, *Kennedy Legacy*, pp. 146–47.

548 *"To think"*: Halberstam, pp. 83–84.

548 *"It was his vulnerability"*: *New York* magazine, April 19, 1993, "Kennedy for President in '63," p. 108.

548 *"the best speech"*: Oral history interview with James E. Tolan by Roberta W. Greene, June 27, 1969, p. 46, RFK Oral History, JFK Library.

549 *"And then he started"*: Ibid.

549 *"I've never been"*: Author interview with Joan Braden.

549 *Later that night*: The New York Times, Aug. 7, 1988, "Recapturing Bobby."

549 *"and then joined"*: Roy Jenkins, *Memoirs of a Radical Reformer*.

549 *"when Kennedy came"*: Halberstam, p. 90.

550 *"If I could have"*: *Life*, April 1993, p. 61.

550 *"Make way"*: Elizabeth Drew, *Atlantic Monthly*, July 1969.

550 *"I don't know how"*: Hersh, p. 310.

551 *"Bobby Kennedy holds"*: Schlesinger, p. 228; Atlanta *Constitution*, Sept. 10, 1960.

551 *"Bob went into"*: Ibid., p. 311.

551 *"That's my farm"*: Witcover, *The Last Campaign*, p. 55.

552 *"It has been"*: RFK to Edward Lewis, Jan. 16, 1967, RFK Papers, Sen. Corresp. Pers. File, 1964–1968. Files: Kennedy, Robert F.: handwritten notes and letters, box 20, JFK Library.

552 *"Won't it be"*: Martin, *Hero*, p. 571.

552 *Author C. David Heymann*: C. David Heymann, *A Woman Named Jackie*, p. 593.

553 *"My heart"*: Ibid., p. 431.

553 *Singer Dean Martin's*: Oppenheimer, *The Other Mrs. Kennedy*, p. 243.

553 *"Why don't you"*: Ibid.

553 *And Peter Lawford*: Ibid., p. 400.

553 *"I remember"*: Author interview with Charles Spalding.

554 *"He was never"*: Interview with Robert Kennedy Jr. by Collier and Horowitz, *The Kennedys*, p. 363.

554 *"She read"*: Interview with Barbara Gibson, former secretary to Rose Kennedy, July 17, 1991, "Geraldo: The Kennedy Women: Public Glory, Private Pain."

554 *"a great white"*: *Theodore H. White at Large*, Edward Thompson, ed., p. 445.

554 *"among the less"*: Sorensen, *Legacy*, p. 153.

554 *"I think what"*: Oral history interview with Stephen Smith, April 16, 1970, p. 12, RFK Oral History, JFK Library.

554 *"I just don't feel"*: Witcover, *The Last Campaign*, pp. 68–69.

555 *"I don't know"*: Ibid., p. 44.

555 *"I can't plan"*: Newfield, p. 31.

555 *"Dad, I'm going"*: Dallas, p. 303.

556 *"We were greatly"*: Oral history interview with Lawrence O'Brien by Michael Gillette, July 21, 1987, p. 11, LBJ Library.

556 *"For every man"*: Oral history interview with Cesar Chavez by Dennis J. O'Brien, RFK Oral History, p. 12, JFK Library.

556 *"Kennedy stood"*: Jimmy Breslin, "The Way He Was," *People*, June 7, 1993, p. 47.

556 *"the young especially"*: Newfield, p. 39.

556 *"I think the country"*: Halberstam Papers.

557 *"exchanged powder"*: Theodore H. White at Large, Edward Thompson, ed., p. 447.

557 *A string of*: Newfield, 286.

557 *"how John Lindsay"*: Ibid.

558 *"stretched out"*: Richard Goodwin, "A Day," *McCall's*, June 1970.

558 *"Hubert had it"*: Oral history interview with Lawrence O'Brien by Michael Gillette, July 21, 1987, LBJ Library.

558 *"and I really hit"*: Breslin, "The Way," pp. 42–43.

558 *"I remember watching"*: Interview with Richard Goodwin, "The American Experience: The Kennedys, Part 2," Sept. 21, 1992, WGBH-TV.

559 *"Joe hated"*: The New York Times, Aug. 7, 1988, "Recapturing Bobby."

559 *"You know"*: Author interview with Kenneth O'Donnell.

560 *"I was waiting"*: Breslin, "The Way," pp. 44, 47.

560 *"Get the gun!"*: Rogers, p. 158.

560 *"an awful sound"*: Newfield, pp. 299–300.

561 *"I happened"*: Breslin, "The Way," pp. 44, 47.

561 *"Bobby's open eye"*: David, Ethel, pp. 203–04.

561 *"Please don't"*: Breslin, "The Way," pp. 44, 47.

563 *McCarthy kept repeating*: Interview with Richard Goodwin by Jean Stein, American Journey, pp. 340–41.

563 *"Next morning"*: Breslin, "The Way," pp. 46–47.

563 *"One of his possibilities"*: Interview with Robert Lowell by Jean Stein, American Journey, p. 344.

564 *"But I didn't think"*: Interview with Rose Kennedy by Robert Coughlan, Coughlan Papers.

564 *"just walking"*: Gail Cameron, Rose, pp. 216–17.

564 *"In Los Angeles"*: Oral history interview with Lawrence J. O'Brien by Michael Gillette, July 21, 1987, p. 8, LBJ Library.

565 *"sheer guts"*: Interview with Ethel Kennedy by Robert Coughlan, Coughlan Papers.

565 *"Oh, why"*: Cameron, p. 181.

565 *"She never wanted"*: Interview with Jacqueline Kennedy by Robert Coughlan, Coughlan Papers.

565 *"When the President"*: Interview with Rita Dallas, "The American Experience: The Kennedys."

565 *"Having had two"*: Interview of Dave Powers by Robert Coughlan, Coughlan Papers.

565 *"Rose concentrates"*: Interview with Gloria Guinness by Robert Coughlan, Coughlan Papers.

565 *"Ted leaning"*: David, Good Ted, Bad Ted, p. 6; Boston Globe, July 10, 1985.

566 *This seems*: Honan, pp. 129–30.

566 *"You're not going"*: The New York Times Book Review, Nov. 7, 1993, p. 29.

566 *"There was one"*: Newfield, p. 302.

567 *"A day or two later"*: Oral history interview with David Burke by Larry Hackman, Dec. 8, 1971, pp. 38–39, RFK Oral History, JFK Library.

568 *"I'm going to show"*: Hersh, pp. 330–31.

568 *Ethel wanted*: Oppenheimer, p. 351.

568 *"The Church is"*: Oral history interview with Frank Mankiewicz by Larry Hackman, p. 56, JFK Library.

568 *"I worried"*: Betty Hannah Hoffman, "Joan Kennedy's Story," Ladies' Home Journal, July 1970, p. 100.

568 *"We felt pretty funny"*: Honan, pp. 171–72.

569 *"with frenzy"*: David, Ethel, p. 237.

569 *In a wide-ranging*: New York magazine, July 29, 1968.

570 *"Jackie first"*: Interview with Shirley Mac-Laine by Jean Stein, Stein and Plimpton, American Journey, p. 158.

570 *"Nobody collapses"*: Interview with Rose Kennedy by Laura Bergquist, Bergquist Papers.

571 *"Yes. But what"*: Interview with Arthur Schlesinger, Jr., by Jean Stein, Stein and Plimpton, American Journey, p. 64.

571 *"Ethel asked Andy"*: Cameron, p. 219.

571 *"As we know"*: Coughlan Papers.

572 *"The crowd"*: Interview with Naida Cohn, American Journey, pp. 250–51.

572 *"I can't let"*: Hersh, p. 330; Collier and Horowitz, p. 364.

572 *As the train*: Sorensen, Kennedy Legacy, p. 19.

572 *"You know how"*: Author interview with Dave Powers.

573 *"We had a reception"*: Jack Sirocco, "The RFK Legacy," New York Newsday, June 3, 1993, p. 63.

573 *"When Bobby"*: Author interview with Benjamin C. Bradlee.

573 *"Bobby, to me"*: Cameron, p. 222.

574 *"there might"*: Author interview with David Hackett.

574 *"He didn't necessarily"*: RFK Jr. on "Sonya Live," CNN, June 4, 1993.

13
THE LAST TORCH

575 *"and since then"*: Author interview with Paul S. Green.

575 *"Jack always"*: Author interview with Dave Powers.

576 *"Can you imagine"*: William H. Honan, *Ted Kennedy: Profile of a Survivor*, pp. 4–5.

576 *"Maybe the country"*: Author interview with Charles Spalding.

576 *"I remember walking"*: Interview with John Tunney, "The American Experience: The Kennedys, Part 2," WGBH-TV, Sept. 21, 1992.

577 *"Once Ted"*: Warren Rogers, *Look*, August 10, 1971, p. 19.

577 *"Dad rose up"*: Ibid.

577 *"It's altogether"*: Author interview with Blair Clark.

578 *"they suddenly"*: Interview with Dun Gifford by Jean Stein, Stein and Plimpton, *American Journey*, p. 315.

579 *"Both of my brothers"*: Theodore Sorensen, "Ted Kennedy's Memories of JFK," *McCall's*, Nov. 1973.

580 *"she collapsed"*: David, *Ethel*, p. 259.

580 *"He loves"*: Meg Greenfield, *Washington Post*, Sept. 19, 1979.

580 *"I served"*: Author interview with James Symington.

580 *"Bobby believed"*: Oral history interview with Aaron Henry by T. H. Baker, Sept. 12, 1970. Clarksdale, MS, Third interview, pp. 4–5, LBJ Library.

581 *"The source"*: Boston *Globe*, June 14, 1991.

581 *"We all felt"*: Collier and Horowitz, *The Kennedys*, p. 368.

581 *"just like Kennedy"*: *The New York Times*, March 29, 1994.

581 *"That's just"*: McGinniss, p. 25.

582 *"It was obvious"*: Mary McGrory, quoted by McGinniss, p. 507.

582 *"Teddy has"*: Califano, p. 331.

583 *"I just think"*: Interview with Rose Kennedy by Robert Coughlan, Coughlan Papers.

583 *"He shouldn't run"*: Ibid.

583 *"Will Edward Kennedy"*: *U.S. News & World Report*, June 24, 1968.

583 *"Nor would they"*: Albert Eisele, *Almost to the Presidency*, p. 351.

584 *"There's a big"*: *Newsweek*, Sept. 9, 1968, p. 35.

584 *"I will never"*: *The New York Times Magazine*, June 17, 1979.

585 *"Basically, I"*: Warren Rogers, *Look*, March 4, 1969, p. 42.

585 *It was also reported*: Garry Wills, *Atlantic Monthly*, Jan. 1982, p. 34.

585 *"Forget about 1980"*: Hersh, p. 256.

586 *"He has no one"*: Joe McGinniss, "The Kennedy Imprisonment," *The New York Times Book Review*, March 14, 1982, p. 23.

587 *"It is thought"*: *The New York Times Magazine*, May 31, 1970, p. 25.

587 *"I knew Onassis"*: Author interview with Larry Newman.

587 *"For God's sake"*: Fred Sparks, *The $20,000,000 Honeymoon*, p. 26.

587 *All through the summer*: *Newsweek*, Oct. 28, 1968, p. 41.

588 *She absolutely*: Author interview with Roswell Gilpatric.

588 *"She was wiped out"*: *Family Circle*, July 10, 1978.

588 *"Jackie, how could you?"*: *Time*, Oct. 25, 1968.

588 *"Jackie was the one"*: Author interview with Benjamin C. Bradlee.

589 *"Money is security"*: Author interview with Betty Beale.

589 *Onassis's former steward*: Christian Cafarakis and Jacques Harvey, *The Fabulous Onassis*.

589 *Teddy afterward*: Interview with Lemoyne Billings by Collier and Horowitz, *The Kennedys*, p. 367.

590 *Once, Senator Strom Thurmond*: *Washington Post Magazine*, April 29, 1988.

590 *"This goddamned"*: Hersh, pp. 450–51; Burns, *Edward Kennedy*, p. 187.

590 *"Teddy, I see where"*: Myra MacPherson, "Kennedy Night at the Hilton," *Washington Post*, Jan. 23, 1969.

590 *"The thing about"*: Joseph M. Mohvat, "There's a Time for the Kennedys," *The Sunday Times*, June 8, 1969.

591 *"Does he drink?"*: Ibid.

591 *"He is the least"*: Burns, *Edward Kennedy*, p. 335.

591 *"He's living"*: Sylvia Wright quoted in David, *Good Ted, Bad Ted*, p. 111.

592 *"His sense"*: Rita Dallas quoted in Honan, p. 88.

593 *"a state of shock"*: Tony Ulasewicz, *The President's Private Eye*, p. 218.

593 *"because he had"*: Robert Sherrill, *The New York Times Magazine*, July 4, 1974.

593 *"if Ted had admitted"*: Author interview with Larry Newman.

593 *"No one told me"*: Marcia Chellis, *The Joan Kennedy Story*, p. 86.

594 *"Teddy had everything"*: Interview with Rose Kennedy by Robert Coughlan, Coughlan Papers.

594 *"I do not understand"*: Interview with Rose Kennedy by Robert Coughlan, Coughlan Papers.

594 *"Jack would never"*: Author interview with Charles Spalding.

595 *"We don't know"*: Reston, *Deadline*, pp. 297–98.

595 *"I think Teddy"*: Natalie Gittleson, "Chappaquiddick," *McCall's*, August 1979.

595 *"After all, when"*: *Time*, Aug. 1, 1969, p. 14.

596 *"But if I had"*: Halberstam, p. 435.

596 *Judge Boyle's twelve-page*: "Judge Boyle's Report," New York *Daily News*, April 30, 1970.

596 *"Each time"*: Wills, pp. 157–58.

596 *"What Chappaquiddick"*: William F. Buckley, "After Chappaquiddick," *National Review*, Oct. 7, 1969; Burns, *Edward Kennedy*, 172.

597 *"There was a gasp"*: *Newsweek*, Aug. 4, 1969, p. 26.

597 *"Over there"*: Interview with Ted Kennedy by Lester David, *Good Ted, Bad Ted,* p. 141.

598 *Some Republican Party*: *Time*, Nov. 29, 1971, p. 18.

598 *"It's my feeling"*: *Newsweek*, Aug. 4, 1969, p. 31.

599 *"After Chappaquiddick"*: Author interview with Richard Whelan.

599 *"Mort Downey"*: Author interview with Larry Newman.

599 *"Oh, Grandpa"*: Rita Dallas, p. 345; Collier and Horowitz, pp. 376–77.

600 *"If God does"*: Laura Bergquist Papers, Special Collections, Mugar Memorial Library, Boston University.

600 *"I wish you"*: David, pp. 24–25.

600 *"You'll see"*: Interview with Joseph Gargan by Burton Hersh, Hersh, p. 32.

600 *Joe Kennedy put*: Oral history interview with Eddie Dowling by Neil N. Gold, #5323, PRCQ, Columbia University Oral History.

601 *"You want kings"*: Interview with Doris Kearns Goodwin, "Geraldo: The Kennedys: The Dark Side of the Dynasty," Feb. 20, 1990.

602 *"Unless you know"*: Honan, p. 5.

602 *"the 28 Democratic"*: Warren Rogers, *Look*, Aug. 10, 1971, p. 20.

602 *"Our people"*: Oral history interview with Cesar Chavez by Dennis J. O'Brien, p. 11, RFK Oral History, JFK Library.

602 *"And all this"*: Betty Hannah Hoffman, *Ladies' Home Journal*, July 1970, p. 70.

603 *"I'll make bets"*: *Ladies' Home Journal*, Sept. 1968, p. 87.

603 *"If he doesn't"*: Rogers, *Look*, Aug. 10, 1971, p. 23.

603 *"I do not think"*: Rose Kennedy to EMK, June 8, 1972.

603 *What Ted Kennedy did not*: Interview with Gregory Craig by Lester David, David, 197–78.

603 *"I try not"*: Warren Rogers, *Look*, Aug. 10, 1971, p. 20.

604 *"Kennedy was"*: William Schneider, "Political Memo, Bridge Led to Detour over 20 Years," *The New York Times*, July 18, 1989.

604 *"It is eerie"*: Lippman, *Senator Ted Kennedy*, pp. 99–100.

604 *"in an open convertible"*: Tom Gerber, "The Non-Candidacy of Edward Moore Kennedy," *Time*, Nov. 29, 1971.

604 *"If he isn't"*: Honan, pp. 19–21.

605 *"except that the way"*: Burton Hersh, "The Thousand Days of Edward M. Kennedy," *Esquire*, Feb., p. 64, Box 12, JFK Library.

605 *Nixon still saw Teddy*: Haldeman, p. 215 (Dec. 5, 1970).

607 *"It was just like"*: Author interview with Marquis Childs.

607 *"Rather than get"*: *People*, May 27, 1991, p. 12.

607 *"I was embarrassed"*: Burton Hersh, *The Washingtonian*, Feb. 1979, p. 102.

607 *"It formed"*: Ibid., p. 101.

608 *When she was arrested*: Interview with Boston *Herald* columnist Norma Nathan, "Geraldo: The Kennedy Women: Public Glory, Private Pain," July 17, 1991.

608 *"This is the best"*: Interview with John Lindsay by Collier and Horowitz, p. 557.

609 *"If Uncle John"*: David, p. 199; *McCall's*, Feb. 1974.

609 *"Teddy doesn't want"*: Tom Mathews, "Ready or Not, Here He Comes," *Newsweek*, Sept. 24, 1979, p. 29.

610 *"I might as well"*: Interview with Senator George Smathers by Lester David, *Good Ted, Bad Ted*, pp. 184–85.

610 *"Vulnerable"*: *Time*, Nov. 29, 1971, p. 23.

611 *"but I think"*: Interview with David Kennedy by Collier and Horowitz, p. 429.

611 *"Because of what"*: *The New York Times Magazine*, June 17, 1979, p. 15.

612 *"He had more"*: Interview with John Gage by Collier and Horowitz, p. 434.

612 *"Well, I learned"*: Collier and Horowitz, p. 442.

613 *"She thought"*: Interview with Norma Nathan on "Geraldo," July 17, 1991.

613 *"Oh, I know"*: "The End of Kennedy's Troubled Marriage," *The Evening Sun*, Feb. 2, 1981.

613 *"He's becoming":* Ibid.

614 *"I don't think":* Ibid.

614 *Vicki told Ted:* David, p. 249; interview with Victoria Reggie's mother.

615 *Chris Lawford:* Collier and Horowitz, p. 452.

615 *"His home was":* Billings Collection, JFK Library.

615 *"We were vaguely":* The Newe York Times, Aug. 7, 1988.

BIBLIOGRAPHY

Abel, Elie. *The Missile Crisis,* Philadelphia: Lippincott, 1966.

Adler, Bill. *The Kennedy Children.* New York: Franklin Watts, 1980.

Alsop, Joseph. *I've Seen the Best of It.* New York: Norton, 1992.

Alsop, Stewart. *The Center: People and Power in Political Washington.* New York: Harper & Row, 1968.

Atwood, William. *The Twilight Struggle: Tales of the Cold War.* Harper & Row, 1987.

Baker, Bobby, with Larry L. King. *Wheeling and Dealing: Confessions of a Capitol Hill Operator.* New York: Norton, 1978.

Baldrige, Letitia. *Of Diamonds and Diplomats.* Boston: Houghton Mifflin, 1968.

Ball, George W. *The Past Had Another Pattern.* New York: Norton, 1982.

Barham, Patte B., and Peter Harry Brown. *Marilyn: The Last Take.* New York: Dutton, 1992.

Belin, David W. *Final Disclosure.* New York: Scribner, 1988.

Bergquist, Laura, and Stanley Tretick. *A Very Special President.* New York: McGraw-Hill, 1965.

Beschloss, Michael R. *The Crisis Years: Kennedy and Khrushchev.* New York: Burlingame, 1991.

———. *Kennedy and Roosevelt: The Uneasy Alliance.* New York: Norton, 1980.

Birmingham, Stephen. *Jacqueline Kennedy Bouvier Onassis.* New York: Grosset & Dunlap, 1969.

Bishop, Jim. *A Day in the Life of President Kennedy.* New York: Random House, 1964.

———. *The Day Kennedy Was Shot.* New York: Random House, 1968.

Blair, Clay, Jr., and Joan Blair. *The Search for JFK.* New York: Putnam, 1976.

Blakey, Robert, and Richard Billings. *The Plot to Kill the President.* New York: Times Books, 1981.

Bohlen, Charles E. *Witness to History, 1929–1969.* New York: Norton, 1973.

Bowles, Chester. *Promises to Keep: My Years in Public Life, 1941–1969.* New York: Harper & Row, 1971.

Bradlee, Benjamin C. *Conversations with Kennedy.* New York: Norton, 1975.

Brandon, Henry. *Special Relationships.* New York: Atheneum, 1988.

Bundy, McGeorge. *Danger and Survival: Choices about the Bomb in the First Fifty Years.* New York: Random House, 1988.

Burke, Richard E., with William and Marilyn Hoffer. *The Senator: My Ten Years with Ted Kennedy.* New York: St. Martin's, 1992.

Burner, David, and Thomas R. West. *The Torch Is Passed.* New York: Atheneum, 1984.

Burns, James MacGregor. *Edward Kennedy and the Camelot Legacy.* New York: Norton, 1976.

———. *John Kennedy: A Political Profile.* New York: Harcourt, Brace, 1959.

Cafrakis, Christian, and Jacques Harvey. *The Fabulous Onassis.* New York: Morrow, 1978.

Cameron, Gail. *Rose: A Biography of Rose Fitzgerald Kennedy.* New York: Putnam, 1971.

Cassini, Igor, with Jeanne Molli. *I'd Do It All Over Again.* New York: Putnam, 1977.

Cassini, Oleg. *In My Own Fashion.* New York: Simon & Schuster, 1987.

Chellis, Marcia. *The Joan Kennedy Story: Living with the Kennedys.* New York: Simon & Schuster, 1985.

Claflin, Edward B., ed. *JFK Wants to Know: Memos from the President's Office, 1961–1963.* New York: Morrow, 1991.

Clifford, Clark, with Richard Holbrooke. *Counsel to the President.* New York: Random House, 1991.

Clinch, Nancy Gager. *The Kennedy Neurosis.* New York: Grosset & Dunlap, 1973.

Collier, Peter, and David Horowitz. *The Kennedys: An American Drama.* New York: Summit, 1984.

Cutler, John Henry. *Honey Fitz.* Indianapolis: Bobbs-Merrill, 1962.

Dallas, Rita, and Jeanira Ratcliffe. *The Kennedy Case.* New York: Putnam, 1973.

Damore, Leo. *The Cape Cod Years of John Fitzgerald Kennedy.* Englewood Cliffs, NJ: Prentice-Hall, 1967.

David, Lester. *Ethel: The Story of Mrs. Robert F. Kennedy.* New York: World, 1971.

———. *Good Ted, Bad Ted.* New York: Birch Lane, 1993.

———. *Jacqueline Kennedy Onassis.* New York: Birch Lane, 1994.

———. *Ted Kennedy: Triumphs and Tragedies.* New York: Grosset & Dunlap, 1971.

David, Lester, and Irene David. *Bobby Kennedy: The Making of a Folk Hero.* New York: Dodd, Mead, 1986.

Davis, John H. *The Bouviers.* New York: Farrar, Straus & Giroux, 1969.

———. *The Kennedys: Dynasty and Disaster.* New York, McGraw-Hill, 1984.

Deakin, James. *Straight Stuff: The Reporters, The*

White House and the Truth. New York: Morrow, 1984.

Dineen, Joseph F. *The Kennedy Family.* Boston: Little, Brown, 1959.

Donovan, Hedley. *Roosevelt to Reagan: A Reporter's Encounter with Nine Presidents.* New York: Harper & Row, 1985.

Donovan, Robert J. *PT-109.* New York: McGraw-Hill, 1961.

Eisele, Albert. *Almost to the Presidency.* New York: Piper, 1972.

Exner, Judith, as told to Ovid Demaris. *My Story.* New York: Grove, 1977.

Faber, Harold, ed. *The Kennedy Years.* New York: Viking, 1964.

Fairlie, Henry. *The Kennedy Promise.* New York: Dell, 1972.

Fay, Paul B., Jr. *The Pleasure of His Company.* New York: Harper & Row, 1966.

Friedman, Stanley. *The Kennedy Family Scrapbook.* New York: Grosset & Dunlap, 1978.

Fuchs, Lawrence. *John F. Kennedy and American Catholicism.* New York: Meredith, 1967.

Galbraith, John Kenneth. *Ambassador's Journal.* Boston: Houghton Mifflin, 1969.

———. *A Life in Our Times.* Boston: Houghton Mifflin, 1981.

Gallagher, Mary Barelli. *My Life with Jacqueline Kennedy.* New York: McKay, 1969.

Giancana, Antoinette, and Thomas C. Renner. *Mafia Princess.* New York: Avon, 1984.

Goodwin, Doris Kearns. *The Fitzgeralds and the Kennedys.* New York: Simon & Schuster, 1987.

Goodwin, Richard N. *Remembering America: A Voice from the Sixties.* Boston: Little, Brown, 1988.

Guthman, Edwin O. *Recollections of the Kennedy Years.* New York: Bantam, 1988.

———. *We Band of Brothers.* New York: Harper & Row, 1971.

Guthman, Edwin O., and Jeffrey Shulman, eds. *Robert Kennedy in His Own Words.* New York: Bantam, 1988.

Halberstam, David. *The Best and the Brightest.* New York: Random House, 1969.

———. *The Unfinished Odyssey of Robert Kennedy.* New York, Random House, 1968.

Haldeman, H. R. *The Haldeman Diaries.* New York: Putnam, 1994.

Hamilton, Nigel. *J.F.K.: Reckless Youth.* New York: Random House, 1992.

Hersh, Burton. *The Education of Edward Kennedy: A Family Biography.* New York: Morrow, 1972.

Heymann, C. David. *A Woman Named Jackie.* New York: Lyle Stuart, 1989.

Hilsman, Roger. *To Move a Nation: The Politics of Foreign Policy in the Administration of John F. Kennedy.* New York: Doubleday, 1967.

Honan, William H. *Ted Kennedy: Profile of a Survivor.* New York: Times Books, 1972.

Humphrey, Hubert. *Education of a Public Man.* New York: Doubleday, 1976.

Johnson, Haynes. *The Bay of Pigs.* New York: Norton, 1984.

Johnson, Lyndon. *The Vantage Point: Perspectives on the Presidency, 1963–1969.* New York: Holt, 1971.

Johnson, Sam Howard. *My Brother Lyndon.* New York: Cowles, 1970.

Kearns, Doris. *Lyndon Johnson and the American Dream.* New York: Harper & Row, 1976.

Kelley, Kitty. *Jackie, Oh!* New York: Ballantine reprint, 1978.

Kennan, George F. *Memoirs: 1950–1963.* Boston: Little, Brown, 1972.

Kennedy, Edward M., ed. *The Fruitful Bough.* Privately published, 1965.

Kennedy, John F. *As We Remember Joe.* Cambridge, MA: Privately printed at the University Press, 1945.

———. *Profiles in Courage.* New York: Harper & Row, 1964.

———. *Why England Slept.* New York: Wilfrid Funk, 1940.

Kennedy, Robert F. *The Enemy Within.* New York: Harper, 1960.

———. *Thirteen Days: A Memoir of the Cuban Missile Crisis.* New York: Norton, 1969.

———. *To Seek a Newer World.* New York: Bantam, 1968.

Kennedy, Rose Fitzgerald. *Times to Remember.* New York: Doubleday, 1974.

Kern, Montague. *The Kennedy Crisis: The Presidency and Foreign Policy.* Chapel Hill: University of North Carolina Press, 1983.

King, Larry, with Peter Occhiogrosso. *Tell It to the King.* New York: Jove, 1989.

Kissinger, Henry. *White House Years.* Boston: Little, Brown, 1979.

Klagsbrun, Francis, and David C. Whitney. *Assassination: Robert F. Kennedy, 1925–1968.* New York: Cowles, 1968.

Koskoff, David E. *Joseph P. Kennedy: A Life and Times.* Englewood Cliffs, NJ: Prentice-Hall, 1974.

Kraft, Joseph. *Profiles in Power: A Washington Insight.* New York: New American Library, 1966.

Krock, Arthur. *Memoirs.* New York: Funk & Wagnalls, 1968.

Laing, Margaret. *The Next Kennedy.* New York: Coward-McCann, 1968.

Lasky, Victor. *JFK, The Man and the Myth: A Critical Portrait.* New York: Macmillan, 1967.

Lawton, Patricia Seaton, with Ted Schwarz. *The Peter Lawford Story.* New York: Carroll & Graf, 1988.

Leamer, Laurence. *The Kennedy Women: The Saga of an American Family.* New York: Villard, 1994.

Levin, Murray B. *Kennedy Campaigning: The System and Style as Practiced by Senator Edward Kennedy.* Boston: Beacon, 1966.

Lieberson, Goddard, and Joan Meyers, eds. *John Fitzgerald Kennedy: . . . As We Remember Him.* New York: Atheneum, 1965.

Lincoln, Evelyn. *Kennedy and Johnson.* New York: Holt, 1968.

———. *My Twelve Years with John F. Kennedy.* New York: McKay, 1965.

Lippmann, Walter. *Conversations with Walter Lippmann.* Boston: Atlantic Monthly, 1965.

McGinniss, Joe. *The Last Brother: The Rise and Fall of Teddy Kennedy.* New York: Simon & Schuster, 1993.

McTaggart, Lynne. *Kathleen Kennedy: Her Life and Times.* New York: Dial, 1983.

Madsen, Axel. *Gloria and Joe.* New York: Morrow, 1988.

Mailer, Norman. *The Presidential Papers of Norman Mailer.* New York: Bantam, 1964.

Manchester, William. *The Death of a President: November 20–25, 1963.* New York: Harper & Row, 1967.

———. *Portrait of a President: John F. Kennedy in Profile.* Boston: Little, Brown, 1962.

Martin, John Bartlow. *Adlai Stevenson and the World.* New York: Doubleday, 1977.

Martin, Ralph G. *Ballots and Bandwagons.* New York: Rand McNally, 1964.

———. *The Bosses.* New York: Putnam, 1964.

———. *Cissy: The Life of Eleanor Medill Patterson.* New York: Simon & Schuster, 1979.

———. *Henry and Clare: An Intimate Portrait of the Luces.* New York: Putnam, 1991.

———. *A Hero for Our Time: An Intimate Story of the Kennedy Years.* New York: Macmillan, 1983.

Martin, Ralph G., and Ed Plaut. *Front Runner, Dark Horse.* New York: Doubleday, 1960.

Mazo, Earl. *Richard Nixon.* New York: Harper, 1959.

Miller, Merle. *Lyndon: An Oral Biography.* New York: Putnam, 1980.

Myers, Debs, and Ralph G. Martin. *Stevenson.* New York: Random House, 1952.

Navasky, Victor S. *Kennedy Justice.* New York: Atheneum, 1971.

Newfield, Jack. *Robert Kennedy: A Memoir.* New York: Plume, 1969.

O'Brien, Lawrence F. *No Final Victories: A Life in Politics.* New York: Ballantine, 1972.

O'Donnell, Kenneth P., and David F. Powers with Joe McCarthy. *"Johnny, We Hardly Knew Ye": Memories of John Fitzgerald Kennedy.* Boston: Little, Brown, 1972.

Olsen, Jack. *The Bridge at Chappaquiddick.* Boston: Little, Brown, 1969.

O'Neill, Thomas. *Man of the House.* New York: Random House, 1987.

Oppenheimer, Jerry. *The Other Mrs. Kennedy.* New York: St. Martin's, 1994.

Optowsky, Stan. *The Kennedy Government.* New York: Dutton, 1961.

Osherson, Samuel. *Finding Our Fathers.* New York: Fawcett, 1986.

Parmet, Herbert S. *Jack: The Struggles of John F. Kennedy.* New York: Dial, 1980.

———. *JFK: The Presidency of John F. Kennedy.* New York: Dial, 1983.

Presidential Recordings Transcripts. Papers of John F. Kennedy, vols. 1–3. The John F. Kennedy Library.

Public Papers of the Presidents of the United States: John F. Kennedy, 1961–63. Washington, DC: U.S. Government Printing Office, 1962–1964.

Rachlin, Harvey. *The Kennedys: A Chronological History.* New York: World Almanac, 1986.

Ragano, Frank, and Selwyn Raab. *Mob Lawyer.* New York: Scribner, 1994.

Reeves, Richard. *President Kennedy: Profile of Power.* New York: Simon & Schuster, 1983.

Reeves, Thomas C. *A Question of Character: A Life of John F. Kennedy.* New York: The Free Press, 1991.

Report of the Warren Commission on the Assassination of John F. Kennedy. Introduction by Harrison Salisbury with additional material prepared by *The New York Times.* New York: McGraw-Hill, 1963.

Reston, James. *Deadline: A Memoir.* New York: Random House, 1991.

Roberts, Allen. *Robert F. Kennedy: Biography of a Compulsive Politician.* Brookline Village, MA: Braden, 1984.

Roberts, Chalmers M. *First Rough Draft.* New York: Prager, 1973.

Rogers, Warren. *When I Think of Bobby: A Personal Memoir of the Kennedy Years.* New York: Harper-Collins, 1993.

Rostow, W. W. *The Diffusion of Power.* New York: Macmillan, 1972.

Salinger, Pierre. *With Kennedy.* New York: Doubleday, 1966.

Salinger, Pierre, and Sander Vanocur, eds. *A Tribute to John F. Kennedy.* Chicago: Encyclopedia Britannica, 1964.

Salisbury, Harrison. *Heroes of My Time.* New York: Walker, 1993.

———. *A Journey for Our Times.* New York: Harper & Row, 1983.

Saunders, Frank, with James Southwood. *Torn Lace Curtain: Life with the Kennedys.* New York: Holt, Rinehart & Winston, 1982.

Schlesinger, Arthur M., Jr. *Robert Kennedy and His Times.* Boston: Houghton Mifflin, 1978.

———. *A Thousand Days: John F. Kennedy in the White House.* Boston: Houghton Mifflin, 1965.

Searls, Hank. *The Lost Prince: Young Joe, the Forgotten Kennedy.* Cleveland: World, 1969.

Settel, T. S., ed. *The Wisdom of JFK.* New York: Dutton, 1965.

Sevareid, Eric, ed. *Candidates 1960.* New York: Basic Books, 1959.

Shannon, William V. *The Heir Apparent: Robert Kennedy and the Struggle for Power.* New York: Macmillan, 1967.

Sheed, Wilfrid. *The Kennedy Legacy: A Generation Later.* New York: Viking, 1988.

Sidey, Hugh. *John F. Kennedy, President.* New York: Atheneum, 1963.

Slatzer, Robert F. *The Life and Curious Death of Marilyn Monroe.* Los Angeles: Pinnacle, 1975.

Sorensen, Theodore C. *Kennedy.* New York: Harper & Row, 1965.

———. *The Kennedy Legacy.* New York: Macmillan, 1969.

Spada, James. *Peter Lawford: The Man Who Knew Too Much.* New York: Bantam, 1991.

Steel, Ronald. *Walter Lippmann and the American Century.* Boston: Atlantic/Little, Brown, 1980.

Stein, Jean, and George Plimpton. *American Journey: The Times of Robert Kennedy.* New York: Harcourt Brace Jovanovich, 1970.

Stoughton, Cecil, and Chester V. Clifton. *The Memories: JFK, 1961–1963.* New York: Norton, 1973.

Sullivan, William. *The Bureau: My Thirty Years with the FBI.* New York: Norton, 1979.

Sulzberger, C. L. *The Last of the Giants.* New York: Macmillan, 1970.

Summers, Anthony. *Goddess: The Secret Lives of Marilyn Monroe.* New York: Onyx, 1986.

———. *Official and Confidential: The Secret Life of J. Edgar Hoover.* New York: Putnam, 1993.

Swanson, Gloria. *Swanson on Swanson.* New York: Random House, 1980.

Szulc, Tad. *Fidel: A Critical Portrait.* New York: Morrow, 1986.

Tanzer, Lester, ed. *The Kennedy Circle.* Washington, DC: Luce, 1961.

Taylor, Maxwell. *Swords and Plowshares.* New York: Norton, 1972.

Thayer, Mary Van Rensselaer. *Jacqueline Kennedy: The White House Years.* Boston: Little, Brown, 1967.

Thompson, Robert E., and Hortense Myers. *Robert Kennedy: The Brother Within.* New York: Macmillan, 1962.

Tierney, Gene, with Mickey Herskowitz. *Self-Portrait.* New York: Wyden, 1979.

Ulasewicz, Tony. *The President's Private Eye.* Westport, CT: Macsam, 1990.

Vanden Heuvel, William, and Milton Gwirtzman. *On His Own: RFK: 1964–68.* New York: Doubleday, 1970.

West, J. B., with Mary Lynn Kotz. *Upstairs at the White House.* New York: Warner, 1974.

Whalen, Richard J. *The Founding Father: The Story of Joseph P. Kennedy.* New York: New American Library, 1964.

White, Theodore H. *In Search of History.* New York: Harper & Row, 1978.

———. *The Making of the President: 1960.* New York: Atheneum, 1961.

———. *The Making of the President: 1964.* New York: Atheneum, 1965.

———. *Theodore H. White at Large,* ed. Edward T. Thompson. New York: Pantheon, 1992.

Wicker, Tom. *JFK and LBJ.* New York: Morrow, 1968.

———. *Kennedy Without Tears.* New York: Morrow, 1964.

Wills, Garry. *The Kennedy Imprisonment: A Meditation on Power.* Boston: Little, Brown, 1982.

Witcover, Jules. *The Last Campaign of Robert Kennedy.* New York: Putnam, 1969.

Wofford, Harris. *Of Kennedys and Kings: Making Sense of the Sixties.* New York: Farrar, Straus & Giroux, 1980.

Wyden, Peter S. *Bay of Pigs: The Untold Story.* New York: Simon & Schuster, 1979.

INDEX